PEACEMAKER

NIGHT TRAP

About the author

Gordon Kent is the pseudonym of a father-and-son writing team, both of whom have extensive personal experience in the US Navy. Both are former Intelligence officers and both served as aircrew. The son earned his Observer wings in S-3 Vikings during the Gulf conflict. After service in the Mediterranean, Persian Gulf, Pacific and Africa, he left active duty in 1999. Both live in the United States. *Peacemaker* is their second Alan Craik novel, following the highly acclaimed *Night Trap* (which was published in the USA under the title *Rules of Engagement*). They have recently completed a third, *Top Hook*, which will soon be available from HarperCollins.

THE ALAN CRAIK NOVELS

Night Trap
Peacemaker
Top Hook

GORDON KENT

PEACEMAKER

HarperCollins*Publishers*

HarperCollins*Publishers*
77–85 Fulham Palace Road,
Hammersmith, London W6 8JB

www.**fire**and**water**.com

Special overseas edition 2001
This paperback edition 2001
1 3 5 7 9 10 8 6 4 2

First published in Great Britain by
HarperCollins*Publishers* 2000

Copyright © Gordon Kent 2000

The Author asserts the moral right to
be identified as the author of this work

ISBN 0 00 651295 X

Typeset in Meridien by
Palimpsest Book Production Limited,
Polmont, Stirlingshire

Printed and bound in Great Britain by
Omnia Books Limited, Glasgow

For those who serve in secret.

Prologue

April 6, 1994

Zulu wore sunglasses and camo fatigues, and he had a star on each collar point that winked in the sunlight. These were not the first things you noticed, at least not as soon as you got close. What you noticed first was that somebody had tried to cut his nose off with a hard downward stroke from above, perhaps as if the blade had struck a helmet first and been deflected a little and gone into the hard bone of his nose almost at the bridge and taken out a chunk of it. Now he had a nose that looked in profile like a child's idea of a witch's nose, a nose that started too far down his face and came straight out before plunging downward. Some people winced when they first saw that nose.

His real name was not Zulu. Nor was it the name on his passport. The men with him simply called him Z.

He had four men with him, also in camo, men like him who were too pale to have been in the sun for long. He spoke to them in French, but, because one of the four had to translate for the others into another language, it seemed that the French was, like their Belgian uniforms, something false. All five men carried side arms and grenades, and they had things like NATO battle helmets and Kevlar vests and fanny packs that they had put on the ground nearby because it was so hot. They had the air of men who were in some place of transit—say, an airport—and who were used to not caring where they were because they would soon be somewhere else. They lit cigarettes and looked around and waited.

Elizabeth Momparu was too shrewd to hang back from the white men, even though she was the only woman. If she isolated herself, even from apparent shyness, she would be noticed that much more. Not that she could be easily ignored; she was a big woman, tall and robust, heavy-boned. People noticed her. Here, the African men noticed her with particular clarity because she was the daughter of a general, a Hutu, and half-sister to Peter Ntarinada, who was a big man in his own right. The European men noticed her because she was good-looking. A green dress that showed off her breasts and hips didn't hurt.

"Peter!" she called. She put laughter into her voice. She made more of the difficulty she was having with high heels and the soft earth out here. Her half-brother turned his head but only made an impatient gesture with his hand. He had pushed himself into the group of Europeans, and he didn't want some woman, even a half-sister, pulling him back out. Peter was aggressive—"proud," Africans said—and very touchy, one of those people who can't conceive of not using power if they have it. And he had some. And he would soon have more, if his plans worked.

Elizabeth Momparu laughed loud enough for the clusters of men to hear. There was a black cluster and a white cluster, with Peter the only one who had crossed from one cluster to the other. Still laughing, she tottered to join him. Peter turned again and scowled at her. She laughed.

They were gathered around the man named Zulu, who was speaking in a language Elizabeth didn't understand to two white men in Belgian uniforms. Elizabeth didn't believe for a moment that they were Belgian, and she

2

didn't believe Zulu was French, but she didn't say so. She merely smiled into Zulu's dark sunglasses and ignored his maimed nose.

The sunglasses stared back at her. Where were the eyes? Zulu looked down at the two "Belgians." He said something, and the men began to unzip two long nylon bags. Elizabeth knew they were ski bags, because she'd been skiing in Switzerland, but she knew, too, that they didn't hold skis. Not in Rwanda.

Another man in a Belgian uniform was murmuring into a radio. He had a short antenna strung, and equipment laid out on a plastic tarpaulin, and he listened and then called something to Zulu and held up a hand, the fingers spread, and opened and closed them once, twice. Ten.

"Ten minutes," Zulu said to Peter. Peter squinted into the sky. He looked at Elizabeth, still squinting. "Keep out of the way," he said in French.

But she moved in closer and watched one of the "Belgians" begin to take pieces of metal out of the ski bag. He began to assemble them. Elizabeth knew that he was putting together a missile launcher; she knew that much from having lived through a war, but she didn't know that it was a shoulder-fired American Stinger.

"You want to help?" Zulu said to her. His voice was uncannily low, and he had an accent that she thought was either American or German. He had been pleasant to her at dinner last night and afterward in bed, and he was being merely pleasant now, perhaps letting his need for her brother's help attach to her.

"Oh, yes!" she said. She didn't feel that enthusiastic, but she thought that enthusiasm was called for.

Zulu took a camera from a bag at his feet. She saw at once that it was a very expensive camera but not of a kind she knew, very flat, square. She recognized the brand name, however. "Oh!" she said, "I have a Canon, too. A cute little one." She began to burrow in her shoulder bag for it.

"This is, I think, the only camera of its kind in Africa." He surprised her by sounding boastful. Odd, such a petty thing in a man who, according to her brother, was so important. Yet, he seemed childishly pleased at showing her his digital camera and how it worked.

"No film?" she said. She tried to make herself seem as stupid as possible—her "Marilyn Monroe act," as she called it.

"No film. No laboratory. I print from my computer."

"Your *computer*! Oh, wild! Oh!" But he was immune to the Monroe thing. It was the camera and the computer that turned him on. He showed her how to work it and then said, "Your part is to take pictures of me. You will be the official historian." His lips smiled. He was used to dealing with men, she thought. This was how he got men to do things. Things like coming to Rwanda and wearing a Belgian uniform and firing a Stinger missile? Yes, almost assuredly so.

Zulu posed with her brother, his white arm around Peter's black neck, his face turned up to the sky. She took the picture. Zulu posed, one foot up on a log, pointing toward a cloud. Zulu went and stood among the Africans and posed, seeming to be explaining something to them. The men were all her brother's soldiers, Hutus, all armed with Heckler & Koch assault rifles, all in camo fatigues and bush hats; now Zulu posed them, one by one, as if he were directing a play, until they stood in a tight group, rifles at the ready, looking this way and that as if on guard. Elizabeth took the picture. It was an odd thing, such an ugly man being so vain, but she knew that he was.

Would she dare try it with her own camera? Better now than later, she thought. She took it out. It was bright pink, hardly something you would seem to be trying to hide. She raised it to her eye. She framed a couple of the soldiers.

"Wait!" Zulu shouted.

She froze, the viewfinder at her eye. She couldn't see him in the viewfinder, so she turned her head to the left, seeing a small rectangle of the world swing by, and there he was. Was he angry? Was he going to do something to her?

"I'm not ready," he said. He ran a hand over his hair and went to the black men, her viewfinder tracking him, and he took the assault rifle from one of them and pointed it into the bush. "Ready," he said, turning his profile so his witch's nose was silhouetted against the shadows. She snapped the picture.

"Okay?" she said brightly.

"Now with my camera, please."

She took that one.

"Now like this." He swung the weapon around and aimed it at her. Right at her face. Right at the camera. One of the Africans laughed, and then he got next to Zulu and pointed his rifle, and then a couple of the others came and then all of them, a dozen, and they stood there, some shaking with laughter, aiming their rifles at her until she took the picture with both cameras. The rifles were loaded, she knew.

Then the radioman shouted something, and Zulu busied himself with the two men who had the missile launchers. He slapped one on the shoulder and trotted over to Elizabeth. "Get pictures when I tell you." He touched her little pink camera. "Put that one away."

"Just one more?" she pleaded. Dipping her knees as children do, making herself smaller.

"Make it quick."

He headed for the radioman, and she snapped one hurriedly, trying to get him and the two shooters; she cycled the film and stepped back, hoping one of them would raise the launcher to his shoulder, but they were busy on the ground.

"Put that thing away!" a voice said behind her. Her brother.

"He said I could take one more." She bounced up and down on her toes.

"This is serious business, Elizabeth! Don't you know what's going on here?"

"It's a *déjeuner sur l'herbe*, isn't it? A peek-neek?" She gave him a foolish grin. "I'm not an idiot, Peter."

"I don't like you taking pictures."

"He asked me to take them! And anyway, if you have your way, it won't matter what pictures have been taken, will it? Besides which, they're all supposed to be Belgians, so what does it signify?"

The Belgians were in Rwanda as peacekeepers. So were the French. Twenty-five hundred of them, keeping "peace" since last August in a country already up to its knees in blood. Now her brother was involved in something designed to start the horrors up again. She knew a lot about it; she was part of the Hutu elite, always on the edges of discussions and meetings. She was trusted because she was a general's daughter and Peter's half-sister, and because all her life she had had privileges and luxuries beyond most of her countrymen's wildest dreams.

"Put that camera away *now*!" he hissed. Zulu was shouting at his men. Somebody was running.

"Oh—poo!" she said. She snapped a picture of Peter looking furious, then swung the camera around and got one of the "Belgians" as he raised the launcher. Then she gave her half-brother a big grin and made a show of dropping the pink camera into her bag and zipping it closed. She laughed into his angry face, then minced across

6

the soft earth, her beautifully coiffed hair bouncing, Zulu's digital camera held like a jewel between her fingers.

Zulu was gesturing at the Rwandan soldiers, spreading them out. "All the way around us!" he shouted. "Both sides! When I tell you, you go! We get out very quick when this is over!" He looked for Peter, found him. "Get them out another fifty meters or so! A big perimeter—I don't want any interference—" He looked around again. "Where's my camera? Ah—" He ran to Elizabeth. "I'll take it now. No, wait—get one shot of me and the guys—"

He crouched behind the two shooters, who had their backs to her with the launchers pointed into the sky to the north. "Okay—take the picture— Good. One more—" He changed his position, waved her around so she was getting him in profile again, cheating a little so his face, his nose showed as he seemed to be directing the two shooters. "Got it? Give me the camera. Many thanks." He gave her the smile again, the smile that worked on the men and didn't work on her. "Well done." Then he was back with the shooters, speaking to them in the other language.

And then she could hear the aircraft. At first, it was an almost subliminal rumble, then a soft roar that diminished into a hiss and a sigh, with a thin screaming of air over wings beginning to descend above the other sounds. She stared into the north sky. The morning clouds had piled up but not delivered their rain; it would pass over them now and fall somewhere to the east. The clouds were bright enough to hurt her eyes; she squinted, trying to make the aircraft out above the trees. She prayed it wouldn't be the civilian plane. *Make it military*, she prayed. *Make it the UN*. Even the French or the Belgians. It could be that it was them they meant to hit. That could be the strategy, to down a UN plane, stir things up. *Not the other*, she prayed. If it was the other, then they would all be in hell.

Zulu rapped out a word, and one of the shooters set his rear foot and hunched. Zulu had seen the aircraft, and she tried to find it in the brightness of cloud. Where? She was looking too far ahead, of course; she was deceived by the sound.

"There it is," Peter said. The others had already seen it.

Then she saw it, too, surprisingly clear and close. It was a civilian 747. *Please, no, God,* she prayed.

The aircraft came on, dropping, on its final approach now for the Kigali airport. The thin scream of the wind cut into her ears. She covered them, screwed her face up, a frightened child.

One Stinger whooshed and roared and smoked from the tube. She followed its trajectory as it seemed to curve away from the aircraft. *Miss, miss, dear God,* she prayed. The trail curled and then swung more tightly up. It seemed to hang there for a long time. *They missed,* she thought. The airliner was screaming down the glide path to their left, dropping toward the trees, and the missile was invisible. Seeking, seeking the aircraft's heat—

And then it hit. The aircraft erupted. A ball of light blew out of its roof, although the craft seemed for a moment to remain intact, to go on flying. Then flame and smoke spread from that white-hot center, and the tail section, independent now, began to fall. The front was almost entirely obscured by flash and fire; another explosion tore it apart; a wing and an engine seemed to slide sideways across the sky, and the fireball plunged.

She found that she was standing on her toes, one hand clasped over her mouth. She was weeping. Peter was shaking her and pulling her away. "Weakling!" he shouted at her. "Weakling! You stupid bitch!"

* * *

8

Everyone aboard the civilian flight, including the presidents of Rwanda and Burundi, was killed. Both were Hutus. Tutsi rebels were blamed.

Then ten Belgian peacekeepers were killed by Rwandan presidential guards.

Then Hutus began to kill Tutsis. The killings were not random. On April fifteenth, more than a thousand Tutsis were murdered in a church by men throwing grenades. By April twenty-seventh, a hundred thousand on both sides were dead. Then the Hutu strategy backfired, and by August the Tutsi Rwandan Patriotic Front was in power in Rwanda, and somewhere between half a million and a million Hutus had become refugees in other countries, mainly Zaire.

The man called Zulu was not there. He had flown out the same day as the downing of the presidents' aircraft. After refueling at Abeche in Chad, an ancient Britannia 252 took him up to the edge of the Mediterranean at Tubruq, then to the military airport south of Belgrade, Yugoslavia. "Zulu" became somebody else who had his own training camp and weapons depot south of the city and whom the authorities in Belgrade feared and disliked, but without whom they could not achieve the ethnic victory in their own country on which their political lives depended.

Part One

The Friends

1

Bosnia, February 1996

The sea was gray, the sky near the horizon pink, between them a line of silver. It looked as cold as dawn in Canada, but this was the Mediterranean in February. Cold.

He felt the bucking of the aircraft, under it the surge of the deck, under that the throb of the ship, felt these things without feeling them because he had been there so long these were normal, and when he got on shore the lack of vibration would feel wrong, something missing in the universe.

"Ready back there, Lieutenant?"

Fatigue perched on him like a big, obscene bird. *Crow picking at roadkill.* He roused himself, realized he had been half-asleep, the pilot's voice in the comm waking him. Was he ready? Ready for one more of Suter's punitive jobs, one more of his humiliations, one more of his demonstrations that he, Suter, was a lieutenant-commander and Alan Craik was only a lieutenant and it had been a big mistake for Alan to show that he thought Suter was an asshole?

"Yo," he said.

"O-kay! And they're off, as the monkey said—"

When he backed into the lawnmower, Alan finished for him. The puck dropped and the cat whacked him in the chest with Gs and the aircraft threw itself at the horizon. It was like the old days for a moment, and he felt the thrill of it, and then it was gone.

They flew into the rising sun, up toward thin strands of cloud like combed-out hair. Alan Craik looked back and saw the carrier, already small, a destroyer just visible in the haze a couple of miles away. Bitterly, he thought that he was off to do an ensign's job, and behind him on the ship Ensign Baronik would be trying to do Alan's job and screwing it up because he was only an ensign, and LCDR Suter would be on him like a weasel on a chicken, pleased that this nice piece of warm meat was there for him to savage. Ensign Baronik hadn't been savvy enough to put space between himself and Alan, and so he was warm meat by association. And he was too young and too scared to tell Suter to back off, as Alan had done.

Alan sighed. God, he was tired. Four hours' sleep in three days and now this. A lose-lose situation: if he didn't work his ass off, Suter gave him every shit detail that came along; if he did work his ass off, Suter took the credit— and gave him every shit detail that came along. For Alan, who loved the job and for whom work was life, it was better to work himself to death and know that at least he'd done his best, but helping Suter's career was bitter medicine. And it was made worse by Suter's having control of his life—of his orders, of his job, of his fitness reports. And Suter hated him. "You're supposed to be God's wet dream," Suter had hissed at him. "You're supposed to be hot shit, Craik, and I know you're not! I see through you! You're just luck and bullshit wrapped with a ribbon, and I'm gonna untie it. People been hanging medals on you like Christmas ornaments—well, no more, mister. No more! You're not even gonna get close to glory this trip— no way!"

What was worse, Suter was good at his job. And smart.

14

"You wanna sleep back there, Lieutenant, go ahead. We got a couple hours, no scenery."

"Would you ask the stewardess to turn down my bed?" Alan said.

"Jeez, I would, but she's busy in first class just now."

Alan smiled, the smile of habit, the sea-duty smile. He started to think about his wife, and home, and what it would be like when this rotten tour was over. He must have fallen asleep, because the next thing he was aware of was the pilot telling him they were five minutes from going dry and he could wake up now.

"Must have dozed off."

"Hey, I thought I had a corpse back there! Feet-dry in four minutes, man. We're coming in over the islands now—" He started to give a guided tour but clicked off to deal with the comm. Alan consulted his own kneepad: Split was off somewhere in the haze to his left; to his right would be Dubrovnik, down along the coast that was now like a smudge from a dirty thumb. Directly underneath, the island of Brac, one of a series of former resorts that step-stoned down the coast to Dubrovnik. Not resorts now, he thought. He had no intel of fighting down there, but the war had been everywhere, the gruesome agony of a nation turned in on itself. Down there were perhaps only shuttered hotels and distrust; ahead on the mainland were horrors. He had already seen some of them. A so-called "peace accord" had been signed a few weeks before, but people who looked alike and had a common history and common problems were still killing each other, like a trapped animal chewing off its own leg.

The weather inland was lousy. Sarajevo was socked in, as usual. The UN food flights had just ended, and NATO had taken over the airfield. Alan watched the cloud tops, felt his eyes close, nodded forward—

15

"Cleared for landing. Check your straps, Lieutenant. You know how this goes—ejection position SOP. Make ready—" He felt the familiar turn and sink, deceleration, pressure as he came against the straps, but nothing like a carrier landing—no hook here, and a runway long enough to land a commercial jet. Alan saw the too-close bulk of Mount Igman, acres of dirty snow, low, dark cloud cover obscuring dark slopes, houses flashing underneath, a burned-out car—

A bang and a screech and they swiveled a degree and back and were down. A radar installation flashed past, two trucks angled to it in a plowed space, high snowbanks all around, a French logo. The plane was rolling now, no longer seeming to scream; they swung left into a taxiway, slowed some more and began the long taxi to the intake building. When Alan climbed down, a cold, wet wind slapped at him: welcome to Yugoslavia.

He blew out his breath. Six hours here. To do ten minutes of an ensign's work. As he humped his pack toward the warehouse building that served IFOR as a local HQ, it started to snow.

The French officer signed for his package and gave him coffee (damned good—bitter, fresh) and asked him to stay to lunch (also damned good, probably, with wine), but a Canadian major with the worried look of an old monkey looked through a doorway and shouted, "That Craik?"

The Frenchman grimaced, winked at Alan. "Just arrived, Major."

"In here, Craik." The worry lines deepened and the major turned away, then looked back and said, "Welcome and—so on. Kind of a mess."

Alan was supposed to sit for six hours and then get a lift to Aviano, sit for four hours, and then get something that might put him near the carrier. Suter's idea.

16

Nothing was supposed to happen here except turning over a lot of clapped-out aerial photos. "Uh—" he said stupidly at the retreating back, "—my orders have me going to—"

"Orders have been changed!" the voice floated back.

Suter again?

Alan shrugged himself deeper into his exhaustion and went through the door where the major had disappeared. There was a battered corridor, black slush on the floor, hand-lettered signs on pieces of notebook paper drooping from map pins like old flags— "G-3," "S&R," "Liaison." He passed a makeshift bulletin board, most of the postings in both English and French. Well, they were Canadians, after all. At the top of the bulletin board, it said "UNPROFOR," the acronym of the UN Protection Force that was in the process of pulling out.

"In here!" The major sat in a tiny office that had been a toilet before the sinks were ripped out. An unusable commode was almost hidden by a pile of pubs. "Francourt, Major, Canadian army. You know about all that." He handed over some message traffic: his orders. Alan's eyes flashed down it—". . . temporary duty . . . CO UNPROFOR/CO IFOR Sarajevo . . . liaison and intelligence support and acquisition . . ." What was this shit?

The major was talking again. "You know UNPROFOR, what we do—?"

"I thought you were IFOR."

The major shook his head. "UNPROFOR. We're going, they're coming." He jerked his head toward the front of the building where the French officer was. "Unfortunately, some of us are still here."

"Yes, sir."

"French and Canadians down here, mostly us and the Italians up above." He looked at Alan. "Tuzla." That was "up above," he meant. There had been a lot of fighting. "We were keeping the peace, ha-ha. You know all that. It says here you speak this African Kissy-willy, that right?" He rattled a piece of paper.

"Kiswahili? A little—"

"Good. And Italian, it says. Good, just the guy I want. We got a problem up there, I don't follow it, but there's a Kenyan medical unit making a hell of a noise, and I haven't got time to deal with it. You've been asked for. Dick Murch—know him?"

His mind was slow because of no sleep, and it was all coming too fast—Yugoslavia, winter, snow, then all of a sudden Kenyans and Swahili. Murch. "Murch. Yeah—Canadian Army intel—"

"He asked for you by name." The major rattled the paper again. "Your boss messaged us you're just the man for the job." The major, a man with decent feelings, glanced a little unbelievingly at Alan. It would be, after all, a shitty job, whatever it was—cold, uncomfortable, fruitless. Alan saw the major understand that Alan's boss hated his guts. The major's voice was almost apologetic: "Well—won't last long. And it's just being a good listener, eh? And you can take those photos you brought in right up to Murch and save us a step."

Well, Alan thought, at least there would be wine with lunch before he left.

"There's a plane going up in—well, it was supposed to leave a half-hour ago, but they never get out on time. One of yours." He meant that the US had re-opened the airport at Tuzla and was moving there in a big way. Alan doubted the jab about being late; the Air Force, like the Navy, ran a tight operation. The major was just pissed because he was still here. "Dalembert'll show you which one." There went wine with lunch. And lunch,

18

probably. A voice in his head said, *This is another fine mess you've got us into!* The voice would have been Harry O'Neill's, doing one of his imitations. God, he wished O'Neill was with him! The bond of friendship would have got him through this crap. He and O'Neill had been two first-tour IOs together five years ago, winning the Gulf War on brilliance and brashness (with a little help from some pilots). O'Neill would have known how to deal with Suter. O'Neill would have known how to deal with Alan, for that matter. *You're good, Shweetheart—you're really good—*

"Got a weapon?" the major said.

Weapon. Weapon? Alan had to concentrate. "Got an armpit gun in my pack."

"Wear it. They're shooting at us up there. I mean, at *us*. Take off your rank, anything shiny." He held up a finger. "Lesson: If you try to help some poor sonofabitch who's being killed by his brother, they'll both kill you, instead." He made a gun with his hands and pretended to squint into a sight.

Alan gave another long, fatigued sigh. He unstrapped the pack and began to feel for the Browning nine-millimeter. This *was* a fine mess.

Fort MacArthur, North Carolina.
The Georgian brick buildings, the green lawns and the old trees looked like a university campus. The classroom looked like a university classroom. The students, in their thirties and forties, might have been university graduate students. But they weren't. This was the toughest school in America, with the highest rate of flunkout, dropout, and just plain exhaustion. This was what people inside the intelligence community called the Ranch.

Harry O'Neill sat relaxed at one of the student desks.

Unlike the rest, he was attentive to the briefing on Africa. The rest were in body positions that suggested that Africa didn't exist for them. The teacher, himself a case officer no longer active, was pointing a laser pointer at a map with the outlines of countries but no names and asking questions with the resigned tone of a man who knew that he wouldn't get answers.

"What's this?" he snapped. When there was no answer, he said, "O'Neill?"

"Rwanda," O'Neill murmured.

"This?" Silence. He nodded at Harry. O'Neill said, "Burundi."

The bright dot moved. The teacher waited, flicked an eye at O'Neill. "Zaire." Then, "Central African Republic. Chad—"

The teacher snapped the pointer off and leaned his butt back against a table, arms crossed, and said, "Okay, okay. You know what's going on there? Want to do a little central African brief off the cuff, Mister O'Neill?"

Harry smiled. "Off the cuff, sir, let's see—two years ago, there was a crash—some folks say a shootdown—of an aircraft with the presidents of Rwanda and Burundi aboard. All hell broke loose, with the two major ethnic groups, the Hutus and the Tutsis, massacring each other. Tutsis came out on top, drove the Hutus into eastern Zaire, where they're now living in big refugee camps that are being run by their own militias, who got out with their weapons and a big blood lust. When the other shoe drops, there'll be hell all over again."

"How come you know all this and the rest of these guys don't, O'Neill?"

Before Harry could reply, a voice behind him said, low and with a snicker, "Cause dat's his *home*, man!"

O'Neill was the only black man in the class.

20

The teacher snapped erect, face flushed. "All right—who said that—?"

But Harry O'Neill hadn't stirred. He only smiled and said softly, "Oh, that's okay, sir. *I* know who said it."

When the class ended, most of them stirred and stretched, but a man named Richmond hurried out the door and started down the corridor. Harry O'Neill was just as fast, however; within a few strides, he had caught up and fallen in with the man, draping one arm around the other's shoulders with what seemed perfect friendliness.

"Richmond, Richmond!" he said. He smiled. He squeezed Richmond's shoulder. O'Neill had been both a Phi Beta Kappa and a starting defensive end at Harvard; the squeeze had authority. "Richmond, next week we have Close Combat Drill three times, did you know that? And, because I'm near the top of the class, I get to pick my partner, did you know that?" He gave another squeeze. "And Richmond—" His voice took on the same thick, fake-black tone that had been heard in the classroom. "Ah picks yew—*man*!"

Tuzla.

Alan tried to sleep on the short hop to Tuzla, but it was no good. They'd put him in a "crash-resistant" seat with enough straps to hold back Hulk Hogan, but they hadn't given any thought to comfort. Most of the huge aircraft was loaded with cargo. The French coffee had lifted him for a little, but that was gone now. He had already had the second surge that comes with real fatigue, the time of being wired, with crash to follow. Except he hadn't been able to crash. At Tuzla, they made one big turn and went in, with another aircraft on the runway ahead of them and another right behind. Like cyclic ops. Alan tried to find an office for UNPROFOR and finally learned

21

that what was left of it wasn't at the airfield; it was beyond the city, and he'd need transport. It was like a demonstration of Murphy's Law. Somebody found him a truck.

The driver was Italian, one of those people who dedicate their lives to not being impressed, so he was not impressed that Alan spoke Italian with a Neapolitan accent. Still, he was willing to talk, so long as it was clear to Alan that he was not impressed by officer rank, either. When they had gone a few kilometers, he stopped.

"Good place to piss," he said in Italian. "No snipers." Alan didn't recognize the Italian word for "snipers" but got it from a pantomime. The second time somebody had pretended to shoot him that day. He got out, and they stood side by side. Lots of other trucks had stopped here for relief; the place was an outdoor toilet, in fact. He climbed back up into the cab, higher than climbing into the old S-3 he had flown in for two years, and they coughed and clanked along. It was an incomparably gloomy scene, as so many land-war scenes are, all dirty snow and mud and artillery damage, and one woman with no teeth and a head scarf and a cow-like stare, watching them go past. Early in the war, a mortar round had landed in a square in Tuzla and killed seventy-one people, most of them children.

The trucker dropped Alan at what had been the UNPROFOR HQ. That was not where Murch was, of course; Murch was in the intel center, in a former school three rubble-strewn blocks away. When Alan had finally humped his pack to the right doorless office, Murch looked at him and said, "Is this the best the States can send us? You look like the meat course in an MRE."

"I'm wiped."

"You'll fit right in." Murch looked worn out himself.

Alan had met Murch a couple of months before down on the coast; they had done a job together and had hit it off. They had found a shared interest in fishing. Murch was convinced there would be fishing nearby when spring came. His only evidence was that Tito had been a fisherman. "Eaten?"

"Somebody gave me a box lunch. I think I ate it. The French were going to give me real food. With wine."

"You want to be walked through the chow line first or you want to crash?" There were cartons and fiber barrels everywhere. Murch was in the middle of moving.

"I'm running on empty, man."

Murch handed him a tan plastic cup of acidic coffee and said, "Ten minutes. Got to brief you. Then—" He looked at his watch. "You can get eight hours and you'll be off."

"What the hell is 'off'?"

Murch jerked his thumb toward the sky. "Up the hill. We'll give you a Humvee and a driver and a gunner. You're going up on a peacekeeping mission—between the Italians and the Kenyans."

Thirteen minutes later, he was asleep.

Eastern Zaire.

The air was damp from rain that had come out of season, making haloes around the gas lamps in the cinder-block building. Insects flew in and out of the haloes. Out in the camp, somebody laughed; somebody screamed. Peter Ntarinada, sitting in the building in the scruffy room he called his office, pushed the gift bottle of Glenlivet across the rickety table. "I want more money and I want more arms," he said.

The Frenchman poured himself some whiskey. He gave a

kind of shrug with one eyebrow. "We don't give something for nothing, Colonel. Lascelles himself said that times are tight."

"Something for nothing! Look how I'm living! Is this *nothing*?" Peter snatched the bottle back, poured more into his own glass. "I'm living like a peasant! I live in this fucking camp that is paved with shit because we don't have toilets—you call that nothing? Anyway, when we get back into Rwanda, you'll be repaid. Lascelles knows he'll be repaid. I have a scheme, you see? To move diamonds out of Angola—"

"Yes, yes." The Frenchman nodded in the way that means, You told me that three times already. "We want you back in Rwanda, Colonel. We want you in the government there. But, we think—Lascelles thinks—in order for us to, mmm, underwrite you again, we need to have, mmm, insurance."

"Insurance." Ntarinada, a man at war, didn't seem to understand the concept of insurance. In fact, he laughed.

"We want to put in a company of real soldiers, Colonel. Oh, I know, I know! Your men are soldiers, yes, yes, they are very good at beating up civilians and fragging people in churches, but frankly, the Tutsis are trained now, and we have intelligence that the Ugandans and the Tanzanians are helping them. So—we need insurance, and you need real soldiers."

Ntarinada's face was drawn tight. He licked his lips. "White soldiers, you mean."

"One company. The best. They'll go through the Tutsis like a knife, then you come behind. Yes, white. Sorry—it's the way the world is, Colonel. They have the guns, they have the training, and they have the recent experience. We'll give you money and guns if you'll accept one hundred of the best. To ease things a little, Lascelles will send a man you already know to run things. A friend of yours. Okay?"

Ntarinada was furious, but he contained his rage. "Who?"

"Zulu."

Ntarinada stared. He was surprised. And impressed.

"Zulu," the Frenchman said again. "The guy who was here two years ago and shot down the—"

Ntarinada held up a hand. "Not even here—don't say it out loud." He let his hand fall with a little slap on the table. He pushed his glass about, picked it up and drank off the rest of it and lifted the bottle to pour more. "A lot has happened since Zulu was here."

"A lot has happened to him. Bosnia. He's been fighting in Bosnia."

Ntarinada nodded. He understood perfectly well how a man like Zulu could be fighting in his own country. "Zulu is a good man. Okay. Tell Lascelles I said okay. But get me money and some guns!" He drank. "I keep overall command," he said.

The Frenchman shook his head. "Sorry. Zulu."

"Never!"

"Insurance." The Frenchman smiled. "How about—*shared* command? You're both colonels now."

Ntarinada looked away into the little room's shadows. He was looking into a century of colonialism, the bitter darkness of working for the whites. "All right," he said. "I'll share command with Zulu." He ran his hand over his thin face, sighed like a man dying of exhaustion. "You bastards."

Above Tuzla.

The Canadian driver loved the Humvee and couldn't stop demonstrating it. Alan got the hairiest ride he'd had on dry land since a drunken Italian had taken him on the Amalfi

25

Drive. He found it oddly exhilarating, maybe from having had eight hours of sleep so deep he didn't even dream. Still, it was nice to know it was a trip he'd have to make only once.

Except that he made it three times—three times up, three times down. And the last time wasn't until the next afternoon.

The trouble up there wasn't something that needed a linguist; it needed a good listener. And Alan was a pretty good listener, like anybody who wants to make it in intelligence. The fact that he knew both languages helped, sure; to the Kenyan doctor in charge of the medical unit, there was a plus in hearing a non-African say that it was *baridi, baridi kabisa*—bloody cold, man. And Alan had been in Kenya and could at least talk as much as a traveler can about the coast and Nairobi and problems up on the Sudanese border. So he learned that the real trouble between the Italian soldiers and the Kenyan medics was not that the Italians were racists or the Kenyans were bad nurses, but that they had all been there too long and none of them felt he had done shit to help the peace and now they were being pulled out and replaced by NATO. To make it worse, the unarmed Kenyan medics felt isolated by language and color and abandoned by the very people who were supposed to protect them, and they took it out in gallows-humor jokes, and some of the jokes were about how the Italians had got their asses whipped twice in Ethiopia—once by the Ethiopians and once by the Brits and the Kenyans.

For Sale: Like-new Italian rifle. Only dropped once.

The jokes had gone stale, then bad; there had been shouting—and, the doctor admitted, a bad fight, a punch that had emptied the benches and become a brawl. Bad.

So Alan got several of the officers from both units

26

together and badgered them into eating their MREs in the same tent—it was lunch, and partway through one of the Italians produced some wine—and, when a shouting match broke out, he got the doctor to calm down enough to snarl that they, the Kenyans, were catching hell from the Serbs, who were just over the newly drawn border two miles away, and the Italians were doing nothing to stop it.

"We can't do anything to stop it, you cretin!" the Italian screamed. Alan translated this as "We do everything we can, sir." The Kenyan hollered, "You were afraid in 1942 and you're afraid now!" which Alan didn't translate at all. Another Kenyan, a senior surgeon named wa Danio, shook a finger at the Italians and told them that it was the civilians, the civilians over there, they were being tortured, maimed, massacred, and the Italians were doing nothing. The senior Italian, Captain Gagliano, threw up his hands and said, "Nothing, nothing—there is nothing we can do! Anyway, we are leaving." After lunch, Doctor wa Danio insisted that Alan come with him to the ward, where he showed him an old man who had had his feet cut off with an axe and who had crawled the three miles to the Kenyan unit.

"You know, Lieutenant, we Africans are supposed to be uncivilized, but this is a horror. This is not stupid men swinging pangas; this is deliberate, organized hell. The Italians think we are savages, but we know those bastards over there are monsters!" He showed Alan a woman who had been gang-raped and beaten. A child with one hand, the other lost when he had tried to keep his already wounded father from being beheaded. Alan had a child. He felt sick, then thought what it would be like to sit here week after week, helpless to stop it . . .

So Alan went down the mountain. On the way down,

he figured how it could be done. A warning bell rang in his head but he turned it off, paid no attention, and instead he listened to an inner voice that said, *Okay, Suter, you want liaison and intelligence support and acquisition. I'll give it to you, right up the nose.*

He told Murch that the problem up there was not language or jokes or nationalities, it was frustration, fighting men and medical personnel who were frustrated and angry and unappreciated. They wanted to go in and make one hit on the Bosnian Serbs who were committing the atrocities before they were pulled out.

"We can't go in there," Murch said. "We're protectors. Not aggressors." Murch's mouth seemed to lose some of its muscle: he was afraid.

"They say there was US armor up there a week ago and it got turned back."

"Mm, yeah, all the women and kids in a Serb village blocked the road, lay down in front of a tank—they're fanatical up there. Leave it."

"Going in to get war criminals would be allowed."

"I'm not at all sure of that, and we don't know anything about war criminals over there."

"The Kenyans say that they know for certain of a house ten miles in that serves as a command center for the butchery. They say it's used for torture. Everybody knows it, they say."

"Oh, Christ, Alan, 'everybody—'" He was afraid of his place, his next evaluation, his career. Fuck him.

"Look, the Italians are good guys and they're hot to trot. They've been sitting up there for two months and their hands have been tied and they've had to watch— to *watch*—while civilians get slaughtered, because of this phony 'border.' They want to do something."

"We all want to do something. Alan, there's nothing—"

28

"Yes, there is." He was feeling pretty good, still. He thought he'd start to sink, but he hadn't. It was two in the afternoon; he felt really good. Not wired, but charged. "Hit that two-bit torture center in Pustarla."

"We can't do that! Al, look, you're exhausted, you're not thinking clearly—"

"If we have intelligence that the house is a center for war crimes, we can go in and hit it. In and out."

"I don't have the authority." Murch's face got stiff. "Canada prides herself on not involving UNPROFOR ground forces." His voice became pleading. "We're out of here! IFOR has the responsibility now!"

"UNPROFOR hit Udbina and took out the airfield! UNPROFOR used artillery in Sarajevo! What the fuck, you're making noise about a goddam hit on one house?"

"Udbina was part of Deny Flight. Alan, please! Go see IFOR."

They both knew that was bullshit. IFOR command was back in Sarajevo, and they'd say it was an UNPROFOR problem, because weren't the Italians and the Kenyans the remnant of UNPROFOR? "The Italians are fed up. Their colonel might say no, but he's taking a few days R and R in Dubrovnik. A company-level hit, that's all they want. We'd need choppers; I think two would do it." He was thinking of his own experience, of being pulled out of a firefight by two marine helos. Of course, these guys wouldn't be US marines. And Alan wouldn't have his wife in command of the choppers this time. "Who's got big choppers? You guys have two brand-new Griffons. No? I'll check the order of battle."

"Alan—we don't have the intelligence!"

Alan stared at him, saw a man who wasn't fed up with bullshit yet, maybe wanted to dedicate his life to bullshit. Why had he thought he liked this guy? He went to the outer office and got the package of photos he'd brought in that morning—all photos that had already passed through his hands once—and pulled a couple and went back to Murch, got a grease pencil, and began to make small circles.

"What the hell is that?"

"This is intelligence."

Murch leaned in close. "Fuck, man—"

"I could do better with a stereo magnifier."

Murch provided one. In fifteen minutes, Alan had marked the house that they said was a torture center, five "suspected grave sites," an outbuilding that the Kenyans' patients told them was a torture chamber. "Crematorium," he said, circling something with a chimney.

"Aw, shit— !"

"You been there?"

"No, but—"

"It's as good as the crap the CIA gives the President." He handed the photos to Murch. "Copies to whoever has to okay the choppers, plus the Italians, plus me, plus the chopper crews; give us blowups of the house and surroundings. You got a problem?"

Murch shook his head. "Man, you're something else." He looked as if he might cry.

"You asked for me." He was checking the order of battle. "The French have five Pumas; they're pretty ballsy—they picked those SAS guys out of Gorazde."

It turned out that Murch wasn't such a bad guy, after all: he said, "Don't ask the French." Alan stared at him. The French had been part of UNPROFOR, were now in IFOR, but a different sector. What was wrong? Murch dropped his voice to almost a whisper. "Just don't ask the French right now, okay?" The two intel officers looked at each other.

Problem—he means there's a problem. *Leak?*

"Gotcha."

While he was getting his materials together, Murch bent over the aerial photos. When Alan was ready to leave, Murch handed him one with grease-penciled circles. "There's two armored cars by a building down the road— has to be the police station. One's in the snow, no tracks around it, so I think it's down. Probably parts; the embargo's hurting them bad." Murch tapped the photo and Alan put it down and looked at it with the magnifier. "I think it's an AML, maybe French-made, but they've licensed countries all over the place. Old, but one of them's operational—look at all the tracks." Alan grunted. "Scout car configuration," Murch went on. "Just machine guns, no cannon—see the shadow?" Alan punched Murch on the shoulder. "We'll need a couple of shooters. Good catch." Murch, he decided, was a *really* okay guy. Just a little— let's use a polite word—*cautious*.

He went back up the mountain. The nineteen-year-old driver was beside himself. The gunner, hanging on the back, was not so delighted; he didn't even get to fire his weapon. Up on the mountain, the Italians were skeptical and the Kenyans wary, but Alan explained how it could be done and asked them to say yes. Two squads plus medics. "Plus me," the Kenyan surgeon said.

"And you?" the hawk-faced Italian captain said to Alan. It was a challenge. These guys were ready to dislike anybody.

"You want me?"

"I want you to believe in your intelligence. Enough to go along, I mean."

What had Suter said? He was going to keep Alan away from anything that even smelled like glory? He grinned. "Count me in. As an observer, of course." He didn't say that he might be risking a court-martial.

31

The Kenyans and the Italians looked at each other.

"When?"

Alan thought about his own orders, about how long it would take Suter to figure something out. "Soon," he said.

The Italian officer murmured, "If I give my colonel time to hear about it before we do it, well—"

The Kenyan surgeon said, "Tomorrow."

"Tomorrow dawn," Alan said.

The three of them looked at each other. They shook hands. He turned the problem of the helos over to the Italian captain and went back to the Kenyan hospital and spent time interviewing the civilians, getting as much hard data as he could on the house in Pustarla. Murch would be putting together a route, he hoped; he should have the latest data on Serb positions and air defenses. Alan's belief from shipboard intel was that there was no air defense, but out in the Med he hadn't paid a lot of attention to this hate-filled line where Bosnian Muslims and Bosnian Serbs were supposed to divide themselves, and people who happened to be in the minority on either side were being terrorized.

Then he went down the mountain again and used Murch's computer to write a report on suspected war crimes and criminals in the Bosnian-Serb Pustarla region, pulling in this and that from Intelnet, creating a nice little package of the kind that admirals liked to be briefed from— maps, pretty pictures, juicy quotes from victims. Murch had marked out a route and made a real briefing packet he could use with the troops. He was liking Murch again.

"You got a journalist in your pocket?" he asked Murch.

"Are you wacko? Jesus, Craik— !"

"Wassamattayou? You never heard of PR? Nothing covers your ass like a news report, Murch."

"Suppose this bombs out?"

Alan had thought about that. "If you've got a journalist in your pocket, it'll come out as a victory no matter what. I'll get some color photos for him, give him the story, exclusive. He'll kiss my ass if I ask him to. Yes or no?"

"My boss—"

"Fuck your boss! Yes or no? If the story is out quick, nobody will dare bitch. 'Brave UNPROFOR Forces Score One for Humanity!' Come on!"

Murch rubbed his jaw. "There's a Brit named Gibb, he's okay, he—"

"Tell him to be at my Humvee in ten minutes. He can watch the prep and he can be there when it's over, first to interview the brave troops and all that crap. He cannot go along. I'm outa here."

Then he went back up the mountain, the journalist Gibb laughing nervously as the Humvee spun mud and gravel into the black gulf at the edge of the road. Gibb was on something, might have been a better companion if he hadn't been, but Alan suspected the man was strung out like everybody else, thought he needed help—whatever gets you through the night. Alan left him in the Kenyans' civilian ward. He spent half an hour with the hawk-faced captain and the Kenyan surgeon and a cluster of men in battle dress, planning. It was going to be kept simple, except nothing involving death is ever simple. The captain was unhappy about the armored vehicle but didn't want to use anti-tank rockets—they had old Canadian Hellers—which he thought might go right through the meager armor without exploding. He was taking bullet-trap grenade launchers with HEAT, instead. Alan frowned when he heard but muttered, "Well, it's your call." Except that he would be there, too.

Two Ukrainian Mi-26s "diverted" from Zagreb would

come in at 0300, and Alan would brief their crews. Off at 0445. Seven hours from now.

He slept.

When he woke, he reached for Rose and murmured her name. His hand felt the grit of the floor and he remembered where he was, a cot in the company office. Through the door, he could see men in flight suits and hear their talk, all charged up. The chopper crews. He had slept right through their arrival. Sitting up, he felt how tired he really was, and he thought, *This isn't a good idea. I'm wiped.* But it was too late.

He put his wallet and his tags in his pack, checked himself for anything that would show he was American. His watch. His wedding ring; it came off hard, and he sucked the knuckle and got it off with the spit. Reluctantly, he put the Browning in the bag; he wanted to carry it, but it had been his father's and had personal engraving on it. Even his skivvies, which had a label. Then he dressed from the skin out in stuff the Italians had given him. No rank marks. This is really stupid, he thought. He pushed the pack toward the Italian captain. "If something happens— I'm anonymous. My people will figure it out." He wrote a couple of lines to Rose and stuffed the paper in the pack and pushed away the thought of what she would say if she could see him. Then he was on.

"It's a short trip, gentlemen—ten miles in, ten out. I figure six minutes' flying time each way, including diversion. The target is a house in a village called Pustarla, just one street and a few houses around it. Problem: there's deep snow everywhere. Roads around the place took a week to get plowed, then some of it was done with horses— we got aerial photos. Only two sure places to put down a chopper, the town soccer field, which I've marked Bravo, and this smaller place marked Alpha, which is cleared—

for a helo, we think, but the helo wasn't there yesterday. We believe no land mines. It's a hundred meters from the target; the soccer field is close to four hundred. The village street is a mess—ruts, ice, high banks. The police station is three hundred meters farther along; there should be ten to twelve guys there, well armed, capable. Respect them! They've got two armored cars, one probably inoperable because it hasn't been dug out of the snow.

"We're going in to Alpha as our primary landing zone; Bravo is backup and will be where the helos go if there's trouble while the troops are at the target. That would leave us four hundred meters to cover on foot to get out." He didn't like that part. Four hundred meters could be a long way in snow.

"If the Yugoslavs scramble aircraft, they're only fourteen minutes away. However, if they do that they're going to get pasted." Deny Flight was still on under a different name, the pilots impatient because nothing much was happening in deep winter. The F-16s and F-18s, Jaguars, Hornets, Tornados, and Fighting Falcons of several countries would love it if the Serbs scrambled so much as a flying chicken.

The Ukrainian choppers had come with crews and their own ground defense, two tough guys each with squad weapons. Alan made sure there would be room for prisoners and material coming back, double-checked with the Kenyans and the Italian ground troops. It would be tight: the Kenyans had insisted on sending two medics per helo; they wanted in on the action. The Italians were sending twenty altogether, two teams they had decided to call Romulus and Remus. Oh, shit, why not? Gagliano had told him that the Dutch had a mortar unit up the hill that was itching to put stuff over the border if the militia there made a move; the Canadians would have two electronics surveillance F-16s in the air, with the new

US Air Force operation at Tuzla on alert. Certain shrugs, looks, and evasions suggested that the operation had been put together the way crucial spare parts were sometimes got—what was called "moonlight acquisition."

"Captain Gagliano will brief you on the operation itself. I want to remind everybody—everybody—of what we're after: intelligence. One, prisoners; two, electronics—computer stuff, direct links, comm, anything; three, records, including photos. We're going to go in, grab what we can, and get out. If we have to shoot up somebody who happens to be a war criminal—" He looked around. "Sending messages is part of intelligence, too. I don't object to sending a message." Somebody guffawed.

Translations were going on all over the tent. The Kenyans and Italians had already got together with the Ukrainians, and they'd cobbled up some kind of signal system, with somebody who could speak English on each team. Still, it would be hairy, he thought. Speed, they had to emphasize speed. Surprise and speed, and baling wire and spit.

The big helos pounded south from the takeoff, seeming for three minutes to be heading back toward Srebnik, as if they might be taking hospital cases out. Then they cut sharply east, then east and north, two hundred feet off the deck. It was still dark, but the first light made the eastern horizon visible. The chopper interior smelled of metal and hot oil and sweat. Somebody passed gas, not helping matters at all.

"Four minutes."

The word went along the helo, *quattro minuti, quattro minuti*.

Alan was in the second helo with the Kenyan surgeon and the hit team, Remus. Gagliano was in the lead aircraft with the Romulus team, which would protect against the police. They had two shooters with shoulder-fired antitank weapons, at least one guy with a rotating rocket grenade launcher. If things went right, Romulus would already be on the street when Alan's helo touched down.

Thirty seconds on the street, he thought, forty-five max if the ruts are bad. How long did it really take you to trot a hundred meters in full battle gear? He shifted uneasily. The Italian body armor felt strange; so did the helmet. NATO gear, but not quite right, somehow. He was too thin for the body armor. He had a 9mm Beretta in a holster, a weapon he'd never liked as well as the Browning. Different safety, different trigger pull. If he had to use it, it would be in close, fast. Not good with an unfamiliar gun. What was he doing here, anyway?

"One minute." *Uno minuto, uno minuto* . . .

He would be among the last out, only the Kenyans behind him, then the Ukrainian rangers who would stay with the chopper. He put his hand on the buckle, ready to unstrap. Where were his gloves? On his hands, of course. It was cold out there. Strange weapon, gloves, Christ—

"Thirty seconds." *Trenta secondi*—

"*Avanti!*"

He watched the Italians bail out; they emptied the chopper like apples coming out of a basket. Alan jumped into the dark after them and hit the snow running, staggered, felt somebody hit him from behind, and he was up and following the dark line of figures ahead of him. They weren't trotting, they were sprinting, or so it seemed. Somebody passed him, too eager. He whispered, "No—" It must be the Kenyan medics. "*Polepole, polepole*—" But they surged ahead of him. Only Doctor wa Danio back there now, floundering a little in the snow.

They came out into the village street. It felt like a tunnel, the snowpiles high on each side, thrown up there with shovels, tree limbs overhead like fingers, then charcoal sky. It was lighter in the east, noticeably so now. Faint lights showed in a few of the houses, maybe not even electric, but they were mostly blocked by the snowbanks. He slipped in a frozen rut and almost went down; ahead of him, the Italians were sliding, lurching. His feet made loud crunching noises, like the other feet, all out of step as he'd briefed them so there would be no pounding rhythm. Otherwise, it was silent. Not a tunnel but a tomb. A tomb with running men, running figures that would have been dark shadows moving through their town if anybody had seen them. Ghosts in NVGs.

A cow was walking down the other side of the road. Its breath came out in steamy puffs. Suddenly, it frisked to the side, stood splay-legged, staring at them. It jumped again, then tried to run back up the street, sliding.

He was hyperventilating now. Only a hundred meters, and he was puffing as if he was running the mile. Too fast, too fast, he thought. He didn't dare look at his watch, fearful he might fall. Then he was at the driveway that ran up to the house, which had been somebody's pride once, a sign of some kind of wealth in this pitiful place. The house stood back among some scruffy trees that were only big enough to make a chopper landing there impossible; it had a low wall around it, the remains of gate pillars, all visible on the aerial photography. Gagliano's team were already spread along the cover of the wall, the two shooters out where they could get at the armored car if it came.

He turned into the drive. No lights showed in the house. They still had surprise. They had wanted to cut off the house's communications, but it had a spindly radio tower on the roof and there was no getting at it easily. They were just going to go in, and the hell with it. Somebody up there had plastique, if they needed it.

As Alan got close, he saw the crouching figures, weapons ready, and two more, only shapes to him, near the house, moving nearer. Several had already put up their night-vision goggles. The two closest to the house would be the sergeant and his partner, he thought. They were to try the door, place the plastique if they had to. If they could go in, they would, stun grenades ready; four more men behind them. The hope was to invade the house before any defense could be laid on. That was the hope.

Alan flopped into the snow facing the door. The Beretta was in his hand. When had he done that? He held his breath. What were they doing up there? The sergeant and his partner had disappeared into a little portico, like something on a cuckoo clock, with a little peaked roof. Alan could see nothing, then made out one of them bent over or kneeling. What the hell was he doing, looking through the keyhole?

The man stood up. "*Aperto*," he whispered. Open. Jesus, the front door was open. Just like a small town anywhere.

The four men got up, ready to go, and there was movement in the portico and suddenly it looked different, blacker, the door open, and the silent figures rushed forward. He wanted to go in. He looked at his watch, couldn't find it because of the heavy glove. The hell with it. It couldn't have been more than a couple of minutes. Surely not. Yet—

A shot boomed from the house. Everybody on the snow tensed; you could hear nylon rustle, a piece of ice crumble. Then hell broke loose, brief hell, loud hell: shots in quick succession, too many to count, and the thud of a stun grenade, the flash in an upstairs window as well as the doorway. A voice. Then somebody screaming, the words not Italian, not one of his. Then he was up and running for the door, and somebody was reaching back for him, hand on his arm, *"Tenente, subito, subito—"* Quick, quick.

"Lights!" he bellowed in Italian. Speed was more important now than invisibility. A flashlight bounced off painted walls, some godawful blue; then a light came on in a corridor beyond, and he was being waved in. Overhead, feet pounded and doors banged, and automatic fire started somewhere outside, maybe the outbuilding in back, somebody hosing. The screamer dropped to a lower key and gurgled, and the Kenyan medics were already inside and headed up a stairway to Alan's left. He shoved ahead, was aware of more shots outside, prayed it wasn't the armored car already but the other building, the torture place. Ahead were bare rooms, what had been some sort of dining room, now an office. He saw two wooden desks, several chairs; a bare overhead bulb threw a sickly light, hardly more than a wash of yellow-gray.

"Get the computer!" he shouted. One of the Italians started to wrestle with the monitor, and Alan pushed the man's hands away, tore out the cords and gave him the computer itself. He didn't know the words for keyboard or monitor. "Only this!" he shouted. The man passed it to somebody else. Alan raced around the room, opening drawers, dumping files. There was a fax machine. Could they take it? Would there be anything worth saving on it? No, he decided, too bulky, must have been the first one ever made, huge. He shoved papers into a pile with his feet, and somebody began to stuff them into a pack. He added notebooks, a weird kind of rolodex, a card file. Then he stood in the middle of the room, for just an instant paralyzed, unable to think. Too much stuff, no way to sort it out. Couldn't read it, didn't know the language—what the hell—

"Tenente?"

The sergeant was framed by an archway, dark wood with things like spools sticking down all the way around. He had a civilian, hands held behind (plastic cuffs; they'd begged them from the MPs). The man was in pajamas, barefoot. Alan made a savage gesture. "Take him!"

"All of them?"

"How many?"

"Three. Sleeping upstairs. One is—" He made a gesture.

"Take them, take them—they can help carry this shit. What's upstairs?"

"Bedrooms. Nothing."

Alan grabbed a flashlight and sprinted up. The stairs went like a square corkscrew, up-turn, up-turn, up-turn. There were heavy doors everywhere, all open. The grenade had left burn marks and the place stank, and smoke drifted in the flashlight beam with dust. He went along, shining the light into each room, the Beretta ready but feeling awkward and too big, sliding the light around the door and then looking. The sergeant had been right; there seemed to be nothing. Graffiti, old magazines, a girl's photo, clothes. Not military, these people. He had done five of the rooms when he flashed the light in one and something pinged and he swept the light back, not knowing what it had been, a shape or a sign, what? And the light showed another anonymous room, this one seeming unused, even austere. But something—

An ashtray. He went in and shone the light down into it. Big, plastic, empty. Wiped clean. Around the edge, "Chicago Bears Football."

Small world. That's what had caught him, something out of place that had put little hooks into his consciousness, like burrs catching a sweater. Chicago Bears Football. Here?

He picked it up with the hand that held the Beretta and with the other swept the light over the walls. Nothing. Yes,

41

something. A color photograph, held to the old wallpaper with transparent tape. He went close and looked at it. Was it anything? A man in camos with an assault rifle raised above his head, standing over what Alan was pretty sure was a corpse. Something written on the too-blue sky with a felt pen, Cyrillic and unreadable. Alan peeled it from the wall and started to stuff it into his jacket, and he saw color on the back as well, another photo, female and nude and—

He saw the movement before he heard the man, and he ducked and swung the light and glimpsed a broad, dark face, contorted by the flinch that meant he was in the act of firing. Alan had time to think that the man was half-dressed and therefore cold, somebody who had been in the house and had managed to hide, and he kept the light moving, meaning to blind the man but in fact giving him something to shoot at. Better for the man if he had been an inexperienced shooter, but he wasn't; he knew enough to aim, and habit makes you aim at what you can see. He had a nine-millimeter CZ that sounded louder than the grenade and made a flash that blinded them both. Alan shot on instinct, on terror, not sure he hadn't yelped. He was slow because of the strange pistol, wrong size, too heavy goddamit take forever to point! But the man was only five feet away. Tap-tap, tap-tap. Four sounds running into two like more grenades, flashes of fire, blood and bone on the wall, the smell of copper and gunfire. Alan reacted away, stepping to the side, moving the light away so he wouldn't be a target; he knew the other man was down, and his ears were dead to sound from the shots, his eyes dazzled, but he knew he had heard something, seen something else out there—a second man?

His heart was thudding. He raised the Beretta again, and suddenly the corridor was bathed in light, astonishingly bright and white to his dark-accustomed eyes.

One of the helos had put on its searchlight. *Why now?* he had time to think, realizing that the light must be moving over the house but registering at the same time a shadow on the corridor wall, then knowing that the light was coming through a window of the room beyond and catching another figure, because what Alan saw was like a hand clutching at the back of his neck. The shadow not human, distorted by the angle, but there was something wrong with it, anyway; impressions cascaded down his consciousness: *kid's game*, the shadows you make with your fingers on the wall, a rabbit, an owl, but this one something bad; then *witch, Halloween mask* and he couldn't figure it out, something primitive whispered *evil* and then the shadow was moving and the light was swinging away, getting watery and fading, and Alan moved to reach the doorway at the side, to put only his hand and an eye out where the bullets would come.

He doused the light and stepped forward, swaying, his balance suddenly all wrong, crashed against the side of the doorway and saw movement. He ducked low and fired, knowing he'd miss because he couldn't see. Flash and roar and then an answering flash from the corridor, something smaller (a .32 or some goddam thing like a Makorov), and he was trying to get the light on again, his hand suddenly slippery, rotating the flashlight to try to find the rubber button, and it came on, and he saw a face, a large, ferocious face, fired, and it was gone. Down low now, he brought the Beretta around and squeezed, and a window exploded outward as somebody jumped through it.

Alan straightened up. Something was very wrong with his left side. He slipped, knowing he'd slipped in the blood of the downed man, tried to run along the corridor and got to the smashed window bent over and leaning against the wall. Thinking, What kind of maniac goes through a window, taking out the frame and cutting the shit out of himself—? and flashing the light down and getting an immediate gunshot flash from below. He doused the light. His eyes were still dazzled. Below and thirty feet away, somebody was leaping over the snow, and Alan had time only to see that the man was naked and barefoot before the figure disappeared behind the old smokehouse that Alan had labeled "possible crematorium" on the aerial photo. He fired two double-taps and shouted for the sergeant.

Where the hell was everybody? He started back down the corridor, bellowing for the sergeant, and almost fell over the man he'd shot, and he thought *The nose, there was something wrong with the nose in the shadow, that's why I thought it was a witch.*

Alan shone the light on the downed man. His own hand was shaking; he could feel sweat on his ribs, jelly in his knees. And pain in his left side. The fucker had hit him, maybe got off a second shot. The body armor had saved him, but he had a hell of a pain.

The man was on his back. Bubbles of blood were coming up. His eyes were open, and Alan felt that the eyes were staring at him, right through the glare of the flashlight.

"Medic!" he shouted.

"*Tenente!* You okay?" The sergeant was at the far end of the corridor, assault rifle at the ready.

"Somebody went out the window! Get after him! Now!"

The sergeant shouted, and Alan could feel more than hear feet pounding downstairs.

"I've got a man down," Alan said, shining the light downward.

"One of ours?"

"Theirs."

"Leave him!"

Shit. Alan inhaled sharply, realizing he'd been holding

his breath; the sound shuddered in his chest. He kicked the man's gun down the corridor and swung the light off him, as if not seeing him made it better.

They had the downstairs almost cleaned out, what little they could take. The sergeant had taken charge, using some system of his own to determine what to take, what to leave. Probably weight. Alan checked his watch. Nine minutes since touchdown. Christ, it seemed like all night.

"You all right, *Tenente*?"

"You guys missed two of them up there."

"They're after the one in the snow, but I told them, no pursuit." The sergeant was a hard nut. He was more concerned about his men than about Alan's lost war criminal. Good for him.

"The guy's naked—in the snow!"

The sergeant nodded as if he had known that all along. "They want you in back," he said. "Then we go." He was old for a soldier, probably ready to retire; he wasn't taking any shit from an American intel officer. A Navy intel officer at that, for Christ's sake.

The other building had been a cow barn. A few of the stanchions were still there in a row down the left side. The walls were stone, laid up without concrete, the floor, a couple of feet below ground level, mostly dirt with a cracked concrete apron at the front end. Three bodies were laid out on the concrete now, all civilians. There seemed to be far too much blood for only three men, but three was all he could see. There was an under-smell of old cow, on top of that fresh blood, and then shit.

"They tried to shoot it out. One was awake somehow; one of our guys took a hit, he's not bad. We took out two people. Not in very good shape." The soldier looked sideways at him. "Really messed up."

45

"Torture?"

The soldier nodded. Alan walked down the room, smelled vomit. He already felt sick, was still hyperventilating. There was old blood on the walls down here, probably a lot more soaked into the dirt floor. The stanchions had been used as human restraints, with handcuffs locked to them high and low. At the end of the room was a single chair by itself, almost centered. It looked like a set for a minimalist play. Against the wall was a big washtub, half full of reddened water, a lot of water splashed out on the floor. Ropes and a steel bar, once some sort of tool, hung from the ceiling beam.

"The airplane," he said. A form of torture.

"They'd cut the eyelids off one guy, then shot him. The doctor doesn't think he'll make it."

Alan got out the point-and-shoot camera and pointed and shot. He felt he was going to throw up. Partly it was almost getting killed, partly it was what he was doing, seeing. And the pain in his side. His hands were shaking so hard he had trouble pointing the camera.

"Tenente! Time to go!"

He ran back to the house and took three photos of the interior. Maybe the newsman could do something with them. He didn't go back upstairs.

Something boomed. He doused his flashlight and started out the front door. The sergeant grabbed his arm, pulled him down. "Police armored car. They're coming up the street."

Alan looked around. It was almost light. There was the sergeant, three soldiers. Him. Flames turned the snow pink, the torture barn on fire.

"Everybody else out?"

The sergeant nodded.

"Go?"

The sergeant pointed, got up. They ran for the gate. One man stayed behind, threw something in the door—*thud*—and the place went up in flames.

A big double boom sounded from the street, probably both shooters at once; flame snicked up through the tree branches like a tongue, then seemed to expand at the bottom, beyond the wall. He was aware of more general firing, faraway pop-pops and louder, more deliberate noise nearby. At the gate, the sergeant thrust out an arm like a traffic cop and held him back, looked, then grabbed him and pushed him in the direction of the choppers. Alan resented it, resented the rough handling and the implication that he didn't belong there, but he knew the sergeant was right. Anyway, bullets were whiffling near him. He got down. Captain Gagliano and half his Romulus team were trading fire with somebody down the street—quite a way down the street, well beyond the burning armored car. The other way, the rest of Romulus waited to cover the withdrawal. On the other side of the street, several bodies lay in the snow. Serb militia, from the town. One man was in striped pajamas. The sergeant waved an impatient hand at him and Alan began to run. The waiting soldiers got bigger, bigger, and then they, too, were passing him backward through their line, as if he was not quite their main concern just then and they just wanted to make sure he was out of the line of fire . . .

He hunched his shoulders and ran for the helos.

The temperature in the big tent must have been close to eighty Fahrenheit despite the cold outside. It wasn't the big propane heater but the press of bodies. Italians, Ukrainians, Kenyans, one American—even a couple of Dutch artillerists who had wandered down, although they hadn't had provocation enough to fire a shot. It was as noisy as a locker room after a winning game, and just about as smelly, although the over-riding smell was red wine, with some Kenyan cane splashed around the edges.

Feeling no pain, Alan thought. He certainly knew what that meant now. The surgeon had given him two capsules, would have given him four or maybe eight if he'd asked, and on top of that there was the wine. It wasn't what used to be called Dago Red, either, but Gattinara from a year long enough ago that the stuff didn't show up in shops any more. Courtesy of Captain Gagliano's colonel, who was shocked, shocked! to hear of what had happened (you had to be reminded of Claude Rains in *Casablanca*) but was so delighted he'd released a couple of cases from his own store. Flown in specially as soon as the message flashed that they were out with only three hit, no dead, and two helos full of goodies.

"Well, not exactly goodies," Alan was explaining slowly to Doctor wa Danio. He spoke with the exaggerated care of a man who has had too much wine, just enough painkiller, and not enough sleep. "We seem to have brought out two oversize sacks of Serb garbage." He leaned closer. "I am not speaking met-a-phor-i-cally. I mean actual garbage. Rinds and things." Along with some more useful stuff like names and addresses and computer disks.

Two Ukrainians were doing some sort of dance to music that sounded to Alan like Afro-pop, but he suspected that everything sounded like Afro-pop to him just then. He smiled at the Ukrainians. When he turned back to the Kenyan doctor to tell him how much the Ukrainians amused him, the doctor had been replaced by Captain Gagliano. Gagliano had a glass in one hand and Alan's neck in the other. "Did we biff them?" he said.

"We biffed them."

"We biffed them!" Gagliano nodded. "I hear you were hit."

"In the ribs."

"Nothing."

"They are my ribs."

"Ribs are nothing. I have one man shot in the neck. The neck is something. One in the arm. He may lose the arm. But your rib does not impress me." He kissed Alan's cheek. "What impresses me is you got us in and out and we biffed them." He leaned his head back and tried to focus. "You want an Italian medal?"

"You can't have too many medals."

The captain nodded. "Or too much wine. You want some wine?"

"I think—"

Then he was sitting on the floor and somebody was smiling at him, God knows why. He tried to get up, thought better of it, and sat there, grinning at the noise and the heat and the uproar. The combination allowed him to remember that he had killed a man, this time without feeling sick about it. Tap-tap, tap-tap. Bubbles of blood.

"Lieutenant?"

He looked up. Way up. A very tall, emaciated man in civilian clothes. The man folded himself into pieces and brought his head down to Alan's level and said, "You look for me, they say." He had a bony, almost skull-like face, and skin cratered by illness or acne long ago. "I am Marco. Translator?"

"Ah." Right. That made sense. But why? Aha. Translator, yes. Alan held up a finger. "*Momento*," he said, forgetting that Italian was not the language in question. Where had he put it? He patted himself, finally found it in the buttoned breast pocket of the Italian shirt he was wearing. Took it out with great care and unfolded it, presenting it to Marco

49

so that the slightly frivolous backside, showing incomplete but naked female parts, was hidden. It was the picture of the man in camos he'd taken from the bedroom in the house. "What's that say?" he asked. At least that was what he hoped he asked.

Marco squinted. "Says, 'Colonel Zulu at the Battle of the Crows.'"

"What's that mean? 'Battle of the Crows'?"

Marco scratched his ruined chin. "Aaah. Well. It's the Serbs, you see? The Battle of the Crows—hmm. Well." He sighed. "It happened six centuries ago, okay?"

That was not okay at all. That made no sense. What was this guy, drunk or something?

Detroit.
Radko Panic dropped his heavy coat on the floor, not even thinking, knowing she would hang it up later, if she knew what was good for her, and glanced out of habit at the crappy little table where she put the mail. Bills, junk, ripoffs, he expected, the same as always, but there was a package and his heart jumped. Even the fact that it was different was enough, but there was the color of it, too, and the feel of the paper under his fingers and the string that held it together. The old days. That rough brown paper, that hairy string—relics, he knew now, of a technology he had left behind when he had left the old places. The postmark was French, but he knew it did not come from France.

She had left his meal for him and he shoved it into the microwave and pushed buttons without thinking, his face split by a big grin. Rare, that grin. Really rare. He saw himself in the microwave window. He'd had a couple on the way home at the Rouge Tap; the grin, pasted on the microwave as if it belonged to the machine and not to him, was happy. Well, why not? A man deserved to be happy.

He took one of her knives and cut the string. He had surprisingly delicate hands for a big man, but he was a precision toolmaker, did things well, deftly, when he was sober. He slit the tape-shiny ends and slid out the box inside, made of a thin cardboard of the kind that used to come inside shirts. It too was held with tape, and he cut that and put her knife aside, thinking without thinking that the knife was getting dull and what the hell had she been doing with it, sharpening pencils again?

Inside was a photograph and something else. He slid the photo out. He left the something else, like the prize in a Crackerjack box. There had still been Crackerjack boxes when he had first come to America. He had loved them.

The photo, grainy and a little washed-out, showed a man in camo fatigues, one hand raised over his head, an automatic rifle in the raised hand. It was too fuzzy to see what kind of rifle it was. At the man's feet was something dark, a bundle, a pile, a—what?

He turned the photo over. Big, black letters said, "YOUR BOY AT THE BATTLE OF THE CROWS!!!!"

She came in behind him then; he heard her, didn't even turn, didn't speak. He grinned at the back of the photo. He had heard the expression "bursting with pride," knew now what it meant. He thought he was going to explode with it.

The microwave dinged and she said something and he grunted at her, and she got the food out and began to arrange it at the place she had already set for him. Her hair in some kind of thing, an old bathrobe clutched around her, her face gray, soft, lined, purple shadows under the eyes.

"Is it—from—?" She had had a sweet voice as a young

woman; now it was wispy. She was afraid of him. With good reason.

He thrust the photo at her. He sat down and picked up the fork and filled his mouth. Seeing her standing close by, he waved her away and she went over to the sink and held the photo up under the light.

He thrust another forkful into his mouth and then put a long finger down into the narrow box and took out the small thing that was in there. It made him grin again. It was a human eyelid.

2

February–April

The succession of naval fleets that guard the Mediterranean is like the turning of a great wheel. Always, at the top, is the fleet in place—one nuclear-powered aircraft carrier, most potent of the weapons in the world, on which the commanding admiral flies his flag; two guided-missile cruisers; destroyers and frigates and submarines; and, around and behind them, support and repair and fueling ships. These ships are six months on station—six months at the top of the wheel—with tenuous lines of communication to the land, to be sure, but alone at sea as ships have always been alone at sea. Then the wheel turns, and the battle group on station turns its bows and heads for the Pillars of Hercules, Gibraltar, and at the same time the fleet that has been forming and training on the east coast of the United States puts to sea and begins its voyage to the top of the wheel. The wheel turns, and the new fleet takes its place on station, and the old fleet goes into port at Norfolk, while another fleet trains and forms and readies itself to sail in six months more. And behind it, at the bottom of the wheel, another fleet exists as an idea and a skeletal organization; it will not sail for a year, but already its flag-rank commander is in place with his most important senior officers; the air squadrons that will deploy with the carriers are designated; ships and ships' companies know where they will be. And even as the wheel turns, other fleets exist, phantom or hypothetical fleets, ideas of fleets that will come into being in eighteen months or two years or five or ten. Other crisis areas, or areas of strategic interest, have their own wheels—Korea, for instance, or the Persian Gulf. Sometimes one area has several wheels.

The wheel turns, and forward into time the fleets move toward their place on the wheel and the six-month period for which they exist: the presence of a battle group in the Mediterranean Sea. It is a figure of life—of coming into being and of going; of being born, and of dying; of existing only as an idea of the future and as a memory of the past.

The battle groups come and go. It is the wheel that is important.

Vice-Admiral Richard Pilchard commanded Battle Group Four. Battle Group Four served off Bosnia, drilled holes in the Adriatic, had liberty in Trieste and Naples. They won no glory, but they held the line, and their aircraft sent a message. Now Battle Group Four is split back into its component ships, in Norfolk, Charleston, Mayport, and Newport.

Vice-Admiral Nathan Green commands Battle Group Five, now on station off Bosnia; it changed its name when it arrived on station and became Task Force 155. It has a NATO name, too, but most people will keep calling it Battle Group Five, or BG 5.

Vice-Admiral Richard Toricelli commands Battle Group Six, now training in the Norfolk area. Vice-Admiral Rudolph Newman will command Battle Group Seven and is organizing his staff. Vice-Admiral Harold Rehnquist will command Battle Group Eight but has only just received those orders and will not sail for almost eighteen months.

Alan Craik is the Assistant Carrier Air Wing Intelligence

Officer for BG 5, which is at the top of the wheel. On station. If not facing the animal, then at least very sensitive to its presence.

LCDR "Rafe" Rafehausen, now finishing a stint at the Naval War College, Newport, Rhode Island, will soon report to VS-49 as its executive officer. LTjg Christine Nixon has already reported aboard VS-49 at Cecil Field, Florida, after her first, abbreviated tour working counternarcotics in Key West, Florida, to become its intelligence officer. Seaman Apprentice Henry Sneesen, Aviation Electronics striker, has joined VS-49 direct from his A school and boot camp in Orlando, Florida. VS-49 itself has existed as an entity with airplanes and men and women to repair them, maintain them, fly them, and fight them for only two months, but 49's place on the wheel has existed for over a year. VS-49 is going to sea as the airborne antisubmarine squadron of an air wing assigned to USS *Andrew Jackson* in Battle Group Seven, commanded by Admiral Newman. And, like every battle group that the US Navy sends to sea, this one will endure wind and waves, merciless weather, stress, and danger, and not all of its members will return. But, unlike most, Battle Group Seven will have to fight.

Fort Reno, North Carolina.
Harry O'Neill was mad, and he had to piss so bad he could feel his bladder throbbing. He was doing a goddam stupid surveillance exercise, and he was still angry about last night's exercise, and he wasn't doing things very well. He hadn't checked this part of the route for johns when he did the prep, only telephones. Would it be a screwup if he stopped to piss? And what would he do if one of the instructors came into the john with him—maybe spoke to him, even challenged him?

"Shit," O'Neill muttered. He didn't say it with any force.

Last night still enraged him. He and a student partner had done a mock recruiting exercise, taking two instructors to dinner and pretending to make the first steps toward recruiting, pretending to have a cover and having to use the fake name and the fake ID and the fake profession. And what had been the instructor's summary of what O'Neill had done? What had the black instructor said about the black student?

"Not credible," he had said. Why? "Has to learn to dress." O'Neill felt outraged. He'd worn the clothes he'd been wearing for years! What was it—the Burberry blazer? the Willis and Geiger shirt? the Church shoes? What the fuck did he mean?

Then he had got to the last line of the evaluation and understood—a lot.

"I don't believe this put-on taste and 'class' in a black man."

Harry O'Neill had seen where his real problem lay.

So he had tried to take out his anger by writing a letter to Alan Craik. He could let Craik, alone among his white friends, see his bitterness. "I been dissed by what I'm sure this bastard would call 'one of my own people'!" he wrote. "I ain't NEEGGAH enuf fo him. This NEEGGAH is 2 stylish 4 him! Jesus Christ, Al, haven't these fuckheads ever seen a gentleman before?"

So now he was driving carefully down a road in Virginia, seething with rage and trying to do well in a surveillance exercise while keeping his bladder from exploding all over the rental car.

He wanted a john so bad he squirmed. He drummed on the steering wheel with his right hand and then jabbed the radio to turn off some sixties soft-rock crap and then jabbed it back on because the silence somehow made his bladder worse. He glanced into the left-side mirror and saw them still back there, the green Camaro with the two guys, nicely on his butt but hanging back. Where was the other one? And which was the other one—the red Saturn he'd seen twice with the dark-haired woman? Or the dark Cherokee with the older guy in the hat? "Shit," he muttered again.

Ahead was the two-lane road down to the ferry. There would be a line for the ferry, but it went every fifteen minutes, and he could get into line and then hit the head at the ticket office and get relief. Yes! Except that his plan was to take the left before the ferry and force the guys following him to declare themselves, both cars, and then when they had done that he could go one-point-three miles to the little hill with the sharp left on the far side, take the left and get out of sight before they came over the hill so that at least one would go straight. If he was lucky. (Luck is not a planning factor, the instructor had said, but it is useful.) No, they would go straight, because the road turned again and then twisted like a snake for a mile, so they'd think he was up ahead. (That was his alternative, to speed up and stay on the road and use the twists to get out of sight. He might do that. In fact, that had been his original plan. But, goddamit, there wasn't a phone with a john up there for six-point-two miles, and if he took the left there was one in point-seven!)

He swung left away from the ferry, trying not to feel his bladder as the road got rough, going deliberately slow so they wouldn't lose him, drawing them along. They must be made to think that losing him was their fault, not his. Then he would make his phone call and leave the message and be out of it.

Phone call first, he told himself. He groaned. He knew that the phone call had to be first. Even if his bladder burst. Duty calls. Ha-ha. Call of nature. Right.

The Camaro was right back there where it should be,

and then well behind it he could see another vehicle, dark-colored. Must be the Cherokee. Okay. Well, that was good, at least he knew who they were now.

He was chewing his tongue, a habit he'd got into since he got in this business. He'd never had nerves before. Now he chewed it almost viciously. The little hill was coming up, then the quick left. If the Camaro speeded up— ! But it didn't. It was okay. Distance was good, speed was good—

O'Neill went up the hill exactly right, wanting to gun it but keeping it just the same speed, not giving anything away (Nice job, O'Neill; thank you, sir, but I'd rather be pissing) and then, just over the crest, accelerated and hit the brake a tap as he jerked it left, a quick skid turn, and he was into the side road and swinging back right and out of sight, and he'd done it.

He'd done it! Nobody had followed him!

"Bladder, stick with me now!" he murmured, and he ripped the last seven-tenths to the convenience store he'd spotted three days before. There were two pump islands and a small parking area, and at the side a telephone he'd checked, and it had been working last time he came by. Please, God. He had the phonecard ready. He winced as he got out of the car and his bladder shifted, and he was sure he was walking bent over as he headed for the phone. God, if there was somebody there ahead of him, he'd crack! Some teenager, giggling and—

Nobody.

He was aware of movement behind. He swung his head, alert for one of the pursuers. No, an old guy in a blue Jimmy. Still, he waited, throbbing. Always be suspicious. The old guy got down. Flexed his knee. Bad leg. Come on! The old guy was wearing a tractor hat, which he now took off so he could rumple up his hair. He looked around. Stretched. Come on! Then he took out a lot of keys that were chained to his belt by something you could have docked the *QE2* with, and he selected a key with the care of a Baby Boomer selecting a blush wine, and at last he jerked the hose out of its cradle and jammed it down into his tank and began to pump. Whistling.

That was okay, then. O'Neill tried not to think of the gas running into the tank, the sound of liquid.

O'Neill leaned into the phone's transparent shelter and heard the dial tone. Inserted the phonecard. The call was to another area code; the numbers seemed to go on and on. Then the ringing. Two rings, hang up. Good. Wait. Don't think about pissing. Listen for the dial tone. Card. Area code. Number. Ringing. One, two, three, four—picked up. No voice.

"Seventeen," O'Neill said. "Yes." Oh, thank God! End of exercise.

He hung up, ready to run for the men's room—and the old guy from the pickup truck was standing there, about five feet from him. The old guy reached into his shirt pocket and pulled out a card and held it up. The card was black, otherwise blank, but O'Neill knew what it meant.

"Oh, shit."

"You left skid marks back at the turn," the old guy said. "C-minus."

O'Neill sagged. "You going to wash me out of the program?"

"That's not my decision. I'll say you did pretty good up to the last part."

O'Neill started to say something, and then his bladder really pulsed, and he said, "If I don't get to pee, I'll wet my pants."

"Oh, we would flunk you out for that." The old guy grinned. "Got to learn to carry a bottle, son." And, as if to prove that he was a mean old sonofabitch, he made a sound: "Pssssssss—"

O'Neill ran.

That evening, he learned that he had made the second cut, despite the low grade on the surveillance exercise. Three others hadn't—two young civilians who hadn't a clue and shouldn't have been there in the first place, and a marine captain whose flunkout was a real surprise. He seemed tough and smart to O'Neill, but he was out and Harry was still in. And Richmond had left on his own hook three days before. The class was shrinking.

Why him and not me? he wondered, thinking of the marine captain. *I stay, he goes. Makes no sense.* He found he wasn't entirely pleased that he hadn't been bounced. Relieved, yes. Ego-relieved. But deeper, no. He wasn't sure he belonged here.

After the posting of the flunk list, they'd put up for the first time a list of after-graduation assignments. The better you did, the better your chances of getting a good one two months from now when it was over. He had identified two he wanted, and he knew he would have a lot going for him in both because of his near-native French and his experience in-country. Paris and Marseille. Wow. You bet. Then all the others, Guatemala, Sri Lanka, Yugoslavia . . . Jesus, Yugoslavia! Surely nobody would send a black man to Yugoslavia!

Would they?

Near Nice, France.
The man called Zulu was riding in the back seat of a chauffeured Daimler and enjoying it. He liked the idea that other people envied him without knowing who he was, some wealthy man made invisible by tinted glass. He

was a little wound-up, not bad, nothing like before a fight or the other—a couple of black pills, pulling him up, then a silver to smooth him out. A civilian dose. He touched his sunglasses, which were very dark and very sleek, wrapped back around his temples like the windows of a jet (Bolle, expensive) and a further step toward invisibility. No, toward disguise. This made him smile, too. Zulu was forty and looked younger. A lot tougher than most men of forty. The disfigured nose was a badge of honor, and some women loved it.

The car purred through electronically operated gates that closed behind it, and it swung right and then curved widely left up a semi-circular drive. A man with a rake and a man with a two-way radio watched it; the man with the rake went back to work on a flowerbed, and the man with the radio murmured something and looked intensely serious.

Lascelles was waiting on a terrace. Lascelles was old, old enough that his face had started to show cross-furrows between other furrows, like the cracks in dried mud where a lake had once been. Lascelles had been a colonel, a mayor, a minister, and the real but invisible head of France's security apparatus. Until he had been forced out. Now he was an angry old man. Not to be underestimated, however. A dangerous, angry old man.

Zulu got out of the big car quickly, his hands just touching the front of his trousers as if he expected the edges of the door to be dirty, swinging his hips out as a woman does, sliding. Erect, he touched the sunglasses and checked his inner self. Was he just a little too high? No, just right. Not nervous. Zulu had not been nervous since he had got big enough not to fear his father's belt.

"You like the Daimler?" Lascelles said, shaking hands. Meaning nothing.

"Very nice."

"You picked a pleasant day." Lascelles's eyes flicked over the almost fresh cuts on Zulu's face, then flicked to his hands. Lascelles missed little. "Yesterday, we had rain. Cold!" Lascelles led him along the terrace, making these human sounds, although neither man was very human, smiling a little smile, as if it amused him to be leading this *creature*, this *thing*, this *gorille manqué* along his terrace. He had used all those terms to talk about the man they called Zulu. Not that he wasn't something of a creature himself.

"Everything is working all right?"

Zulu used silence for his answer. If everything was not all right, he would speak.

They went in through a door to a big, pleasant room full of soft colors like those on the terrace, fabrics with a sheen, a couple of good but unassertive oil paintings. The room did not smell quite right. "I have a task for you," Lascelles said once they were inside, as if in there it was safe to get serious.

"I need some things, too." Zulu reached into his jacket, took out a folded paper and handed over a computer-printed list of weapons.

"Well—" Lascelles sat, motioned toward an armchair. "Tit for tat. I have something I want you to do, fairly big." His face furrowed still more deeply. His head was round, bald, mottled brown. It drew back into his collar.

"My plate is full at home."

"Nonsense. They have this 'peace accord,' NATO have drawn a wavy line on the ground, you are all at peace." He laughed. "The Americans are putting their nose into something and I need to slice the end off. That will not offend your sensibilities, I think?"

"You know what I think of them."

"Exactly." Lascelles went off on a rant that Zulu had heard before, on and on—moral decay, the Jews, Brussels,

NATO, the UN. *Etcetera, etcetera, etcetera,* Zulu said to himself, his thoughts invisible behind his tinted glasses, although he had his own reasons for hating NATO and the UN.

"I am an exile in my own country," Lascelles was saying. "I! An honorable exile! A patriot!" His face was red. Like all the French of a certain kind, the ghost of Napoleon always hovered close by him. "The current government of France is deeply unpatriotic, completely subverted by the world state!"

"What do you want me to do?" Zulu said, letting his impatience show.

"Africa," Lascelles said.

"Africa, oh, shit— Not again!"

Lascelles leaned forward. "The UN patched together some of their internationalist crap and stopped the Rwandan genocide before a satisfactory conclusion was reached. That's how they work, to put their army in place. Now they are setting up subversion centers all over that part of Africa. The Americans have satellites up above there, too. Hand in glove. But central Africa is *French* territory. It has always been French territory. One cannot be soft about such matters. One must be *hard*. Whatever one's humanitarian feelings, one must be hard. For the greater good."

"Absolutely."

"The UN and the Americans must be driven out of central Africa. I will put Africa back together later, after the threat is finished. They will welcome me, you will see. I—we— have old friends there, old clients, I need only speak a word—" His eyes narrowed. "*Mobutu!*" he whispered. "Very powerful. Very rich. Absolutely my client."

"Oh, God, Africa." Zulu rolled his head on the back of the couch. One day in and out, shooting down that airliner, that had been all right. Once in a way, it was all right. Still, he needed weapons. And his war in Bosnia

63

was on hold. "NATO-compatible weapons this time. No old Russian stuff, Lascelles."

"Yes, yes, yes— !" Lascelles waved the list. "I don't do these things *myself.*" He sounded whiny, at the same time arrogant. *I give it to some underling,* he meant. Arms dealing was a detail, he meant. "You will get your weapons."

"Soon, it has to be soon, or no deal. To go to *Africa,* you know—"

Lascelles's eyes looked shrewd. Like a child saying a naughty word, he said, "One of your centers in the Serbian zone got knocked over, I heard, is that what I heard?" His eyes flicked over Zulu's face and hands again. "You were there?"

Zulu made a face. "A little one, nothing." It definitely had been more than nothing, but he wouldn't admit it to this old spider; it had outraged him, some bunch of shitkickers from UNPROFOR driving him out of one of his own places. Forcing him to jump through a fuck-ing *window* with some American shithead shooting at him! The amphetamines pushed his anger up and he almost let it show, but he brought himself down, stayed quiet. Pretended to deal with it. "Pustarla, big deal— ! The fucking UN!" He flexed his right knee and felt the pain of the long gash he had got, jumping through that window.

"Internationalism!" Lascelles cried. "You see? You see? *It's all part of their plan!*"

Zulu didn't in fact see. He didn't care a dog's fart about internationalism. He believed that Greater Serbia could exist in and of itself, separate from the world, above the world. When they had exterminated the Muslims, when the Croats were subdued, when Greater Serbia was a clean and pure state, then they would close their borders and be themselves. To hell with the UN and the US, was his view.

To hell with Europe. And fuck France. But, just now, he needed Lascelles.

"What do I have to do in Africa?" Zulu said.

"For now, go back to Serbia and select good men. Say two companies. Elite. Then I will need to send you down there to start things, and if it really explodes, I will need you and your men there perhaps for a month. White troops go through Africans like a hot knife."

"Money?" Zulu said shrewdly. "White men get good money to fight in Africa."

Lascelles's furrows folded in on themselves a little, as if he were pulling into himself. This was his version of a smile. "France will be fair."

He meant that *he* would be fair, but he thought of himself as France.

He put his head back, closed his eyes. The meeting was over.

Zulu waited a few seconds to show that he couldn't be dismissed like a flunkey, but Lascelles ignored him, and he got up and put on his sunglasses and went out to the terrace. As soon as he got out there, the air was sweeter. The odd smell inside was Lascelles.

Zulu went down the terrace, thinking about his war and the loss of the place in Pustarla. *Him*, the commander, being forced to go out a window and run through the snow like a naked girl. Some goddamned American shooting at him— he'd heard the voice, knew that accent all too well. Rage surged up again and he let it go this time. Rage was good for him, he believed, a rush like a drug. He could do a lot on rage. *Africa*. For a little while, maybe, while things were quiet back home, until the "peace accord" fell apart. But he had to *stay focused*. Not get sidetracked by Lascelles's adventures in Africa. A means to an end. There was no rage for him in Africa. *The American who forced him out that*

65

window. Yes, he felt rage about that. *Greater Serbia*. Yes, there was rage. The fucking Muslims, the goddam Croats. Lice. Vermin. *Things*. Rage. Rage.

The Med, aboard USS *Jefferson*.

Alan had Ensign Baronik working on the squadron IOs brief, the intel specialists prepping the visuals, and his senior chief cruising the ASW spaces in case there was any chance of running anything against a real target. He felt a pang of envy for the guys who would do it if he found anything. Alan had been a pretty good back seat not so long ago, and he'd run a line on a Russian sub that had almost got his S-3B goosed with the periscope when it had surfaced. Great days. Great for a young man, anyway. Now, he was a senior lieutenant, about to become an acting CAG AI, in—he checked his watch—six hours and thirty-nine minutes.

Because LCDR Suter was leaving.

Leaving his IO's post, leaving the ship, leaving the Navy. To take "something better," he'd said with that sneer-smile he used, as if the something better was *really* better, and none of you merely mortal shmucks would understand how much better. Resigning usually took six months to a year.

Alan's guess was that Suter had had a greatly accelerated resignation because somebody out there, somebody with real clout, wanted him enough to twist arms.

The raid on the torture center in the Serbian zone seemed like a distant memory now, except for flashes of the man he had shot and of that shadow on the wall—the witch. Or gargoyle. Or whatever that had been. And the name *Zulu*, which had been on the photograph and which the men who had been tortured there had spoken with fear.

He had got some medals out of it, for what that was

worth—one from the Italians that said *Coraggio e onore,* and a letter from the Canadians, commending him for "extraordinary efforts in intelligence support and acquisition." The Kenyans had been downright embarrassing ("glorious achievements to enhance our medical work under the banner of the United Nations").

Had he done well? Had it meant anything, that dawn raid? Men had died; he had killed—what had it accomplished? They had saved two men from more torture, he supposed. One of the victims they'd brought out had had a fractured sinus, wa Danio had said, a broken nose and broken teeth, three broken ribs where they had kicked the water out of him. One had died. One of the bodies had had both eyelids cut away. And for what? Nobody seemed to know. For being young and Muslim. When he thought of the man who had had his eyelids cut off, Alan thought, *How can a human being do that?* and then he felt a revulsion and anger that gave the Bosnian raid a bad taste.

He had tried to write to a friend who was a Navy cop, Mike Dukas, about it. *What kind of people do these things?* Maybe a cop would understand. *Mike, it's you guys they need there, not me. They need law.* Was that what peacekeeping was?

Now, back on the boat, Alan was going down the list of classified pubs for which Suter was responsible, because Suter was leaving and had to sign off on the classified pubs in his care. The list had already been done and checked by Suter himself, but Alan knew that Suter would screw him somehow if he could. So on and on he went, Alan sinking lower and lower in his chair, until, as he had feared, he found two titles that had been checked off by Suter but that in fact couldn't be found. Alan wrote a memo and put it in the folder, and then he indicated the missing two as unaccounted for on Suter's sign-over receipt, initialed the two, signed "with exceptions as noted," and sent the pages off to Suter. Another stack arrived shortly after.

Suter put his head in at 1717. "I'm out of here in a half-hour."

Alan went on signing.

"I hear you found two docs missing."

"Yes, sir."

"They were there this morning when I did them."

"They're not there now."

"You know they'll turn up."

"Yep." He went on signing. "I'm sure that right now they're under somebody's rack, and when we do a final fore-and-aft sweep before hitting the beach, they'll come out on the end of a broom and we'll get them back." Scrawl, flap.

"Why not just sign off for them now, then?"

"Because they're not in my possession, and that's what I have to sign for." He looked up, grinned. "It's the law."

"You know, Craik, you're the most arrogant cocksucker I've ever had to serve with." He sounded almost genial.

Alan finished signing and pushed the orders across the desk. Later, he would wish he had thought to say, *Clearly, I don't have your experience with cocksuckers*, but he didn't. "You'll miss your flight if you don't hurry, sir," is what he said.

Suter stared into his face, Alan into his. Finally, Suter uncrossed his arms, picked up the orders, and straightened. "Jesus, I'm glad I'm leaving the Navy," he said. He started out. "I hope you fall on your ass trying to do my job, Craik."

Alan stopped by the mail slots and found a letter from his wife, which he read in the quiet of the maintenance office, with Senior Chief Prue thoughtfully giving him some space.

Everything was good at home—Mikey was growing like a weed; the dog had eaten part of a sweater Rose's mother had knitted specially; Rose thought she had a line on a great posting for her next tour, some project called Peacemaker. He headed for a briefing with a grin on his face.

Near Atlanta, Georgia.

Mike Dukas was thoroughly pissed. He had just taken part in a bust that was supposed to be a big coup for the FBI and his own agency, the Naval Criminal Investigative Service, and all they had got was an empty house, five hours of tedium, and a U-Haul full of computers and computer disks. Never mind that the disks were loaded with pornography; nobody knew that yet, and, anyway, the porn wouldn't have any significance to him for months.

And it was all Alan Craik's fault. No, be honest; not Craik's fault—*his* fault, his, Mike Dukas's. It was the frayed end of an old operation that had started with Al Craik years before, and Dukas couldn't let go of it. In part because he was nuts about Craik's wife. And thought of Craik himself as a very, very close friend.

Oh shit. Dukas felt lousy. A day wasted, and for what?

He sat in his rental car and thought about driving to the airport and waiting for the plane and flying back to DC and having nothing to report. What was he accomplishing, anyway? And what waited for him at home—three AWOL sailors, five domestic disputes, two incidents of racial hatred? This was what a Navy cop did?

So he took from his pocket a letter he had just got from Craik and read it over again, and he was envious. It was all about some raid Craik had been on in Bosnia, shooting and everything. Helos! Grenades! Prisoners! And what the hell was Dukas doing? Sitting on his ass in a rental car and mooning over a busted operation.

And a line that went right to the heart. *Mike, it's you guys they need there, not me. They need law.*

It was like an order from a friend: *Get involved.*

But how?

Well, he was a cop—a Navy cop, sure, but a cop. They must need good cops in Bosnia. They must have criminals. War criminals. Hey, there was an idea. Catching war criminals—what could be a more honorable duty for a cop than that?

War criminals. Now, who was hiring cops to go after war criminals?

He started the car. The UN. No, it wasn't the UN who went after war criminals; it was the World Court. Somebody he knew must know somebody over there. Somebody—

Langley, Virginia.

At CIA headquarters, a man who disliked Alan Craik as fiercely as Dukas and O'Neill liked him was, for a moment, thinking about Alan. His mind flicked over the subject of the young naval officer on its way somewhere else— flicked, felt distaste, moved on. Alan Craik was one of his failures: he'd tried to recruit Craik, had told him only a little lie, and Craik had gone all moral on him and humiliated him. The little shit.

George Shreed leaned on his stainless steel canes, looking down from the window of his new corner office and, after touching Craik as you'd touch a sore spot and flinching away, thinking that it was time to do something big. Something really big. *A riiiillly big shew,* as that asshole used to say on television.

He had been kicked upstairs. Downstairs, his former assistant had his old job. She had betrayed him, too, and now she had his old job, which she was already making a mess of. Good. He must see to it that she *really* made a mess of it.

In the meantime, he was going to launch something big.

A light flashed on his desk; he hobbled to it and hit a button and a woman's voice said, "Lieutenant-Commander Suter is here."

"Send him in."

He waited, standing behind his desk, his weight on the canes. He had a handsome face made haggard by constant pain, a long body with big shoulders from heaving it around on his hands. He had probably risen as high in the Central Intelligence Agency now as he ever would, and he knew it, and he was going to start having his fun.

The door opened. Suter paused in the doorway.

Shreed smiled. "Come on in." He propped the canes against his desk and swung himself into the armchair. "I was going to call you, anyway. You settling in?"

"I know the route from my car to my office, anyway."

"I have a task for you," Shreed said. "You ready?"

Suter bobbed his head, cocking an eyebrow; it was a kind of acknowledgment or recognition.

Shreed took his time in settling himself at his desk. He leaned the steel canes against a spot that had held them so often it was worn. "I took you on," Shreed said, "because I figured you're my kind of bastard. Isn't that what you figure?"

The faintest of smiles touched Suter's face. "We seem to have a kind of meeting of the minds, yes."

"You're getting a late start here. I've pulled you in above a lot of other people who therefore hate your guts. Hate is good for a career. You just have to keep ahead of it. You're used to being hated, I'm sure. Where did you get that suit?"

Suter was wearing a dark-blue rag that had nothing to recommend it except the crease in the trousers. He reddened and named a department store.

"It looks it. Anyway, I'm sending you someplace else— a place called the Interservice Virtual Intelligence Center." He grinned. "I've made a deal with the devil. You're going to see he keeps his part of the bargain. That may be just the suit for the devil." He waved a hand. "Sit, sit; this is going to take a while. What do you know about a project called Peacemaker?"

Atlantic Fleet Headquarters, Norfolk.

"Project Peacemaker!"

In Conference Room B of LantFleet HQ, Alan Craik's old squadron-mate LCDR "Rafe" Rafehausen was having a briefing. The briefing was part of a larger planning conference for Battle Group Seven, now in its formative stages as it prepared to join Sixth Fleet late that year. Consisting of the CV *Andrew Jackson,* a Tico-class missile cruiser, and associated destroyers, subs, and support ships, it would carry the flag of Admiral Rudolph Newman aboard the *Jackson* with Air Wing Five. For Rafe Rafehausen, this would be a make-or-break cruise: he was to join VS-49 as XO only three months before the battle group put to sea, with the awesome certainty that if he did the job well he would become skipper of the squadron two years after he signed on. At the moment, he was sitting in on the planning conference as a guest of the current VS-49 skipper and exec.

The briefer was a captain. Everything about him said he was a hardnose. He was laying it out as if he had been up to the mountain and got the plans on stone. He summarized: "And so this cruise will have two primary responsibilities— Project Peacemaker, in Libya's Gulf of Sidra in December,

72

and the ongoing support of blockade and air ops in the former Yugoslavia.

"Project Peacemaker will require that we secure the Gulf of Sidra for the Peacemaker launch vessel. This will be a major undertaking involving air and surface elements within fifteen miles of the Libyan coast. We will do a complete, repeat, *complete* fleet exercise that will mock up the entire operation. Fleetex is currently scheduled for October of this year. That is six-plus months to prepare for units that at this time are not in a high state of readiness!" He glared around the room. Full commanders avoided his hard eyes; lieutenant-commanders blanched. It was no secret that the fleet was below full manpower and that training was behind.

The captain held up a fist, from which an index finger pointed upward like a preacher's. "Fleetex, Bermuda, October 96." Another finger pointed. "To sea, November 96." A third finger. "Peacemaker, Gulf of Sidra, December 96!" He glared. "Questions?" He said it like a man who dared anybody to ask a question.

A courageous commander murmured, "Is that date for Peacemaker firm?"

"Why wouldn't it be firm?" the captain shouted.

A rash lieutenant, one of the few people in the room below lieutenant-commander, stood up, and Rafehausen groaned inwardly. The lieutenant said, "Bosnia and Peacemaker, that's it, sir?"

"What else would you like?" the captain snarled.

"Uh—sir, Africa is ready to—" Rafehausen groaned silently again and thought *Oh, Christ, another Al Craik!*

The captain barked like an aroused Doberman. "Africa's not even on my map! Bosnia and Peacemaker! Any *other* questions?"

Rafe had a question, but there was no point in asking it

of this guy. It was a question that only Rafe himself could answer, anyway: *How am I going to get an under-manned, inexperienced bunch of guys ready for sea in six lousy months?* He looked at the man who would by then be his skipper. The guy had a reputation as a screamer and a morale-destroyer. *My fucking A!* Rafe thought.

Norfolk Naval Base.
"Peacemaker? The hell with it!"

Vice-Admiral Rudolph Newman was the flag commander of Battle Group Seven, which was beginning to take shape. "We're going to do this right, for once," he said. He sounded angry, as he always sounded, even when he wasn't angry. "No Mickey Mouse!" he said.

"No, sir." His flag intelligence officer was the hardnosed captain who had done the briefing where Rafe Rafehausen had sat in. With the admiral, however, he was sweet as honey. He had served with Newman twice before and knew what the man was like.

"Nothing we can do about this Peacemaker crap," the admiral growled, "so we'll have to do it. Keep something in the Fleetex script about it. You know how they scream if somebody's pet project doesn't get its due."

"Yes, sir."

"But I want a fleet exercise with *guts*. I want the men and officers who serve under me to know who the enemy is, and I want them to have this experience so they'll be ready!"

"Yes, sir."

"Victor-II class submarines. MiG-29s. I want my subs hunted by whatever the latest is that the Soviets have got—the Helix A?"

"Mmm—KA-27PL."

"Well, extrapolate an upgrade. You know as well as I

74

do the Soviets have one by now. The best, understand? Kirov-plus cruisers. I want an exercise against their best. I don't want any of this 'real-world' crap. 'Real-world' means unreal world. Get me?"

"The, um, LantCom Planning Office is scripting a scenario. I've been picking their brains. They're thinking, um, one threat as Libya and the other as Yugoslavia."

"Negative! See, that's exactly what I mean. That's what they'd call 'real world.' We can lick those pathetic bastards without a rehearsal. Negative that. You script me a Fleetex that puts me against the Soviets in waters where they can bring their good stuff to bear. Get me?"

The IO nodded. He cleared his throat. "I'll leave it to you to deal with LantCom, sir?"

"Yeah, yeah, yeah, yeah."

Interservice Virtual Intelligence Center, Maryland.

"Peacemaker?"

Colonel Han was Chinese-American, an engineer. Suter, fresh from his briefing by his acidic new boss, George Shreed, disliked Han on sight. Han, he could tell, was Mister Nice Guy. Well, screw that.

"Let me put you in the big picture first," Han said when he had settled behind his desk. "You know what IVI is, or you wouldn't be here." He pronounced the acronym for Interservice Virtual Intelligence like "ivy." *The halls of IVI.* His round face smiled on Suter.

"Communications research," Suter replied, "which is why it falls under the Agency's umbrella."

Han grunted. He was turning a ballpoint pen in stubby fingers. "The Agency's mandate inside the US is communications, right." He smiled again, but Suter suspected he disliked Suter on sight as much as Suter had disliked him. "So your responsibility will include keeping communications separate from anything else, anything that isn't part of the CIA mandate. Right? I mean, that's partly why you're here. Right?"

"What're you getting at, Colonel?"

"You don't want your agency to get involved in things outside its bailiwick, right?"

"I'm afraid I don't follow you."

Han looked up at him and they stared at each other. Han dropped the pen. "Come on, I'll show you around."

They started at the top floor of the three-story building, where there was a suite of offices and meeting rooms that would have suited one of the new high-tech, high-risk companies. Suter thought that there was something vaguely pushy about the place, a bit too much of a good thing. "We entertain up here," Han said. Our friends in Congress, he meant. At least that was the way Suter had heard it from Shreed.

The next floor down was a work floor, endless cubicles, an outer ring of small offices, some sort of atrium that looked down at the security desk and the lobby and up at the rain that was falling on a glass dome. In the back was a big, windowed cafeteria where people were already sitting drinking coffee. Again, there was the feeling of a start-up, lots of very young people, jeans and T-shirts, few neckties. "We hire them for their brains," Han said. No explanation.

There were three floors below the surface. Each had its own security check and a security lock where, for a few seconds, they were held between closed gates. "If you're claustrophobic, you're not for us," Han said. He held up a card to a television camera while they waited inside the lock, and a voice said, "Now the other gentleman, please." Han moved Suter forward with pressure on his arm, and

Suter turned his face up to be seen and then held up the temporary pass he'd been given. "Thank you," the voice said. Suter couldn't tell whether it was a human voice or a computer.

Down there, attempts had been made to disguise the fact that it was underground, but you couldn't make windows where the outdoors was solid earth. It was bright and colorful, but at the end of a day a lot of people would breathe fresh air with real hunger. The spaces, as if to try to compensate, were larger, the cubicles fewer. The people were older, more male than female; Suter thought he recognized the look of ex-military. Uniforms, he knew, were not allowed.

The second below-ground level had at least two laboratories and a model-making shop. Han made this part of the tour pretty perfunctory, as if these were nuts-and-bolts places, not where the real work went on. Then they got in the elevator and started down to S3.

"So," Han said. "What do you think?"

"Where's Peacemaker?" Suter said. "It's the reason I'm here."

They got out of the elevator and went through the security check and into the lock. When they stepped out of the lock, Han said, "I think I'll take you right to the general and let him explain Peacemaker to you."

Suter asked a couple of questions as they walked along the central corridor, but Han didn't answer. He didn't like pushy questions, was what he was saying.

A few women could be seen down here. Suter eyed them, looking for a hit. He had been married, now was not. In fact, it was the end of the marriage that had freed him to leave the Navy—no, actually, freed him to let loose the ambition he had been holding in check. She had never liked the ambitious Suter. *She made me a different person.*

Limited me. With her, I was just another nice shmuck. It never occurred to him to wonder what she had thought about it, or if she had been another person in the marriage, too. He was simply terribly glad to be rid of her. Except for the sex, so he was now looking around.

"The general" was Brigadier Robert F. Touhey, USAF, a small, round man about fifteen pounds over a healthy weight, with shrewd blue eyes, a sidewall haircut, and just a touch of the Carolinas in his voice. He was wearing a white, short-sleeved shirt and a blue tie, as if it was summer; when he stood up, he was several inches shorter than Suter, but he had a handshake like a Denver boot. They made polite sounds, and Touhey let go of Suter's hand, and Han muttered something that caused Touhey to give him the briefest of cold looks before he said, "Sure, okay, you take off, Jackie." Then he motioned Suter to a chair.

Suter sat, opening his coat. The room was hot. Touhey plopped back into his desk chair and said, "What'd you do to old Jackie? He don't like you."

"No idea. What makes you think he doesn't like me?"

"I can tell." Suter leaned back. Touhey's face was made for smiling, and, even in repose, it seemed to have the beginnings of a smile. Touhey seemed to be smiling at Suter now—but was he? "So," Touhey said. "How's my old buddy George Shreed?"

Suter nodded, smiled. "He sends his regards."

"Regards!" Touhey laughed. "What'd George tell you about me?"

"He said you were the best empire-builder in the American military."

Touhey guffawed. "And you better believe it! Alla this—" Touhey waved a hand that included the office, the building, the idea "—is my empire. I grabbed it; I rule it; and

78

I'm gonna go on ruling it. Administrations come and go; Touhey endures. How'd you connect up with Shreed?"

"He got in touch with me."

"What about?"

"Somebody who was going to serve under me."

"Good or bad? Come on, George don't dick around; what'd he want?"

"He wanted to warn me." In fact, George Shreed of the CIA had wanted to tell him that Alan Craik was a thorough-going shit, and Suter should be careful. Shreed really hated Craik. "We had lunch, hit it off."

"He recruited you?"

"I guess."

"Don't guess, okay? I don't like vague shit. I'm a scientist and a politician, call me a scientific politician. Vagueness is for people got time to dick around. I don't. George recruit you?"

"Yes."

"Right there, one lunch? Man, you came cheap. So, what—he pulled strings, got you outa the Navy quicktime? Musta wanted you. If George Shreed wanted you, I better watch my ass." Touhey smiled.

"He was moving up to a new responsibility. He wanted to reorganize."

"Right. 'No contingent trails.' Okay. He sent over a file on you; you look okay. The impression I get is, you're the kinda man can always go into the woods and find a honey tree—am I right about that? I think I am. Divorced. No kids. You a loner, Suter?"

"Maybe. I never thought of it that way."

"'He travels the fastest who travels alone.' Kipling. Okay. Whatta you know about Peacemaker?"

Suter was sweating. Could he take off the suitcoat? He wasn't quite sure how to handle this highly intelligent redneck. He decided to wear it and sweat. "I know it's just coming out of the closet. That it's a low-earth-orbit satellite system. That it's part of an intelligence-communications effort. That it's controversial. That it rang Colonel Han's bells when I mentioned it before he did."

"Go on."

Suter shifted his weight and a rivulet of wet trickled down his right side. "Shreed told me it's a weapon."

"Ri-i-ight! By which you mean, it's a weapon in this room, but you say it anyplace else and it's deny, deny, deny. Old George is with me on this one; we see eyeball to eyeball. Common ground down someplace where his ideology and my theory about intelligence come together, although it's like an ox and a bear hitched to the same plow. George and I want this thing for different reasons, but we don't see any purpose in killing each other just yet, and we're kissy-kissy around Congress and the White House so's the project will succeed. You being George's boy, I expect you to go along one hunnerd percent. Right?"

"Yes, sir."

"Damn right. Let me tell you about Peacemaker. No! Let me tell you about intelligence. Intelligence and the modern battle. Now, you're an intel guy. Wha'd you do in the Navy? Carrier intel—what do you guys call it, CAG AI? Right. You got lots of intel from this source and that, you patched it together and strained it and shaped it and you looked at the target lists and the briefing books that Uncle provided, and then you made up something comprehensible for the jet jocks, and they took off and did what B.F. Skinner tried to get pigeons to do, which is use your intel to carry a weapon to target. Now, that's asinine.

"Here's my theory of intelligence. Intelligence and force projection in the electronic world are the same thing. To have a thought should be the same as to use that thought. Idea is action. Stay with me here: the usual model, the model you used on your aircraft carrier, is pre-electronic. It's all about the failure of intelligence that's built into slow communication. The great example is the Battle of New Orleans. The British come up into the swamps and Andrew Jackson and a lotta people shoot the ass off them, and the British tuck their tails and go away. Only trouble is, the war had been over six weeks before they started.

"When you got slow communications, you in effect got no intelligence worth the name—everything happens the night before the battle, the day of the battle, the moment of the battle. The intel guy is just some no-respect major who can read maps. Who matters is the guy who has the muscles to carry the weapon.

"But come up to the 1980s. Now I can take a photo and have it come up simultaneously on a missile that's already in the air. The missile don't need any pigeon to drive it; it's got the electronic brains to drive itself, using satellite positioning and my photo. I drive it to the target. Me—the intel guy. But do they let me do it? No—they turn it over to the guys who used to carry the weapon and still want to get their rocks off.

"Now come to the 1990s. What're we doing, mostly? We're giving jet jocks briefing books and briefings and kneepad maps and photos and satellite coverage, and they fly off and make the same fucking mistakes that they and the pigeon could have made without all that help. Who's still the least respected officer in a squadron? The intel guy. But who's the one knows the most about the target? The intel guy.

"So, here's my theory of intelligence: cut the crap. Cut out the middleman. Put your intel guy where all the electronic fields come together, and give him the button.

81

"That's what Peacemaker is—the world's first intel-driven killer. War with an arrow and no archer. George tell you how it works?"

Suter shook his head. He was a little dazzled.

"See, the problem that we saw was, you put stuff into a high orbit, you got a major launch involvement, and *still* you got a hell of a weight problem. You can put up your electronics, sure, but conventional weapons are heavy stuff. So we come up with something out of a sci-fi novel, no shit. What makes a conventional weapon heavy? Fuel and explosive. Okay, do away with both a them, you got your problem licked. Whatcha got out there in orbit instead of fuel for your weapon? *Gravity.* Whatcha gonna put up there instead of explosives? *Manmade meteorites.* Like a goddam cafe-curtain rod, only made of either ceramic or spent uranium, we ain't decided which—doing tests next month from the high-altitude research aircraft out in Nevada. I favor the uranium, because I know that at Mach 5 that stuff will *explode* hardened concrete, I mean not just knock pieces off it, but fucking explode it!

"With the weight problem solved, we conceived Peacemaker as a low orbiter so it can be launched any old place. But low orbit means it won't stay up long, maybe five days. Long enough. Peacemaker 1 will carry forty rods and will be in-orbit maneuverable plus or minus five hundred klicks. Above the range of all known missiles and aircraft. It'll carry an onboard computer not much shabbier than an early Cray, plus receivers *direct* for optical, side-look, satellite TV, infrared, or digital data. I won't say the thing will be able to think, but it'll be able to compare and prioritize, and it will always be in direct contact with *here.*"

"Expensive," Suter said. What he wanted to say was, *That's the greatest thing I ever heard.* "Awfully expensive."

"There's enough pork in the Star Wars budget to do this

little old thing ten times over. There's so much pork, I oughta get some hickory sticks and start me a barbecue place. 'Touhey's Hog Heaven'!" He laughed. He was excited, too, just talking about it. "That's why I need George. George can carve a pig about as good as anybody in Washington."

"How far along is the project?" Suter found that his voice was hoarse.

"We're going to prototype in six weeks; legal is cleaning up the contracts. They got a model upstairs, I expect Jackie whisked you by that, but you're welcome to see it. I want to test the end of this year."

"But—"

"Go ahead."

"It's destabilizing as hell."

Touhey grinned. "Direct contravention of the ABM treaty. That's my view of it, although there's controversy in-house. I'll let the lawyers work that out. Frankly, I don't give a shit. Neither does George, who's in it—between you and me—precisely *because* it's destabilizing. It fits old George's ideology, and he ain't exactly over there on the far left. But you hit the sore point, yeah, and that's why the only word we've leaked on Peacemaker is that it's an intel-comm satellite. *Not a weapon.* That's the way it's gonna stay for the public and part of the Congress for the foreseeable future. But sometime we gotta go public with the weapon part, because what this is, is a weapon of fear. It don't do squat if people don't know about it."

"A deterrent."

"Well, wouldn't you be deterred if you knew somebody could position an untouchable machine over your house and drop meteorites on it at Mach 5?" Touhey leaned back and began to scrabble in a drawer, coming up with a pack of cigarettes. "That's why we're gonna sell this as

83

a support to UN peacekeeping. Our likeliest demo will be Yugoslavia—pardon, the former Yugoslavia. We're gonna put a Peacemaker up in the Mediterranean, current plans are the Gulf of Sidra, coordinate with Navy's Sixth Fleet— I expect you to be a help there—and we're gonna put it up and juke it around in orbit over some of their real estate and *suggest*—merely suggest, meaning we're gonna do a little discreet leaking—that this little toy might be compatible with some kinda weaponry. We think it'll get their attention. Meanwhile, in secret, we're gonna drop some rods on a pile of rock in the South Atlantic and see what survives." He fiddled with a ball of paper. "You can imagine the UN debate if it's the UN that thinks it's gonna benefit. They won't know whether to shit or go blind."

"*Give* it to the UN?"

"Now, you know we'd never do that. We may say we will, but we won't. Remember Reagan's offer to give Star Wars to the world? Like that. But we'll use it in a good cause, you bet, and I for one am not at all happy about a set of tough guys kicking ass, including women and kids, in the name of what they call ethnic cleansing, when their ethnic ain't much to look at to begin with. And we need the PR, 'cause this is gonna be one mother of a fight when it goes public."

"I'm supposed to be part of that."

Touhey grinned at him. "You're gonna be the targeting officer." He grinned even more when he saw how startled Suter was. "George wants you to be. You're gonna be the oversight on his investment. You got an office on this floor for the duration of the project, plus you'll get space at our DC connection. You're gonna ride along with me on some trips up there. You play golf?"

"Some."

"'Some' don't get the hay in. Learn to play. We get a lot

of our support over a good game." He smiled. "Not *too* good, mind." He stood. He had worked a cigarette out of the pack, was now holding it in his fingers and getting ready to work a lighter with the other. There were No Smoking signs all over the building. "You're gonna liaise with George, but in-house here you're part of the targeting and data flow ladder. You can be useful there. Work hard."

"I always work hard." Suter said it proudly, but it brought an unreadable glance from Touhey—maybe slightly challenging?

"We're about to expand. You're part of the expansion. In the empire-building business, if you don't keep getting bigger, they cut you off at the knees and all of a sudden you're small."

The lighter flared.

The Med.

USS *James Madison* was going home.

The great wheel turned, and in the Adriatic, the carrier battle group began its move toward home port; in Norfolk, the outgoing battle group that would replace them, BG 6, was making its final preparations to sail.

Not that very moment. Not even that day. But the *Madison* had turned her bow away from the Bosnian coast, and she had headed down the length of Italy and around the boot, and her crew knew they wouldn't come that way again, not this tour. Some of the tension in the ship began to ease, as if all at once people had got a good night's sleep and nobody was quite so down.

Alan Craik was going home. His air-intel team was finally turning to leave the Med, and just in time. The men and women were tired; the machines were tired. They had really pulled together after Suter had left— Alan didn't kid himself that it was his presence that made things better; Suter's absence was most of it—and now they were efficient and smart, but they were worn out. They were good kids; their shiny newness had worn off under the strain of constant planning and activity, and the N2, with Alan, had quickly repaired their gun-shy (or Suter-shy) attitudes. Alan had preferred to let them learn with minimal chiding. Now they were a solid team, and Alan reflected wryly that, like most military organizations, they had hit their stride just as their duty together was coming to an end.

Peacekeeping was wearing. There wasn't anything to strive toward; it was all just *keeping on*. There would never be any gongs for them for "winning" the war—or the peace—in Bosnia. It just went on. *And would go on*, he thought. *We'll be back*, was what he thought but never said to his people.

So the *Madison* rounded the toe of the boot and charged up to Naples, and when they pulled into the bay for their last run ashore, the whole battle group seemed to put Bosnia behind them. They poured ashore by the ferry-load and dispersed over the streets like ants on spilled honey. Alan, walking up toward the Royal Palace, could hear some of them whooping a block away. Bad PR, but— get a life!

That night he took his gang to a small restaurant called Pappagallo. They pushed a lot of tables together and shouted back and forth, and some unabashed flirting went on between the men and women that had been suppressed on the boat. *A couple of Italian songs and half of them will be in bed together*, he thought, and he turned the subject to Bosnia and peacekeeping. It was always the great subject, and it had the same effect now as a cold shower. On the boat, it had almost led to people's not speaking to each other—Why are we here? What's our duty? Are we the world's policeman? What's wrong with the people in the Balkans? Why can't we bomb the fuckers?—but now the tone was elegiac, as of people who had done their best and had to leave with things no worse, perhaps no better. Baronik summed up for them. "There's hope," he said. He was a little drunk, mostly a bit more laid back than usual, but maybe showing off for the benefit of LTjg Mary Colley. "Folks, there's hope! Look at all the other places that have had this kind of shit. Neighbor killing neighbor! Village burning village! It does come to an end. It does! Strong government and economic prosperity can break the chain of violence." His voice was passionate. Seeing doubt in some of the faces, he said, "Look at the Anglo-Scottish border between the fourteenth and the eighteenth centuries!" Somebody groaned. "Look at the Norman Vexin!" Everybody groaned.

"Look at the time," Alan said. He waved for the check.

"It *will* happen, Al!" Baronik said. He glanced at LTjg Colley.

"Of course it will." Alan remembered the torture chamber in the Serbian zone. Well, maybe it would happen.

Washington, DC.

Mike Dukas pushed open the door of his apartment with a foot and heard his mail, just as it did every night, scrape along the floor as the door pushed it. As he did every night, he thought that the door was a stupid place to put a mail slot. Bending, groaning because he was a short, wide man, he picked up the mail and threw pieces of it at the wastebasket as he crossed the living room. Junk, junk, bill, junk, credit union, bill—*and bingo*!

He felt his heart lurch. The top of the envelope had a return address for the War Crimes Tribunal in The Hague. When he tore the envelope, his hands were shaking. *Why did it matter so much? Christ, he didn't get this nervous with a woman!*

" . . . your very impressive résumé . . . hope to set up an interview within five days . . . speed of the essence because . . . suffering . . . criminals . . . a need for leadership and your professional skill." There was a telephone number that he was asked to call during business hours ASAP.

Dukas was grinning. *Sonofabitch!*

He pulled the door shut and trotted to his car and drove the five miles to the mall where he knew there was a Borders. There, he leaned into the high counter and said to the very young, pretty attractive woman there, "How you fixed for a Bosnian dictionary?"

"Bosnian?"

"Yeah, like the country formerly known as Yugoslavia."

"I know what it is." She smiled. "I read the papers, you know. But I don't think Bosnian's a language. It's an ethnic group, but—" She was talking to the computer with her fingers. A really smart woman. "Uh-uh." And smiled again. "We got Serbo-Croat, though!"

"Whatever!" Dukas said. He reached for his credit card. He felt like a kid.

Fort Reno, North Carolina.
Harry O'Neill paused with his fingers on the envelope, a prayer on his tongue. But it was too late. Last-minute prayers wouldn't change what was inside.

He put his left index finger inside the flap at the end where it was ungummed, and it tore; he used the finger to tear raggedly the length of the envelope. He glanced around to see if anybody was watching him, but anybody from his class who was there at that time would have his own envelope and would have sought his own alcove in which to open it. O'Neill leaned still closer to the window, shielding himself almost inside the window drapes. He took out the single sheet of paper and unfolded its three sections.

His assignment for the next three years. Paris? Marseille? Or—?

He almost groaned when he saw it. He stifled real sound but wailed inside. He pressed his forehead against the cool glass.

How will I ever tell my father? and then an instant later with a different kind of shame, *How will I ever tell Al Craik?*

3

June

Norfolk.
Home is the sailor, home from the sea. He had never learned
much of the rest of it. Something about the hunter—"and
the hunter home from the hill." But he wasn't a hunter.
Dukas was the hunter. He was the sailor. And O'Neill? Had
he been looking for O'Neill—?

Alan woke. He was home. Relief and gratitude flooded
through him. What had he been dreaming—sailor, hunter?
He smelled his house, his bed, his wife. His left hand slid
across the wrinkled sheet and found her. She made a
pleased sound without waking. His hand went up her
hip. Squeezed. The dog raised his head. The dog slept on
the floor of the bedroom and would have got on the bed
in a moment if he'd been encouraged. When Alan wasn't
there, he slept on the floor next to Rose, and he would
wake when she did, just like this, raise his head, look at
her eyes as he now looked at Alan's.

"Walk?" Alan whispered.

The dog's tail thumped on the floor. Alan slipped from
the sheets and padded to the bathroom, then to Mikey's
room, the dog following, springing, ready to bark so hard
the effort would carry him right off his front feet if Alan so
much as murmured *walk* again. Alan hushed him with
a hand on the huge head, caressing the ears, the side

of the jaw. He got a big lick on his bare wrist in return.

His son lay on his back, seemingly asleep, but his eyes opened when Alan leaned over him. The light from the hall glinted on the eyes, and the child smiled. Alan's heart turned over, broke, put itself back together. *So this is what it's like.* He had been home for ten days. One night on the ship, drinking coffee on an all-nighter, a shipmate had told him about coming home from a sea tour, always finding his children changed, new. Kids who might one day, unless you were careful, remember mainly that their father was "always away." He touched his son's face.

He put on the coffee-maker and got the dog's leash, and the dog began to prance. The dog wanted to bark; cautioned to stay quiet, he sneezed. His head went up and down so enthusiastically that Alan could hardly get the leash on him. Then they were out the door and into the dawn; he had a momentary flash of dawns on the carrier, one morning when there were no air ops and the great deck had stretched like a field, and the eastern edge of the sky was a bright line like a hot wire. Did some part of him miss it already?

The dog pissed on every vertical object between their house and the end of the block and then got more discriminating as his supply ran low. Beyond the second street was a wood with a kind of stream in it. He let the dog run. Walking along the dark path, listening for the scuffle of the dog in the old leaves, he thought about the dawn when they'd gone to the Serb house in Pustarla. He thought about it a lot, couldn't get it to settle down into the understory of his mind. The smell of old blood. The tub full of bloody water. The victims. *Shooting that guy.*

He clipped the dog's leash to the ring on the collar and started for home. The dog's pissing had now become purely symbolic—lifting a leg to show what he would do if he could.

"You remind me of some guys I know," Alan said. The dog grinned. "You ready to eat?" Alan said. The dog surged forward. "Let's go!" They ran.

Rose was up. When she saw him, her face opened into a lovely smile, a smile you could dream about at sea. He wondered if he did that for her. Rose did her time at sea, too—exec of a helo squadron, a lieutenant-commander who ranked her husband. They kissed. It went on a while; he wondered if they had time to— They did not; she had a meeting at 0830.

"Maybe come home early?"

"We've got company, remember?"

He groaned.

"Feed the dog; it'll take your mind off your troubles. Your idea, having old friends over for a last get-together with O'Neill—remember? I have to shop; it's Mike and Harry and the Peretzes, that means no red meat, jeez, I dearly love Bea Peretz, but what the hell does she have to go vegetarian for? Can you eat chicken?"

"How about soy burgers?"

"Fuck you and stop that, there isn't time. Boy, do I come back from sea duty like this? Mike's bringing somebody. I don't think it's serious."

Something he had been dreaming about. Mike, the hunter— Mike was in love with Rose; everybody knew it, and everybody knew it was hopeless. "Mike's serious about you," Alan said. He put down the dog's water bowl, and the dog made sounds in it as if a duck was trying to take off.

"He's doing Greek salad and hors d'oeuvres and I'm doing the main stuff, and yes, I think he's in love with me and I guess that after you he's the next one I'd want to be that way. That okay?"

Alan grinned. "So long as I'm first."

"You're always first." She cocked her head, listened.

"Mikey's awake." She started out, turned back to him. "If it's any comfort to you, just having you in the house makes me so horny I want to scream." She started out again, swung back. "Correction—moan, not scream. 'Bye."

In the Serbian zone, Bosnia.

Zulu nodded, and Radic swung his fist and it hit the bound man with a sound like a ball hitting a glove. Zulu remembered that sound, the old catcher's mitt heavy on his hand, his father's throw making it ache even through the thick, old leather.

Radic looked at him. Zulu nodded again. Radic swung; the bound man screamed as the same sound struck. And again. And again. And again.

And now the Americans were here. The first ones had come in March to replace the UN. Zulu hadn't fought them yet, perhaps never would, but he wished to. He remembered that American voice shouting in the house at Pustarla, then the running through the snow, naked, that voice and the gun booming behind him. Humiliating.

The bound man looked like raw meat. He was stripped to the waist. So was Radic, from whose sleek muscles steam rose in little wisps, like ground mist. It was still cold up here.

"Is he still alive?" Zulu said.

Radic lifted the man's drooping head and felt in the bloody mess of his throat. He nodded.

"Cut him down."

The men from the little pigsty of a village watched Radic. Zulu could smell somebody's shit. They were terrified. That was the idea.

The bound man lay on the ground. Blood soaked into the dirty snow. Zulu handed Radic a sledgehammer. He nodded.

Radic swung the sledge and blood and brains spattered, and the village men began to wail.

Zulu decided that Radic was all right. He would add him to the Special Unit for Africa.

That evening. Norfolk.

As it turned out, Mike Dukas's date had canceled and he came alone, a little sheepish that he had been stood up but probably glad, really, that he had more time in the kitchen with Rose. Alan could imagine Mike's mental pictures of himself in their house, a kind of uncle to their child (who had been named after him), a kind of protective presence to Rose. Alan was not sure that those pictures had much to do with reality, except that Mike was a very good friend and they had been through a very tough time together and almost got themselves killed. Now, he listened to Mike and Rose chattering in the kitchen about food, and they made him happy.

Then O'Neill came, and he and Alan made a lot of noise because they hadn't seen each other in eight months or so. O'Neill was hardly in the door before Alan lunged toward him; O'Neill swayed back and said, "Oh, I say, old chap!" and shook Alan's hand. Then they boogied for three seconds, then gave each other high fives, and then fell on each other, squeezing and whacking and saying, "Hey, that's fat, man, you put on *fat*!" and "Muscle, that's muscle!" and each told the other he looked great, and they held on to each other and just grinned. Rose came in and smiled at them and kissed O'Neill, and Dukas asked him how the Ranch had been. O'Neill made a face and they all laughed.

"Can you eat vegetarian lasagna?" she said. She sounded worried. O'Neill was big and looked as if he ate whole cows or roadkill or something.

"If I could eat grits, I can eat anything. They gave me grits every goddam morning. I think it was a *test*!" He and Alan began to remind each other of horrible food they had eaten on the boat. They did a lot more happy shouting. Dukas and Rose looked at each other and shrugged and went back to the kitchen.

The Peretzes were late. The Peretzes were always late. Abe Peretz had been a kind of mentor to Alan, even though his own Naval career had ended when he hadn't made the cut for commander. Now he worked in the J. Edgar Hoover Building and made sad jokes about being a G-Man.

"How's the G-Man?" Alan said as he took their coats a few minutes later. They were embracing O'Neill and asking him how the Ranch had been. Alan grinned at Bea. "How's Mrs G-Man?"

"He got a promotion!" Bea shouted. Bea shouted everything. She was handsome and noisy. "Tell them about your new job!" Bea was wearing black pants and a pale yellow, shiny blouse with a huge saxophone on it in green— the saxophone was a bizarre touch, some kind of joke? Some reference he didn't get?—and enough buttons left unbuttoned so her very attractive cleavage showed to good advantage. She seemed very up, maybe too much so.

Abe shrugged. "So I got a promotion."

"To what?"

"I don't know; it's classified."

Bea bounced into a chair, bounced right out again. "You make me so damn mad, Abe, I could kill you! He's been made department head. I hate false modesty!"

Abe kissed her. "Nobody would ever dare accuse you of it." He began to explain the organizational structure of FBI headquarters, which was so complex that Alan wondered if he'd finish before the evening ended. Then he realized that O'Neill was chuckling and that what Abe was saying was an elaborate shaggy-dog story, an invention. He began to laugh, too, and Abe, seeing he'd got the joke, roared.

Then Mike and Rose came in with wine, and they all got noisier, and the dog made his rounds, poking his big nose into everybody's crotch and spilling a wineglass, and there was a lot of loud talk. Dukas told a couple of his Clinton jokes, and Alan glanced over at Rose and saw her face shining, and she gave him a wink and he was glad that Mike's girl or woman or whatever she was hadn't come, because these were the people he most liked to be with. He and O'Neill sat next to each other and started saying, "Hey, remember when—" and the others tuned them out. When Alan started listening to them again, Rose was trying to talk Abe Peretz into doing his two weeks of Reserve duty at her new station, someplace called Interservice Virtual Intelligence.

Peretz whistled. "Interservice Virtual Intelligence! Wow, how'd you like them apples? Virtual intelligence, that's for me! If you can't have real intelligence, by all means have virtual! What do they do, Rose, teach monkeys to talk, or something?"

"I don't start for another week. All I know is, it's a great-looking place, they've got a fantastic cafeteria, and they're hungry for analysts."

O'Neill squinted his eyes. "As a trained interrogator, I sensed a missed step there. What is a helicopter pilot doing in something called 'virtual intelligence'?"

"She's hiking her ass up the ladder toward being an astronaut. I need space-related duty for my next tour."

O'Neill looked at Alan and swung into his WW-II-Japanese-officer voice. "So, American flygirl, your intelligence is space-related!" And then to Humphrey Bogart: "You're good, Shweetheart, you're really good, but there's something you aren't telling me."

Rose batted her eyes. "It's something about satellites, Mister Spade, and I can't say more because it's classified."

And O'Neill swung into his Big Badass voice and growled, "Who you callin' a *spade*?"

"That kind of joking makes me nervous," Bea Peretz said. Rose and O'Neill laughed, the indulgent way that people laugh about their parents, and Rose began to shepherd them all toward the table. When they were all seated, there was a sudden silence, everybody looking at everybody else, and Bea said, "I think the CIA sucks."

"I'll drink to that," O'Neill said.

"Yeah, that's about how I'd put it," Dukas said. "You got a way with words all right, Bea." He smiled at her. "So how'd our boy O'Neill do at the Agency's finishing school?" he said.

"Well, our boy O'Neill got through," O'Neill said. "But not first in his class." He twirled his wineglass. "Folks, I want to be pampered tonight, because I just spent three days with my parents explaining *why* I wasn't first in my class. I mean—it was *expected*."

"Ah, why would anybody expect you to be first at that zoo?" Dukas said.

"God, yes," Alan said. "You're the wrong type, O'Neill. Harry's an aristocrat," he told the others, as if that explained everything. He had heard this theory from O'Neill in the long days and nights on the carrier, years before.

"I thought the CIA was the Old Boys' Club for Ivy League graduates," Bea said. She was shoveling down vegetarian lasagna. "William F. Buckley was CIA. George Throttlebottom Bush was CIA. I thought the CIA was the Washington branch of Skull and Bones."

"Yeah," O'Neill said, holding out his wineglass as Rose went around the table with a bottle, "but I'm a *real* aristocrat. My father's a federal judge, my mother's a partner in quite a good law firm. One of my ancestors was a governor during Reconstruction. I went to Harvard, not Yale, which is a far, far better place, and you're talking about the CIA of fifty years ago, which is where I would probably have felt at home, *except* there was the problem back then of my, um, *hue*." He sighed. "My mother thinks I'm slumming."

Rose did her imitation of O'Neill's mother. "I just *wish* he'd meet a nice Spelman girl." More laughter.

"Anyway," Alan went on, "you got through the course, which is better than about eighty percent of the people do. So, did you get the orders that you wanted?"

O'Neill raised his eyebrows. "Not quite. No-o-o-t quite. In fact, as the Brits say, not by a long chalk." He speared a floweret of garlic-sauteed broccoli. "I'm afraid I promised my parents that I was going to France. They thought France was where I deserved to go, being their son, and so they made up their minds that I was going there as a glorious addition to the giddy whirl of Parisian embassy life. But that's not where Harry is going, and Harry can't bring himself to tell them."

There was a silence. "So where *is* Harry going?" Abe said to break it.

"Well, I was able to tell them a, mm, partial truth. I told them that it was classified and secret and terribly hush-hush, and so I couldn't say much, but I could say that I was going where the people spoke French. They kind of winked and smiled and looked at each other and were real pleased. So I let it go at that."

Alan grinned at him. "But you're going to the *other* place where they speak French. Montreal?"

"Umm—close, but no cigar." He gave a half-smile. "Africa. The middle part."

After another silence, Dukas said, "Well, there's a certain logic in that."

"What logic?" Bea roared.

"I know you never noticed, Bea," Dukas said, "but Harry is black. So are the people in Africa."

"That's sick!" she shouted.

Did Dukas and Bea dislike each other? Alan wondered. Maybe at base there was something sexual—an attraction gone wrong?

Rose jumped in to make peace, and Abe said something to his wife, and Alan poured more wine. *Uproar, uproar,* he thought. Well, it was friendly uproar. So far. Trying to make peace, Dukas muttered, "Well, at least Africa's kind of quiet just now."

"Like hell," Alan said. "I'm worried about him already."

"I thought the good guys took over in Rwanda and the bad guys got shoved out and the killing was over."

"There aren't any good guys," O'Neill growled. "What there is, is three-quarters of a million refugees who've crossed into Zaire, which is ready to go up, anyway, and Uganda and Tanzania thinking it's a great opportunity for them to make out, and there's me in the middle of it. Thanks for being worried, Al." He took more lasagna, to Rose's obvious relief. "They offered me a choice, Bosnia or Africa. I took Bosnia, because I thought I could do the Jugs a spot of good, as the Brits used to say. So they sent me to Africa."

"Sounds like the Navy." He knew that under his jokes, O'Neill was worried. Probably about his parents' reaction. They demanded a lot of him, and getting a posting to Africa would be "disappointing"—as in *We're disappointed in you, Harold*. His parents would have preferred even Bosnia, was the implication, because it was in Europe—a place with a history and civilized people who just happened to be massacring each other. Alan thought of the torture barn and the man who had been on the "airplane."

They were into dessert—Sicilian cassata from a recipe of Rose's mother's—and the uproar had quieted down when Bea got on the subject of Israel and then of Jonathan Pollard, the man convicted of turning American classified materials over to the Israelis.

"Pollard is a hero!" Bea cried.

"You don't know what you're talking about," Dukas growled.

Bea threw down her napkin. She was goddamned if she was going to listen to anti-Semitic crap, she told them all.

"I don't have to be an anti-Semite to think an American who sells out his country is a traitor, Bea. Get a grip."

She scrambled to her feet and her chair tipped over. "I take this seriously!" she cried. Abe was on his feet and waving them both down, saying Don't, don't, and they were out of the room.

"You guys shut up," Rose said. "She's stressed out about something." She went after them; seconds later, Abe came back.

"I'm sorry. Jesus, I'm sorry—Al— She's upset, it's been— She found that Jessica's on the pill, okay? Just found out today."

Jessica was fourteen.

Dukas reared back. "I'm sorry, Abe. I won't take that crap about Pollard from anybody."

When Rose came back, they were all looking at their hands. "She's going to lie down for a little. Lighten up, guys."

"The perfect hostess," Alan said, smiling.

"Yeah, somebody compliment me on the food, or something. Wonder Woman Cooks!" She picked a crumb of cassata from Bea Peretz's plate and ate it. "Not bad, if I do say so myself."

Dukas looked whipped. "I ruined your dinner."

Rose came around the table and kissed his balding head. "You didn't ruin anything." But Alan felt a chill, as if an unwanted future had put its hand on him. It was as if Bea's daughter, growing older out of his sight, out of his awareness, had become the cause of the break. He thought of his own son, sleeping upstairs: was he, innocent, a kind of time bomb? He found himself thinking, *Why can't things just stay the same?*

They all did the dishes and then poured out more wine, and Rose went to check on Bea and Mikey.

"I feel like shit," Dukas said.

"Shut up about it, it wasn't your fault."

They were getting a little drunk, Alan decided. He'd better make coffee.

"I've put in for a transfer," Dukas said. "I'm leaving, too."

"Good God, why—you love NCIS," Peretz said.

"It's Al's fault—he wrote me this letter. About Bosnia." He looked accusingly at Alan. "You said they needed cops like me! Well, now they got one!" Now, almost apologetically, Dukas said, "I've volunteered for a war crimes unit. NCIS would have sent somebody anyway."

Alan went to the kitchen to make coffee, shouting back to Dukas to talk loud so he could hear.

"I got no family, no kids, so what difference. Mainly I'll put together this unit and try to go after some of these bastards." He talked about the program he was joining, mostly a sop to the conscience of NATO. "Don't get your hopes up," Alan said, coming back. "You can't save the world."

"I can do *something*."

"We were there six months, what did we do? We did Operation Deny Flight, did we save the old man who had his feet cut off? The guy who was tortured so badly he died of pneumonia? The UN set up enclaves, so-called safe zones, 'safe havens,' they're where some of the worst fighting has been. Now they've signed a so-called 'peace accord' and divided Bosnia with a line like a snake's intestine that makes ethnic cleansing permanent. It's a rat's nest. The Serbs aren't the only assholes, either. Fucking Croatians are not exactly saints. The Bosnian Muslims are in bed with Iranian Intelligence. You can't save them from themselves!"

Dukas was stubborn. "We have to do something."

Peretz put on his skeptical face. "Who made us the moral guardians of the world, Mike?"

Dukas stuck out his lower lip. "We're the most powerful nation on earth. It comes with the territory."

"Maybe it comes with the territory to *try*. What doesn't come with the territory is succeeding. It always works in sci-fi novels—you hover over the uncivilized planet and you say, 'If you guys don't stop the bullshit, the Moral Federation will squeeze your planet down to a bowling ball,' and wham-bam, they all turn into good guys! Magic."

Alan sighed. "Maybe that's what we need—magic."

"A magic weapon."

"Interplanetary ballbuster."

"Right. Meanwhile, we can't keep one old man from getting his feet cut off."

"Well—I gotta try, guys. I gotta try." Dukas looked up, his eyes agonized. "You judge yourself by what you have the guts to do—not what it accomplishes in the big picture. If I stay here and do my job while all that shit goes on, I'm not a moral person." He seemed embarrassed by using the word "moral."

"A guy can get killed," Alan said.

Dukas half-smiled. "I'm just so sick of shit. Like the Pollard shit. I want to—take a stand on something!"

Alan had a flash of the photo he'd found on the wall of the house in Pustarla. Colonel Zulu. *He* had been taking a stand. "Ever hear of the Battle of the Crows?" he said.

"What about it?"

"It happened six hundred years ago, and the Serbs lost. And it's the biggest thing in their mystique—like the burning of Atlanta to the Daughters of the Confederacy. Those people have a long memory, Mike. Long passions."

"Those people are insane," O'Neill said.

"Some of 'those people' are Americans," Alan said. He told them about the Chicago Bears ashtray in the house at Pustarla.

Dukas was taking out a little notebook and a pen. "There's Americans all over that scene. No shit; I been reading the traffic. Fucking Croatians have a special-forces unit is two-thirds American—skinheads, Nazis, Aryan Nation, crazies—because they give them a historical link to Hitler, no shit." He was making notes—Zulu, the ashtray, Pustarla. "Maybe it's like the Pollard thing and it's why I get so mad—people with two loyalties. You can't have two loyalties; you got to decide. This mercenary, *Soldier-of-Fortune* shit sucks. You're an American, you should act like an American, you don't go someplace else and chop people's feet off and rape little girls." He was writing, talking to himself. "Maybe I'll run into him, who knows? 'Colonel Zulu at the Battle of the Crows.' What an asshole." He looked up as Rose came into the room, Bea a step behind her. His face broke into a smile when he saw Rose. "You light up the room, Babe."

Bea was carrying a tray with a bottle of champagne and six glasses. Her eyes were red. "There's six of us, nobody will get very much—it's late—" She put the tray down. "But it's a going-away." She looked around at them. "I'm sorry about what happened."

"Hey," Dukas said. He went to her and put his arms around her. "Hey, me too."

Rose poured the champagne into the tall tulip glasses. When she was done, she stood holding the bottle and looking down. "When we drink this—it's kind of over, isn't it. I think I'm gonna cry," she said. She and Bea had an arm around each other's waist.

"Don't," Dukas said.

"Harry's going to Africa, and Mike's going to Sarajevo, and I'm off to this new job, and in a few weeks Alan leaves the air wing— We're all going—like pieces of paper, or something."

"Except Bea and me," Peretz said. "We're not going anyplace."

Alan took his wife's hand. "We all volunteered." He meant, *It comes with the territory.*

She sniffed and smiled and picked up a glass, and with eyes shining she raised her head. "Let's look on the bright side! A year from now, we'll be riding high! It will all have been swell, and everything will be great!" She sniffed again. "Somebody for Christ's sake make a toast!"

Harry O'Neill stood. Alan and Dukas stood, and the six of them made a circle, their wineglasses almost touching in the middle. O'Neill said, "Good food—good wine—good friends." He grinned. "I read it on a restaurant menu."

"Friends," they said together, and they drank. Then Rose did cry, and O'Neill looked across her head at Alan, his eyes wet, and Dukas sniffed.

Time seems to freeze, and he is able to look at them and think but not to move, and he sees that they will never be like this again, not merely never so young again but never so comfortable; nor will life seem so easy. It is a turning-point, and what he senses but cannot put into words is that time brings trouble and pain, and it is coming to them. And, as if the effort to warn them causes time to run again, he moves, and the moment is shattered.

It is for such times that you keep a dog, because when it pushed its head into the circle and sneezed, everybody could laugh, and the mood was broken.

They wanted the others to stay the night in case they'd drunk too much, but people gulped coffee, and O'Neill said he had to get back and pack. He went out the door, drawing the others like leaves in the track of a car. Then Rose and Alan stood together in the driveway, watching them get into their cars and start them up, and they told each other they were okay. The tail-lights diminished down the street and disappeared, and they held each other in the warm darkness.

"We're all going our separate ways," Alan said. It saddened him. "You blink and everything's changed."

She pulled him closer and then rocked them both with her shoulder and hip, as if shaking him to make him forget such things. "How'd you like to take a horny helo pilot to bed?" she said.

"Girls get pregnant that way."

"Yeah, I'd heard that." She tipped her head back. "I sort of had it in mind."

"Really?" He smiled back. Rose wanted six children, she said, a houseful; he thought three, max. They had only one.

"It works out just right if we're quick." Motherhood and a naval career could be made to mesh, she meant. "We might have to work at it all weekend."

"You're on." They walked into the house with their arms around each other's waist. Inside, the six empty glasses stood in a circle.

Part Two

Turning the Wheel

4

June–July

After the dinner that was supposed to have been O'Neill's farewell but that became before it was over a farewell for everybody, they all went their ways. O'Neill was the first to vanish, into what he called "the wilds of Africa." Dukas was suddenly too busy to answer his telephone. Bea Peretz had a long talk with her daughter and took her away for a week at Disney World, where she turned out to be the daughter she'd always loved.

Even Rose went away. Her new duty station was in Columbia, Maryland, a "new town" originally beyond the Washington, DC sprawl and now part of it, a suburb that was like stepping into some mediocre planner's dream of about 1960, a small town the way a nature walk is nature. It was too far from Little Creek for her to commute, and so while Alan finished his tour with the air wing, Rose got herself a furnished apartment and tried to cover her lack of a home life with work. That was Rose's solution to all problems—work.

Left to himself, Alan put their house on the market and got to know his son again. He drove around, too, getting his land eyes back, as he thought of it—learning that the world was not only gray p'ways and crowded rack rooms, and not only young people in blue and khaki, but that it had both the very old and the very young, the slovenly and the neat, the male and the gloriously, non-militarily female. The "boyz in the hood" look had really taken hold while he was away; every male under thirty and a lot of females, black and white, seemed to be wearing baggy pants and oversize T-shirts. He loved it. It was so different from the boat he wanted to sing and often did, just driving around with the radio on, singing and whacking his hands in time on the steering wheel.

In a little while, he would go to the new job at the Pentagon. He and Rose had agreed that they would take their time finding a new place to live, somewhere between his new post and hers. When he drew a circle on a map that touched Columbia and the Pentagon, the center was out there somewhere in Maryland. He figured it couldn't be worse than Little Creek. Still, he wondered what it was like to live where you really wanted to.

She came home on weekends, and after several of them she said she was pretty sure she was pregnant. Mikey, Alan, and the dog were all delirious to have her around. He asked her if she felt like a queen and she said no, after all it was only what she deserved.

They saw Mike Dukas a couple of times before he went to Bosnia. Alan saw him in Washington when he was going back and forth between his old duty and the new, as well. Mike was rushing around, learning a little Serbo-Croat to go with his Greek, getting outfitted by the marines in something approaching combat gear, getting briefings at State and DIA. He was pumped. Alan felt the nipping of envy, morosely aware that he was heading into three years of briefing admirals and putting together dailies. It was a good career move, but it wasn't *action*. He told Dukas so at their last meeting.

"You're a fucking action junkie!" Dukas said to him. They

were wolfing down crabcakes. "Where'd you get it from? Life isn't a goddam comic book, Al!"

"I'm not an action junkie!"

"You're an addict. An adrenaline-rush addict."

"Bullshit."

"I've seen you!"

"Well, I'm going cold-turkey for three years, okay? And you, you Greek slob—!"

Dukas picked a bit of shell out of his teeth and put it on his plate. He leaned his round head toward Alan and growled, "I don't want action! I just want to do some good!"

The next week, he was gone.

O'Neill was apparently in Africa, but Alan didn't hear from him.

He had almost three weeks' leave, but when his leave time was up and he went back to the air wing, it was a ghost. There was a lot of cleaning-up to do, old reports and pubs and general crap, but the life was out of it. He haunted the offices for a few days, thought of reporting to his new job early, resisted that (already leery of it, flinching from it) and volunteered to fill in at Atlantic Fleet Headquarters to keep himself from going bats in an empty office.

It gave him several days on a different point of the great wheel. He was sent to the intel sections where they were planning the next battle group's pre-deployment "fleet exercise," called officially Atlantic Fleet Battle Group Exercise 3-96, known now to everybody in the place as Fleetex. It was an interesting point to intersect the next BG, he found—looking at it not from the point of view of somebody on the carrier, but of somebody one step away from the strategic thinking of the Joint Chiefs.

Fleetex 3-96 existed then as an idea, expressed in a

two-inch-thick, ring-bound planning book, five subordinate planning guides, and a rapidly increasing roomful of transparencies, viewgraphs, computer projections, maps, and graphics. He worked on one detail, and one that tickled him: figuring aircraft fuel consumption for eight dispersed supply points, of which one was to be a deep-draft, ocean-going oiler whose skipper was already designated in one of the pubs—Captain John H. Parsills, who, as a then commander, had been the first squadron skipper under whom he had ever served.

Wow! Skipper Parsills on an oiler! Here was the great wheel in one of its odder turns. Between being commander of a squadron and the captain of a carrier, a new O-6 had to have experience as a deep-draft-vessel skipper, and the battle group's oiler was often that ship. Fifteen years in the air, three years in the water!

Alan smiled. He didn't even mind totting up fuel-consumption projections. Parsills had been a great guy, perhaps the finest CO he'd ever known. Helping him out, even on paper, was good.

Fleetex 3-96 was like a vast war game, with real ships and real aircraft for counters. It could best be understood by placing its master transparency, BG3/96-LL1, over its wide-view map (Exhibit 5). The map showed the Western Atlantic down to part of the Caribbean and north to the Carolinas. The transparency showed the Mediterranean, from Tripoli, Libya, north to the Adriatic and Venice. You put the transparency over the map, lined up the registration points, and saw the game scenario: Libya's Gulf of Sidra thus became a bay in the outer Bahamas; Gibraltar was a spot in the northern waters, Bosnia both somewhere out in the Atlantic and, for hands-on bombing, the island of Vieques south of Puerto Rico. Reference to one of the planning books would reveal that a Canadian frigate and a British destroyer were to play opposing (Orange, read "Libyan") forces, along with four smaller Bahamian gunboats, out of Nassau. (*Nice duty*, he thought.) Opposing-force air strikes would come from Marine Corps and Navy F/A-18s at Cherry Point, Beaufort, and Jax, with refueling by USAF KC-10s, mostly reserves, flying from East Coast bases. The focus of two of the three phases of the exercise was a point in the Bay of Sidra that looked, to Alan, dangerously close to Libyan territorial waters. Designated merely "Alpha," it had on at least one viewgraph a ship's symbol. Without going through the stack of binders, he could see that what Fleetex 3-96 was going to mock up was some sort of provocative action involving a US or NATO vessel in Libya's Gulf.

This was not merely a game. You didn't get that specific in a game.

It looked to him to be an interesting undertaking— "interesting" understood to mean dangerous, with serious international implications. Not to mention military: the Fleetex Phase One and Phase Two were scripted to stage an event at Point Alpha while running opposing-force actions against the battle group from two directions, which might as well be understood as Libya and Yugoslavia. *Yugoslavia?* With a wild card thrown in for good measure, representing either other Islamic nations in the region or somebody with the ability to do force projection in the southern Mediterranean. *Meaning, it's going to piss a lot of people off!*

On his third day at his desk in a big room full of desks, somebody suddenly shouted, "Flag officer on deck!" and Alan, like everybody else, jumped to his feet and braced. Moments later, a remarkably tall man came in with an urgency that carried him to the center of the room before he even looked around. He was trailed by a captain, two commanders, and a smarmy-looking jg with chicken guts on his shoulder—somebody's nephew who had got staff duty instead of a destroyer. *Flag puke*, as his friend Rafehausen used to call them—not the ones who had earned their way there, but the ones who were doing it on Daddy's nickel.

The admiral stared around him and then made for the big table where the master chart was. While he was turned away, the guy at the desk next to Alan's mouthed "BG" to him, and then something that Alan figured out as "Newman," the name of BG 7's admiral. It was The Man himself.

Admiral Newman leaned over the big chart. He must have been six-six, Alan thought, towering over everybody else, a rather gangly man who looked somehow untidy even in a spotless uniform. He had tough eyes and a not very forgiving jaw, and as he leaned over the chart, Alan could see him in profile. He was not looking at a happy man, he thought. And he was right.

"Where's the nuclear sub?" Admiral Newman said in a raspy voice.

Somebody said that was being handled over uh there, and they all walked over there, and a female jg started to explain that Libya had diesel subs and so they were working on the scenario that—

"I want a nuclear sub in the opposing force. Victor II. Do it." But he may have said the last words to one of the O-5s with him, although the jg staffer almost wet himself trying to show how willing he was to do it if only somebody would explain what a Victor II was. Alan looked at the guy next to him and winked.

The admiral took an O-6 by the elbow (either his flag captain or his chief of staff, Alan guessed) and came to the center of the room and said in a low voice, as if he thought they couldn't be overheard, "—gotta have more

Soviet-style Orange forces; these guys don't get it. *This is not acceptable!*" Then he strode out.

The room relaxed. Everybody seemed to think this was a pretty funny scene. The guy next to him said, "Oh, he does that about once a month. He wants to fight *Commies*!"

A couple of days later, Alan went back to the air wing offices and began to wind up his affairs. A week later, he was to report to the Pentagon. The experience with Fleetex remained as an interesting sideways look at the wheel, at least until he discovered what Rose's role would be in what was to happen at that dot in the Gulf of Sidra designated Point Alpha.

Dar-es-Salaam, Tanzania.
The Dar chief had a very fine job and thought he was a very fine fellow, one successful in an admirable line of work. He was clearly not so convinced of O'Neill's worth, although willing to give him a little time before a final judgment, probably negative, was made. His name was John Prior, inevitably called Jack; he was white (hence not Black Jack); he had got as high as he would ever get in the Agency but didn't yet know it. Fiftyish, lean, furrowed, he looked as if he might have a second career in modeling low-end fishing and hunting underwear.

"I understand you didn't want to come here," he said.

"Not exactly—"

Prior went right on. "Lots of people think they don't want to come here. It's stupid. You go where Uncle needs you, right? Well." Prior had a very pleasant corner office in the embassy, with an American receptionist sitting outside (also Agency, minimally trained but capable). He had a good house and a fine car, and he lived in clear—that is, no assumed identity. O'Neill would not live in clear, at least some of the time.

"Locals'll get on to you but not tight, you know? They live and let live, so long's we share a little and pass some bucks along. That's my bailiwick, dig? Don't get into it. Leave it to me. They won't hassle you much. How good's your Swahili?"

"Excellent." O'Neill had done a six-week immersion course.

"Bullshit." Prior's Swahili was terrible, therefore everybody's must be. "Don't get smart and try to go native or something. Black guys confuse them. Give yourself a year to fit in. Hey?"

"Well, I've looked at the files—"

"Yeah, yeah, yeah." He shoved a pile of folders across his desk. "These are Requests for Information from DC. I've tagged five of them for my attention. You get six and seven; they're softballs, so you can learn on them." He stared at O'Neill. "Don't recruit anybody until I say so. The word is 'Go slow.'"

"I would have thought—"

"Don't think yet. Go slow on that, too. Your predecessor tried to set the world on fire and all that caught was his own pants. I had to get him out of the country before the whole place went up. This is a country where we got things working good for us. I don't want it screwed up."

The whole western fringe, O'Neill knew, was in turmoil because of things that were going on in Rwanda and Zaire; there was a neo-Marxist, anti-Mobutu group of Zaireans that had been living in Tanzania for a decade and were supposed to be getting ready to invade their own country; Tanzanian military forces were supposed to be lining up behind them. This was to be ignored?

"Kabila and the Zairean Tutsis—" O'Neill started to say.

"You keep out of that. I've got that under control. I

116

want you to focus on the economy. Secondary focus, trans-shipment of drugs from southern Asia."

"My predecessor had some good contacts in Rwanda."

"MacPherson *inherited* some contacts in Rwanda, and he blew them. They're gone! He was an asshole, I told you. Let it lie." Prior tried to stare him down, and O'Neill let him. His new boss, after all. "Rwanda is another country," Prior said, his voice deep with significance.

"'And besides, the wench is dead,'" O'Neill said. He smiled. *Get it? No, you don't get it. Oh, shit.* But he was saved, because Prior didn't listen to what was said to him by subordinates unless he had asked a direct question.

"Repeat, Rwanda is not in your domain."

"You don't want me to even try to contact them?"

"I want you to work with what you got. You got two good clusters of econ-intel contacts that MacPherson didn't screw up; just stay with them. There's a couple of business guys that I met socially I'm passing on to you; I want you to bring them along. Thank God, you strike me as the kind of guy might get along here if he behaves himself—you dress well, you talk well, you look okay."

Okay? There was a compliment for you.

"You play tennis?" Prior said.

"Of course."

Prior glanced at him. Prior, he guessed, had not grown up in such a way that "of course" he played tennis. "You got a doubles date tomorrow with Amanda and one of the business guys I told you about." Amanda was the receptionist. "I was supposed to go but I'm going to say I'm suddenly down with a turned ankle and you're taking my place. If you can beat them, do it; the guy'll be impressed. He's in the blue folder."

"How real is my cover job?" O'Neill said.

Prior snickered. It was a beginner's question. "Your job is

117

being a case officer. Period." So much for being the Deputy Attaché for Trade.

O'Neill hugged the folders to his chest and started down the corridor toward his temporary office. Go slow, read the RFIs, and play tennis. It wasn't quite like being James Bond.

The Pentagon.

Alan Craik walked down the long, long corridor, past a stand of flags and a wall of framed photographs of admirals, past door after door after door. It was early; a hundred, a thousand other men and women were also walking this corridor and all the other corridors exactly like it in the concentric pentagons that gave the building its name. Now and again, through an open door, he could see right through to windows that gave on the vast inner courtyard, and, across it—over the trees, the walks, the tables—other windows, other walls.

He held his attaché case with his orders tight against his right side. His morning coffee burned in his throat. *Christ, I'm all tensed up*, he thought. *Why? This is going to be a piece of cake.* Tense because he had already persuaded himself he was going to hate it, he knew. All during that mostly sleepless night, he had told himself not to pre-judge it. Don't anticipate. Be ready to be pleasantly surprised. Try to love it. If you don't like your job, there's something wrong with you, not the job.

He found the right door at last and turned his orders over to a yeoman, and eventually he was led to an office where a woman full commander with a pleasant face shook his hand and said Welcome aboard and Boy are we glad you're here! We're three slots short!

She took him around, introduced him. Sketched the roughest outline of the job—reading nine sets of dailies, compiling, writing five summaries, editing, briefing. A big smile. "Could you run a classified package out to the Agency for us? Got a courier pass? You get one up on four—Jackson'll tell you how. Get it there before lunch, okay?" Big smile.

He had hardly settled behind a desk he was told was his (he was not sure; there was a brassiere in one otherwise empty drawer) when a woman in civilian clothes leaned in his cubicle door. "Hi. I'm Jan—I'm a plans editor. Not why I'm here. Subject: your turn to make the coffee." Big smile. "Your turn started two minutes ago and the natives are getting restless."

Not exactly James Bond.

IV.

Suter had been away at the major contractor's in Texas, and after that Touhey had had him trotting around congressional offices in Washington, so he hadn't been at the Columbia location for almost two weeks. He was getting the feel of the job and the place, and he almost wished he had come there directly instead of by way of the Agency; the place had an enormous feeling of things happening, of energy. He found that he admired Touhey, even while his allegiance was to Shreed. Of course, that could change. But it was early days for any of that; for now, he was back, getting to know the offices, some of the people, getting to understand the complexities of the compartmentalization that kept Peacemaker's secret-weapon function utterly separate from its public, intelligence function.

He had found early on why Han had rushed him through sub-level two. There were, in a limited-access lab, mockups of the modules that latched to Peacemaker's main unit. Most people in the know referred to the main unit itself as Peacemaker, the modules as "the intel pack" and "the weapon." Officially, these three were called the Low-Orbit Maneuverable Satellite, or LOMS; the Acquisition and Radiation Module, or ARM; and the Direct Application Module, DAM. Everybody agreed that the weapon module should somehow have had the ARM acronym, but that wasn't the way it had worked out. Actually, DAM sounded not too shabby as the nickname of a weapon.

Part of the design problem of Peacemaker was Touhey's requirement that ARM and DAM attach to the LOMS in exactly the same way and have exactly the same shell. Visually, it would be difficult to tell one from the other; the observer would have to get close enough to read the legends on the latches. Touhey had planned way ahead. What he wanted—and got—was a device whose artist's renderings could go direct to the media without compromising its real nature. That was where they were now, releasing generalized pretty pictures and PR sweet talk, visiting pet congressmen (they were all men) and handing out information packets. They'd made the evening news as a "ground-breaking short-term satellite to plug holes in America's surveillance grid." Meanwhile, at a minor contractor in Indiana, the DAM module was being built in drop-dead secrecy.

Suter spent twenty minutes with Touhey, reviewing some of George Shreed's questions about the project, and then he went up to the cafeteria for coffee. He tried to be seen up there, to get them accustomed to him as a real member of the team. As usual, the big, windowed space had young people dressed like athletes at most of the tables. Suter looked them over, thought they weren't very interesting, then snapped his eyes back to a woman he didn't recognize, who had been turned away. She was dark, shapely, truly pretty. *Eye candy*, he found himself thinking.

She was sitting by the window so that the outside glare made him slit his eyes to see her. *Nice.*

He walked toward her, pretending to look for a place to sit and covertly looking at her again. *Really nice.* He was going to walk right up to her and ask to sit at her table because everything else was full (although it wasn't) when somebody called, "Hey, Suter!"

It was Han. Suter smiled. It paid to stay on Han's good side, he had found. People *liked* Han, God knows why.

"Hey, Colonel." Suter sat down where he could look at the woman.

Han grinned. "This is a side of you I didn't anticipate," he said.

"Sir?"

Han grinned some more. "If your tongue hangs out any farther, you're going to wet your tie. She's married."

"Who?"

Han laughed. Suter, he said, was something else.

Suter glanced at the woman. *Married.* Oh, well—so what?

Sarajevo.
Mike Dukas was standing by a window in the newly painted office of Sarajevo's Associate Deputy Chief of Police for NATO Liaison. New office, new title, new man. The guy was a Bosnian Muslim, a desk cop, doing what he did best—managing information. In this case, he was briefing Dukas.

Dukas had been in Sarajevo for twenty-two hours. He was still groggy from jet lag and he didn't have an office of his own yet. He was looking down into the courtyard of a small apartment building next door and wondering what the long heaps of earth like graves were.

When the Associate Deputy Chief shut up to take a

breath, Dukas said, "What are those?" He pointed down. "The things that look like graves?"

The Bosnian hesitated a moment, then suddenly became human. "Those are graves," he said quietly.

Dukas looked at him—disbelief, questioning.

Entirely human now, the Bosnian cop gave him a sad smile. "We couldn't get to the cemeteries because of the bombardments. The snipers. We buried the dead where we found room. I buried my mother in her rose bushes."

Welcome to Sarajevo.

5

July

IVI.

Her name was Rose Siciliano, and she was a lieutenant-commander in the Navy. Suter was amused by that, because when he'd seen her Friday, she'd been wearing blue jeans and a Redskins T-shirt. The clothes had meant she probably worked on Upper Level 2, where the whiz-kids played and things had low security classifications. Suter had been surprised to learn that in fact she worked on S1, the first underground level, where security classifications were high and Peacemaker got a lot of its work done. But the S1 location meant she knew Peacemaker only as an intelligence satellite and was walled off from DAM.

He had been back a total of nine hours, four of those spent with a lot of boring crap about British real estate in the South Atlantic that might make potential test targets for Peacemaker, and more spent with the general and some with Han, and he'd still found time to ask about the woman he'd seen at the cafeteria window. He'd thought about her at home, thought about her on the drive in.

She was the just-designated Seaborne Launch Officer. Her arrival signaled Peacemaker's move from mockup to launchable prototype.

He managed to catch her in the cafeteria by making three trips there his second morning back. He was supposed to be reading targeting pubs, getting up to speed on the flashiest way of using Peacemaker. He was a speed reader, very good and very smart, if he did say so himself; he could spare the time to chase this wonderful-looking woman. And, the third time was the charm: there she was, in the same chair by the window. This time she was wearing a dress and looking like a businesswoman. Even more terrific.

"Mind if I join you?" he said. "I'm Ray Suter."

She sort of smiled, but also looked a little pained.

"I'm a little lost, and I could use some sympathy. I'm new here."

"Sure, sit."

She was not an easy piece of work. Her eyes were amused by him, not charmed. She also had an innate toughness that surprised him; it hadn't been evident on Friday. Maybe it had been the T-shirt, the suggestion of somebody young and naive.

"I thought you were one of the computer kids," he said, trying to sound like a man who was embarrassed by some small stupidity. "I noticed you Friday."

"Friday's Casual Day in my place," she said. "Today we're just regular people. I gotta go." She was on her feet, tossing her Styrofoam cup into a plastic receptacle.

"I'll see you again," he said. He stood.

"Probably." She looked him up and down, still not charmed. A very tough woman inside that softness. But she smiled. "It's a small place," she said.

That afternoon, he called up her personnel file on his computer. He could do that because of Shreed's influence with Touhey. He had access to everything. Almost the first thing he saw on her file was that she was married to Alan Craik.

His first response was that it was a real kick in the ass. The second was that something might be made of it. After all, taking Craik's wife to bed would be killing two birds with one stone.

But it would take time. Well, he had time. Launch was still five months away.

IV.

Rose loved the work at IVI. She was surprised. Desk jobs were usually a pain in the ass, something to be got through because the detailer said it was good for your career, but this one was both exciting and demanding. Two or three days a week, she was on the road, either visiting the contractors or hitting offices in the Navy department. She was going to be launch officer on a ship, and she didn't know zip about ships, except what you had to know to land a chopper on one. More visits, more reading. She set herself up for a week's cruise on a survey ship of the kind they would be using.

Alan was living in a short-term rental house in Falls Church, with Mikey and the dog. He hadn't sold the Norfolk house yet and fussed about it—somewhat childishly, she thought. She missed him, but when the chance came to go to Houston to watch a missile launch from Mission Control, she went and lost a weekend with him. And Mikey. And the dog. She was pregnant but made little of it yet. *In a few months*, she told herself. When, at an IVI planning meeting, Touhey had talked about moving the test launch date up, she had found herself regretting the pregnancy. What if she had to take childbirth leave and they brought in somebody else and that's when the launch went? Then, guiltily, she scolded herself. *Where are your priorities?*

East Africa.

O'Neill was getting the hang of it pretty well. Prior had told him so. Prior was fairly generous with compliments, actually, applying some version of the pop psychology the Agency rented from its consultants—"Motivate Your Subordinates," "Catch More Flies with Sugar," "The Four Steps to Excellence." Or was it five? Or three? Mostly, what he said was, "God, at least you're better than MacPherson!"

MacPherson fucked every female agent he could get close to and some of the men, I really believe it, Prior had told him. *He had no more idea of how to behave than my golden lab.* And the files and the stories around the embassy showed that, indeed, MacPherson had been one of God's great fuckups, a possibly unique creation. Worst of all, he had let sex come into everything, which was not morally wrong but was, in O'Neill's view, a mistake because sex was too powerful to use; it ended up using you. He would never make that mistake, he was sure.

O'Neill had a tiny house on the mountain slope outside Arusha, but he was seldom there. He also had an office in Arusha, but he was seldom there, either. The office ran itself, thanks to three female in-country employees who were vetted yearly out of Dar. Mostly, O'Neill was on the road, touting the wonders of capitalism and making contacts, but really driving, driving the roads to work out surveillance routes and trying to apply the lessons of the Ranch. The lessons were a bad joke in Africa, having been designed for cities and developed countries, the Ranch's idea of the terrain of espionage being the shopping center and the parking garage and the supermarket. Now, O'Neill drove hundreds of miles, trying to establish routes from here to—where? That tree? This village without a telephone? That abandoned cement factory? This overgrown sisal field?

Thus, the Rotary Clubs and the Chambers of Commerce and above all the colleges and schools became major waypoints. His excuse for going there was his canned pep talk on Africa and the Free Market Economy. He thought of it as the Flea Market Economy but didn't say so. He was a good speaker, and educated Africans in particular took to him because he reminded them either of their own days on an American campus or their days in England. English education was still the ideal, and Cambridge O levels, although abandoned in England, were revered here, and O'Neill, with his good clothes and his manners and his cultured voice, was very like those African academics who were more British than the British. They wore dark suits and had morning and afternoon tea in the Common Room, brought round by tea ladies pushing metal tea carts. Like academics everywhere, these were suckers for flattery and money, and the two in combination got him a lot of likely recruits. The trouble was, would they know anything worth squat or would they just want to spout off?

Mostly, they were merely excuses for trying to lay out detailed routes.

He had a five-year-old Toyota LandCruiser. Most of his travel was in the north and east of the country, where the modern economic activity was, but he made reasons to go west to the shore of Lake Tanganyika and up to Bikuba, where there were signs of military presence, because he knew that Rwanda was going to be big, no matter how cautious Prior was. He was also going nuts from the frustration of doing nothing important. On weekends, he came back to Arusha and sat in his nearly empty house. He wrote letters to Alan Craik full of up-to-date, inside stuff and sent them in the diplomatic bag. He reviewed the old files left by his woeful predecessor and the far better man before him,

Hammer, who had set up the networks that MacPherson trashed.

He knew that there should be survivors out there who could be wooed back. To get the files, he had to drive to Dar, sign the files out, drive them to Arusha, read them, and drive them back and sign them in before his workday started on Monday. When he pointed out that the files could be sent via e-mail because Tanzania had no means of monitoring transmission, Prior told him that the official Agency position was that e-mail is not secure.

O'Neill selected what he saw as Hammer's best three agents in Rwanda.

When he next went west, he left a sign at three places, and then he waited.

One agent was dead. One was terrified, living under a new name in Zambia. The third would respond.

6

August

IVI.

Rose had stopped going to the cafeteria for morning coffee because there was too much to do. Or that was what she said—and believed. An outsider might have said she had found work to fill that time. An outsider might have said she liked to boast of never having a minute, even for the cafeteria.

Suter stopped by sometimes. Rose found she rather liked him. She knew he was coming on to her. Many men did. So?

"At it again," he said, leaning in her office door. "Got a minute?" He always had some excuse for visiting her. She didn't discourage him. She learned stuff from him. And was flattered by the attention. Suter was a good-looking guy. Unlike Alan, however, he was aware of it. Vain.

"*Half* a minute," she said. "I'm swamped."

He had learned to bring his own coffee. Hers was terrible, made by some Seaman Apprentice first thing in the morning and left to cook down to its acidic worst all day. He told her some bit of detail about adjustments in the launch angle and said, "So you want to be an astronaut."

"Sure do." She was writing notes to herself about the launch angles.

"Ride the Vomit Comet? Join the Team of Heroes?"

"You got it."

"I might be able to help you there." She looked up. Her face was expressionless and did not give him the encouragement he wanted. "I know some people in the program."

"I like to make it on my own," she said.

"That's not how it works."

"That why you left the Navy?"

He had never mentioned his Navy career to her. It irritated him that she knew something like that without his having told her. "How'd you know that?" he said.

"My husband."

Of course! That shithead Craik had told her all about him. He could picture the letters Craik had written home from the boat, full of self-pity and bitterness. He felt better. "I can imagine what he said about me," Suter said with a smile.

"Really?" She had been writing, finished, looked up. "Actually, he didn't say anything. I was the one who mentioned your name, and he put two and two together and guessed you were his old boss."

"And *then* what'd he say about me?"

"Nothing." She seemed surprised that he'd ask.

Well, of course he couldn't believe that. Craik *must* have given her an earful. That was okay; bad press was better than no press. Maybe she found her husband just a bit of a shithead, too? "At least you mentioned my name to him," he said with a grin.

"Valdez!" she shouted. She had a hell of a voice when she needed it; Suter resisted jumping out of his chair at her sudden bellow. Somebody had passed behind him out in the corridor. *What the hell?* he thought. A male voice behind him said, "Yeah," and Rose called over and through Suter, "Show me how to acquire the Orbit Adjustment file

130

out of White Sands, will you? I keep getting some message saying I'm committing an illegal act and I get closed down. It hurts my feelings."

"Yeah, ma'am, I told you twice already." He came in, a compact, dark, near-teenager in blue jeans. "Hey, how ya doin'?" he said to Suter without looking at him. He went right to Rose's computer.

"Valdez is my resident geek," she said. The words had a final tone to them, as if she had said something like, Oh, look how late it's getting, meaning it was time for Suter to go. She turned away from him and toward Valdez, who was leaning over her computer.

"Uh—" Suter was annoyed. He didn't like being dismissed. He liked even less being dismissed in favor of a Latino kid who had barely finished high school. "Maybe I'll stick around and learn something," he said.

She gave him a dazzling smile. "Valdez is the smartest computer jock in LantFleet. He's got Silicon Valley after him—don't you, Billie?"

"They jus' want me for my body," the kid said. His head was close to hers over the keyboard. Suter saw that he had a tiny tattoo behind his ear. Suter hated him.

Late in the day, Rose and Valdez caught a flight out of BWI to Houston. She was starting to ride herd on the thousands of details that affected the ship and the launch hardware; from Houston, they would go to Newport News to pick up the civilian ship for her week's orientation. Go and go and go.

It was not enough for Rose to be assured by somebody else that things were going well. She had to see it for herself. She had to see the drawings, the mockups, the prototype. That first launch was not going off without her understanding *everything* about it. Valdez went along

131

because he was her personal computer whiz—requested by name from her old squadron, where she had learned almost everything she knew about computers from him.

"How come you know so much, anyway?" she said as they flew over West Virginia, for once not using the flight to press her nose against the screen of her laptop. This was not a sudden desire to relax; Valdez was showing signs of unhappiness, and if her computer geek was unhappy, she knew she was going to be unhappy somewhere down the line.

"I'm a genius." He meant it as a joke, but it was literally true, if you went by IQ scores.

"You weren't born a computer geek, Valdez."

"No, ma'am, I was born a spic. I was goin' to be a criminal mastermind, but Mister Carvarlho got to me first."

"Okay," she said, "I'll ask—who was Mister Carvarlho?"

"We called him 'Mister Horse,' because *caballo* means horse. You say 'Carvarlho' fast, it sounds like *caballo*—horse, okay? I hated him. He was PR, half black, he always wore suits, he was a born-again Christian with an attitude."

"Not your ideal."

Valdez laughed. "My *nightmare*! That guy was the opposite of everything I was gonna be. I was a gangbanger at eleven; at twelve, I was carrying a gun. No kiddin'! I had this Rossi .38 special, nickel, real shiny—I thought I was cool. I shot it *once*—I'm runnin' the street at two a.m., just for the hell of it I shot it. Blam! I only had five bullets, that's what it held—like a Chief's Special, right, only a Rossi?—it was light, nice, but a lotta recoil for a little kid. Anyway, I carried that; I had a place I put it outside the school, I'd leave it in the morning, pick it up as soon as I got out. I was bad."

The Navy didn't like people who had been *ba-a-a-d*, she

thought. He must have got awfully good awfully quick. "You never got caught?"

Valdez hesitated. He was slumped down in his seat, his left knee and calf pressed against the back of the seat in front. He was frowning. "My dad caught me. Him and me didn't get along then. My dad—" Valdez squirmed upright. "He was workin' two jobs, sendin' money home, didn't speak English—I came in drunk one night, he was comin' home from his night job—I'm twelve years old, remember—and the gun drops out on the floor. He just looks at it, and then he starts to cry. I thought he was a jerk. I di'n't know, you know? I see it now—the guy was worn out, beat down. But Jeez, to be a hotshit gangbanger and see your old man cry— ! I thought I was so cool, man."

Valdez plucked at a little packet of salted peanuts that had been put in front of him. "You understand about bein' Latino?" he said. "In *Cleveland*?"

"Probably not."

Valdez sniffed, like a bull inhaling. "Couple days later, I'm walking down the hall in school—I'm in junior high, seventh grade through ten are all together—and this hand comes outa nowhere and grabs my shoulder. I was gonna deck the guy. *Nobody* touched me—tough guy, huh? That's when I found Mister Horse was one *strong* born-again Christian. One hand, he held me, I couldn't move. 'Come in here, young man,' he says. Whoosh! I'm in his room. He holds me like a frigging vise! When I'm quiet, he says, 'You are the newest member of the Computer Club. Welcome to the Club.' I think he's loco—I think he's lost something up under his hair. Later, I find him and my father are in a Bible-reading thing together. My father has told him about the gun. Mister Horse sits me down in front of my first computer and puts a joystick in my hand and he turns on a simulation game.

"I'm hooked."

He chewed on his peanuts. He shrugged. "Couple months later, I was doing simple programming."

"How's your father now?" she said.

"He died." Valdez chewed. "He took my gun, he threw it in the river. I hated him. Then he was dead, I understood him a little better. Too late. Sad story, huh?"

"Well, yeah."

"Lotsa sad stories. World is full of sad stories. Let's change the subject." Valdez squirmed again, shot a glance at her. "I'm not real happy with this job," he said.

That was a surprise. A shock, in fact. "It's a great job!" she said.

"Great for you, maybe." He shook his head. "They're not giving me stuff."

"Who?"

"Them. Whoever." He waved a hand. "In computers, what difference is *who*? Difference is what, Commander. Lemme put it in Navy: 'Insufficient data are being provided to Petty Officer Valdez.' See? No *who*."

"Insufficient data about what?"

"If I knew that, I'd have the data, woul'n't I? What I mean is, there's too much code for the stream I'm getting."

"How can you tell?"

"I can *tell*. That's like me asking you how you can tell a chopper is loaded wrong from the way it flies. I can *tell*."

She was already protective of Peacemaker. "You don't have a need to know," she said primly.

"Bull*shit* I don't have a need to know! You think I'm gonna trust my work on a system where I'm closed out of part of the data stream? I might as well ask for a transfer right now."

"Valdez!" She sat upright, turned on him. "What's this 'transfer' crap?"

"I might do it." He looked like a stubborn child. "I believe in freedom of information."

"This is the goddam US military, and information is classified, not free!"

He rolled his head toward her. He had large eyes the color of dark chocolate. "You know what MP3 is?" he said.

"Are you changing the subject on me, Valdez?"

He shook his head. "MP3 is the way you download music and play it through your computer so you listen to what you want, when you want—no CDs, no albums, no nothing decided for you by somebody else. That's freedom of information. You know what open source code is? Same kinda thing. I *believe* in those things. I also believe in the US Navy, but if the Navy gonna put me in a position where I got to knuckle under to somebody else's idea of what comes through my computer—" He made a horizontal chopping motion. "Finito, man."

She was angry—she recognized that she was getting on top of the job because she was beginning to get angry about it more often, *caring*—but she controlled herself and said, almost but not quite flirting with him, "Valdez—you wouldn't desert me, would you?"

But he wouldn't look at her. The movie had come on and he was watching it without headphones. "You find out what's bein' kept from me," he said.

Rose sat back, arms folded. Problems, problems.

On the flight to Newport News two days later, it was as if settling into the seats and snapping the seatbelts put them back where they had left off. Nothing had been said in the interim; in fact, they had hardly seen each other. But clearly, the earlier conversation had been somewhere on

135

her mind, because the first thing she said after they took off was, "Can I ask you something personal?"

"Sure, why not?" He flashed her a grin, all teeth and big brown eyes. "Maybe I won't answer, though."

"What's that tattoo behind your right ear?"

"Pachuco."

"What's that?"

He didn't believe it. "You don't know pachuco?" He laughed, made the face that means, This is fucking incredible! "You know *Zoot Suit*." He said it as a fact, not a question.

She was laughing now—at herself, at both of them. "What's *Zoot Suit*? I'm sorry, Billie—"

"You don' know *Zoot Suit*? Edward James Olmos, man! Luis *Valdez*!" Now, he was pleading with her to know. Then it was too much; he threw himself back in his seat and gave up. "I'll bring you the video." He started to take out his earphones, then turned to her again. "I saw *Zoot Suit* when I was a little kid. Another kid put the pachuco mark behind my ear; most guys got it on their hand, here, between the fingers so it doesn't show. Then I did him. We weren't gangbangers yet; we were being cool, big-time, but— It meant something to us! Zoot suits!" He shook his head. "It was a Latino thing. I kind of gave it all up when I went to Jesus, but, you know, it's part of me, man."

"Are you a born-again now?"

He folded his arms and stared at the seatback. "Yeah, and yeah, and finally no. I been to Jesus so many times I get frequent-flyer miles. You not laughin'? That's one of my best lines, Commander; guys always laugh, 'cause it's cool." He slouched lower. He was a small man and the seat fit him. "Jesus got me out of the gangs and He got me through high school and into computers, but I couldn't take church. Jesus, *si*, His people, no way, Jose. So, Jesus and me got our own church." He looked at her, his head now lower than hers. "Okay?"

"Your mom and dad disappointed?"

"Yeah. Big-time. But after my old man died, my mom, she kind of toned it down. Maybe one day she'll go back to the priests, I think—one of those little old ladies in a black shawl, goin' to mass every mornin'. She believed the pentecostals because he did, I guess."

"How did he die?" Rose asked gently.

"Fell off a scaffolding. Tired out." That was enough of that; he wriggled upright. "Hey, did you find out what I ast you?"

"About the data stream?" She shook her head. She was a little embarrassed; the truth was, she didn't understand the question well enough to ask it.

"Okay, I tell you how we goin' to get the information. The Peacemaker electronics bein' done on the cheap—off-the-shelf. That's fine; there's good stuff out there. But what it means is, someplace there's a contract for all the software. You get that for me. Once I see all the software laid out, I know what's goin' on." He pulled down his tray-table. "You want to keep your computer geek happy, remember, Commander." He started to put on the earphones, then held them away for a moment. "You get me the list of software, I get you a video of *Zoot Suit*."

Right. One more detail to take care of.

Washington.

At home in his rental apartment after Mikey went to bed, Alan had started "flying" a simulator on his PC. It was like a parody of the idea of going to flight school. It was a mockery of his desire to get out of his job. His old squadron friend Rafehausen had asked him to

137

visit him at the War College at Newport, where he'd give him a real flying lesson, he said, and Alan had so far refused because he had had some dumb idea that by staying home he was being loyal to Rose. Or something.

One night, he crashed a Cessna three times in a row on the virtual ramp of his virtual aircraft carrier, and then he telephoned Rafe and said When should he come up? They made a date for it, and he told Rafe that he'd just learned that his board had deep-selected him for O-4 for next year. It wasn't like telling Rose, but she was on the road somewhere.

Off Hampton Roads.

The USNS ship *Grace Orbis* rolled in heavy swells and took enough water over the bows to splash against the bridge windows as if it had come from a monstrous bucket. Below, Rose and Valdez made their way along a narrow corridor whose steel bulkheads were studded with rivets, their path partly blocked by "knee-knockers," those unmovable metal uprights—fire-hose connections, corners of lockers, sills of watertight doors—that put bruises on the shins of everybody before a voyage is over. The ship's roll swayed Rose against a bulkhead and then out again, and she giggled. Ahead of her, Valdez was walking with his feet wide apart and his hands out at each side to keep himself off the bulkheads. He looked to her like a mechanical toy. She giggled again.

"Well," she shouted over the storm, "you wanted a change!"

"Hey, man, this is too much like being a sailor!" he bellowed.

They were doing a quick familiarization cruise. She was air Navy; now she had to learn more about what the despised line officers did. The *Grace Orbis* was a much smaller ship than *Philadelphia,* the one that would launch Peacemaker, but *Philadelphia* was at Newport News being refitted for the launch. She figured that if she could stay upright aboard *Grace Orbis*, *Philadelphia* would be a cakewalk.

A ladder led up to a watertight hatch and the deck. To Valdez's disgust, she wanted to see the storm close up. She gave him a shove. "Move it!"

Valdez started up. The bow rose and he swayed back and she thought he was going to come down on top of her; she put a hand in the middle of his back and pushed. The bow started down and he swayed to vertical again, and she started up after him. He was at the hatch, reaching for the big white handle, and she was halfway up the ladder when the ship made a more abrupt move to starboard, the bow going down and the deck swinging far over to her right. She started to make some sound to show she wasn't scared, the sort of sound you might make on a roller-coaster, and then she felt Valdez sway back and down and into her, and her feet were going out from under her, sliding, and briefly she was airborne and then slamming against the metal rail. She slid down, banging her shins on the ladder, feeling a sharp, horrible pain in her gut and then hitting hard on the bottom step and bouncing once more to the steel deck below. Valdez was beside her in two jumps.

She thought *I've hurt myself,* and then almost at the same time, *Don't show it, don't show it!* and she was clutching his arm, feeling the bow come up, taking her with it, swaying; she clutched his arm and said, "I'm all right— I'm all right—" She clawed herself halfway upright. The pain flashed down her abdomen and into her thighs and she thought she would fall again, and she held on to his arm with both hands, staring into his brown eyes so she wouldn't pass out. "I'm really all right— !"

"Oh, Jesus," he was moaning, "oh, help us, Jesus— !"

"Get me up straight—I've got to stand up straight—I'm all right, I'm all right— !"

7

August

East Africa.

O'Neill sits beside Lake Victoria. He is waiting for her—the female agent who responded to his sign.

O'Neill is at peace, perhaps for the first time. He has found he likes Africa. He understands now what Craik meant about its size, about its smell, the look of it. He has no feeling of coming home; to the contrary, it is the most alien place he has ever been. Yet it brings him peace.

She will wear green, and if something is wrong she will also wear a red scarf. This is not the sort of tradecraft they taught him at the Ranch, but Ranch tradecraft is not designed for Africa in the 1990s; it is designed for Europe in the 1970s. He smiles to himself. The wonder of it is that any of what they taught him actually does work here. The cops-and-robbers of counter-surveillance, for example. Most of the psychology of recruitment. It is like being a Boy Scout and finding that what the Boy Scout Manual says about building a fire really does make flame, even if nobody in his right mind would ever make it that way.

Perhaps, when he goes back, he will teach about Africa at the Ranch.

He sees a green dress coming toward him. It is still far away, but he can see the swing of her, her size, and he can see that she does not wear a red scarf.

O'Neill rises and goes to meet his future.

Which is Alan Craik's future.

Near Newport, Rhode Island.

"You're over-controlling." Rafe's voice was calm, devoid of criticism, an LSO voice.

Alan eased up on the stick, flexed his hand, and tried to keep the little gauge that measured rate of climb centered on zero through the turn. The single-engine plane wobbled slightly, very like a horse that knows it has a novice at the reins.

"See the runway?" The question seemed superfluous— the ancient runway of Quonsett Reserve Naval Air Station almost seemed to fill the viewscreen. "Center up. Ease up on the stick. The plane will fly just fine without you."

Rafe spoke to the tower one more time, but Alan's entire concentration was on the airplane and the runway. The runway, which had seemed miles long a moment before, now seemed to flow beneath him at the speed of light.

"Throttle down." Rafe seemed to be running a checklist. Alan looked at his flaps and saw they were at full. His momentary glance broke his concentration on the stick, and the plane wobbled. He corrected automatically and was delighted to find that he had recentered. The plane dropped lightly; the altimeter ran slowly down toward zero, and the plane touched, less than a third of the way down the runway. Alan wanted to shriek with joy, but Rafe smiled wickedly and said, "Full power."

Alan reacted automatically, running the throttle to full before the speed fell below thirty knots.

"Touch and go. Flaps up." Alan ran the flaps all the way up with one hand, trying to watch the airspeed while keeping the plane centered on the runway. The airspeed needle passed through fifty-five knots and he pulled back lightly on the stick. His eyes flickered to the rate of climb; he was trying to hold on five degrees, with reasonable success. The plane began to climb away. Rafe spoke to the tower again and turned to Alan. "Nice job. You might have a stick hand, at that. Now ascend to 5500 and turn on course 172 for Naragansett. We'll land there for lunch."

The plane was Rafe's. He kept it at Quonsett while he attended the War College. As a senior O-4 with no kids and a busted marriage that so far hadn't cost him alimony, he could maintain the sleek Cessna 182 in top condition and decorate the dash with gauges that were meaningless to Alan.

"You landing on the altimeter?" he asked casually, fiddling with the pocket on his windbreaker.

"Is that wrong?"

"Unfortunately, it just broke." Rafe grinned and taped a piece of cardboard—he had been planning this, the sonofabitch—over the altimeter dial. "You liked flying with me off the boat, you get to learn my way."

Rafe's way was unnerving. Alan watched the ground, then started to glue himself to the angle-of-climb monitor. The airfield was down there, visible, and Alan was well into the approach, yet he felt lost. He kept waggling the wings to get a better view of the ground, and once, he almost panicked when he saw that he was in a 15-degree descent instead of being level, but he fought the machine and himself and at last achieved lineup with the runway.

"How's Rose?" Rafe asked.

Alan took a deep breath. "Rose was pregnant," he said. "She lost the baby."

He watched the runway and made a minute correction.

"Never try to correct so close to the ground!" Rafe shouted, and the wheels touched. He modulated his voice. "Nice landing, Buddy."

"She fell down a ladder during sea trials on her new project." Alan was thinking of Rose, the pale face on the hospital sheets, the limp hand in his, the averted face. No tears. *Rose.*

"Fucking A, Alan, that sucks." With the engine at idle and no slipstream, the utter honesty of Rafe's comment struck him. That was how it had been at the squadron. Confrontation, joy, sorrow—all right there. Not a lot of bullshit. "She taking it out on you?"

Two nights before, he had tried to make Rose talk about it and he still saw her gesture—hands raised on each side of her head, fingers spread, blocking out sound, sight, him; her voice, *I'll deal with it! Just let me deal with it!* The hands, the voice shutting him out—

It was Rafe's turn to try to smile, wryly now. "You don't hide things very good, Spy." He unbuckled his harness. "Get a hundred hours' real time and you can solo in my plane. You'll be a good pilot. Just stop paying such close attention to everything."

Words to live by. *Just stop paying such close attention. Right.*

Houston.

Rose tears down the corridor and out a fire door, banging the handle with both palms to get it out of her way. The rental car waits in the parking lot and she almost runs to it. Drive as fast as she dares to the airport, dump the car;

144

run to the check-in, only ten minutes to spare, slam down the ticket, run for the departure lounge—

If only I can stay busy. If only I can move fast enough. If only—

Work is a drug. She hates the evenings and the nights. Evenings, there isn't always enough work to keep her mind from going back to it. Nights, there is never enough sleep, always the waking, the thinking, the pacing around the house or the hotel room. It is better on the road, because there is no Alan beside her there to remind her of what they have lost. Because of her. Because of going too hard, trying too hard, wanting too hard—

It was her fault. Not Valdez's fault. Valdez had fallen on her, but that was because she had been hurrying him up on deck. Trying too hard. Going too fast. Her fault.

Now, so as not to remember, she tries to go faster. Cursing the people ahead of her in the aisle of the plane, the ones who left their overhead crap until the last moment, the ones who have to chat up the flight attendant, the ones who can't walk fast enough. She hurries around them, almost running toward the terminal, toward the new rental car, the new offices. If she can only go fast enough—

Late that night, she calls Alan, as she does every night. She feels exhausted but doubts she will sleep. She hopes she has enough paperwork to last until tomorrow. She keeps her voice light, nonetheless. She must succeed in making everything seem okay, because he talks of other things: His job bores him. He has had lunch with Abe Peretz. He has heard nothing from O'Neill or Dukas; he is worried about them. What are they doing?

She tries to enter into his concern. Maybe it will get her through the night. What are O'Neill and Dukas doing?

What are O'Neill and Dukas . . . ? All she can think about is the baby and the accident, and she turns on the light and begins to memorize the launch-parameter codes for Peacemaker.

8

August

East Africa.

Harry O'Neill had made a mistake.

In fact, he had made the biggest mistake a case officer can make.

He had fallen in love.

With one of his agents.

All case officers, it is said, sleep with their agents—surely an exaggeration—but they don't fall in love. It is the falling in love that is the mistake.

And he knew it was a mistake, and he was happy. He was happier than he had ever been in his life, happy in a way that reconciled him to his father's snobbery and his ex-wife's nastiness, to his own self-doubt and to the dangers of his mistake. If his life ended tomorrow, he told himself, he would say it had been worth it.

"I love you," he said to her. "You make me happy."

Elizabeth Momparu looked at him. Her eyes were slightly swollen from sex and sleep and fatigue, and when she half-closed them to look at him, they seemed to turn up at the corners. She had a fair idea of how she looked to him but no notion of how she really looked to him—the most beautiful, the most wonderful, the most enchanting woman in the world. She had had a lot of men, white and black. Some of them had said they loved her. She had thought she had loved three. She had never known one like Harry.

"I like being with you," she said. "I like being safe with you."

They were sitting on the terrace of a game lodge in eastern Kenya. Night was almost there, coming fast; the retreating day had left a reddish light that made everything—waterhole, thorn trees, sky—seem like an old color slide that had lost all its blue and green. In front of them was a low wall, and a dropoff of twenty feet to an artificial waterhole that would be floodlighted later. For now, only rock hyraxes the size of gray squirrels were there, scrambling up over the wall and taking crumbs from the tourists. It was a safe place, she was right; O'Neill had looked for a long time before he had picked it. None of the Hutu Interahamwe would ever come there.

"Why don't we get married, and you can feel that way all the time?"

"Harry— !"

He smiled, shrugged, as a man who has asked the question before will shrug. He would go on asking it, too. One day, as they both knew, she would say yes. He touched her fingers, and she twined hers into his.

The reason it is the worst of mistakes for a case officer to fall in love with an agent is that he endangers his very reason for being when he does so. An agent, cut it how you will, is expendable, but a lover is not. At the same time, the agent is rarely unique, is more likely part of a network. When the case officer wants to fold the agent into his real life, he destroys both of them, and often the rest of the network, too.

O'Neill knew these things. He was thinking of them as he sat in the near-dark and seemed to watch the hyraxes. He had already decided that he didn't care, at least not about

148

the theoretical part—his job, his career, the Agency. He did care about disentangling her from her role as agent.

"I don't want you to go back," he said.

She squeezed his fingers. "I have to."

"I want you to fly to Paris. I've made a reservation for you."

"Oh, Harry—"

"You'll be safe. Somebody will meet you."

She was silent for so long, she seemed to have forgotten. "You know I can't," she said at last.

He knew she wouldn't go. He had to do it, had to make the arrangements, as if she would. Maybe she would. But of course she wouldn't. She wouldn't for the reason—one of the reasons—that he loved her: because she wanted to stop the killing. She had first allowed Hammer to recruit her because once she knew what he was doing, she thought that helping the Americans would bring their power and what she saw as their idealism into it. The Americans would stop the killing, she had thought. But the Americans hadn't stopped the killing, as it turned out.

"I have to go back there," she said. "You know you need me there. Six months, then maybe—"

"I'll get somebody else." He knew he wouldn't, couldn't. She was close to the leadership; he'd never find anybody so close, with all the turmoil. It would take years to replace her. That would be somebody else's problem.

"Maybe," she said, "things will change next year."

Things wouldn't change in a hundred years. They both knew that. But it was what people told themselves all over central Africa: maybe things will change. Meanwhile, the uneasy truce in Rwanda had become a preparation for war in Zaire, using the refugees there as a weapon. O'Neill had agents in Uganda and eastern Tanzania and Zambia now, and they all said the same thing: a splinter Zairean group in Tanzania was going to be supported in a takeover of Zaire. The other nations would all profit, grabbing slices of territory—buffer zones, minerals. The Hutu refugees were a kind of shield for all sides, behind which the Interahamwe sheltered and the potential invaders hid their intentions.

"What if I quit my job and we went home?" he said. *Home* was the States. She had been there on a holiday— Disney World—but she couldn't think of it as home.

"You're being silly. People like us don't have a home. Nobody in my country has a home any more. We're all refugees, even me, and I own a villa. You made yourself a refugee when you took your horrible job."

"I'm an expat, not a refugee."

"Yes, you're American. Americans can't be refugees, can they. They own the world."

"I told you, I'll quit the horrible job."

"No, you won't."

They sat another twenty minutes. By then, it was black dark. Lights had been turned on in the trees below them, but no animals had come to the waterhole yet. They stood to go in to dinner. When she was facing him, close to him, she said, "I—" and stopped. She wasn't looking into his face, rather down into the trees.

"What?"

She had a habit of pushing out her lower lip and pushing her tongue up against her lower teeth when she was challenged, getting an expression faintly like a chimpanzee's. She shook her head. "We'll talk about it later."

She ate greedily. She was a big woman and she liked to eat. She did many things greedily—making love, talking, shopping—and he loved her for it because the greed extended to him.

*　　*　　*

The place was laid out with winding paths that ran along the curved front of the single-story buildings that housed the guest rooms. At night, guards were available to take guests to their rooms because animals came in from the bush, seldom anything more dangerous than a baboon, although a baboon can kill a child, maim a grown man. Elizabeth was afraid of neither the dark nor the animals, and she strode along, the low lights with shades like conical hats shining on her ankles, leading Harry by the hand as if it were he who needed her protection. Once in their room, however, she became tentative. She stood with her blouse partly unbuttoned, as if lost in some idea. Then she moved to the closet, took the blouse off, hung it up, and turned back—and stood there. When he put his arms around her she moved away, said, "No. Not yet."

She continued to undress slowly. Wearing bra and thong panties, she took a cigarette from her purse and stood looking at it. He had been astonished that she smoked; he still didn't much care for the taste of cigarettes on her. In Africa, everybody smoked.

"I want to tell you something," she said.

He thought he had heard all her revelations. The ones about other men had been hard on him. He had shucked off a lot of immature bullshit, coming to grips with them, coming to realize that love in this case required accepting whatever had gone before. It had taken him weeks to come to it. Along the way, always, was the possibility of AIDS. He had coped with that, too.

"Is this place really secure?" she said. She had been tapping the cigarette, tapping it and tapping it, and at last she struck the lighter he had given her and put it to the end. "Are you sure?"

"Absolutely." He had scoped the room and made sure it was clean. Kenyan security were not on to him. They

151

would sometime, but just now he was not of interest to them. She was on a false passport he had got from the embassy and not interesting to them. They were secure.

She strode up and down. She was nervous, more nervous than he had ever seen her. After several minutes, she turned on her little radio, stubbed out the cigarette and took out another. When it was alight, she said, "I want to tell you something I haven't been able to tell anybody else."

Harry O'Neill prepared himself.

She sat on the bed and took his hand and drew him down next to her. They were both big, both mostly naked. She said, "I have something I didn't give you. Business, you know." *Business* meant in her capacity as agent. Harry felt immense relief. Not another lover, then. She swallowed noisily and smoked and said, "I couldn't tell the guy before you. And Hammer—"

Hammer had been in his forties, overweight, and he had driven his Range Rover down to Ruaha in the rainy season, and they had found him after he'd been missing for two days. The vehicle had got stuck in a vast mudhole and he'd had a heart attack.

"Hammer died two years ago. I had this—something to tell him—but I couldn't for a while; it was the bad time, the really bad time, you couldn't travel and there were killings everywhere and everybody on the move, and— By the time I thought it was safe to send a signal, he was dead. Then that idiot came in and I couldn't trust him." She looked at him. "I just couldn't trust him, Harry!"

Their bare shoulders and arms and thighs were pressed together, but O'Neill knew that he was supposed to sit and listen. This was one of those times when love and sex didn't go hand in hand.

She got another cigarette. "I couldn't tell you until I was

sure. Even when I loved you, I wasn't *sure*. It takes time, Harry, to trust somebody." She meant, she had lots of lovers she had liked, spent time with, but she hadn't *trusted* them. Well, he should be flattered, although he wasn't. "Now, I'm going to tell you. But you have to promise me—promise, *promise* me, Harry—that you'll protect me. It can't get back to me!"

"You know I'll protect you, my Christ—"

"I know, I know!" She put her fingers on his mouth. "I know, you have to protect me as an agent, I know all that. But I'm going to put my life in your hands, Harry. This isn't like anything else I've ever had. Okay? You promise?"

"Yes. You know I do."

She bent her head as she talked and picked, as if doing so was important, at a small patch of crusty skin on her leg. "On the sixth of April three years ago, the airplane with the two presidents in it crashed coming into Kigali. Everybody says now it was shot down." She sighed. She sounded hopeless. "I was there."

He knew a lot about that event, certainly knew exactly what she was talking about and its importance to the weeks of genocide that had followed. He knew, or at least had had reliable information, that two missiles had been used to shoot the plane down, and he had a less reliable report that the shooters had been white. Still, he didn't get it. "Where were you?" he said. He thought she meant at the crash.

"I saw the missiles fired," she said.

"Jesus."

"There were four Europeans. The missiles were in ski bags; I recognized them from Davos. Two of them fired the missiles, one gave the orders; the other one had a radio. My brother had set it up."

The half-brother was Harry's nightmare, one of the leaders of the Interahamwe.

"Maybe he hadn't set it up; he acted as if he had. I think that at least he provided his personal guards for protection. They were there, twenty or so of them, around the missiles with their guns."

"What the hell were you doing there?"

"I was just *there*. I just went along. They had come in the night before, the Europeans—"

"How?"

"Air. A big airplane, somebody said it had flown in from Angola. Probably running guns to UNITA."

"Do you remember anything else about the plane?"

"Four engines. Fans, you know—what do you say?"

"Propellers? *Propellers?* Okay, okay." Some old plane, then— turboprop?

"I don't care about that. Let me get through it my way! They came in and we met them at the airport. Out at the end, not by the terminal—they got off way out on the runway and then the plane taxied back. We had two cars. The head European got in with us. Then we went home; we had a kind of party, some people of my brother's, then dinner."

And next day she went along, meaning— "You went to bed with him?"

She blew out smoke, nodded. "That was before you, Harry, I didn't care so much. I wanted him to like me. Next day, I just got in the car when everybody else did and we went out to this place in the bush. I didn't get it until a small plane went over, landing, and I knew we were on the flight path. Everybody knew the presidents' plane was due in. I saw the ski bags, I knew what they were going to do." She let out her breath in a great gust. She looked down at herself. "I took pictures."

"How?"

"This guy, the European, had a camera. He *wanted* me

154

to take photos! I just took out my own camera and took some, too. I had this hot-pink point-and-shoot. I thought, If they stop me, okay. Nobody cared."

"Your brother?"

"Oh—" She hugged herself. "He's always bad-tempered; he was no worse. Anyway, he was being a big man for the Europeans. So, anyway—" Her mouth was trembling. "They shot the missiles and the plane crashed. Like that."

Like that. And then the killings started. A hundred thousand in three weeks. The plane crash had been like a match thrown into a puddle of gasoline.

"Where are the pictures?"

"Safe. At home."

"How good are they?"

She shook her head. "I didn't dare have them processed. Somebody could have seen them, or the shop could have been burned or bombed. Anything. Those were crazy days."

"It may be no good because it's been so long. The heat."

"I know."

"Still, I should—"

"I'll get it to you, Harry. Now that you know everything, of course, the photos are for you. Just don't let it come back on me!" Her hands were shaking and one knee was bobbing up and down like a shuttle, from tension. "He'd kill me."

"No, no." She was safe, he was sure of that; he would put the film and the Agent Report in the diplomatic pouch and it would go straight to the Agency, highest classification. It would be a bombshell, though. He went through it with her again, the case officer now. He asked more questions, drew out things she thought she had forgotten. They had called the top guy Z—just Z. Z had had a horrible nose—grotesque. The whites had worn Belgian uniforms, but they weren't Belgian, she said.

"Can you be sure?"

"They didn't speak French. The top man spoke French, but with an accent; I couldn't place it. Among themselves, they spoke something else."

"Some Belgians speak Flemish."

"I don't know about that. All the Belgians here speak French."

"Maybe American?"

"No."

"German?"

She hesitated. "Maybe. Possible."

The third time through, she remembered that she had glimpsed one of the pilots through the big aircraft's windscreen. He was white. She remembered details of the Europeans' weapons and equipment. The missiles sounded from her description like Stingers. Put together this and that and he agreed with her that they didn't sound like either Belgians or French. Mercenaries, maybe, with a mixture of NATO and some other gear. There were a lot of Russians around, other Eastern European military left over from the Cold War.

He let her run down. There was no love-making; she was profoundly shaken, almost in shock. He helped her to lie down and rubbed her neck and her back, and he gave her a pill, and after half an hour she slept. O'Neill lay in the dark room, smelling the rank, unfamiliar cigarette smoke, wondering how he was going to get her out of it. Get them both out of it. It would be easy for him; he'd resign. He skipped the hard part, getting her out of Zaire. He tried to concentrate on the good part: They'd marry, and he'd take her home and he'd get a law degree or go to med school or study business or some goddam thing. That would be easy.

He'd started out in the Navy. Once, he'd told Alan Craik that he was going to be CNO: he'd spend a tour each in Air OPS, ELINT, HUMINT, and SIGLINT, and then he'd cut a swathe in the military intel establishment. He'd been wrong. He was burned out already. All he wanted was home and her.

He'd thought he was hot stuff and his plan was a good one, do everything and be CNO, why not? But even then, secretly, semi-consciously, he had seen that Craik got something out of it that he didn't. Some lift, some rush. He hadn't realized that the rush was essential.

Craik was his best friend, whatever that meant. Kids have best friends; adults don't, really. But he and Craik were close, despite O'Neill's being envious of Craik's dedication and his—what? His luck? And—admit it—of Craik's reputation and his awards. Craik made things happen, got medals pinned on his chest. O'Neill had wanted some of that, too, some of the glory stuff. That's why he'd resigned from the Navy and signed on with the Agency. Now he realized that Craik had a need for risk—that was his "luck," that hunger for risk—that he lacked. Craik had flown, even though he had been a squadron IO; O'Neill, also a squadron IO, had never gone up. Craik, in his view now, had some error in his core program that made him foolish about danger. The truth was that they should switch roles: O'Neill could still be a good IO, Craik a good spook.

Now none of that mattered. What mattered lay beside him, terrified. He'd get her home. Somehow. For once, he didn't care what his parents would say. Love had done that for him, too. He saw now that the first time, he had married a woman his mother had picked out, and it hadn't worked. His wife had thought she was slumming because her husband was a military officer. She had been a sour-minded snob. Incapable of being happy. What a curse. The marriage hadn't lasted two years.

So he would send the Agent Report and the film, undeveloped, in the diplomatic bag. Then he would get her out and give her a new identity and send her somewhere, and then he would join her and they would go home.

But he would have to persuade her, first, to give up the idea that she could stop the killing.

Sarajevo.

The two men walking in the Bascasija looked somewhat like the others who had survived the war years, but a veteran could probably have seen that they were not local. Here, deep in the oldest part of Sarajevo, they were not quite out of place, but not quite of it, either. For one thing, they smiled.

Dukas had a local sort of face—his ancestors, after all, were from not far away, and he shared some of the locals' genes. He wore a traveler's nylon raincoat, the kind that folds into its own pocket, which was not in itself wrong, but it looked both too new and too touristic to have belonged to somebody who had survived the siege of Sarajevo and now wanted the latest, the coolest. He looked, in fact, like a blue-collar worker on holiday. The trouble was, he was sure he fit right in.

With him was a slightly shorter man whose face and body seemed to be all angles, made to cut the wind like a sailing ship. He, too, wore nylon—a short jacket in blue and copper—and any Parisian would have looked at him and thought, *Flic*. And they would have been right: he was a French cop.

"I like this," the French cop said. He meant the part of the city where they were walking. "When I was here in eighty-four, I came down here all the time. It has *character*." He smiled. "In Paris, we would say it is an Islamic slum."

"What were you doing here in eighty-four?" Dukas said. His voice was hoarse from a cold. His nose was stuffy, his nostrils red.

"The Olympics."

"The Olympics! You were in the Olympics?" Dukas looked aside at the smaller man. His name was Jean-Luc Pigoreau; he was a senior lieutenant in the Sûreté. Dukas did a quick calculation—a dozen years ago, could this small tough guy have been an Olympian?

"A skater, Michael." Pigoreau's English was almost unaccented, very American, only the "R" sounds betraying his roots. "Not a dancer like the *pédés* in the fancy shirts. A speed skater. Eight hundred meters."

"Wow." Dukas didn't know what to say. He had never met an Olympian before. "Did you, um, win?"

Pigoreau laughed. He laughed the way people laugh in movies when they're showing wild abandon, head back, mouth wide open, big smile. "I was very, very good—but not good enough. You know how it is, to be very good, but not good enough?"

Dukas's view of himself was that he was probably not very, very good at most things, and certainly not good enough to win the gold at anything. Still, with a guy who had actually made it to the Olympics, you were talking about a different way of not being good enough. Dukas tried to say something consoling and sounded perfectly stupid. He laughed at himself when Pigoreau gave him a funny look, then started coughing. Pigoreau stood with him while he gulped cough medicine from a bottle. "That sounded pretty stupid," Dukas said. "I meant, I'm sorry you didn't get the gold."

"I have nothing to be sorry for," Pigoreau said. He was

159

very serious. This was something he had thought all the way through, perhaps many times. "I was just so good— so—" and he indicated a height with a hand—"and I lost, so—" and the hand went up a little—"and now I know exactly how good I was." He dropped his hand and shoved it into his jacket pocket. "Most men, they do not dare find that out. To know exactly how good you are." He turned a little and stared across the little plaza-like widening of the streets, what the locals called a *mejdan*, and looked off toward the mountains to the north, visible only as a dark mass between the red-tiled roofs, with the narrow spire of a mosque splitting it like a tear in paper. "It was all *very* beautiful in eighty-four, Michael. And *exciting*. This city was so *alive*, so—clean! They were all very proud of Novi Grad, Novi Sarajevo, all that new stuff that is so full of holes out there now, all those walls without glass. But I liked it down here. This is old Sarajevo. This is Turk, you know? This—" He turned around, gesturing with a hand. "This was the market. Big! Blocks and blocks. Now—" He shrugged and hunched down in his jacket.

"I gotta meet somebody," Dukas said.

"I know. Just another street or two here. I think I remember." Pigoreau grinned. He was trying to find a memory. "You know, you visit a place for one week, you come back twelve years later, you forget."

"Not to mention some sonofabitch blowing the shit out of it with artillery."

Dukas had been in Sarajevo a month, and he had seen most of the damage. The Holiday Inn. The UNIS Towers. The old National Library, a gutted shell. More discouraging, as he stayed longer, was the damage to the modest buildings where people's lives had been destroyed, the only evidence an exposed interior wall with the faded outline where a picture had hung, or a second-story bathroom, still intact but with no outer wall, the bathtub an astonishing pink. He had seen empty shells of apartment houses where curtains still blew in glassless windows, cellars that stank of wet plaster and rats, a sodden dining table lying on its top, its carved legs in the air like a dead horse.

"Well," Pigoreau muttered. He had a habit of making little ttt-tt-tt noises with his tongue and the roof of his mouth. *Tt-tt-tt*, he said to himself. "It was along here." He was looking for a restaurant he remembered from 1984. *Tt-tt*. "I am getting old, I think."

Dukas and Pigoreau were finding that they liked each other. They were both cautious men, but they were spending a lot of time together, not all of it demanded by the job. On paper, Pigoreau was commander of what was called— on paper—the Counter-Intelligence Unit; in fact, he was already becoming Dukas's second-in-command. Wary of intimacy, experienced in cynicism, the two men had circled each other and come closer and liked what they saw.

"Ah!" Pigoreau cried. He grabbed Dukas's sleeve and pulled him to the right, down toward the river. "Just along here—" And he pulled Dukas around a corner and drew up across the street from a bombed-out ruin. "And there it is. Well." Shrugging himself into his jacket. "It was stupid of me to think things would not change, eh?" His restaurant was a hole between damaged buildings.

"You can't go home again," Dukas said.

"I was young there, Michael. Now I will tell you something foolish. I had a meal there before I won my first race in eighty-four. So I came back, for the good luck. Then I lost." He laughed, the way a man laughs at himself so somebody else will not think him self-pitying. "Maybe I thought I would see myself in there, still eating a meal and praying to win. Eh?" He ran into the street, dodging a run-down Fiat, and looked into the ruin. Dukas crossed more cautiously; Sarajevo drivers, he had concluded, were not to be trusted. He, too, looked into the ruin—bricks, weeds, one wall with some white tiles halfway up that may have indicated where the kitchen had been. "I want you to be careful," Pigoreau said. "You have a gun?" Clearly, he wasn't talking about the ruin.

"Yeah, yeah."

"*Tt-tt.* They're on to who we are now. They won't like it when we actually go after somebody. You're in charge; they could have targeted you already."

"Nah."

"Don't sit outside. You see anybody on a Vespa, get off the street. Anybody parks a car and walks away, run." Pigoreau had headed an anti-terrorist squad in Lille. He knew a lot about assassination.

"I'm just going to meet a woman," Dukas said. He blew his nose and groaned.

"You are going to meet a *Serb* woman. I could still call in a couple of minders."

Dukas grinned despite himself. He loved "minders." The first time he had heard Pigoreau use the word, he had thought he was kidding. "Nah," he said. He looked at his watch. "I gotta go. Sorry about your restaurant."

Pigoreau shrugged. "I am a big boy, Michael." *Tt-tt.*

Dukas nodded. "So am I." Dukas slapped the French cop on the upper arm and walked away. When he reached the corner, Pigoreau called after him, "You should be in bed!" and Dukas growled, "I don't know anybody to go to bed with," and walked on. He went down toward the river and waited with half a dozen people for the tram to Novi. The others stood a little away from him, not because they knew he was a cop but because they sensed he was different. When the tram came, they moved toward the back and Dukas sat alone, facing into the car. It swayed along its tracks. He nursed the cold and thought about these people. They were tough but tormented, often clinically depressed. They had been under siege, a literal artillery bombardment that had gone on sporadically for years. One stretch of the city was called Sniper's Alley because men had hidden in the ruined apartment blocks there and randomly shot down civilians. Perhaps people they had once known, perhaps even people they were related to. Now the siege was over and the city had segregated itself into zones more rigid and more hate-filled than the old Muslim-Christian or Turk-Austro-Serb. Now it was a city of forty percent unemployment, its economy down by eighty percent from prewar levels, a city of splendid destruction. A few years before, it had been one of the most beautiful small cities in Europe, a sparkling, modern bracelet around an ancient core. Now—

He got down in the shadow of a bombed-out modern tower in Marijin Dvor and stopped next to a still-operating bakery to study a map. The woman—he knew it was a woman; she had said so in the note—had drawn a crude map on a piece of ruled paper from which a child's drawing had been erased. Paper was in short supply.

Figuring his direction, he crossed the tram tracks and headed toward the river and the distant mountains. The apartments here had been fairly modest, like something from the sixties in the States. A lot of aluminum sheet and glass, the glass now gone, the aluminum twisted. People were living in some of them, God knew how, he thought.

Her map was all right. He found the church she had drawn by the oddly truncated steeple; he went to the left of it as she had indicated, then down a flight of steps and into a small park with a cinder running track around a half-sized soccer field. Some children were kicking a ball. The air felt warmer here, more like summer, and he unbuttoned the raincoat, then peeled it off and threw it on his right shoulder. She was sitting where she had written she would be, all the way across the soccer field. When he came toward her, she stood, as if to welcome him, and he saw she was beautiful.

Pigoreau had seen the map, so he didn't bother to follow Dukas closely. Nonetheless, he kept him in view after he got off the tram. Pigoreau was not at all sure that Dukas could take care of himself. Dukas was an investigative cop, after all, not a hammer, as Pigoreau was. And Dukas was older by a good eight or ten years. Even the gun Dukas carried—a revolver! It was like something in a Humphrey Bogart movie. In fact, it was a Ruger .357 Magnum, but to Pigoreau, all revolvers were antiques. He carried a Browning High-Power 9 millimeter and thought it a minimal, but modern, weapon.

He cut across a diagonal of Dukas's route and made a wrong turn and, cursing, had to retrace his steps and then follow Dukas's own route. He knew the destination, a small park he had checked out yesterday. At least it was an unlikely spot for a drive-by assassination because of a fringe of trees and several small buildings around the running track. By the time Pigoreau got into the trees and could see without being seen, Dukas was already standing at the far side, and with him was the woman.

She was not Pigoreau's type. She looked, at this distance, plain and dumpy—a peasant. Pigoreau liked small, dark, intense women like his wife, an urban shrew who made half his life suicidal and the other half intoxicating. Pigoreau thought that the woman with Dukas looked like a cow. And maybe a Serb decoy.

*   *   *

164

Dukas was thinking, *She's too casual; she should be scared*, but he knew he was blushing because he thought she was beautiful and he was excited. Dukas's luck with women was terrible, and the worse it got, the less cool he got around them. He was like a high-school boy.

"Would you like to walk?" she said. She had a strong accent, but her voice was better than nice. Warm. She was nearly forty, he thought, with little lines around her eyes, and skin that had been exposed to too much wind, yet she was lovely. Strong bones, very full lips, gray-green eyes a little tilted, like a cat's. And big. She was almost as big as he was. That was a plus. She was wearing some kind of stretch-fabric pants, like old polyester, blue, the fabric pilled from age, and a long-sleeved maroon shirt that showed off her big shoulders.

"Do *you* want to walk?" he said. It was what he always did with women: they wanted decisions, he asked for more input.

"I will walk if you like," she said.

Here we go again, he thought. Dukas the jerk. "Siddown," he said. *The hell with it, this is business.* He jerked his head toward a bench. He plunked himself on the hard iron seat; she settled next to him more gracefully. The thought flashed through his consciousness that she was light despite her big body, would be a good dancer, and he said, "You wrote to me you got information."

"About war criminals, yes." She smiled. "You are after war criminals, yes? WCIU?"

"Yeah." He was head of WCIU, he meant—the War Crimes Information Unit, pronounced "Wicky-U" by those who tried.

"I have information about four of your criminals."

They had a list of 237 "strong suspects," Croat, Muslim, and Serb. About a third of the names were still secret, another fifty or so treated as "eyes only," meaning there had been no press contact on them yet. The Hague court had indicted seventy-five. Nine—nine!—were in custody. He found himself thinking that she had worked very quickly, to locate him within a few weeks of his setting up an office. As so often in the past, Dukas the callow high-school boy was running neck-and-neck with Dukas the cynical cop. "How do you know they're war criminals?" he said.

She was a little flustered. "Well—everybody knows. Yes?" She smiled, all that warmth again. Was she coming on to him too obviously? "You have hundreds. Haven't you?"

"Who told you that?"

"Oh— Everybody knows. The newspapers, the TV." If she watched Serbian TV, all she got was Belgrade—no Serb war criminals there. He continued to look at her. She looked away, made a nervous gesture with one hand on her knee, looked back at him. "I have a friend."

A friend, holy God. *A leak? Already? Maybe Pigoreau is right about her.* Dukas had had snitches before, lots of them; in that respect, being a Navy cop was little different from being any other kind. In a sense, the woman was coming to him as a snitch, but the context turned her into something closer to an agent. If, that is, she had real information and she could go on providing it.

"What's your name?" Dukas said. He leaned a little toward her.

"Draganica Obren. I am Serb. What is your name?"

Dukas was caught off guard. He laughed, first to cover, then with real humor when he glanced at her and saw she was laughing a little too. "I'm supposed to ask the questions," he said.

"Yes, you are the policeman."

"Exactly. My name is Michael."

"Oh, I like that name." She said it as if it was a great relief—as if she had feared disliking his name and thus ruining everything. "You are American."

"Miss Obren—"

"Mrs."

He glanced at her. She was suddenly serious. *Okay, something about being married—the husband doesn't know she's here? The husband is a war criminal?* "Mrs Obren, why did you approach us the way you did—no name on the note, meeting like this?"

"Because it is a secret." She might as well have added "of course." She said it the way you say something obvious to a child.

"Why is it a secret?"

"Because they will kill me if they find out. Everybody knows that. Especially in Republika Srpska. They say there you are the enemy and anyone who goes to you will be dead." Republika Srpska was the Serbian zone on the other side of the wiggly line that was officially known as the IEBL—the Inter-Entity Boundary Line.

"What are you doing in Republika Srpska?" His voice was harder.

"I live there. I am free to come and go, like anybody. I go everywhere." She looked defiant.

"Yeah, everybody's free to do anything, and everybody else down here in the Federation is terrified to cross the IEBL. So why aren't you?"

"I am terrified. But—so?"

So she was a Serb from the Republic, coming to offer him information from the goodness of her heart. It stank. "What d'you want?" Dukas said.

"I want what every woman in a conquered country wants from the conqueror."

167

"You're talking riddles."

She smiled, not very pleasantly now. "Chocolate—cigarettes—silk stockings—"

"Money?" It was a kind of relief to say the word, although he was disappointed in her. He had been liking her. *Jesus God, she wants money. What the hell was that crack about conquerors? Oh, I get it—the army of occupation turns nice girls into whores. Okay, lady.* There were already hundreds of newly recruited prostitutes in the resorts along the coast, put in place by the international gangs that had flocked into Bosnia while the ink was still damp on Dayton.

"Money—of course, money."

"How much?"

"How much do you pay?" She was trying to be flirtatious all of a sudden; the effect was unutterably grim and for the first time made her seem grotesque because of her age. She knew at once how she seemed, and she looked away across the soccer field. A boy in red shorts was dribbling the ball around two other, bigger boys. She nodded as if approving his skill. She clasped her hands between her knees and looked down. "My husband disappeared two years ago. I must find him."

"So you want money?"

She nodded. "Money and help. You can help me."

"How?"

"You know how. You are police; you look for people."

"That's the business of the High Commission. Or the Red Cross. UNHCR. Amnesty—"

She was shaking her head. "They are no good; they want to find graves, or prisoners, or papers—I have been to them. Do you think I have not been to them?"

Dukas tried a guess. "They told you he was dead?"

"They 'made a negative evaluation.' A lot of hearsay, guess-work. He is not dead. He is *not* dead. If he is dead—"

She put her elbow on the back of the bench and rested her forehead on the hand, rubbing her temples with her big fingers. "Let me work for you! Help me! The money itself will help; I can buy information, buy officials in the Republik. I must be paid in Deutschmarks; you must give me identity so I can pass into the French sector as somebody else. Then I will give you good information."

"Now, just why am I supposed to believe that?"

She reached into the V of her blouse with two fingers and took out a slip of paper, probably from her bra. Dukas was aware of its warmth as she passed it to him. He opened it, recognized two of the four names on it. "Two of these guys are Bosnian Muslims," he said. They were on his list.

"So? The Muslims are war criminals, too!" She meant that she knew that the UN and the United States were prejudiced against the Serbs and favored the Muslims.

"Twenty-five dollars a month," he said. Sarajevo cops made thirty. It was ridiculous—a drug dealer could buy a whole squad for the US price of a cheap suit.

"In Deutschmarks. Cash."

Dukas hated all the Mickey-Mouse about signals and drops and cutouts and all that *shit*, but he knew she would have to be able to communicate. He sighed. "How well-known are you in Sarajevo?"

She shook her head. "I came here only to see you. I stay with a friend—" She waved her fingers. "Near the airport. Ilidja." She was telling him too much, he thought; was it significant?

He thought of different people he might hand her over to, knowing all along that he would run her himself. He had to try her. He thought she was a plant or a double, but she was the first one who had come to him, and he knew he had to see where she would lead him. "Why don't you give me a call or a visit next time you're in

Sarajevo? We're interested, you understand, in any local information."

In his mind, she was already his agent. He would run her as Petra, a name he had taken from a list of the names of ancient cities. They had a safe house, actually a deserted apartment, in Novi Sarajevo; he would work with her there. She would have to have some sort of comm plan. If she was a plant or a double, she would be secretly amused. If she was the real thing, she would be risking her life. He wanted to go to bed with her and thought he probably would, because if she was a plant, that would be part of the deal, and if she was sincere she would do anything to find her husband.

When he looked at her, she seemed excited, at the same time disappointed, as if he had given her exactly what she had come for but had withheld what she really wanted. Maybe she thought he would, like the conqueror, turn her into a whore that very day?

Pigoreau followed her when she and Dukas separated. After walking for five minutes, she looked around, looked at him and through him, not appearing to see him, and then stepped into the street with her arm up, and a yellow Yugo swung in with a screech and she all but fell in. Small car, big woman; the door banged, and it squealed away.

When he got back to the WCIU office, Dukas was waiting for him. "So, did you find where she lives?" he said. Pigoreau stared at him, then burst out laughing. So did Dukas.

"Michael, I didn't think you would see me. You're pretty good."

"You were dead easy; I was expecting you."

"I thought you had eyes only for the lady."

"Oh yeah. Oh, sure. Listen—" Dukas jabbed a finger into

170

Pigoreau's chest. "She knew more than she should about us, so I think we got a leak already. Check around." He smiled in a way that was not at all a smile.

"I thought you were making a conquest."

"Yeah, I think that's what I was supposed to think, too. We'll see. Where'd she go after she met me?"

"She walked and then got in a car."

"Rendezvous?"

Pigoreau shrugged. Sometimes, without his knowing it, he was like somebody playing a French cop. "Maybe. Maybe not. Anybody with a car here, they can make money picking up passengers."

Dukas sniffed. He got out a wad of tissue, peeled some off and began to straighten it so it would fit around his nose. "See what IFOR has on people up in RS. Maybe phone books, voter lists—I don't know. She says her name is Draganica Obren, so check that. Also the last name for a guy, the husband. I'll get more out of her next time. Maybe even the truth." He blew his nose to hide the fact that he wanted to see the woman again.

It occurred to him that he might be making a big mistake. Dukas was less intellectual than Harry O'Neill, but he had better instincts when it came to women.

In Republika Srpska.

Zulu found his way in the dark to the bathroom and urinated and pushed open the window to ease the stink of the place. The woman was a sloven, or the sewer had backed up. Maybe both; what he had seen of the little apartment last evening had shown him disorder. Zulu believed that one's outer world reflected one's inner self—cluttered room, unfocused mind. His own surroundings were always austere, even monastic. Yet he liked a certain sluttishness in women other than his wife, and this one's flat, with its clothes strewn over the floor and its dirty cups and plates, had suggested to him—correctly, as it turned out—a sexuality little restrained by convention or the marriage she kept talking to him about and the husband she wanted to find.

He went back into the bedroom and sat on the few inches of free space on the only chair. His neatly folded clothes lay on some of it, her castoff garments, that might have piled up over weeks, on the rest. He began to dress in the dark.

She had been lying with her back to him; now she rolled over and lay looking at him, or at the dark space where she must have known he sat. He was a careful man, but he supposed he had made small noises.

"Going?" she said.

He liked her husky voice. It was what had attracted him at the party. He was recruiting in RS. He usually paid for a party in somebody's house so that he could invite the possibles and harangue them as they got drunk. He had his local contacts make sure there were women, too, loyal Serbs who understood that soldiers, even would-be soldiers, needed sex. This woman was rather old for the job. Surprisingly, he had picked her for himself.

"I asked if you're going," she said.

He grunted.

"I can fix you food."

"I'll eat on the way." He had a car and a driver and false papers. The Americans were all over up here, setting up roadblocks, interfering; but he was going only thirty miles, and then there would be a house where he would be welcome, food, and then horses to go where there was no road.

"I will do anything," she said. "Please help me find him."

172

"I know."

"My husband—"

"You told me. Several times, Mrs Obren." It was an old story to him. Lots of women were looking for their husbands or fathers or brothers. Lots were willing to trade sex for help in finding them. A paradox—the loyal wife is disloyal out of loyalty. Still, some of them were glad for the excuse, he thought; this one was sincere, but when they had made love she had made a sound of pent-up release that had surprised him. The husband was a good Serb, she had told him between bouts of love-making; he had been in a militia, active against the Muslims; he had disappeared; she would do anything to find him. Then she had initiated another round of sex. Then the questions again: What could she do so he would help her find him? What did he want her to do?

Zulu stood and zipped his jeans and began to button his shirt. "I will put his name on a list," he said. "It is Mister Obren, yes?" His voice was sarcastic.

She boosted herself up on her elbows. A little light came in the window; he could just make out the shape of her, one breast with inky shadow below it. "I can find things out for you," she said.

There was little he didn't know, he thought. He grinned, unseen. "What things?"

"What the Americans are up to." Her voice had an edge—of what?

"Which Americans?"

"Any of them." She was going too fast, making it up as she went along—some fantasy of spying she had seen in a film. "The ones who come through from Tuzla in the tanks. The ones who set up the roadblocks. I get around, looking for my husband. I can make notes of what I see—when they are such-and-such a place, when they are not. Patterns. Anything you think would be of use."

"I'm a soldier, not a spy-master."

"Soldiers need information."

He grunted. He went into the other room and found his warmup jacket by feeling over piles of old magazines, clothes, dishes. He could feel filth and dust—was she never here to clean the place? Disgusting. Still, a good, sluttish woman in bed, and maybe a good source of information because she was not stupid and because she got around. Maybe it was not such a bad idea. The UN had got together some gang of do-gooders who were going to arrest what they called "war criminals"—a bad joke, that—and he had heard that they already had their spies out. Maybe having some of his own would not be so stupid. Anyway, if doing that helped her to be a good Serb, what was the harm? He put on the jacket, aware of her as a bulk in the doorway. He kissed her, meaning nothing, and caressed one breast.

"You're a good woman. I'll try to remember your husband, but—you know, there are thousands. If you get useful information, sure, pass it along." He told her whom to give her information to, a schoolteacher in the town. The information about tanks and roadblocks would be useless, of course, but later, who knows? This war would go on for years. Maybe they would need spies. The husband, he thought, was dead and in one of the Croats' mass graves.

"And—do I simply tell him? No secrecy, no, well, codes?"

He smiled in the dark. "Whatever the schoolteacher wants. Just tell him it is for Z." He kissed her cheek. She smelled slightly gamey, warm, female. He would not have tolerated the smell on his wife, but he liked it on this woman. He would come back to her next time he came this way.

174

"My spy," he said, and he squeezed her breast and left her.

Sarajevo.
She came back to the city after a week away. In the "safe house" on Radovan Street—actually an empty apartment in a mostly deserted building—Dukas let Pigoreau and a British member of the team deal with Mrs Obren. They went over and over her story, challenged her with the bits they had got from Civil Affairs, had her in tears more than once. Pigoreau caught her in two small lies. He told Dukas she should be dropped.

After a grim lunch of stale sandwiches, Dukas took her quickly through an overview of signals, barely enough for her to communicate if they were to use her. Then they took a walk, and he talked to her about looking out for trackers and doing the likelier thing, which was making sure your trackers didn't lose you, so you could deceive them some other way. He found himself liking her despite Pigoreau's recommendation and resisted the feeling, because he was increasingly persuaded she was working for somebody else. The business of spying didn't seem to surprise her enough.

In the afternoon, they sat in an almost empty room and went over the list of war criminals. They had two folding chairs, a broken card table, and cardboard cups of coffee that had got cold. He went through the list name by name, alphabetically. She knew only the four she had already given him. It was boring for both of them. At the end of the list was the name he had got from Alan Craik, the man who had run away through the snow.

"'Zulu,'" Dukas said. "A man who calls himself 'Zulu' or 'Colonel Zulu.'"

She shook her head, for perhaps the two hundredth

time. Nothing else showed—no body language, no change of breathing, nothing to indicate it meant anything to her.

"Z for zip," Dukas said to himself. She looked puzzled. He wondered if he should try her for a couple of months and realized what he was really wondering was how he could see her again. How he could get her into bed.

"Come home with me," he said. She looked relieved.

9

August

Naval Air Station, Norfolk.

Seaman Recruit Henry Sneesen stood at attention in the hot Virginia sun and watched the two distant figures shake hands and salute. Sneesen held himself very tight so he wouldn't touch the black guys on each side of him. Black skin gave him a creepy feeling, like he ought to wash afterward.

The old skipper was giving way to the new skipper—Darth Vader, in his terms, giving way to Screaming Meemie. Like most of the men in the squadron, he hated Screaming Meemie with a passion; as XO, Screaming Meemie had single-handedly drawn the brand-new squadron's morale down to knee level. Now, as skipper, he would probably drive it right down into the deck.

Sneesen, however, wasn't depressed. And he knew what depression was. The real thing, the black thing. The thing they give you medication for and muttered to your parents about institutionalizing you for. Sneesen had had his black years, all right. Now—joke; he smiled, standing at attention on the squadron grinder, shoulder to shoulder with blacks—now he was having his white years. He was wearing his dress whites, and so was everybody else, the officers in choker whites, red-faced in the sun. The old skipper even had a sword on. Cool.

But it wasn't the whiteness of the spectacle (white sun bouncing off the concrete like a fantasy blade bouncing off magic armor) that made him happy now. It was the man in choker whites standing behind Screaming Meemie. He was the new XO, name of LCDR Rafehausen, and Sneesen worshipped him. Rafehausen had been on board five days, and Seaman Sneesen worshipped him.

It had happened the day before yesterday: Rafehausen had suited up for an ASW training flight in a squadron S-3B, and just before he taxied out toward the runway, the TACCO had called the back end down. Screaming Meemie had happened to be nearby when Rafehausen reported it, and he had blown his stack as he always did at every goddam thing that happened, big or little, and he began to scream at Rafehausen over the comm.

Sneesen didn't understand even now why he had run out to the aircraft. He just had. Terror of Screaming Meemie, maybe. (Terror of that contorted face, the huge voice, the monster from the computer game that morphed into his dreams as The Great Arch Fiend.) He had waved at the copilot and climbed up into the aircraft, and, sitting in the TACCO's seat while the half-scared, embarrassed female jg (Nixon, the squadron intel officer, not really black but colored, also Japanese or something—creepy) stood over him, Sneesen had punched buttons and stared at the unwilling screens and then, right there, using only the non-issue tool kit he always carried around, he had fixed it. Took the cover off the AN/ARS-4 ref system and unscrewed the two anchor bolts of a black box he could see was out of line—who the hell had installed that, anyway?— and pulled it out of its slot and pried up the contacts and checked the leads, cleaned this and that and taped a length of frayed cable, and when he put it back into its slot, it came up sweet and sweet and the whole crew cheered.

"Hey, genius, what's your name?" Rafehausen, the new XO, had hollered at him from the front seat. Rafehausen was just as loud as Screaming Meemie, but for some reason, Sneesen wasn't afraid of him.

"Sneesen, sir." He was wearing blue shirt and dungarees, no rank designation. "Seaman Recruit, sir."

"Well, goddam, Sneesen, if everybody in this squadron is as good as you are, this tour is gonna be a piece of cake! Okay—let's take this bag of bolts for a ri-i-i-de!"

Not Screaming Meemie's style at all. Screaming Meemie's idea of praise was not saying something bad. He didn't know what praise was. While Rafehausen, with a single sentence, had won Sneesen forever.

Band music played over the squadron PA. It sounded like fifty old men playing Sousa on beer bottles. Still, it gave them a cadence, and they began to march off the broiling tarmac. Sneesen loved this part. This was the Navy. This was his new life, in which he was one of the guys. No need to wear weird clothes now; no need to hear the jocks snarl "fag!" at him as they passed. That was all that time ago in high school. Now he was a new guy. Him and LCDR Rafehausen.

10

Carrier Quals, Early September

Norfolk Naval Base.

In the turning of the great wheel, BG 7, the battle group that was to sail for the Med in late October, was readying itself for sea. Qualifying pilots to land on the carrier was an important step in that process. Three squadrons of fighter aircraft were designated: VFA-149, VFA-161, and VFA-132, flying F/A-18Cs, due in from Cecil Field; VS-49, flying S-3Bs, with the multiple missions of ASW, tanking, and "Sea Control", also at Cecil; VAQ-6, flying EA-6Bs, tasked with electronic warfare, currently en route from Whidbey Island, Washington; VAW-6, flying E-2C early warning aircraft, the largest planes in the wing, now at Oceana Naval Air Station, Norfolk; and VF-22, flying F-14s, also out of Oceana. They were at varying stages of readiness, flying aircraft of varying ages and states of art. VS-49 had the lowest ratings for overall readiness and the second-oldest aircraft of the air wing.

Carrier quals had been scheduled for the CV on which the squadrons would deploy, the *Andrew Jackson*. In two days, she would start unzipping troughs off the Carolinas, putting her nose into the wind while nervous pilots tried to put down on the flight deck without getting bad grades (or worse), then heading out again to do it all over. For the nugget aviators, and even for some of the veterans, it would be hell: three acceptable landings, or scrub. For the carrier's skipper, himself a pilot, the carrier quals would also be a time of tension—a new command for him, a crew that was eight percent shy of manning levels, and ready rooms crowded with pilots strung out by the thought of having to put a multi-million-dollar piece of tin down on a postage stamp at a hundred and fifty knots. The CAG, an old friend of the CV's skipper, was worried because he didn't have enough trained Landing Signal Officers (LSOs), and his Air Boss, he thought, was a vain horse's ass who didn't believe in Murphy's Law. And the Air Boss was worried because— well, because he was the Air Boss.

On the twenty-ninth of August, the *Jackson* was secured to the dock at Norfolk to take on those squadron personnel who wouldn't be flying aboard with the aircraft. Rented school buses pulled up on the dock, and everybody aboard them stood up and started to grab his gear and make space with butt and elbows. It had been a hot ride over from NAS Norfolk, and a long, cold ride up from Cecil in a leased 747 for the crews from Florida squadrons. After part of a night and a day cramped up, the sailors of VS-49 were cranked, wired by seeing the carrier loom over them like a vast gray cliff. Sailors boiled out of the buses.

Sneesen, last off his bus, swung his sea-bag up on his shoulder and got in the line between two other white guys, then dumped the bag on the concrete when the petty officer in charge told him to, braced, checked his spacing, all that shit, and then gratefully swung the bag up again and headed up, up toward the hangar deck, which seemed from that angle to be somewhere on the roof. He fucking *marched*; he humped his sea-bag like a weight-lifter. He wanted to look *Navy*.

His section leader had told them three times what to do, and Sneesen had gone over it and over it. *Don't screw up,* he had told himself. *Don't make yourself a dork. Don't call attention to yourself.* He turned at the top of the ladder, a little out of breath, and saluted the fantail, where the flag he couldn't see was supposed to be, then saluted the deck officer, who was some ensign who wasn't even looking at him. "Sneesen, Henry, Seaman Recruit," he said, too loud, but the petty officer checking the list didn't even look up but muttered, "Move along, move it—" Ahead, guys were swinging their sea-bags on the conveyor of the metal detector.

Sneesen dropped his bag on the conveyor and walked through the detector, allowing himself just a hint of swagger, and just after he got in the clear a shrill alarm went off, and everybody perked up and a black chief petty officer with an armband and a pistol belt said, "All right, who the fuck is *Sneesen*?" He had one of those scowling, Mike-Tyson faces. An intimidator.

"Oh, shit, *Sneesen*!" somebody groaned behind him.

His bag had set off the metal detectors. *Oh, shit, indeed.*

"Empty it," the CPO said. He grinned. He seemed to enjoy Sneesen's humiliation.

Sneesen yanked and pulled and piled stuff on the deck until his tool kit came out. *His tool kit! Metal!* His personal tool kit that he had had since tenth grade, with the Leatherman tool and the really cool combo wrench he had stolen from a Brookstone store and the set of Allen wrenches that had been his dad's, and his Belrin sixty-five-part computer tool kit (bought with real money, sixty-nine ninety-nine, *great stuff!*) rolled up in a canvas thing he had bought at a yard sale. He hadn't even thought about it, putting it in. It was *him*, that tool kit. "My tool kit," he mumbled to the chief. He had to look way up to see that black, scowling face.

"I said *Empty it!*" The chief grabbed the bottom of the

182

bag and with one hand upended it, and Sneesen's life
fell out on the deck, paper blowing away, metal rolling,
clothes scattering. Guys started to laugh. They bellowed.
They loved it!

Sneesen choked. Inside, a voice screamed, *You fucking rotten nigger! If I had my way—if things were right—if, if, if—* !

Off Norfolk.
Aboard USS *Andrew Jackson* as it headed out to sea for
carrier quals next day, a representative cluster of the air
wing's officers and the BG flag staff were getting their sea
legs—and their first sense of dangers ahead, as they went
into a week at sea. In the flag briefing room, Admiral
Newman was surrounded by his staff.

"LTjg Christy Nixon will now give the intelligence portion of the brief."

Christy Nixon had black hair that she used to wear
painted down her back and now wore short. She had
skin the color of chocolate powder, the eyes of a cat, a
broad forehead. She wasn't quite black and she wasn't
quite Asian, but military people looked at her and guessed
her heritage: a child of the Vietnam War, of a black father
and a Vietnamese mother. Pretty, ambitious, smart, she
was the AI of VS-49, the S-3 squadron to which Rafe
Rafehausen had just reported.

Nixon hugged her arms to her chest. She was freezing
cold—shipboard cotton khakis were insufficient for standing directly under the air-conditioning vent in the flag
briefing room. "Good morning, sir. I'm LTjg Nixon of the
Rat Catchers, and I'll be—"

"I know your name," the admiral said. He added, to his
flag captain, "Jesus, Hank." His tone was not savage, simply
bored. Admiral Rudolph Newman, seated, sprawled in all
directions. Nixon collected herself and went on.

"I'll be briefing the Fleetex scenario as it now—"

The admiral raised his hand. "Everybody shut up!"

Silence. Even the soft whispers from the back ceased. In the port-side passageway outside, however, voices continued. "What's up, dude? Man, that was some fucking landing, you know— !"

"Hey! Chief! You got to sign—"

"So I downloaded the stupid thing off the web and, bang—"

The admiral unfolded himself, stood, seeming to threaten the overhead. He jabbed a finger at the passageway. "Shut them up!" Then, to everybody around him: "From this moment, the blue-tile passageways are off limits to all but flag staff. All! Tell everybody else to go around. I want silence and *I will have respect!*" He sat down.

Christy Nixon tried to imagine walking all the way around the combat information center to the starboard passageway and back across, then twenty frames forward again, merely to get from her squadron ready room to the intel center. Was he kidding?

Everybody was looking at the admiral. He looked at her and raised an eyebrow. She continued. "As it is now constructed, the exercise—"

"Jesus, Nixon! Do you always interrupt admirals?" The admiral glanced around at the ship's captain, the air wing commander, and the chief engineer. "I'll *tell* you when to talk. Carry on, Miz Nixon."

"Yes, sir. The exercise is designed to represent—"

"Who the hell drew that map?" The viewgraph showed a map of Libya superimposed over the central Caribbean.

"I did, sir."

"I don't know why you chose to draw Libya on the map when we're going to exercise against the Russian North Fleet. Fix it."

She stared at him.

The F-18 skipper jumped in. "Sir, it was my understanding that we were going to do a freedom-of-navigation operation inside the Libyan flight intercept region in the Gulf of Sidra."

"Yeah, Palmtree. FONOPS in the FIR. What about it?"

"Sir, I believe LTjg Nixon's orders were to brief that scenario."

"I've already made this point clear. I want a proper Fleetex with an opposing battle group—a Kirov-class, high-value-unit surface-action group. I want to practice for a real fight. *Not* dicking with A-rabs. And I can't really believe that this bright-looking young woman thinks she can come in here and flout my orders."

"My error, sir," CAG AI murmured. "The scenario we received was from LantCom."

The flag N-2 was looking embarrassed—no, scared. She got it. He hadn't passed on the fucking changes!

The admiral shook his head. "Don't send that female up here again. She's clueless."

Off Cape Hatteras.

By the third day, anybody on the *Jackson* who wore scrambled eggs on his hat was also wearing a worried look on his face. Nobody said outright that the admiral was angry, but the frowns hurrying in and out of blue-tile country let everybody know he was, and that unhappiness ran down the chain of command like a lightning strike. The CV's captain was definitely unhappy about the way his ship performed since a refitting; the CAG was definitely unhappy about the way the Air Boss was unhappy about the pace of carrier quals, which seemed "slow and irregularly paced," according to a memo from the flag. The squadron skippers were unhappy about what the CAG had told them. The pilots were unhappy because of the way their skippers behaved and because, as a group, they knew they were on their way to posting a new record for carrier-qualification misery. Three aircraft had already had to head for the beach because their pilots couldn't put them down on the deck. The one thing they had avoided was a crash.

At the Landing Signal Officer's stand aft of elevator number four, however, the duty LSO refused to be unhappy. He was a lieutenant and he was doing a job he loved and he was damned if he was going to let the big bird sit on his shoulder just because the Air Boss was snarling into his earphones, "Rhythm! I want to see a rhythm out there! Recovery is ragged! Move them!"

Chris Donitz was old to be a lieutenant. He was a rare bird—he'd had a job after college, chucked it to join the Navy and fly. He had a degree in economics, not aerospace engineering, and he was contemplating where he might be on this sunny evening if he had kept his nose to the grindstone as a senior, fixed-income analyst in a major stock security firm, rather than, say, an LSO calling landings from a portside platform of a Nimitz-class carrier in the Cherry Point operating area. *I got rhythm*, he hummed to himself. Loved Gershwin. Maybe the Air Boss loved Gershwin, too; maybe that's why he wanted rhythm.

The Air Boss was supposed to be one of the best fliers in the Navy and a damned good LSO in his day; it was just that now, he was tensed up, like everybody else. *Except me*, Donitz thought. *I refuse to play Get the Guy Below You.* He grinned at the half-scared junior pilots who were putting in their first orientation sessions on the platform.

Everything stank of JP-5, and the roar of aircraft on the deck was a counterpoint to the louder roar of aircraft punching off the catapults up forward. Donitz's face was already sunburned a bright cherry red because his flight deck helmet had no visor, and the speed with which aircraft were being landed, cycled, and launched kept him always at his post, which had no shade. He had three so-called assistants from other squadrons, but it was all his responsibility.

"Fuck, that guy sucked!" bellowed the junior guy from the FAG squadron as an aircraft flashed past and all but bounced as it snagged the one wire. And he had. Some EA-6B guy fresh out of flight school; two power calls and a lame lineup.

"No grade!" Donitz shouted. He watched as it was written down. Poor bastard. Chris Donitz hated giving poor grades, especially to new guys. Those grades and comments would go up on the greenie board in the squadron's ready room. Bad enough that most of his squadron-mates would have watched his lousy landing on the plat-camera relay to the ready-room TV. Donitz remembered all too well the demoralizing consequence, the loss of faith. But the guy's landing had been impossible—at one point almost a ramp, then almost a waveoff, then a first-wire. Dogshit. Donitz hated humiliating people, hated making them miserable— but he hated more the idea that a guy who couldn't come down in the groove and catch the three wire in the daytime was going to have to do it at night, no beach to fly to, combat conditions. Better to wash out now than screw up the entire ship on deployment.

Donitz peered into the haze, then looked at the board. Two F-18s to go and one S-3. The first F-18 was right in the groove already (*Hey! We got a rhythm!*) and looking good, a nice change after three days of landings that had filled the ready rooms with shouting, helmet-throwing, clutch-your-head-and-try-not-to-cry skipper tantrums. Donitz didn't have the experience to fathom just how bad this air wing was, but he knew it was not in the same league as the wing where he had been a nugget. Too few old guys here, for one thing. So few that he, a second-tour pilot, was standing on the platform pretending to be a senior LSO. Too many no grades. Too many power calls. And too goddam fast!

The F-18 guy still looked good; hadn't even waggled his wings. He was seconds away now, and Donitz relaxed.

"Three wire and okay!" he bellowed, even before the tail hook caught the wire. The juniors looked impressed.

Christy Nixon, recovered from her run-in with Admiral Newman, was enjoying her first flight off a carrier. She hadn't got airsick; she'd survived the cat shot and Rafehausen's personal air show; and now they were heading into the break, something she had watched from the flight deck but never really understood.

"Tricky?" Rafe said over the intercom.

"Sir?"

"What's the break for?" *Could he read minds?*

"No idea, sir."

"Bleeds off airspeed." Was he showing off? Coming on to her? Teaching? "It's also fun to do. It also serves the pilot as a start to a landing routine, okay? I'm going to call off the numbers. We come over the carrier in the break so that we can start the geometry problem of landing the same way every time. Copy?"

"Yes, sir." Did the new XO give this much attention to every jg who flew in the back seat? She doubted it. She had already wondered if his smile was just a little wider for her, his attention in the passageway as they passed just a little more focused. She looked sideways at the SENSO in the other seat and caught a slight smile and guessed that he was wondering, too. No, the smile was more as if he had stopped wondering and had made up his mind.

"We'll stay hot-mike." This was Rafehausen, maybe for everybody's benefit, maybe for Cutter, the newbie aviator in the righthand seat, whose own attempts at landing the day before had been so bad he had gone round and round, and somebody had said in the Dirty Shirt that the puddles on his side of the aircraft when he finally got it down were sloshing higher than the CV's bow wave. Everybody had laughed, but the guy was a wreck.

"Tricky?"

"Sir?"

"Once we're in the break, we start to go dirty—know what that means?"

"Uh—gear and stuff down?"

"Cool. Hang on, guys—goin' for a r-i-i-i-de—"

The S-3, not one of the sports cars of naval aviation, made like a Lotus as it suddenly propped itself up on its port wing and seemed to pivot on the wingtip. Tricky felt the G-force build on her body and her lunch, and forgotten objects flew past her face. *Lesson learned.* Out her tiny window she watched the sky, a perfect sunset just amber pink in the part of the sky that swung past. She turned her head to the left and saw the carrier slide past the SENSO's window. The turn seemed to go on forever, and it was like an amusement park ride, and she found she loved it.

"No whooping in my plane!" Rafehausen called. Had she whooped? She looked over at the SENSO. He gave her a thumbs up. He was smiling that smile again. She guessed she'd whooped.

It was Sneesen's first full day on the flight deck. He loved it. He loved the air and the noise and the light. He was standing close to the island, tense and almost shivering because he was afraid he would screw up. Just now, he wasn't supposed to be doing anything, but the parking chief stopped every few minutes to explain what *he* was doing, which Sneesen thought was really cool. He knew that nobody trusted him to do anything important yet, but it was enough to be there, enough to have the chief take him seriously. And the chief was a great guy, older, serious, with pale blue eyes that really *looked* at you.

But it was all so fucking fast! Planes landed—no, trapped—and launched after only the briefest check. Guys moved the planes around a lot, hauling them with tractors that moved like waterbugs; other guys got the hook of a newly landed plane off the wire, then walked (often ran) the plane to a spot on the deck where it waited or got turned off, and at once other guys chained it down. At the run. Mostly, today, the newly landed planes were moved straight to the catapults—no, *cats*—and readied for re-launch. Sneesen understood that this was all done to train the pilots and to test them, but it also served to train the flight-deck guys, like him. So far, the deck was to him like a chessboard to somebody who doesn't play chess, the positions meaningless, the movements purposeless. He had only the foggiest notion that there was an Air Boss in a bubble high up on the island directing this perilous game; he had no sense that the nonskid under his feet was new and that after three months of daily ops it would be worn down to slick steel; he did not know that only three squadrons were actually on the boat today so that cyclic ops could go almost nonstop, or that, if the whole air wing had been there, the deck would have been full and the hangar deck crowded.

But Sneesen wanted to learn. He wanted to do right for LDCR Rafehausen. He had been on the deck when Rafehausen had come out to pre-flight his bird, and Sneesen had hovered nearby. Rafe had spoken to him—even remembered his name. Said, "Hey, there's my man!" Then the female jg had joined him—the Alien, Sneesen thought of her as, because she seemed very foreign to him, *different, untrustworthy*—and Rafehausen had turned away to talk to her. Sneesen thought she was distracting Rafehausen from his job. He didn't like her.

But just now, he was so frustrated he was angry. Everything on deck was happening *too fast.* He wanted to join in, but he was afraid that anything he did would be wrong.

Then the plane-spotting chief with the great blue eyes came over, took a big hit off the water bottle, and whacked him on the shoulder.

"Want to try getting the tail hook off the wire, next trap? You don't touch anything! Just get your ass down where you can see and give me this sign when the hook is clear, got it? Just the way I showed you." He made the "hook free" sign.

Sneesen felt his stomach drop. He nodded. *Oh, Jesus!*

"Okay, that FAG in the groove, he's your bird." *Fag?* Sneesen thought. *Why's he a fag?* "Garrett, catch a break! Drink some water. Sneesen's gonna spot the FAG." Garrett, who was built like a jock and had a lot of friends, gave Sneesen a wave of thanks. Suddenly, Sneesen was *a guy.* He moved out on the deck with the chief, unconsciously moving just like him.

The F-18 came roaring in as if it was going to hit them. Sneesen, seeing it for the first time from out on the deck, was sure the plane would hit the ramp, then that it would miss all the wires. Instead, it dropped with a tremendous whack and caught the three wire twenty feet away and surged to full power; Sneesen knew enough already to know that you hit the power when you *trapped* in case you *boltered* or had to do a *waveoff.* The seemingly huge aircraft ran out the wire as if it was going to tear it right out of the boat, and then it decelerated as if a big hand had caught it by the scruff of the neck. Sneesen got hit with a wall of heat, and adrenaline rushed like an injected drug.

"Go!" the chief hollered over the aircraft noise, and Sneesen raced out as he had watched Garrett and the others do. He squatted by the wing, clear of the jet blast as the pilot ran his throttle down. Sneesen got his ass really low, the seat of his jeans just off the deck, loving the tension in his thighs; he watched, then heard, the wire tension drop as the hook moved and the wire dropped free, and he gave the sign to the chief. *Made the sign! I did it!* The chief waved his paddles and the plane rolled forward, clear of the wire and toward the waiting number three cat.

Sneesen trotted back to his spot near the island as if he had just done a space-jam. He thought somebody might high-five him or something. But Garrett was nowhere in sight and the chief was still out there with his paddles, and suddenly Sneesen had no idea what he was supposed to do next. He felt momentary anger, and then he remembered what the counselor had told him, *Try to look at yourself from outside,* and he saw that it was okay. Everybody was doing his job. *He had done his job. He had helped the pilot bring his plane up the deck. They couldn't have done it without him!*

He looked up and saw another F-18 in the groove. Okay. Same deal. No problem. Cog in the machine.

Then the chief ran up. The look on his face startled Sneesen. The chief plugged in to a comm set and started to jabber. The F-18 they had just spotted was parked behind the jet blast deflector, the big wall that hydraulics moved up out of the flight deck to protect planes ready to take off from the jet blast of those actually launching. Sneesen had watched it all day because he thought it was really cool; somehow, it made the whole launch sequence look like something out of sci-fi. He knew now the rhythm of the launch: plane forward; deflector up; engines to full; bang of the cat. But the plane on this cat wasn't moving, and its engines were not at full power.

Sneesen looked at the aircraft near him, trying to look over them, through them, to see the pattern of the deck. He hadn't believed they could get this many planes here. Planes were parked with their tails out over the water, lining the whole deck edge. As he watched, an EA-6B moved out from a parking position and rolled up behind the just-trapped F-18, adding to the clutter near him. But the chief seemed even angrier now, holding his right ear cup and shouting into the mike. The words were carried away from Sneesen by the wind.

The incoming F-18 was well into the groove now.

Sneesen thought the deck looked full. But what did he know?

Down and across the deck on the LSO platform, Donitz watched the incoming F-18 and wished he could have more landings like the last one. This guy's wings rocked back and forth like he was flying in a hurricane, and he was chasing the ball all the way. Donitz touched the mike at his throat and kept the pickle switch high in his right hand. This guy might need it.

"Power," he murmured. In his headset, he heard (and tried to ignore) the Air Boss say, "Paddles, I don't want this aircraft waving off." *Well, Jee-zus H. Christ, Big Guy, do you think I do?* "Power," he said again quietly. "We've had too many waveoffs," the Air Boss pontificated. *Yeah, yeah, yeah*— Then all of a sudden the Air Boss was gone, leaving Donitz only the ghost of his voice saying something about Catapult Two. *Not my problem*, Donitz thought.

The F-18 got its nose up and looked better. The kid seemed to have the ball, now. Donitz looked over at the three wire, but some inconsiderate bastard had just parked a giant E-2 Charlie right over their platform and he couldn't see the deck. At least the E-2's tail gave some shade.

Way off at the edge of the haze, the unmistakable, ugly bulk of an S-3 was turning upwind toward the groove. Nice. Donitz had liked his break, too. *Has to be Rafehausen.* Only fucking pilot in that squadron.

"Power," he said seductively to the F-18. He didn't want to scare the guy.

One mile astern of the carrier, Rafe had just explained to his captive audience that a pilot wanted to exit this turn lined up with the carrier, in the groove at six hundred and forty feet altitude and around one twenty knots air speed. He and Cutter Sardesson, his newbie copilot, had counted out together the distance from the break to the turn. Rafe liked the fact that the backseaters thought the lesson was for Ms Nixon. Only Rafe and Cutter knew that the lesson was for Cutter, an otherwise sharp kid whose three no-grade landings demanded tutoring. He'd already spent two sessions getting screamed at in the ready room by the skipper. That came with the territory, but Rafe figured a little quiet teaching from the XO wouldn't hurt.

"Call the ball."

"Roger, Ball." Cutter gave the boat their fuel and weight.

Rafe scanned the instruments and liked what he saw. He was dead on. He looked out over the high instrument panel at the boat. Good lineup. Good angle of attack. Something on deck—hard to tell in the haze and dusk. Deck would deal with it.

Rafe loved landing at this hour. Light enough for visibility, dark enough to count as a night trap. A free landing. Rafe was past needing such a crutch, but the feeling remained from his first cruise. He was smiling. He turned to see if he could flash this smile at Nixon, but the view was blocked. He'd hoped she might be craning around to watch him.

Half a mile ahead, Sneesen fidgeted as the chief shouted into the mike. The incoming F-18 was only seconds away; last time, at this point, Sneesen and the chief had been out on the deck, ready for the trap. Was somebody else going to take this plane? Sneesen had no clue. He moved closer to the chief.

In the tower high above the deck, the Air Boss perched on the edge of his big chair. He glanced at the incoming F-18, which looked to be a few seconds from another botched but safe landing. He shrugged and moved his attention back to what seemed to be chaos at catapult two. Colored shirts were massing around it. Broken shuttle? What was the fucking problem? He already felt that he was behind the deck, its choreographed action threatening to slip out of his control. He needed a second to think. He heard the petty officer in charge of spotting planes on the deck trying to get his attention, but he was fixed on the mess at cat two. Was the goddam plane there on fire? Smoke seemed to be coming out of the cockpit. *That wasn't a broken shuttle, that was an electrical fire.* The F-14's canopy opened and smoke burst out with the two aviators. A swarm of deck crew with extinguishers surrounded the plane. A fire party raced toward it.

"Cat two down!" the Air Boss called.

"Sir, I, um, that EA-6B is—"

"Shut up!" The Air Boss had no time for parking problems. "Plat camera on cat two!"

The Air Boss could see that the movements of the badly parked EA-6B had created a traffic jam near elevator four, but that situation hadn't reached crisis level yet, and he moved back to watching catapult two.

Sixty feet below, the chief gave up on his attempt to solve the parking problem, grabbed Sneesen and raced toward the F-18. It had already trapped, and they were fifteen seconds behind the action. He shoved Sneesen toward the plane, and his mind registered that the kid knew what to do. *Smart.* The chief looked to their right, toward the bow. Still no room to move the just-landed F-18. He looked aft. The inbound S-3 was much closer than he expected. Sneesen gave him the sign and he began to wave the F-18 forward, but the inexperienced pilot had throttled down too far and was having trouble getting his plane to roll. The chief hit his mike.

"Foul deck!"

He knew he was already too late.

Sneesen heard it, and he looked around. It sounded important, the way the chief was shouting it. Crouched under the F-18, he couldn't see the incoming S-3.

The F-18 he was squatting under was blocking the landing area, that's what the chief's "foul deck" meant. Time stopped for Sneesen. In a way that he would always remember, the whole meaning of the flight deck abruptly became clear to him: suddenly, he saw it all, as if all the rules and the moves of chess had come to him at once. It was like being blind, and then seeing. *The LSO couldn't see that the deck was clogged.* That E-2 was in the way.

The F-18 and whatever else the chief was yelling about were clogging the landing area.

The S-3 was seconds away. The pilot should have been able to see the F-18, Sneesen thought. But in the falling dark, he knew in his guts that the chaos on deck might be invisible from the air.

And he knew that the pilot was Rafehausen.

Up in the tower, the newbie, second-class petty officer finally yelled at the Air Boss.

"The deck is *foul*, sir!" A more experienced man would have grabbed the Air Boss and made him look. A more experienced man would have made him look forty-five seconds ago by using a certain tone of voice, when it still would have been a small crisis. A more experienced man might even have fixed the problem himself, ordering the S-3 waved off and risking the chewing-out that would come if he was wrong. A more experienced man would have known, with dead certainty, that there was no master plan any more, that the deck was clogged with aircraft and had been unsafe for several minutes. But all the more experienced men were in other jobs, preventing other crises. This ship had too few veterans and they were spread too thin.

The newbie's fear finally outweighed his caution. His call was a shriek. "*Foul deck!*"

Seconds too late, the Air Boss turned to look at the incoming S-3 and the F-18 still on top of the wire. He froze. Sixty feet above the deck, entropy triumphed over training.

Six hundred yards aft of the stern, Rafe's head was briefly down on the instruments as he continued to explain his descent and the concept of angle of attack to his crew. His approach was perfect. But something still bugged him and kept his hand on the throttle.

From the LSO platform, Donitz watched the S-3 with contentment. The deepening dusk would be full dark soon, and this S-3 was his last call. He admired the landing, too.

While the turbofan engines could be responsive, the S-3 was notoriously hard to steady up. A rock-solid approach like this was a pleasure to watch, and Donitz had already alerted his three LSOs to pay attention.

Sneesen was still squatting. He could see under the F-18 to the E-2; beyond the E-2 was the LSO's platform. He didn't know how he knew that, but he knew it. He couldn't see Rafehausen's S-3 but he knew it was there, and when he glanced back and saw the terror on the chief's face, he knew what was about to happen. Rafehausen would come down on top of the F-18, and a fireball would take out all of them.

Sneesen threw himself forward under the F-18. He wasn't a runner, but fear and hero-worship and adrenaline drove him. He didn't even think what would happen if the F-18 started rolling at that moment; he only knew he must go, dig into the nonskid and go. He tore across the deck, threw himself under the E-2 and felt something rake across his back like fire, and he hit the nonskid on his hands and elbows, and his face struck, but he scrabbled with hands and feet and kept moving—

"Foul deck! FAG in the wire! *Foul deck!*" Lieutenant Donitz heard the cry even through his protectors. He swung his head. The assistant LSOs had their mouths open. Donitz realized that he was being hit by a small enlisted man who was pounding his shoulder, who had apparently fallen or jumped off the deck on the LSO platform. What got him moving was that the kid was crying.

Donitz didn't think. He had been an LSO too long; some of it was merely reflexes now. His thumb hit the button on the pickle switch and his voice was already roaring.

"WAVEOFF!" He must have busted Rafehausen's eardrums, he thought.

Rafe had his hand on the throttle ready to go to full power, two hundred yards and four seconds from the deck when the cut lights went and the voice roared "WAVEOFF," just as his sixth sense finally told him that something was definitely wrong in his landing area. The deeper dark down there in the dusk had to be another plane.

Smoothly, without hesitation, he ran the throttle forward to full power. Power is altitude. His airspeed was low, just above stall speed at this altitude—perfect for landing, shit for maneuver. Maybe five knots to play with. He lifted the nose by an adjustment so slight as to be unnoticed by the horrified watchers on the deck and felt the slow load of the S-3 respond. The turbofans charged and screamed in response to his throttle, and he edged the nose up another fraction, slowing his rate of descent. He still needed the aerodynamic edge of the flaps to keep him from stalling, so he discarded the notion of retracting them to get speed. Speed is not *always* power and altitude.

Three seconds from the ramp, Rafe remembered that he had a brand-new SENSO and an AI with no experience in the back, and he realized that neither would be ready to eject even if he had time to order it.

He could see the length of the deck now—no room even to touch and go. He uttered one word.

"Gear!"

Thank God, Cutter got it. He slapped a switch and turned his head, but Rafe never saw the look that Cutter gave him, mixed awe and terror. The landing gear began to retract, half a second and sixty feet from the ramp.

Later, and forever, both men would remember that

Cutter, who had had three bad landings, had obeyed and acted.

More power came.

The S-3 was game, and so was Rafe, and her descent stopped as her nose crossed the line of the stern.

Sneesen watched his idol in slow motion as the S-3 roared toward the deck. It was all so clear, so final. He saw, with utter attention, as the landing gear twitched and began to retract. He saw the nose go up a fraction and the shallow dive bottom out at the stern deck edge. He even saw Rafehausen's head, bent forward, dedicated. Then the E-2 mercifully blocked his view and he heard a sound like a cannon shot from the flight deck and all the LSOs threw themselves flat.

Sneesen's chief watched from a prone position on the deck as the S-3's high wings cleared the vertical stabilizers of the trapped F-18. The retracting landing gear missed the cockpit, because the plane's nose-up attitude held the gear clear. The tail hook, however, slapped down on the F-18's body and dragged up the length of the canopy. It cut a gouge in the airframe and in the air wing's legends that would outlast every man and woman on the deck, before dangling into empty space fourteen feet off the deck. It still dangled there as the S-3 sailed down the centerline, perfectly trimmed, just clear of the deck. The Air Boss watched it go by below him, fighting for altitude. By the time it reached the bow, Rafe had got it sixty feet higher.

Any emergency on the flight deck communicates itself like a wave of light throughout the ship. On the deck itself, every sailor was either face-down on the nonskid or crouched behind the largest metal object he or she could find. Below decks, men and women were drawn to the plat camera images that could be seen on TV monitors in every space. As the S-3 clawed upward and away from the bow, eight thousand lungs exhaled simultaneously through four thousand throats, none less roughly than those of the Air Boss, who was muttering to himself *Oh Jesus thank God oh thank God*—

And aboard AG 703, Rafe continued to pray for altitude, but the battle had been won for ten long seconds. His grin was not relaxed, but it was genuine. He winked at Cutter, who was as gray as the plane, and called to his frozen backseaters:

"Everybody want to try that again?"

Sneesen got a commendation later, and the plane crew bought him a fancy Walkman with stereo speakers when they all hit the beach. But the best thing he got was one of those little plastic figures that have captions on the bottom like "World's Best Golfer" and "World's Best Grandad." Rafehausen had somebody in the squadron shop fancy it up and re-do it so it read "World's Best Sailor," and he gave it to him in a ceremony in the ready room. Afterwards, Rafehausen took him aside and was utterly serious, looking right at him, and he said, as if he was eighty and not thirty-two, "You're a very brave young man."

From then on, Sneesen was ready to kill for him.

11

September

The submarine base at Murmansk, Russia.

An expected but long-delayed summons came to Alexandr Petrovitch Suvarov, Captain First Class of the Russian Navy, on a late afternoon whose perfect, golden beauty was going unnoticed by the captain and his harried crew. Captain Suvarov had requested a real cruise, a deep cruise, both to try his boat and to justify why an officer of his seniority was commanding a single submarine, and the high command had put him off and put him off, stroking him, lying to him, bullying him. Soon, Sasha. Very soon, Sasha. Not today, Sasha. Now, today, suddenly, it was *Report, Sasha!*

The dockyard workers were shit. Under the empire, under the Soviet system, workers at Severodinsk had been the best, and they had got special privileges, like scientists, to manhandle the titanium and maintain the fragile systems. Now they were shit-eating idiots, like men who built refrigerators and cars. Not for the first time, or the last, Suvarov grunted his hatred/admiration for the Americans' casual assumption of technical competence at every level, and he went back to reviewing every inch of every machine part delivered from the factory. The last factory. The one remaining defense plant that produced the fine-machined parts that made the reactor hum.

Suvarov welcomed the summons, because it gave him an excuse to air his rage at headquarters, and because it gave him a chance to test his new second officer, an unproven quantity who lacked sufficient sea time for his seniority. Suvarov gave him distinct orders, winked at his engineer, an older man who ought to be in semi-retirement at Malachite or Lazarit, and went down the ladder to his stateroom to shrug his heavy shoulders into a regulation tunic. Suvarov had avoided the tendency of Russian officers to add weight with rank. He lifted weights and he ran, and he was sometimes mistaken in the dark for a Spetznaz officer, which of course always displeased him in a pleasant way. And he had avoided the tendency to add acolytes; when he went to a naval office, he trailed no tail of junior officers to show his importance. The truth was, Suvarov was a bit of a puritan. Even a bit of a prig.

Even in the best of times, North Fleet Headquarters had been on the drab and industrial side. This was probably for the best, as now, in hard times, there was no real change to either the exterior of the buildings or their interiors. Indeed, the number of new computers and the haze of concealing cigarette smoke combined to suggest actual improvement and modernization. Suvarov cut through the legions of flunkies and doorway guards with a deceptive swagger, a pose he used only, contemptuously, on functionaries. He made it to the admiral within five minutes of entering the quarterdeck.

"First Captain Suvarov of the *Shark*," an aide murmured and withdrew.

"Sasha!" The admiral rose from his chair, embraced him swiftly but sincerely, and waved him to a chair, a fine eighteenth-century chair at odds with the massive official furniture. The admiral occupied its twin, which protested faintly under him.

"Sergei," smiled Suvarov, after the embrace. They were still Sasha and Sergei; that was good, considering that the boy who had been his guide and tormentor through the Nakimov Academy was now Commander, North Sea Fleet. Same age, same training, utterly different types: one lean, honed, trying to seem younger; the other overweight, bearded, avuncular. Suvarov was the better sailor, the admiral the better politician. The difference explained their difference in rank.

"Sasha, I have a cruise for you! An old-style cruise."

Come, thought Suvarov, this is promising. He doesn't open with an admonition for the recent past. No criticisms for landing the Navy in hot, hot water for a little violation of Swedish neutrality. And a cruise? Too good to be true.

"North Sea?" he said, hopefully. "Iceland?"

"Better!" the admiral said. "Much better. And between us old boys, Sasha, it will be a long time before the President sees fit to allow you anywhere near a Nordic country, you understand?"

Ah. The sharp knife rather than the thick bludgeon. "The American coast?"

"No, Sasha. Your old hunting ground. The Mediterranean." Sergei beamed with pleasure. Well he might. Suvarov had longed to return to the Mediterranean. Too seldom they showed their ships and submarines in that strategic water. The Americans had begun to sneer, and Suvarov with them. Blue-water navy. Where? Within fifty miles of Mother Russia? But they are sending me. And I'm known to be dangerous. Splendid. What's the catch?

"Are you ready for sea?"

Sasha snorted, meaning, In these times with such slip-shod crap, I am never ready as I was taught to be ready. The admiral leafed through Suvarov's orders, which sat

204

on his lap in a blue plastic folder that was grained to look like leather and embossed with the gold seal of the Naval Command. "I say this to you privately, as it was said to me, Sasha. We are trying to make a point, not start a war, yes? We lack the muscle to demand that the United States give up a godawful weapon, an against-the-balance-of-power toy their scientists have given them. Do you know what I am talking about?"

Suvarov did not. Once he might have. Once upon a time he would have read all the intelligence reports for himself, back when he did not need sleep. He shook his head, trying to make it look like the angry no of a man who hadn't the time.

"Don't worry, Sasha, I'm not sure they would have given you these reports anyway." The admiral made a face. "It is an American program, called Peacemaker. A wonderful name, because it is absolutely as peaceful as any other force America sends to destabilize our sphere of influence and destroy our empire. It is like Coca-Cola and the free market, eh? It is like—" He was going to go off on a hobby-horse, and then he saw what he was doing and he caught himself. "Peacemaker is supposed to be a spy satellite that can be deployed by a theater commander, fired from a ship or a submarine. It is to be in low-earth orbit and capable of being maneuvered in orbit—not unlike, let us say, some sort of aircraft, perhaps. Only eighty miles up. To 'surveil.' To 'fill in the temporary gaps in the satellite network.' That has been the story for two years; it's in the newspapers, some of it. Now, our intelligence people think maybe too much is being made of too little— that, even in an open society, the Americans are being very, very public about their Peacemaker—because they're hiding something. You have read Poe—*The Purloined Letter*? Like that.

"It has occurred to a committee at the National Academy of Sciences that Peacemaker could in fact be something else, maybe something left over from their so-called 'Star Wars'—perhaps a prototype satellite hunter-killer, a weapon to destroy other nations' satellites. Not only our spy satellites, Sasha, but communications. Information warfare. Which we hardly even understand, yet, and the Americans may be getting ready to wage it."

"If they develop one, then we will develop one."

"Oh, Sasha! You are a brilliant commander and also a little fool! American technology is so far beyond the rest of us— ! Have you read that Englishman, Fuller, as I have asked you?"

Suvarov made a little hissing sound, the sort of noise a kid lets escape him when he is scolded. "Not yet, not yet—"

"Bah. You are unchanged since school. You read Poe, but you don't read strategy." He reached way forward, leaning over his own gut, to tap Suvarov's thigh. "Sasha, defensive weapons make for security. Our 'attack boats' can defend our boomers, our ballistic missile submarines. Thus, they defend stability. Yes?"

"Sergei, I do not need to read this 'Fuller' to understand the basics of nuclear strategy and diplomacy, I thank you."

"Then listen. Space weapons that destroy, let us say, communications satellites, change the balance of power too fast and too much. They make other nations spear-waving barbarians against the cartridge rifle. Understand?"

Suvarov turned this over in his mind until he was satisfied. Yes. Reaching out into space to destroy another country's communications satellites would cost the user nothing but money. It would make the concept of a national fortress—one achieved by geography, by air defense systems, by armed perimeters—irrelevant. He nodded heavily.

"They have scheduled a test launch from a ship, in the Mediterranean. The test itself violates the ABM treaty. They know that, of course they know that—probably why they're doing it so soon, a year ahead of the schedule they made public in '95. We want them to know we want the test stopped. I am sure that the drunkard in the Kremlin will be telling his pal the US President the same thing; so will our people in the UN, but our command believe the message should come from us of the Navy, as well— in the form of action. In the form that their command will understand—eh? So." He folded his big, heavy hands over Suvarov's orders, as if keeping them secret until Suvarov had been lectured. "You will shadow a US battle group now assembling in Norfolk and tag them as you see fit. You must allow yourself to be detected from time to time but not held, so that they get the message. You must seem a potential danger and an angry comment. If you can embarrass them by penetrating their screen, please, those rules are removed. But Sasha—" and here the admiral turned his bulk on the tiny chair, and the hard gray eyes had little of friendship in them. "Sasha, please understand me, and Moscow. You do not start a war. You back down if threatened. You make our comment and then you are the reliable old adversary who usually plays by the rules. Things are too fragile now. We cannot afford a real incident that would lose us the IMF money or the German heating oil." He made the same face. "Or the Coca-Cola."

Suvarov nodded. He was already pondering places he knew like old friends in the twisty currents of the western Mediterranean.

"Any surface ships?" he asked, hopefully.

"A Sovremenny group. Just a couple of destroyers and some support ships, and something to watch their test. And those ships mostly not worth a crap."

"They're handy if they make noise in the water at the right times."

"And they give the American admiral more to think about. Yes. By the way, you're in luck—it's a man named Newman, his first flag—two years ago, he commanded the *Fillmore* and got so rattled in the South China Sea, you remember? Very bright, but unwise, if you understand me. You'll sail rings around him. Anyway, that's all in the briefing book. Would you like to meet the commander of your task force?"

"Is he senior to me?"

"No."

"Then Sergei, let me command the task force from the *Shark*. Come, we have practiced this. In peacetime, it can work."

Sergei smiled, but warmth did not lift the corners of his mouth.

"Perhaps. Let me take it up with Kandinsky and the rest." He held out the blue folder. "Ready for sea in fourteen days, and we will meet for dinner. How is your second officer?"

"Splendid."

"Good. He does not have enough sea time. Make sure you give it to him with honor and glory, old friend. It is time he went up the ladder."

The second officer was the admiral's son. Suvarov wondered if the admiral's son was there to watch him, or whether he had gotten this beautiful cruise because of the golden boy aboard. No matter. He was taking to sea the finest ship ever built by the Soviet Union, and he was being ordered to take her in harm's way, on a mission that mattered. It would be complicated; it was political. No matter.

"I must see to my ship."

The admiral returned his salute.

Ten minutes after he boarded his boat, his mood had infected every sailor aboard. He had a picked crew, a professional crew, and now they smiled and joked and sang. He watched them carefully and turned up the discipline a notch.

If this was his last time, it would be the best. A great game at sea, with an American carrier battle group as the opponent, and with that element of profound risk that made it worthwhile.

12

Fleetex

Fleetex 3-96 had been planned for four months, but it had been planned one way by Admiral Newman and another by the rest of the Navy—the way Alan had glimpsed when he had put in those four days at LantCom in Norfolk. The Navy's way had been rehearsed on paper and in computer simulations. It had been trained for by ships and squadrons.

From ten hours before it ever started, Admiral Newman's way was a disaster.

The *Andrew Jackson*, with her battle group, had sailed again from Norfolk and was positioning itself in the Bahamas.

At 2330 on the calm night preceding the storm that would be Fleetex 3-96, the ASW module was deserted except for the watch stander, an aging black warrant officer named Charlie Hamilton, and LTjg Nixon, who was squeezed comfortably between two computers, digesting a two-month-old copy of *Jane's Defense Weekly* and trying to overcome the anxiety of her first big at-sea operation. Since the carrier quals, the skipper had been on Rafehausen; Rafehausen had been on everybody else; the admiral had loomed over the lot like a mountain balanced on a rock. The only thing she felt no anxiety about was her part in it: she was rock-solid on the LantCom scenario, could have briefed it in her sleep.

Admiral Newman, she knew, was at war with most of his battle group over the terms of the Fleetex. He kept changing the scenario. Only that morning, he had exploded at the flag navigator, a full captain, during the final flag briefing on the exercise. In a tantrum, the scuttlebutt said, the admiral had torn up the briefing charts and demanded that the navigator revise them to fit Newman's idea of a war-at-sea exercise against a "traditional" adversary.

Now, she glanced over to see Hamilton pressed against the chart table that filled the center of the ASW module, leaning forward to stare at a bank of radios attached to the beam above the table.

"Eagle, this is Osprey, over?" came clearly over one of them. Charlie stabbed a key. A small green light went on. He turned to Christy and made a chopper-blade sign with his right hand.

"Osprey, this is Big Eagle, over?" Charlie said carefully into the handheld mike. "I got you loud and clear."

"Big Eagle, this is Osprey. I got a periscope V in visual."

Christy wasn't sure what she'd heard. Did he actually mean—?

"Osprey, this is Big Eagle. What's your location and the bearing and range to periscope, over?"

"Big Eagle, we are in Bow Guard, one nautical mile dead ahead of Big Eagle. Periscope is 000 relative, range from me two nautical miles. Range is approximate."

These guys were seeing a sub's periscope only three miles ahead of the carrier?

"Roger Osprey, copy that periscope is three nautical miles 000 relative to Big Eagle, over?"

"Roger Big Eagle. Confirm three NM, 000 relative."

WO Hamilton put a mark on the chart. "Fuck, eight hours until Startex!" he muttered. "How the hell can that helo see a periscope two miles away—?" Christy

211

was thinking of what two miles looked like from the air, at night; even low down, a couple of hundred feet—could you really *see* a small bow wave?

There was a squawk from the radio.

"Big Eagle? Big Eagle? This is Osprey. I see three, four new periscopes same bearing and range. Repeat, four new contacts!"

Suddenly Hamilton was bellowing into his hand mike, "Break! Break! This is Alpha Xray over! Osprey, *are you looking at breakers*? Over!"

Breakers? The word was so far out of the context of the emergency that Christy didn't even know what he meant. Then she got it. Breakers, as in surf. As in beach. As in running a huge ship aground.

"*God!*" The helo sounded spooked, even over a mile away. "Osprey—yes, shit—Jesus, we're seeing a whole line of breakers. Do you copy, Big Eagle? Line of breakers at 000 relative, range two nautical miles!"

Washington. Startex minus three.

"Good morning, sir. I'm Lieutenant Alan Craik, and I'll be briefing the Fleetex 3-96 portion of today's presentation."

He stood, as usual, in front of the projection screens of the CNO's briefing room. Today, Alan was presenting a major fleet exercise, not the sort of thing usually covered by the news services. He had wrestled with the intricacies of the exercise for days, read through mountains of message traffic, and even had the heady experience of asking his wife, who worked on the exercise's centerpiece, Peacemaker, for advice. As the exercise developed, other briefers would cover each "battle" and sortie in detail; Alan was doing the setup, so that over the coming days the CNO and his staff would be familiar with the complexities of the exercise. It was pretty small, considering the giant all-NATO exercises Alan had seen as an ensign, but the multiple threats and the need to conduct the complex "exercise within an exercise" of practicing the Peacemaker launch would keep BG 7 busy.

The CNO nodded. Alan had learned that this was his way of indicating that he had absorbed the last brief and was ready to continue. Alan turned down the lights of the auditorium and began.

"Sir, Battle Group Seven, centered around the USS *Andrew Jackson*, a Nimitz-class carrier, is steaming south from the Cherry Point operating area and was last located an hour ago here." Alan illuminated the battle group's position near the Bahamas on the large-screen monitor. A separate monitor displayed the battle group's composition: USS *Andrew Jackson*, CVN; USS *Fort Klock*, Tico-class Aegis cruiser; USS *Isaac Hull* and USS *Steven Decatur*, Arleigh Burke-class Aegis destroyers; USS *Lawrence*, Oliver Hazard Perry-class frigate; AO supply ship; and USNS *Philadelphia*, scientific research and launch support vessel. A small photo of each ship was displayed next to its name.

"The battle group has just completed carrier qualifications and is now entering the exercise area. They are expected to be on station for the first phase of the exercise in five hours.

"The exercise will be held in three phases. In the first phase, the exercise area will be configured as shown," and Alan added an overlay that superimposed the outline of the western and central Mediterranean on the Caribbean between Cuba and Puerto Rico. "Exercise Orange forces, representing the Islamic Republic of Orange, will sortie from harbor with strong land-based air cover represented by USAF F-16s and attempt to isolate and destroy the battle group's picket ships. The timing of the attack has been left to the Orange Force commander. His objective is to disrupt or destroy the USNS *Philadelphia*."

Which has my wife on board, and thank God it's only an exercise.

"Phase Two will be a practice of the countdown of the Peacemaker system in preparation for actual launch in the Gulf of Sidra during deployment. During this phase of the exercise, all assets will take up their stations for a missile test. The Aegis cruiser USS *Fort Klock* will act as range monitor, and the air wing will provide observer, chase, and closure aircraft in positions as noted on screen three. USNS *Philadelphia* will be the center of these proceedings, and she will conduct a full countdown and mock launch to engine start on the missile. Please note that, as Phase One can be conducted at any time by the Orange Force commander, it is possible that Battle Group Seven will be forced to conduct the exercise while repelling the Orange Force efforts.

"Phase Three is meant to represent possible threat-force reaction to the launch of the Peacemaker system. Orange forces will be regenerated and supported further by the units listed on screen one, including Canadian and UK diesel submarines, B-52s representing Backfire bombers, and an increased surface threat centered around a small surface-action group. Battle Group Seven will be required to resist Orange attacks while supporting an exercise UN peacekeeping force against the Balkan Republic of Green, co-located with the Puerto Rico bombing ranges. An information warfare exercise will be conducted jointly by the USAF and National Security Agency, targeting selected US Navy facilities noted on screen two, to represent off-board powers reacting to the launch."

He went into detail about correspondences to the battle group's actual deployment, including ongoing operations in Bosnia and the implications of the proposed launch so close to Libyan territorial waters.

"Phase Two will commence on Day Two, when the Peacemaker exercise launch is initiated. Phase Three will commence six hours after the exercise launch. Phase One will initiate when Orange chooses to attack."

Alan paused. The CNO's voice floated from the darkness. "Alan, can I see the battle-group composition slide again?" The CNO was renowned for remembering names. Alan keyed the first slide back up.

"Is Peacemaker on schedule? Looks like we're giving Newman a lot of work if this new toy isn't ready to fly when he deploys." Alan knew the answer, from Rose, but he had learned to wait. The pause lengthened and a voice from somewhere in the room said that he had to check.

"Sir," Alan said a little tentatively, "I believe that Peacemaker is right on schedule." Alan knew that it was in fact ahead of schedule, and Rose had said that the scientists and engineers were put out at waiting for the Navy exercise to begin.

"Thank you, Lieutenant. How do you know that?"

He tried to remain deadpan. "My wife is the launch operations officer, sir."

There were some chuckles. These were the closest to human reactions Alan had seen as a briefer in this room.

The CNO spoke up again. "This is a pretty tough exercise. Is Battle Group Seven ready?"

Alan raised the lights. He had to stay for his windup and in case any questions were asked, and this sort of discussion in the middle of a briefing was new, in his experience, but he felt that lights were probably a good idea.

A tall admiral in the second row leaned forward—Pilchard, former flag of BG 4; Alan had met him once.

"Sir, the *Jackson* had a near-fatal flight-deck accident

during its carrier quals." He was angry and was trying not to show it. "Yesterday they had a serious navigation error that put them several hours behind their exercise plan, and they seem to be moving to a different part of the op area than expected. Admiral Newman seems bent on changing the exercise to a more traditional Orange Force threat-on-threat exercise and has repeatedly asked that the Orange forces be augmented to be a 'fair match' for his battle group."

"How serious a navigation error?"

A moment's hesitation, then, blurting it out, "The *Jackson* came within a quarter of a mile of running on a barrier reef." Somebody gasped, and Alan heard a whispered *Jesus* from the back. "They were saved because the ASW watch officer was on the ball."

The CNO looked around. He remained calm—too calm, unless you had served with him and knew what that calm meant. "Anybody else?"

An officer in the back row cleared his throat nervously, glanced to his left as if hoping that someone else would speak for him, and rose to his feet.

"Sir, the battle group, uh, they have departed consistently from the op plan since last Tuesday, sir. And the admiral has relieved his navigator since yesterday. The Phase Two coordinator, Captain Cobb of the *Fort Klock*, has asked four times for clarification of 'changes' to the exercise, sir. We, uh, think that Admiral Newman has changed the exercise on board and not informed us."

There was some nervous movement at the back of the auditorium. *Lucky Rose, sailing into that.*

"Has Newman voiced disapproval of the exercise through channels?" The CNO sounded serene, but what Alan heard in his inner ear was *Why hasn't anybody told me this before?*

Another admiral down front spoke up. "Yes. He has. We

216

explained that his group's principal responsibility was the Peacemaker launch. He didn't seem to disagree. I believe his word was 'augment' for what he wanted to do."

One of the CNO's staff officers scribbled a note and handed it to him. He read it, winked at Alan, and headed for the door. "Good brief, Lieutenant. My conference room in two hours. I want to see the whole exercise brief again, and I want to see the op plan. Somebody get copies of the pertinent message traffic. Okay, this is not the forum to discuss this fully." The CNO paused at the door. "Is there something wrong with this battle group? I don't need any more accidents."

The tall admiral, Pilchard, spoke up again. "Newman's what's wrong, sir; he won't obey orders. And he's stuck in the nineteen-eighties."

Startex plus five hours. Aboard USNS _Philadelphia_.
"Zero minus eight hours and holding."

Rose blew out her cheeks and stared at the computer monitor. "We've been _holding_ all day. What the hell is going on?"

Valdez raised his hands and let them drop. "There's too much data stream."

"Shut up about the data stream."

"I'm tellin' you, there's more here than they—"

"_Will you shut up?_" She put her hands on her head. "Ohhh— ! I'm sorry, Valdez! I'm sorry I screamed at you."

"I'm used to it."

"Just don't tell me about the data stream for five minutes, okay? I know there's more data than you can explain. I'm working on that. Please, please, _please_ don't mention it again just now!"

"Okay, I get you." Valdez sounded grieved.

Rose looked out the window of the launch-command

center that had been built on the deck of the *Philadelphia*. It had big windows and lots of equipment, with a central console and four computer screens, one of which was getting most of Valdez's attention. Behind the console were two big chairs, one for each of them, hers high enough so she could see over the console to the deck and the launch pad. The missile was still flat on the deck, the satellite and the module swathed in silver plastic at its far end.

The hold at eight hours was a convention. The countdown, in fact, had not started. "Eight hours and holding" was a way of saying that nothing was happening.

On the *Jackson*, Rafe walked around his plane one more time before crawling up through the hatch. The plane looked good. The morning did not.

Cutter Sardesson was deep in his kneeboard cards and didn't seem to notice Rafe's arrival. The auxiliaries were already up and running; Rafe completed his seat check and moved on through his preflight without much conscious thought.

"Rafe?"

"Yeah, Cutter?"

"What are we doing this morning?" This was the kind of new-guy question that Rafe hated—the kind that showed a guy who hadn't done his homework. Cutter didn't seem the type.

"You were at the brief. You tell me."

"Yes, sir. We are giving gas to a formation of F-18s so that they can conduct a war-at-sea strike on an enemy surface-action group. We have one buddy store to give gas and one Harpoon simulator plug in case we need to shoot."

"Great! You get it. What's the problem?"

"None of it's on Nixon's schedule." Christy, as squadron intelligence officer, had posted a full Fleetex schedule and briefed it to the squadron two weeks before. Rafe had convinced the skipper to invite the maintenance chiefs and officers as well. It seemed a good idea that everybody know what to expect.

Rafe sighed. One of the really hard things about the transition from the Junior Officer's Protection League, as the world of lieutenants and lieutenant junior grades called themselves, to the responsibility of command, was the need to support incomprehensible decisions by seniors instead of complaining about them.

"Cutter, the whole Fleetex has been re-engineered since Tricky briefed it. Deal with it."

Cutter was not a stupid man, and he had ambition. Simple answers were not enough.

"Rafe, the missile-shot exercise is going down in ten hours! We don't have anyone on the flight schedule to support it. I thought we were acting as the range closure support? I mean, all these kneeboard cards are frequencies for range clearance." He banged his kneeboard.

"Yeah, sir." That voice belonged to a new naval flight officer flying today as the TACCO, Sharon Dietz. "Like, where is this surface-action group? Does it have emitters? I asked LTjg Nixon and she just shook her head. She usually so far behind?" Dietz had just stepped off the COD last night, the latest in a stream of new officers intended to bring VS-49 up to strength.

Rafe tried not to sound overbearing; more important, he tried not to sound defensive about Christy Nixon, who seemed to be taking on too much importance in his own inner life. "Tricky Nixon is one of the best AIs in the air wing. The changes to Fleetex have all of us a little behind, Lieutenant Dietz."

Rafe finished his checks in a slightly resentful silence. He and Cutter moved the plane from its parked position to the line on catapult two and began the run-up for launch. When they were silent on the preflight checks, just waiting to roll to the cat, Dietz spoke up again.

"Sorry about the crack about Nixon." She sounded embarrassed. Rafe credited her with more sense than he had just then. "But I'm just baggage back here unless we have radar and ESM targets. Are we flying against exercise ships, or completely fake ships? Like, does anyone know? Air Ops didn't. The ASW module didn't."

Rafe had never shared the NFO passion for this stuff—he liked to plan a strike or fly a plane. He knew the rest was important, and he had always assumed that somebody like Alan Craik or Christy would feed it to him. Now he was the XO, and people came to him for those answers. He grimaced as the plane rolled forward on the cat.

"Bear with us, Dietz. The exercise is screwed up. Let's just fly for now." He turned his head and looked out over the deck and gave a crisp salute.

Startex plus ten hours. Washington.

Alan was deep in reports of renewed ethnic violence in Rwanda when someone in the corridor shouted "Attention on deck!" It might be the Pentagon, but it was still the Navy: Alan got hurriedly to his feet, braced, and waited. When nothing more happened, he snuck a look outside and found that Admiral Pilchard had descended on the briefing center. The unit commander was brown-nosing for all she was worth, but Pilchard was standing down at the far end, looking around him with quick movements of his head and waiting for a pause in the word stream. Something positive registered in Alan's semi-consciousness: the admiral wouldn't humiliate a subordinate, even when she was making an asshole of herself.

"I'm looking for the guy who briefed the exercise this morning."

"Yes, *sir*, that would be, uh—"

A chief muttered in the commander's ear.

"Lieutenant Craik, sir. I hope nothing was—"

"I'd like to see him."

They started down the corridor.

Alan swallowed and rogered up. Admirals seldom entered the briefing area, and it was never good news when they did.

"This is Craik's office, sir."

"Yeah, give us a minute, will you?"

The commander looked into the tiny office, seemed deeply skeptical, although Alan had managed to get on his uniform coat and was standing at attention and said, "Yes, sir." She backed away a few feet. The admiral moved into Alan's doorway, a tall, thin man with a narrow head that seemed to have pushed all his features to the very front, giving him a big, thin nose and a profile like an axe. The axe blade turned toward Alan.

"Can I help you, sir?"

"You came aboard to brief me when Nate Green took over from BG 4, right?" Those quick head movements took in the office, the stacks of briefing books, the old squadron photos and decals, the pictures of Rose and Mikey and even the dog, my God, that seemed pretty dumb suddenly to Alan. The admiral smiled a little, nothing very warm; he didn't seem to think much of the dog photo, either. "Weren't you Jack Parsills' AI in the Gulf War? Mike Craik's son?"

There it was; Mike Craik's son. To the admiral's generation, he'd never be anything but Mike Craik's son. And some remote briefing during turnover in rota. "Yes, sir."

"How'd you end up in this job?"

This was not a topic Alan was prepared to be entirely up front about, certainly not with a senior officer. "Detailer recommended it, sir."

"Parsills said you were some sort of Africa expert, am I right?"

Alan felt that the questions were coming a little fast.

"Not really an expert, sir."

The admiral leaned over Alan's desk and started leafing through the notes on Rwanda. "Right."

The commander was still in hover mode out there in the corridor. "Is there anything I can do for you, sir?"

"I want to pick this guy's brain." The commander backed away.

The admiral pulled up Alan's desk chair and sat down, started to read again and waved a finger at the straight chair that was half hidden by the file cabinet. Alan sat down, a guest in his own office. The admiral scanned another page and tossed the papers aside. "It's Alan, right? Alan, are you *sure* that Peacemaker is on schedule?"

The question took him by surprise. Another change of subject. He had to move his brain to the new subject. Not Africa. Peacemaker. Briefers are always short on sleep at the Pentagon, and his son, Mikey, was not being very cooperative lately. And had to be picked up from day care in an hour.

"Yes, sir. Rose—that's my wife, she's a lieutenant-commander on collateral duty—she implied that the techs are impatient to get through the Fleetex tests to start the final process."

The admiral looked away. He ran his hands down his

immaculate uniform trousers and stood up. Alan stood up.

"Tell me what you think will happen in Rwanda. Make it short."

Alan took a deep breath, changed mental directions one more time, and launched.

"Sir, as you probably know, the Tutsis have regained control of Rwanda. They're still being hounded by remnant Interahamwe forces operating out of UN camps in Eastern Zaire. They're having limited success interdicting attacks on both their own ethnic tribesmen and on Hutus."

"Why would the Hutus attack Hutus?"

"To terrify them into support of the Interahamwe, sir. To show them that the Tutsi government can't or won't protect them. To drive them out of the country and increase their power base in Eastern Zaire." It was like a digest of O'Neill's letters.

"Okay. Proceed."

"Sir, at some point, the Tutsis, and their allies the Ugandans, will take some step to eliminate the Interahamwe. Or they'll attack the Hutus in Rwanda, for ethnic cleansing purposes, or both. The Rwandan People's Army, that's the Tutsis, are pretty good. They could probably accomplish anything they want. France and Russia back the Hutus. That's an over-simplification, sir. We back Uganda, who backs the Tutsis. That's another simplification."

"How will this affect the next ten months?"

"Not my department, sir."

"Guess."

He wasn't prepared, but he made a prediction, anyway. "Sir, I think the Rwandan Tutsis will find a pawn and use him to cover an attack on Eastern Zaire. They'll annex Eastern Zaire long enough to eradicate the Interahamwe. If Zaire, and thus Mobutu, and his ally France, react, it will be a fairly hot war. With a bunch of US NGOs—nongovernmental organizations—in the way. That will mean an evacuation operation."

"When?"

Alan hesitated, then went for it.

"Any day."

"During BG 7's deployment?"

"If not sooner."

The admiral summoned the commander, who had not drifted very far. She frowned faintly at the chummy scene in Alan's office, which was so small that the admiral's and the lieutenant's medals were almost touching. "Sir?"

The axe head turned toward the commander. "I'll square it with the CNO. I'd like this guy to brief the Rwanda crisis tomorrow. Get some support from DIA. Okay? Great." Pilchard looked back at Alan, touched the pink ribbon that was a little off by itself on his chest. "What's that?"

"Italian, sir. Humanitarian contribution."

The admiral shot a look into his eyes. The look was inscrutable—a little amused? Did he know about the adventure with the Italians and Kenyans in Bosnia? "See you tomorrow."

Admiral Pilchard went through the door like a launch off the catapult. Alan called a babysitter and asked her to pick Mikey up from day care. The commander poked her head into his cubicle as he called a guy he knew at DIA.

"What crisis in Rwanda?" she asked.

Day Two, Startex plus 34. On the flight deck of the *Andrew Jackson*.

Rafe stood next to the aircraft and stared down the deck at the JBDs. Cyclic ops were going on as if things were normal, and things weren't normal, and he didn't know what was going on. He did know that his squadron had for the second time that day failed to be on station to provide fuel, and two F/A-18s had had to divert to the beach at Guantanamo, one of them almost dry when he touched down, and Rafe himself had just dumped fifty thousand pounds of fuel because he had been hundreds of miles from anybody who could have used it.

He suppressed the idea that it was Christy Nixon's fault. But a traitorous part of his mind whispered that if Al Craik had been the squadron AI, things wouldn't have happened this way. But Craik wasn't a pretty woman who was turning Rafehausen's head, either.

It was bad. It was very, very bad.

Startex plus 34.30. Langley.

George Shreed spent five minutes on the telephone, listening to General Touhey burn with a flame so hot it could have welded steel. Touhey hated the Navy as a matter of course, but today he hated it with a passion that was epic.

The Navy had screwed up his project. Peacemaker had aborted.

"I'll call Wick," Shreed said for the fourth time. He said it again twenty seconds later. "I'll call Wick." Wick was his man at the White House. Touhey also had a man at the White House, Red, a figure of some note on the National Security Council. Thirty seconds later, Shreed said, "You call Red. I'll call Wick." He hung up, grinned, and called the White House.

Day Two. Washington.

Alan got to brief Rwanda *and* Fleetex. The commander cited Alan's experience and kept her favorite, the ops briefer, out of what appeared to be a very contentious issue.

The Rwanda piece went early in the briefing cycle and

passed almost without questions. Alan showed some tape from a recent BBC piece on the ethnic struggle there while he went through a two-minute summary of the events in the region since 1994. He used the rest of his five minutes to lay out his theory, as modified by a harried CIA analyst and an excited DIA guy who seemed glad that anyone was interested in Africa at all. His suggestion that an evacuation operation might be necessary passed without remark. One admiral asked how many Americans were in the potential conflict area and Alan gave the CIA figure of about six hundred. That was it.

The rest of the brief, about BG 7, went smoothly, too, because everyone knew that an explosion was coming and nobody wanted to be in the way.

Alan didn't like briefing this disaster that was occurring in the Caribbean. But he did it, and he did it well. He showed a nice slide with ship positions and noted in passing and without comment that Battle Group Seven was now several hundred miles off station. It was only when he reached the umpire reports from Phase One that the silence from the audience became oppressive.

"Lieutenant Craik, do I understand that Admiral Newman has suspended the Peacemaker exercise launch indefinitely?"

"Yes, sir."

Alan turned up the lights. Most of the officers were now sitting at attention.

The CNO shook his head. He, alone, looked composed. He turned to Admiral Pilchard, who sat two rows behind him.

"You were right, Dick." He stood. "Get down there and clean it up."

With those words, although he did not yet know it, Alan began to get back on the wheel.

Day Two. Aboard the *Andrew Jackson*.

It was quiet on the carrier—eerily quiet. The ship made all the same noises—propulsion, laundry, maintenance—but air ops were canceled and everybody seemed to be holding his breath. Waiting.

Sneesen was in the ship's electronics shop on the third level, trying to stay out of everybody's way. He was also trying to extend the life of an aged transducer that nobody else in the squadron wanted to tackle. He was doing it because CDR Rafehausen had asked him specially. You couldn't refuse a request like that. And he had asked— not ordered. And down here in the shop, nobody was screaming that the fleet exercise had gone one hundred percent to hell.

Sneesen had pretty well decided the transducer was hopeless, but he was going to go one more step, just because it would be so totally great to fix it. He had found himself a spot on a bench behind a floor-to-ceiling bank of steel shelves that were loaded with electronics equipment, a kind of cubby-hole. He wanted some space.

Now he worked in his little cubby-hole and hoped for a miracle. He was trying to get into a black box that wasn't meant for him to get into, when he heard the door open and at least two people come in. At least there were two voices, both male, and he thought he knew one but couldn't place it. The talk was low, the sounds rumbling, meaningless. Then the door opened again and there was a silence and then a new voice, tenor, almost shrill, said, "Borne! So this is where you guys hide!"

Borne. He knew Chief Borne—the guy who'd been managing deck traffic when Rafehausen's plane had almost piled in! The great guy with the blue eyes.

Something was wrong out there. Sneesen could tell from the tempo of the talk. It changed the moment that new voice struck in, and the tones shifted—louder, a little more assertive. He couldn't understand Borne, but he recognized his bass tones.

"Chief, don't bullshit me! I've got a bullshit detector! I want that guy's draft fitrep and I want it today. Get me? Get me?"

Sneesen peered at them between pieces of old equipment. He could see Borne's back and the face and hat of a very young jg. He must have been all of twenty-three, Sneesen thought—half Borne's age. Ship's company also—not a squadron officer. What was he on Borne about? Borne was a great guy, in Sneesen's book.

"You get me, Chief? *Do—you—get—me?*"

"I get you. Sir."

The jg smirked. "Then get to it, Chief. Today, or it's your ass."

Sneesen ducked. He heard the door open and then close, and then Borne's deep voice said the words that would change Sneesen's life: "Yes, sir, Lieutenant Jew-nior Grade Jew-Boy!"

It struck Sneesen like a slap. Of course, that was what he hadn't liked about the jg—he had one of those Jewish faces. But what Borne had said—Jeez. Hadn't he had sensitivity classes? You just weren't supposed to say stuff like that, even if you thought it. Which everybody did, but—

He must have made some sound, scuffing his foot in the silence after the guffaw that had followed Borne's outburst. Something had alerted Borne, anyway; a moment later, his face appeared in the gap between the pieces of equipment, and he said, "Who's back there?"

Sneesen waited, feeling himself go red and hot. "It's only me, Chief." He stepped to the end of the equipment rack where they could see him. He was trembling. He swallowed.

228

Borne looked at him. Hard. Then he glanced at the other sailor, a ship's company sailor Sneesen didn't know, and he rumbled, "Give us some room, will you, Billy?" He waited until the other man had left and then he stepped closer to Sneesen, and he said, "Don't I know you? Aren't you the kid that saved that S-3 on the deck?"

"Yes, sir." Sneesen looked as if he was going to cry. "Sneesen, sir."

And then Borne smiled.

Borne had a wonderful smile, made more so by the terrific frown he usually used. His pale-blue eyes seemed to glow when he smiled, as if they had been lit from within. "I guess you heard what I said just then, didn't you, Sneesen?"

Sneesen wanted to lie. He had told a lot of lies, in high school and to his mother and like that, but he thought that if he lied to Borne and got caught, he wouldn't get out of it the way he used to. Hardly breathing, he muttered, "I guess so."

"Sure, you did." Borne's smile stayed just as bright. "You know I can get in trouble for saying that, don't you, Sneesen." It wasn't a question.

"Yeah, but I won't say anything! Really!"

"Why's that?"

"I just won't. I don't care. If you wanta say stuff about— you know—what the hell. Not my business."

Borne studied him. Borne's smile slowly went out, and the face that replaced it was more thoughtful than threatening. Almost fatherly.

"Son," Chief Borne said, putting his hand on Sneesen's shoulder and looking into his eyes, "do you believe in equal rights for white, Christian men?"

Fleetex, Day Two, Startex plus 47. The *Andrew Jackson.*

The COD made a perfect landing, and the thud of the wheels on the deck was exactly matched by a bosun's whistle over the ship's loudspeaker and a voice saying "Admiral, US Navy, arriving."

All through the ship, men and women waited. It was night, but people were wakeful and edgy. The cyclic ops that had been scheduled were on hold; the intel and ASW spaces were not empty but were silent. Activity around the blue-tiled area had come to a standstill three hours before, and, ever since, the ship had seemed to hold its breath.

Down the passageway in the ready rooms where the aircrews fidgeted, conversation was stilled, waiting for an explosion. Everybody knew when Admiral Pilchard and his staff of one came down the portside passageway from the ATO. Hundreds of eyes watched Admiral Pilchard enter the admiral's briefing room.

The hatch closed behind him.

There was no explosion.

In Admiral Newman's quarters, the flag commander of the failed Fleetex waited. He felt almost light with relief, and he admitted that relief to himself. The exercise—yes, even his proper role—had escaped his grasp. He had failed. The failure would haunt him, later. Now he was mostly happy it was over.

His flag lieutenant ushered Admiral Pilchard into the day cabin. Pilchard was a smaller man, only six feet, and his face was relaxed, easy. Newman stood as Pilchard entered, and they shook hands with apparent warmth.

"Nice to see you, Dick."

"Sorry it has to be like this, Rudy."

Newman glanced around the day cabin. Everything that

mattered to him was packed. The rest was somebody else's problem, now.

"Go a little easy on my people," he said. "They were following my orders."

He put on his cover and went out. This time, there were no eyes in the passageway to watch.

Months later, sitting at the breakfast table with his wife because there was no point in hurrying any more, he would suddenly blurt out, "I know what I did wrong!" It would have come to him in the night, as revelations will. "I tried to make it perfect!"

And, with this essential truth of leadership at last in his brain, he would prepare to accept enforced retirement.

13

September–October

Norfolk and Washington.
The *Andrew Jackson* had thirty days to repair the errors of
Fleetex before it began its cruise. The battle group ran a
reduced version of the LantCom scenario without Phase
Three, and, with prayer and baling wire and spit, they got
through it and almost believed they were competent.

The squadrons flew back to their bases and set to work
to correct what they had learned about themselves. For
Rafehausen, this was to be days and nights of exhaustion,
trying to bring too many new people up to standard. For
Christy Nixon, they were days of self-doubt and outward
good humor; she knew she had made a disastrous mistake
for her squadron in the Fleetex, but she could not see what
she should have done differently. She was hardly alone.

Admiral Pilchard went back and forth between the
Jackson and his offices in Norfolk and the Pentagon. He
could not replace Newman's flag staff without reason, and
the spelling-out of reasons meant wounded, sometimes
finished careers. Nor could he do it without Newman himself, and so there was the delicate, sometimes embarrassing
matter of regularly consulting the man he had replaced on
the culpability of his own chosen aides. Pilchard knew he
would have to go with some of them, and he let those
who had been farthest from the Fleetex debacle in rank or

function stay on. For his own chief of staff, he pulled from another duty with BG 7 a man whom both he and Alan Craik knew: he requested, and got, Captain Jack Parsills, once Alan's S-3 squadron skipper and now captain of the BG oiler. He let Newman's flag captain and lieutenant stay. He let the O-4s and below stay. Still, blood flowed. He judged and cut, and he judged and cut again, and he waited and reasoned and examined, and, only days before he was to sail, he reluctantly axed the flag intelligence officer and his assistant.

Rose was in constant motion during those days. Threatened by what she saw as a black mark on her career, she tried to work still harder. She started with the defense of the *Philadelphia*. If she could help it, nobody was going to sink her launch ship again, BG or no BG, even if she and Valdez had to stand out on the deck with crossbows. She requested weapons. She requested a squad of marines. She went looking for some Stingers that might have been left around someplace.

For his part, Alan briefed and analyzed and fretted. He was delighted to tell Rose what he could about MANPADs and ship-fired chaff pods and light explosives. He still had time to worry about O'Neill and Rwanda, which looked to him more and more menacing. Admiral Pilchard asked him twice to brief his staff, and Parsills came to see him for a long talk. The African situation had been thrown at him by the admiral, who had some interest of his own in the continent and so was for once ahead of the Gnomes of Langley in sensing what was about to happen. To Parsills, however, a crisis in Africa was something from left field. His questions to Alan were troubled, half-angry: Why should they care? What was the US interest? What might happen? What were the implications of an evacuation plan?

"Maybe a marine division to be put ashore, for starters."

Parsills came back twice more. He had thoughtful questions that clearly disturbed him, and he wanted to discuss them with somebody other than the admiral: What happened to the battle group if they had to oversee an evacuation from Zaire? Where was the CV? The missile cruiser? Who was minding the store in the Med? What were the constraints on the use of air power? What were the implications of the notoriously short legs of the F/A-18 if they had to fight in two oceans?

Alan felt close to BG 7 because of Parsills and Rose and his part in the old Fleetex. From his office in the Pentagon, he grieved that he was not a member of the wedding.

Like the rest of them, Electronics Tech Third Class Sneesen worked overtime in those days after Fleetex, trying to play catch-up. Screaming Meemie was everywhere, bellowing and threatening; Rafehausen came behind him, trying to pick up the pieces, help morale, keep the squadron together.

It was a tough time for everybody, but for Sneesen it was also a time of intense learning. Chief Borne had given him four pamphlets and a book about the threats to traditional American values to take home with him and study while he was off the boat. They had titles like *Aliens from Earth—Immigration and the Final Battle*, and *The Children of Satan and Eve: How the Jews Push the Anti-Christ's Agenda*. Sneesen learned a whole new vocabulary from them—spawn of Satan, mud-people, blood in the face. God's plan for America. The Jewish specter behind sex music and so-called black culture. Jungle music. Gorillathletes. He learned whole explanations of things that had always been mysteries to him—why God sent AIDS via Africa. Why most so-called athletes are black. Why the Jews own the movie industry. How American so-called education rots the minds of America's white, Christian children.

It was all so goddam logical. It all made so much *sense*. Things that had bothered him but seemed to have no cause now hung together. There were plans, both divine and satanic; there were agendas, mostly bad. He'd been waylaid by political correctness—that "sensitivity" crap. Bullshit about diversity. Now, here was the truth—why he *instinctively* flinched from Jews. Why *fundamentally* he knew blacks were dumber. Why he *knew in his gut* that God was male and white.

It was the most intense and exciting intellectual experience of his life.

Without even thinking about it, he began to isolate himself from the black guys. When they spoke, he only grunted.

The world, which had always bewildered him, was becoming clear.

Tanzania.
Harry O'Neill hadn't heard from her, and then he had a report from an agent on the Zaire side of Lake Kivu that he should look for a message, and he thought it would be from her. What he really hoped was that she would bring it herself, but he was almost certain she wouldn't. If she did, he would try to make her stay.

The drop was just outside Kigoma on Lake Tanganyika. He had been driving fake runs over there once a week or so, timing the distance between points, looking for places where he could check for surveillance, doing the boring stuff he had been trained to do. He would drive over, never varying his route, stopping at a technical college and visiting the library, then going on to the Kigoma Chamber of Commerce, and getting to the lakeside in time to eat the lunch he'd brought in his car. He always did it the same, and he knew the surveillance was getting sick of watching him.

The lake had a lot of traffic, both licit and illicit, and, despite the heavy presence of intel people and military from several countries, it was wide open. Most of them were waiting for something to happen, but nobody was quite ready yet. Harry had heard too many truckers talking about some sort of build-up south of here—real logistics, going to soldiers who sounded pretty professional. Harry wanted to either check it out in person or pay a trucker to do it for him. His chief had told him, bluntly, to keep his hands off.

Harry watched the other people near the checkpoint. He thought several looked remarkably like Rwandan People's Army officers in drag. They weren't interested in him. They were waiting. Everybody seemed to be waiting. He thought they weren't going to wait much longer.

He went about his business there quietly, not acknowledging the surveillance, which was not very clever and not very enthusiastic and today was only one man in one car, not enough to follow the Yellow Brick Road, much less a case officer. He thought that they'd about given up on Harry O'Neill.

He found the spot on the lakeside where he could eat his lunch and watch the drop, a *hoteli* near a private dock where some of the lake's fishermen kept their boats. He sat in his car. The young man from the Tanzanian police watched him from what O'Neill thought was too great a distance for him to see anything useful, but that was his business. When the boat O'Neill was looking for came in, he waited, his head aching from hoping too hard, but the person who got off was a man, not her at all, and, although he wore the red hat that O'Neill was looking for, he was a disappointment. The man went up to the *hoteli*. After five minutes he came out, looked around, and walked down to the water's edge.

O'Neill got out of the car, wiping his hands on a towel he always had in the front seat, tossed it back in and looked up at the sky. Seeming to judge that it was sunny, he reached back in and got a baseball hat, also red, and walked down to the *hoteli*. The toilet was in the back, nothing but a bombsite in the concrete with a water tap next to it, but there was a lock on the door. He pissed, ran the water over his hands, and came out.

The young plain-clothes cop had followed him down, and he went into the toilet the moment O'Neill was out, leaving his car parked in front of the *hoteli*. The man in the red hat was gone. When O'Neill got back to his car, he found a roll of film in the glove box.

Two days later, he was in Dar-Es-Salaam with the roll of undeveloped film and the Agent Report encrypted on a floppy. Both went into the diplomatic bag for secure shipment to Washington.

In Republika Srpska.

Z believed he had found Draganica Obren's husband, but he hadn't told her so. There was a patient in a "mental ward" (meaning a kind of human warehouse) near Banja Luka who was officially known by a number but who had had a letter to Obren in his pocket when he was picked up two years before. He had no memory, was sometimes violent and had to be restrained, according to Z's informant.

Z thought she would be better off if she never learned about him, never let her hopes rise. Whoever he was, her husband or just somebody who happened to have picked up a letter, he would die some day, and nobody would care.

237

But that was not his decision to make, Z decided. Draganica Obren should make her own decision. She should have the right to get herself to Banja Luka and look at this madman and see for herself if he had once been her husband.

So when he was near her village in RS, he went over, meaning to tell her. He saw the schoolmaster first, the one she reported to, and he told Z about all the good information she brought back from Sarajevo, most of all about the War Crimes Unit. Names of its officers, where they lived, what their security arrangements were. "We could kill some of them," the schoolmaster said with a grin. "Make a statement."

"That's not my department. Anyway, not yet. You think she's worth keeping on?"

"Yes, my God—! She's the best."

So he didn't tell her about the man who might be her husband. He spent the night with her and left her some money and said she was doing a good job for Serbia. He didn't tell her he was leaving soon for Africa.

Langley.

George Shreed was scrolling down the weekly summaries, bored, unhappy with himself, changing his position every few seconds because his spine ached despite his medication. He was trying to avoid the thought that something more was going on back there than the usual smashed disks and ruined nerves. A grin flitted across his mouth, his response to the irony of his caring if there was something there like meningitis or cancer—he, who could hardly walk! He, the human ruin!

But there is a logical inconsistency in anybody's thinking he is better off dead.

Now and then he saw something on a list that seemed

promising and he would click on it, and it would appear on a screen in another office, and somebody would come to see him about it in a day or two. *Like a spider in his web*, Shreed thought. *A metal-legged spider*. He didn't think of his legs as legs any more. The steel canes were his legs. *My war trophies*. He had been a pilot once, a very good pilot, and he had crashed.

He was scrolling through Agent Reports Received and something caught his eye and he scrolled back, not knowing quite what it had been— Yes, that one. In the African section. "Eye-witness reports missile shootdown of civilian aircraft. Reliability One. (Photos)."

Photos! That would be rather interesting. He knew exactly what shootdown was meant, from the date and the place. Rwanda. *With photos?* He wondered why it had taken three years to get the stuff here. Probably a fake, somebody trying to make some money. Still—

He knew the unverified reports and the rumors, and the belief in part of the community that the French had been behind that shootdown. Agent reports like these were rigidly guarded, but his clearance was so high he was qualified to see them. It was not unusual that he would open one, as he was doing now, although normally he would have got the material in a digest, rewritten so that the agent's identity was hidden. Now, however, he read the report, and he saw at once that it was probably genuine and that the agent could be easily identified by his or her (he thought her—why?) access to one of the Hutu Interahamwe generals. Very high-risk action. Dynamite.

He clicked on the report and brought up another screen and blue-lighted four names and clicked again, and the report popped up on the encrypted mail of four of his analysts. He sent the usual terse message—read and report, prepare to discuss implications, all that.

Interesting.

He downloaded a fifth copy of the report to a disk. Later, from another computer, he mailed it to an internet address. No record of this transaction would exist.

Shreed left at a little after six and drove himself home in his specially equipped car. He always looked forward to getting home—a good sign in a smashed-up man, he thought. Life can't be too bad if you're glad to get home. Home was a sprawling four-bedroom in Falls Church, where they'd lived for twelve years. Every year, the commuting got worse, the neighbors got younger, and the neighbors' kids' problems got more serious—drugs, AIDS. His own kids were grown now but would have survived what his neighbors' kids could not; his kids had grown up in places like Macao and Jakarta and had the expat child's blend of toughness and despair that made for survival, the result of being both feared and cosseted in alien places. His house was a kind of island for him in the oily sea of the Washington suburbs. It was supremely comfortable and, thanks to his wife of twenty-seven years, elegant in a slightly dated way he liked, vaguely colonialist, evoking the warren in Europe of some retired senior civil servant homesick for the places where he had spent his real life. Shreed entered it with relief—the Javanese shadow puppets in the foyer, the ranks of barrister's bookshelves in his study, the real Kilims, the lingering odor of Straits Chinese curry—and kissed his wife, scratched the cat, massaged the dog, had two drinks and ate his dinner.

"I am the most ordinary man in the world," he said to her. And winked.

"You're going online?"

"Only for a bit."

"You've become an addict." She meant it as a joke, but it had edge. She was a tall, handsome woman with soft gray hair that fluffed out around her head and down her shoulders. From the back she still could have been taken for a girl. But menopause had been hard on her; intercourse was no longer possible, or not possible without pain that made it out of the question, and other kinds of sex were usually distasteful to her. She took their near-celibacy harder than he did and was always ready to think she was losing him and deserved to.

He kissed her. "I won't if you don't want me to." She shook her head. They had reached that age when nothing comes without a sliver of imperfection that may prove to be, with horrible speed, only the thin end of some terrible wedge. "I have some reading to do," she said. She taught history at a community college, confused him by seeming to enjoy it.

He had some quite special software that did not appear as itself when the hard disk's contents were called up. It had other, quite innocent names—a defragger, a zip program. Now, he booted up one of these.

Shreed stared at the screen for some time. His wife came in, kissed the back of his neck; he reached back and touched her. "Going up?" he murmured.

"I'm going to read."

"I'll be up."

When she was gone, he turned back to the computer. He called up the African report from the place where he had stored it and, using one of the masked programs, translated it to an encrypted form that was compressible to a single pixel. Then he called up from a file called "Books Read" a color photograph of a naked woman performing a fairly common sex act with another woman. He told the computer to embed the compressed data as a pixel in the photo, which it did through random selection, locating it in one of the women's left big toenail.

241

Shreed then consulted a list on another computer, sent the digitized photo from one computer to the other, and then sent it over the internet to the selected address. And, like that!, it was gone.

Seconds later. Tehran.

The digitized photo was intercepted by an Iranian monitoring its destination in Dubai. The operator found the pixel that contained too much data. He expanded the pixel that had resided near the toenail of the darker of the two naked women and transferred it to another computer, whose operator activated a decryption program that would run for nearly forty-eight hours before either decrypting the pixel's data or admitting defeat.

Within half an hour, a message about the interception of the pixel was on the desk of Yuri Efremov, the former Soviet KGB colonel who had sold his skills to Iran when the Soviet Union self-destructed. After studying the memo, he put it in a "To file" basket and turned to other matters: to date, they had not succeeded in decrypting anything that had come through this channel.

But this time was different. Thirty-one hours later, he was given a copy of the single page that had been decrypted—a low-resolution photograph (*JPG file*, he thought to himself, *nature of the transmission?*) that showed several white men with a shoulder-fired missile, and black men standing in the background. If that had been all, it would have been merely tantalizing, but the picture had been taken by one of those little cameras that print a date and time on the image itself. And the date told him, without his even having to look it up, precisely where the picture had been taken and what the men with the missile were doing. *Rwanda, April 6, 1994*, he thought.

"Remarkable," he said to himself in Russian. "Remarkable." He had the photograph scanned and sent to his home computer.

Four seconds later. Beijing.

After receiving the photo from the transfer site in Dubai, and unaware of its interception by Iran, the deputy head of signals had to wait two days to see the Chinese Under-Minister for Defense Munitions. He had outlined the subject of his visit in making the appointment. It was not, therefore, surprising that a Chinese he did not know, probably a diplomat or just possibly a lawyer, was also present. Immediately interested in the report and its photographs of several whites shooting a Stinger missile, he murmured apart with the under-minister, and a few minutes later the two began to shoot questions at him—Where had it come from? How reliable was it? Could it have been faked? Who were the whites in the photographs? How had the photographs been taken? What nations had the greatest interest in such a report?

Two hours later, they dismissed him. So far as he could tell, they thought a man named Lascelles would be the most productive buyer of the report.

One day later. Cannes.

Lascelles looked down at the papers and photographs spread on the library table before him. The photographs were not of the best quality, being computer-printed, but they were clear enough. His old man's face was blotched with red. His breathing rasped.

"Get me Zulu," he growled. His head snapped around toward the two other men in the room, who looked blank. *"Get me Zulu, you stupid filth!"*

One day later. Belgrade.

Zulu had spent the morning organizing the movement of his two elite companies out of their barracks. A couple of TU-109s were on their way from Tirana; by the time they landed next day in Dehibat, his agents there would have housing and office space available. It was all tremendously hurry-up. The Libyans were cooperative, a good deal more so than usual, either because Lascelles had thrown money at them or because they wanted to get rid of Zulu and his men—officially, Libya was anti-Mobutu. He didn't care about the reason. He was so angry at what Lascelles had said to him that he didn't care about any of it: *You get your Serbian ass down there and make it right! You let some fucking American agent take your photo, you shit, you filth, you pig's cock, and you'd better make it right or I'll have you killed! I'll have your children killed! I'll— !*

Z wouldn't take that kind of abuse. He wasn't a child, no matter how big a man Lascelles was in his own mad world of Napoleonic fantasy.

But, of course, he would do as he was ordered.

His men had been training for Zaire for four months. There was big money in it and more weapons. He would have to find a way to deal with Lascelles's infantile insults later.

Z drove home. His wife knew at once that something was up—knew it from his face, knew it from the way he fondled his children, knew it from his voice.

He sat on the bed and drew her to him, pressing his face into her belly. "I have to go," he said.

She started to weep, quietly, no sobs.

"Africa," he said.

She knew it was too late to ask questions. He started to pack. She sat on the bed, and he told her what the arrangements would be for mail through Libya, people to call in Belgrade if there was an emergency. Finally, when he had got out his pistol and was checking it, she said, "Why now?"

He shrugged. He worked the slide. "Some American. Some American CIA shit did something and the balloon is going up." He let the slide slam shut and put the pistol into its holster and began to get into the shoulder harness. "I'll be back in two weeks. It's only a matter of pushing some blacks back across a border into a place called Rwanda. They won't know what has hit them."

They kissed. His children cried.

Next day. The Pentagon.

Alan Craik didn't know about Z. However, he did see a reliable-source report next day that two planeloads of Serbian mercenaries, with battle gear, had landed in Dehibat, reportedly in transit south. He inferred correctly that they were going to support Mobutu in Zaire, and so advised Admiral Pilchard.

The balloon was about to go up along the Zairian border, he said.

He continued to worry about O'Neill.

14

October

The Uganda–Zaire border.

O'Neill had crossed into Zaire twice a couple of months ago, both times by air, heading for Kisangani to do something that the resident in Kinshasa couldn't get around to. Airplanes generally took you well above trouble, whatever their bad reputation for disasters. Flying at thirty thousand feet, he could look down and see the chain of lakes that used to separate French Africa from British Africa, pick out the length of Lake Tanganyika and, north of it, Lake Kivu, like the dot on an upside-down exclamation mark. On each side of Kivu were extreme danger and death—the camps at Bukavu and Goma, enough blood to have turned the lake red. Flying over, however, he had seen only brilliant blue water, fields, and the steep mountainsides and forests of Zaire. It was like a theorist's view of war, very clean, very safe. A nice way to do spook work.

This time, however, he was going in by road, and he didn't like it. Elizabeth had at last asked to be taken out. He had suddenly had a message from her two days ago, plus a report that she had been seen as far south as Uvira, then up north near Goma. Then the "Get me out" message, the comm plan's emergency cry for help.

She was staying close to the leadership of the faction to which her half-brother belonged, he thought, but trying to keep herself clear of the fighting in the camps. Her one report, three weeks ago, had been crisp, fact-filled, unemotional. It had told him what other people had heard but she could verify: the Interahamwe were growing more violent, more desperate as more and more Hutus tried to return to Rwanda from Zaire. The Rwandan government broadcast pleas for them to come home and assured them that they would be safe; the Zairians were sick of them and wanted them gone; the only food was coming from the aid agencies, and there were too many people for the camps.

He had to wonder how she had stayed alive and still been able to get such stuff, unless she had taken part in some of it. Maybe she had had to. Maybe that was how she had got close enough to know for sure.

Anyway, it was over for her. She had sent him the message that she had to get out.

He hadn't seen her since they'd been at the Kenya game lodge. If anything, he loved her more, not less. He wanted her all the time; the nights without her were miserable, tormented. Now she was coming out, and the moment he had her safe in Arusha, he would send in his resignation and they'd be away. The air reservations were made.

There was only this sticky part of driving into Zaire a few hundred meters to get her. That she had had to do it this way suggested that things were tight for her. O'Neill squeezed his left arm against the gun in his armpit for the twentieth time. He had never had to carry the weapon before; now, ending his brief career as a spook, he hoped he wouldn't really need it.

The road he was taking was a mess of rubble and potholes, some as wide as the road and deep enough to break an axle. The road had until 1990 been a mere track that ran down along the flanks of the Ruwenzori to Kasindi, the one-dog border town between Uganda and Zaire. Only the locals had used it, along with people sight-seeing in that part of the Queen Elizabeth Park, until Idi Amin had ruined the parks and even that use had stopped. Then the first wave of genocide had struck Rwanda, and all the heavy trucks that every day had pounded the main road from Kigali into Goma had had to find a new route. They went north into Uganda and nosed around and found the border crossing at Kasindi, so many of them that the road had had to be paved, meaning that a one-inch layer of asphalt had been laid down over dirt. It was broken to bits almost before it hardened, but the fact that it was paved brought still more trucks, and after two years it was the worst road in Uganda, which is saying a lot. Most of the trucks then stopped using it, it was so bad.

Now O'Neill was headed down it, nursing the dust-white LandCruiser into the huge holes and out again. He was able to go around some; others spread so wide that their verges had become bottomless sand pits. He thought of Hammer, who had died trying to get his vehicle out of a mudhole. Maybe he should have brought somebody along, in case he got stuck. Three times, he was astonished, then terrified to see dust boiling toward him; after the first time he knew that the dust hid a sixteen-wheeler coming up from Zaire. They drove as fast and hard as they could on this road, as if they could mash the road into condition. If he hadn't got out of the way, they'd have flattened him, too. He came across one truck stranded in a hole with an axle broken and the drive wheels deep in the sand. The driver waved. He had been there for two days, he said. No, he didn't want a ride; somebody with a big tractor went up and down, making a living pulling trucks out. He'd be along.

It wouldn't matter, once he had her. He'd put up with this road coming back. He'd walk, coming back, if he had to. Getting her was everything.

Things seemed normal. The trucks, the dust, the quiet. Prior had told him yesterday that there were reports of a lot of activity down around Kigoma, but up here everything was quiet. Anyway, this was Uganda.

The town was nothing. On the map it appeared to be something; in reality, there was a border post, and a few houses scattered along a couple of hundred meters of the road. And a *hoteli*, where dispirited prostitutes were standing around looking at nothing, waiting for the truckers to come back. Two of them ran out when they saw his car. He didn't stop. The border post was tougher than he had expected, even though he'd been warned. The Ugandan military had a lot of spunk because they'd won a good part of their war and were still doing pretty well in the north, and they hadn't been back long enough for real corruption to set in. They had AKs and razor wire, and they weren't taking any shit from anybody, not even an American businessman like the one O'Neill was supposed to be. They gave him a hard time, but they let him through. He laid the groundwork for his return with Elizabeth: he was only going to pick up his wife, he said, who had been spreading God's word in Beni. The grunts were not impressed. He hoped they'd be more impressed by her false passport when he brought her back.

The Super Ten Moteli and Monumental Strip Bar sat on the left side of the road a couple of hundred meters inside Zaire. It had no motel and, so far as he could see, no strippers. It was a truckers' rest stop, with some beer cases and a low building with rooms like chicken coops, by the hour or the night, and five stringy women.

He was to park his car there and walk in a hundred paces. He would come to the remains of a colonial house—the former Belgian customs officer's residence, in fact. Next to it would be a soccer field. He was to walk down the soccer field where she could see him, and, when she knew it was he, she would come out. She would be wearing green. Then they would go home. He was aware that he was following her directions. He had been trained never, ever to follow an agent's plan; always insist on your own. But this was Elizabeth.

O'Neill pulled in next to the bar and set the parking brake and squeezed the gun with his upper arm. Either she was still very afraid, or it was a trap. He had had that thought all along—that it could be a trap—but he wanted her so much, he did not allow it to be a trap. Anyway, nobody trapped American CIA people. The retribution was too terrible. Anyway, it couldn't be a trap, because the signals had been right. Everything checked out. It couldn't be a trap.

He got out of the car and locked it and told one of the resident women that he was sorry, but he couldn't enjoy her services because he was a man of God, which amused her a good deal, probably the best thing that had happened to her all day. She gave him a sales pitch that used several words he hadn't learned yet to describe things he probably had heard of in English. His heart was pumping so hard from getting ready to see Elizabeth that he could hardly hear her, and finally she gave up and shrugged. O'Neill unlocked his car, wiped the sweat away with his towel, and locked it again. It couldn't be a trap, he told himself. It couldn't be a trap.

He shifted the gun a little, moving the butt farther out from his arm so he could get at it quicker. He would rather have had it in the front of his pants, cross-draw, but you don't do that with a Beretta and hope to drive a car. He remembered that Craik had hated the Beretta, and now he had to agree. It was a really lousy concealed gun. He was wearing a half-belted khaki shirt that was sort of like a short-sleeved bush jacket; it was an idiotic garment, very touristy *à la* Hemingway, but it was the only thing he had that halfway concealed the Beretta.

The customs officer's house had fallen in and was growing bananas through its roof. It had been a fine house of that style, one-storied with a metal roof and verandahs, and windowless hovels out in back for servants. Now it was too far gone even for squatters. O'Neill walked past it, sweating buckets, and turned the wrong way and had to go back several steps before he came to what he figured out was the soccer field. It was untended, and nobody had played soccer there in years. Only the remains of something gray that had been used as a goal told him that he was there.

O'Neill prayed. He prayed for her and he prayed for the two of them. He prayed that it would be okay, and in twenty minutes he would be laughing with her about the horrible road back up to Katunguru. Please, God. Just this once.

He started down the field. Tall, dry grass whisked at his legs like broom straws. A cool breeze was blowing down from the Mountains of the Moon, drying his sweat, but he never noticed it. He was keeping his eyes moving to see everything, trying, as he had once heard a pilot say, to read the whole instrument panel at once. Then he saw her, down at the end, wearing a green pantsuit that he thought he remembered, and his heart turned over. She waved, and he waved, and he began to run.

There were thornbushes down at the end of the soccer field, and when he got down there, panting, she had disappeared behind one of them. He knew that wasn't right, and he put his hand on the gun and prayed and stepped around the bush where he thought she had gone, and there was nobody. He knew it was a trap, then.

He stood still. There was loud insect sound, a buzzing like cicadas. The wind. A truck on the road—not that far away.

"Elizabeth?"

He pulled the gun out.

Something moved at the edge of his vision. He turned, and he saw her.

He wouldn't have recognized her because of what they had done to her face, but he knew the size of her, and her body. She was staggering. She had lost her sense of balance and perhaps couldn't see, because she put one hand a little ahead of her and one out at the side, but nothing worked in coordination with anything else and she half-fell and walked first one way and then another. She was naked. Dried blood covered the inside of her legs.

O'Neill heard himself gasp. He heard himself squeal her name.

"You like her?" a high-pitched voice cried. "You *love* her?"

Men appeared behind her. O'Neill knew it must be her half-brother. He carried a machete. Then another man, this one white.

O'Neill raised the pistol and managed one aimed shot before something struck him on the side of the head, and he was grabbed from behind and the right side, a hand over his face and then another coming over his forehead from the back, going into his eyes. He fired three shots but he couldn't see, three shots at nothing. There were four men, he thought, holding him as he struggled, prying the gun out of his hand by breaking his fingers. He did what he had been taught. He caught somebody in the gut, and he kicked a chest hard enough to stop the heart, but one man is no match for four. They held him and beat him and then swung him around to look at her.

"You like her?" the brother said again in that high voice. "You like her *face*? You like her *hair*? Lots of men like

252

her! She had one hundred and twenty-three men since yesterday! Some twice! Okay—I *give* her to you!"

She had wandered forward a little. He got behind her and put the machete at her throat, pulling her head back by the hair; O'Neill roared, and her half-brother cut her throat with a single long stroke, deep, deep, and arterial blood gushed out, down her body and forward on the dry ground. He twisted her as she fell, holding the hair, and swung the machete and cut deep again into her neck and then, letting go, he hacked at her until her head was off. He jabbed the point of the machete deep into the severed neck so he could lift the head and brandish it. Blood was running down from the neck over the machete, over his hand and his wrist.

"I give her to you!" he screamed. He ran forward. When he was a dozen steps away, he stopped. "You piece of American shit!" he screamed. Down the field, the white man was looking at Elizabeth's headless body. "You did it! You shit Americans, you pushed the Tutsis on us and now they're killing us and you're right behind them!"

It was the first O'Neill knew about the invasion of Zaire. It must have started overnight, was what he was thinking, but he didn't get very far with the thought. The man ran at O'Neill, swinging the machete with her head on it like a club. The head hit him on the left temple and the top of his own head with a great cracking noise. The head split, the machete coming out through the right cheek and jaw, and the half-brother lifted it again and brought it down on O'Neill, again and again until the machete cut through the bones and it fell off, and he hit O'Neill with the blade, but he was unconscious by then.

15

To Sea, October

The day was fine and bright. Captain Cobb, of the Aegis cruiser *Fort Klock*, thought that it was an autumn day worthy of New England. The sea was the rich, deep blue that it saved for special days, and the sky overhead was deeper still, seeming to grow up and out from the bright horizon to the overhead depths of space. The sun was rising out past Hampton Roads, and the bright disk reflected off the wave tops in a shining path to the east. The *Fort Klock*'s bow wave showed a perfect, crisp white against the water as she cut a path toward the open ocean. Cobb leaned out over the portside bridge wing and looked back along the column.

The solid bulk of the carrier was next in line. Aside from a battleship, no human invention gives a deadlier air of menace and danger than the ominous gray box of an aircraft carrier. The morning sun caught the wingtips of the dozens of aircraft parked at the deck edges and painted the haze-gray wings and fuselages a healthy orange.

On board the carrier, LCDR Rafe Rafehausen stood near the bow, next to the plane that carried his name. He thought of traditional things—the woman who more and more filled his mind, the gas bill he had forgotten to pay, the fact that he had left his short-wave radio behind. He also thought that these were the mornings that made a man proud to be a sailor, when the armed might of the fleet showed to best advantage and the world smiled on those who went down to the sea in ships, or planes. He tried to think of a way to say this to the men and women of his squadron around him, but all that came out was "Hell of a morning, folks." To himself he said, half in prayer, half in promise, *It's going to be all right. It's going to be fine.*

Several yards away, EM3 Sneesen kept sneaking a glance at the new crow ironed on his shoulder that meant that he had been promoted to petty officer third class. He longed to get back to work, to get 705 in really great shape for LCDR Rafehausen, to make the back end sing and fix the sluggish controls and earn more praise, more slaps on the back. He treasured the new knowledge of the world he had got from Borne's books, caressed it in his mind, counted it over like money. It was like—power. Knowledge was power.

LTjg Christy Nixon put aside her troubles and simply let the wind blow over her face. No more exercises. No more impossible decisions. The real thing. She felt like singing. *It'll be okay.* She looked at Rafehausen. He'd been cruel about her fuckups in the Fleetex. Yet— *It'll be okay.*

On the flag bridge, high above the flight deck, Admiral Pilchard looked out at the sunrise between scribbling notes for his staff. His second deployment in eighteen months was not acceptable to his wife, nor could he blame her. He knew how to do so many things better, this time, and he knew how seldom any admiral got two shots at battle-group command. His pen stopped as he noted, for the tenth time, that he didn't have a flag intel officer. *Got to fix that. Ask Jack—move up the CAG AI? Kick the thing downstairs?* So far, he was leaning on the ship's N-2, and the N-2 was delighted to help, for now. In time, the workload of doing both jobs would kill him. *Tackle that problem later.*

He looked down over the deck, down over the massed planes, past Rafehausen's S-3 and the tiny figure of Sneesen, of whom he had actually heard because of the carrier-qual save, and the tiny figure of Rafehausen, whom he had already chatted with, to the bow and the sea beyond it and, through the early haze, the might of the *Fort Klock*. Admiral or no admiral, he was still a sailor, and he felt it in his throat and his gut. *Please, Sir, make it all right. Give us the courage and the intelligence and the strength to make it all right.*

He reached for a clean sheet and started to write.

Battle Group Seven, at sea . . .

That day. At sea, north of Sweden, on the *Poltava*. Captain Suvarov had given a pre-sailing dinner, just like the old days. He had invited all the officers of his little group, and he had passed the wine and the vodka round and round and led them in roaring out old songs. He had given a little time for hard heads, and in the morning he had held a briefing and made his plans clear.

Now he was on the bridge of one of his destroyers, spanking through the water on a day that would delight any sailor. No commander of a battle force could resist some little lift at such a scene—his force deployed around him, bow waves in their teeth like white bones, a blue sky and a fair wind that lifted whitecaps on the indigo water of the Barents Sea. He was momentarily one with every commander who had ever sailed—even his enemy, who was coming to meet him. It was his first multi-vessel command, and it would probably be his last command at sea.

His plans were simple, as resources and old ships forced them to be simple. The surface-action group comprised two Sovremenny-class DDG guided-missile destroyers, the *Poltava* and the *Okrylennyy*; one antiquated Udaloy-class

ASW frigate, the *Borozdin*; and two auxiliaries. They lacked air cover, they lacked big missiles, they lacked good supplies and reliable equipment, but by the time they had been at sea five days they did not lack morale or leadership.

He stood on the bridge wing of the *Poltava* and exercised them again and again in air defense, ASW perimeter, anything he could think of to prepare them to look like a threat. Somewhere west of Africa was a Balzam-class spy ship, a specially designed scout that would track the American battle group mercilessly—and legally. The American battle group was now moving through the Atlantic toward the Mediterranean, as he had been told they would, but fleet intelligence believed they would divert or divide to cover central Africa, where they seemed to want to contest French hegemony. They would have to re-form to launch their new weapon in the Gulf of Sidra, off Libya in the Mediterranean, in March, probably when whatever was going on in Africa—a place Suvarov had never been and had no interest in—would be over. He must be there to contest that launch; until then, he was to "send a powerful message."

Suvarov was not a political officer. Life on shore confused him, and fleet politics gave him a headache. But at sea he was a different man. The doubts that affected every tiny action in port, every request for supplies, did not exist for him at sea. At sea, he was the master.

Despite his orders, he was not going to meet the Americans in the Atlantic. He was going to take an apparently peaceful "show the flag" surface-action group—no Akula-class submarine evident—into the Mediterranean and, if the diplomats could arrange it, take his men ashore for liberty in Tunisia or Algeria. The Americans would not suspect his real mission.

He would then take the nuclear submarine *Shark*, alone, to "visit" the American battle group.

Down the coast of Africa, where no rules applied, where submarines almost never go. He doubted they would be watching for anything as dangerous as his *Shark*. He would penetrate their screen, scare them, and slip away. That was the hard part, the escape, but he would do it. Then he would sprint north, back to his little group of ships, and, when the Americans came, he would be waiting, waiting to use his favorite and familiar waters in the Med. They would have to react.

First, however, he had to move his group three thousand miles from the tip of the Nordkapp to the Strait of Gibraltar. And the American battle group would then be, if intelligence was right, another three thousand miles farther south, off the coast of Zaire—except he believed that they dared not go that far. Somewhere north of there, let's say— perhaps the Bight of Benin.

At ten knots, his group would see Gibraltar in twelve days.

He looked at his route, already approved in Moscow, cutting between the Faroes and the Hebrides, passing through the heavily traveled shipping lanes west of Ireland in broad daylight. That would send a message, too.

And what were the Americans doing? Where would their battle group go? They were turning south in the mid-Atlantic, but how far south could their commander go and still support an exercise off Libya? Sierra Leone? There was good, deep water off the coast of Ghana, with dozens of isothermal layers to confuse and distort the American sonar. Would the Americans go so far south? Ideally, Suvarov wanted to wait for them in ambush, silent and deadly, letting the escorts and the hunters pass ignorantly overhead.

Five years before, while the empire fell and Moscow was in chaos, North Sea Fleet had sent an unprepared Victor II to the Mediterranean with a poor crew and a bent and squealing main-propeller shaft. The frightened men on that ship had endured day after day of relentless prosecution from NATO planes and ships. They, and the entire Russian Navy, had been humiliated. Suvarov had not been aboard, but he still felt that humiliation to the core of his being. Now, he wanted the Americans to have to search for him and not find him, to have the feeling that they were naked to his 63cm torpedoes and his anti-ship missiles, that he held their carrier in his fist, just as they had done to the crew of the Victor II.

He had a new intelligence report in his cabin that suggested one new factor, although he did not take it with any great seriousness. The Americans had replaced the commander of the battle group at the last minute, apparently over some balls-up in an exercise. The new man was reported to be much better than the old—in fact, given the highest rating, with "maximum future rank potential." This report pleased Suvarov. He wanted to match their best. So—good. Let us see how well he deals with the most advanced nuclear submarine in the Russian Navy.

Suvarov bent over the chart table and lit another cigarette. He motioned the navigator to him.

"As soon as we weather the Nordkapp, we will pass these orders in radio silence." He gestured at the chart. "Please prepare charts with these alternatives. Am I clear?"

"Yes, Captain."

"Carry on."

Out in the perfect autumn evening, two sailors chipped away at the twenty-seven layers of perfect enamel that sealed the 76mm bow turret from the weather—and kept it from rotating or functioning in any way. Up until now, the appearance of the *Poltava* had mattered far more than the reality. But their orders were clear, and they chipped with gusto. They had helped put the last layer on only six weeks ago; now, off it came. A paradigm of military life.

And, tomorrow, the gun would work.

Suvarov saw them as small figures. He knew what they were doing. He knew the consequences of what they were doing: there is only one purpose in freeing a gun, to make it ready to use.

And the only purpose in making a gun ready to use is using it.

How far would he go?

He had asked himself the question a hundred times since Sergei had handed him his orders. *Do not start a war.* But there were levels and levels short of war, and at one of those levels waited revenge for the humiliation of five years ago.

Two days later. Battle Group Seven, at sea.
They had been underway thirty-eight hours when word came of the push into Zaire near Bikuba. The reports were scattered, and later the Agency would be excoriated for not having reliable assets in the area. Hutu refugees had been on the move for days, some answering the Tutsi call to come home, some moving away into eastern Zaire, and the Interahamwe militias had been more and more savage. They were trying to cow their own people, and although in the end more than a half a million of them went home, in the short term they were terrified, and horrible things were done.

Word reached the Tactical Flag Command Center at 0237 Zulu that communications among the front-line Zairian (FAZ) units along Lake Kivu were going down. This was held by the duty officer until 0630, when it was felt safe to tell the flag lieutenant, who, if he wasn't awake should have been, that there was priority message traffic. In fact, Parsills had already seen it by that time and was using it as breakfast conversation with the admiral. In other words, they hadn't yet worked out when the admiral was to be rousted out of bed and when he wasn't.

They tracked the situation for the next nine hours. By then it was clear that the major upheaval that Alan had foretold was taking place.

O'Neill's capture hadn't been discovered yet.

Eastern Zaire.

Zulu stood at the intersection of two roads that were little more than streambeds in the pouring rain. His Toyota was axle-deep in mud; ahead of it, two old Bedfords were mired for good. His driver looked at him with the strained, frightened look of a boy fearing punishment from his father. "I can't go around, Colonel—no room— !"

Zulu waved at his communications officer and then tried to get a fix with his American-made GPU. He couldn't find a third satellite in the heavy cloud cover, then got it briefly and tried to pick off coordinates. "Where the hell is Djutzic?" he snarled.

"He's near a small village, he says, but he doesn't know which one. His map is no good."

"Oh, shit!" Zulu smacked the GPU with his palm. Nothing was working. He had expected to be pushing ahead into Rwanda by now; instead, they had been mauled behind the Zairian border and were withdrawing, or trying to, into an area they had never expected to have to fight in—no good maps, no recon, no local guides. "Have you raised Colonel Ntarinada?"

"No, sir. The last contact I had, his ADC was headed west of Masisi."

261

"Masisi! That's sixty fucking kilometers west of the border! Those shits! They're running!"

A gnarled captain, years older than was usual for his rank, trudged back from the mired trucks, his boots so thick with mud he seemed to have a tree-trunk at the end of each leg. He came up to Zulu silently and stood looking at him, rain dripping from his helmet and running down his face. "We'll have to pick another route," he said. "The trucks are hopeless."

"What's your status?"

"We lost three men right off. I've got six wounded in the lead truck. Those fucking Hutus, they deserted us! We were up against Rwandan regulars, they went through the Hutus and the FAZ like they weren't there; we held, and when I looked around, we were all by ourselves! I didn't think we were going to get out." He wiped his face with a bandaged hand. "This isn't what I thought, Colonel. These Rwandans are as good as anybody we fought in Croatia. We can take up a position, but—"

They both heard it at the same time, the scream of an incoming artillery round; Zulu pulled both men down and the round passed over them and exploded with a thundering *crump* that shook the soaked earth.

"Get your people out of the trucks and get moving! Put the wounded in my pickup—Jacov, back my truck around, get the boys to lift it out if you have to—we're going up the other road—" He pulled the communications officer off the road and knelt as they heard another round come in and explode farther away, his lousy map, something sold by the Zairian Triple-A ten years before, spread in a puddle.

"Get on to the other company and tell them to make for Masisi. *Masisi*—it's on these shitty maps, so just tell them to get their asses there and take up a position. Then get on to Colonel Ntarinada or any of these Hutu shits you can raise and ask him what the fuck he's doing! Tell him for me I can't hold the Rwandan army alone!"

Another round whistled in, and Zulu stepped into the mud of the road and stood there, shaking his fist at it as it went over, as if daring it to come for him.

After it had exploded, he began to shout at his men. "Well, move out! Move out—move out— !"

Two hours later. The Pentagon.
The African message traffic was on Alan's computer when he sat down to work. He went through it grimly, knowing where each place mentioned was, watching the Rwandan professionals going through the Zairian troops like a scythe through hay. He had no doubt now of a report about South African mercenary involvement; they must have gone in during the night and neutralized whatever early-warning system the Zairians had had. They would already have pulled out, he suspected, their job done. A report of black South African special forces heading home would not surprise him. Nor would one about the white Yugoslav mercenaries showing up in the battle.

He sat in front of the screen, chewing a knuckle, asking himself *Where is O'Neill? Where the hell is he?*

That afternoon. The flag deck of the *Andrew Jackson*.
Parsills found the admiral in flag plot and comm'd him that another Priority message was in, this one Urgent and Eyes Only. Admiral Pilchard elected not to take it up on the island but came shooting down into TFCC, read the message, scheduled a staff conference for 1600, and went forward into the flag quarters and his own office. Parsills was already there.

"Okay, the other shoe has dropped. A hell of a lot sooner than I thought. What's it mean for us?"

The message announced that a CIA case officer had disappeared and his abandoned car had been found in Eastern Zaire. Nothing more was known, but the Director was already calling for "all appropriate measures" to get their man back.

Pilchard wanted to know if those appropriate measures included BG 7.

Two hours later. The Pentagon.

Alan Craik did not hear about O'Neill until somebody at the Agency who knew both him and O'Neill told him. She had taken over Shreed's old job, had once been Shreed's assistant when they were all involved together. Now, she told him to get on a STU, and then she read the messages to him. "The Director's frantic, they say. Everybody in Ops is going nuts. They said they'd never let it happen again—the guy who was killed in Lebanon, remember? Alan, taking an Agency case officer is *bad news*."

"Oh, Christ," he said. "Oh, Jesus, poor Harry. Goddamit!"

"To hell, yeah. We'll get him back, Al. We'll get him back if we have to send in the marines." She tried to make him feel good about how quickly it would happen: Whoever took him must already know they'd made a huge mistake. They'd probably thought he was a tourist. The State folks had already been on the blower to the French, who were propping up the Hutu militias. They'd damned well make things happen or Washington would really put the screws to Paris. They'd have him back within twenty-four hours.

"Just his car? That was all they found?"

"There's a million stories; it's only been a couple of hours. And we haven't got anybody there. It's local cops or somebody. One story is the Ugandan military crossed the border there and found it. You hear all sorts of things. We've got a team on the way and they're sending people from Nairobi and Dar, plus FBI. It's only a matter of time, Al." She hesitated. "Unless he was meeting an agent, and the Dar guy says he didn't have any agents yet." She waited. "We'll get him back."

"Yeah. Thanks for calling me."

He sat with his head in his hands. He tried to call Rose, but she was away from her desk. He tried to get Abe Peretz at the Bureau, but he was in a meeting.

He felt so *futile*.

Next day. Sarajevo.

The news about O'Neill's capture got to Dukas via the local CIA chief before it appeared in an intelligence report. He called Alan in Washington from a secure Air Force office and was able to talk openly over the encrypted link. Even through the digitization of the machine, Craik sounded to him keyed up, almost frantic. It wasn't just O'Neill, Dukas thought. His job? Not Rose, surely.

"How's the world's most beautiful woman?" he said.

"Better. Working too hard. But—"

Dukas waited, but no explanation of the "but" came. She was okay, but—depressed? Manic? "She'll get over it," he said.

"Yeah, of course. Sure."

Again Dukas waited. When nothing more came, he searched for something to say, some change of subject. "How bad is the thing with O'Neill?" he said lamely.

"Bad and getting worse. Every day it goes on, his chances lessen. If he's still alive."

"Jesus, Al, that's not like you."

"Get real. If the Hutu militias have him, what are they going to do with him? The RPF have started a major push eastward and are driving half a million refugees ahead of them—good mine-sweepers, right? The militias are running even faster. No matter how good an idea it seemed at the time to snatch a CIA officer, now they're beating their heads against the wall because it was the stupidest thing they could have done. Suicide! Instead of a hostage, they've got a target. The easiest thing is kill him. Worst thing is, any group stupid enough to do it in the first place are stupid enough to kill him."

"They won't do that."

"Sure they will. We're trying to keep him alive by spreading the word that we'll deal for him. The French are on our side, for once—they're blown away by it. The militias start snatching Big-Power intel guys, they're cooked."

"Oh, Christ, the French! Well, my guy Pigoreau seems a straight arrow."

"Something smells bad in Paris—you remember that little op I did in Bosnia, the guy who went through the window when we went in by chopper? I had a warning about the French then."

"Zulu, you mean. Yeah, he's on my list, but—*nada*. So, how are *you*?"

He heard Alan sigh, wondered how a sigh got digitized. "I feel like shit. First Rose, then Harry—now I sit in a goddam office while you guys are doing stuff— Change the subject, for God's sake."

"Uh— Hey, Africa! I got a report of some Serb troops in Africa. That make sense?"

"Yeah, a couple hundred went through Libya last week—mercs, off to help Mobutu, which is pretty funny when you know that the Libyans are supporting the RPF. Somebody's making it worth the Libyans' trouble, I suppose. So? That's it? That's your change of subject? Some sparkling conversationalist you are. How's your love life?"

"Oh—you know—"

"No, I don't know. I read in the dailies that Bosnia's overrun with German pimps and a lot of local talent. That true?"

"There's a lot of outside money, a lot of poor people. A lot of girls, yeah—it's a pretty sick scene."

"And you?"

"I'm fine."

"I mean you and the girls. Rose says you got a girl."

Dukas felt himself blush. He cleared his throat. Yes, he'd written something to Rose. "Woman, not girl," he said. "Well, I'm not so sure. One of those things, you know. Here today, gone tomorrow."

"Rose said you sounded serious."

Dukas mentally kicked himself for having told Rose. No, that wasn't fair; he had wanted Rose to know, to sanction it. "Oh, you know—you think it's something, and then it isn't." He searched for another change of subject, thought it was a hell of a thing when you called somebody specially and spent all the time trying to find something meaningless to talk about. He went back to O'Neill: How had they snatched him? From his house? The street?

Alan told him what he knew. "It's bad, Mike—there's no logic to it, which makes it worse. As if they simply took him for the sake of doing it, for the hell of it. Unless it was personal. Then it's even worse."

"What's 'personal' mean?"

Craik hesitated. "He said a couple of times in letters that he'd met a woman—'a real woman, at last' was what he said."

Oh, shit, Dukas thought, *O'Neill, too*. "They wouldn't grab him over some woman. Would they?"

"Who knows what they'd do? It's a civil war—that's a hell of an opportunity to kill somebody. The official

267

Agency story right now is O'Neill walked into the middle of something by accident and got snatched in the 'turmoil of civil war,' to quote their talking head. That's bullshit, and they know it's bullshit, but they're trying not to scare whoever's got him into killing him. If they didn't do that five minutes after they snatched him. Meanwhile, I'm sitting here with my thumb up my ass, briefing admirals on five-year projections of Ukrainian air power."

"Well, I'm sitting here in Sarajevo with my thumb up my ass, trying to write a report on all the swell things we've been doing while we haven't been catching war criminals. We're a great pair, Al. Christ, this call is cheering us up so much we better hang up before we kill ourselves."

Days later, the local CIA guy told Dukas that there was a story that a headless female body had been found near where O'Neill had disappeared. Dukas lay awake at night with the image of that headless woman before him. Fear that he would cause such a thing to happen to Mrs Obren was the other side of his suspicion of her, the case officer's guilt at sending the agent into a place where civilized rules didn't apply, and beating, rape, and mutilation were tools of war. The thought that he might do that to her tormented him. The headless female body became hers.

Three days later, she came over from RS. He had decided, he thought, to terminate her status as an agent and simply try to keep her as his lover, but she brought what seemed like good information on a suspect, and next day Pigoreau told him that it had checked out; they even had sympathetic police in the target area, and they could start planning a raid. She came to Dukas's apartment as a matter of course, and when she undressed he forgot his doubts and his reservations, marveling at her big, robust body and its power to arouse him. Sex in those days, in that place, was the only haven from the miseries of peacekeeping—sex and booze, and Dukas was keeping a tight rein on his drinking—and it had rare value for all of them. Pigoreau, he knew, went off to the whores, terrified of AIDS but needing something; Dukas guessed that some of Pigoreau's suspicion of Mrs Obren was jealousy. Dukas suspected that it was that way with her, too—coming to him for a small piece of rest, even joy, in an otherwise bad life.

Lying in the dark with her, Dukas got her talking about her husband. He wanted to know enough to prove the man was dead. She had a terrible eagerness when she talked about the man, almost childlike. Dukas was hurt.

"What will you do if I find him?" he asked.

She pulled him against her, wrapped a leg over him. "I will be so grateful," she whispered. "I will always be for you."

"If I find him, then you'll have *him*. He's your husband."

"I have room in my heart for two men."

The picture in his mind was not of a heart with two men in it, like some sort of comic valentine, but both of them between her legs—two men, ignoring each other, pumping away, and she lying back, smiling. It was worse than the picture of the headless woman.

Aboard the *Andrew Jackson*.
Admiral Pilchard sat in an armchair in his office, his chin on his hand, one leg swinging slowly up and down. Parsills came in; an aide disappeared. The two men looked at each other. The capture of the American CIA officer by unknown forces in central Africa had changed everything. Now, it was not merely the possibility of having to repatriate Americans from a war-torn African country that faced them; now, it was the possibility of direct, angry, CIA-driven American involvement.

"That staff meeting was pretty pathetic," Pilchard said.

"They'll be up to speed tomorrow."

"By tomorrow they won't be up to speed! They'll just have caught up with today. What's happening?"

"Things are still breaking. It's pretty confused. Nothing on the missing CIA guy. Something called the RPA is supposed to be thirty-five miles inside Zaire, but they deny they're there. Uganda says they aren't there, either. Mobutu says his army is throwing back the invaders and may have to move into Rwanda, tomorrow, if not sooner. All dicked up."

"Just like us. Jack, that was one of the most pathetic meetings I've ever sat in on! This is supposed to be a goddam flag staff, not the Moe and Curly show!"

Parsills sighed, then grinned. "You know what's wrong, Dick. You know how little these guys have been together. Give them some—"

"I don't have any time to give!"

"I was gonna say 'slack.'"

Pilchard took an angry turn up the room and back. "Using the ship's N-2 for intel won't work."

"I told you that last week."

"I know you did. You were right. That doesn't help us. Shit! What's the expectation for the next twenty-four hours?"

Parsills looked at a binder that held a thick sheaf of messages. "CIA have teams going in. State is leaning on Mobutu, or trying to—he's in Monte Carlo having his hair done, or something. Actually, he's got cancer and is there for radiation. There's a lot of confusing stuff about the guy who was taken and what may have—" He looked up as Pilchard waved a hand. "Okay. NSA have intercepted some French traffic that indicates the French are serious about trying to help. Instructing their embassy in Kinshasa—that's Zaire—to lean on the Hutus. Jesus, Dick, you need a goddam program to keep these guys straight—the French are in Kinshasa, but the CIA guy was snatched by Rwandans a thousand miles away, but the fighting's a hundred miles south of there in Zaire!"

"What're they asking of us?"

"National Security Advisor wants an estimate of steaming time to the mouth of the Congo, how many marines 'and others'—ha! what's that mean, you and me?—we can put ashore, maximum perimeter of controlled air space. Can we secure the major airfield in Kinshasa for air transports? Ditto Kisangani, which is four hundred miles up the Congo, ditto Lumumbashi, which I haven't located yet but has some American missionaries and engineers—"

Pilchard held up a hand.

"Is there a bottom line?"

"Not yet. Too fluid."

Pilchard looked at one shining shoe tip. He waggled the shoe. "Ask Sixth Fleet for an estimate of the consequences if we don't enter the Med."

"Whole BG?

"Whole BG and also only part. Part better be the *Fort Klock* and others, meaning if we keep the CV outside regardless and somebody has to take up the slack over Bosnia."

"Will do."

"Then get me somebody who's ahead of the curve on Africa and can up readiness so that we know what's breaking before it breaks!"

Parsills looked at Pilchard with his head down, looking up almost slyly through his heavy eyebrows. "Well, I have a candidate." He waited. "You know him."

"Okay, say it."

"Craik."

"I knew you'd say that." He made a face. "Mike Craik's kid."

"Yup."

Pilchard thought about it. He got up, put his hands in his pockets. "He's awfully young."

"He's the best intel officer in the fleet! He's good enough on Africa that you picked him out of a shopful of experts to brief your people. He's not just up to speed; he's ahead of the curve. Nobody else is."

"But he's on a shore tour. He's got a family. He just came off sea duty. I don't want somebody who resents me for tearing him up by the roots!"

Parsills shook his head. "*You* just came off sea duty! He won't resent you, Dick. O'Neill—the guy who got snatched—is his best friend. O'Neill was the Prowler AI when Craik worked for me; they were a team. Right now, I promise you, Craik is trying to find a way to get to his buddy."

"I don't know." Pilchard shook his head. "He impressed the hell out of me, but—" He looked at the other man with shrewd eyes. "Would you go to the wall for him?"

"All the way." That meant, *Even to the end of my own career*. Then Parsills said, "Would you?"

Pilchard hesitated. "I back my decisions to the hilt. I haven't made a decision here yet."

"Time's a-wastin'."

"Jesus, Jack—he's only a lieutenant."

"Deep-select for O-4 last August, effective next year. You say the word, and he'll come aboard as a lieutenant-commander. Flag intel. Our best hope!"

Admiral Pilchard looked out one of the ports that gave light to this almost elegant office. Outside, the gray Atlantic rolled, and, far in the distance, a destroyer almost faded into the haze. Pilchard tapped his big finger three times on his mahogany desk and then gave it one decisive rap.

"Make it so."

The Pentagon.

A round-faced female jg made her way across the inner court of the Pentagon and into the other side of the building, then up two levels. She carried an attaché case, which she swung with some of the pleasure in the movement that kids feel sometimes in swinging a bookbag. She loved the Pentagon and she loved Washington, and she felt sorry for the person she was going to see. She had looked at the message she was carrying and she had seen it was a set of orders, and, cheerful as she always was, she felt really sorry for somebody who was going to have to give up duty at the Pentagon to go to sea.

She was astonished, therefore, when she had delivered the papers and had left the man's little office and taken no more than a few steps down the corridor, to hear from that very same office a yell of delight that could have broken the eardrums of a mule.

16

October

Visualize modern warfare at sea as a set of interlocking circles. At the center of each circle lies a ship, a submarine, or an aircraft; the circles radiate from them and indicate their capabilities. One is the "far-on" circle, which shows how far a ship might go in any space of time—a minute or an hour or a day. Sub-hunters use the far-on circle, for example, when they have lost contact with a target. The far-on circle shows them the farthest that the missing submarine may have gone, in any direction, from the moment that contact was lost.

Another circle is the range ring. Any ship or plane or submarine may have several range rings, which radiate from it like irregular waves. The *Fort Klock*, for instance, a Ticonderoga-class guided-missile cruiser, has one circle for the range of her defensive surface-to-air missiles, another for her Harpoons, still a third for her Tomahawks, but some of these are for land attack and some for ships, and so their circles, too, may be different. Smaller rings represent the ranges of her 76mm gun and her CIWS 20mm anti-missile defense system and still lighter weapons.

Yet it is not range, but targeting, especially over-the-horizon targeting, that drives the combat problem. A ship cannot shoot another ship two hundred miles over the horizon or even two hundred meters away in fog, no

274

matter how vast her range circles are, if she does not know that the other ship is there. To target, the ship must see, but it "sees" with radar and sonar and satellite down-links. Radar extends vision to many miles, but it is limited by the same geometry that limits sight—the straight line of emission and reflection, and the curved surface of the earth, which line of sight touches as a tangent that we call the horizon.

A swimming man has a horizon of a few hundred yards. A man at the top of a thirty-foot mast has a horizon of almost twenty miles. Lookouts used to climb the highest mast of a sailing ship to get the widest horizon: a higher mast meant a wider circle, which was extended even farther if another ship's mast-tops stuck up above that horizon. So modern targeting circles leap from each ship, laid down around each one by a geometry based on the ship's and its target's heights. And, as with the two sailing ships, the modern lookout has to remember that to see, is to be seen.

But, nowadays, one unit can target for another. It is possible to be out of the other ship's targeting circle altogether and yet fire at him, so long as your targeting circle is extended by somebody else's—a plane's or a satellite's, most likely. Using datalinks, aircraft or ships can extend another's targeting circle out to the limit of weapon range, and a ship can hit something it can neither see nor detect with its own sensors.

An aircraft is a hugely extended mast, one with a sophisticated communications suite and a radar; cruising at thousands of feet over the water, it can see hundreds of miles, and it can tell the ship almost instantly of everything it sees. The aircraft runs the same risk as the lookout, however—what can be seen, can see. And so the aircraft is returned to the game of circles, and aircrew members have computer banks and kneepad cards and memories to help them know which potential enemy has a long-range surface-to-air missile, and how fast that enemy is moving and can move, and whether it has detected the aircraft, and where its far-on circles reach.

Enemy and friendly sea- and land-based aircraft and ships further complicate this laying-down of circles, until the ocean's surface and the sky above it become a maze of interlocking curves, a madness of arcs, a puzzle scribbled by a child gone berserk with a pair of compasses. The amount of data to be assimilated at a glance during a naval battle becomes so immense that the human being finds the world not simplified by electronics, but confounded by it, and the decision-maker still has to have some part of himself that trusts his intuition, aided by training, complicated by prejudice, muddied by desire; and the human commander continues to make decisions and to suffer with their consequences as commanders have since Drake.

And then there is the surface on which the compasses scratch their puzzles, the sea: water, spray, waves that tower to mast height and roll hundreds of feet between crests; roaring storms that strip radar masts from enduring hulls; fog and rain and snow that attenuate radar emissions; heat and cold and salinity and whales and shrimp and krill that interfere with sonar. Decks still pitch; horizons still tip; weapons still fire into and across currents and gales. The gunner sighting down the bronze barrel with his linstock in his hand, waiting for the wave to lift his target into view, would understand: these are moving puzzles, in all three dimensions.

Battle Group Seven pushed across the gray Atlantic. The range rings of her ships pushed invisibly ahead, projecting offensive power far beyond the visible horizon. The targeting rings of her radar expanded and contracted as operators shifted their focus; through satellite-fed datalinks, these coordinated with other data, and the group's knowledge of its path illuminated it for a thousand miles.

The sky was wintry, and a raw, damp wind blew across the decks. On the smaller ships—the destroyers *Decatur* and *Melward*, the frigates *Hull* and *Macon*—spray smashed up from the bows and across the decks. The ocean-going tug *Frank Balducci* rode the waves like a toy boat, up, cresting with a smash; down, rolling, and up again.

For the new flag intelligence officer on the flag deck, there was little sense of this outer weather. Twenty-four hours after touching down on the carrier's deck, he stood above a datalink display and studied this new task as if the screen might tell him how he would function here, separated from the familiar ready rooms, the ship's intelligence center, the cluster of AIs. Here, his job was not to be the day-to-day conduit of tactics, but the eye and part of the brain of the flag. His long, intense face was lit from below by the glow of a computer terminal. Its predominantly green hue made his eyes sparkle and gave his intensity an almost demonic edge. His compact, wrestler's frame was hunched with concentration and his dark hair was almost invisible in the surrounding dark.

The computer terminal was set to show the disposition of the battle group, and he saw it from the point of view of the flagship, the range and targeting circles as clear to him as if they were really on the screen: the *Andrew Jackson*, tagged CVN, occupied the center of the screen. There was no Aegis cruiser on the screen; the Ticonderoga-class cruiser *Fort Klock* had parted company the day before, with *Isaac Hull*, an ASW frigate of the Oliver Hazard Perry class, as escort. They would enter the Mediterranean and cruise between Nice and Naples before rendezvousing with the

USNS *Philadelphia* and the Peacemaker twelve days before the Peacemaker launch; long before then, the flag intended to have the rest of the battle group in the Mediterranean, as well. The other Arleigh Burke-class ship, the *Steven Decatur*, was two thousand yards astern of the carrier, her robust surface-to-air missile capability describing a circle that covered the entire battle group. Two older frigates of the FFG 7 class covered the flanks, providing both ASW and anti-missile protection. They did not have the radar capability of the *Decatur*, but, in combat, Alpha Whiskey, the air warfare commander on the *Decatur*, would control their missiles and use them as an extension of his own radar via datalink.

Together, these ships would protect the battle group from air threats well beyond the visual horizon, and, with an E-2 Hawkeye from the carrier aloft, their range and detection would be still further improved. Each unit supported and fed the others, increasing the battle group's circles of defense and attack to hundreds of miles. In an emergency, the carrier could send out a rotating series of tanker aircraft, called a chainsaw, that would allow projection of the battle group's force to thousands of miles, as fighters and bombers flew out along the chain of tankers, getting gas at each one and carrying on to a distant target.

An oiler, USS *Ajax*, trailed the *Decatur*, her captain an aviator preparing to command a carrier by doing a tour on this deepwater ship. Farther astern, the helicopter carrier *Rangoon* held station several thousand yards away. *Rangoon* carried a marine expeditionary unit, which had its own air group of choppers and VSTOL Harriers, as well as tanks and marines. If Zaire really blew up, they would be the teeth of the US response. *Rangoon* had her own escort, as well, an older destroyer, the *John P. Melward*, which had been updated with a state-of-the-art ASW module and related weaponry but which lacked *Decatur's* radar and missile power.

Alan knew that if he walked down to the ASW module, he would find that several of the surface ships had SQR-19 passive arrays—sonar "tails"—deployed, protecting the battle group from the intrusion of potentially hostile submarines. Every ship had an SH-60 Lamps III ASW helicopter, as well.

The battle group sailed today in a formation codenamed Cheetah. It was spread over twenty-one miles from flank to flank, eleven miles from the bow of the forward ship to the stern of the last. The formation was itself a response to the nuclear age: if all defenses fail and a nuclear missile or a nuclear torpedo hit, dispersal might protect some of the ships. They communicated electronically.

It all came together on the flag bridge.

Alan studied the computer screen and wondered if he would be able to grasp it all before the crisis came in Africa. Very much on his mind was the absence of the *Fort Klock* and its escort from the battle group. The decision had already been taken to split the force and leave the aircraft carrier and its escorts outside the Strait of Gibraltar. *Fort Klock* was thus denied air cover; the *Andrew Jackson* was denied the cruiser's missile punch. It was a calculated but unavoidable risk: there had to be a force in the Atlantic off the African coast until the Zairian upheaval calmed down. And there had to be a force in the Mediterranean.

Split in two, the battle group sailed on, each part weakened, yet projecting circles of confident power on the ocean.

Alan had returned to the warm and smelly embrace of life at sea as if he had never left it. It helped him that many of the crises awaiting him in the flag operations

279

room were the same crises he had been briefing at the Pentagon—Rwanda, the snatching of O'Neill, the advance across Zaire—as well as familiar ones of long standing—Bosnia, Iraq, movements of the Russian Navy, the latest a new report of a surface group coming out of Murmansk.

He had barely had time to notice the process of moving into his stateroom, although as a latecomer he had had to take a small one located amidships on the O-3 level, close to the jet blast deflectors and their noise; normally, he would have bitched and tried to maneuver himself into a better one. He simply had no time or energy for it, however. A little grimly, he reminded himself of Rose: no time for herself. His consolation was that he had very little gear to move into it and he was hardly ever there, anyway.

He had dropped his helmet bag that first morning on the desk chair. There it sat for days, like a castoff. In its depths, the H & K P-9 lay in darkness, unused and unwanted.

He had hung his flight suit on the back of the door, distributed a couple of photos of Mikey and Rose in the small open patches between the pipes, thrown his flight jacket over the back of the chair, and put his laptop on the desk. That was about it, because at that point a yeoman had appeared at his elbow, saying that, uh, sir, the admiral wanted to see him.

17

October

Sarajevo.
Mike Dukas was watching his war-crimes unit turn into a functioning police entity. It was like building the ideal police operation from scratch—or trying to, because it wasn't ideal, and conditions were shit, and support from the UN and IFOR was cautious. Nonetheless, they had put together a sort of intelligence unit, called among themselves "Stein's guys" for the German who ran it, and an administrative function, and a liaison function that was all in Pigoreau's brain, and an operations unit that was hot to trot but so far hadn't had a single operation to test itself on. The division into separate functions was in fact so much smoke and mirrors; everybody did everything, and Dukas himself ran both intelligence and ops. He was reluctant to put much of it on paper or to wave organization charts at anybody, afraid that if he did they would all start to believe what was on the paper instead of what was on the street, and they would quickly become just another little bureaucracy, in business to keep themselves in business.

But they hadn't caught any war criminals. They hadn't even tried. They had no hard leads. In fact, they all knew that it would take three years to build a working organization and an intelligence network, and the big arrests would be made by the people who followed them in their jobs. But Dukas kept pounding into everybody's head that he wanted to score—a couple of arrests, a couple of the names on The Hague's list, something that would make CNN. Then the world would take them seriously.

He and Pigoreau had recruited two people over in Republika Srpska to act as cutouts for Mrs Obren; one of them, a farmer, drove his tractor over the border through a purported minefield to bring information and pick up American goods to sell back in RS. The other agent was an electrician with a girlfriend on the Bosnian side and a wife on the Serbian side; they got him a contract with the Air Force at Tuzla so he had an excuse to come across the border. Dukas guessed correctly that Yugoslav intelligence busted him at once and that thereafter he was a double, but he turned that to advantage by having Mrs Obren send her material through the farmer, while a third recruit left false messages for the electrician to carry over. Later, the Air Force let the electrician do some clumsy stealing of dumb stuff like open-comm frequencies, and they used him to feed crap to the Serbs.

Mrs Obren remained a problem, mostly Dukas's problem. Pigoreau told him she was a double for sure, and Dukas, although not so certain as his now-close friend, knew she was dangerous. By then, however, he had been to bed with her several times and he had come to depend on those nights when she would come to Sarajevo and they would lie in the dark and talk and make love and eat food she got up to cook, sometimes at two or three in the morning.

"You are in love like a teenager," Pigoreau said with a grimace. "Like a fourteen-year-old. Haven't you ever fucked anything before, Michael?"

"Buzz off."

"Bosnia is full of whores, my God, you can have your

pick! I can even find you one without AIDS. Some real beauties, nice girls, as they will all tell you, not a professional among them, all forced into it by war. Heart-rending stories. For a cop, they'll even do it for free."

"You're a cynical bastard, Pigoreau."

"She's got her hooks into you and you're losing your objectivity."

"Shut up about it, will you?"

"She's a Serb double, Michael!"

"I know what she is, and right now she's what I want. She's giving us better information than anybody else we've got, so shut up about it."

"All doubles give good information. If she's being run by a Russian, which is very likely, she's giving wonderful information! That's the way the Russians are, they always give good stuff."

"Then you've got no beef. If it's good, then it's good; who cares where it came from?"

"Michael, in the name of almighty God! She's using you!"

"Prove it."

But Pigoreau couldn't prove it. All he could do was repeat the same worries, nagging, wearing down their friendship. Dukas came close to disliking him, but then the Djejevic Thing happened and they both had other matters to think about.

The Djejevic Thing was named for Radovan Djejevic, a name from the war-crimes list, somebody who had been running a small prison two years before near Srebrenica. His was one of the names that Mrs Obren had recognized, and over a couple of weeks she sent messages about him— that somebody said he was living in the French sector, that he was now a policeman, that he had a new name. Then she came over herself. Dukas debriefed her before he took her to bed, and she told him that Djejevic was now calling himself Radko Mslava and was a cop in the village of Ustar in the French zone. Dukas told Pigoreau and then went home with her; when he got to the office the next morning, Pigoreau had already looked into it, and it checked, and they had a target for their first operation.

"I thought you didn't approve of my source," Dukas said, not unkindly. He was pleased, full of good food and good sex, liking his friend again.

Pigoreau shrugged. "Sometimes, like I said, Michael, they feed you good stuff. We see how it plays out."

It didn't play out well. There were five of them, in a Humvee and a LandCruiser, and they had to accept a squad of French grunts to be allowed to make a raid inside the French zone. Then they got to the zone border, early in the morning, ready to go, and they could see the French troops assigned to them waiting on the other side, and the French soldiers at the border crossing wouldn't let them cross. They were held up two hours, and when they finally got across and connected with their French support and made their way to Ustar, Djejevic was gone.

"It was a setup, Michael!" Pigoreau hissed at him. "She made a fool of you!"

"It's the French fucking zone, wiseass!"

"It was her! It had to be her!"

"It didn't have to be her! We got fucked at the border by your people! Explain that! You're so fucking busy looking at my sex life you can't see beyond the end of your goddamned big French nose!"

They were toe-to-toe, really into each other's face, chins only inches apart. But Pigoreau didn't swing at him as, later, Dukas admitted he hoped he would, because they both were gut-deep angry and a fight would have suited

284

both of them. But Pigoreau was a cop, a hell of a good cop. "We will see," was all he said.

Later, Dukas understood that Pigoreau had connections in French intelligence that weren't on his résumé. Maybe, in that sense, Pigoreau was a sort of double agent, too— maybe they all were. At any rate, Pigoreau came into his ratty office eight days later and closed the door and put on a radio he had brought with him to frustrate any eavesdropping and told Dukas that the operation had been blown by another Frenchman on their roster.

"Rampon," Pigoreau snarled. Rampon was from Lyon. He was a good worker, a little stolid, something of a boozer off-duty, but he pulled his weight. Now, Pigoreau said that Paris intelligence could trace the tip-off of Djejevic back through a captain in French military intel to a Frenchwoman with diplomatic status on the UN staff, and from her back to Rampon.

"They think Rampon was planted on us from the beginning. He tells the woman diplomat, she tells the intel captain, he arranges for us to be held up at the border and then he warns Djejevic." Pigoreau made a face. "You were right, Michael. I couldn't see beyond the end of my big French nose. I will resign, of course."

"Like hell."

"He is my countryman."

"This is a mixed goddam unit; nobody wears his flag on his shoulder; he wasn't your guy. But one thing, Pig—you gotta tell me this wasn't a French operation. You follow me? You gotta tell me this wasn't some part of French policy. Because if it is, you're cooked."

"I assure you, this is not French meddling! This is not my country's policy. Rather the contrary; my contacts think this was some, what do you say, rogue?—rogue operation, some people in France who put Rampon in place at the beginning. Not French people pursuing French policy, but French people pursuing their own policy." He spread his hands on the greasy gray plastic of the desk. "I am a patriot, Michael. I am not a plotter or a falangist."

"What's in it for them—these French people who aren't French?"

"They are French, they are, but—ah, you are making fun of me. Of course. Well, I deserve it. What is in it for them is some separate arrangement with the Serbs, which means with Belgrade. Maybe paying an old debt, maybe keeping their side of an arrangement. Yes? It is not some little shit like Djejevic; they don't care about Djejevic. It is maybe doing something to look good in Belgrade. What is it the British say— to 'show willing'? I think these people, this, mm, this cabal, let us call it—you know 'cabal'?—wanted to show willing to Belgrade, so they saved Djejevic."

"A pretty well placed cabal," Dukas growled, "if they had a diplomat and a military intel guy."

Pigoreau shook his head. "Much bigger than that, Michael. Much bigger. These are very little fish."

"Who says?" Dukas thought he knew who said, but he wanted to hear Pigoreau say it.

"My friends in Paris."

"Good friends?"

"Contacts, Michael, nothing more. France is not like the States; a French cop has to work with the national security guys. It's all the same, right? But Michael—I am not an agent of the Deuxième Bureau!"

"You better not be." Dukas leaned across the desk toward Pigoreau. His mind was working quickly; what did Pigoreau's "assurances" mean? Pigoreau was right: France wasn't the US, and the French didn't cut the security pie the same way; if you were a cop, you did what the national security boys wanted—if the Deuxième Bureau farted,

286

you said Excuse me. But did it matter? After all, Dukas himself had friends in American military intelligence like Al Craik, friends at the FBI like Abe Peretz. Every man in the war-crimes unit probably had connections in his home country. "I don't want you to resign," he said. "I need you. Anyway, you're my friend."

Pigoreau stared at him, then jumped to his feet and threw himself on Dukas in a fierce embrace. "You are a big man, Michael—a great man! I will do anything for you!"

"I don't want you to do 'anything'! I want you to get rid of Rampon and I want you to shut up about Mrs Obren, okay?"

"Anything!" Pigoreau struck himself on the chest. "You are in my heart, Michael—friends forever!"

Two days later, Pigoreau planted a false operational plan on Rampon, and when it turned up with the French diplomat, Rampon was arrested. The diplomat made a quick, and permanent, trip to Belgrade. The French intel captain had been walled off and was left to dangle, with a security specialist from Paris planted on him as an enlisted word processor. Pigoreau reported that the man's computer, telephone, and mail were monitored, and it was hoped he would ultimately lead them back to his masters in France. "Already, we think they use the internet to communicate—we don't know how, but they think they have identified at least two web sites that are some kind of, mmm, intersections. What we call 'switch points'—you understand?"

"Pass-throughs. Electronic cutouts. I get it." Dukas grinned. "So, your French buddies going to screw us any more?"

"Never again, Michael," Pigoreau said. "I assure you! The next operation we have in the French zone, we will be treated like the angels!" He grinned. He told Dukas a joke. He said everything would work out. It was only later in the day that Dukas heard him murmur, apparently to himself, "Still, Mrs Obren could very well have been part of it."

At sea aboard the *Andrew Jackson*.

"Mud-people are imitators, like monkeys," Chief Borne said. "They can seem really, really smart, but it's all imitation—you understand what I'm saying? But the Jew, he's smart, and that's because he's descended from Satan, and as we know, Satan is smart—the first among the Lord's angels till he fell. You with me here?"

Sneesen nodded. His eyes shone: the world was becoming clear.

"So the Jew, because he's smart, uses mud-people to corrupt us. How? Music and sports. Who's the big names in them?—mud-people. Who owns the big record companies, the big teams? Jews. Check it out—every one of them. Y'ever listen to mud-music, Sneesen? ''Course you have— how could you miss it? Thud-thud-thud, ump-ump-ump—it's sex music, am I right? 'Fuck me, fuck me.' I even heard some, it's just some mud-woman breathing like she's coming. 'Do it, do it.'

"So how does this serve the devil's plan? By turning white, Christian men away from their true destiny and toward things that corrupt them. What can the devil want more, Sneesen, than for white men to get into mud-women and produce mongrel babies? Because a mongrel child is a mud-child—bad drives out good. So don't you do it, you understand what I'm saying? Don't listen to the music; don't watch their so-called athletes; don't mix with them. And don't think you can get into the pants of one of them and get away, because I tell you, Sneesen, I'd sooner put my dick in the flame of a propane torch than a mud-pussy, because Satan's hand is in there, just waiting to get a grip. And he never lets go."

Sneesen swallowed hard. "So—should we try to help a white Christian man who's got some mud-woman after him?"

"What d'you think the Lord wants, Sneesen? What d'you think your duty as a Christian white man is? Figure it out."

Suburban Washington.

George Shreed was not immune to bad temper, despite his being a man of power, maturity, and sophistication. Perhaps those things in fact made him more vulnerable to his temper, not less. Physical pain didn't help, either, nor fatigue, nor disgust with the world in which he felt he was forced to exist.

It was time to act, he thought. His own government had worn his patience to the bone: he and Touhey had been making the rounds of the Senate, pleading and joking and cajoling to get Peacemaker more money. And more money and more money. *Assholes,* Shreed thought. *Why do the people keep electing absolute assholes?* The question confounded him. He believed in America to the depths of his soul, but he despised every person who got elected to its government.

Shreed hobbled to his study after dinner and, once confident that his wife was in bed, again booted up his computers and called up his special programs. Reaching with one of them into an Agency network, he withdrew a file and left no track; from that file he selected a report, deleted the rest, and then edited the report to remove any specific data that would trace it back to its sources. What was left was a description of Peacemaker, detailed enough to make its capabilities clear, but merely verbal and therefore not specific enough to make replication possible. Enough, that is, to scare the daylights out of any reader but not to give much hint as to what the hell he could do about it.

Again, Shreed prepared to encrypt the document and embed the result in a pixel.

Again, he called up a pornographic image, this one of two male bodies, so twisted together they might have been wrestling, on examination shown to be engaged in mutual oral sex. Shreed did not even glance at it.

The report proved too long for a single pixel. He encrypted the first, and longer, section, reduced it and embedded it in one man's eye. He was setting up the remainder for encryption when he became aware of two things simultaneously: that someone was standing in the room behind him, and that she had been there for longer than a breath.

Shreed turned. It was his wife. Her face was uneven, as if she had started a smile and it had gone wrong.

He looked back at the screen, saw the image of the two men, hit a key, and it vanished.

When he turned back, she was gone.

"Janey— !" He tried to struggle up. His canes were a long reach away, and he flailed. "Goddamit— !" He threw himself back in the chair as the canes rattled to the floor, then sat there with his face in his hands. He was trembling with anger, with frustration, with hopelessness. When he got control of himself, he turned back to his work, his inevitable antidote to failure.

And he looked at the screen, and realized that he had sent the second part of the document.

Unencrypted.

He put his face in his hands again.

Eleven seconds later. Tehran.

The operator intercepted the message early in his shift. It fit the parameters, from the correct address and aimed at the site in Dubai. The program detected two expanded pixels in a somewhat garish photograph of two men performing fellatio on each other. The computer operator was scandalized and said aloud that it was certainly American.

One pixel contained encrypted data that was opaque to the decryption program. The other, however, came through in clear, causing consternation: Was somebody on to them? Was this a joke? A message? A virus? Two of the operators, studying the image, decided it was a message, and an insulting one, at that.

They turned it all over to Efremov, who took it home, where he did his best work and nobody except Anna, his mistress, bothered him.

The unencrypted page of the intercept appeared to be part of an agent's report on a weapons system codenamed Peacemaker. Efremov was initially confused by the name. Then, as he read the material, things got clearer. This was the American surveillance system that was in the public media—indeed, the Americans were making rather a lot of its peaceful intentions and its usefulness to the world— hence its name. And yet, according to this report—

Sensing its importance by the change in his body language, Anna came and folded herself on a pillow by his chair. Her autumn-leaf hair fell to the floor and pooled upon it as she threw her head back to watch him. That was what made him trust her: that she never rushed to look at his affairs, but only at him. If she had other priorities, she hid them well.

"This is interesting, darling. Somebody is passing what appears to be a classified report to an untraceable recipient. I think the recipient is in China, but that is what we brilliant analysts call a 'guess.' The report is on a piece of military reconnaissance hardware. You understand?"

"Like a satellite?"

He smiled. Anna was uneducated, but she was not ignorant.

"A temporary satellite. Of course, they're all temporary, but this one apparently falls out of orbit after a week. But what is interesting about this one is that, I think, it is also meant to carry some sort of weapon."

She said nothing. She had nothing to say. She waited.

"It's American, of course. So is this document—an intercept, did I say that? Another from the pornographic site. I told you about it." He looked down at her.

"The site you own," she said, a little mischievously.

"Well, my ministry owns it." He had had them buy it when he had discovered that the site functioned as a pass-through for at least one Chinese agent. Physically situated in Dubai, the site got ninety-two thousand hits a day from the sexually challenged—perfect cover.

He read some of it a second time. "Hmm. Well—you see, the Americans have by-products from their Star Wars program. This must be one—a temporary, low-orbit satellite that can provide local photographic coverage as well as detect radar transmission within a fairly broad band. That by itself would be useful. But this seems to be a weapon, as well. It can target the transmissions, identify them, log and locate the point that made the transmission and—and what? That is where it ends!"

She scowled. "A nuclear weapon?"

"Oh, I wouldn't think so. Too big, too heavy. But it refers to 'the test,' so they're apparently ready to test the weapons capability when they test the rest of it—soon, if I remember; it's no secret."

"What will the Chinese do?"

"What a good question. What good questions you ask, darling!"

He ran a hand through her hair and laughed. "The Chinese are inscrutable, which is simply a way of saying they have a different culture. They use time as a defensive weapon; therefore, they will go slowly. It is now weeks before this test; they will slowly stir, murmur, contact this country and that. Then, very late, they will appear very big on the world's screens and they will be very loud. A speech at the UN, I suppose. Perhaps call home their ambassador to Washington. Even perhaps cut off trade, but I doubt that." He grinned. "But I will tell you what they won't do. They won't say that they *know* that this thing is a weapon or how it works, because if they do that, they will reveal their source—and the source is far more important than the facts."

In truth, he wasn't as confident as he seemed. The fragment seemed to him of the first importance, and he was frustrated by all that he didn't know—who had sent it and why (A spy in the American defense establishment? How useful to identify him!); how this weapon worked; where the test was to take place.

"Come to bed?" she said, mistaking his stroking of her hair.

"In a minute." He put on his glasses and began to touch the keyboard, giving orders to the computer operators downtown: try more decryption; gather and prepare a digest of all data on Peacemaker and an upcoming test launch; list all files re US "Star Wars" programs; flag agents in Beijing re awareness/response to US space/satellite/weapons development—

He called the duty officer at his headquarters, had himself put through to an encrypted answering recorder so that somebody would start working on things as soon as the first shift came in.

"I want to know what agency or office in the United States is responsible for a new satellite device called Peacemaker. Identify the managing office.

"Then I want a list of all employees.

"Then I want that list sorted for the following criteria: one, Chinese ancestry or connection by marriage; two, experience in weapon targeting; three, new hires by that office over the last twelve months; four, prior service with the so-called Star Wars program." Efremov stopped, stood with the telephone in his hand, staring at the doorway in which Anna had appeared, not really seeing her. He was thinking about the earlier intercept, the African shootdown photo; since then, they had had a report of a CIA case officer's disappearance in the Rwandan push into Zaire. *Suppose*, he was thinking, *the source of the first one was somebody in the CIA—that is sensible, that it was their photo, got somehow by one of their agents, maybe this one who has disappeared—*

"Yuri?" she said, very softly because she knew how he hated to be distracted when he worked.

He paid no attention. When he had been in the KGB, they had said that there were five moles in the CIA: three were their own, one was Israeli, and one was a mystery. *Suppose—*

He spoke again into the telephone. "Five, sort for any connection with the Central Intelligence Agency. Then— new task here, give it to somebody else—I want to check the Peacemaker's managing entity for any links with the CIA—advisory, financial, shared committees—anything. If you find something, try to get names of individuals. End of message."

He hung up. He thought for some seconds. He looked at her. "That color suits you," he said.

18

October

At sea—the *Andrew Jackson*.

Even without the press of fourteen-hour working days, it took Alan a week to find where his laundry went. On his old carrier, the *Jefferson*, laundry was bagged, tagged, and left outside the stateroom door. On the *Jackson*, it had to be left in the ready room—if you were squadron personnel, and he wasn't. It took him about six hours of homesickness to get over wanting to hang around the squadron spaces, because it was quickly apparent that he didn't belong there—nothing personal, nothing even overt—but he was a lieutenant-commander and he had a staff marker, and despite his background with S-3s he was from up there in blue-tile country and, suddenly, an outsider.

His new duty-mates became individuals over several days, but he had no friends up there as yet. Captain Parsills, maybe, but Parsills was working even longer hours than Alan and spent his working life elsewhere. The admiral was a familiar presence but hardly a friend—not even, properly, an acquaintance. He greeted Alan that first day with a handshake and a quick smile and a "Let's get on with it," and that was the beginning of a full-court press that was still going on. It took him a day to discover that he had an assistant, a ship's-company, senior jg glommed from communications by Parsills. "Thought you'd need help in this zoo," Parsills growled and introduced LTjg Kravitz, a ship-driver who had already had his own command (granted, not much bigger than the average bass boat) and who brought to flag intel a knowledge of ships and water that Alan didn't even know he lacked. In the same way, air warfare was a mystery to Kravitz. "Well, our ignorance is a good match, anyway," Alan said and set Kravitz to swotting up the data on ocean conditions, including isothermals, from the Bight of Benin down to Walvis Bay. Oh, and by the way, keep track of that Russian surface group and just make sure they stay out of our water, okay?

And then he had no clean shirts.

The discovery came in the middle of the afternoon, a week after he'd come aboard. He'd been getting a whiff of his own sweat for some hours; now, back in his stateroom, he wanted to change, and where the hell was a clean shirt? There *were* no goddam clean shirts. He tunneled through his bags, tore the locker apart, went into his dirty laundry (a pile beside the rack) hoping to find something better than he was wearing, and found nothing. This was what you got for going to sea on short notice, smartass. He saw the helmet bag on the chair, went into it, thinking that maybe, somehow, he'd stuck a shirt in there. No, but he did encounter one of the plastic-wrapped parts of the gun, and he thought, *I ought to put that in the armory,* and immediately forgot about it.

Shirts. That was the subject, shirts—in the squadron spaces, you could wander around in a flight suit; blue-tile country was different, felt different. Same people, most of them, having been squadron personnel last tour, but now they seldom flew and the boss was an admiral, and you dressed a little up to the job. So he put on a different shirt instead of a clean one, hustled down to the head and washed the collar and the underarms of the one he'd been wearing, using hand soap, and wrapped everything else into a bundle and put it outside his stateroom door.

That was when he found that they didn't pick up the laundry outside your door on the *Andrew Jackson*. What they did if you put your laundry outside the door was leave it there, and other people kicked it out of their way. If the people were other officers and they saw you and connected you with the laundry, they said things like, "You expecting room service, too?"

This small change in custom came as a shock at the end of a fourteen-hour day of trying to dummy-up a French order of battle because the admiral, on his advice, wanted it. The French were an unknown quantity *vis-à-vis* Zaire. If they got their backs up, and God knew the French could, what might their submarine capability be down there? Did they have any boats down there already, or did they have to send them from Toulon? Should *Fort Klock* be listening for them? Did they have a specific sonar profile? And what about French air power—aircrews from the *Jackson* should be able to reel off speed, far-on circles, radar frequencies, weapons, in case they met French aircraft, plus everybody would have to know French IFF or NATO ID code. And a great deal more, for which he had a stack of pubs under his arm and another sitting in his cubicle in the flag spaces. And now to come back and find his shirts, socks, and underwear scattered over about twenty yards of corridor! Stepped on. A lot! He was tired enough to think, *This isn't fair; I have important work to do; I'm the*— And he caught himself, and he thought, *Yeah, and I'm certainly capable of being small-minded. Hump your own fucking laundry, asshole!*

He slung the laundry bag over his shoulder and walked down to the S-2 locker near the Dirty Shirt wardroom, just forward of his stateroom. It was ship's nighttime, past 2200 local, and a single, rather harassed-looking petty officer third class was playing a Game Boy. He looked up when Alan entered but didn't seem to focus.

"Hey! Petty Officer—mmm—Sanchez." Alan was reading the nametag with difficulty. "Where does laundry go?"

"Oh, yeah, sir. You new? Gotcha. Air wing? Ship's company?"

"Flag staff." It still embarrassed him to say that. It sounded as if he meant the staff the flag flew on: *Hi, I'm on the flagpole.*

"Uh, I think you got to drop it in the flag wardroom. Or in a squadron ready room."

Alan pondered this. It was a week until next laundry day.

"What are my chances of getting it done right now?"

"Sure. Just take it down to Laundry yourself. Fourth deck forward. They'll maybe do it while you wait." He was an optimist—why not? It wasn't his laundry.

"Thanks." Alan ducked out of the duty closet. The process struck some kind of memory in him; he had once taken his own laundry down when he wanted his shore-going shirts ironed on the *Jefferson*. Not a problem.

Twenty minutes later, he was wandering from berthing area to berthing area on the fourth deck. As most of the crew was asleep, the entire lower deck area was lit only with dark red lamps. He couldn't see to read frame numbers on hatches, and no one seemed to be awake to give directions.

As much as possible, the Navy tries to have enlisted men of similar ratings bunk together, as they work together. The addition of women has changed this somewhat, as women require separate berthing areas and often don't comprise the numbers to allow all female air-warfare petty officers, for example, to bunk in the same space, but the custom is continued as far as possible. It has a practical aspect, as well: dental technicians tend to be a different breed from steamfitters, often with different hours, different rhythms.

Pure luck now led him into the intelligence-specialists' berthing area of the ship's company. Equally lucky, somebody was awake and watching a John Wayne movie on ship's TV. Alan walked up hesitantly: officers are discouraged from intruding into enlisted berthing areas.

"Ah—excuse me. Petty Officer, mm—?" It was too dark to read the nametag.

The man looked up with that hint of slowness that suggests that he could have moved faster if he had wanted to, but he didn't want to because he wanted to watch this fucking movie, sir. The man had a big head, the face still in shadow, although the light from the TV glittered on two shrewd eyes. He didn't get up. He took in Alan's collar pins, his flag marker, his decorations. The decorations seemed to require a second look, and then he suddenly uncoiled from the chair and stood and said, in a cigarette-roughened voice, "Help you, sir?"

"Don't I know you?" Alan said. He'd seen the intel-specialist badge, now took in the iron-on SEAL patch—a trident and a pistol—on the left breast of the blue work shirt. Alan grinned. "You're Petty Officer Djalik." People had already told him about Djalik, the only former SEAL in CVIC.

Djalik was the work-center supervisor for the CVIC, a man with the natural authority that comes from being big and hardened. He had a square body and a long, leonine head. He spoke very softly, in a manner calculated to make officers and teenagers pay attention, with a lot of dropped final g's and some t's and d's that suggested, maybe, Chicago. Alan already knew the story: Djalik had been a SEAL until his knees began to go and jumping became too painful. What he lacked in professional knowledge about intelligence he made up for in leadership, and he kept the intel center running with high efficiency. A lot of people admired Djalik. Some envied him his SEAL pin. Alan wasn't immune to the mystique: he found himself resisting admitting to the former SEAL that he was lost.

A stupid male reaction. He bit the bullet.

"I'm looking for the laundry."

Djalik smiled. "You're not too far off, sir." Was he amused? Was he going to have a little fun? No, he was thinking, because now he said, "You'd be Lieutenant-Commander Craik, I guess. Am I right about that?"

Alan held out his hand. "Can't deny it."

"I heard about you."

I heard about you. What had Djalik heard? he wondered. CVIC didn't waste a lot of grief on flag-deck personnel. "Want some coffee, sir?"

Alan didn't think it was right to linger in IS berthing, but he had work to do later and he had been climbing around for a while.

"Got a cup handy?"

"Oh, roger that, sir." Djalik poured coffee into a mug from a thermos, picked up his own cup and headed toward the far hatch. "Wanna follow me, sir?" He started out. Alan took a slug before following. The coffee was rich and mellow and had just a hint of sugar. It was the best coffee he had ever tasted on shipboard.

As the hatch to berthing closed behind him and they entered a well-lit stretch of passageway, Alan caught up with Djalik.

"Great coffee."

"Yeah, I make it myself. Brought the beans. I spent a bunch of time in Colombia, you know? They may all be

300

drug lords, but they sure do know coffee. And you gotta keep the filters clean. The coffee in the intel center tastes like they strained it through their jockstraps."

"I always get my coffee in the ASW module. It's habit." Actually, it was strategy—get your coffee in ASW and you get free, off-the-cuff ASW briefs from the experts.

"Oh. Right. Yeah, theirs isn't so bad. I tell the peons in CVIC, keep the filters clean and I'll be a happy guy, but they don't get it. They're kids." Djalik was Alan's age, maybe a year or two older, looked in some lights older than that. "Here we go, sir."

Alan had forgotten the noise and the size of the ship's laundry. He felt a little stunned. Djalik, unfazed, took charge. Djalik would take charge of anything, Alan decided, that wasn't nailed down; he had that kind of straight-on machismo.

Djalik was staring around the chaotic space, which was more like a factory floor than the ship's spaces Alan knew. Every section in the ship had to contribute junior enlisted people to laundry detail, and twenty men and women were at work here, even though it was the middle of the night. Djalik scanned them until he saw a small Asian kid.

"Hey, Lew!" Djalik bellowed. The kid turned and made his way quickly across the deck. As he came closer, Alan read the nametag. Lu, not Lew. Made sense. Lu looked scared—Djalik, or Alan? Officers, especially lieutenant-commanders, were rare in laundry, but, then, so were ex-SEALs.

"Hey, Lu, how's it going? This job suck, or what? Hey, man, only one more week and you're out of here and back in CVIC where you belong, okay? I've been hearing good things about you from Chief Roberts."

"Thanks, Petty Officer Djalik. Everything is okay." *Okay*

was made to sound as if it meant one step up from unendurable.

"Listen, how about you help out Commander Craik, here? Some idiot forgot to pick up his laundry." When Lu hesitated, Djalik said, "I'll square it with the chief."

"Can do, sir. Give it here, please." His intonation was odd, but his English was good. Alan tried to place him.

"Malaysia?" Alan said.

Lu grinned. "Indonesia, sir."

"Jakarta?"

"East Timor." He continued to smile, but Alan read the silence. *Another Rwanda, another Bosnia.*

"Thanks for taking the laundry, Seaman Lu."

"No problem, sir. Stateroom number?"

His laundry bag was an old one from the *Jefferson*, its frame numbers wrong for his new ship. Lu burrowed in a box and came out with a black magic marker and handed it over, and Alan squatted and started to black out the old numbers. Lots of numbers. A real mess.

"How about I have Lu bring your stuff up to the O-3 level when it's done?"

Again, Djalik had that little smile. As if he was enjoying Alan's discomfort? "Have him bring it to CVIC, okay?"

"Sure, that'll work."

"I'll send him back with an apple pie from the Dirty Shirt for the laundry guys." A plump woman in a T-shirt went by, male eyes following her. "And women."

Djalik grunted. "Don't get me started on that."

Djalik walked him back through the enlisted berthing, saying nothing, twice indicating a turn with a pointing hand, the fingers together and straight, the way a Masai points. It was like being guided through Africa in the dark. Alan wondered if the former SEAL thought of it that way. When they had reached a lighted p'way that seemed brilliant after the red-lighted sleeping spaces, Djalik pulled up by a ladder and pointed that same, straight-fingered hand up.

"Thanks a lot." Alan held out his hand.

"No problem." Djalik shook hands.

Alan was going to go up, but he was intrigued by that image of Djalik as a jungle guide, and he stepped back down and said, "Ever been to Africa?"

"Nah. South America, mostly. Philippines, once. You have, I hear."

Alan dipped his head. "You hear a lot." He tried to make it pleasant.

"I hear we're maybe going there. Africa."

"Well—ships are full of rumors. I wouldn't lay out a lot for a bush jacket just yet."

They were talking about something else, but Alan wasn't sure what. Something between the two of them, an odd sense of speaking in code, rare enough with a stranger, more so with officer and enlisted man. It was as if they might be involved with the same woman, and just finding out about it.

"Well, thanks for the help. And the coffee." He held out the mug.

"Any time. Sir."

Alan went up the ladder. When he got to the top, he glanced down, and Djalik was still standing there, holding the two cups, looking after him.

A couple of days later, he found that Djalik had several years before been awarded the Silver Star for something in Colombia. Alan had one for Africa, and he thought it was that ribbon that Djalik had been looking at when he had first looked up in the enlisted berthing space. That was the possible link between them, maybe the subtext of that last conversation. Whether what Djalik was showing was rivalry or comradeship, however, he couldn't say. Perhaps both.

Sneesen had been scheduled for duty in the laundry, but his new rating got him out of it. He was too valuable fixing things, he figured. They needed him. He hated the laundry, with its noise and its heat. Too many mud-people, too, even though that was where they belonged, the sort of work they were born to do. But white men shouldn't have to work alongside them.

The only bad thing now was that Chief Borne was gone. They said he'd gone to the *Rangoon* because they needed somebody experienced on the flight deck. He'd left Sneesen a note: "The Lord has sent me where he needs me more. Do the Lord's work."

It scared Sneesen that he would have to do that work alone.

19

October

IVI, suburban Maryland.

Abe Peretz was on his two-week Reserve duty at IVI. He had followed up on Rose's long-ago suggestion and got himself assigned there, in good part because she was there. Like all Alan's friends, he enjoyed the company of Alan's wife. IVI itself "tickled" him, to use the word with which he described it to his own wife, Bea, after the first day. It was so focused, so gung-ho, so high-tech; after his own very staid department in the Hoover Building, it was almost frantic.

Rose was away in Naples on the Monday when he reported. She got back Tuesday afternoon, and for the rest of the week, Peretz and Rose met every morning for coffee. The second morning, he asked her what Peacemaker's offensive capability was.

"Offensive? Like, in weapon?"

"Yeah, offensive, as in offensive."

"Zero. Peacemaker's a short-term surveillance and comm satellite."

"Yeah, I read the PR handout." Peretz had a constantly amused eye and an ironic manner, both of which had played a part in his early exit from the Navy. Now, he fixed the eye on Rose and said, "You believe everything you read, Pollyanna?"

"I'm too busy to do otherwise, Abe. What's on your mind?"

"You buy your food at the company store, too?"

"Just what's that supposed to mean?"

Peretz cocked his head, grinned; her voice was more defensive than he had expected. Peretz believed that people should be amused by the organizations they worked for, not impressed. "I mean, you kind of buy into the party line here, don't you?"

"Look, Abe, I'm real busy. I don't waste my time asking no-go questions. What are you trying to say?"

"My, my." Peretz smiled at her again. He tried to make the smile paternal, because he was ten years older and she was his friend's wife. "My, my. Well. What I was trying to say, Commander, is that for a nonoffensive device, Peacemaker has me collating an awful lot of targeting data. You, know, targeting—as in drop bomb, go boom?"

"Peacemaker isn't big enough to carry bombs. Sorry, you're making things up. Look, this is a great place to work; the general's a standup guy with a great idea and a lot of hustle; I'm making points on the way to being an astronaut. Don't ask dumb questions, okay?"

"Why are you so defensive?"

"I'm not defensive! I just—" She ran her hands through her abundant black hair. "I'm up to my ass in work, Abe. Okay?"

He smiled again. "'Don't bother my pretty little head about it?'"

She started to get angry then, caught herself and said instead, "How does Bea put up with you?"

As she walked away, she was thinking that now there were two people on her case about Peacemaker, first Valdez and now Abe Peretz! It didn't occur to her to ask if they might be right. In Rose Craik's world, if you did your job well, there wasn't time to ask if the kooks were right.

Next day, Abe joked around the subject and the tone between them was light, although he did say quietly, "Sure is a heap a target data, Miz Scarlett," as they parted. On the Friday morning, however, he was frowning as he carried his coffee over to her table. He put the cup down and sat quietly, all but ignoring her greeting, and then he said without irony or humor, "Rose, I'm not kidding this time. What's going on with this project?"

"Abe, for God's sake—"

"No, I'm serious, Rose, you're not going to frown me down. There's something screwy here. I'm doing PDAs—Projected Damage Assessments—on damage zone restrictions that don't match any bomb I know. And with virtually no collateral damage, as if this is pinpoint targeting of something low-yield, except at the point of impact. Tell me that part's so classified I should shut up, and I will. Hmm?"

"Shut up."

"No, no, that's not good enough. I mean, tell me you know what's going on and it's okay and I don't need to know."

She looked grim, and he knew she was again ready to be angry. She *liked* Peacemaker, he realized, somehow identified with it, perhaps because she had an important role in it and it was a step up for her. She was going to say something ugly, he thought, when he saw her eyes flick over his shoulder at something, somebody beyond him, and she said, "The very guy who can straighten you out, thank God! Ray—hey, Ray—come on over— !"

She introduced a tall, somber man as Ray Suter. He was also ex-Navy, she explained, but a permanent fixture at IVI. "Ray," she said, "explain to this eager beaver that Peacemaker is exactly what we say it is, will you? Tell him that what he sees is what he gets? He's driving me nuts."

"What seems to be the trouble?"

Peretz was ready to dislike Ray Suter. He didn't like having his time with Rose interrupted; he didn't like Suter's almost patronizing tone or a sense, maybe because he had sat on Rose's side of the table, just a little too close to her, that he somehow claimed Rose. "Only some of the stuff I'm working on." His tone minimized it. "Seems kind of bang-bang."

"Bang-bang?" Suter made it sound like a child's prattle.

"Oh, he means the surveillance plan is full of targeting data that we got from Touhey's Air Force buddies," Rose said. Her head was down and one hand was shaking out her hair. "Abe thinks it's offensive stuff."

"Offensive?" Suter said in the same tone.

"Yeah, as in 'offensive.'" Peretz cocked his head. "You understand 'offensive'—like 'offensive manner'? Or offensive weapon?"

Suter's face flushed. He was one of those people, Peretz saw, who come on very strong and then back off as soon as they're challenged—but not for long. Not somebody he'd like to know any better, he decided.

Now, in a milder tone, Suter said, "Peacemaker's strictly an intelligence project, I can assure you of that. No question. I have access to elements of the project that don't impact Rose, and I can tell you absolutely that there's nothing offensive there. What we're keeping compartmentalized is tech data, especially some of the computer and missile details, that are really, really sensitive in today's world picture. If you'd like more reassurance, Mister Peretz, I can set up an interview with Colonel Han, who's our honcho on the big picture."

"Well, I'd certainly like to meet a honcho, especially

one on the big picture. But, no, I'll take your word for it." Peretz flashed a smile. Suter did not return it.

"We don't want anybody asking the wrong questions," Suter said. "We certainly wouldn't want you expressing those questions outside these walls."

Peretz stopped smiling. He began to gather up his things. "I know how security works. Any doubts I have, I'll express here or nowhere." He grinned at Rose. "Okay?"

"Okay." She patted his hand. "Just remember, I'm too busy to listen."

Peretz laughed and went back to work. He thought that was the end of it.

At sea.
Alan had started a letter to Rose three times and not got to finish it. It began, "Only a week since I got here and it seems a month! I've been going so hard I—" Then somebody had called him into ASW, and when he next looked at the letter it had been two days since he had written the first sentence. He finished the sentence and added a couple more about Rafe and the admiral and the food, and then he had to go; he left the letter on his desk, where he could finish it that night.

Five days later, he got back to it. It seemed callous, letting it lie there; he *missed* her, how come he couldn't find the time to tell her so? Guilty, he sat down and wrote for twenty minutes—the laundry story; Kravitz, who was really working out well despite still having to stand watches in ship's comm; his first dinner in the flag wardroom— He stopped and looked at his watch.

"Time to go! I love you! Write! More later!"

He stuffed it in an envelope as he ran to flag ops, intending to post it that day.

Two days later, he found it under a pile of pubs.

Sarajevo.

To Dukas in Sarajevo, the worlds of O'Neill and Alan Craik and the Navy were dim. He wrote a few letters, but he was not really a letter-writing man; aside from short notes to Rose Craik, he settled for picture postcards with ten or a dozen words scrawled on them—"Still here, everything okay!" The postcards showed the new Sarajevo and were a credit to entrepreneurship, color photos of the ruined library, bomb damage in the old market, rebuilding in Nova Sarajevo, and old faithfuls like the Olympic Mountain. The postcards were an afterthought, however; all his concentration was on the frustration of hunting war criminals where many of them lived openly but were beyond his reach.

He remembered the story that Al Craik had told him about Kenyans and Italians in Bosnia, walking around in a perpetual rage because they couldn't do anything against an enemy that openly mocked them. He and his people were like that. The failure in the French zone had bruised their morale. Two of them had quit, gone back to police work in their countries, where the problems were the same but there were lots of other cops to make you feel good about things.

"We got to have more intelligence," he told Pigoreau. "Put out more money for snitches. I'll get it someplace."

"I handle it? My way?" Pigoreau didn't believe in the niceties of Agency-style espionage, the things O'Neill had learned at the Ranch—recruitment, seduction, training, comm plans—but in old-fashioned bribery.

"Any way that works."

Mrs Obren remained his best source. She sent him rumors, gossip, occasional snippets about an identified name on his list that might one day lead to an arrest.

Washington.

Suter walked toward the door of the conference suite where the Ops/Plans Committee were meeting, wishing that he weren't there but was instead out at IVI, where his real life now seemed to be. He enjoyed it, of course, because Rose was there, Rose now a fixture in his mental world, on the way to becoming an obsession; but he enjoyed it, too, simply as itself—the park-like campus, the atmosphere, Touhey—and the project, which still excited him. But he needed to talk to Shreed, and Shreed was inside there, sitting through one of the seemingly interminable meetings that took up most of his days. Shreed had wanted to be Deputy Director for Ops/Plans but would not be, or so he said; how did he know? You knew those things, Suter supposed. Or maybe they told you outright—some enemy at your level or just above, telling you with relish that he or she knew for a fact that you'd never have your heart's desire.

The door opened, held by a guard, and through it Suter could see a male receptionist and half a dozen people with attachés and notepads, a few of them with obvious aides, hangers-on, lingering close as if it might be necessary to wipe the great one's nose or bottom, as if they tended small but very rich children. As he looked, Shreed's canes hove into view, first the tips, aslant like silver arrows, then, as the canes rose to vertical, the fierce face and *en brosse* hair. Shreed looked down at the floor as he planned his next assault on gravity, picked his spot and swung forward. Somebody spoke to him from the group but he made no acknowledgment, swung forward again and looked up and, seeing Suter, nodded. He placed the canes outside the door and swung through.

"Something's come up," Suter said.

"Fucking idiots," Shreed grated. He was in either physical or intellectual pain, perhaps both; his face was contorted. He was on his way to another meeting halfway across the building and up another floor. Suter knew his schedule, was there because this was the only time to catch him. He started along the corridor, but Shreed swung himself against the wall, reaching out for Suter, hissing, "I'm sick of fools."

Shreed's hand clutched Suter's right arm like a claw, and, for the first time, Suter was aware of Shreed's age. There was something ancient about that grip, like some very old but powerful man's hand clutching at him for momentary balance. "None of their crap matters," he heard Shreed growl. His voice was intense, almost too soft to be heard. "Operations—little men moving other little men around. *Trivia*. No big thoughts." Suter remembered Shreed's saying—when?—that only station chiefs had power, meaning that only operations had power; what was he talking about now? It seemed like a contradiction. If Suter had been a more reflective man, he might have thought that Shreed was contradicting himself because he was suddenly old and suddenly in the position of the old man who believes that somehow he will recover all his missed opportunities with one last, great achievement. His ear was good enough, nonetheless, to hear the subtext that said that Shreed was separating himself from the rest of them.

"Don't think small," Shreed was muttering in his ear. "Have great thoughts."

Suter felt he was supposed to say something. "There's Peacemaker," he muttered. People were going by in the corridor. Nobody looked at them, because people muttered secrets to each other along here all the time.

"That's small, too," Shreed rumbled. "It's only a step." He

312

began to laugh nastily. "Crippled steps for crippled feet," he said. "What do you want?"

"There may be something going on. I wanted you to know."

"Spit it out."

"Rose Siciliano came to me today with somebody asking about targeting data for Peacemaker."

Shreed's hawk's eyes fastened on him. "And?"

"Somebody's been laying off the idea on her that there's too much attention being given to targeting for Peacemaker to be passive."

"Meaningless."

"It's somebody she listens to. Some friend she got to do his Reserve duty there. He's full-time FBI."

Shreed leaned back against the wall. His deeply lined face seemed to sink in on itself for two seconds, giving him briefly an almost peaceful look. "Just chat, or has he got the wind up?"

"She was bothered enough to talk to me about it." Suter had been delighted that she had called to him, in fact, although he wouldn't say that to Shreed.

"Tell Touhey."

"Touhey's in Houston for a week. I thought of going to security, but they'd just make it worse. They'd underline it by going after it."

Shreed nodded. "How concerned is she?"

"Not very. She compartmentalizes. If I tell her not to worry about it, she won't. But this other guy—"

"Who is he?"

Suter had already checked. "Peretz. Ex-Navy. Like me. LCDR. Intel, didn't make commander, got out. He's in the FISA office in the Bureau. Not a fool. A friend of hers. And Craik's."

"Two weeks' Reserve duty?"

"He's just finishing the first week." He didn't need to add, So he's got another whole week to cause trouble.

Shreed pushed himself away from the wall. "I'll take care of it. You deal with Siciliano. Can you assure me you can stay objective about her? If she starts to get ideas, I don't want you making excuses because you want to get in her pants."

Suter let silence speak for him. He knew that Shreed would believe him less if he made some flossy protestation.

Shreed hobbled up the wide corridor. People hurried around him. "Don't report it to your security people out there. Let me handle it." He went two difficult strides down the corridor and then turned and started back, and Suter hurried to him.

"No, you handle it," Shreed said. "I'm being stupid—martyring myself. Ego. You do it. Here's what you do. There's a full commander in ONI named Harley Ohlheim. My secretary will have the number. Set a meeting and see him today. Tell him to pull this Peretz in someplace else for the second week of his Reserve duty; we don't care where it is, so long as he never goes back to Ivy. Don't take no for an answer. Ohlheim thinks he's going to be DNI one day, which is laughable, but it's a useful weakness to play on. He'll come around." Shreed leaned his left elbow on his cane and scratched his nose. "Maybe this Peretz will forget all about Ivy. If he doesn't—" He shrugged. He meant, Then we'll do something else.

Suter rather hoped that Peretz wouldn't forget. He liked this sort of maneuvering, the sense of something slightly underhand and therefore risky. The sense of being where things really happened, even if they were what Shreed had dismissed as trivia. And even as Shreed was distancing himself from such things, Suter was trying to get closer to them. He liked Shreed; more importantly, he admired him. In fact, he wanted to *be* Shreed. This is an ambition in an underling that is theoretically admirable but in practice extraordinarily dangerous.

20

October–November

On board the *Andrew Jackson*, at sea.
Time began to blur, as it does all too easily in the routine of the sailor. Pizza night, a Friday on the *Jackson*, came and went and came again. Seaman Lu returned to duty at CVIC, and he and Alan smiled. Petty Officer Djalik became a fixture in his routine, always visible in CVIC.

The flag captain suggested to him after a week on board that he really ought to eat in the flag wardroom because business got done there, and Alan realized that there was more to being on staff than met the eye.

Much more. For one thing, the flag N-2 (intel) functioned as the admiral's ambassador, when the admiral trusted him, so in his first weeks aboard he flew off once to Walvis Bay, the huge tanker port on the Namibian coast, to check on what they might be able to make available in avgas and ship's fuel; and once to Rota, Spain, to talk about juggling the Deny Flight duties over Bosnia because all the BG's aircraft were still in the Atlantic.

He tried to keep up-to-date on O'Neill, but O'Neill had dropped down a black hole, and the sad but very human fact was that O'Neill dropped through a hole in his attention, as well: he was too busy to grieve. There was simply no news: the CIA had closed in on itself; the State

Department was silent. So, as flag intel, and prodded by CinCLANTFLEET, he began to prepare for the possible evacuation of Americans from Zaire, a huge operation that made the plight of one missing intelligence officer a mere blip. Such an operation would necessarily involve the marines, and the *Rangoon*'s intel officer came aboard for a day and a night of briefings that took all Alan's attention, and he deputized Kravitz to do the morning brief, fearing the worst, but Kravitz was okay and the admiral didn't read him out.

At the same time, the *Jackson*'s air wing staff was preparing a bombing campaign against Libya. Alan believed that such a thing wouldn't happen this cruise, but none of the young intelligence officers knew this, and they prepared target folders with the sort of humorless concentration that accountants bring to tax preparation. He was aware of Christy Nixon in CVIC during this effort, once watched two or three minutes of one of her briefings on a television screen. She seemed pretty, competent, a little flirtatious, not his type; he couldn't see what was getting to Rafe about her. But you never could see what your friends saw in women.

Three days later, he was in CVIC getting viewgraphs so he could do a composite for the admiral, and Nixon was there. She gave him a big smile, a little wave. *Don't do that*, he thought, but there was no reason why she shouldn't. The truth was, she irritated him. Probably it was because of Rafe, for Rafe's sake—absurd, as Rafe hadn't asked him to be irritated on his account. She was working on Libyan SAM sites, and he was aware of her, some questions she asked, stuff she was getting for a brief she was going to do—thorough, patient, but spending too much time on the trivia. She just didn't go about it the way he would have. When she was leaving, he said, "Mind if I walk along with you?"

"Not at all!" Again, the too big smile. Alan had learned at the Pentagon that these warm smiles were more a defense than anything else.

"Rafe talks about you a lot!" she said as they headed down the p'way. She had a bunch of pubs squeezed against her chest, like a kid with schoolbooks. Alan didn't pick up the cue about Rafe; instead, he said, "Can I give you a bit of advice?"

She turned and raised an eyebrow. Advice was never a good thing, to junior officers. "Yes, sir. Go ahead."

Alan stopped at frame 133, where he had to cut across to the flag N-2 office, and they stood there, squeezed a little against the bulkhead so people could go past. "Focus," he said. "You learn fast, but it looks to me like you keep trying to learn *everything*. What you want to do is figure out what the essentials are, learn those, ditch the rest. They don't pay us to be perfect. They pay us to be right." He looked at her and smiled at her earnestness, thinking *Lord, was this me?*

She looked back. There was a lot going on behind her eyes, although the earnest smile stayed firmly in place. "Am I in trouble?"

"Absolutely not. You're a very good intel officer. Learn to scan the material and you'll be even better. Look, I'm not in your chain. But you screwed up during Fleetex because, in the end, you couldn't see the forest for the trees, right?"

Small nod. Smaller smile.

"Right. Now, you're learning the whole history of air defense so you can give one brief to the admiral about Libyan SAMs. Predict, Christy, predict. Guess what he'll ask. Learn that. Guess what he needs to know. Learn that. Ditch the rest. What's the most important thing about the Libyan air defense?"

"The big stick. The location and range of their big missiles." She was crisp, with no hesitation.

"That's what's important to aircrew, right. But to the admiral?"

She looked flustered, and he felt for her, cornered in a passageway, but this was the Navy. She shook her head.

"Maintenance. Infrastructure. Do the damn things still work? How old are they? Stuff like that. That helps the top echelon make big decisions."

He saw in her eyes the spark of understanding.

"Okay, sir. I get the point. But sir? I like to know everything. Really." She seemed to give a small jerk, as if the words had pulled her up, and she covered by shifting the load of pubs.

That was the way Sneesen saw them, rounding frame 133 and starting up the p'way. He barely remembered LCDR Craik from the flight from Bermuda, knew he was a friend of CDR Rafehausen's. He recognized *her*, though. And he saw that she was at it again, curving her body like that, looking up into the guy's eyes—just the shit she laid on Rafehausen.

He went by them, hating her. In his head, he didn't say the n-word, because Borne had told him that was stupid and got in the way of right thinking. Instead, he called her what she was: *mud-bitch*.

Washington.

For Rose, Alan's absence was a relief, at least at first. It was hard to admit it, but she liked coming back to the empty house and having nobody else's emotional needs to deal with except the dog's. She had to confront this unexpected part of herself, this place where she wasn't a "real woman" but simply wanted peace. Privacy. A place of her own.

Then that passed. She missed him. She missed him physically, became as horny as a teenager for a few nights, got over it. Then a letter came from him, written in spurts over several days, not very coherent, not written with his full attention, and she felt such a pang of loss that she wept.

That was when she knew she was getting better.

At sea.

One morning, after he had briefed the admiral and was closing his laptop before leaving, the admiral said, "Did I understand it's your wife who's the launch officer on this USNS ship we're going to ride shotgun for?"

"Yes, sir."

The admiral spun a piece of message traffic with a finger. "We just got a request for a squad of marines to protect her ship. What's that all about?"

"She asked some of us what sort of protection she ought to have. I suggested that the Bay of Sidra was a good place to have to deal with Libyan patrol boats, which don't necessarily think their authority ends twelve miles from the coast. Plus they're looking for something to take the world's mind off Lockerbie."

"You suggest she take marines?"

"No, sir."

The admiral looked at the paper and made a note. "I'll authorize four, not a squad. We're going to need every marine we can get if we have to evacuate people from Zaire." He looked at Alan and nodded. "Thanks for not trying to ask favors for her. Make a note for the CAG AI: I want a *short* précis of the cover we're giving the *Philadelphia* once it hits the Gulf of Sidra."

*   *   *

320

Mornings, he briefed the admiral, then the staff. Then he hit CVIC and ASW, met with the CAG AI, went back to his own cubicle and did the message traffic, then went through the squadron spaces hitting the highlights of the air wing's day. Nearly four weeks after he'd come aboard, the admiral told him to make up a list of possible liberty ports along the African coast, because they might not be getting into the Med as quickly as they'd hoped. Alan had already decided the same thing, and so had most of the ship; there was a tension on board that came from five thousand people cooped up longer than they'd bargained for.

By then, they should have hit the same ports *Fort Klock* had—Nice, Naples, Antibes—and been as happy about it as *Klock*'s crew were. Instead, they were still outside the Pillars of Hercules, steaming up and down, carrying out cyclic air ops that were really raising the squadrons' readiness but that were also driving a lot of young sailors with strong hormones nuts.

For Rafe's sake, Alan was just as glad there were no liberty ports. He believed that Rafe and Christy Nixon couldn't go ashore without heading for the nearest hotel. That was how far they'd come. He'd seen them in the squadron ready room together; there was sexual tension there, anticipation. They were both playing it cool, but you could tell. Everybody could tell, he feared. Despite his advice, Rafe had put her in his own aircraft. And maybe the atmosphere of the S-3 would be an anti-aphrodisiac: boredom, body smells, pissing in a bag, working as parts of the machine. Maybe routine flying would de-glamorize her. Maybe cows would give Ben and Jerry's chocolate.

For his own sake, he wished they'd hit Naples tomorrow. He and Rose had planned to meet there. He'd had several letters from her, and he saw that things were getting better. Naples would have been wonderful.

21

November

The Strait of Gibraltar, aboard the *Shark*.

Suvarov smiled at Lebedev, who was his admiral's son and his chief sonarman and who excelled at his job. Right now his job was to identify the USNS *Philadelphia* among hundreds of other merchant ships in the eastern Atlantic. As usual, he was doing a superb job.

"Dead ahead, 010 relative, four thousand meters," Lebedev said quietly. "Two escorts, one Ticonderoga-class, one Burke-class."

"How far from the Rock?"

"Fifteen thousand meters."

"Make revolutions for three knots. I want to be dead ahead of the *Philadelphia*. I want her to pass directly overhead. Helm, place us bow up in the layer. Weapons, set up a passive torpedo attack, bow on." The weapons officer looked appalled.

The tension on the bridge was like a layer of cigar smoke. It could be felt; it certainly had a smell. Suvarov watched Lebedev. He wasn't rock steady, but he was solid enough. He conned the ship carefully. Suvarov watched the screen as he mentally counted the seconds. He didn't need the sonar to feel the placement of the ships. He was taking an unholy risk: that the Americans did not have a tail deployed. They were about to transit the Strait of

Gibraltar and he hoped they had no idea that he existed. If one American destroyer had an acoustic tail deployed, he might very well be caught, and that would ensure humiliation and might mean the end of the mission. *Protest* meant showing the Americans that he could have taken action had he desired. That was the language of the Cold War, and sailors spoke it better than anyone. Especially submariners.

He felt the ship slow, felt the change in attitude as Lebedev changed the internal ballast and pointed the bow a few degrees up. The crew was silent. They did not need passive sonar to hear the big American ships passing. While every hand on the bridge sat glued to his screen, many white-knuckled, Suvarov watched them, looking slowly from man to man. They were not bad, and in that moment he loved them, even little Rubinov who was trying to hide his hyperventilation.

"Prepare revolutions for twenty-six knots," he said, very quietly. The last American ship was almost directly overhead. The tidal race would start in forty minutes, a period of acoustic chaos.

Lebedev raised his head sharply. He laughed, two small barks like a lapdog. "It is a game!"

Of course he had never intended to fire. He had simply said hello. *Protest, not fight.* That was in his orders. The surface ship captains knew, but he wanted to give his crew this taste of the past, a knowledge of themselves.

Suvarov smiled. He turned to the engineer. "Run," he said, and made a small gesture. The engines sang out and the *Shark* leapt forward. Suvarov knew that every sonarman on the American ships now knew his location. Their officers would get the message.

I was under you. I owned you. Welcome to the Med.

The protest had begun. So had his revenge.

Off Africa, aboard the _Jackson_.

"So," Alan was saying to Kravitz, "this is right up your alley. List every deepwater port from here to Cape Town. We gotta be able to take on water, fresh foods, probably fuel— check with the Texaco [ship's slang for the oiler that trailed the CV] on what they've got and what they'd need—and if the people are going ashore, the port has to be cleared. Check with the NCIS office here on the carrier. Think AIDS. Think terrorism. Okay? You see the scope of the problem? Give me a first draft by tomorrow."

All in all, things were going okay.

Then they got _Fort Klock_'s pos con on a probably Russian high-value submarine, and everything went up for grabs.

They were just entering the African littoral when _Fort Klock_ sent them the set of sonograms that indicated a possible contact on a Russian submarine near Gibraltar. Alan didn't see the tapes, but he got a précis, and he and the other senior intel officers discussed the possibility of a Russian sub's coming into the Med again. Russia was a sagging old fighter, on the ropes financially and socially, but its navy still had punch, especially undersea. The early third-generation Victor IIIs were high-quality nuclear boats, and the Akula-class was among the best in the world. Early in a cruise, when people weren't up to speed, you didn't want to have one nearby, no matter what had happened to the Cold War.

It was some time since the Russians had sent a submarine to the Mediterranean, and this one had clearly sent a challenge, and then just disappeared, but it had apparently passed close to the _Fort Klock_.

A month into the cruise, Alan had learned to become a regular at flag-wardroom dinners, where much of the staff's business was discussed and where things were often settled with Admiral Pilchard over coffee. Still eating, Pilchard was that night going through message traffic and asking Alan and the flag captain to comment. The admiral made no bones about sharing his worries with his staff, and he was worried about many things, to which the *Klock*'s possible contact was an unwelcome addition. After going through the message stack, he finished his food, waved to the messman for dessert and coffee, and fell silent until they appeared. Then he cleared his throat for their attention.

"Gentlemen, I want to direct your attention to our situation, and then I want to discuss our options. We're in a bind: *Philadelphia* transited Gibraltar yesterday and is on the way to Naples, right on schedule. We're at Launch minus thirty days—one of our two primary responsibilities on this cruise.

"The situation in Africa is going to hell in a hand-basket, and fast. To put it as baldly as possible, LANTFLEET wants our battle group in two places at once—in the West Med to cover the Peacemaker launch, and in the Bight of Benin to watch Zaire." He looked around the table. The flag captain and the logistics officer were fully engaged; some of the other staff tried to look fascinated; some listened out of politeness. Strategy was not their problem, and they had been over this before, hadn't they? Alan listened but let part of his mind go elsewhere; he'd heard it an hour before dinner, and he was worried about the NEO, about Rafe, about O'Neill—

"Craik has been working very hard to keep us up-to-date on Africa, but, Alan, I need more information. I'm putting us on our African station in another day, well up toward the Côte d'Ivoire, where we can run north in a hurry. If I can, I want to run to the Med in time to make our port call in Palma twelve days before Peacemaker. If that works, I mean to leave the *Rangoon* and her escorts down here, but

I'll only do that if the situation warrants—if Zaire's calmed down by then, the whole BG meets up in the Med, and we're home free. Until then, however, LANTFLEET seems unable to decide which is more important, Peacemaker or Africa, and if it's Africa, is it an NEO or an intervention? They're asking us for clarification." He looked at Parsills. "What happens if we have to intervene?"

Parsills rolled a bit of bread between his fingers. "Likeliest, the *Rangoon* puts her marines on the beach, we get *Fort Klock* down here for bombardment. Probably we scrub Peacemaker."

"You mean, we *ask* to scrub Peacemaker. That's not our decision. There's a lot of pressure to launch that thing; I'm not sure where it's coming from. Maybe Congress." The admiral glanced at Alan, undoubtedly reminded that Craik's wife was a key player in the launch, but he went on talking to Parsills. "Ask LANTFLEET to get an assessment of how a postponement impacts BGs eight and nine. If one of them gets it added to the scenario, it's going to screw something else up." He looked back at Alan. "Where do we stand on a liberty port if we don't make Palma?"

"Kravitz has done a good job of narrowing it down. The fact is, there's nothing between here and Cape Town that makes it."

"Jack, could we send the *Rangoon* and its folks down to Cape Town while we keep station, then trade with them?"

"Divide the BG into three? Come on. That's two thousand miles."

"Twenty-four hundred," Alan said. "Kravitz did the fuel, talked it over with the Texaco. We'd need another oiler, tank up at Walvis."

"Shit." Pilchard put the spoon on the plate with a clang. "They've got us between a rock and a hard place, gentlemen. We're going to have some very unhappy ships here

326

pretty soon; you can say they're soft, but this isn't wartime. Sailors want liberty. And they deserve it; I've been working their tails pretty hard, this last month. Well—" He looked up at Parsills. "Liberty's the safest thing to forgo."

"You bet."

"Ships don't sink from lost liberty."

A voice from the end of the table said, "I'd recommend we put the *Rangoon* off Zaire, keep them ready down there while we stay where we are. Fuck a liberty port. From here, we can chainsaw air cover into the Med if we have to."

Alan had his head down. He was picking at a small defect in the linen tablecloth. "Two aircraft," he said.

"Two! More like ten! Have you done the math?"

"Yes, sir. Two F-14s and the S-3 to tank them, and if it's in the eastern end of the Med we'd need a KC-10 or everybody goes into the water."

Mutterings and groans. Some of them would do the math over, not believing him because he wasn't part of their faction, nor an aviator. It was a political table, with pro- and anti-Pilchard factions, and pro- and anti-Parsills factions, and some nutcases who had been held over from Newman's regime and somehow wanted him back. Alan wasn't used to this way of massaging ideas; most of his experience had been down where the ideas got translated into tactics. Nonetheless, he knew his role: to supply facts and to suggest reasonable ideas. Now, he said, "We could send part of the aircraft to the Med to cover our asses up there. Shore-base them at Sigonella."

"Negative that!" a deep voice boomed from the back. It was the staff plans captain, a diehard carrier pilot who had hated leaving the squadron level. Mildly, the admiral said, "We're not going to negative anything just yet, Tommy." He gestured toward Alan. "Craik means that we're supposed to make a contribution to air cover over Bosnia, along with everything else—that'll come up at appropriations time, or it will if we haven't performed. Tommy, see what you can do with it—maybe one F-18 squadron and a couple of Prowlers?"

"I don't like it," the deep voice said.

"Neither do I. There's lots of things I don't like."

The admiral picked up the spoon again, tasted a quarter-inch of ice cream on its tip, then pointed the spoon at Alan. "How much of a factor is this Russian sub?"

"If it's a late-generation boat, it can give *Klock* a lot of training real fast. It may be coincidence, but there's a Russian surface group in the Med, too, liberty-porting in Algiers, the last Kravitz looked. A high-value sub with a surface group would be unusual for the Russians in the Med, but—" Alan scratched his head. "I'd like to hear what other people think about the idea that this could be connected with Peacemaker."

Several of the other staffers looked at each other. One winked: the staff intel officer was off on another wild hare, he meant. The idea was not new to the admiral, however; indeed, he and Alan had discussed it as soon as *Klock*'s pos con had come in. "Tell 'em your idea," Pilchard said, spooning out a larger bite of ice cream.

So Alan laid it out: the Russian Navy wanted the US Navy to understand that launching Peacemaker annoyed it. They would express that annoyance by putting a high-value submarine nearby and causing the BG to wear itself out on ASW. The surface group, if connected, would provide a complicating element.

"There's no evidence for that whatsoever," a commander from operations said. Speculation bored the shit out of him.

"No, there isn't," Alan said, turning a little away from the table because the man was behind him.

"Then why are we going on about it?"

"Because," the admiral said, "I think it's important." There was a little silence: somebody had shit on his face. Another commander cleared his throat and said that he didn't see why the Russians would care enough about a missile test to go ballistic.

"They aren't going ballistic," Alan said. "If this is a gesture, they're showing a lot of restraint. So far. Look, gentlemen, most of us have played games with Victors; it's good training and it's good, clean fun. Maybe that's all this is, too. But remember that Peacemaker isn't a missile. It's a satellite *put up* by a missile. It's low space, and if you're paranoid, you think that the Americans are at it again, violating ABM treaties and trying to push Reagan's Star Wars agenda. And trust me, the Russians are paranoid."

One of the lieutenants at the back said, "What's the idea with the Libyan bombing plans?"

"That's just to keep people busy while we bore holes in the water," Parsills growled.

"Peacemaker isn't a device so we can bomb Libya?"

Parsills was going to say something sharp, but the admiral looked at him and frowned. Alan jumped in and said, "I wish I'd thought of that, Fred. No, Peacemaker's going off from the Gulf of Sidra to show the Libyans that they don't own the Med. I really think that's all of it—except that the orbit brings it back over Libya several times, maybe as a reminder to them."

"I don't see the Russian connection," somebody else said from the other side of the table. "I don't buy it."

Alan glanced at the admiral, waited for an okay, which came in the form of a nod, and said, "There's a Russian Balzam-class surveillance boat off the Canaries. It's just what you'd want if you were going to carry out SW ops down here."

"You said in the Med!"

"The Russians have more than one high-value submarine. If that boat up in the Med is an Akula, its presence means something serious. It left port with the surface group. We know that. If there is a second boat, it would be a major deployment."

People leaned forward. Suddenly, the atmosphere changed: were they talking *serious* business here?

The admiral was now actively enjoying the puddle of melted ice cream and strawberries. Turned out he liked ice cream that way. "Alan, you better prepare for a two-ocean ASW effort. Gentlemen, it looks to me like a major deployment already. We have to take the Russians seriously." The remnants of the Newman faction exchanged glances.

"It's in hand, sir. I could brief it Friday morning."

The admiral put his spoon down. "You're not going to be here Friday morning. We'll talk about it."

Stunned, Alan looked at Parsills, who winked.

"Staff meeting, 0800 tomorrow," Pilchard said. "I want recommendations on the issues of keeping the BG split, pulling it back together before Peacemaker, and keeping ourselves viable in two oceans. Tommy, be prepared to discuss sending aircraft to Sigonella. We *will* reach a decision before the meeting is over." He rose. "Gentlemen, enjoy your coffee without us, please. Alan, we need to talk. Jack, you come, too."

The admiral's suite had a form of living room that served as study and office, with chairs only a little less comfortable than those in the squadron ready rooms. A young white messman (the new Navy, those old racial habits finally breaking down) was setting out a tray of coffee when they went in; with a nod from the admiral, he was gone. Without preliminary, the admiral sat down and, after offering a box of pretty good cigars, said to Parsills, "Tell him, Jack."

"There's a feeler on your friend O'Neill."

Alan, still recovering from the admiral's *you won't be here on Friday,* which had sounded to him like a career-ending announcement of failure, now felt a thrill of anticipation. "That's great!"

"From the French."

The admiral was working on a cigar before lighting it. Now he sniffed it. "For once, things went our way. The ambassador down there is away—called back 'for consultation,' as they say, which means in diplomatese that Washington is fed up with Mobutu. So a feeler came through French military intelligence—*military,* which is why it didn't go to the CIA first. Somebody French and military in Kinshasa contacted the naval attaché—not an accident, because these guys apparently know each other. Anyway, before he reported through channels, he told me, as US military commander on the spot."

"Where's O'Neill?"

Parsills picked the story up. "He doesn't know. What's happening is this, and it's changing fast: French military intel is leaning on whoever snatched O'Neill to cough him up." He raised an eyebrow at Alan as he accepted a cigar from the admiral. "Any idea why it would be military and not civilian intelligence, by the way?"

"Maybe—there's some sort of rivalry. Or worse. When I was in Bosnia, they said you couldn't tell the French things, there were leaks. Or maybe it's just that the military are the diehards who want to hold on to Africa. Except that now they're the ones who seem to have come to us, and we're the bad guys, if you're French."

"This French mil guy—whoever he is—told the attaché that they want O'Neill handed over. *He* doesn't have

O'Neill, that's apparently certain, and he's not going to get him. The word we got is that French military intel is trying to pressure the kidnappers to give him up to the Kinshasa embassy."

"God, that would be great."

"Don't get your hopes up. This is all second-hand."

The admiral stirred in his deep chair. He exhaled cigar smoke. "I want to send you on another little trip—to Kinshasa. The ostensible reason is to pay a courtesy call on the embassy and get the local read on the situation. Actually, I do want you to do that. It's damned important. But I also—" He blew smoke out the side of his mouth and knocked ash off into a big ashtray. He looked tired in the room's low light. He was twenty years older than Alan and kept just as tough a schedule. "You've done well since you got here. Better than I ever hoped. You're a damned good officer. Consider this my way of saying thank you: I thought you'd want to be there if your friend comes out."

Alan found it hard to swallow. "Thank you, sir."

"Take a good uniform. Talk to the station—the CIA people—if you can. I suspect they'll be doing the negotiation; he's their guy, after all. If you can go along, do it—after all, you'll be the only one there he knows. Or who knows him."

The flag captain rolled his cigar between his fingers. "Kinshasa's pretty chaotic, sir. I'd like Craik to take somebody with him."

The admiral looked at Alan, then up at Parsills. "What'd you have in mind—marines?"

But Alan already knew what he wanted, and, before Parsills could speak, he said, "If I may, sir— There's a guy in CVIC, ex-SEAL. He's intel, he's smart, he knows a lot. Good guy in a chaotic city."

"Officer or EM?"

"First Class Petty Officer, sir. Silver Star."

The two older men looked at each other. Pilchard shrugged, nodded; Parsills reached across to use the ashtray, said, "Suits me," and that was that.

"When do I go?"

Pilchard smiled. "You'd go right now if I had a plane on the flight deck for you, wouldn't you? Late tomorrow, if things don't change. We can't speed things up beyond that, but we might put it off if there's news. You just be ready, and stand by for changes." He stabbed the air with the cigar. "You be careful, but get me some straight dope. I know O'Neill is your first reason for going; okay. But use the trip to get us some straight dope. Anything that will clarify what we're doing out here. Get me the embassy's call on the possibility and timing of an NEO or an intervention—that's *my* priority." He looked straight at Alan. "Do I have to say, 'Don't do anything stupid?'" He answered his own question. "You know Africa; you've been in harm's way there and come out in one piece. This should be routine. However—" He slipped down a little, became less formal. "Y'know, I was an attaché a long time ago. Unless embassies have changed, they're awful places. They don't think like we do. So, this is an order: don't take any shit from them. I'll write your orders broadly enough so you have a little discretion where O'Neill's involved, and I'll make it damned clear you're there to get their input, so they won't pull some 'need-to-know' crap on you. Can Kravitz cover for you for, mm, let's say five days?"

"With the CAG AI to help, yes, sir. Okay if Kravitz briefs you a couple of times?"

"Well, his style is boring, but the stuff is good. We'll survive." He straightened and prepared to stand, the sign that Alan was being dismissed. "Talk to those people. Get me the truth. Get your friend. Then come back and write us an op plan and we'll go on with this damned cruise."

Alan faced the two older men, both standing now. The room was blue with cigar smoke. He tried to think of something to say, and finally he said what was simple and honest. "Thank you, sir."

When he was gone, the two older men looked at the door where he had vanished, and the admiral sat down, and after some seconds he said, "How far will he go to get his buddy, if he has to?"

Parsills, who had known both O'Neill and Craik in the Gulf, thought about it. "Pretty far. Real far."

The admiral nodded. "Good for him." He seemed to be talking to himself, looking inward at—the past? "Good for him . . ."

22

November

Sarajevo.

The cold in Sarajevo was vicious. There was no heat in Dukas's apartment building, or so it seemed; he slept in quilted underwear and a marine winter bag and he was always cold. Pipes froze; civilians died of carbon-monoxide poisoning from trying to stay warm with charcoal grills; the UN Officers Club was the only place that always seemed warm. Dukas dreamed of Florida, Hawaii, California. He wrote himself orders to Naples to confer with the NIS officer there, and Naples was almost as cold as Sarajevo.

"Spain, maybe?" he said when he got back. He was sitting at his desk, wearing a down-filled coat, his breath making vapor trails between his freezing hands.

"The Seychelles," Pigoreau said. He had his hands shoved into his pants pockets. He wore a fraying sweater over several turtlenecks, but somehow he looked dapper, while Dukas knew that he looked like a slob. Pigoreau had a cigarette dangling from his lower lip, as if he had learned to smoke by watching French movies. He bobbed the cigarette and elevated an eyebrow and made a quick head movement to look around his own smoke cloud. "Michael, I have something to tell you."

"Good news, I hope." A tip Mrs Obren had given them had actually resulted in an arrest. Two of Dukas's cops were

335

in The Hague, delivering the suspect—had it gone wrong?

"You told me to spend some money on informers, Michael."

"Snitches, yeah. And it's paid off." They were finally building a network; another two years, they would be on top of it. But Dukas wanted something now, something soon.

"I have a report, Michael. You will not like it." Pigoreau shrugged.

Mrs Obren. He knew it at once. Pigoreau had an expression when he talked about her—a cynical snarl, a slight grin of apology because his friend was involved with her. Using that expression now, Pigoreau put a closed file on his desk.

"Just give it to me, Pig."

"Michael, I would rather—"

"Give it to me! Summarize, for Christ's sake! I'm not a kid, Pig."

Pigoreau shrugged. He removed the cigarette, scratched his nose. He looked out the small amoebic shape of clear glass of the window, the rest of which was thick with frost on the inside. He flicked a bit of ash, holding the cigarette at his side. "I hired a guy in RS. I swear to God I didn't target her, Michael. He was some pal of Dubricoviz the farmer, the guy with the tractor. Last week this guy sends in a report a Serb was recruiting up there for a militia, about the time the partition line was drawn and he killed somebody, or he gave the order to kill somebody. Then he came back, and there was some kind of party, a lot of 'Greater Serbia' bullshit, the guy goes home with a local woman. My snitch thinks that the point of this is that the guy is a war criminal because somebody got killed." Pigoreau threw the dead cigarette to the floor and went into his turtlenecks from the top to get at the pack. "What interested me was he gave the name of the woman."

"Mrs Obren."

"You got it." Pigoreau was bent almost double, trying to get at the pack of cigarettes. When he straightened, he had one between his fingers. "That's part of it." He flicked a lighter, looked through the flame at Dukas. "The guy who was recruiting was called 'Colonel Zulu.'" Pigoreau smoked, waited, then said, "American military alphabet, Z is Zulu."

"I got it, Pig. I'm not as stupid as I look." Dukas was dead calm, colder now than the room he sat in. "Is that it?"

Pigoreau shook his head. "I went up there and saw my snitch. IFOR was running routine patrol in a couple of Bradleys, I hitched a ride, made a meeting with some Serb cops for cover. My guy says Colonel Zulu has an agent in the town. Schoolteacher. Obren's got very thick with the teacher's wife, goes there at least once a week. Reporting, I think."

"That's it?"

"Details are in the file."

"You didn't get all that in a week. How long you had her surveilled?"

Pigoreau shrugged.

"Goddamit, Pig— !"

"All along, okay? Michael, she's feeding us! That was a treat she brought us—a 'goodie,' you guys call it. She's being run from over there in RS!"

"Zulu."

"Maybe not. Zulu has gone away, my guy says. He doesn't know where, but he's gone. Anyway, he's not from RS, he's from Yugo; he thinks Belgrade but he doesn't have any proof." Pigoreau inhaled deeply of the cigarette and snatched it from his mouth and held it at his side again. "I'm sorry, Michael."

Dukas opened the file. He read quickly, reports written on Pigoreau's laptop and printed on a failing, aged printer and stored on floppies because they were afraid their desktop network was insecure. Pigoreau wrote good reports. They didn't take long to read.

"Bring her over," he said. "Cook up some excuse—a bonus for the guy we picked up, tell her we want to pay her a bonus, that'll do it. Don't scare her."

In his mind's eye, the two men between the woman's legs had become three. But one was dead or missing; the important two were Dukas and this other—the man called Zulu? He felt a surge of revulsion.

23

Late November

Kinshasa, Zaire.

Alan looked at Djalik, asleep in the webbing next to him, without envy. The vibration and noise of the aircraft drowned rational thought, which was just as well.

Alan dozed off himself. It was not the change in propeller pitch, or the rumble of tires on runway that woke him; this was a different homecoming. He felt the temperature change first, and as he swam up out of his noisy nap he felt he was surfacing from the cold, slightly mildewed life of the Navy, but as his eyes opened, his senses detected the differences: warm, moist air; delicate sweet-and-sour smell overlying the aircraft smell and the JP-5. Exhaust fumes from leaded gas. Garbage and spice and rampant vegetation, hurrying its way from bud to rot. Africa.

Alan rooted through his helmet bag as the pilot entered the terminal leg of his pattern into Kinshasa. Under 1000 AGL, he was already sweating, pumped with adrenaline. Waterproof matches. Condoms. GPS. Flashlight, the old Navy knife, twenty-five US dollars in ones. H & K 9mm and twenty-five rounds—probably against embassy regulations, but they had to catch him. Did Djalik also have something from the armory? He burrowed some more: Energy bars. Airport novel. Where the hell was his passport? Ah, side pocket. Fishing kit.

On a COD, there are no cabin services. No one talks to the passengers, who all too often sit facing the wrong way, contemplating the number of CODs that fail to survive launches or recoveries. The last plane in the US inventory designed during WWII, or so someone had once told him. Alan tried to see out the small window, as he always did, and, as always, he decided it had been designed so that he couldn't see a thing out of it.

He had been to Kinshasa during a get-acquainted trip around Africa in '93. Parsills had wanted him to take an armed marine? Kinshasa would fall pretty soon, nerves were probably running high, and the sight of even one set of US BDUs and Kevlar on the streets might have what some Africa hands still called the Liberia Effect. No, it was better to have Djalik.

There was talk he didn't like black people. So Alan had asked him, and Djalik had shrugged, "No problem," and that had to be good enough.

In Alan's experience, one gun wouldn't help much if things went bad. On the other hand, he really doubted if anything would go bad in the next four or five days. Most Africans were super-careful about Americans.

He saw a flash of landscape out his useless window just as the wheels struck the runway tarmac. BAM. BAM bam BAM. Okay, not a lot of tarmac, at that. The pilot was clearly trying to avoid the potholes, old shell holes, and other excitements that runway 140 at Kinshasa held for the visitor. They crossed 270, which was freshly re-macadamized with French asphalt by a French construction company. He wondered if only "friends of France" were allowed to land there. BAM. The pilot was doing pretty well. They were slowed now and the taxiing, while a touch erratic, was quieter.

"Screw it," Alan muttered aloud and fumbled with the

odd, non-ejection-seat toggle. He'd used these things only about fifty times. There. He stood against the swaying of the aircraft, just starting to turn on a smoother taxiway, and made his way to the window. Smog and a visible haze—fear made visible, or the fog of war? But the green, green riverbank, the brown river. The once gaudy terminal, clearly an attempt to outdo the simple strip-mall approach adopted in most African airports: Mobutu Moderne. Now it looked badly used, unmaintained, desperate. So did a great many African airports, but they had flowers and trees and beautiful women meeting the plane. Not this time. Kinshasa had the sinister air of Mogadishu in '91.

Alan didn't care. It was green; it was Africa.

They taxied to the civilian terminal. A green Chevy Blazer drove out to the plane and pulled alongside before the pilot could cut the engines. After a moment, it occurred to Alan that the pilot wasn't going to cut the engines—he didn't need gas. He'd just turn around and launch.

A crewman emerged from the cockpit area and started opening the rear gate. Alan waited as the ramp deployed, drinking in the bright sun, the glare and the shade of it. He hefted his bag. He stripped his helmet and handed it to the crewman, and the ramp hit. Alan made his way back to the two seats and put his hand on Djalik's shoulder. Djalik woke, peered down the ramp, and fumbled with his webbing as Alan walked to the rear and continued down.

They were about a hundred meters from the terminal. No customs, no immigration. Djalik appeared, fully alert now. Alan led the way to the Blazer, and the passenger door opened and Alan got in. Djalik got in the back.

"Craik?" The man was short, broad and powerful. He reached across the transmission to shake hands. "Ralph Halland. I'm with the embassy." He was wearing a short-sleeved khaki shirt and shorts and was deeply tanned.

"I'm with the embassy" means he's not with the embassy, Alan thought. *I'm* at *the embassy but I'm not* with *the embassy. What was going on? The Agency, that's what's going on.*

"Alan Craik. Navy. Anything new on O'Neill?"

"You'll be briefed." He turned to the back seat, where Djalik was arranging himself next to another man, also overweight, also in shorts—a standard, State-Department-issue American?—who shook hands all around as Halland put the Blazer in gear.

"Arnie Molnar," the second man said. "Diplomatic Security." *Meaning, not Agency, so with the embassy, and not with Halland but riding herd on him. Uh-oh.* Embassy security was handled by the Diplomatic Security Office—DS—local intelligence by the Agency. The two didn't necessarily get along.

Djalik was looking Molnar over.

"Ever train at Little Creek?" Djalik said.

"Oh, sure."

"Team Six?"

"What about it?"

"Navy SEAL."

Halland turned to Alan. "They're exchanging secret handshakes." Not said with merely guileless humor, but rather with some edge—personal dislike? Or professional distrust? *Uh-oh.*

Alan smiled, rather taken with him despite his own prejudice. "I thought *we* were supposed to do that." They chuckled, not with any real amusement.

Halland drove fast. Despite what appeared to be a fresh bullet hole in the hood, neither Halland nor Molnar appeared really stressed—no guns at the ready, no frightened eyes. Halland opened the glove compartment, took out a Coke, all while driving down a runway. He left the glove box open.

"Have one." He pointed at the glove box with his Coke can. Inside the box, next to a water-beaded can of classic Coke, was a gleamingly new Beretta.

"Not just now, thanks." Alan closed the glove box.

"Got one?" Halland muttered as he leaned back.

"Mmm, as a matter of fact, I do."

"Don't tell—" Halland's eyes flicked to the rear-view mirror.

Alan glanced in the mirror to see what Halland saw. Djalik and the DS guy were deep in some reminiscence about bars in Little Creek, Virginia.

"You bring courier stuff from your ship?"

"Yes."

"We'll talk more later." He rearranged his body on the sticky seat and, with it, his attack. "How're the Caps doing?"

Alan hadn't been asked a basketball question since he left his first cruise, but he was a good guest and had a few sports factoids at hand. Even Molnar leaned forward from the back to listen.

Alan watched as Halland turned off the runway and drove straight through a gate in the airport security fence. Bored black soldiers in ragged camos and berets watched him without interest; no weapons twitched in their direction—a nice experience at an African checkpoint. "Armed teenagers scare me," Alan said as they breezed through. Halland guffawed.

They turned down what appeared to be a major thoroughfare and drove at what Alan considered a reckless speed. Zaire's infrastructure was shot to shit—streets potholed, sewers clogged, buildings no longer maintained. Lots of uniforms were on the streets, mostly ragged; their wearers had been rioting for back pay only a week ago.

Alan turned to Halland. "Kinshasa dangerous?"

Halland laughed. "Fuck, what's dangerous? Yeah, you can get popped out there. Probably not if you're white and look tough. Planning to sight-see?"

"My admiral wants a report on local conditions."

"Get it from us." Alan wasn't sure whether this was an offer or an order.

Alan smiled. Time to do secret handshakes. He nodded at the crumbling city. "Reminds me of Mogadishu."

"You been to Mog?"

"Before it went to shit. June."

"Yeah? Ever eat at that canteen by the Canadian HQ?"

"Yeah, once or twice. Real fries, as I remember."

"Ever meet the Queen?"

Alan was puzzled for a moment. Then he got it.

"Yup. I went fishing with her off Mombasa."

Halland smiled and looked at him differently. Mostly, Agency guys had used to eat in that canteen in Mog. The Queen was a famous figure in very limited circles. They both knew it. Halland had to know who Alan was already, but, in some undeniable way, Alan was now, he thought, more acceptable. Still, he didn't like the atmosphere, the lack of play between Molnar and Halland. *And O'Neill is depending on these guys.*

The deputy ambassador's working office was not the most cheerful of rooms; indeed, the metallic official furniture, drab walls, and lack of pictures smothered any cheer that the deputy himself might have shown. The flag in the corner was the only splash of color, and it seemed faded by the strain of competing with the surrounding drabness. The two Navy men in their sage-green flight suits fit right in.

If Alan had expected a welcome, he was destined for disappointment. Within seconds of shaking his hand (and *not* shaking Djalik's hand) the deputy ambassador began a harangue about a lack of cooperation from the military. He was a weary-looking man of about fifty, probably working twenty-hour days with the ambassador away, and probably worried about how he was going to get his family out in time. Still, he was doing the obligatory State rap: he suggested in what he probably thought were civil terms that Admiral Pilchard should have visited the ambassador in person. Alan tuned out for that.

"—and that brings me back to you, Lieutenant. I don't really see why you're here."

"Lieutenant-Commander." He smiled. "My rank is lieutenant-commander."

Addicted to protocol, even capable of inventing some if required, the deputy got flustered.

"Sorry, Christ, Lieutenant-*Commander*." He smiled and looked at his watch. "Anyway, I'm still trying to see a role for you here. You don't, um, intend to mount a military expedition, do you?" He laughed, but it was clear he had just voiced his real concern. "We have to convince the Zairians that our work here is peaceful."

"I believe that my presence might be helpful solely because I know the victim and can identify him."

The ambassador snorted. "How hard can it be to identify an American in Africa?"

Alan smiled his gentle, combat smile. "Mr O'Neill is a black American."

The deputy's face fell. He was running on empty, and he was making mistakes, and obviously he despised himself for doing so. "I'm sorry," he said. And he sounded sincere. "I knew that; I just—" He looked at his watch.

"I have several classified items for your chief of station. I assume that you and he have a plan to deal with whoever has O'Neill. I don't want to interfere. Petty Officer Djalik and I would like to go with them to identify O'Neill, and, given the situation in the city, we'd like to move him to the battle group's hospital on the carrier if he needs care." The confidential tone seemed to soothe the deputy. Alan went on. "Sir, I know you're a busy man. If I could meet with the chief of station, perhaps he could get back to you—?"

The deputy ambassador cleared his throat and looked grateful.

"Yeah, right. Do that. I'll speak to Tom later and we'll see about the contact. We can't have any appearance of dealing with the factions—you understand, Lieutenant. Uh, -Commander. It jeopardizes our standing with the government." He cleared his throat. "The legitimate government of Zaire."

Alan thought that Laurent Kabila had so thoroughly jeopardized the whole of Mobutu's government that the ambassador could rest easy about who was legitimate and who was not, but he kept that thought to himself, nodded his head, kicked Djalik, and escaped.

Halland's boss, the Agency honcho, was an Old Africa Hand. He wore khaki shirts and shorts and had a tan so dark and tinged with red that it declared that the wearer seldom checked UV levels and never wore sunscreen. A large-caliber revolver in a vest-like rig hung on the wall behind his desk, where, in other offices, the President's portrait hung. Alan wondered if this was some sort of political statement. Otherwise, the man escaped being a colonial stereotype only by not offering him a drink. He was on the phone when Alan entered, and his prolonged conversation gave Alan the chance to glance at his books. *The Scramble for Africa. The Washing of the Spears.* Kind of colonial. Kenyatta's *Facing Mount Kenya* and a play of Ngugi's. Not so colonial.

"Sorry to keep you waiting, Commander. Enjoy your time with His Assistant Excellency?"

Alan smiled, said nothing.

Neither did the man in khaki. Alan lost. "I have messages for you, sir." He rifled his helmet bag and came up with two double-wrapped envelopes.

"Fuck, don't call me sir. It's Tom." He started to rip open one of the envelopes, glanced at the security stamps on the inner wrap, tore at it. "Halland says you're okay."

"I thought he was probably okay, too."

Tom guffawed. He looked around, found a glass, and poured himself a dark liquid. He raised the bottle. Alan thought, *Ooh, shit, here comes the booze*. "Iced tea?"

Chastened, Alan accepted an iced tea. Tom read his secrets and put the two envelopes aside. "Let me put you in the picture. This city is a zoo. Kabila's troops are still four hundred miles away, but the smart money is that Mobutu is finished."

"He's surprised a lot of people before."

"Yeah, well, the surprises are over. Some of the French hard-liners from the old days aren't very happy, but fuck 'em. We think they're still trying to turn the clock back. There's wheels within wheels here, Craik—good French and bad French, good Zairians and bad Zairians—and it's all been stirred with a stick. It's a mess. See, the French from the old days always backed Mobutu and the Hutus, and now they're out of the government in France, they're limp dicks up there, but they're still at it down here. Backing the Hutus, among other things."

"And the Hutus have O'Neill."

Tom grunted. "O'Neill was probably in the wrong place at the wrong time, but they really fucked up big-time, grabbing him. Now they're losing the war, and we hope they're trying to lighten the load, so they'll turn him over." His eyebrows went up and down, and he guzzled more tea. Then he looked up and said, "We're negotiating."

347

"I can identify him."

"Yeah, I was pretty excited when I heard that. Frankly, I can't believe they'd dick around with us, but they were stupid enough to grab him in the first place, and they're pissed off because the Tutsis and the Ugandans are beating the shit out of them. Ralph Halland says you've got a gun."

Alan's face gave him away.

Tom studied him and grinned. "Keep it."

"You got a plan to get O'Neill?"

"I'm waiting for a meeting that's supposed to give us a place; we've picked three spots we've already scoped out, close to Kinshasa but where the people who have him won't feel too threatened. I'm going to ask the embassy to lift the firearms restriction—right now, we're not supposed to leave the compound armed—and get me a couple of shooters to cover the meeting without going ape-shit. You ever do a hand-over? A lot can go wrong—one guy gets nervous, all of a sudden everybody's shooting. I want it to go quick and easy and then I want to get rid of O'Neill. That's where you come in and it's why I don't mind you being here: you fly him out to your carrier before it makes any press and that way everybody is happy, for once. Okay?"

Alan allowed himself a grin. Everything *was* going to be okay, and this guy was going to let him play. And he'd pick up some information to take back to the admiral. Now, if he could just suppress the tremor that was making his right calf vibrate like a jackhammer, he'd be fine.

That afternoon, Tom and Halland let him read their finished reporting, going back four weeks, and he used those reports to write an informal situation summary for the admiral. He showed it to Tom and watched him wordsmith it for an hour. He wanted to object but realized that Tom had political concerns; Tom controlled its release, so he could only accept the changes. Still, when he and Djalik sacked out that night at the Marine House, he had filed a situation brief via message traffic that might cut through some of the confusion coming from LANTFLEET—although what the message really said was that the confusion was in the embassy itself.

While Alan was still typing, somebody—not Tom and not Halland, and Alan never found out who—returned from the meeting to set up O'Neill's release. Alan went to sleep on the thought that Tom seemed to want to get O'Neill out and was apparently being as forthright as anybody who was distrusted by his boss, surrounded by violence, and unsure of Alan himself could be expected to be. Sporadic gunfire sounded through the night, although always distant. Some of it had to be coming from across the river in Brazzaville, he thought. Would they have to plan and run two simultaneous evacuation operations?

Djalik and Alan both slept late and were alone in the mess hall at 0900. Alan downed a small steak and a stack of really good pancakes, while Djalik seemed bottomless, consuming eggs, bacon, steak, and corned beef hash with a reckless disregard for the consequences. A shower and the American breakfast gave a great sense of well-being, of a protected, American-style life. The embassy compound was a little enclave, a little fortress in a very sick city. Out there were chaos, unpredictability, want; in here were order, cleanliness, plenty. Alan understood why people flocked to embassies when everything fell apart outside. But with the feeling of safety came a feeling of apartness, then inevitably of contempt.

He waited to talk until they had both finished their second cups of coffee.

"Djalik, you got a gun?"

"I understood I was here as an IS, not a shooter. Arnie says nobody here is allowed to carry, anyway." Arnie was his buddy from the back seat.

Djalik didn't ask if Alan had a gun, and he was going to tell him about the H & K when he realized that Djalik might not want to know—might not have asked deliberately. That way, he could be honest with Arnie. Meaning that if Lieutenant-Commander Craik had a gun, that was his business and he, Djalik, wouldn't be the one to rat to the embassy. Only later did he notice that Djalik had evaded his question.

He glanced at Djalik, wondered how well he knew the man. He would have to tell him before they actually went in to get O'Neill, if that's the way it went down. But better to tell him just before they went in—and after he'd lost contact with Arnie.

Alan buttered a last bite of toast and shook his head. He had lost interest in the adventure part of this. He wanted to get his friend, get on a plane, and go back to the carrier.

24

Late November

Kinshasa.

The first hint of trouble when Alan entered the office was Tom's face. He had seen it deeply tanned; now it was blotched red. Ralph Halland was leaning in a corner next to a bookshelf, and even with his arms folded he looked as if he was standing at attention.

"Morning," Alan said, nodding to Ralph. They ignored him.

"What the fuck is he thinking about?" Tom roared. This had nothing to do with Alan Craik, everything to do with embassy business. Alan started to leaf through Tom's message tray; Tom put his hand over it. "No." Alan looked at his eyes. It was a complete turnabout. Overnight. "We've been directed that you don't access our information."

This was the treatment he had feared yesterday. Today it made no sense.

Ralph spoke from his corner. "The deputy ambassador is not pleased with the message you put out last night. He said that it reflects badly on the mission here and suggests that Zaire is unstable. He also said that it was highly biased and indicated that we had misled you. He was particularly incensed by the suggestion that American and certain French interests were at odds."

Alan digested this, wishing he had another cup of coffee. "For Christ's sake, that's exactly what you told me!"

"Yeah, and that's why I'm being punished. I'm out of the loop on getting your guy back." He slid a message paper across the desk. "You didn't fuck up the whole thing. Your fucking admiral did." Alan looked at the message. Under all the headers was a short Pfor— "personal for"— LCDR Craik. Clearly, Pfors were not considered private in an embassy.

Good stuff. Get a headcount of numbers and concentrations of US, UK and Canadian citizens for possible NEO planning Kinshasa and Brazzaville. Get mission view on timeframe of possible Kabila ETA.

Get O'Neill soonest.

Regards to all. Pilchard.

Tom's face had got less red. He leaned across the table and looked Alan in the eye. "The deputy ambassador thinks any discussion of a Non-combatant Evacuation Operation is premature, here even now or in Brazzaville any time. He thinks that the admiral sending notes to his inferiors rather than messages to the embassy is rude. He wants to know why your admiral is taking so much interest in things here but not communicating with us. I don't always see eye-to-eye with him, but I kind of agree with him."

"When an admiral sends his flag intelligence officer, he *is* communicating."

"Not if you're a tight-assed Foreign Service officer! Anyway, that's history. What's bad is, my request to carry weapons to the meeting to get O'Neill was nixed. The deputy ambassador says that, to Africans, America is the land of guns, and that image needs to be changed." Tom held up a hand. The hand was quivering. Tom's face was getting blotched with red again. "I know, I know—a few of the Africans out there have guns, too, but we won't go into that. Apparently the deputy ambassador means to change America's image right now." He stood and put his hands on his hips and stared out the window for several seconds. "He's not sending us to get your guy. He's sending a junior Foreign Service officer 'to avoid misunderstandings.' *No* guns, *no* shooters, *no* backup. I hope that suits you." He glanced at Alan, shrugged. He looked ready to explode. "It may work. I view it as a recipe for disaster and made the mistake of saying so. We don't even get to *take* this young pup to the meeting. A DS guy is doing that."

Alan swallowed. "Am I going?"

"As of now, no." Alan felt outrage, suppressed it as Tom went on. "If we explain that O'Neill was a personal friend, I suspect he'll let you go—as a scapegoat if anything goes wrong, if for no other reason. That's for sure what I'd do. If you have an ounce of sense, you'll refuse. I've cabled the Director for help, but we won't get a reply before the meeting goes down."

Alan thought of O'Neill. Alone, as Alan had never been alone. Humiliated at having been taken, probably beaten, maybe maimed, maybe sick. Alan thought of what it would be like to be out there alone, and who would look out for O'Neill in this divided embassy. O'Neill had always looked after himself, but what shape would he be in after weeks with the Hutu militias?

"I want to go. Please." The words were said before the thoughts were done.

Two hours later, Alan regretted his impulse. It had become clear that nobody wanted to be part of the retrieval. Nobody wanted to be in charge, but everybody wanted to keep Alan out of that role. Nobody was doing any planning.

The green Chevy Blazer was sitting in the courtyard. The appointed embassy officer, a young blue-blood named

Thorn (*Thorn in my side?*) who sounded more English than American and seemed a little too afraid, was waiting to go. Djalik's new pal Arnie was to be the driver. The chief of embassy security was rumored to be trying to wriggle his vehicle and his man out of the whole thing, but nobody would confirm that. If he succeeded, what were they going to do, hitchhike?

Alan thought of the time that went into planning an air strike. Teams of planners. Maps. Briefings. Here, there was nothing—not even a chat over coffee. Alan knew from Harry that the Agency didn't do things this way.

He tried unsuccessfully to see the deputy ambassador, and then he tried, first through Ralph and then through the military attachés, to send a message to the boat. He met a freeze: the attachés were out doing their jobs. Two were on home leave. He was what is officially called SOL—Shit Out of Luck.

Alan found himself sitting in an empty Navy office, wishing the attaché were there to help him and staring at a telephone as if he could make it produce its owner. Then he realized that the ALUSHNA, the naval attaché, had left his key in his secure phone. Alan turned the key. Nobody came on to ask questions or to challenge him. He dialed a digit. The phone waited for more. Whom could he call who could patch him to the boat? No way to patch a telephone to the boat—unless it was to the pay phone sailors used to call home. *Well, any port in a storm.* He dialed the twenty-four-hour watch number at LANTCOM.

It took him two minutes to persuade a harried petty officer to let him speak to the senior watch officer, and the senior watch officer to connect him to the INMARSAT line to the *Jackson*—the satellite hookup to the public phone on the squadron personnel's level. After eleven seemingly endless rings, he got a junior bosun's mate, and he persuaded him to walk up three decks and find somebody from the intelligence center. Finally, he heard movement at the other end of the phone.

"Commander Scott." The CAG AI.

"Sir? This is Alan Craik."

"Jesus, Alan, where are you? What the hell are you doing calling on the—"

"I'm on the beach. Where I'm supposed to be. This is an open line."

"Got it. What's happening?"

"Sir, I'm going to retrieve my package and I'm not too happy about the mission planning and the strike package, if you get me."

Long pause—Trans-Atlantic transmission time via satellite, then thought.

"Okay Al, I think I read that. What can I do?"

He wanted to say, *Tell the admiral I'm in over my head,* but the words wouldn't help anything, and he wasn't sure he should even say "admiral" on an open line. "Tell my boss that the situation within these walls is such that I can't send any more faxes, and I plan to get out of here as soon as possible."

Long pause.

"That bad? Our guys or their guys?"

Long pause.

"Not guys in uniform. Not strangers."

Long pause.

"I got it. Do what you have to, Al. Do you need anything?"

Long pause.

"A COD at 2130. If I need it sooner I'll call back. Give me the number where you are, sir?"

"Wait one. Uh—hold it— It's scrawled down the side.

01131236571119. Does that sound right?" Longer pause, with echoes. "The guy behind me in line says it's the right number. His ombudsman handed it out before cruise. Why don't *we* have an ombudsman?"

"Thank you, sir." Alan waited. He felt tied to his ship, to his whole way of life, by that scratchy thread of sound.

"Keep your head down and get your ass back here, mister!" Hanging up sounds.

Alan took a deep breath. He put the number in his wallet. *Okay*—the COD would be here to whisk them back to the ship. Now he had to try to get O'Neill on it. He looked at his watch. The meeting—if there was a meeting—was supposed to go down in two hours.

He went back to the Marine House and changed into shorts and the khaki shirt he had bought at REI, way back—when? A month ago. Seemed like ten years ago. *Rose. Mikey. Saying goodbye*— He put on athletic socks and light hiking boots. Grabbed his helmet bag—gun, cartridges, first-aid kit—flashlight, GPS, fishing kit, *What the hell is the fishing kit for?*—jacket, boonie hat, bug repellent—malaria pills— Swiss Army knife—

Then he went back to Tom's office. Empty.

Alan looked for Ralph Halland, for a secretary.

Nobody. Conveniently away. On the wall next to Tom's desk was a clump of local cell phones. Several had names taped to them, one still wrapped in its original plastic, no name on it. *Mine, now.* He dropped it in his helmet bag, followed it with a battery. *You never knew what you might need away from the embassy compound.*

He went down to the vehicle and found Djalik already there, dressed very much like Alan, in Africa-practical civilian clothes, baggy shorts. Was now the time to tell him about the gun?

"I called the boat. We got a COD at 2130."

"No problem."

"This could be the biggest cluster-fuck since Little Big Horn."

"I figured that out, sir." Djalik held up a plastic box the size of a laptop, with a red cross taped on it. "Medical kit. You never know." He smiled. The smile was ambiguous—was it really a medical kit?

He wanted to say more, but the DS driver, who was checking something under the hood, smiled at Alan. *Meaning he's supposed to keep an eye on me. The theory is that Djalik is already no problem.*

Djalik lowered his voice. "Commander—you packing?"

Alan thought about it. "Not on my body."

"In the helmet bag?"

"That's right."

"You better give it to me." Djalik seemed to be merely stating a fact. He was wearing sunglasses; he now turned those expressionless surfaces toward him. "That's the first place they'll look."

"They'll be Hutu militia. They won't find it. I've put cigarettes on top; that's all those guys will want." He sounded, he thought, more confident than he looked.

"Commander, if you want to trust your life to a pack of cigarettes, that's fine with me. I don't." He held out his hand where Arnie, at the front of the car, couldn't see it. Alan was going to argue—he'd never had anybody find squat at an African checkpoint. (But, then, it was true that nobody had ever been motivated to look very hard.) And then he thought about which of them would really be better with the gun if things went to hell. He had played a fair amount of playground basketball in his youth. He had never been able to shoot, not close, not far. He had learned to take the ball in close and pass, even if he was open to shoot. Any SEAL could shoot better than he could,

357

and it was probably the last chance to pass before the game ended.

And then Arnie slammed the hood, meaning he was getting ready to go. Alan thrust his hand down into the bag and handed the H & K to Djalik.

"Don't stand in the line of fire. If I give you a shove, go." Djalik put the pistol down the back of his shorts.

"Jeez, that's cool," Alan said. "They'll never look there, right?" He was angry. At that point, Arnie joined them.

"You guys ride in the back. Mr Thorn will ride up front with me."

Thorn came out carrying a briefcase and wearing a seersucker sport coat, unconstructed, very Eastern Establishment. He looked as if he might be heading for a weekend at Bar Harbor. He also looked scared shitless.

Nobody saw them off. No ambassador, no team. No backup. No plan, no fallback, no counter-surveillance. Just Mr Thorn, who couldn't have been a day over twenty-five.

They rolled out of the compound, the local rent-a-cops at the gate staring at them while the hydraulic gate came up as if they had just arrived from Saturn. Djalik's friend kept reading a map on the steering wheel; after twenty minutes he handed the map back. Alan looked at the route that somebody had drawn in grease pencil—well, at least there had been that much planning.

Nobody had told him where the meeting was to be. Now he saw that it was well out along the river, and he saw, too, that they were going to be late. He kept his silence and continued to pretend to himself that these people knew what they were doing.

Around them on the dirty, crowded streets, crowds moved with purpose. The car drove by an army unit doing some sort of PE, strong, tall men, running smoothly through the streets.

Finally, they cleared the city. Badly paved streets gave way to a badly paved road. Shanties pressed against one side, and, on the other, tiny plots of tilled ground and small teashops, mostly built from crates, started where the broken macadam gave way to dust. Whenever the traffic stopped them, small boys waving bottles of Coca-Cola approached the car. Ignoring Thorn's disapproval, Alan rolled down his window and bought four bottles. A cleaner Africa entered as the air-conditioning escaped.

The Coke was too sweet. Thorn refused to drink it, anyway. No doubt Thorn, bringing the siege mentality of the embassy with him, believed that the local version came right out of the nearest gutter.

Then they got stuck facing a wall of what he took to be refugees streaming down the road from Kanindi. They still had ten miles to go.

"We're late." There, he had said it.

Thorn didn't even turn his head. "They have to know their place."

Alan didn't quite know how to react to this. *Place? Did he—could he—mean place, as in, knowing your place?* "What place is that, Thorn?"

"They don't represent a country, or a recognized negotiating platform. This is not an official meeting. They need to know that we aren't following their schedule." Thorn's fears were muted in his voice, but very much present. Alan thought he was parroting instructions.

"Why?"

Thorn turned his head and looked at Alan with adolescent scorn.

"You have no function with these people except to ID your buddy, and I don't believe you know what the stakes are here, and I'm fully briefed. Don't interfere. I'm in charge."

That's what parents spend their money for at places like Choate and Andover—for people to teach their kids to speak with utterly convincing authority, even when they're scared witless and hardly out of diapers and don't know shit from shinola about what they're saying. It was an ability that kept the British Empire going for half a century after it should have fallen down.

Alan smiled back—pleasantly, at least to anybody who didn't know him very well. "Please tell me if I can help in any way."

The silence that seemed to follow Alan around Africa filled the car.

They were more than an hour late when the car emerged from the stream of people at a bridge, passed through a Zairian Army checkpoint where the young soldiers seemed to have given up hope, and turned right up a smaller, red-earth road. Alan figured that they traveled a mile before they saw the building. It was large, made of corrugated iron, and it, like Zaire, had seen better days. Two men in fatigues were smoking outside. Alan was relieved that they weren't wearing hoods.

Thorn rolled down his window, and a blast of afternoon Zaire entered, completely replacing the dry cool air of officialdom that had filled the car. Alan could smell wood smoke and vegetation.

"Mr Hatusis sent me," Thorn called out. The two men looked at each other. One went inside and the other stood without reply.

Djalik and Arnie had seemed like different men since they had left the city. Their eyes moved constantly, little movements, economical but thorough. Djalik spoke without moving his head.

"Guys in the grass on the left."

"Got 'em. Ain't friendly."

A whistle sounded, dimmed through the auto glass. Men stood up around the car. Many were dressed in rags. Most had guns. Alan noted with some relief that many of the guns were AK-47s with no magazine in the receiver. Still, enough seemed to have magazines to kill all of them several times over.

One man approached the car. He was small, round-headed, balding, seemingly embarrassed, but he wore a suit and a tie, and he had shoes on his feet.

"Which of you is Ralph, please?" he said in very clear, if accented English.

"I am Mr Thorn." Thorn sounded piqued, as if someone at Mummy's party had failed to recognize him.

"Please, then, get out of the car, Mr Thorn. We have to take a small trip."

"No trip! The meeting is to take place here."

"Yes, yes—trip. Small trip."

"What trip? Where? Show me on the map."

"I am sorry, sorry Mr Thorn. But—no. Please get out of your car now, please." The guns were steady, whether they had magazines or not. Alan could see that Thorn's neck was trembling.

Alan got out of the car. So did Djalik. His friend Arnie did not, because two men were leaning against his door. The DS guy appeared relaxed behind the wheel, nonetheless, as if he was just in there because he meant to take a nap and not because two tough ones were holding the door shut with their buns. Alan wondered then if he was armed, remembered the ambassador's orders, wondered again if the guy was either so obedient or so butt-stupid he wasn't packing. *Some security.*

Somebody came up to Alan from behind and ran a hand

down his back and between his legs. Alan felt a gun barrel in his back. Very real. *Little Big Horn*. Another man stood in front of him and pulled open the helmet bag and looked in; seeing the cigarettes, he grinned. He pulled at the bag; Alan pulled back; he swung his AK up.

Thorn emerged from the car, still bitching.

The small man who spoke English hurried over to Alan and struck down the AK, said something to the soldier, the words coming rat-a-tat, and the man let go of the bag; the small one took it from Alan and said with what seemed to be sincerity, "I will take care of this. It will be given back to you afterward—no question. No problem."

Right.

Djalik was being searched by a soldier who knew his business better than the one who had run his hands down Alan's back. This guy found the H & K in the back of Djalik's shorts in about two seconds. He said something and another man laughed, and the small one came over, holding Alan's helmet bag open as if he was collecting for the needy, and the H & K disappeared into it. "No need," the man said to Djalik. "No need whatsoever. Unwise." He took Djalik's medical kit and opened it and walked away, studying the contents.

Alan looked at Djalik. Did he shrug? And if he did, what did it mean—nice try? Better luck next time? C'est la goddam vie?

He began to look around him. He noted two other cars, an ancient Citroën and a slightly less old Land-Rover. There were at least twenty soldiers—FAZ—Zairian Army, he thought, not Hutu militia.

Thorn was unhappy and got strident when the man who spoke English put a bag over his head. Cloth, maybe once a pillowcase, ancient stripes now faded to gray. Thorn tried to take it off, and another man held his wrists the way Africans hold the wrists of an out-of-control child, not chastising, keeping it from hurting itself or somebody else.

Alan looked at Djalik. Djalik looked serenely back.

The English speaker approached them.

"We are going to take you to the meeting now, please. You are also from the embassy?"

Alan took the plunge. "I am here to identify the man who is to be exchanged."

The man turned to Djalik. "You are medical?"

"I'm all they got," Djalik growled. Alan thought that it was the best half-truth he had ever heard. Behind him, somebody was climbing into the Blazer from the passenger's side with a gun pointing at the DS man's head. The two who had been leaning against the door had got out of the way and were looking on with interest, one of them apparently getting ready to crawl into the back. It looked as if Arnie was going for a ride. Alan looked at Djalik. Djalik made one of those ambiguous faces: *He can take care of himself, I guess.*

"I have to blind you, please. Not long." Alan thought the blinding was a good sign. It suggested that they were not going to be killed. Or did it make killing them easier?

They moved toward the Citroën.

The car seemed to go very fast, and the potholes were thick, and they bounced, whacking down to the bottom of the springs, then up so that once he hit his head on the roof. Alan began to be able to see through the thin black cloth, just a little light and not much more. He wondered where Thorn was, why he was in a different car. It didn't matter.

Time passes differently when you are deprived of sight. He had no idea how long they drove, and he thought he might have dozed off. He wasn't sure. Not likely. Djalik was snoring deeply—real or fake? At any rate, the ride was a lot longer than "not long," and he figured they might have come thirty or forty miles—that maybe it had been an hour, over bad roads, at an unwise speed.

The driver ground the gears going into reverse. Alan heard him set the emergency brake and get out, then the English voice telling them to get out. As Alan emerged, someone took his shoulder and turned him, steadied him, and then lifted the hood away. The light made him blink, even the beautiful pre-evening light of equatorial Africa.

They were by a river. The grass was brown. That was what he saw first. A baboon was screaming in a tree across the river. Doves were cooing close by. He looked around.

They were parked by a tiny airstrip—a line of red dirt angled at the river. He saw a small, two-engined plane on the field, recognized it as an ASTRA Nomad, the all-purpose African workhorse. A man was tinkering with one engine. As Alan watched, the man turned and watched as another car, the green Land-Rover, pulled up and Thorn was led out. Their Blazer was pulling in behind. Alan and Djalik headed that way, nobody trying to stop them. In fact, everybody seemed focused on Thorn. *They think he's the Agency guy, poor bastard. Better him than me.*

The new lot of soldiers here looked very different from the last, good uniforms and boots, every man with a weapon and clips, several with side arms. Hutu Interahamwe.

The man who spoke English said, "We will now all board the aircraft, please?"

Thorn looked at him, his mouth slightly open. He shook his head. "Where is the American—O'Neill?"

"We take you to him."

"Bring him here."

"That is not the arrangement."

Thorn turned on Alan. "Turn around and start walking back to the car. Ours is the last in line."

Alan looked at the plane. He watched a bird, off beyond the runway, circling slowly in the still air of the evening. He leaned past Thorn and directed his question to the man in the suit. "Where are you taking us?"

"Nowhere!" hissed Thorn. "We are walking away."

"Vicinity Kisangani," said the officer. "Long flight, but—" He looked at the aircraft, made a face. "Not too uncomfort-able." Pronouncing it *uncomfort-able* and then giggling.

"These people have no diplomatic standing!" Thorn said. His voice was going up. "I don't have clearance to travel out of Kinshasa, and I won't!" He started to walk away. No one moved to stop him, and Alan guessed that nobody had instructions for this behavior. They were here to take the Americans to get the CIA man, period; if the Americans didn't want to come—well, if the French were pushing them into this, they'd have done their part, even if the Americans hadn't, right?

Djalik had one eyebrow raised in question. Alan supposed that the Hutus wanted to turn O'Neill over in their own territory, up where there was no danger of retaliation. Maybe stage some kind of minor tantrum to show that they couldn't be pushed around. Kisangani was where the bulk of Mobutu's defense forces and all of his Hutu allies were, as well as half a million Hutu refugees who had been swept ahead of the soldiers as they retreated westward. He thought about this, tried to put himself into the Hutus' place.

"Djalik, I'm going. You go back."

Djalik wiped his face with his whole left hand, a habit Alan was learning indicated frustration. Djalik shook his head, then looked beyond Alan at the two Americans climbing into the Blazer. He scratched at his crotch.

"Sir, my ass is grass if I leave you here."

"I'll make it an order. Give me something I can write on—"

Djalik turned and stood very close to Alan. Alan could feel his breath on his face, smell it—slightly sour. "You get in that aircraft with those ape-faces, you're dead meat. Sir."

"Djalik, he's my friend and I can't leave him. You can." He was patting his pockets, looking for a piece of paper. "For you, it's just duty. For me, it's my best friend. And duty comes second to friends." Alan was surprised by his own words. He meant them, but he hadn't measured them before they came out. "Give me some paper, I'll write you orders. The COD will be in tonight; you can still get on it. Tell the *Jackson* I'll communicate after I get O'Neill."

The small man in the suit looked at him and then at the Chevy Blazer, where Thorn and Arnie were already sitting, and he gestured with his chin toward it. "That man?"

"He says he can't exceed his instructions. He can't go. Mine were different. I'm an officer in the US Navy and I will come with you. Do you have a sheet of paper?"

The question flustered him, but he went into his pockets and came out with a folded, not very clean piece of paper and a ballpoint pen. He scratched out some words at the top of the paper.

"And your companion?"

Alan was writing, using Djalik's back as a desk. *You are ordered to proceed immediately to Kinshasa embassy—* "I felt it better that he return to the embassy. I am writing his orders."

The soldiers were getting on the aircraft. Alan had to raise his voice to be heard over the engines. He handed

Djalik the paper and, grasping the elbow of the small black man, started toward the plane.

When he turned back at the entry hatch, Djalik was boarding behind him.

25

Late November

Zaire.

"Why'd you come, Djalik?"

"You need a keeper."

"No, Dave, I don't. I've done this sort of thing before."

"Yeah? Me too. A little more often. And sir, with respect, you strike me as a dangerous glory hound. Someone without enough training to be in this shit."

They were crammed in the back end of the plane. Two of the soldiers sat facing them. Nobody seemed to care that they were talking, or that their position was anomalous— not well-treated guests, but not prisoners, either.

"Dave, I'm going for my friend. That's all."

"I got a wife and two kids, sir. And don't call me 'Dave' when it suits you. I got out of this business so that I could look my wife in the eye and tell her that I'd come back. And I don't give two shits about your friend! My family comes first. You're going for friendship! Great! Tell my wife about it. Because I *have* to come with you. Hear me? If you scrape through this and get another medal, and you leave me face-down in goddam Africa, go tell my wife it was for your friend. I'm sure she'll understand."

It was the most he'd ever heard Djalik say. Outside, true night fell.

* * *

After three hours, they were blindfolded. Even with a full moon, the night was so black that they might have been flying over water, and Alan knew he would never have been able to pick up a landmark, anyway.

Then he thought that they flew for another hour before he heard the flaps move and knew they were beginning an approach. The plane turned twice, both times to the left, and then began a sharp descent. He felt them go through some invisible barrier where the ground could be sensed, where the air had moisture and taste, even inside the black sack. Then the wheels hit and they were down.

When the plane stopped taxiing, he heard scrambling from the soldiers and then he was grabbed and forced to his feet and marched out to the hatch and down the ladder. He heard other airplane motors and what sounded like the whine of helicopter turbines. He could smell wood smoke, strong, acrid. Then he was pushed into a vehicle. Something bumped his head.

They didn't drive for more than a minute before the vehicle stopped. Again, hands grabbed him and propelled him through a door that he hit with his shoulder. He was pushed into a chair, his hands left free. He decided to try removing his blindfold. Nobody stopped him. He and Djalik were seated in a small room. Battered folding chairs leaned against the walls. They looked at each other. "Here we are," Alan said. "Wherever 'here' is."

The door opened and a small, very black man in button-less green fatigues entered with a tray. He gave them both coffee, then shuffled out in sandals made from old tires.

"Coffee's not bad," said Djalik.

"You didn't have to come." Alan sounded more aggress-ive than he had intended.

"Belay that." Djalik sounded serious, but no longer angry. "What's going down, you think?"

He thought they were in some small airfield building, maybe a hangar, because the voices from the other side of the wall echoed. Beyond the voices were the sounds of aircraft, the high whine of the helicopters continuing, as if they were waiting but staying ready to lift off. Beyond the aircraft sounds were distant pops of small arms, intermittent and impossible to read, but in the middle of the night, people up here didn't shoot for fun. The powerful wood smoke smell meant that they were in the midst of the refugees, whose fires were probably visible from the air, the reason they had been blindfolded. He told Djalik all these things. "I think they mean to turn him over. They wouldn't bring us this far just to dick us; the word is they have to get rid of him. So I think we play it straight, probably listen to a harangue, keep our mouths shut. This is one area where I know more than you, okay? If there's talking to be done, let me do it. I don't want any—"

Two voices were shouting in French beyond the sheet-metal wall. Alan's French was rusty, not great at best, but he could hear tone, and he thought that what he heard was anger. Was it O'Neill? Somebody shouting at O'Neill? Or somebody arguing about O'Neill? There were two voices, one high-pitched and enraged, the other deeper, colder, but equally angry.

"What's up?" Djalik said.

"Something about the helicopters. One of them keeps shouting 'Blancs, blancs'—whites. Maybe he means us."

"He doesn't sound happy."

Alan listened. He thought he heard *lâche*—coward. Maybe plural, cowards. White cowards? Were he and Djalik white cowards? Then the high-pitched voice came through loud and clear, "*Allez, allez, sauvez-vous! Foutez-vous, lâche blanc! Laissez-nous à notre afrique sanglante, traître!*" And then a crash of metal—something thrown? Dropped?

And then silence.

"The one with the high voice told the other one to go fuck himself, go away, um—something about bleeding Africa—save yourselves, you white cowards—"

The small man came in and took a stack of the folding chairs, a look of terror on his face. Alan got up and walked to the door. There was, in fact, a hangar beyond it.

The hangar was made of sheet-iron over a rusty welded frame. It must have been an oven when the sun was overhead, he thought. There was a door, permanently open for so long that the dirt had piled an inch higher than its bottom edge, and inside it the remains of a concrete floor. Lots of oil had been spilled on it over the years, and lots of birds had been up in the rusted framework, adding their droppings to the mess below. All the way across the hangar from the small door where he stood, the big doors through which planes were meant to enter were almost closed, and through the opening between them he could see darkness.

There were no aircraft in the hangar. There were parts of what might have been aircraft, or perhaps old cars, or just possibly agricultural machinery from the Bronze Age. All were the leavings of the wrecked, what was left after, first, abandonment, and, second, repeated looting. What was remarkable about the hangar was not anything about aviation, in fact, but about civil war: a table stood in the very middle, and the man with the chairs was arranging them like seats in a French court. There was one light, the kind of yellow work light that cops set up at an accident scene, and now the muffled pucket-a-pucket-a of a generator. A flag that Alan could not identify was hanging from a steel rafter above the table.

In the far corner of the hangar, out of the light, a tall black man and a muscular white man in a dark uniform were scowling at each other. Half a dozen black soldiers by the opening in the big doors looked tense, maybe frightened, and two white soldiers behind the white man actually had their fingers on the triggers of their assault rifles.

He stepped back into the little room. "I think we got a problem. There're white mercs out there; that's gotta be what the shouting's about. I think they're pulling out."

"So?"

"So let's hope they go before somebody starts shooting. Zairian Army started shelling one of the white barracks last week because those white guys are pulling down a couple thousand American dollars a month each, and the locals haven't been paid their ten bucks a month for a year." He chewed his lips. "Bad timing."

The shouting stopped. When he looked out again, neither the tall black man nor the white one was there, and Hutu militiamen were standing by the opening in the doors, trying to joke, smoking cigarettes that Alan guessed were from his helmet bag.

Then the small man who spoke English appeared. "Come, please."

There was a man in one of the folding chairs, way over against the hangar wall, out of the light. His hands were secured in front of him, but he was slumped over so far that there didn't seem to have been any point in restraining him. In fact, he looked asleep or dead. He was only a shape, but Alan guessed that if O'Neill was really there, he was this wretched figure in the chair.

They were prodded into place, facing the table. They had two guards, each with an Ingram M-10 submachine gun. Djalik studied one of them with a professional's interest, even flashed the guy a smile. No response.

Black men in green fatigues began to fill in the chairs,

five of them, and the tall, angry man who had argued with the white man walked slowly to the table, and the hangar fell silent. He sat and all of the other men sat. Alan's and Djalik's possessions had appeared on the table in front of him—helmet bag, first-aid kit, H & K P-9. There was also a rough stack of papers.

The tall man began to speak in French. The English speaker, standing between Alan and the table, translated.

"He tells you he is Colonel Peter Ntarinada of the Grande Armée Rwandaise. He has summoned this court-martial to try a man here, Mr Harold O'Neill, for espionage and treason against the Hutu people and the people of Rwanda." He pointed at the unconscious figure. "Over there, that man."

So that was Harry. Alan tried to make out something, but the figure was in near-darkness.

The tall one, Ntarinada, ruffled through the papers.

"This man O'Neill, he, um, claims to be an American, we allow—*are* allowing you to watch these, ah, happenings." The translator knew this word was wrong but didn't have the right one. Alan silently supplied *proceedings*.

Alan thought of Thorn and played his part, but in a flat voice, almost as if he was translating from another language, himself. "I must protest. I was not told of these proceedings, and I am not here as a representative of the American embassy. If your prisoner is an American, I request his instant release."

He braced and looked Ntarinada in the eye as his words were translated. Ntarinada smiled, spoke. "We have a, um, *pas compris*, um, miscomprehension. If you are not here for the embassy, you have no wish to see the prisoner?"

Alan smiled and pretended a confidence he did not feel. "If the prisoner is an American, you have no right to detain him, sir. America is not a combatant here."

Ntarinada's voice rose until he was shouting; his right

hand banged on the table, found the H & K, rested on it. Alan got the drift before the translator did. "The prisoner is a traitor to the people of Rwanda. He seduced a woman into betrayal of her blood and people. He attempted to prevent the liberation of the Hutu people. He is an agent of the Central Intelligence Agency and the so-called Rwandan People's Army. He has admitted guilty to all charges. We have his confession, many times. Do you understand, sir?"

There was movement in the opening of the big doors. Alan began speaking, but his eyes flicked aside and saw the same white man come in, with two others behind him. The black soldiers got out of his way. Alan went on, but he watched the whites, because the atmosphere had changed as they appeared. Something flared outside and he saw the man's profile. *The witch's nose.*

"Please address me by my correct military title, if you please. I am Lieutenant-Commander Alan Craik of the United States Navy."

Several of the officers murmured. He had intended that the rank legitimize him for them, move them toward the exchange, military to military. For a moment, it seemed to; even Ntarinada looked impressed, perhaps relieved. Then the white mercenary was coming forward into the light. There was a little rustle of movement, as if a wind had scattered dry leaves across the broken concrete. Alan felt Djalik push against his right side. *What the hell?* He didn't get it. The pressure came again, harder, and he remembered, *If I move you, go*, but he was thinking *He doesn't have a gun, what does he want to clear the line of fire for?* Even as he was swaying to the left, then taking a half-step, feeling the tension around him rise.

Ntarinada had been haranguing them right through this; the translator started on what he'd said:

"—an apology from your government to the Hutu People, you will write, you will, um, make your signing, your name—for the United States of America—if you do not make apology, I will kill him."

"*Pardon, mon Colonel—n'est pas le projet—*" It was one of the others at the table. Now the white mercenary was listening, too; he had a stake in this, it seemed. But his eyes flicked back to Alan, and now their eyes met. For Alan, it was like watching a dangerous animal in the wild, not knowing why there should be enmity but feeling it. *Alan flashed on the dark corridor in Bosnia. Crooked nose.*

Ntarinada shouted in Hutu. His tone was savage. The other man shook his head.

The other officers wanted to release Harry. *This is not the plan,* the officer had said. To kill Harry, he meant.

The white merc went closer to Ntarinada. "*Dépêchez-vous; il faut partir.*" *Hurry up; we have to leave.* As if he gave the orders there. Ntarinada's head snapped around and he snarled something. They were isolating Ntarinada—dangerous.

"I am prepared to offer an apology," Alan said smoothly, "but I have not seen any evidence of a crime." He didn't know what the ramifications of apologizing might be, but if the other officers at the table wanted to get an apology and turn over O'Neill, he was going to throw them a bone; the hell with protocol. *That white man was the war criminal, Zulu.*

The pop-pop sound of shooting was far away, but it made a steady background to the transaction. The soldiers in the opening were growing restive, staring out into the dark and fingering their weapons. One of them turned, called something into the hangar. Men started to get up from the table, and the one who had already spoken said something to Ntarinada, pointing at the slumped figure against the wall and then at Alan, making an insistent gesture, and Alan raised his voice over the noise and said, because he could feel it going out from under his feet like sand, feeling the pace accelerate and the tension rise, feeling it go to the brink and then start over, "Please— !"

And the white mercenary whirled on him and started to draw his side arm from a flapped holster, and Alan had time to think only, *It is him,* and he saw Ntarinada move, too, startled by the white man's move for his pistol, and he reached for the H & K on the table.

Then Djalik's hand was in his groin and then out and he shot the first guard in the head, the snout of a Colt Mustang pressed against the temple, and he stripped the man's machine pistol over his head as he fell. Birds rose in the rafters, a great clatter of wings. Djalik shot the second guard before the first hit the ground and before the mercenary's pistol had cleared his holster, another head shot at point-blank range, and he turned with the second man so that he had the sagging body between him and the table, and the mercenary fired into the guard's body trying to hit Alan, and Djalik shot once and dropped to the floor, bringing up the M-10. Other shots roared and echoed in the metal hangar, and in the gloom beyond the circle of light the shots flashed in inches-long tongues of fire. Ntarinada rolled away from the table, into the confusion of officers panicking behind him, but Alan was diving at the table, at one man still trying to get to his feet. Alan's weight threw the table over and he landed in a tangle with them, the table between him and the white man as he was thinking, *Zulu.* Djalik was moving again. One of the guards behind the table fired, and the other tried to get his muzzle up toward him, but Djalik stepped inside the arc of the barrel and shot him from inches away and then shot his partner under the third victim's arm. Those were the five rounds from the tiny .380, and the first body was still thumping on the floor.

Alan had no idea whom he was fighting. They had all landed in a heap, and he was fighting the way a marine gunny had taught him, with his elbows and knees and fingernails, trying to tie them down so they wouldn't shoot Harry. There were three of them. Alan got his left hand on a face and thumped it savagely on the floor. A knee hit him in the groin and the world exploded and he was flung back against the tabletop. He held on to a pair of shoulders and heard two more quick shots. Nearly blind with pain, Alan had no idea that Ntarinada had just shot the English translator, trying to hit Zulu. *Oh, God, Harry!* he thought—that slumped figure, helpless in its chair—

Djalik fell on his back, with the body of his third victim on top of him, and fired the M-10 into the clump at the hangar doors.

Alan found a pistol under his thigh and pulled the slide, pointed it blindly and fired. His breath was coming in gasps and his vision was tinged with red. The kick to the groin hurt like fire. His victim's last breath was hot and foul in his face. Alan thrust with his legs and pushed himself toward where Harry should be. Ntarinada was gone. Alan fired at a white man going out the hangar door, hit a second who had turned to fire.

He looked around the side of the table, breathed, and shot at a black man who put his head in the opening in the hangar doors.

Djalik was slamming a new clip into the M-10.

Silence and cordite hung in the moist air. Then the moans started. Alan continued to watch the opening. The world hung suspended.

"Nothing behind us, Djalik."

"Hangar secured, sir. Where'd that white motherfucker go?"

Alan scuttled on hands and knees toward the figure who was supposed to be O'Neill, fearing he had been shot, seeing him on the floor, the chair tipped over. *Christ no*, he prayed. His groin hurt; he pushed through it and came to the quiet body and put his hand out.

"Harry?" He felt for a pulse. The man stank, urine and shit and clothes that had been slept in for weeks. Alan raised his head, feeling the matted hair, holding it, gripping it as if the twisting of the hairs would wake the man.

"Harry?"

He thought then that it wasn't Harry, that it was a joke, a trick. It certainly didn't look like Harry. The face was swollen, the lips so enlarged they looked like grotesque balloons. The right eye was swollen mostly shut. Alan rolled the head to see the other eye and was nauseated by what he saw: a red, staring eyeball without lids. The socket had infected and the skin above it was swollen with pus, crusted with blood and scabs. He had seen it before, in the torture chamber of Pustarla. Zulu.

"Oh, Jesus, Harry, what have they done to you!" he cried.

He put his face against the bruised cheeks. He felt tears on his face, knew they were his own. "Harry—Harry—" And he reached down into his memory for the word that would wake this wreck, and said, "Creole? Hey, Creole— it's Spy— !"

The good eye cracked open. The eyeball rolled toward him.

"Oh, Harry— ! Goddamit— !"

Djalik's voice cut in. "We gotta move outa here! Some

asshole's gonna roll a grenade through that door—" The light went out. "Come on, let's move— !"

Alan tried to move back to the opening in the combat glide the gunny had taught him, but his knees were still shaky and his balls ached. Djalik had closed the door to the room where they had waited, then blocked it with two bodies. Somebody Djalik had shot moaned and gave a little burbling scream. He was gut shot, and the contents of his guts added to the hangar's reek. Djalik, his eyes on the area outside the hangar, stooped by the wounded man, drew the man's side arm, and shot him in the head. He had never even looked down.

"That your friend?"

"Yeah."

"He gonna be able to walk?"

"I don't know."

"He goddam well better be able to walk; they aren't flying us outa here after this shit. Anyway, they're all shooting each other out there now. There's two white guys dead out on the concrete; I didn't put 'em down."

Alan took out his magazine. He had somehow ended up with his own pistol. Where had he fired nine shots? He sat by the hangar entrance and pushed cartridges from one of the downed guards into the magazine.

"Why did you shoot that wounded man?"

"You can't turn your back on them. Come on, sir, let's get your guy and go."

Alan wanted to praise Djalik, to tell him how stunned he was that any one man could take on so many and win, but the words didn't come. He found it hard to praise the killing. Finally he said, "Thanks. Nice job."

He felt his way to the upended table, flashed his light, found his helmet bag. Everything in it was intact: the little man who had spoken English had kept his word. Not even the cigarettes. A small man of honor, who had wanted these white outsiders to see that his people were upright, too. Alan flicked the light around, found the man's body. A decent, small man who had got between the killers. Alan thought then of the white man who had started the shooting and wondered what had gone on between them that had been so deadly—between him and Alan, him and Ntarinada, Ntarinada and Harry; Hutu and Tutsi; white and black—and a small man with the decency to keep his word had got a bullet in the temple. Alan moved the flashlight and saw Ntarinada, lying dead at the small man's feet. He had been hit repeatedly. Perhaps his officers had had enough.

He gathered a couple of the weapons clips. "We need water," he said.

"Belay that." Djalik went to Harry, flashed a light on him for one second, then stooped and raised his torso. Alan took the legs; they propped Harry up, and Djalik bent his knees and lifted him in a fireman's carry. "We're outa here." Alan got ahead of him—through the small room, out the back, into the darkness. They settled again into a metal outbuilding fifty yards along.

Alan shone his own light on Harry's face. His eye was open.

"Harry?"

The ruined mouth twisted. Tears were coming out of both eyes, the giant red one and the other. Alan knew that the monster eye was the result of the eyelids' having been cut off.

"Let me," Djalik said. "Stay by that door and shoot anybody comes close. You shoot an AK?" He handed over an AK-47. There was more shooting outside now, and Alan could see movement on the airfield. There was little light and no moon.

"Keep your eyes moving," Djalik said. He had the medical kit over by Harry and was swabbing Harry's arm. "I'm giving him a lot of morphine. I mean a *lot*."

"Can we wash him?"

"Sure, and serve him ice cream when we're done. His pants are full of shit because somebody beat him up, probably yesterday. He isn't gonna die of shit. Neither are you. Sir."

"How bad is he?"

"No idea. Tell you tomorrow. Tonight, I just got to get enough painkillers in him to get the fuck out of here. Enough morphine, you can walk on two broken legs if you have to." He detached the needle and threw the squeeze-syringe away. "Here—wait two minutes, then give him another. Just stick it in and squeeze. I'm gonna look around."

Djalik sounded mad as hell. And with good reason, Alan thought. This wasn't what he'd signed on to do—none of it. He wished he could wash Harry, but there was no water. The little flashlight gave a white, harsh light in a one-foot circle; the picture of Harry's terrible eye in its light was too much for him. "Anything we can do for this eye?" he called. Djalik was prone by the opening. Djalik rolled toward him, said, "Tube of three-way antibiotic; squeeze half of it all over the area," and rolled back. By the time Alan was through doing that and giving the second shot of morphine, Djalik was there.

"All hell broken loose out there, Commander. I don't know the players, but I'd say the white guys are trying to take the helicopters and leave and somebody else is shooting things up over there east. Couple good thumps, sounded like mortars." A nod toward Harry. "He conscious?"

"Now and then."

"Shot of speed. It'll either kill him or get him on his feet. Those bastards really worked him over." Djalik was containing his anger better now. "Scout a back way out of here."

Alan moved toward the door, turned back toward the little circle of light. "Why didn't you tell me you had another gun?"

Djalik paused, but only for an instant. "You might have acted different, let them know."

"What the hell did you take my gun for, then?"

"For them to find."

The amphetamines had had an effect, because when he had been around the shed, Harry was sitting up against the wall and shouting, the words muffled and tangled by his battered lips, "Fuck you! Lousy cocksucking Hutu bastard, fuck you!"

They watched the airfield in moonlight, with fireworks laid on by several sides. They saw several white men and quite a few black soldiers, some running, a few dying, several dead. The other troops he assumed to be Ntarinada's "Grande Armée Rwandaise." They had full camo, full webbing, good hats and boots.

Another hangar stood almost two hundred yards down the field. Figures kept flitting past them; they could hear shouts, even babies wailing. The refugees were being driven in by some attacker, he guessed. Three Russian Mi-8 helicopters stood near the other hangar, two with their turbines singing, one on fire, illuminating the whole scene down there.

They watched white soldiers emerge from somewhere beyond the northern hangar, carrying rucksacks and duffel bags that they began to load into the helicopters. Others, in camo, stood watch and continued to exchange fire with the GAR troopers out in the dark.

"I could get hits from here," Djalik said, sighting down his AK-47. Alan looked for Zulu. Alan felt a new feeling; the desire to kill. He had never felt this personal need to kill a particular man before, not even with the traitor who had betrayed his father to his death. He wanted Zulu. But the range was long, and the light uncertain.

"Are any of the whites the officer who started shooting in the hangar?"

"Nope. Something about him I should know, Commander?"

"He's a wanted war criminal in Bosnia. I shot at him, once."

"You do get around. No, I don't see him."

"We won't get out alive if we shoot, anyway."

"Yeah, that's why I'm not doing it. I figure we're not their main concern tonight."

"Djalik, I think the white guys are pulling chocks."

Djalik watched the drama below through the iron sights on his rifle.

"Good time to go."

"They say I was a slave and the child of slaves," O'Neill said out of nowhere. His voice was thick, and his consonants were slurred by his beaten mouth: s sounded like sh, th like h. "That my ancestors were slaves. Fuck them. White fucker!"

"Yeah, Harry, fuck them. Harry, we need to be quiet right now."

"Yeah, right, quiet." He was quiet for about three seconds, and then he screamed, *"Foutez le camp, salauds!"*

Djalik laughed. "It's the speed. What'd he say?"

"'Fuck you, you bastards.'"

"Yeah, well, I'm with him there. Okay, you ready?"

"Ready."

"You're recon."

That was the agreement—Djalik commanded any fighting, Alan picked the route and did the recon. They both supported Harry.

Alan duck-walked out and stood against the building, accustoming his eyes to the starlight. His groin was a large, dull ache, but adrenaline was keeping him up. A great many people seemed to be moving around him. When he could see as well as he ever would, he moved forward until he found a thorn fence, the wall of the enclosure. He began to trot down the outside of the boma. When he reached the corner, he turned north and continued to follow it. Occasional firing came from within the boma, and random shots whispered through the thorny wall beside them. Alan felt very exposed, but logic told him that they weren't shooting at him—not much help if a stray bullet hit him.

Beyond the boma was a field where plastic tents flapped like ghosts. People were running past them, and he watched them clump up and then disappear into the forest. There had to be a trail there, and it was going in the right direction, west. He retraced his route back to the hangar.

Djalik had Harry on his feet.

"Can he walk?" Alan said. Even in the dark, he was shocked all over again by this stinking hulk.

Djalik put a surprisingly tender arm around O'Neill's waist. "Sure he can, can't you, Bud." He moved Harry a step. "That's the way—that's the way—there we go—" O'Neill began to totter forward.

Part Three

The Ignorant Armies

26

Late November

At sea, the flag deck of the *Jackson*.
Captain Parsills didn't wake Admiral Pilchard early to tell him that Alan Craik and Dave Djalik hadn't made it to the COD they'd laid on for Kinshasa. The matter wasn't yet a crisis—less than twenty-four hours late—and Pilchard was weary; let him sleep. The COD pilot was apparently testy about lying over in Kinshasa, but that's what he'd been ordered to do. *They'll come in tonight,* Parsills thought. Hoped.

He told the admiral over breakfast. A spasm of concern passed over the tired face and then was gone. "I hope I didn't make a mistake there," he said.

"We're trying to find out from the embassy what happened. They're not right quick about responding."

"Those— !" Pilchard waved a hand. "You know my views." He turned his attention back to breakfast. "Better have *Rangoon* prepare an extraction plan, just in case."

"We don't know where he is."

"Well—some radius from Kinshasa. Shit, Jack, do it!"

The flash of old-man's temper was briefly ugly, then gone but not apologized for. Parsills' manner didn't change; he remained cheerful, solid, maybe a little unimaginative. As he was leaving, he said, "I'd already got on the *Rangoon* for an extraction plan."

Pilchard nodded. "Stay on it." He was going through message traffic.

That afternoon, they got a message from the embassy: their man had come back because of "unacceptable risks and threats;" the two naval personnel—no names, probably in fact forgotten by whoever wrote the message—had got into an unidentified aircraft with "unknown and unverified local militia without authorization or embassy clearance" and disappeared.

Parsills asked for clarification and passed the message to the *Rangoon* so that they would expand the radius from Kinshasa for possible extraction. The chief of staff rejected the idea of informing the missing men's families. It was too soon.

Sarajevo.
It had taken five days to lure Mrs Obren out of Republika Srpska. Not that she was suspicious, but their system was not very fast. Somebody had to go over the border and leave a message; she had to see the sign, wait until it was safe to pick up the message, then make arrangements to leave.

Dukas worked on what he had come to think of as the "other two"—her husband and the man called Zulu. He had sent a priority message to the States for the file on Craik's raid, when the Serb had gone out the window into the snow and he had found the photo with "Colonel Zulu at the Battle of the Crows" on it. Dukas had gone to intel at NIS to request searches for any contacts or reports on a Z or a Zulu. He had remembered talking to Craik about Serbs in Africa and had put that together with Pigoreau's information that Zulu was "away." Could that be why he had been recruiting, even after the shooting in Croatia and Bosnia was over?

Dukas called Pigoreau into his chilly office two days after they had sent for Mrs Obren. Pigoreau had been avoiding him, came now with obvious reluctance, his head down like a dog's who expects to be scolded. The weather had broken, something like a thaw setting in; the office was damp and dead, but Dukas felt energized, maybe because he was drinking in the morning again and had a false sense of himself.

"Sit," he said. Pigoreau sat. Pigoreau was tough and never took any shit from anybody, but this was different because they were friends. Dukas looked straight at Pigoreau until he looked back. "Okay?" Dukas said.

"What okay?"

"You know what, for Christ's sake. It's done, Pig. You did the right thing. It's hard on me—she really got to me. You know. But you did right and it's over. Okay?"

Pigoreau looked wary. "Okay." He began to burrow in his chest for a cigarette.

"How I read it, Pig, it's the husband. She'll do anything, fuck anybody, to get the husband back. Zulu's using the husband, just like I was, I guess. So run a check on Serb militias and see what officers' names come up with Z." Pigoreau groaned; they had done that twice already. "I know, I know; try it again. Run it past somebody who knows what the hell is going on in Belgrade. French intel— can you trust French intel?"

Pigoreau made a mouth for whistling and blew out smoke. "They are sorting that out, Michael. I think I have a contact guy who is okay."

"We want to know who's been recruiting and who went from Belgrade to Zaire via Libya. Your guy got contacts in Libya? If not, go to the Italians. I wanta know what the Yugos got there—maybe an office? They flew in and out—they keeping aircraft there? Servicing them? Friend

389

of mine said it was weird the Libyans supported anybody going to help What's-His-Name—the dictator with cancer—?"

"Mobutu. Yes, peculiar but not impossible; money talks, plus we got old friends in Libya."

"We?"

"France." Pigoreau put his elbows on the desk. The cigarette dangled from a corner of his thin mouth. He was enjoying himself, Dukas realized—two cops, two friends again. "Where does Mobutu go when he gets sick? France. Where does he look for help when his pathetic dying dinosaur of a country is attacked? France. But France says, 'Well, Sese Seko old friend, you are welcome to bring your cancer here because of old times, but not your dinosaur. Times have changed. We don't take pet dinosaurs any more. Sorry. Your dinosaur is dying; let it die.' So Mobutu goes to certain particular old friends in France and he says, 'Boo-hoo, my dinosaur is dying, help me! You owe it to me because of old times.' And these particular friends, because they do not want to admit that times have changed, and because they believe that saving dinosaurs is what the French *gloire* most requires, they say, 'Sese Seko, *copain*, your cause is my cause, we will save your dinosaur.' And they take a few millions from Mobutu and send him back to his luxury clinic, and they put out the money in Belgrade and Tripoli, where they have other old friends from the days of the dinosaurs, and *Voilà!*, Serb mercenaries appear in Zaire."

"I think one of them may be our man Zulu. Just a hunch." They looked at each other. "We'll ask Mrs Obren."

Later, he thought of trying to contact Al Craik, who knew a lot about Africa. He rejected the idea because he was sure Craik was sitting on a boat somewhere, far from the actualities of Zaire.

At sea, the flag deck of the *Jackson*.
On the second morning after Alan Craik and Dave Djalik had disappeared, Parsills watched as Admiral Pilchard drafted a harsh message to the Kinshasa embassy. It demanded details of what he called the "abandonment" of his men by the embassy; it demanded current intelligence information from the chief of station. It threatened reporting of non-cooperation via the Chief of Naval Operations to the White House.

The embassy, however, had the fine-tuned diplomatic art of ass-covering on its side. The embassy's version of the matter was that an uninvited military officer had pushed himself in where he wasn't wanted and had disappeared as a result. That was the classified story they had already begun to spread through channels in Washington. There was no press reporting on the matter.

Washington.
Ever since he had left IVI, Abe Peretz had been thinking about Rose and Peacemaker, even as he went about his normal work at the FBI. The abrupt end of his own time at IVI had angered him: what had seemed a pleasant two-week reserve duty had turned into one pleasant week and one wasted and stupid one sitting at a temporarily empty desk at the Air Medical Evacuation Training Office at Fort McNair. His objections that he knew nothing about air medevac and was a Naval intel specialist, not an Army doctor, took three weeks to resolve, and by then of course he was back at his regular job. The only answer, given to him over the telephone by a foolish-sounding lieutenant, was that somebody had been needed in a hurry at Fort McNair. Otherwise, it was shut up and do as you're told.

Peretz had been suspicious. He got an excellent fitrep for the week at IVI, but he still smelled a rat. The rat looked like the guy who had come to the table while he and Rose were having coffee—the ex-Nav named Suter.

So, Peretz had started to do some checking. Peacemaker's interest in targeting data would have remained only an anomaly if he hadn't been so abruptly transferred. Now, he was curious—*real* curious. On his lunch hours, on odd times when he could work by telephone or the internet from his office, in the evenings at home, he began to examine IVI and some of the people who worked there. Suter particularly interested him.

A surprising amount of information is available in a free society. Much of it is buried in government documents. Some of it is on the web, often in the form of self-puffing web sites for agencies. A lot of it is in Congressional documents, which the Congressional Record Service will cough up if you have a Congressman who will front for you. Peretz could do even better than that: one of the people he played tennis with was a senior congressional staffer. She also liked Peretz a lot—enough to worry Bea Peretz.

"What's on between you and Mindy Goren?" Bea said. It was a challenge; Bea spoke mostly in challenges, proclamations, and outraged denials.

"I'm meeting her twice a week at the Quick-Fuck Motel."

"Abe, I'm warning you— !"

So he had told her. Bea was outraged for his sake, had been outraged for his sake by the transfer from IVI, now was outraged for his sake that he suspected something behind the transfer. For both sympathy and self-protection, Bea joined the quest and became his go-between with Mindy and the Congressional Research Service.

Two lines of investigation had quickly emerged. They would sit by his computer or at her desk after dinner, their daughters' rock CDs thumping down the stairs as background; each would nudge the other or grunt when something good came up. First, it was the contracting history for Peacemaker; then it was the committee hearings where Peacemaker was discussed. Abe learned to track Peacemaker through classified hearings by looking for General Touhey's name; often, to his surprise, George Shreed's would be there, too.

"What the hell has Shreed got to do with Peacemaker?" he grumbled.

"Who?"

"Shreed, Shreed—the Agency guy Alan got into trouble with in Africa a couple of years ago—remember?"

"Oh, *that* shit."

Bea had taken on the contracts. They were an interesting relief from the homework assignments of her fifth-grade class. There were hundreds of them. But they were on the record—or most of them were. They all had numbers, very long numbers, and one night Bea shouted "Gotcha!" when she found a nineteen-digit gap in the number sequence.

"Got what?"

"I don't know, Dummy, I just found it!" But the gap was real, and more searching didn't fill it.

"Secret," she said. "They've got secret contracts."

"Lots of contracts are secret."

"No, asshole—lots of contracts have secret *contents*. A bunch of these are just marked 'Classified,' but their numbers are there. This is a gap in the *numbers*—they just aren't there!"

"Clerical error."

"Come on— !"

Abe was still working on the committee hearings. Armed Services, Intelligence, Appropriations—those seemed normal for a standalone entity like IVI. He could see in the pattern of Touhey's testimony that IVI was a one-man monolith, carefully crafted by somebody who knew Washington's civilian and military back rooms. IVI also seemed to have its own lobbyist. Peretz wanted to get him on the phone, but Bea wisely dissuaded him and reminded him that before you went behind somebody's back, you first exhausted legitimate resources.

"Maybe I ought to call that bastard Suter."

Now it was late in November. Peretz debated a couple of days and then called Suter at IVI. He wasn't there, a crisp female voice told him; he was at the Washington office. Peretz called the number she gave him, and a Southern female voice told him that Mistah Sutah wasn't theyah; had he tried the Maryland office? He played this game of telephone tag for two days and then decided that Suter was out of town, until he found a Ray Suter in the Virginia telephone book and called that evening, and that remembered, arrogant voice answered.

"Sorry, wrong number," Peretz said, automatically dropping his voice an octave.

"Why the James Earl Jones imitation?"

"Instinct. I thought—Hide yourself from this guy."

"I thought you wanted to talk to him."

"I did, until I find he's home when I can't get him at the office. I don't get it."

"He works part-time."

"No, no. This guy's hot to go."

"He's got another office."

"You mean—three? No, no, Bea, nobody has three offices— Unless—"

Peretz called the government information number and gave Suter's name. Two numbers came back. One was IVI. The other was not. He had Bea call it, and she reported that it was a number in the Operational Planning Directorate of the CIA.

"Bingo." Peretz made a wry face. "George Shreed's bailiwick. Suter must be Shreed's guy at IVI—but why?"

The next day, he called Rose. He told her about the missing contracts and the apparent connection between Suter and Shreed. He repeated his suspicion that Peacemaker was a weapon. They didn't talk about Alan. Neither of them knew that he had been missing for forty-eight hours in Zaire. They both thought he was at sea. Rose was in her final days at home before going to Naples to join the *Philadelphia* for the launch. She was busy, focused, and annoyed.

She took Peretz's questions to Suter.

Suter called George Shreed.

At sea, the NCIS office aboard the *Jackson*.

Most carriers have two Naval Criminal Investigative Service agents, who are crammed into an office with their files and their computers and their worries, two civilian cops in a big military community. They are often harried by trivia.

"Oh, shit," one of the two on the *Jackson* was saying. "Oh, *shit*!" He held up a sheet of paper and shook it at his partner. "Guess what!"

"You got a secret admirer in the marine detachment."

"*We* got another Christian-identity creep! Listen to this—'I feel the Lord pushing me to reveal the satanic matchinations'—misspelled—'of a mud-woman against a Christian white man.' Oh, Jesus H. Christ and the Seven Fucking Dwarfs! We got rid of that Borne guy, I thought that was it!"

"Where'd you get it?"

"Chaplain."

The partner, a slightly older guy with a paunch and an air—not necessarily justified—of greater experience, said, "Cry for help, right?"

"My ass."

"Yeah, well, we already got skinheads; let's find the guy.

It's gotta be a guy; it's always a guy—'Christian white *man*,' right?"

The other was reading silently. "Hey. Listen to this— 'this female mud officer—' Huh? Officer? How many black women officers we got on the ship? Huh? Should I check it out?"

His partner nodded. "You check it out. Makin' a list, checkin' it twice—kinda an NCIS job description, isn't it?"

At sea, the bridge of the *Jackson*.

Admiral Pilchard was on the bridge with the *Jackson*'s captain when the flag lieutenant grabbed his arm. There was damned little protocol to the gesture; the sailor at the helm nearby visibly flinched. The lieutenant put his mouth close to the admiral's better ear and muttered something, and a quick, boyish smile flashed over the older man's face, for a moment wiping away the wrinkles and the fatigue.

"They sure?"

"Absolutely. Scott's down there now."

"Can they patch it through to here?"

"Uh—it's the INMARSAT telephone on the second deck, sir—they're trying." He smiled uncertainly. "It's my understanding he's in a tree."

"I don't give a goddam if he's in Disneyland! What's the situation?"

"Sir, I didn't—"

With that, somebody smacked a headset on the admiral, and he heard Commander Scott's voice, tinny because of the double telephone-to-wireless transmission, and then Craik's voice in a hail of static.

"Craik! Craik—this is Admiral Pilchard! Do you read me?" He turned to the flag lieutenant. "Get Captain Parsills—patch in CVIC and get this on tape, every word—"

"Yes, sir."

The crackling got louder. There had been better transmissions from the moon, and that had been a quarter-century ago.

"Craik, where the hell are you?"

"I'm in clear, sir—I hate to give coordinates—"

"Got you, okay—" He thought about it. "Fuck clear. How's the other man—from the boat—?"

"He's good. Invaluable."

"Did you get what you went for?"

"Yes, sir. He's—we had to carry him the second day. We need morphine, sir. We need food, too."

Pilchard was writing—*airdrop—morphine—MREs—radio—*"What the hell happened?"

"Meeting went bad, sir."

"Where are you?"

"Near Kisangani, sir. I can provide UTM or LAT LON coordinates."

"Can you get to the FAZ base in Kisangani?"

"Sir, I'd rather not do that. The folks who were holding our friend had the same boss. There was some shooting."

"Casualties?"

"Not on our side, sir." *More trouble with the embassy,* Pilchard was thinking; *he's shot up the local troops; all the embassy will see is in-country criticism.* "Is the shooting over?"

"We think there's pursuit. Hard to tell—we have refugees all around us—"

"Craik, I understand that this is an open line. Tell me anyway what happened."

"The people holding the American citizen were Hutu soldiers. They shared a camp with a lot of refugees and some white mercenaries and Zairian regulars. The exchange went bad, we think because the mercs and the Hutus had a falling-out. We had to shoot our way out."

"Wait one." Somebody was gesturing to him, and he

397

was handed another headset; it was Parsills, passing on a message from the *Rangoon*. "Craik?"

"Sir?"

"Find a good extraction point and give us coordinates and time. Can you do that? Is your SAR card up to date?"

"Roger that, sir. Sir, the white mercs are a Serb outfit led by a wanted war criminal called Zulu. Please pass it, sir."

"I will. Now get moving." A tone, less stern, crept into his voice. "Take care of yourselves."

He handed back the headset. "Get the chief of staff. My office, five minutes." He apologized to the ship's captain, said he'd get back to him, and hurried out. Going down the p'way toward blue-tile country, he was dictating orders to the flag lieutenant, on one side, and the flag captain, who had appeared on the other. "I want air cover for those poor bastards, get on it! Harriers from the *Rangoon* are closest, get 'em in the air, but they're short on range, so fire up our CAG and get him moving. I want a flight plan for a three-day air cover; if we extract tomorrow, as we goddam well ought to, we'll pull it back, but tell CAG we gotta be ready to push this thing through."

"The embassy, sir—"

"Fuck the embassy! These are our guys in there, they're not keeping us out!" He turned back to the lieutenant. "Tell the Zairian Air Force or whatever the hell they've got to stay out of the air. Don't put it just that way, but—clear this with Parsills and CAG AI, Christ! I wish I had Craik here to do this—make it clear that we're going to shoot to protect our people, so they're not gonna go in and do air strikes within fifty miles of our guys, okay?"

They were in the flag suite by then, and the admiral led them to his office, waved Parsills to his side, and said, "Coordinate this with the French. They've got air assets in-country; tell them the situation—the truth, the truth, it's their intel people started this—and tell them not to mess with us. Just stay the hell away, got it? And let's get a message off to the Agency. Put in this Serb mercenary report, but use it as a vehicle to convey that we have contact with their guy and we may need to take action. Those guys can be good allies, even if we have to ruffle some feathers." He looked up. A determined-looking EM was standing in the doorway.

"Well?"

"Sir, ASW reports possible submarine contact from the *Melward*. Russian Akula-class grams, sir."

Pilchard looked at Parsills and suddenly laughed. "Well, of course! What else would it be?" He clapped Parsills on the shoulder. "Get on it, Jack. Gentlemen, we have work to do! I want those guys out of Zaire by this time tomorrow, or else!"

As the flag captain and the flag lieutenant left, they heard him say, "What's one Akula-class sub between friends, anyway?" He sounded twenty years younger.

"There's that ghost again," WO Hamilton said, chewing on an unlit cigar and crouching forward over his tiny light table. Displayed on it were the sonograms from the SQR-19 tail of one of the fig-seven frigates, as well as two of the battle group's S-3s, taken that day. Hamilton traced two lines with his thumb and forefinger for the Tactical Action Officer and his flag counterpart. Both craned over the table to see what he was showing them because the lines did not leap to the eye.

"*Here* and *here*. This was 0920 this morning. Then the FFG-7 has it at 1140, here." Hamilton peeled the sonograms off the table to reveal a stained chart with dozens of marks and erasures. Hamilton had a computer that supposedly did all this, but he stuck with the technologies he understood.

"Then at 2135 AG 707 has this contact here. These are the strongest lines."

The flag TAO ordinarily deferred to him. "Hamilton, you know your business. But, er, I don't see anything."

"Hell, I'm not sure, myself. I've never worked a third-generation Russkie before. But that's what it ought to look like, I figure. Look, this is a 688-class, a quiet one, taken from an S-3. We got this cut during Fleetex. What do you see?"

"Nothing," said the TAO, who couldn't read a sonogram, anyway.

"Exactly. Not much to see."

"But you think something's out there."

"Yes, sir, I do."

"Okay, Hamilton, I'll tell the admiral. And we'll lay on some more S-3s and alert the helos. Has this ever happened before? Soviet subs in the Bight of Benin?" Like many sailors of a certain age, he always thought of things Russian as Soviets.

"I got the S-3 AI looking at it. Ms Nixon. She'll brief you."

They finished their coffee and left through the undogged hatch to CIC. "Do you buy it?"

"Fuck, yes. *Fort Klock* got a cut on something third-generation last week. They must have a couple of subs out."

"It's like the eighties!" He didn't sound particularly unhappy.

He was not happier after the dapper and competent Ms Nixon had reviewed Russian naval deployment history for him. The Russians had visited the area before, but not in many years. Not since the wall fell and Glasnost changed the balance of power. The TAO ordered Christy to polish her information to brief the admiral and the captain, wrote a long note in his actions log, and spent the rest of his watch wondering what the hell the Russians were doing. Was Newman right? Everyone said the Russians were dead. That brand-new, very quiet ghost contact was probably one of their best subs.

The Russians were flat broke. They didn't have money, or power, for wild adventures. They were smart, too. He knew that. They weren't following him around the Bight of Benin for nothing.

What the hell were they doing?

27

Zaire.

"Last one." Djalik tossed the MRE to Alan. "Sir, if you get the soup and ham hot with the heating packet, I'll see to Mr O'Neill's eye."

"Right." Alan didn't mind being reduced to cook. He was tired, more tired than he could ever remember, but he had Harry and he hadn't lost anybody. Yet. He used the water bottle in his helmet bag to start the heater in the MRE. In seconds the soup packet was hot, and then he heated the ham. He poured the rest of the water into his stainless-steel cup and made coffee. It wasn't great, but it was hot and sweet.

The three of them shared the soup, and Djalik fed O'Neill the ham a bite at a time. Harry had lost three teeth and had two broken ones in front, which Djalik had patched up from a dental pack in the first-aid kit. Today, he could totter along on his own, but he was still bad.

Djalik gave each of them a Snickers bar. Harry looked at his with his one good eye, then put the candy in his shirt pocket. He was still filthy, still smelly. Djalik had covered his lidless eye with Second Skin and gauze, which at least kept the flies off—and made it invisible to the others.

Alan and Djalik ate most of what was left. They ate every cracker, finished the thick peanut butter, ate the jelly, and rifled every packet of the MRE until there was nothing left. Djalik produced more water and made the Kool-Aid and poured some into the foil pack Harry was using as a cup. "Poo—poo—" Harry tried to speak through his battered lips. "Poo—yee—" He swallowed. "Poo-yee Foo-wee-say."

"What's he say?"

"He made a joke. About wine. He's feeling better."

Alan buried the plastic wrappers.

Around them, the forest was moving.

28

The End of November

Sarajevo.

Mrs Obren came in from Republika Srpska by bus. Dukas had her tailed from the station. She came straight to their meeting-place in the park; he embraced her, smiled, chatted, and she smiled the smile that enchanted him, and he wanted her and knew he was never going to have her again.

He drove to the flat in Radovan Street and told her they had to go in for a moment, something about her check. She seemed unusually happy; maybe it was the money. Dukas took her up, holding her wrist in one big hand, apparently a gesture of affection. He got an "Okay" sign from the woman who had tailed her, meaning there had been no counter-surveillance.

Pigoreau and two Brits who had done anti-terrorism interrogation in Ireland were waiting inside the flat. Dukas felt her try to pull away and heard her changed breathing, and he knew she understood. He didn't look at her face.

"Get everything. I want it all—every detail, every name, every word that was said. Break her."

She started to weep and spoke his name. He let go of her wrist and went out. Down on the street, he leaned against his car and gulped in big breaths to keep from being sick.

At sea, the flag deck of the *Jackson*.
They didn't make the extraction within the twenty-four hours that the admiral had demanded. They had aircraft over the area, and the embassy was screaming about it, but they couldn't find their people. The pilots who went low reported seeing hundreds, maybe thousands of people. If there was pursuit of the Americans, it was impossible to recognize it. The few roads were clogged; there was no transport—half a million people were moving through the forest down there.

One F-18 locked on a French Jornada, but the E2 Hawkeye told him to for God's sake back off; the guy was flashing NATO IFF. A little late, but he was flashing.

Admiral Pilchard demanded to know why Craik wasn't in touch. Commander Scott, who had taken Craik's phone call before the admiral got on, explained that Craik had a cell phone, and Zaire didn't have coverage outside the cities. That was why he had gone as close as he had to Kisangani—to get within cell-phone coverage. "Now he's on the move again, sir."

"On foot," Pilchard said, as if being on foot was a moral failing.

"I guess so, sir."

The admiral threw a pen.

Zaire.
They had come to a deserted village. Alan walked past the first hut with his rifle up, then a second, and a third. He looked in each door. In the third, an old woman was sitting on the floor. The banda smelled pleasantly of smoke. Alan remembered that smell from the past. Smoke and unwashed bodies. Smoke and urine. Smoke and smoke. He smiled at the woman.

"Habari ya leo. Bonjour? Uh—bei gani?" He tried various

combinations. She sat on her haunches. She still didn't say anything. Alan pulled his head back outside and approached the other bandas, looking past the hide flap of each one. Nobody.

Djalik was waiting in the center of the hamlet. "All clear," he said. "I walked all the way around. Tracks goin' off north. What'd you find?"

"One old woman."

"What the hell's she doing here?"

"Left behind."

These little villages emptied ahead of the refugees. The refugees were scared, hungry, angry. They came like locusts.

Djalik went back and helped Harry up to the village.

Alan descended to the pragmatic.

"There's a good aluminum pot in that banda. All we need is a chicken."

Harry's chest moved. He seemed to be coughing; then it appeared he was laughing. "Ev-er—" he started. "Ever—eat—rat?" He actually smiled. His voice got stronger. "I did. Caught it, smashed it, skinned it, ate it." The words were mushy, but his mouth was not so swollen today. "Not so bad."

Alan tried to keep him going. "Patrick O'Brian always has the midshipmen catching rats as a treat."

Harry's chest heaved again with what was probably laughter. "Yeah, but—but—they get to—cook them."

Djalik nodded down the ridge toward the river. "There's a Gould hand pump, product of the USA, just over the hill. I'll fill the canteens. Put in purification." He looked at Alan. "We're running low." He glanced at Harry significantly. "On lots of stuff." He meant the morphine.

Then they heard the chicken. She croaked more than she clucked, but she was an actual chicken. Possibly a sick

406

chicken, because Djalik caught her after one run around a banda.

Alan shook his head. "These people are poor as dirt. I hate to take their chickens."

"This chicken is a fucking miracle. You believe in miracles? After this chicken, I do." Djalik held its neck and spun the chicken's body, and it was dead.

In the end, Alan cooked and Harry watched. They tried to share the bits of tough meat with the old woman, but she didn't have teeth and she simply looked at the food. They left her the aluminum pan with some of the broth in the bottom; Harry begrudged her even that, because he said she was going to die, anyway. Alan cut some sisal rope from the back of the banda and rigged straps to carry his helmet bag. When he was done, he had both hands free for the first time in three days. Out of guilt, meaning it the way Africans mean gifts, he put three fishhooks and some line on a mat, as a kind of payment, or maybe propitiation. He picked up the rifle and left the old smoke of the hut. The woman was still staring at the untasted chicken broth.

They walked three more hours before dark. The GPS said that they had made twenty-one miles since the battle at the airfield.

Sarajevo.
Pigoreau called Dukas thirty hours after they had started interrogating Mrs Obren and said she was being tough but was starting to give. She was still trying to bargain for news of her husband. "I'm not sure she is quite sane, Michael."

Well, that made sense. Dukas hadn't thought of it before. "How long?" he said. He was drinking scotch from a coffee cup.

"She's tough, Michael."

407

"Tell her if she doesn't give to us I'm going to throw her in prison and she won't get to go looking for her husband for five, ten years. Tell her we'll try her in the States, which she'll believe, because the fucking Serbs think America is the Evil Empire and can do anything. Tell her I'll get her twenty years in an American women's prison full of black dykes where she won't fuck anything more interesting than a broomstick until she's too old to care."

"Don't make it personal, Michael."

Maybe he wasn't quite sane, either, he thought. Maybe that was why they had been drawn to each other. "Okay, cut the last part. Just scare the shit out of her and get me some information."

He arranged with the Bosnian border cops to make up a sheet on her, charging her with having false documents, which Dukas knew was true because he had given the documents to her when he had recruited her. The paper trail said she had been arrested at the border and was being held in the women's jail. The word would get back to RS, then to Belgrade.

Thirty-six hours later, two of the female cops took her to the train station and north to the UN jail at Stobranica. They were going to keep her for a few weeks while they set her up as a double and turned her back to RS. Dukas watched them from his office window. She looked thinner and pale. They hadn't marked her; they were too good for that.

The transcripts of the interrogation made up a thick file. Most of it was shit. She was an instinctive agent; she may not have known the theory of interrogation, but she had surely known how to weave and dodge and backtrack and confuse. After she had started to talk, most of what she said was small stuff—the schoolteacher who was her contact, Serbian cops in RS whom she fed information on her neighbors—but she got good on the subject of Zulu. He came last. It was as Pigoreau's snitch had said: she had taken Zulu home twice, had been a hostess for a recruiting party, had informed to him on Dukas and the WCIU.

Did you tell the man Zulu you were having an affair with Mister Dukas?

Yes.

What did he say?

He said to keep it going, to keep him happy.

Late in the interrogation she had started to make things up again and the transcript got incoherent. She was a natural liar, to be sure, but by then she was trying to please them and she was making up things she thought they would like to hear.

I know his name. I know that man's name.

She didn't call him "Zulu" or "Z." She called him "the man" or "the man who came to my flat" or "the recruiter." She must have been saving that, and they never got in that far.

You went to bed with him but you didn't know his name?

Yes.

You spent the night with him? What did you call him?

I didn't call him anything.

Dukas remembered his delight in hearing her speak his own name. She said she loved the name Michael.

Then, at the end, she had started to let it go.

I know his name. I know that man's name.

What man?

That—the recruiter—the one who comes to my flat—who I said before. Didn't I tell you before? NOTE: Subject not entirely coherent from lack of sleep and other factors.

What is his name?

It is on his arm—top of the arm—you say—?

Shoulder?

No, here—here—

409

Upper arm.

Yes, I see it when he is—nude? Without his clothes. His name.

What is his name?

It is Italian name, not Serb. Maybe he is spy? Not a name I know.

What is his name?

His name is Semperfi. NOTE: Subject spelled name here. This appears to be invention. Name does not check in standard lists.

Well, Dukas thought, it wouldn't. And no reason for a couple of Brits to recognize it.

He printed the name on a pad in front of him. Then he drew a line between two of the letters.

Semper/fi.

Semper Fi.

Had she known? Or was she simply crazy? She must have known the man wouldn't have his own goddam name tattooed on his arm. No, she was being smart—smart even when she was exhausted and hurting and frightened, smart because she suspected everybody and she thought that somehow what she said might get back to the Serbs. So she had handed over this bonbon as if she didn't know what it was—handed it over, Dukas knew, to him. Because he would know what the tattoo meant.

Know that Zulu had been an American marine.

At sea, the flag deck of the *Jackson*.
"Sir, I'd like to start the battle group west now, rather than wait another week."

"What's on your mind?"

"The Russian sub, sir. We've lost it—had it four days ago and we lost it. I'd like to move away from the deep water here and the trench off Gold Coast, and get out to where our guys have a better chance at detection. I wouldn't mind getting to where P-3s out of Rota could support our ASW effort, too. We're wearing the S-3 guys mighty thin, flying them around the clock."

"How far do we need to go?" Admiral Pilchard knew the answer. He wanted to make sure that everybody else did.

"I'd like to head for a point south of Cape Palmas. We'll be closer to the Med and still within range of Zaire. We'll set up a set of cleared boxes in the water, here and here, and move between them at high speed to make him run to catch up. Then we'll hear him."

"Make it so." The admiral went back to his message traffic.

It was a good plan. Except that the *Shark* was already eight hundred miles away.

Zaire.

The morning of the fifth day, they found a place where a helo could get in and where Alan could make contact via the cell phone. Djalik knew what the helos needed for an extraction site, and he did the scouting while Harry slept and Alan watched, worried about insecure communications going through a cell switch in a town overrun by Hutus. He was worried, too, by the volume of refugees in the woods. Too many, and the helicopter would not want to land if he couldn't claim the area was clear.

As soon as Djalik was through, muttering that the site was crap but the best they could do, Alan had the coordinates on the way to the boat. Transmission was horrible, but he kept at it and at it, waiting for the battery to go down, but finally he believed he'd got the coordinates through and had heard a time.

"0630," he told the others. He thought that was what he'd heard, anyway. "Now we wait."

At sea, the flag deck of the _Jackson_.

Parsills was waked by the flag lieutenant with the news that the extraction was on. The admiral wanted to see him, he was told; he pulled on clothes, brushed his hair enough to make the loose ends lie down, and went forward. Pilchard was awake, up, sitting in one of the leather chairs in a navy bathrobe, looking rather elegant. He was going through paperwork, and there was a stack beside him on the floor.

"You're working too hard," Parsills said.

"Can it, Jack. " He held out a page, a transcript of the last exchange with Craik. "This cell-phone crap sucks. We've got to get a radio to him if the extraction bombs." He looked up. "_Rangoon_ gives it one-in-three of succeeding. The position is too close to a town, too close to reports of FAZ units. They think Craik's desperate, because the site is crap."

"We're doing our best."

"And it isn't good enough! Or won't be if we miss him." He held out another page. "Pfor to me from CNO—he got a call from some tame columnist on the _Washington Post_, guy says State is ready to put out the story. 'Navy Team Lost in Zaire.' That'll cook it—once you get the media on it, our guys'll be hunted like rabbits."

"Jesus, they can't do that—"

"Yeah, they can. But they're willing to deal: we stay out of country, they'll sit on the story. The embassy's denied us over-flight as of 0800 tomorrow. If we violate it, they'll blow the story." He sipped at coffee that must have been cold for an hour. "An embassy can do that—legally, they're on solid ground to keep us out. We're supposed to abide by their rules. Practically, in a situation like this, we're usually allowed to take care of our own people, so long as we're discreet and don't scare the horses. Did you hear one of our guys lit up a French aircraft yesterday? French went ballistic. Apparently that got all the way to the White House." He held the cup in front of him like a sick man. "CNO wants me to go along on this, Jack."

"Christ. Jesus, this is our last chance, then."

The admiral put the cup down. "Not yet. CNO's Pfor had a suggestion, off the record. There's a black Agency operation down south whose people still believe we all work for the same government, thank God. They'll make an air drop for us if we get out of it otherwise—it's a three-way deal—us, the embassy, the Agency. If the extraction doesn't take, it's our best hope. So, get on this now: Send an S-3 with everything we want airdropped to Craik. Specifics're in the Pfor—country clearance on the way, route that has to be strictly abided by, no mistakes, no assing around. No over-flight of Zaire."

"The S-3 squadron XO," Parsills said. "He's burning to do something." He looked at his watch, saw how little of the night there was left. "Jesus, don't you ever sleep?" He reached for some of the message traffic. "I'm a morning person, myself."

Zaire.

Alan heard the rotor blades before he saw the helicopter coming low along the ridge. Early light made any kind of identification difficult. The three of them were in a small brush pile in the corner of a big field that had once been planted to sisal. He had a very patchy signal from the cell phone, but they had wanted the cover, and they were well hidden from anyone down toward the town. He pressed the Send button and was connected, after a painful delay, to the *Jackson*. In seconds he had been switched through Air Ops and was talking to the helo.

"Stranger, this is Big Bird, over?"

413

"Big Bird, I can see you."

"Roger, Stranger. Say the words."

"Roger, Big Bird. Stranger had a big mongrel dog called Bayard; Bayard was deaf."

"Roger, Stranger. I copy."

Djalik heard a burst of fire over the rotor blades and grabbed at Alan's arm.

"Shit!" Probably terrified deserters, shooting at anything. Alan shouted into the phone. "Big Bird, you're under fire!"

The helo turned sharply and climbed the ridge away from the fire.

"Stranger, roger weapons fire. Please wait—gotta check how bad."

The second helicopter had stayed well back and now came in, firing a heavy machine gun from the door. The marine choppers were well equipped for this role, but there was a lot of firing coming from the far side of the old sisal field. This wasn't a few guys with guns, but half a company, maybe even with squad weapons. Djalik was motioning to him.

Alan had to make the decision.

"Can you hold them off, Big Bird?"

Could you hear regret over a cell phone? "We have orders not to return fire, Stranger." *Well, what the hell was that you were just doing—pissing?* There was more firing from the other chopper, but the aircraft was hanging back, trying to impress rather than suppress. He knew what they were afraid of: if one of the choppers went down, the shit would hit the fan in Kinshasa, and in Paris, and in Washington.

And now figures were moving through the patches of sisal toward them.

It was already too late. He said the words that made him sick.

"Abort, Big Bird, abort. We have to move on."

"Confirm abort."

The big chopper swung toward the trees.

"Hang in there, Stranger."

The helicopter swung over the trees, then disappeared behind the treetops, leaving only the diminishing sound of its rotors behind. Djalik already had Harry on his feet and was moving him away along the escape route. Alan was drained by the failure, his hopes dashed in one minute of gunfire.

Djalik was worried by a different aspect: the volume of fire. Very professional. Djalik thought of the white mercenary called Zulu and the look that he had exchanged with Mr Craik.

29

The End of November

Zaire.

Zulu was sitting on the ground with his head in his hands, fever making his shoulders and neck ache. If it didn't get worse, he would get along. It couldn't be malaria, he thought; he had taken his medication, still had pills. But even those were running out.

He heard the helicopter coming in, and he looked up, his eyes red and watery. His own chopper had been rolled off the improvised pad and more or less camouflaged, but it was a half-assed job because there weren't enough men, and the FAZ soldiers hung back, looking on but not helping. *Not helping at anything*, he thought. *As useless at this as at fighting*.

The helo winnowed down and touched, sending up spray from the puddles that stood everywhere in the rain-soaked field. Zulu shuddered and got to his feet as a man dropped to the ground and splashed toward him, ducking his head as everybody does, as if he feared the rotor blades would take it off. He was a white civilian, Lascelles's best man in central Africa.

His best man, Zulu thought, *and look where we are.*

"Eh, Jackie." Zulu put out his hot hand. "Welcome to nowhere."

"Thank God for global positioning—the only way I found

you—what would we do without the Americans, eh?"
Jackie was in his forties, thin, small, red-faced. He had
been Lascelles's intermediary with Peter Ntarinada—until
Ntarinada had died. "What the hell are you doing here,
Zulu? You look sick. Malaria?"

Zulu waved a hand a little weakly. "Some fucking bug.
Africa." He wiped a hand over his forehead, running his
little finger into the hollow where the bridge of his nose
should have been, as he always did. "We need to talk,
Jackie."

"No, we don't. I know what you want to say: It's over.
Right?"

Zulu was surprised. Maybe it was the fever. He had
expected a fight. "I want you to tell Lascelles I have to
take my boys home. What's left of them."

Jackie led him under a tree, as if it were more private
there. "He already knows. He's willing."

"I still get my money? It isn't our fault, what's happened!
The fucking blacks, they won't stand; the troops are okay,
Jackie, but the officers are a joke! See that lot over there?
I could make something of them, give me a month or two.
But their captain's a kid from Kinshasa whose father is
some buddy of Mobutu's; the kid's shitting himself that
he'll get shot at. The only part of his uniform is dirty is the
seat of his pants." Zulu wiped his face with a hand again,
unconsciously felt the old knife wound on his nose. "We
did our best. Better than our best. Jesus Savior, I've lost so
many guys—"

Jackie put a hand on his shoulder. He was a little
man, but he behaved with the physical ease of a big
one—clearly not scared of Zulu, not scared of Africa.
"What the hell are you doing out here in the nowhere,
Zulu?"

"Following three fucking Americans who started all that

417

trouble at the airfield. Where they killed poor Ntarinada. Shot him down."

"The Hutus say your boys did that."

"Like hell! There was a shootout, these American Navy guys showed up, killed Ntarinada, and took off with a prisoner. I'm not going to let them get away with it. I'm after them."

Jackie looked at the bigger man's flushed face. "You'd be better off in bed. Listen, Zulu, I don't care who killed Ntarinada; it's too late to care. Don't bother. Let them go."

Zulu looked at him, looked away at the helo. "They know who I am." He shrugged. "The prisoner—"

"The black CIA guy."

Zulu nodded. "I worked him over; he'll remember me. Plus, you see, one of the American Navy guys, we'd run into each other before—I've got a face people remember, Jackie—"

Jackie patted Zulu's shoulder. "The way Lascelles figures it, you were going to take all three Americans and use them as hostages, and it went bad and Ntarinada got killed. Okay, who cares? It's too late. Kabila's people are going to take Bumia any day, and they'll take Kinshasa, so we've lost this round and we'll have to come back in a year, two years." He lit a cigarette, offered one to Zulu, who shook his head. "Lascelles is willing that you leave. On one condition."

"I don't bargain!" Zulu cried. "He owes me— !"

"Lascelles has one job for you to do on the way home. You and ten or a dozen of your men. Libya."

"Fuck that. We're going home."

"Of course you are, but you're going by way of Libya and you're going to stop there for twenty-four hours to do a job, very quick, fairly easy. If you don't do it—" He waved a hand. "Lascelles is a little angry with you, Zulu.

He can withhold your aircraft. He can withhold your money. He can fix it so you rot in Zaire."

"No, he can't!" But Zulu knew he could. His head was aching now. All he wanted to do was lie down.

"Here's what you do, Zulu. You go up to Gbadolite. That's Mobutu's home territory, and there's an airfield that will take big jets there. Lascelles will tell Mobutu you're up there to guard his homeland from the rebels. You train up there for ten days to two weeks for this mission in Libya, then we send in two cargo jets for you and you're out. Okay?"

"I've got wounded men in bush clinics all over this goddam country. I can't leave them."

"You've got two weeks. Use your helo. I'll lend you mine for a day or two if you need it." Jackie dropped the cigarette on the sopping ground, stared at it, at last put a toe of one boot on it. "Well?"

Zulu stared at him. "You know the FAZ shelled us? *Us?* Because they hadn't got paid, they said, and we're millionaires! Eh? I lost three guys. Christ!" He wiped his face. "What's the job in Libya?"

"Board an unarmed merchant ship and kill the crew, bring the ship into Tripoli harbor. That's it. The ship will be hit by a limpet mine; you pull up in speedboats, board, it's yours. I'll have the plans of the ship waiting for you in Gbadolite; that's what you'll need ten days or so to train on—we'll lay out a mockup on the ground, you get to know it like your own flat. Then the day comes, it's a walk."

"It can't be that easy."

Jackie shrugged. "It's a US ship. Civilian, but Navy control. Part of an exercise."

"Shit! No! Do you know what the—?" He stamped several steps, splashing mud and water. "Aw, shit! I can't think." He spun around. "Jackie, for God's sake, let us go! We're running on empty."

"There will be a missile on the ship. That's what you're after. A quarter of a million extra, dollars, when you get it into Tripoli harbor."

The FAZ soldiers began to stir a little. Two small black men had appeared among them, two men in ragged civilian clothes but carrying AKs. One talked animatedly to the FAZ captain, and then a sergeant started across the wet earth toward Zulu.

"This ship is unarmed?" Zulu said.

"I assure you."

"What's to keep the US Navy from towing it away?"

"It will be inside the twelve-mile line. The Libyans will have warships out, aircraft aloft. Much uproar in the press—US intervention in the Mediterranean, violation of Libya's territorial waters— It will work, Zulu."

"But—a missile?"

"Some sort of test. And how hard can it be? A small crew, some scientists. Your men will knock them over like birds."

The black sergeant stood near them. Neither man paid any attention. Zulu shivered. "I can't think," he muttered. "All right. But we're out of this shithole as of now—we're through."

Jackie turned on the sergeant. "Well?"

The sergeant saluted, even though the message was for Zulu. "They find the track of the three white men, Colonel. The *shenzi* say they are twelve kilometers away, going west."

Zulu straightened. "Can we hunt them with the helo?"

"*Shenzi* say no, Colonel. They going deeper into forest, keeping on small trails. Soon, gone altogether."

Zulu waved at his own men, only a handful, weary,

dispirited. They began to gather up weapons and buckle equipment.

"I have to get these American bastards," Zulu said. "I have to go."

Jackie gave a half-salute. "See you in Gbadolite, then." He gripped Zulu's arm. "Two weeks, and you'll be out of it."

Zulu stared at his tired men, at the reluctant FAZ. "If you dick me, Jackie, I'll kill you."

Jackie seemed to find this charming and funny. He ran for his helo.

Tehran, Iran.

Yuri Efremov structured his day like a businessman's, going each morning to an office in a pre-revolutionary building on Dedication Square. It gave him a feeling of normality to put on a Western suit and a white shirt and a really good tie, one of those he had bought in London or Rome when he was still based in Moscow. Then he would have his car brought around, and he and a bodyguard would be driven down to somewhere near the square, and he and the bodyguard would get out and walk the rest of the way to the office through crowds of men in less elegant suits and, often, no ties at all, and women in whatever politically correct covering the regime was enforcing just then. Efremov liked jostling through crowds and flower sellers and street vendors in the streets of Tehran, crossing the parks and construction sites and evidence of fifteen hundred years of imperial culture and fifteen years of religious attempts to redefine it.

Various groups followed him, and he once wondered with a detached amusement if the sales of coffee and orange juice along certain streets actually improved when he chose to walk them. The agents of the Revolutionary

Guard followed him; the agents of rival agencies stalked him; behind them were his own agents. And behind them? Americans, Russians, Israelis, Chinese?

The office was a cross between a command center and a front company. The sign on the door said "Executive Security Services" in English and Arabic. His employees were rigorously screened. In Iran, rigorous screening usually meant qualifying for a certificate of religious devotion, but, to Efremov, it meant a deep background check and several interrogations. Americans still used the polygraph. Efremov had been interrogating men and women for thirty years. He didn't need a machine. Anyway, if he had had one in Tehran, it wouldn't work or the operator wouldn't really know how to use it, or somebody on the Council of Fidelity and Truth would take it from him.

Efremov had been a colonel in the old KGB. He had been good. But his loyalties hadn't survived the collapse of the Soviet Union. Sometimes, now, he wondered why; it was possible, obviously, for somebody like him to make a lot of money in Moscow nowadays. Maybe he should have stayed. Except that money hadn't been all of it. "Power" was the buzzword now; well, he had had power, but perhaps not as much as he had wanted. But that hadn't been all of it, either. Some sense of betrayal. The title of an old book about communism—the god that failed. Well, yes. Except he hadn't believed in God and he thought he hadn't believed in communism, but how what people called capitalism revolted him! What slaves to moneymaking Americans were! He'd have done anything to avoid that. He'd seen it coming to Russia. A vision of the state where everything was for sale, as in fact somebody had written about ancient Rome. So he had defected to the Islamic state, where only some things were for sale and the rest were narrow-minded and rigid. Oddly, the

Islamic state suited him, or suited him in his privileged position as a foreigner who could have a mistress and a private compound and a credit line at the Swiss embassy shop, so long as he kept bringing in better intelligence than the regular state agencies.

Today, the sun was pale, as if the light were coming through a rainy window, and a haze of dust hung in the air. Downtown Tehran bustled, in that way that third-world cities do—incredible noise, stink, movement, but a lot of sense of waste motion. He supposed it was no worse than Moscow now, perhaps better, in fact—maintenance of buildings, for example, was actually quite good. He looked to the side, saw his car moving slowly along, the driver waving other cars and people out of the way. And everybody got out of the way, despite the hectic traffic.

What I do not have, Efremov thought to himself, *is the privilege of anonymity.* It was a paradox: in his KGB days, he had had multiple identities, lived in the shadows, spent a large part of his life under cover. Here, he might as well have been a film star. One day, he knew, he would get sick of it and go underground again and surface somewhere completely different. Not yet, however. Just now, there was Anna. Anna the Complication, because she had been furnished as a perk, and he had fallen in love with her.

Miss Rezai was waiting with her appointment book, as always. She was single and anxious to stay that way. Having a job that paid well was her security against a domination far more severe than that of theocratic Iran. Dark, plump, with heavy circles under her eyes, she was not attractive to him, but she was good at her job and she amused him with her strategies for escaping the sumptuary laws, above all a collection of silk scarves that went up, down, on the head, over the shoulders; now across the face, now over the hair, now on one arm—Miss Rezai's

423

scarves were like semaphores that signaled the religiosity of the atmosphere. They also told him at a glance what strangers might be in the office at any moment.

"The naval interview is due in twenty-five minutes," she said. Not a religious zealot, he could tell; her Hermès knock-off was knotted over her left breast and worn like a shawl. She carried a tray of coffee into his office ahead of him, like a priestess carrying the censing tools of her trade. He sipped café nero while he went through the internet editions of the London *Times* and the *Guardian*. He had lived in England as a case officer for a while, had never got over the habit of English newspapers. Then he went to the briefing room and prepared it himself, setting out more coffee, several packs of good Western cigarettes, and replacing the Impressionist prints he preferred with scenes of naval battles. He had the conference table removed and replaced by two wingback armchairs facing each other at a slight, non-confrontational angle, with a low table between that did not intrude or block gestures between the two seats. Miss Rezai brought flowers with the same faintly gloomy enthusiasm that she brought to the rest of her job, implying that nothing this nice could last.

Efremov's guest arrived precisely on time. He was not in uniform, but his tailored blue blazer and khaki trousers spoke not only of his rank, but also of his foreign training. They shook hands like old friends.

"Commander, may I record our meeting?"

"Absolutely." His confidence was surprising. Few men met Efremov with confidence.

"I did not get much from our phone conversation beyond that you wanted to speak to me."

"Yes." They spoke English, Efremov with a Russian accent, the commander with a distinct American one over-laid with Iranian. "It seemed best that nothing go by telephone. I have no idea if it was important, or even if it was a test. I waited, but no one said anything. I didn't want to report it to our people. I'm with the Revolutionary Guard, now, and they do not trust any of us who went to school in America. And then, my wife had seen your, mm, companion at the Golestan mall—"

Efremov had ceased to wonder how well known Anna had become. She did not hide, and he did not hide her. Anna was liberating and dangerous—perhaps the reason he had fallen in love.

"I have the utmost respect for your counter-intelligence in the Guard," Efremov said. It was unlikely that this polished man was some IRG provocateur, but anything was possible. Their CI branch was in fact a haven for brutish fanatics, and Efremov had no respect for them whatsoever.

"Yes, well. Mmm." His guest was looking above Efremov's head, perhaps working too hard at looking above Efremov's head. "Are you a devotee of naval history?" He was staring at a print showing the USS *Constitution* engaging HMS *Guerrière*.

"In a small way. Indeed, I started my career in Russia as a naval officer, although I don't spread that too widely."

"At sea?"

"I was, and in fact I made a cruise in the 1970s that brought me quite close to here. We visited Bandar Abbas. Iran was so different then." That was the line that Efremov had wanted to deliver. *The bait is out.*

"It was, yes, it was. You know that I joined the Navy under the Shah."

"I assumed so. Though to end up a commander in the Revolutionary Guard—"

"They need me—to drive their mini-subs. And keep them repaired. Otherwise they spit on me. And I on them,

425

you understand. A few are sailors, the rest useless. Half of them want to die gloriously but can't perform simple maintenance. The other half, well—"

"I see, yes—" Efremov had his man. "More coffee?" *Old school*. Loyal enough, but nostalgic for the old days when women wore short skirts in the streets and scotch could be purchased in the stores. He had a very good record since the revolution, nonetheless. With his American education and Russian submarine school, he should have been unpromotable in the Guard. Clearly an exceptional fellow.

"Are those really Dunhills?"

"Do help yourself."

"As I was saying— I don't know if what happened—what I am going to tell you about—was a test, because of my background, or a genuine offer. Anyway, almost two weeks ago now, a foreigner approached me in Bandar Abbas. He said he had taken the hydrofoil across from Dubai just to meet me. I thought he was Egyptian. Maybe he wasn't. He charmed my wife, certainly; Egyptians have that rather— oily attack, you know? He brought me a bottle of scotch, which I have finished, and my wife a bottle of scent, which may last the rest of our lives. Allah be praised." The last was delivered in a manner so devoid of humor it must have been meant as humor. The local sense of a joke still baffled Efremov. He smiled. The commander smiled back.

"Should I have turned the gifts in?"

"What do you want me to say? You know the law. On the other hand, are you asking if I care? I don't."

"At any rate, he represented himself as the owner of a marine salvage operation. The Mediterranean, although maybe I assumed that; I don't remember. He explained that he was expanding operations and meant to purchase several small submersibles and was looking to hire experienced men to maintain and pilot them."

Efremov sipped his coffee. Some of the confidence was bleeding out of the commander as he told the story.

"I told him that I did not think I could get an exit visa. He brushed that off. He wanted to talk price. I told him that I was not available. He knew a fair amount about my situation—that was why I thought it might be a test, he seemed to have so much information about me. At first, he offered me a thousand dollars a week plus expenses, and a bonus when the first operation was completed." He blushed. "You know what kind of money that represents in Iran! It was already too much—you understand? Then he volunteered that the first operation would be near Libya and asked if that would make it easier for me to get an exit visa."

"Sounds like a perfectly genuine offer." Actually, it did not, but Efremov saw no reason to show interest. He thought he knew what was happening, now.

"Wait, wait, you haven't heard the rest. I refused. I claimed age. He pressed me hard and finally admitted that he needed me for just that one operation. Then my alarms went off, I can tell you! I said that I was not a mercenary. He began to offer more money. I sent him away. It got crazy—he was offering me one million dollars on completion! He got really angry when I asked him to leave. He suggested that someone had promised him that I would agree." He bent forward toward Efremov. "Who? Who?" As if he were saying, *You? You?*

Efremov shook his head. Someone close to this patriotic commander was an agent of another government—not Egypt, was his guess. That person had volunteered his name and had been wrong. Later, Efremov would enjoy ferreting out the traitor in the ranks of the fanatic Guard and holding him up to ridicule. No; forget the minor pleasure; turn him and have another agent inside the Guard.

With a little luck, he could make this old-fashioned sailor a hero, get him promoted, and gain another ally in the supposedly impenetrable Guard at the same time. What was it the British called it? Shooting a left and a right.

"You will excuse me for one minute, please."

"Of course." The commander lit another Dunhill and poured more coffee. Efremov watched him for a moment from the next room. He didn't fidget or look at his watch. He looked at the naval prints with evident interest. Efremov had seen his type before, in the Spetznaz, in the submarine fleet, in the American Navy. All too rare here.

He returned with a black three-ring binder. The commander had no way of knowing that it had come with Efremov when he had fled Russia. He opened to a tab and began to turn pages of photographs for the commander. After half a dozen pages, his bushy brows went up theatrically and his finger descended like a falcon on one picture.

"Sure?"

"Yes, yes—he is younger here, but he is unmistakable. That smug look. He's even fatter now."

Not Egyptian at all, but French, with an Algerian grandmother: André Malmaison, born in Algiers, moved to Nice with his parents when De Gaulle gave up Algeria. A teenage *pied noir* who had got involved early on with the diehards who had tried to assassinate De Gaulle but had never been prosecuted, because either he had given secret testimony against them or he had been a plant all along. At any rate, from age seventeen an agent of the old guard in the Deuxième Bureau, and tossed out on his ear when they were in the 1980s.

And still, Efremov thought, working for one of them.

Lascelles, he thought. He must be eighty now, and nuts. What the hell is he up to, wanting an expert on mini-submersibles in Libya?

It might be a fine item to pass along to the friends in Libya.

Zaire.

He had lost the cell-phone signal. He thought the battery was gone, but they were out of range of a tower, anyway: the last message had told them to move to a location farther west and wait for an airdrop. No explanation. Airdrop, not extraction. He thought he knew what that meant.

Alan had built a fire in the night and stood watch. Despite lack of food, Harry seemed better again this morning, although he was still in pain. Djalik said he was sure the lidless eye was blind, but he was pumping antibiotics into Harry to try to fight the infection that raged there.

They heard the small aircraft engine vibrating against the trees, coming and going for some time. Alan built up the fire with everything he could find and threw damp grass and ferns on it to make smoke. They never saw the plane itself; the forest canopy was too thick. But something crashed through the canopy within yards of their position and dangled, far above them, from parachute cords. The aircraft noise receded. Each sway of the cords caused the package to dangle a little closer. Alan went up the tree, dizzyingly high, even though he wasn't at the top, and cut it loose.

It was better than Christmas, with food and medicine and weapons and maps and two radios. Two Berettas and a .22/20 gauge survival gun. A thousand dollars in South African gold coins. Batteries and a solar charger.

They looked at the maps as they consumed an MRE to its last plastic pouch.

The best map of the area, a TPC, had three small airfields marked on it. The first was twenty miles to the west, with the others spaced roughly thirty miles apart beyond it. They were, he assumed, potential pick-up points, but there was no message; that would come via radio.

Djalik had separated out the medical supplies and divided them into three; each of them took some. He brandished several at Harry. "Percodex. Tylenol with codeine. Seconal. We're getting you off morphine before you turn into a junkie, Bud." They both grinned. They had developed an odd relationship, Djalik and Harry.

Djalik didn't tell Harry what he'd already told Alan: they had to save a little morphine, in case somebody took a bullet.

Alan got on the radio. One only received—weather, canned messages. It gave him codes for the two-way, and that told him the news that he relayed to the others.

"There's three possible extraction points ahead of us— twenty, fifty, and eighty miles. As of now, the BG's out of the extraction business, but they're trying to set something else up, but it's gotta be rock-solid from our end—no hostile fire, good landing area, no witnesses."

Harry laughed. His speech was quite clear now. "Whom are they sending in, American Airlines?"

Alan grinned. "Air France. Let's go."

He wasn't entirely kidding. The French evidently wanted the task. At that point, Alan thought he'd hop into the Red Baron's Fokker tri-plane, if it could land near him.

That evening, Djalik calmly reported the bad news.

"We're being followed. I kept thinking we were unlucky."

Alan felt his pulse race at the thought. Alan was tired, his knees and back hurt, and he wasn't sure how many more small crises he could handle. He raised his head slowly and looked at Harry first. Harry was better, but he still wasn't fast.

"Are you sure?"

"No, I ain't. But I'm pretty sure. I'd like to drop back tonight and check."

Alan wondered what Djalik was made of. He didn't seem tired. He also appeared to do twice as much of the work and acted as scout, often traveling twice as far as Alan or Harry every day. Alan wanted to volunteer. He felt that as leadership had devolved on him, he ought to be in front. He was also realistic enough to realize that Djalik, and even Harry, had survival and combat skills he lacked.

He hated to be in charge of people better at their jobs than he was. He had always led through energy and skill, his ability to learn any task swiftly. Now he was the leader by custom and assumption, but Alan knew that any of them could have led. Alan thought for a moment and looked out over the darkening forest canopy below them. The open country to the south was golden red in the setting sun.

"Is it Zulu?"

Djalik nodded. Harry's head came up, fast.

"If you have to go, do it. You don't need me to tell you not to take chances, though. I don't think we'd have made it this far without you."

Djalik merely looked at the ground for a moment and grunted.

Djalik moved easily through the trees. He had expected dense vegetation and lush jungles, but this part of Africa seemed mostly dry red dirt and thorny, open trees with massive hills set in the plain. They were camped at the base of one of these hills. Djalik moved quickly down their back

431

trail for almost a mile, making only a minimum effort at concealment. He had a pretty good idea where the enemy was. Novices spent lots of time sneaking in the woods. Djalik used speed first.

He was surprised by Craik's praise. Djalik had sized Alan Craik up and found him to be a glory hound, the sort of officer that got guys killed and got medals. Djalik shook his head minutely as he took a break in a small gully and pulled at his chin several times as if fingering an invisible beard. Craik hadn't lived up to his glory-hound impression. He took a swig of water, rolled it slowly in his mouth, and spat. Then he checked his weapons and began to move. Now he was moving slowly and carefully.

They weren't as close as he had expected, and he still wasted almost an hour moving along slowly in the dark, moving from vantage point to vantage point to check the ground ahead as the darkness became total. He checked his map twice, but mostly he navigated by an internal picture that was seldom wrong.

They had sentries out, but they were noisy and confident, and far too close to their camp. He moved up close to the sentries, close enough to kill one without making enough noise to matter, but he didn't. He couldn't understand their language, but he was damn sure it didn't sound African, and when one man lit a cigarette, Djalik could see why. They were white. Despite their odd, foreign clothing and weapons, Djalik's first impulse was that they had to be some kind of extraction team. Caution and experience warned him otherwise. He waited, lying silent, until the biggest man moved, breaking a branch and cursing. Djalik didn't need to understand the language to get the gist. They were Serbs, the same Serbs as those at the airfield. They had fired on the helicopters, too. The big shape was the one Craik called Zulu. Djalik lay and listened.

Zulu was not just a big man, he was a killer. Djalik had seen it at the airfield. A trained partisan. Djalik just couldn't see Craik coming up against this guy in the dark and getting away alive, but clearly he had. And at the airfield, Craik hadn't been brilliant, but he hadn't been dumb. He'd created a big ruckus jumping the guys behind the table. Not a shooter, but good enough, as long as his luck held.

Djalik heard the big man speak several more times. He was thorough, checking where his men were sleeping and chatting with each one. He visited the sentries, approaching each one as silently as Djalik. He was too good to be some typical merc. Zulu's apparent contempt for his quarry had clouded his group's wariness, but otherwise they were a pretty good outfit, for mercenaries, a group for which Djalik had a special contempt. There were no more than fifteen of them, and they carried only light weapons. Djalik toyed with trying to take them. If he had one more shooter . . .

With a jerk, Djalik realized that there were other men moving. He lay very still, listening to the sound of his heart in his ears, and heard the movement. It was over to his left. Djalik began to inch backwards, cursing that his rifle was strapped to his back.

Then the man moving called something and rose to a crouch. The nearer sentry whispered a reply. They were changing their sentries. The man who had called out had clearly missed the post in the dark. Djalik turned his head to make sure no one had moved behind him and began to move backward again.

Djalik extracted himself very slowly. It took him more than an hour to get out of earshot of the two men watching the camp, and almost as long to get a safe distance away before he could trot. Then he moved quickly. He missed his way twice, but never for long. Before the moon set he was back in the camp.

Craik was still up, sitting with his back against a tree and his weapon across his lap.

Djalik moved until he was breathing in Craik's ear before whispering.

"Fifteen men. Serbs. That guy who tried for you at the airfield."

Craik's thin face was relaxed. He had been tense before he knew Djalik was there; the prospect of fifteen men out to kill him seemed not to bother him. Djalik watched him for a moment. Craik was silent, looking out into the night.

"I think we should ambush them right here. It's a good place. They'd hit us about half an hour past light. If they thought we were dangerous, they'd have kept a better watch."

"Is that really better than just heading out right now?"

"I think so, sir. If we can knock three or four down, they'll stop. Whatever the hell they're after, it won't be worth taking real hits. If you and I and Harry can each get one right away, that should do it."

Alan shook his head. He smiled crookedly, still not looking at Djalik, but the smile was gone when his head turned back and his eyes were dull in the dark.

"He's after me. Because I can finger him as a war criminal. Lousy break for us. Okay, we'll try it."

Djalik smiled invisibly in the dark and moved away to plan.

30

End of November

Washington.

Adams-Morgan is an urban Washington neighborhood that tries to be the Greenwich Village of the capital. It is multi-ethnic, edgy, artsy. It is a relief from the suburbs for people who don't like to live in their cars. It is interesting and exciting—and, sometimes, dangerous.

Abe Peretz lived in Adams-Morgan, the choice Bea's. They had most of an old house on a side street that was always lined with cars, theirs included. They had Latino and Oriental neighbors and rented their top-floor apartment to a dour Ethiopian. Every morning at six, Abe came out the front door, checked his car to see if the tires had been slashed or the wing window broken (both things had happened in the two years they had been there) and then turned left and started jogging toward DuPont Circle. He wore running shoes and green shorts, a zippered purple nylon vest, and a red-and-white hat with a small visor. He had forgotten his gloves, which he should have worn because the temperature was in the forties. Checking his watch, he crossed the street and turned south.

Five blocks south, two men lounged on a corner. The corner was usually empty at this hour, he knew, because he ran the same route every day and could have been clocked at points along it. The two men did not seem to be waiting for him, but when his distant figure appeared, bobbing past the trashcans in front of a Brazilian restaurant, one of them muttered something and stirred.

Both men were black, both in their thirties; both wore the urban uniform of oversize pants, oversize sweatshirt, untied basketball shoes, and backward-facing baseball hat. They were supposed to look like locals, but something indefinable about them was not local, just not quite right. Maybe they could have walked the walk and talked the talk, but Mike Dukas, could he have seen them, would have known they were out of place.

Abe Peretz came closer. When he had glanced to his left and started across the last side street before their block, one of the men plunged across the sidewalk and leaned against a telephone pole with a peeling poster that said *March to fight oppression in ———stry!*

Abe came up over the curb and jogged down toward them. He was breathing easily, running a little hunched. As he came close to the two men, he smiled. He started to run between them.

"Hey, m'man!"

Abe turned his head.

"Hey, man, you got the time?"

Abe did not quite stop running as he raised his left wrist and stared at it. He swung toward the man to give the time.

Behind him, the second man stepped away from the telephone pole and raised a sawed-off baseball bat.

Zaire.

Alan had started at so many nature noises that the sound of voices and the soft crunch of a boot on a rotten stick came as a relief. Now it was real. It was just after dawn. His AKM, with a fur of orange rust down the receiver, was

436

balanced on the branch in front of him. Alan sighted down the barrel and saw a figure in a dark green coat of rags with bright brass buttons crouched on the trail. FAZ. The army of Mobutu Sese Seko. Officially, the US Navy and the FAZ had nothing against each other. Did this guy know that?

The first figure crept back up the trail and Alan lost him. The voices were renewed. His heart began to pound, a mixture of fear and anticipation. The voices went on. Wait for Djalik to shoot.

Another figure moved up the trail with the first, the FAZ guide. Alan's eyes widened over his gun sight. Should he lean out? He had only thirty rounds. *Wait for Djalik to shoot first.*

A long *braaat* from his right answered the question for him. Harry had an M-10. They had picked spots after Djalik had gone over the ground in the dark. Now, maybe Harry had panicked, or maybe his hate was too powerful. At any rate, Alan recognized the sound of the M-10, then Djalik's AK. The newcomer spun to the side, maybe hit. The guide was clearly out, knocked back by the hits, and he plunged backward, disappearing out of the patch of light on the trail that was Alan's chosen sighting area. Other weapons were firing, then stopped; the shooting had lasted only seconds. The man behind the guide had been white. Alan tried to pant silently and looked for something to shoot.

Movement in the trees to his left, somebody attempting to get behind them on the north of the trail. He rolled over a downed log. One shot. He lay still and listened. Then he wriggled down the log. Two men were moving slowly, parallel to the trail, nearly invisible when they stopped, only their movement betraying them. His rifle was trapped against the log, and it took him slow, panic-edged seconds to move it, a fraction of an inch at a time, up his body, over his head, and into sighting position, waiting for them to see him, shoot him. He was hyperventilating. He was drenched in sweat and the red dust and bits of the log stuck to his hands, his face, and the rifle.

Good sight picture *crack* and the rifle tore at his shoulder. The man closer to the trail grunted and slammed into the tree beside him. His partner looked around wildly. *Crack.* This man screamed when he was hit and kept screaming. The forest seemed full of yelling and then there was a long yell and a burst of fire from the south, on the other side of the trail, and then there was more movement. Sweat flowed from Alan's forehead, pumped from his chest and ribs, and he could feel his heart beating fast, heavy hammer blows. He rolled swiftly to his right and tried to point his rifle down the log to his left flank.

Alan crawled in short bursts, expecting each move to be answered by a hail of shots. He stopped when he could see along the trail again. It was a short distance, but his intense concentration gave him a giddy sense of disorientation. He had no sense of time, didn't know where he was or where to expect movement. Then he saw the guide, who lay a few feet from him, the exit wound in his back huge and glistening and already covered in flies. Somebody moved in the forest, coming up the ridge, and Alan saw him and shot too quickly, missed, and Djalik's AK barked almost from his feet; there was return fire from three places and Djalik grunted and stopped shooting. A flash of green. Alan couldn't remember firing fifteen, but when he pulled the trigger there was no shot. He had to change magazines, and the whole time he forced his trembling hands through the process he watched a pair of legs sticking out behind a mound of earth, tried to ignore his gut-wrenching knowledge that he was out of ammo and Djalik was hit. *Take your time.* Alan brought the rifle down too quickly and a shot hit his tree. He moved the sight picture up the legs and fired. There was a cry, a horrible, pitiful mewling cry and the legs flopped, and fire tore up the ground near him. Alan did not twitch away from the fire. He watched and returned a single shot. His hands and feet were cold, and he could taste salt running off his unshaved face and into his mouth.

Djalik had been covering Harry. Alan could see Djalik now, only feet away, blood pumping from his left hand. *If you leave me face-down in Africa, Commander—* He saw Djalik draw a pistol with his right hand, work the slide one-handed against his hip, and place it near him. Then he started to work a tourniquet on his left arm. Harry was pumping shells into a shotgun, the M-10 exhausted beside him.

A face flashed around a tree he had been watching, but much lower than he expected. Alan fired. Nothing. Several of the downed men were screaming or moaning. Alan thought that at least four were down. The man behind the tree swung out at ground level and fired a burst. The man was big and his hat was gone and *it was Zulu* and he fired without aiming, wasted shots throwing clods of red dirt in the air. The man twisted wildly and got back behind his tree.

Zulu. Alan waited for the head to appear. Instead, he saw an elbow materialize slowly, right down near the ground. Alan shot once. There was a long red smear on the tree. *Should have waited for the head.* Zulu, if it was Zulu, made no sound. His heart crashed in his chest, seeming to pound against the huge tree he was pressed against. Zulu who tortured. *Zulu who tortured Harry.*

Alan watched the forest, tensed, his reason and his hatred perfectly balanced. Reason said that he was the only man firing, that he was responsible. Hatred pushed him, hatred and rage, to rush the tree. Zulu had to be hit.

Maybe down. Alan wanted him dead and he crouched, his breath seeming a great shout against the silence, his mind stretched in indecision. Nothing was moving, and the wounded made the only sound. Harry crawled to Djalik and twisted the tourniquet. The wrist had been smashed by a large-caliber round. Djalik was bleeding heavily, and Harry finally gave up on the tourniquet and simply lay in the red dirt, holding the veins with his thumbs. Alan knew his duty then, and he did it. He waited.

After two minutes, nobody more came. He heard movement from the tree he thought was occupied by Zulu, and then behind it. After more long minutes, he thought the patrol had fallen back. He hoped so. He knew that really good soldiers would simply wait. Alan didn't know when he would have waited enough, and he made the decision coldly, weighing further silence against the need to tend to Djalik. He moved. There was no fire and he joined Harry.

"They may get reinforcements," he said. Harry nodded and crouched there until Alan came and tied the tourniquet Harry was holding.

"They were Zulu's." Alan was suddenly gulping air. He had just killed three men. He was very, very glad to be alive.

Harry nodded. He was choked with emotion, and his face twisted with hate, the same hate as Alan showed.

"I saw him and I couldn't . . . I just shot and shot. Like a green kid. *He cut my eye.*" And Alan could see that all of it, rage and hate for the humiliation and the pain, had poured out of the barrel of the M-10 with the bullets. Harry looked better.

Djalik gave a croak meant as a laugh.

"Arrogant bastards. We downed what, five? Maybe ten?" His voice died away in mutters.

Alan could only hope that it would be enough to stop the

pursuit. He looked at his watch, thinking it had stopped, but the second hand was still moving.

"We've got to *break off*, sir," Djalik said, clearly. The words had some special meaning to him. Harry looked at Alan over Djalik's head.

"He means that if we move fast now and lose them, they have to fear another ambush because they lost us and that will slow them. I learned that much at the Ranch." Djalik nodded, too used up to speak. Alan socked back some water and moved carefully down the trail. No shots were fired. Then they began to limp away as fast as they could. Now Harry supported Djalik.

IVI.

Suter was coming out of a meeting when he heard about Peretz. Somebody—he didn't remember who it was afterward, he was so stunned—caught him literally in the doorway and, squeezing past, said the sort of thing you say. Remember the Bureau guy who was here in the summer? Well, did you hear about him? Then telling the details of the beating with relish. "They don't think he'll live, according to the *Post*."

He understood then what Shreed had meant about ruthlessness. He hadn't thought about violence, only about the sort of job ugliness that took place within the really quite civilized bounds of government offices—threats, pressure from above, maybe some hint to his security people that he was a risk and had been talking. But, Jesus, to have him beaten—so badly that he might not live?

He thought about it for a few minutes over coffee and decided it didn't bother him, neither the brutality of the beating nor the responsibility, should he ever need to take it. In fact, something about it excited him, not visibly but far inside, way down where some people had what used to be

441

called a conscience—wherever morality hibernated. Down there, some different beast twitched and moved, roused from sleep by a fascinating dream.

Suter was missing several degrees of what was thought of as "warmth," including any sense of a common humanity. Nonetheless, brain death was something he feared, loathed; the idea of lying there in a vegetative state—*and perhaps knowing it*? —frightened him. Even at second hand, even when it was somebody he hardly knew, like Peretz, it stunned him.

That was what Shreed had meant by ruthlessness and taking responsibility.

He worried then about Rose, and what she knew or guessed.

Paradoxically, the beating of Peretz gave him his first moments of intimacy with her. She was miserable, and she came to him almost instinctively to talk about Peretz, about Peretz's family. Suter relished her unhappiness. What she told him about the Peretzes—two daughters, one going through some kind of crisis of puberty, the mother apparently identifying too much with her—seemed like exotic fiction. What was real was Rose's suffering. Her husband was away and he was taking Craik's place.

Rose wept on Suter's shoulder, telling him about it. He had an erection. He could see the way to bed.

Zaire.
By the third day after the ambush, they were getting close to a town called Yahuma, a tiny gathering of concrete huts south of the main refugee flow. The long rains had started, daily downpours that fell most of the afternoon, then seemed to rest overnight as clouds built up hugely again in the west. It was in the rain that they came to a road.

They saw it first down a long, deforested hillside, an orange stripe along an old valley floor. It was packed with people, moving north and west. They would have to cross it.

Alan had seen it first because he was in the lead. He brought them to a halt and led them back into the trees where the rain fell less fiercely.

"People on the road. More camped along the hillside. Lot of temporary crap and some overturned vehicles. No military."

"I think we gotta just push across with as little fuss as possible," Djalik said. He was taking the morphine now, was in pain, anxious to get to a pickup point.

"People on the road will remember two white men," Harry said. "And the black guy with the eye."

"Can't be helped." Alan shrugged. "We don't know they're behind us."

"Fuck it, let's go," Djalik said, and he started down the hill into the rain. He gave a wave with his left arm, the bandage grimy and bloody and looking like a stump. They started across the open ground toward the road.

Alan realized that they had reached the point of fatigue where they were making mistakes. Djalik walked out into the open without a glance. Alan reached inside for some reserve, and didn't find one. He stumbled after.

As they moved down the spine of the hill, some of the refugee flow continued, but groups and individuals, like rivulets from a main stream, began to separate and move off into the forest. A few people simply lay down or hid at the edge of the road. Alan and Harry and Djalik looked like soldiers—guns, no women or children.

They kept walking. Djalik was heading for a stalled vehicle that had got trapped in a water-filled hole up to the door-handles, a nun standing in the road in front of it. The vehicle was hopeless, they could tell that before they ever got to it. As they trudged closer, Alan saw that there were several nuns. Two were white. He would have crossed farther along, away from the vehicle, but Djalik was in front and boring straight on because he was in pain. Djalik looked as if he meant to slip past the woman, but she moved right in front of him and stood there, hands hugging her elbows, rain pouring down her face.

"Vous vous dépêchez pour tuer plus des noirs?" she said. *In a hurry to kill more blacks?* She was perhaps forty, rangy, strong-voiced; her French had an atrocious accent.

Harry, right behind Djalik, said, "We're in a hurry to get off this road, Sister."

"So that you can kill more," she said. Her English had a Scots accent.

Djalik looked up the road. "We gotta keep moving," he said.

"We're Americans," Harry said.

"Worse and worse. Who did what to your eye, then?" She was already reaching up to touch the bandage, peel it a little back. She stared. "You ought to be in hospital," she said.

Harry laughed. "What hospital?"

"Have you got antibiotics, then?" she asked him.

"Some."

"Give me some, for the love of God. These people have nothing. Some painkiller—please, God!"

Alan started to say that maybe they could give her a little, and Djalik barked, "Negative that!" Alan looked at Harry, who shook his head. "We need what we've got."

The other white nun, older, less strident, reached for Djalik's hand, and he pulled it away. "What did you do?" she said.

"Bullet."

"Let me see—"

Djalik put the bloody hand behind him. "I'm not one of your Africans." He looked at Alan. "For Christ's sake, let's get off this road!"

Alan was going through his first-aid kit, looking for medicines he could spare. He made a little handful of small compresses, merthiolate, a package of aspirin. He held it out to the first nun. "I can spare these—"

She must have seen the word *aspirin* on the label.

"Aspirin!" she cried. "You got the gall to offer me *aspirin*?" She struck the things from his hand and they fell in the muddy water. "Look at them," she shouted. "Look at them!" She pointed up the road at the thousands of people. "You make this, and then offer me aspirin!"

Alan hurried after the others. Her voice followed him as he scrambled up the bank and into the trees. "This is Africa! This is *Africa*!" He heard the sound when he could no longer make out the words.

Washington, DC.

In a cubicle inside the Naval Investigative Service head-quarters, a female analyst disposed of a tasking order, took a quick break for the restroom and a bottle of water, and sat again at her console. Quickly looking down the cover sheet of a new order, she began to enter data. It was a little more interesting than others she had dealt with that day; it had a gamelike quality that intrigued her. Lately, she dealt with deserters' files, and the tasks were no more interesting than adding new data to existing files. In this case, however, the search was for a name that might or might not be that of a deserter.

She skipped the redaction that had been done by some-body up the line and went to the originator's request at the back of the hard-copy file. Here, rather than the search

445

terms prescribed by the faceless person above her, was a cafeteria of suggestions, hunches, and outright questions: *Name or nickname "Z" or "Zulu;" please search for names beginning Zul or something like that. Not African-American. May have been born or raised Chicago area. May have had a Bears ashtray. May have left Marine Corps at time of Yugoslavia breakup—1990 or 1991. Now mid-30s—may have re-upped at least once. Check for disciplinary action re hate-group activity or membership, esp. anti-Muslim, including African-American Muslim. Maybe left Corps if ordered to Kuwait (Islamic country). Appears to have good leadership and military skills; may have been senior enlisted or officer.*

She looked for the initiating agent and saw that it was Mike Dukas. Barb had worked for him once, and was ready to go the extra mile for him, because he was one of the rare agents who seemed to know that people like her existed.

She began to run searches using the prescribed search terms—last name beginning with Z; birth date 1958–1964; service period 1978–1992. As usual, too many people matched. A surprising number of ex-marines had names beginning with Z. What didn't come up, however, was somebody who had deserted in 1990–91, was an E-4 or higher, and came from the upper Midwest.

She tried Z, Chicago. Nothing. Same for Z, Detroit, and Z, Cleveland. Was Cleveland even in the upper Midwest? She went to the web, logged on a map page, and looked at the Midwestern states. Made a list of cities. Logged off, tried them. Nada.

Zul. Names starting with Zul. This merely limited what she already had (names beginning with Z) but didn't help noticeably—eighteen Zul-'s had left the Corps c. 1988–1992 and were more or less the right age.

So she tried first names beginning with Z.

From Chicago.

From Detroit. And got: *Panic, Zoltan, b. 1961, enlisted Detroit, MI, 1980; to E4, 1983; E6 1986; reduced to E3, 1987, fighting and distribution of racial materials on federal property. To E4, 1988. AWOL 1990, Naples, Italy, en route Saudi Arabia; declared deserter, 1990. See File P805937DE for sightings and possible contacts.*

She went on searching, and she compiled a list of a hundred and thirteen possibles, with nineteen likelies, but for her money Zoltan Panic was the man. She attached a little yellow sticky to the packet with her reasons. Then, because it was Dukas, she picked up the phone to call the field office in Detroit.

Zaire.

They pressed on after they crossed the road. It was one of their best days for mileage; Harry could walk pretty well now, and Djalik, although having trouble with his knees, still seemed strong. Alan had to be the scout, now. He was the only one near fit.

The next day, they came to the first of the airfields that had been marked on the map.

It was covered with refugees. There were Luo from the lakes, and Hutus from Rwanda, and even Banye Melenge families, Tutsis caught on the wrong side of the war by affiliation or bad luck. There were people from Kisangani and further east. There were Katangan shopkeepers. Every one of Zaire's forty tribal identities could be found on the long, dirt strip.

Staring eyes. The hollow look. Vacancy. "Refugee" is what people are called when everything has been taken from them; family, homes, work, love. Perhaps so little humanity is left that it becomes easier to kill them, rape them, or ignore them. In time, if not shot or raped, starved, or beaten to death, they recover something and return to

447

life. None of the adults on the former missionary field at Djolugana had reached that stage yet. They were corpses that breathed. Only the sound of children, laughing, crying, hungry, hurt, or curious, showed that any life remained. The children always recover first.

The missionaries, of course, were long gone.

The refugees lay where they had come to a stop, all over the field and in the tiny hangar. The smell of shit was everywhere. The feeling of fear was everywhere. Soldiers had carried a girl away last night. No one knew who they were or where they had come from. Events had narrowed to these defenseless people. Anyone with a gun would harm them. Fear, and despair, ruled absolutely.

The faces of the people on the field were far worse than Alan's first glimpse of Harry back at the hangar. They would never leave him. He couldn't drag his eyes away, couldn't keep himself from looking, but he didn't even stop walking. He couldn't ask anybody to bring a plane in here, and it would be mobbed before it stopped rolling if he did. Djalik, however, looked uncertain.

They slung their rifles across their backs and started looking for another track going west.

Washington.

Rose had been in Houston when the call came about Abe Peretz. Bea had called late at night, at first calm and then hysterical. For Rose, it was an almost distant pain, muffled as if it came through some thick wall. She had enough of her own—the lost baby, still a horror; Alan at sea; the tension of the job. Now, her friend's grief was almost alien.

"How is he?"

"How is he? He's almost dead, for Christ's sake!" Bea started to cry. "I didn't mean to shout at you. Rose, I'm losing my mind. What will I do without Abe, Rose?"

"But he's alive, Bea—he'll be okay—"

"He won't! He's dying. They won't tell me, but I know he's dying. I've seen him. Like a little old man. What'll I do, what'll I do—?"

This was a new Bea. Rose knew noisy Bea and aggressive Bea and abrasive Bea pretty well, but she had never understood how heavily those Beas leaned on Abe. She flew home next day, telephoned at once, and got the pretty daughter who had been in Israel and had gone on the pill at fourteen (and then off because "Sex sucks"). Bea was at Holy Cross hospital. Abe was in surgery.

"On his head," the girl said. She sounded calm, more mature than her mother. "He has a hematoma. Pressure on his brain. I told my mom it would be okay because if they have to go into your head, this is the most common surgery they do, but she's a basket case."

"Want me to go sit with her?"

"I think that would be a good thing to do."

Hospitals at night are foreign places, deserted except for those swept there by crisis. Rose felt the alienation again, hearing her heels ring against the walls of the empty corridor. In three days, she was supposed to join the *Philadelphia* in Naples. Now, Bea's suffering threatened to pull her away from that anodyne, to sensitize her, as if the howl of one woman would rouse another. Rose didn't want to weep and shout about woe. She wanted to lose herself in work.

The two women embraced. They were alone in a waiting room big enough for thirty people. The magazines—sports, gossip, homemaking—were useless. Bea sat upright as if she must be alert for some message.

At two in the morning, a nurse murmured Bea's name and they moved out into the corridor. A doctor was coming slowly toward them, head and shoulders bowed with fatigue. And defeat, Rose thought. She began to pray, returning to the Catholic girl she had been.

The doctor came close. He was young-looking and dark, unhandsome. He took Bea's hand.

"Piece of cake," he said sadly. He sounded on the verge of exhaustion. "He's a strong guy. He'll need four months to recover, so don't expect a lot of jumping around for a while."

"He's going to be—okay?"

"Oh, sure. Maybe hearing loss in the right ear; the drum was ripped, that sensitive area around the anvil was crushed, but—hey, he's got two ears. No paralysis. I'm gonna keep him here a couple weeks, though. He got good insurance? I don't wanna be second-guessed because of cost, but sometimes hospital care—"

"We'll pay—anything!" Bea began to babble. The doctor, looking sadder and more hopeless than ever, patted her hand and told her there was nothing to worry about.

It should have been Bea's role to be paranoid and suggest that Abe's beating had some connection to his investigation of IVI. Bea, however, was too relieved, too exhausted, and she somersaulted and became too happy. It was Rose, driving out to Maryland next day, who found herself thinking, *Who mugs a jogger? Joggers don't have anything to steal*, and then thinking quixotically of the last phone call she had had from Abe, and Suter's angry tone when she had relayed Abe's concerns.

She wished she could call Alan. He would know. But he was busy on the boat. Maybe she could e-mail Dukas.

As she drove, Rose thought about what Alan and Dukas might say. They had the habit of intelligence, a kind of heightened awareness that was, from a different point of view, skepticism, even cynicism. She had the habit of

450

execution, doing what was asked in the best way possible. They asked questions; she avoided questions.

In two days, she would be starting the last phase before the Peacemaker launch. She had already sent the dog to the kennel. She had meant to be stripped for action, lean and mean, no entangling alliances.

Now this.

Ray Suter's face kept popping up between her and the road. She had actually wept on his shoulder.

Now—

Now she wanted to ask some questions.

At sea, the flag deck of the *Jackson*.

Parsills walked into flag comm, where a female jg from one of the squadrons was doing the morning briefing. That she was pretty hardly registered on him. There was just too much to do. She was winding up, pointing at a view-graph, making some point she'd already made, and the moment she was done Admiral Pilchard thanked her and turned toward his chief of staff.

"No go on the pickup at our first possible site, sir." The admiral looked a question at him: why? Parsills went on: "I quote Craik directly, quote, 'I'm ankle-deep in shit and there are people dropping more all around me as I'm talking. There are about ten thousand people in the pickup area.' Unquote."

The admiral nodded. "Keep trying," he said and turned to other matters.

Detroit, Michigan.

Naval Investigative Service agent Marvin Burke had never met Mike Dukas, but the analyst in DC had and said Dukas was a good guy. So Burke had put Dukas's request on the top of his case file and had used it as a reason to get out of the office. It was an unseasonal day, almost springlike, and even the grungy old streets out near the St Clair Flats looked good to him. Here were block after block of little houses on little lots, with here and there an old car in the yard or an unkempt lawn, but most of them painfully tidy, with a lot of statues of the Virgin, some in upended bathtubs, some by miniature grottoes of concrete and lake stones. He saw window boxes with plastic geraniums, homemade wooden cutouts of fat ladies bent over from behind and of little boys with their pants down. He saw a few signs that said *Get us out of the United Nations!* and *Neighborhood Watch* and *Drug Free Zone*. He knew without looking at the people that this was a white neighborhood; he knew that it was heavily Slavic, a lot of the residents retirees or nearly so who had come here in 1956. He knew that people here had used to send their kids straight into the Ford plant, lifetime employment assured, and now that was over and the kids fled as soon as they could and got jobs in other cities, lived in suburbs, laughed when they heard Detroit called the Renaissance City.

Burke went up the walk of a neat house with a neat white porch and combination storm-screens, and he thought that if he went down into the cellar of this house he'd find a woodworking shop and power tools, but he'd look for a computer in this house in vain. A big TV, yes; FM radio, no. Maybe not a newspaper; maybe some fringe "newsletters" that came by mail.

He rang and waited. He heard footsteps. White fingers parted the thin, taut curtains of the window next to him and a frightened eye appeared. Burke smiled. He waited. The gap in the curtains widened to show a small female face framed by gray hair. The expression was still frightened. The woman shook her head. Burke smiled some more. He held up his badge.

He counted three locks on the door as she opened them—a chain, a deadbolt, and the bolt that had come with the seventy-year-old door. She kept the storm-door between them even after the wooden door was open.

"Agent Burke, Mrs Panic—Naval Investigative Service." He waited. "It's about Zoltan."

She shook her head almost violently. "My husband ain't here!"

"It's about Zoltan, Mrs Panic. Your son. I just want to talk to you." He held up his badge again. The woman was apparently terrified of her husband, perhaps terrified of the world. But she was more terrified of the US government and its desire to find her deserter son. They never gave up, she knew; she watched a lot of shows about criminals who were wanted, and some of those things were twenty-five, thirty years old. They never gave up.

Burke put on his "if-you-don't-let-me-in-somebody-even-worse-will-come" smile.

She unlatched the storm-door. "We don't hear from him. We don't know nothing," she said.

The living room had a little fireplace with a gas log, and brown-and-green tiles that had been put in in the 1920s. Above it was a mantel in dark wood with lots of varnish, and on the mantel an array of photographs, some clearly older than the house. Burke looked at one and saw the Cyrillic printing in the corner and said, pointing to another photo, "This must be your mother."

"My husband's."

"Before you came to the States."

She nodded. Her hands twisted each other's fingers. "Back in the old country."

"Zoltan isn't a Yugoslav name, is it, Mrs Panic?"

"I was from Slovenia. Lot of Hungarians there. My father's name."

453

Burke smiled and manufactured a cough. Another cough. "Could I have a glass of water, Mrs Panic?"

As soon as she was out of the room, he reached for a color photo that had no frame and leaned against the wall behind the other pictures. It showed a man in camouflage with a gun of some sort raised over his head.

Burke turned the photo over. On the back, an aggressive hand had scrawled, "Your boy at the Battle of the Crows!"

That was what he had come to find.

It was when he was leaving that he found out about the computer. She had said, with the anger of the terrified, "You're supposed to phone before you come here. Next time, you phone."

"I did, Mrs Panic. I tried three times, yesterday and the day before. Nobody answered."

Her anger fled, and she was the terrified little woman again. "I don't hear so good," she said, twisting her fingers. He remembered the loud television. He started to reach for the doorknob, and she murmured, "You should better phone my husband, but you can't get him no more. That internet!"

He had actually had a moment of wondering what she meant—what's an internet? he was thinking, because it was so out of context—and then it clicked, and he took his hand away from the doorknob, and he said, "Your husband has a computer, Mrs Panic?"

He knew she had told him something she wasn't supposed to, but it was too late. She looked stricken.

Zaire.

Djalik's hand was getting bad. It didn't look so bad—swollen, too white in the thumb, too red in the area around the wound—but it was still bleeding and they couldn't stop it.

454

"You keep that tourniquet on, I'm gonna lose the hand from gangrene," Djalik said. "I'm not gonna lose this hand!" It was only part of a hand, at best; the two outer fingers were gone, and a lot of the meat up to the wrist, blown away by the bullet in the fight on the trail. He looked at Alan with a stare that took him back to the flight out of Kinshasa: *If you leave me face-down in goddam Africa, you tell my wife you did it for your friend!* He started to say, "I'm not a doctor," and he got only a couple of words out when Djalik shifted his glare to O'Neill and said, "*He* understands."

O'Neill grunted.

Djalik was sitting on the ground. His ruined hand was held out, the arm resting on one knee, as if he meant to beg from passers-by. "Cauterize the fucker," he said to Harry. It was between the two of them, then; Alan was out of it. He said something about trying to tie off the artery, but they ignored him. He knew they were right. He couldn't see any artery in that ruined meat. Only blood.

They found one of the half-abandoned villages where it was at least possible to build a fire, and O'Neill heated a knife blade in the coals. Djalik sat nearby, staring into the heat.

"Going to give you morphine," O'Neill said.

"No! Save it!"

O'Neill looked at Alan. The knife blade was cherry-red. Djalik looked at Alan. "Hold me down." Alan looked at O'Neill, and he nodded. Alan grabbed Djalik by the shoulders and pulled him back until he was flat, and abruptly O'Neill was there with one of their morphine tubes, and he put the needle in and squeezed before Djalik even knew it, and Djalik swore. Alan supposed he had to be grateful, somewhere inside.

"You ready?" O'Neill said a couple of minutes later.

"Yeah, Bud. Listen—you got to let it spurt, so you know

where the artery is. Then tighten right down so the blood stops, okay? Then—burn it." He was sweating, but then, they all were. "Make it quick, if you can, Bud."

The people who hadn't left the little village looked on. They might have been looking at something inconsequential, even boring.

O'Neill put one big hand on Djalik's shoulder. "Think of your family. Okay." He loosened the tourniquet. Blood shot across the dirt. O'Neill peered at the hand. "Think of your wife. Your kids. Are they all there?" He nodded quickly at Alan and at the tourniquet, and he tightened, screwing the stick into the fabric on Djalik's wrist. "Look real hard—look hard—look right into their eyes, Dave—concentrate on their eyes—"

There was a smell of grilling steak. Djalik convulsed under them, and one of the villagers looked away, and the smell filled the air.

31

December 1–2

Sarajevo.

In the depths of a dry season, an unexpected bonus landed in Dukas's message traffic: he had put out a shotgun request in the American intelligence community for hits on the names Zulu or Z, and he had learned that the CIA "inferred" that a mercenary called "Z" had been in Africa two years before. No source was given to Dukas, and he could not know that the inference was the result of pressure within the Agency to come up with information about O'Neill's captors. An alert analyst had made the connection with O'Neill's report of Elizabeth Momparu's story, and someone higher up in the Agency had channeled a vetted version of the analysis to Dukas.

Message traffic went back and forth, and at the end of the day, Dukas had a cropped photo of the man who had been called "Z." Not quite *Eureka!*, or even *Bingo!*, because the photo wasn't very good, but certainly, *Hey, maybe!* The photo had been taken at a distance (by Elizabeth Momparu, although he was not to know that), and it was fuzzy, but there was a face. He compared it with the face of Zoltan Panic from his Marine Corps file—could have been the same, he thought, but there were years between the photos, and the African one had something wrong with his nose that didn't show in the marine.

In his own mind, it made sense: Zulu could have been in Zaire in 1994 to shoot down the aircraft, and perhaps Zulu was there now. But there was no proof. If he could get proof, he could report Zulu-Panic as a deserter; he might also get some action in Zaire, although from all reports it was a chaotic mess, with military from six countries and two guerrilla armies flailing at each other, and half a million refugees fleeing across the battle zone. A line from a poem learned in high school had stuck with him, because it seemed so often apt for his profession—"where ignorant armies clash by night." From the sound of it, that was Zaire.

So, he wanted proof that Z was Zulu was Panic. That, he decided, was what he was going to use Mrs Obren for.

"Michael, she'll run! She'll spill her guts." Pigoreau was snarling around the eternal cigarette.

"Maybe. So we won't give her any contacts—nothing she can sell. She goes in, she gets what I want, I meet her at the border and debrief her, we're through with her."

"You're going to send her to Belgrade with no escape plan? No contact?"

"You got it."

Pigoreau stared at him, his eyes half-closed against the smoke. "You're a harder rock than I ever guessed, Michael. What's the big deal?"

"Zulu's a heavy hitter, and I'm gonna nail him." Dukas tapped on the desk with a fingernail that needed cutting. "Zulu's in the middle of something. The guy has his own web site, only not under that name. The way I know, the FBI grabbed the old man's computer. See, the NCIS guy who went out and talked to the old lady, he was, thank God, smart. She blabbed that the old man was on the internet all the time; the agent wanted to get at the computer right then, but he knew he couldn't, not legally, so he says to her something like, 'Well, we'll just let that be your husband's toy,' or something, hoping she won't say anything to the old man because she's so scared of him. And she didn't, because when they grabbed the computer—it took two days to get a warrant, and they were on to me three separate times for verification of war crimes—everything was intact. And I mean everything— the son's web site was right there under Favorites; he had three e-mails from him in his Delete bin; and he's got files they're still going through, stuff he's downloaded that they think came from Zulu. The old man's a Serb nationalist; he's nuts on the subject, so he's got all this hate shit and a lot of stuff he's downloaded from all over the net; we don't know yet what came from his son and what from elsewhere. But it lets us look into part of what Zulu's doing. He's a player, Pig. He's not just a thug. He's an operator."

"And this is the same guy your friend shot at in Bosnia?"

"I can't get to my friend to confirm it."

"A torturer. And you're going to send a woman you've— Michael, when you've been to bed with a woman, you can't—"

"What, suddenly you're concerned about her?"

"She'll know how dangerous it is. She won't do it."

"Yes, she will." He looked straight into Pigoreau's eyes. "I've found her husband. She'll do anything I want to get him."

They stared at each other. Pigoreau shrugged. "Okay."

Dukas met Mrs Obren at the safe house. At his insistence, Pigoreau and one of the female cops were there. It was clammy in the apartment—an icy comment on their lack of success, because they so seldom had use for the place. Dukas sat on a hard little chair, the chair turned backward so that his gut pushed against the ladder-back. Everybody had coats on. Ms Obren wore mittens and a wool hat and looked as if she was dressed for traveling. Nothing passed between them: she understood the situation perfectly.

He laid it out for her. She was to return to RS, spend two days explaining that she had been picked up and held by the rotten border cops, and then she was to go to Belgrade. There, she was to try to contact Zulu.

"But I don't know how to contact him!"

He ignored the voice, what it used to do to him. "I'll tell you how. He's living under the name Zoltan Kousavik—his mother's maiden name." He didn't tell her that NCIS had found the phone number in the father's computer, tracked the address and the name from there. "He's got a wife and two kids. He's got an apartment in a suburb. You go try to contact him."

"But—" She licked her lips. They were chapped and peeling. Her skin looked dry. "He will know. Why would I go to see him?"

"Because I told you to. Because I gave you his address and told you to take a message to him. The message is that he's a deserter from the US Marine Corps, and if he'll turn himself in to me and undergo interrogation, I'll promise him they'll go light in the States."

She was standing. Everybody was standing but Dukas. She looked hopeless. "He would never do that."

"Anyway, you say he isn't there. You told us he's gone away. If he's gone away, he won't be there and you won't have to tell him anything. So, instead of giving him a message, you get me some information. I want to know where he's gone and when he's coming back. I want you to set it up so you're told where and when he returns. You find that out for me."

Her mouth hung a little open. She looked dim-witted. "How?"

"You go to the wife. Become her friend. She'll tell you."

"I can't! Get somebody else!"

"There isn't anybody else."

"I won't! No!"

"You will, or you'll never see your husband again. I know where he is. If you don't do this, I'll see that he's put where you'll never find him. Not ever. If you do it, I'll give him to you."

Pigoreau and the female cop were expressionless, like nurses who stand by while the doctor gives bad news. Working hard at alienation.

"You *know*?"

"He's in a hospital on our side of the line."

Her face changed, illuminated and hopeful. "How is he?" she cried.

"I'll tell you when you get back from Belgrade."

Pigoreau's jaw showed a momentary spasm, as if he had started to flinch and thought better of it. In fact, his alienation had slipped. Dukas was an even harder rock than he had thought.

At sea, aboard the *Jackson*.

Sneesen was holding himself together pretty well. That was how he thought of it—holding himself together, so that he wouldn't fly apart like a spring that had been coiled and let go.

But it was hard. Nobody much spoke to him, even the white guys. They didn't get it. It was just as Chief Borne had said; they were all sucked in by the bullshit about diversity and getting along, and they didn't want to listen to him, they just wanted to pretend to be

461

mud-people, pretending they could do hip-hop, jive, play b-ball. Mud-shit.

Today he'd found that the skipper was a Jew. It made a lot of things fall into place, but it was hard. Nobody else realized it, but Sneesen could tell from the way in the ready room the man dropped Jewish words—*chutzpah, mushoogeneh, tuchus*—and kept touching the top of his head, where they wore little beanies when they were with each other. It explained a lot—why the mud-bitch always flew with Commander Rafehausen, and why now there was a mud-man, McAllen, supposed to be a hot-shit ASW enlisted guy as SENSO, but he couldn't be, so it was part of the whole thing to surround Commander Rafehausen with them and suck him down.

He could see it. Why couldn't anybody else see it?

Sneesen prayed a lot now. He prayed that God would open white guys' eyes to the truth. He prayed for Rafehausen. He wrote another letter to the chaplain.

Washington.

Rose was sitting in her office at IVI. That, in itself, was unusual. More unusual was that she was rolling a bit of paper between her fingers and then, when it felt like a smooth ball, throwing it at the wastebasket. Then she would tear another bit of paper off an envelope without looking at it and start rolling a ball. Two days before she joined the *Philadelphia* in Naples, and she was rolling paper balls.

Valdez looked in. He seemed about to say something, then stopped himself. "Hey, man," he said. He was worried about her now. He was afraid she'd crack.

"What?"

"You're not *doing* anything. I don't think I ever saw you not do anything before. You sick?"

"Hey, Valdez."

"Hey, Lieutenant-Commander Siciliano." He came in. "Hey, you okay? Why don't you take some time off, go—"

"Listen, Valdez, what happened to the noise you were making about the data stream for Peacemaker?"

"You told me to shut up about it." So she was going to stiff his sympathy. Okay.

She tossed the paper ball at the basket, watched it bounce from the rim. "Did you do anything more about it?"

"I asked a couple questions. I got told if I was smart I'd stop asking."

She frowned. "Or what?"

He shrugged.

"Remember when they tried to transfer you out of here?"

"Yeah."

"That was when you were asking questions."

"Yeah. I figured that out all by myself."

She started to roll another paper ball. "It was Suter tried to get you transferred."

This didn't seem to surprise Valdez at all. "I figured he didn't want me around, he got the hots for you, pardon my Spanglish, but then I start putting two and two together, I think maybe it's the questions about the data stream, not having the hots for you. I told you when they called me into Security and asked me, then you went to bat for me. They're fucking Nazis; they wanted to polygraph me, I told them I got twelve-year-olds I could find on the streets could beat a polygraph. I think all that was Suter. It seemed a lot to do because he got the hots for you, so I decided my questions really did push somebody's buttons, and I shut up."

463

"You remember Mister Peretz? The guy who was in here for a week on his Reserve duty?"

"Yeah, he got the hots for you, too. Nice guy."

"*He* asked a lot of questions. He got transferred out of here after one of his two weeks." She looked up. Their eyes met.

Valdez grinned. "Do I begin to see a pattern here?" he said. "Like, former US Navy Lieutenant-Commander Suter called somebody and got him transferred?"

"Last week, Peretz was beaten up on the street."

"You told me. Too bad, but—what's the connection?"

"Think about it."

"Kind of a long time since he was here asking questions."

"Maybe a long time since he was here, Valdez, but he was still asking questions just before he got beaten up. He called me four or five days before and asked me a lot of stuff about Peacemaker. And Suter."

Again, their eyes met. She said, blushing, "I told Suter about it."

"Oh, man— !" Valdez threw his arms out in a big gesture, as if he were asking a crowd to witness how idiotic this woman could be. "Why didn't you tell *me*? The guy's asking questions about Suter and you go and tell *Suter*? In the very best possible interpretation, Suter is a two-faced asshole, and you *tell* him stuff all the time! You got the hots for him or something?" He brushed his hair back, blew out his breath. "Jeez, now you got blood on your hands."

"Oh, God, Valdez— !"

"Hey, hey, hey— ! I didn't mean it; it's just a way of talking. The guy, Peretz, he's gonna be okay, right? Right?"

"He had surgery last night; they say he'll make it, but it'll take a long time."

"Well, then. But my God, that's kind of heavy, beating on a guy because he asked questions."

"We don't know that."

"Well, I don't *know* that lions eat Latinos, either, but I don't climb into the lion cage at the zoo. Hey, listen: what's really on your mind? What's the playing with the paper balls about? I never seen you like this."

She rolled the paper around and around in her fingers, then rolled it between her palms. "I wonder what it is we're not supposed to ask about Peacemaker. All of a sudden—it's late, I know it's late, Valdez; I've like been in denial— I didn't want to hear anything, you know—distracting— Now I'm worried."

"You so worried you gonna bail out?"

She tossed the paper ball into the center of the wastebasket. "Not on your life." She stood. "I'm in for the long haul. Tomorrow, you and I are going to do our last dry run on the launch and then we're heading out to Naples to meet the *Philadelphia*. But first I'm going to talk to Ray Suter—and you're coming along as a witness." She didn't say, *And I'm going to stop being snowed by the guy's b.s. because his attention flatters me*, but that was what she was thinking.

Suter was in, and he was happy to make time for LCDR Craik, his receptionist said. Rose marched through the IVI corridors like a woman with a mission, Valdez scurrying to keep up. They were an odd but familiar pair—she slender, lithe, head-turningly pretty; he squat, muscular, bullish. Neither had an expression that would encourage other people to mess with them.

Rose went into Suter's office first, and Suter came around his desk and was already raising his arms to embrace her—capitalizing on her weakness at the time of Peretz's beating—when Valdez came through the door.

"Wait outside and close the door," Suter snapped.

465

"Stay here, Valdez." Rose sidestepped Suter's advance. "But maybe it's a good idea to close the door."

She stood near the big window that looked out over the rolling industrial campus, where Maryland's weak imitation of winter was taking hold. Valdez, arms folded, stood apart from the two but apparently ready to step in.

"Okay, Ray," she said, "let's cut the bullshit. You've been feeding me a line since I got here; now I want the truth. Who hit Abe Peretz?"

Suter hesitated the millisecond that showed his shock at the question, and then he tried to take the high road. "Rose, what the hell? Peretz—who's Peretz?"

"The Reserve officer you got transferred because I told you he was asking questions about Peacemaker and targeting data. Come on, Ray—what's your problem with questions?"

"Has your boy here been telling you more stories about the data stream, or what? I thought we settled that."

"You settled that, I didn't—and don't use the word 'boy.'" She compressed her lips, and for a moment it seemed she might soften. "Ray, I liked you. I liked the fact you were attracted to me. But you took advantage of that."

Suter glanced aside at Valdez, started to protest.

"You lied to me," she said. "You *lied* to me."

"You have no need to know certain things about Peacemaker."

"I'm the launch officer! I've got a top-secret clearance! I *do* need to know!"

"That's not your decision and it's not mine. You're a military officer. You accept these things."

"Is that why you got out, because you accepted these things?"

"My experience is not relevant."

"Your experience is key! Goddamit, Ray, I told you what

Abe Peretz was finding out on his own about Peacemaker, and four days later he got beaten so bad he almost died. Tell me the truth!"

"Rose, God, look—let's talk this out somewhere without—" He glanced again at Valdez.

"He stays. Ray—*you told people about Peretz and he got beaten*. Who did you tell? Who did you tell?"

Suter seemed to debate his choices, and real anguish showed on his face as he seemed to understand that his feelings for Rose were being ignored, perhaps crushed. He cleared his throat. "It was a security matter. I'm sure I told Security. Otherwise, I, uh—I don't know—"

"Did you tell George Shreed?"

Suter's face suffered a spasm, something like pain, perhaps suffering—or it may merely have been the anguish of being found out. It caused Valdez to mutter "Yeah!" and grin, and Rose made a motion to him to shut up. She crossed her own arms now. She was in charge. "What's your relationship with George Shreed?" she demanded.

"I'm not going to answer these questions. These improper questions."

"Is it because you and Shreed both hate my husband? Ray, George Shreed is bad news—what the hell are you doing, working with him?"

"I don't work with him! I don't even know who he is. Where are you getting all this? This is wild guess-work, Rose, it's crazy—I'm not going to dignify this any further with my participation. I think you'd better leave. *Both* better leave. I'm very disappointed in you, Rose."

She shook her head. "George Shreed will chew you up and spit out the pieces and never even blink. Ray, Shreed is exactly the kind of man who'd do what was done to Abe Peretz—or who would have it done by somebody else, because he gets other people to do his dirty work for him. The way he got you to work on me. And on IVI, if I read it right. Now—what's going on with Peacemaker?"

Suter swallowed, then went back and sat behind his desk. "This interview is over. If you have any further questions, please address them to General Touhey directly. That's final."

She stared at him. It was the end of the interview— and of what he had hoped would become a relationship, and both knew it. "Okay," she said, "I will."

And she marched herself and Valdez down to Touhey's office, but by the time they got there, Suter had already talked to Touhey, and the receptionist told her that the general would give her two minutes and that Valdez was not welcome. In the general's office, Rose was made to stand, was reminded that she was a military officer subject to the rules of security and classification, and she was told by Touhey that if there was any aspect of Peacemaker that made it impossible for her to perform her duties, she should resign them now and let the Standby Launch Officer assume them.

That would be the end of her career. And the Standby was Ray Suter.

"I wish to ask one question, sir," she said.

"Ask."

Her voice was crisp, official. "Are all orders to be given to me about the launch and Peacemaker legal orders as that term is understood in the Uniform Code of Military Justice?"

"Affirmative."

"I'll hold you to that, sir. Thank you for your time."

Outside, she pulled Valdez into her wake and started for her office.

"So?" Valdez said as he hurried to keep up. "So what do we do?"

"We go to Naples day after tomorrow, we meet the ship, we go down to the Gulf of Sidra and do our job."

"Just like nothing happened?"

Her jaw set in a line that Alan would have recognized and been wary of. "That's what doing our job means."

32

December 2

Zaire.

They had made it across a small dirt track and down a wide trail that had once known wheeled travel to the edge of a small lake. Two thatched lodges were falling down at the west end of the water. It was an old white hunter's camp, still kept going by a couple of ancient Luo poachers. They would have guns.

Alan moved warily onto the open ground where once trucks had parked and called softly for the M'zee. After a little, an old man came out of the closer lodge, holding a single-shot, 20-gauge shotgun. The barrel was pointed at his gut, although the old man's eyes were nearly white with cataracts. He understood Alan's pidgin Bemba/Swahili well enough, although he pretended not to. He understood the color of the gold coins much better. The old man agreed to feed them.

The ground sloped gently toward the lake, with the two large bandas standing at either end of what had once been a beach and was now a small, even reed bed. Across the lake, two great hills rose from the plain, each showing a rocky outcrop like giant teeth against the dark green of the forest. In the foreground, flowers grew in an outrageous burst of color between the lodges and the water's edge, gaudy in the rain; after more than a week of the sameness of the forest, the riot of color in the light of day was as loud as a gunshot. At the foot of the lake to his left were two brilliant red flowers that looked like hollyhocks. He cut one blossom and pressed it in the day book from his helmet bag for Rose. Because it was so strange.

Harry and Djalik emerged into the clearing between the two rickety bandas. Alan helped them get their packs off, and the three of them sat in a thatched ruin that had once been the bar. There were still actual chairs. Djalik sat down and fell asleep.

They ate wild impala until their hands and scraggly beards were covered in grease. The impala had been alive an hour before, he thought, shot—illegally—to feed them. It was, right then, the most delicious thing he had ever eaten. He and Harry washed themselves in the lake, making jokes about bilharzia and dinky, but in fact the lake water was icy cold, far too cold for either organism.

Harry tried his Tutsi on the women who cooked the meat and failed. He told Alan later that these people were "honorary" Banye Melenge. They didn't speak any language he or Alan knew, except enough Bemba and Swahili and Creole to bargain with Alan. They were not in the least afraid, either; he saw other figures on the far side of the lake, young men with rifles, and he thought that these people were accustomed to having things their own way here.

Harry found Alan in the last rays of the sunset, casting his hand line into the lake from an ancient concrete dam at its head. The afternoon rain had ended, and the air was misty now, golden. As Harry approached, Alan's bobber disappeared in a splash and Alan began to haul in the fish. Harry laughed as he helped Alan land it. They were both soaked, but the women had taken their clothes to dry and they were wearing pieces of old cloth, like sarongs. Alan whacked the fish on the head with his knife hilt until it stopped moving.

"That's a trout!" Harry said.

Alan shrugged and smiled. Whatever it was, it bore some resemblance to a trout.

"How's Djalik?"

"Asleep again." Harry hesitated. "I think he's running a fever. It's the hand."

The old man and a boy built a big fire of downed wood, saying it was "the way things used to be done." They were able to spread out for the first time in a week. The wilderness they had lived in always seemed cramped, full of refugees, or enemies. The Zairian forest was either desert dry or damp, and there was rarely a flat spot to lie down, much less spread out. Fallen trees, bog, undergrowth, puddles were everywhere. Just seeing an opening in the woods, seeing the fire and the reflection in the lake cheered them.

While they sat, Alan cut up a length of old canvas that had once been a tent. He was making bandages to wrap his bare legs as high as the knee. He made a set for Djalik, as well. They drank tea from old Coke bottles and stared at the fire.

That was the time to give them the bad news. Alan laid the map on the drier dirt near the fire pit and moved a kerosene lamp near it so that the paper was lit from both sides. "The old man says that the second pickup point is being used by the FAZ. He as much as said that it's the field where he used to move illegal stuff like rhino horn. The FAZ are using it the same way now—stuff they've looted, weapons, foreign-aid goodies. That makes it unsafe for us."

"So we give it a bye," Harry said.

"Right."

472

"How much farther?"

"He thinks three days to the third of the airfields, but I don't think he's ever been there. When he says three days, that means at his pace. The way we're going, four—maybe five." Alan tapped the map. "My idea is we lie over here another day and a night and then go for it."

"Negative that." It was Djalik. His face was contorted by the firelight. He knew that he was the one who was supposed to rest.

"You're worn out, Dave."

"I'll be the judge of that, Commander."

Alan bit back the reply he had started to make. At least Djalik hadn't said "no problem." In fact, he hadn't said it for some days.

"Okay. Get some sleep. We're off at first light."

Naples, Italy. December 3.

The streets of Naples were shiny with rain, and the few people out were running for cover as Rose's taxi moved down a main thoroughfare toward her hotel. Along one stretch from the airport, the sun had been shining even as the rain fell, and she had wondered which—rain or sun— was the omen for her mission. She had thought she would be meeting Alan here, but his ship was still in the Atlantic, and she hadn't had a word from him in weeks.

Beside her, Valdez was quiet. It was their third trip to Naples.

"Third time's the charm," she said. It sounded stupid to her as she said it.

"Where do we meet these marines?" Valdez, a solid presence that she depended on, was in no mood for chitchat.

"*If* Suter didn't interfere at the last moment and *if* the Navy didn't tie itself up in red tape, they should be on the beach before we are."

473

"I wanta see them. Seeing is believing."

She agreed, but she didn't want to confess her own anxiety. Many things could go wrong with the launch—the ship, the missile, the weather, the unexpected—but it was the marines she wanted, as if their presence would guarantee success. She had got a medal a few years before for flying a bunch of marines into hostile territory to lift out three Americans (one of them her husband), but she knew that all the heroism had been theirs. Now, she wanted that with her.

And, thank God, there was a message at her hotel. She called the phone number, got another hotel a few blocks away, and was put through to Gunnery Sergeant LaFond.

"Good morning, sir, LaFond speaking."

The voice was even, low. It projected competence, no-nonsense performance.

"Gunny, Lieutenant-Commander Siciliano."

The faintest hesitation—had he not known she was a woman? "Yes, ma'am."

"I just got in. Everything go?"

"Ready to board, ma'am. I got three of the best, we're here checking out our, um, emergency gear." *Weapons*, he meant. She felt a lurch of excitement and thought, *It's going to be okay.* "I'll be right over," she said.

"Uh, ma'am, the boys are, uh—"

"You tell the boys I'm not there to conduct an inspection, but I'm coming over!"

She took a taxi, even though their hotel was close, she was so eager to see them. When she got into Gunny LaFond's room, she laughed out loud. The four marines had spread combat gear over every available surface, and the place looked like a small-arms depot with a view of Vesuvius out the window. The marines were in T-shirts and jeans, and she thought, *They're so young—so goddam young*. But she had thought that about the ones who fought before, and they had always come through.

"The management know about this?" she said to LaFond. He was a thin, short man with sandy hair and the kind of hard face that gets cast as a redneck rounder's.

"We don't want to get thrown out, ma'am. Or arrested."

She saw night-vision goggles, Kevlar battle armor, six handguns, of which only two were issue Berettas, a number of knives, two axes, and what looked like an old-fashioned cutlass. She picked it up and looked at LaFond with raised eyebrows.

"For luck," he said. "I got it in a junk store here in Nap. To repel boarders." He gave her a grin and a look, and she saw that LaFond could be a problem but was trying not to be. *Cajun*, she thought. He was looking at her with eyes that saw women in a particular way, and it wasn't a way that gave them command. But he was fighting it.

He reported quickly on the gear that had been sent direct to the *Philadelphia*: two Mark 19s with belts of HE, APHE, and frag; their four issue M16A2s; grenades; and six Claymores, which, LaFond said apologetically, he couldn't see much use for, but they were all he could get in the explosives line. "I thought maybe I could glom on to something on the black market here in Napoli."

"Belay that; we don't have time, and I don't want you guys in trouble with the local cops. That's all I need, to have you guys in the brig when I'm down in the Gulf of Sidra. Anyway, we sound good to go with the stuff I have on the ship." She told him that all she'd been able to get Touhey to sign off on was an LAW (Light Anti-tank Weapon), which would have been okay against the light tanks of the 1960s, if they should meet any at sea, but probably not much use against anything that floated. On her own, she'd moonlight-req'd two 12-gauge streetsweepers for the ship's company and four Steyr AUGs, one in submachine-gun mode that she had marked for herself. "You guys ever fire a LAW?" she said.

LaFond grunted. "I fired one of everything, ma'am. If not in anger, at least in some school or other." Now, he slitted his eyes at her and said, "What're you expecting, with all this firepower?"

"I'm not expecting anything, Gunny. I just don't want to be surprised. You heard about Fleetex?"

He gave a thin smile. "Ma'am, I was there—on the flag deck."

"It's not going to happen again."

He looked at her with the same hard squint. "Nothing personal, ma'am, but are you the Siciliano who was a chopper pilot that flew some gyrenes into Sudan and out again a couple years back?"

"That was me."

LaFond turned to the three other marines. "She's the one, guys." He held out his hand to Rose. "Honored to serve with you, ma'am."

The hand was dry, the handshake quick and almost painful.

"See you at the boat at 0800. Enjoy Naples." *See Naples and die*, she thought. She gave them a big, big smile.

At sea, aboard the *Jackson*.
Rafehausen was in his pilot's seat, going over checklists before a flight. She came in and gave him that big smile and went back to her seat, and he felt the sense of her like something embarrassing, a hot flash, something other people would see and laugh at. He kept himself under tight controls these days, not only with her but with everything. With Screaming Meemie most of all, whom he wanted to punch in the mouth and whom he probably

would punch in the mouth when they were back on the beach.

Maybe everybody on the boat was under tight self-control—too long without a break, too long boring holes in the air, troughs in the water, waiting for something to happen.

He heard her swear, and then she was on her knees just behind him and to his right, just at the end of the tunnel. He made the mistake of looking back. She was there, head bent, picking up something. Gathering papers. And for an instant, the temptation to reach out and touch her hair was irresistible, and, afterward, he thought his hand had even moved, but he caught himself, feeling dizzy, and he almost said, *Christy, I'm in love with you.*

But didn't. Couldn't. If he did, the squadron would explode. The ship would sink. The Navy would cease to exist.

Discipline first, or chaos is come again.

Belgrade.

Draganica Obren was sitting in Z's apartment. She was frightened but didn't show it. Her nerve was shaken by the interrogation she had gone through, but she had a reserve of strength. She would survive, she knew, if she could get through this.

Z's wife sat facing her. She was smiling. She was a little plump, a little aged by having his children, a nice housewife. At first suspicious of Mrs Obren, she was open and friendly now, because Mrs Obren had the power to charm.

Mrs Obren was selling cosmetics. Or that was what she said when she appeared at the door. She had a free gift, she had said, for every woman who would look at her catalog; the gift was an expensive lipstick and eye shadow she had bought with her own money in a Belgrade store. The woman, this nice woman, this smiling cow, couldn't resist the gift.

And now here she was. She needed only to find a way to turn the conversation to the husband. She knew how; she would introduce the subject of the schoolteacher and say that he was a friend in common, what a small world. And the pleasant cow would agree, and they would talk of people they both knew—Do you know So-and-so, she lives in RS, too? Do you know X? Do you know Y? And then she would talk of husbands: My husband does this; my husband says; Does your husband—?

And then, Where is your husband?

The cow smiled.

Mrs Obren sipped her sweet tea and smiled. She had praised the children, the tastefulness of the room, the smell of baking bread. She smiled. *Now,* she thought. Sweat trickled from her underarms and moistened her brassiere. *Now, I will mention the schoolteacher, and she—*

A sound like a rat chewing, a kind of scratch, then a single knock. The wife made an exasperated sound and went to the door like a woman who knew who it was and didn't want to see him.

She opened the door.

It was the schoolteacher. He came in, all the way into the room, and only then did he look at Mrs Obren. They looked at each other, and in an instant she understood: he had been following her ever since she had crossed the border into RS.

"What is this woman doing here?" he demanded.

33

December 5–8

Next day. The border of Bosnia and Republika Srpska.

Dukas is waiting for her. He has been waiting for two days, and she is overdue, and in another three hours it will be dark and she won't come and it will be over.

He is sitting in a collapsing farmhouse that was hit by an artillery round in the last days of the war. The ground slopes down from the remains of the farmyard to the border, which is only a string of signs here that warn of a minefield that may be real or that may simply have been a cruel invention of the Serbs as they pulled out. One day soon, NATO will get to it and sweep it, but for now it is real and made more so by the bones of a dead horse through whose pelvis the border runs. Dukas has been watching a crushed-stone road and the border posts along it—one down at the bottom of the hill where Bosnia begins, and another a hundred meters along where Republika Srpska starts. This is the American Zone, both sides, and the American forces come and go to patrol both sides—equally, they say—but when they go into RS they go in Bradleys or tanks or armored Humvees.

If she comes, she will come here. That was the plan, the only plan.

He waits. Next to him, Pigoreau waits. Pigoreau is

there mostly to keep Dukas from doing something stupid when—if—she appears. Pigoreau has convinced him that Zulu or people near Zulu will use this opportunity to kill Dukas. It is a perfect setup, with Mrs Obren the perfect bait.

"She's not coming," Dukas says.

Pigoreau shrugs. Pigoreau hopes she isn't coming. To Pigoreau, she is nothing but trouble.

They wait another twenty minutes. The shadows of the trees up the hill in RS are getting long, painted across the melting snow in dirty lines. A bus appears on the RS side.

"There's the bus," Pigoreau says. "Late, of course." He lights a new cigarette. They have been seeing the bus go back and forth every day.

After twenty minutes, the bus gets through the checkpoint and starts down the hill. At the bottom, it stops at the Bosnian checkpoint and the American soldiers get aboard and look around. Dukas studies the bus with binoculars and his heart lurches because he sees her by a window. "There she is," he says.

"Shit," Pigoreau says.

"She made it. By Christ, she made it!" Dukas grins and starts to get up, saying, "It worked, it's going to be okay," but Pigoreau pulls him down and back, away from the window.

They watch the bus come through the checkpoint and stop again and let three passengers off. One is Mrs Obren. Dukas, watching her in the binoculars, sees that she is smiling. She looks happy. Happy because she thinks she is going to see him? No, that can't be. Why is she happy?

A green Yugo has pulled up at the far checkpoint, pulled over by the side of the road. Dukas sees it but does not think about it. Pigoreau, however, is watching it intently

480

in his own binoculars. Below them, one of their men is getting out of his car and is walking toward Mrs Obren. Pigoreau insisted on doing it that way. The man is Belden, a young Brit from Cardiff. He is wearing a raincoat. From here, he looks like Dukas, and that was what Pigoreau intended.

"It's the schoolteacher," Pigoreau says. He is looking at the green Yugo. He sounds grim. He pulls a radio from his belt and flips it on and snarls, "Belden, get out—get out—!"

Dukas sees Belden hesitate, and then he and Mrs Obren vanish in an explosion of flash and fire, and the concussion wave rolls up the hill, bending the leafless bushes and small trees, and a man who had got off the bus with Mrs Obren flies sideways, blood squirting over the snow; the green Yugo turns back into RS and disappears; and the sound hits the ruined farmhouse like the thump of a great drum, or a heart breaking.

Sarajevo.
After a false spring that had lasted only three days, Sarajevo was cold again and plunged back into winter. A little after five in the afternoon, dark already falling, and Dukas stood by his window, reading the last of a stack of files. When he had started reading, he had gone to the window for light; now, it was darkest there, but he read on, hearing the hiss of the snow against the glass but not noticing it. Pigoreau had brought the files in and left; he had stuck his head in twice, seen Dukas still reading, and left.

Now, Pigoreau looked in again and Dukas, without looking up, waved him in. Burrowing in his pullover for a cigarette, Pigoreau took one of the two chairs, crossing the room bent over like somebody playing a servant in bad Chekhov.

481

"What d'you think of the forensics? Hold up in court?"

Pigoreau shrugged. "They're Hungarians. Who knows?"

"Ask them to do some more stuff on trajectories—the side of the bus, they didn't do much on that. Ditto the flak jacket; see if we can get it for evidence and keep it, and ask them to get a statement from the soldier, exactly how he was standing, stuff like that. This isn't for now; it's for three, five years from now, when we get Zulu. I want to bury him in proof on this one. I know it's Zulu."

"It was the schoolteacher."

"What'd IWCT say about him?"

"No to making him a war criminal. This was terrorism aimed at us, is their position."

Dukas folded his hands over his gut and blew out a long sigh, his cheeks puffed like a trumpeter's. "That's the way I'd read it, too. How long before we have to turn him over?"

"Now. Tomorrow at the latest. Federation cops wanted him since yesterday. US military want him. Your FBI 'demand' to have exclusive access to him. Everybody wants him. Maybe we should sell him."

"Maybe we should kill him, the sonofabitch. Okay, keep him at least until tomorrow, even if you have to move him again. Tell him this: it was real cute to use a detonator with an Islamic manufacture, but it won't work. It was remote-detonated, Mrs Obren was his agent—we can prove it, tell him that—and it wasn't suicide. Tell him that's a nice soap opera, he has a very inventive mind, but we don't believe he was up there in his car because he was worried about her mental state. He killed her, and this is why we know he killed her: Mrs Obren's husband was in a prison for the criminally insane until the day before she was killed. Then he was moved, on forged orders, to a doctor's office in Republika Srpska. She visited him there."

"We don't know that."

"I know that! Why the hell do you think she was so happy? Then she comes down here and he blows her up, to get one of us. That's Zulu. I don't know how he did it, but he did it. The schoolteacher doesn't kill people on his own hook. Tell him if he cooperates, we'll turn him over to the US military. If not, it'll be the Federation cops. Remind him that one Bosnian was killed in the explosion and one lost an arm and an eye. Show him the pictures."

"He's a fanatical pro-Serb. He thinks he's a hero."

"I don't care if he's a fucking holy martyr. You let him have any idea of himself he likes. Just find out about Zulu."

Pigoreau went out, and Dukas started through the files again. He was still there at one in the morning when Pigoreau threw himself into the other chair. "He's giving us shit. Nothing, he won't crack."

"Give him to the Federation. Right now. Give him to that Bosnian detective, what's his name? —Rago—Raguz. The big one with the shaved head. Tell him if he gets the dope on Zulu from the schoolteacher, we'll drop a Bosnian name from our active war-criminal list." Dukas looked at Pigoreau, gray-faced in the bad light. "Yeah, yeah, I know, I'm being a bad cop. Well?"

Pigoreau stood up. "What you do is okay with me, Michael. Just between you and me, I think Raguz himself should be on the war-crimes list."

Two days later, Dukas met Raguz in a cops' café and was told that the schoolteacher said that Zulu himself had set up the murder of Mrs Obren, which had been meant to kill Dukas, by e-mail from Africa. "I believe him," Raguz said. "He tells *me* the truth." Raguz grinned, showing a gold tooth.

"The FBI want to talk to him. What condition is he in?"

"For a man who jumped out a third-story window, not bad." Raguz said it exactly as if he believed it. "Now, you keep your word, Dukas—you take Bosnian name from war-crimes list?"

"I can't do anything but take one from my active list. The Hague draws the indictments."

Raguz got up. "I send you the name."

That day, Pigoreau had the results of a paid French hacker's probes into Zulu's web site (information provided, not quite intentionally, by NCIS via Dukas). The hacker had made a hit on another web site belonging to a French corporation called FranTek, and from that on a man named Lascelles. "I want to go overnight to Paris, Michael—I think this is something very big."

Dukas stared at him with what seemed like hostility. "Reporting in to the boss?"

"It isn't like that, Michael." Pigoreau waited for some sort of blessing, didn't get it. "They can help us, Michael."

"They haven't helped us so far. Nobody much has helped us so far, have they? The CIA drops us a crumb and doesn't send us what they've really got; you know they've got files, hunches, more photos— ! You'd think we were fucking pariahs. Security risks! I'm a security risk to your people because I'm American; you're a security risk to my people because you're French. Okay, go to Paris. Tell them what we got. But look—" He seemed embarrassed. "Don't give them Zulu on a platter, okay? He's ours."

Pigoreau had been there when Mrs Obren was killed. "He's yours, Michael," he said.

Paris.

Pigoreau rolled quietly off the bed and began to look for clean clothes, still in their old places, although he'd hardly been there for months. He was quiet, but she heard him, and she rolled toward him, her cat's eyes glittering at him.

"I have to go," he said.

"You are always leaving me. You bastard." She was slipping into one of her angry moods, of which she had quite a variety. They made her life interesting to her, he thought—to him, too. His groin felt exhausted, hollow; he had had no sleep because of love-making. That made their life interesting, too.

"You've been with women in Bosnia," she said.

"Are you sure?"

She laughed, a nasty, tough little laugh. "You bastard. If you bring me AIDS, I'll kill you. I will, Jean-Luc! I'll wait until you're asleep and kill you with your own gun."

"Jealous wives use knives. *Crime passionnel*—a pretty woman like you can get off if she uses a knife. A gun—" He stuck out his lips and rocked one hand back and forth.

"I wouldn't go to trial; I'd have killed myself. Poison. I rather fancy poison. Something horrible—lye, I think. It burns you up from inside. Pain like the fires of hell." Her eyes were bright. Sophie was a self-dramatist, not, he sometimes thought, an entirely sane one. Interesting to be married to, nonetheless.

He bent and kissed her. "Drive me to the Quai d'Orsay."

"No."

"Do it. For love."

"Love, what do you know about love—? You bastard, you're gone all the time, fucking other women, big Slav peasants with butts like car upholstery! I won't drive you anywhere."

"Sophie—" They kissed. And kissed. Her mouth on his, she opened her eyes and saw his open. "Love me?" she said.

485

"Too much. I feel as if somebody's opened a tap in my feet."

She scrambled from the bed. "I know you, you bastard; you'll be at it tomorrow all over again." He heard the shower. In three minutes, she was out, dressing in clothes that were strewn around the room. She sniffed several of the things, rejected them, sniffed at something else. Finding a clean blouse, or at least one that passed the olfactory test, was the toughest. Pigoreau watched all this with affection. He hadn't married her for her cleanliness. When he parted from her, they embraced for a long time, and she whispered, "I love you so much, you tough bastard. Come back to me." Sophie was a statistician; she made better money than he did. The only really bad thing between them had been that he had been a cop in Lille, which she hated; now, with him in Bosnia, she had moved to Paris and was—not happy, because Sophie was probably incapable of happiness—but less unhappy. He squeezed her and got out of the car.

At the Quai d'Orsay, the bureaucrats made a fuss about his getting in; he was just a cop there, and he had to send in his name and fill out a form and wear a special badge, like a boy who's done something wrong at school. Still, he finally got up to the special-intel section, where he was led along a corridor and into Belloc's office. Belloc looked fatter than ever, balder, wearier. He held out a pudgy hand and waved at a green chair.

"So?"

Pigoreau told him what had happened with Zulu—the killing of Mrs Obren, the unproven connection between Zulu and the 1994 shootdown in Rwanda, the computer trail.

"That prick," Belloc growled. He muttered into a desk

phone and rubbed his forehead, offered Pigoreau coffee to fill the time, and, when a thinner, younger man came in, made Pigoreau tell it all over again. Then he introduced the man as Hamy. Just Hamy—no rank, no first name.

"So," Belloc said. "What's it mean?" He looked first at Hamy, then at Pigoreau. Both men looked at Pigoreau.

Pigoreau shrugged. "It means he was working for Lascelles when he shot down the plane in ninety-four. It means he's in Africa now, working for Lascelles." He began to search for a pack of cigarettes. He shot an eyebrow up. "You got anything on that?"

"That's our business," Hamy said, but Belloc waved a hand at him and muttered something about white mercenaries working for Mobutu. "Not ours," he said.

"You assure me that this Zulu is not your guy?"

"Absolutely."

Hamy scowled. Clearly, he didn't like being absolute about anything.

"Then he's the Old Guard's guy, right?" Pigoreau lit up, blew smoke in what sounded like an exasperated sigh. "Lascelles. Right? Well?"

Neither of the other men was going to commit himself on that point; even the name Lascelles seemed to make Belloc unhappy. Still, they didn't dispute it: everybody had a good idea where the troglodytes were in France, and who led them.

Belloc began to draw invisible pictures on his desk with the back of a ballpoint pen. He had his coat open, and Pigoreau could smell his sweat all the way across the desk. Belloc's pen moved, moved, and finally it seemed to have written words that Belloc could read. "If we could get something definite, we'd move on Lascelles. What we need is a hard connection. If this Yugo, this—?"

"Zulu, also Panic, also some other names." Pigoreau

waved a hand, meaning, a long story, boring. Hamy took one of Pigoreau's cigarettes and began to smoke.

Belloc went on. "If this Zulu could be connected directly to Lascelles, placed inside his compound, even, we could do something." He looked at Hamy. "Couldn't we?"

Hamy shrugged, as close as he came to saying yes.

"You have somebody inside?" Pigoreau said. Hamy flinched; Belloc frowned. "Inside Lascelles's place, yes, that's what I mean. Come on, Belloc! I wasn't born yesterday—you *must* have somebody inside Lascelles's. Well? If you have, he can ID Zulu and place him there, and you have a connection." He took out photos of Becque/Zulu from several sources—the Marine Corps, the wall of the torture house at Pustarla, the CIA analysis.

Belloc picked up the photographs, glanced at Hamy. "I have to go to the chief with this."

"When will you move?"

Belloc shook his head.

"What? What's the matter? Lascelles is too big a fish for the Quai d'Orsay to catch?"

Hamy cleared his throat and leaned toward Pigoreau. He had an odd voice, almost a whisper, as if something was seriously wrong where sound was produced. "Somebody's been putting together a crew for a mini-sub. Somebody leased a mini-sub and had it shipped to Tunis. The whole department's upset about it because the Americans are doing some stupid missile business down there, and it's big trouble, because it's in our lake. If it's Lascelles, and he makes shit that the Americans blame on France, the government will roast our asses."

"It isn't like you guys to care about the Americans."

Belloc grunted. "Money. We can't afford to have the US pull out of Bosnia. Them and their goddam hamburgers." Belloc made some more circles on the desk and said,

"Thanks for bringing this to us. I'll see what they say up the line."

Pigoreau laughed. "That's it—thanks?"

Belloc opened a hand, as if to show how empty it was. "You want to make a speech to the President?"

"No, I want this asshole, this Zulu! My unit has turned themselves inside out to get this bastard; my boss, a fine cop, a great cop, he's destroying himself over the bastard! He tried to kill us, *did* kill one of us, remotely detonated bomb! Come on, Belloc—"

"We haven't got him."

"No, but you have somebody inside Lascelles's place, and you've got people all over Africa, still!"

Hamy cleared his throat again and leaned close. His voice sounded as if he was strangling. "If we had him, we'd have to terminate him. Too dangerous. The man must know a lot."

"He's a war criminal. He's going to trial, if we get him."

"Too dangerous."

Belloc shot up, a quick move for such a fat man. "Don't argue about a man nobody has yet! It's no good. Maybe he'll stay in Zaire, who knows?"

But Pigoreau wouldn't let it finish with that. "He's a fanatical Serb; he'll come back to Serbia. We want him."

Belloc shrugged, wriggled, tapped a pudgy hand on the desk. "I'll do my best."

"You owe me."

"I know, I know. I said, I'll do my best."

Pigoreau had to be satisfied with that. He rose, shook hands with both men, and went out, retrieving his cigarettes from the desk at the last moment and beginning to burrow in the pack as he went through the door.

* * *

489

When Pigoreau was gone, Belloc looked at Hamy, then picked up the photos and dropped them in front of the other man. "Show these to Benoit, find out if this is the 'Quebecois with the ruined nose' who's visited at Lascelles's place. If it is, I'll ask for a *congé judiciaire* to move in. Put a team together—helo, two cars, civilian clothes, body armor underneath—you know. Benoit to meet us at the gate and let us in. We'll take Lascelles out by helo, maybe a medevac—lay one of those on, too—he's an old man, I don't want him dying on us. Go."

Hamy stood. "What about that one?" he said, jerking his head toward the door where Pigoreau had left.

"Mmp. We'll see how it plays. He's a good man, but—" He shrugged. "Maybe we can throw him a bone."

Tehran.
Efremov and Anna worked in harness, patching together the conspiracy and its target from tiny bits of information, rather like two devoted archeologists reassembling a shattered vase from the tiny flakes that they dug, each day, from the ground outside. Anna was taking to the kingdom of the World Wide Web as if she was to the ether born. Efremov excelled at puzzles.

Anna had little to do in a house run by servants. She was a courtesan, and she spent hours each day on her body, coating it in glittering artifice and honing it with exercise. Efremov had begun to buy her loyalty when he got her a martial arts instructor. Martial arts were, as far as Anna was concerned, more exciting and more fun than calisthenics and Western aerobics. She settled on Aikido. It gave her a chance to meet the Japanese executives who came so often to Iran. Her lover appreciated what she told him. She enjoyed doing something well that didn't require sex. She also enjoyed Western fencing. This was a contest where she could meet Efremov on level ground. He had years of fencing experience. She was becoming very, very good.

The internet was her second achievement. She had hours at home. She could research things by herself, then show them off at dinner. Her languages were good, her typing nonexistent, but Efremov gave her a tutor in typing and sent his secretary, who had a degree from London University, to teach her the basics of computing. Anna loved the anonymity of the net. She chatted on chat rooms and lied about her gender, her bias, and her profession. She asked questions of Western universities and often got answers. Twice in a month she acquired classified information from the West by chatting with a scientist. Increasingly, she was not only Efremov's mistress, she was also his researcher. And she had no loyalty but to him. That he knew.

When Efremov got the information about Lascelles and the mini-sub, it already had a framework in which to lodge. Anna had found the movement of a French-flagged merchant ship from a Pakistani port that matched Efremov's sourced report of a North Korean sale of a mini-sub to a false end-user certificate in Karachi. Anna knew from a pimply teenager in the Loire valley that he had hacked the plans to the USNS *Newport*, a sister ship of the *Philadelphia*, from the Merchant Marine Academy web site.

And then, there it was. Some of it was still supposition, but the theory was well supported with fact: Lascelles, once the pillar of the French intelligence system, was going to try to grab the Peacemaker missile from the *Philadelphia* just hours before it began its launch sequence. He had surrogates from Sri Lanka. He had a boarding team from Yugoslavia. He had a mini-sub from North Korea. And he was running the whole thing through Libya. In two days.

But Lascelles did not concern Efremov tonight. What concerned him was the possible mole in the CIA—somebody who was sending data to Beijing disguised as porn.

He set out five dossiers. They held the results of the questions he had sent his analysts earlier.

"So," he said to Anna. "Which one?"

She looked at the dossiers, each labeled with a name. She had read them and done her own research.

"This one is dead," she said, putting a folder labeled *Dvorkin* aside.

"Good."

"This one has not been with the CIA long enough, and before that he was in the wrong arena." She put aside the folder labeled *Suter*. Efremov nodded.

"Of the other three, I can't choose—not enough data." She looked up at him with a cautious smile. "But I have a feeling."

"Feelings are for fools," Efremov said. "Well, what does your feeling say?"

She put her hand on the folder farthest to her right and looked up at him again.

Efremov grinned. "My instinct agrees with your feeling," he said.

The folder was labeled *Shreed*.

Zaire.

They walked. The rain fell like a curtain, shutting them into their own world. O'Neill was stronger, and Djalik weaker. When they stopped, he sank down and stared into the rain and sometimes fell asleep, sitting there. They filled him with antibiotics and dressed the hand, but his temperature went up and the hand looked dead. Djalik could no longer feel it.

They made sixteen miles. Then eleven. Then six.

Alan was often gone. Now he was the scout, the man who walked twice as far. Sometimes, the first two days, O'Neill and Djalik talked. O'Neill was spilling out the ideas that had been forming all those weeks he was a prisoner, weeks when he had to walk day after day, moving west with the retreating Hutus. Now, ideas about tribal warfare and ethnic cleansing bubbled up, and Djalik listened, and they were as serious as two old men solving the problems of the world.

"—the *family*. That's always the bedrock of primitivism. It's very African. You help your relatives, you take graft so you can parcel it out among the family—"

"Clan?"

"Yeah, like the Scots. The tribe. It gives new meaning to the expression 'blood relation.' Because it always ends in blood, my family against some other family." They were slopping through mud, the rain teeming down.

"The Hatfields and the McCoys."

"Or the MacDonalds and the Campbells, or the Hutus and the Tutsis, or— It's bullshit. Murderous fucking bullshit."

"I'd put my family ahead of anybody," he heard Djalik say.

"Then you're a dumbfuck. On the surface of it, I suppose it makes sense to think your family is closer or more valuable or something. At least you know where they're coming from, or something. But it's bullshit. There isn't a reason in the world why your family or my family or his family is any better or any worse or any different from any others."

Djalik said, "I love my family and I'd die for them."

"Of *course* you would, but that's *love*. That's not mysticism! You mean you'd die to save your wife and your kids and your mom and dad. Right? But your uncle? Your

493

second cousin? Your mother's brother's daughter's fourth child by her second husband, whom you've never even met? Come on! You're going to stand in the doorway with an M-16 in each hand and a grenade shoved up your ass to protect strangers who don't even have the same name but are 'the same blood'? That's the kind of bullshit that got all these people moving across half of Africa!"

And, later or the next day, "—because you're an American and you're not a goddam *peasant*, which is what we're talking about. Primitives are *peasants*. The Interahamwe are *peasants*. What's-his-name, the dictator in Belgrade—"

"Milosevic—"

"Whatever, he's a *peasant*. Peasant means you live a life of social paranoia, trusting only the people you're related to. It means that the mysticism surrounding language and religion defines your existence—*my* God, *my* words, *my* accent—and anybody who's different is an enemy—kike, nigger, wop! The peasant is the embodiment of narrow-mindedness. He's never been anywhere, he's never really talked to anybody, he's never dared to think, because if he did any of those things, he'd have to open up and let in some of the enemy and he's sure they'd stab him and steal his women. *That's* peasant. That's ethnic. That's the intractable crap upon which ethnic cleansing is based."

And, later, "You can't believe in democracy and be a peasant."

And then, because Djalik said nothing, "In a democracy, people are political more than they're familial. Get it? They believe in politics. Political parties. Consensual politics. Yes?"

And then, because Djalik said nothing, "You can't hate politics and be an American. See?"

But Djalik said nothing.

Next day, they had to carry him.

Zaire–Dehibat, Tunisia.

Zulu was flying out of Mobutu's homeland with the remains of his two companies. He could have got all the ones who could still walk into one aircraft. His men, like him, were bitter: a quarter of them were dead, most from disease or bad medical care. A third were in hospitals in France and Yugoslavia, most of them, again, because of disease, not wounds. They had been in two major battles and been on the losing side in both; they had been shelled by their supposed allies; they had reached the point where they couldn't turn their backs on the Hutus for fear they'd be fragged or shot. Now they were pulling out, leaving half a million dollars' worth of loot behind. And seven men killed by Americans.

Shits, cowards. The FAZ was worse even than the Hutus; if they were protecting your flank, you were dead. They'd just fade away.

Acceleration pressed him back into the seat and he heard the wheels of the Fokker clunk into the wells and he felt relief. *Goodbye, Africa. Fuck you, Africa.* That was all he could think of on the long, boring flight to Chad, during the layover, then on the long, boring flight to Tunisia with the long wound down his arm burning all the way to his mangled elbow. *Fuck you, Africa. Take me back, Serbia.*

He was always in a rage these days. All because of Africa. It had been a failure from the beginning. He had believed that white troops would smash through black ones, that one trained white man was worth twenty blacks. But the Rwandans and the Ugandans had proven to be tough soldiers. It was his men who had been smashed. On the other hand, if they had been fighting the Zairian Army, they would have triumphed as he had expected; the FAZ was shit. He was on the wrong side, that was all. And that, too, was Lascelles's fault.

He moved in the seat, flexed his injured arm. That last morning—the ambush. His own stupidity. And the American had shot him again. The white American he had thought was the one from Pustarla, that bastard who had driven him into the snow. And the other one, who had had a gun and was the fastest shooter he had ever seen. And then that shit Ntarinada with his prancing and his posturing; if he had simply given the American back as he'd been ordered, at least that would have been all right. But he had wanted drama! What he had got was full-scale war between Zulu's whites and his blacks. The Yugoslavs had hardly got out of there in one piece, and as it was they had left half their heavy equipment behind.

The Libyans were waiting for him when he stepped off the plane in Dehibat, the stupid Tunisian airport where they had to land because of the stupid international embargo on Libya, and everything should have been all right then, all the bad part over, only one last stupid mission to do for Lascelles, and then home.

But these weren't the right Libyans.

There was a limousine for him; there were trucks for his men, just the way there should have been—but the people he expected weren't there. He had thought he would be met by Lascelles's usual people—bribed military officers. But he wasn't.

The ones who met him this time hadn't been bribed and they weren't Lascelles's. He felt it like a sickness in his gut: it wasn't going to go right.

They were polite but firm. Two squads of soldiers in full battle dress, with a couple of armored cars, blocked the plane. The Tunisians stayed away; this was some sort of done deal, carried on out on the runway, no Tunisian customs or cops or anything. The Libyans cut him out while he was still on the aircraft and took him off first, and then they told the others to come out or they'd blow up the planes. His men came down the stair, depressed, angry, allowing themselves to be disarmed with little fuss.

"Where are you taking my men?"

"They will be returned to Yugoslavia. *When* depends on you."

"Where is Major Al Benyazi?"

"He is under arrest."

Two of the Libyan soldiers searched Zulu with a thoroughness that was almost a compliment and pushed him into the limo. The last he saw of his men, they were lined up on the tarmac, and one of the sergeants was calling them to attention to salute him as he went by. He was driven over the border into Libya.

Aboard *Shark*, south of Naples.

Suvarov had worked hard to place *Shark* where she could intercept the *Fort Klock* and her group wherever they went after Naples. He waited near the Strait of Messina. He joked to his friend's son, his second officer, that they were between Scylla and Charybdis. When this met with a blank stare, he went to his cabin, fetched a copy of the *Odyssey*, and brought it back. Suvarov could not tolerate ignorant officers who knew nothing but the sea. Neither could Lebedev's father, the admiral. The younger Lebedev was a competent, even gifted, subordinate. But submarine knowledge was not the only kind. "Read this," he said. Lebedev pretended enthusiasm.

He waited for days, cruising off to the south as far as Lampedusa and as far north as Palermo, but always returning to the strait. By his second repetition, Sergei's son knew the reference. By the third, he was quoting the *Odyssey* as often as he could work it in. Suvarov gave him the *Iliad*.

He almost missed them, they stayed so long in port. Twice he had surfaced to get reports from Moscow because he had lost faith in himself and assumed the *Philadelphia* had gone the long way around Sicily. When they finally came, he was too ready.

The little group passed almost directly overhead. The escorts both had their tails deployed. They were looking for him. Good. There was plenty of noise here to hide in.

He followed them some fifteen miles astern. When he had a good set of hydroacoustic conditions, or when his hunches told him the time was right, he would sprint for a kilometer or two and close the gap. On the surface, the weather was deteriorating, increasing his advantage. By midnight he was close. Two thousand yards behind the *Fort Klock*, he increased buoyancy slightly, to drift toward the surface while barely maintaining maneuvering speed. He raised his periscope and his radio mast and fired a burst transmission toward a distant Russian satellite. Then, according to plan, he submerged twenty meters, retrieved his periscope with a beautiful photograph of the storm-tossed *Philadelphia* in the cross hairs, turned sharply to port, and roared off to the east at twenty knots.

Aboard the *Fort Klock*, a sailor woke Captain Cobb in his at-sea cabin. "The Russian sub is back, sir. We detected him within the formation."

Cobb rubbed the sleep from his eyes and looked out his porthole at the black water.

"Bastard," he muttered. "Inform the flag. Increase the ASW screen." *Bastard*, he thought again. The Russian's games were using up his assets. And he didn't like losing.

Nalut border crossing, Tunisian–Libyan border.
December 7.

"What were you coming to Libya for, Colonel?"

"To rest my men. Spend some time at the beach. Spend some US dollars. It was agreed, Captain. We have done this before."

"You brought two plane-loads of weapons, Colonel."

"It was messy at the end down there. Mobutu's finished; we were getting out. The weapons represent money to me."

The captain nodded. The man with him fidgeted. Zulu couldn't place him, but he was no Arab peasant. It was clear from his face that he followed the conversation in French with ease. A Frenchman? Maybe some colleague of Jackie's?

"You have heard of Lockerbie, Colonel?"

He made a gesture: *Get on with it.*

"You are here to get on a hired Libyan speedboat. No, no, don't deny it—Major Al Benyazi told us all about it. We weren't as easy-going with Major Al Benyazi as we have been with you—so far—but we needed to have what he knew in a hurry. We've found the speedboat and have impounded it and, mmm, arrested its captain. Now— in your luggage was a dedicated radio with codes for communicating. Eleven of your men told my colleagues, while we drove here, that they have been training for two weeks to board a ship. This suggests, I am sorry to say, a conspiracy to commit piracy." He shook his head like a man who was infinitely sorrowed by the thought of conspiracy. "In Libyan waters, at that."

Well, Lascelles's scheme was blown, that was obvious. And not his fault that it was. He was almost cheered: sometimes things happened for the best.

"What do you want?"

"I want to know everything about your mission. Explain your plans in detail. If I am convinced, and if what you say checks out, I will have you driven to Tunis and put on a plane for Belgrade. Your men—and your weapons; we are not thieves—will follow within thirty-six hours. Or, you may choose to be heroically silent, and I will send you on a different plane to an air base that the Italians share with the American Air Force, and the FBI will be waiting there to ask you the same questions. You see how attractive the second plan is to me: if I willingly turn you over to the Americans, then Libya is that much less a terrorist state and Lockerbie is that much more obscured. So, *persuade* me that I should not turn you over to the Americans, Colonel Zulu."

He talked. An hour later, he was driven to a luxury hotel.

The officer who had interrogated Becque did not return to Tripoli but went to a scrambler radio-phone in a military scout car. There, he got in touch with a civilian intelligence office in the Tripoli suburbs and made his report. When he was finished, he said, "I think we can go forward. A dozen men to replace the assault crew is all we need. I know, I know time is short— No, I think we simply get rid of him. No, no, not like that— better if he is alive, but not here, not in Libya. You see? He represents this foreign plan to exploit Libya. Let me suggest a procedure to you. The French officer, Duboucq, sat in on the interrogation, so we have shown our cooperativeness; now he knows about this plot that has originated in their country, about this old man, this Lascelles. So, you see, we let this Zulu or whatever his real name is start running. Yes, a running target is always interesting, yes—you see my point. But the timing must be just right. Yes, exactly—the French will be grateful; we will take the American missile; the Americans will be humiliated—" He was persuasive. It seemed like a fine idea.

34

December 8

Zaire.

They had carried Djalik all day on a litter they had made out of branches and soft things from their packs. He was unconscious—not raving, never a sound, always asleep. His temperature was pushing a hundred and four and his hand had a smell that they agreed was probably gangrene.

They came down a hill through the mud of what had been a path, the trees dripping from the rain that had stopped only minutes before. Alan got the rank, vegetable smell he'd first caught when he had landed at Kinshasa— a million years ago. *Ripe and rot.* He was exhausted, but he didn't know how Harry was keeping on at all, because he had been weaker to start with. Yet on he went, plodding, not talking any more.

He was afraid of what he would see when they got to the airfield. More refugees, more tents, more humanity? He had thought they were ahead of the flood of people, but he was no longer sure.

They didn't see the airfield until they were almost standing on it. There was no view over it from the path, only a descent to the plain and then more trudging through scattered forest and openings rank with grass. And then, suddenly, brightness through the trees, and a sense of everything opening out.

It was a graveled strip that had been built with care, plenty long enough for the short takeoff Nomads or light planes like the Cessna. The strip looked new. It was perfect.

No refugees. No tents, no stench of excrement, no noise of babies and anger.

But, parked on the runway five hundred feet apart, two big earth-working machines so old they looked as if they should have been steam-driven. They effectively turned the strip into three five-hundred-foot gravel patches. The only thing that could land on this strip now was a helicopter.

It had to be deliberate. A way, surely, of keeping the FAZ and its smuggling out of the area. Dog in the manger.

"What d'you think?" Harry said.

He was looking far down toward the end of the airstrip. "I think somebody's pointing a rifle at us, is what I think."

The sun came out and steam began to rise from the mud, and they put Djalik in the shade of one of the earth-movers. Alan tried to raise the boat on the radio while Harry, weapon at the ready, watched the guy with the rifle. From the new vantage point they could see that there was a small building down there, too, probably one of the cave-like, windowless houses built of concrete block that represent a step up from the mud banda here.

"Big Bear, this is Bear Cub, over." He checked the comm plan he'd scribbled in the first-aid book. Yeah, these dumb codenames were right. If this was a day divisible by two, he was Bear Cub. "Big Bear, this is Bear Cub, over."

Harry sniffed. "I smell cooking." They hadn't eaten in almost two days.

"Big Bear, this is Bear Cub, over."

503

"BEAR CUB THIS IS BIG BEAR, WE HEAR YOU LOUD AND CLEAR OVER." He held his ear and adjusted the volume. "Big Bear, this is Bear Cub, I'm at Point Three and it is no-go on conventional aircraft, do you read me?"

"Read you no-go on conventional. Confirm."

"Confirm no-go on conventional, Big Bear. Choppers okay. Choppers okay. We, um, haven't checked the site, but there's no bandits and no locals, nobody. One guy. Do you read me?"

"I read you okay on choppers, no site check yet, no people. Over."

"When can you get us out?"

Pause. Then: "We're working on that, Bear Cub."

"Goddamit, I've got a man dying of gangrene here! Jesus, we're at the designated point, why the fuck—" He'd lost it. Harry was staring at him. He made himself calm down. "Big Bear, we need to get lifted out. I have a man who hasn't been conscious in twenty-four hours; we think he has gangrene. Do you read me, over?"

"Loud and clear, Bear Cub. They've put a lock on over-flights. We feel for you, man. Over."

He wanted to shout, *Stop feeling for me and start flying for me!*, but he made himself breathe slowly, and he said, "What about the French? I thought that was an option. Over."

"Bear Cub, most of them have moved across the river, and apparently it's now falling apart over there. Maybe— You just have to give us a little time. Over."

He stared at the little radio. "I don't have any time. We're about done." He clicked the mike, then clicked it back on and said, "Over."

The silence was like a deafness, which filled with an enormous whirring of insects, then shrill cries of birds that sounded as if they were being tortured. He and O'Neill

504

both looked at Djalik, then at each other. "What if they can't do it at all?" O'Neill said.

"Maybe we can walk to the Congo. Find a boat. It's seven hundred miles to the coast, at least two sets of cataracts. Kinshasa and Brazzaville war zones when we get there." He sat down with his back against the big road-grader and felt so tired he thought he'd never get up again. He hung his head between his knees, his arms stuck out in front of him. For a moment, a voice was saying *It's over; it's hopeless; they can't do it*— He sighed. He struggled to his feet. "I see a Coke sign on that building down there, so I guess it thinks it's some kind of store. I'm going to stroll down and see what they'll sell us to eat."

"That guy is still there with his rifle."

"Well, you're going to be the guy up here with his AK-47. If he shoots, waste him."

Alan walked down toward the building. When he got close enough, he could see that a name had been painted, somewhat crudely, in big white letters across the front of the building: *Grand Super-Store A Go Go*. It looked to be the size of a one-car garage.

"*Arrêtez!*" the man shouted.

"Aw, shut up," Alan mumbled. He shouted back in his mediocre French that if the man fired his gun, he would be eliminated by an automatic rifle. At least that was what he thought he said. "*Je voudrais acheter de la nourriture! J'ai de l'argent! Je payerai!*"

When he said he would pay, a woman appeared in the doorway of the building. She was big, majestic, got up in the cleanest clothes he'd seen in weeks. She said something to the man and walked right into the line of fire.

"You English?" she said. In English.

"American."

"You got money?"

"Yeah. Sure."

"American dollar?"

"Yeah."

"Okay, I make you very nice food. Ten dollars US."

Good God, you could eat all day in Africa for ten dollars. "For two men," he said. Djalik wouldn't eat any more.

"Twenty dollars US."

"Chicken," he said.

"Rice," she said. "Rice, ten dollars. Also peas, ten dollars."

"Forty dollars for rice and peas for two?"

She smiled. Big smile. "You got it," she said. "Okay?"

"Coca-Cola?"

"Ten dollars."

Sixty dollars for rice and peas and a Coke. He might as well be back in Washington. He reached inside his shirt and felt for the gold coin he'd taped there. When he had it, he held it out.

"Dollars," she said.

"Gold." He wanted to hold on to his goddam dollars. Anyway, he wasn't sure that they had that much any more. She came close to him and took the coin and bit it, sniffed it, weighed it in her hand. "Okay."

"Like hell okay, that coin is worth more than a hundred!" He reached for it. She waved him off and disappeared into the store, and when she came out, she had a gold scale. She had everything, he thought; there was probably a computer in there with a direct link to Wall Street. She weighed the coin and figured on her black skin with a matchstick and said, "Ninety dollars, this coin. I cut it for you." And she did, with a chisel and a hammer, giving him a good deal less in change than he thought he ought to get.

"You cheat your own people like this, too?" he said.

"These are not my people here! I am from Nigeria!" She made herself seem to expand. "People here are *his* people." She jerked her head at her husband.

The rice and peas were wonderful. And there were a lot of them. The Cokes were warm and were in cans that had been manufactured in about 1960, but the contents were the right liquid. After they had stuffed themselves, they put their bowls near the door and went back to stand by Djalik, whom they'd carried down to a patch of shade by the building, which was both house and store. Alan had peeked inside and seen sacks of rice and beans, machetes, matches, cloth. "With prices to match," he said to Harry. "She's going to greet the refugees like the witch greeting Hansel and Gretel when they get here."

Then they looked at the sky. At the earth-moving machines. The husband was watching them, squatting by a tree, his back against it. The bolt-action rifle leaned next to him.

Alan kept looking into the sky. "It'd be a piece of cake to drop a chopper in here," he said.

The female entrepreneur was standing behind him. "You want to buy an airplane?" she said, smiling.

The plane was on another airfield a mile away. It was the old airfield; the one where the road-graders were sitting was the new one. Both belonged to a French oil company, and when they had flown their big plane away two weeks ago, they had flown the little one to the old field and hidden it there.

The Nigerian woman told them all this as they walked to the field, Alan and O'Neill carrying Djalik. She had contempt for the whites who had left, contempt for her husband, who had stayed. "He calls himself the police! The manager! Because they gave him an old rifle and told him to keep an eye on things." She spat. She was one tough bird.

When he saw the plane, he knew he could fly it. It was the French version of the Cessna 182, built by Reims, filthy dirty now; they'd probably thrown mud on it to camouflage it. But, as he walked around it, he saw that it was probably okay. "How much?" he said.

"How much gold you have, darling?"

He shook his head. "Uh-uh. You have to tell me. And I want the keys, and petrol. I'm not going to buy it from you a piece at a time. No hundred-dollar-a-liter petrol."

"I got the keys." She reached into her front, pulled them out. At the same time, she'd taken an ancient Star M .45 from somewhere and was pointing it at him. "Don't mess me, darling."

"Oh, for Christ's sake— ! How much?"

"Five hundred in gold for the plane. Three hundred for the petrol. One hundred for the keys."

"No deal until I see if the engine works."

She insisted on getting in beside him, the gun still in her hand, as if he might fly away with the aircraft that wasn't hers to begin with. He was taking part in a theft, he thought. He found it didn't bother him in the least.

The engine resisted, coughed, backed, then turned enough to show it had compression, and then it fired and the prop spun. He revved it up, pushing the throttle forward, feeling the plane try to go as the engine roar deepened. The Nigerian woman screamed. He laughed at her and cut the engine.

"Deal," he said. "Half now, half when we leave."

She wasn't going to let it happen that way, but he took the gun away from her and made her sit down, and he counted out half his SA gold pieces and dropped them in her lap and told her to amuse herself counting them.

"Petrol!" he said. She pointed at a sunken spot a hundred feet away. There was a shovel and three machetes in the plane, left from their bringing it in, and he took the shovel and dug until he hit a jerry can, and he wrestled it out and opened the cap and got a good whiff.

"Tie her up," he said. "Then go back and get her husband and tie *him* up. Then you dig up the gasoline and find something to strain it through—that cloth she's got her head wrapped in will do—because I sure as shit don't want a plugged fuel line when we're over the middle of nowhere."

Harry stared at him. "You really going to fly that thing?"

"I sure am."

"Alan—*can* you fly that thing?"

"Can you?" He jerked his head. "Tie her up. I'm going to do the landscaping."

He took one of the machetes and started on the runway. Probably the greenery hadn't been too bad before the rains started; maybe they had kept it cut. But there was grass now, and tough little bushes, and wild bananas that were over his head. He kept himself from looking the length of the runway, because he figured he'd never do it if he knew how far he had to go; instead, he put his head down and started cutting. He had thought he was exhausted when he started, but that was the middle of the day, and he went up the field, swinging and cutting and throwing crap aside for five hours. The rain came in the afternoon, and it was like a blessing on his back.

He let himself straighten now and then, fire running across his shoulders, but he went back to it. His right hand blistered, so he went to his left, then back; the blisters broke, bled. *I'm getting us out of here; I'm getting us out of here,* he told himself over and over and over. When something like a sob broke from him because he

509

hurt so much, he dared to raise his head and saw that he was thirty feet from the end. He looked at his watch. How could he have done that? All that! He looked at his raw right hand. It hurt now to grip the machete. He gripped it anyway and swung at a banana plant and bent, pain singing up his back and across his shoulders. This was the kind of work some people did all their lives, all day, all week, all year. He hit the stalks: *all* day, *all* week, *all* year. Sugar-cane workers. If they could do it— He came to the wall of bush at the end of the field.

He tottered back down the field and threw the machete into the slash. He dropped and lay there, hurting all over.

"When do I get my money?" the woman said. Harry had tied her to a tree near the aircraft.

"You'll get it." The rain was falling on his face. He didn't want to move, ever again. But he had to move.

"Let's gas it," he said to O'Neill. Harry had to help him up, then help him get up on the wing so he could fill the tanks. The forty-pound jerry cans tried to tear his arms off each time he lifted one. Eighty-eight-gallon capacity—except they didn't have eighty-eight gallons. They had about sixty. Well, he'd deal with that when the time came.

He slid off the wing, staggered, and poured the drops from all the cans into one, holding them until his arms and back screamed for him to stop. He wanted every drop. Then he screwed the cap down on that one and threw the others to the side and walked back to the Grand Super-Store A Go Go. It was getting dark by then. There were three small children there, frightened of him, missing their parents, and he tried to get them to go with him, but they stood by the edge of the forest and wailed. He took a dozen cans of food and four cans of Coke and carried them back, showing the woman and dropping some of his American bills in her lap.

510

"Not enough!" she cried. "You are cheating me!"

"Yeah."

"Give me more dollars!"

"Dream on."

He opened a can of beans and a can of spinach, and they ate that, leaning against the plane. They each drank a Coke. He opened two more cans and put them down by the Nigerian and her husband; when they wouldn't eat, he dumped the food out because it was the cans he wanted. He poured some motor oil in each one and set them in a row by the aircraft, crawled up into the plane and tried to sleep. "Call me at four," he said to O'Neill.

"What am I, the night watchman?" O'Neill said.

"You got it."

He couldn't wait. He was awake at three, lay across the seats with things jabbing him, miserable and wanting to go, but he was afraid to take off in the dark. At four he climbed down from the aircraft, smelled the sweet night air. Harry was awake, singing to himself, touching Djalik's forehead, whistling. The tied man and woman were more or less asleep. The children had found their way here and were asleep around them.

He poured the dregs of the gasoline into the cans with the oil and then tore up the woman's head scarf and put a piece in each can, then walked the length of the airstrip with only his little flashlight to comfort him against the dangers of the African night. He kept thinking of snakes, but there were no snakes. There was something big that went crashing away, caused his heart to pound. The refugees would wipe out the wild life, when they came. Down to the mice and the shrews.

He put four cans at the far end of the runway, in a line across it. He put a can on each side at two places where the runway actually rose and then fell, because the airstrip was not level but was a very shallow V with these two bumps in it.

There were puddles and mud.

Harry bandaged the blisters on his right hand. Alan put antibiotic on Harry's dead eye, and together they cleaned pus from Djalik's hand and put on antibiotic and injected him with penicillin. He didn't wake. Alan's hands were trembling with anxiety and the desire to go.

At quarter of five, a little breeze came up, and, as if the sun was pushing that puff of air ahead of it, the first graying of the east.

"Let's do it," he said. He couldn't wait any more. He felt it as an urgency, a pressure, and he thought that if he didn't go now he would explode. O'Neill tried to slow him down, and he lashed out. "We're going! Nobody's coming to get us; there are no helicopters, there's no extraction! It's us! Nobody else! Let's go!"

"But Jesus, Alan—they said to wait, maybe—"

"I didn't walk across fucking Africa to die of old age waiting to be lifted out! I'm going! You're coming with me!"

"Yeah, but—it's *dark*. Why can't you wait?"

"Because I'm not going to leave Djalik face-down in goddam Africa! Because I'm a glory hound! Because I'm a fucking action junkie!" He turned away, suddenly empty. "Take your pick."

O'Neill grabbed him. "Jesus, don't you think I'm grateful?"

He hugged O'Neill's neck. "It's just all so screwed up. All so screwed up."

He grabbed his lighter from his helmet bag and strode down the field, then started to run. At the far end, he lit the four cans, the gasoline hitting with a puff and a flash, and then ran back down the field, going back and forth to light the other cans, not even thinking of snakes now, sliding, sprinting back. In the east, there was a line of gold.

He took the coins from his helmet bag, a heavy weight in his hand. He threw coins in the woman's lap, and she scrabbled for them. O'Neill tossed the cartridges from their guns in one direction, the Star and the rifle in the other. The kids started crying.

"Let's get Djalik in."

"He's in."

O'Neill had loaded Djalik in by himself. Alan felt ashamed that he blew up—and why, at the man who was the reason for his being here in the first place?

He went around the little aircraft, checking with the flashlight, trying to remember the three flying lessons he had actually had. Mostly remembering doing these pre-flights with other pilots—Rafe, Surfer, Skipper Parsills. Computer simulations didn't include this part. No chocks, so he put rotten logs in front of the wheels and was startled when a scorpion crawled out of one into the flash-light glare, a semi-transparent, skinny thing four inches long.

"When I tell you, pull those logs away from the wheels, then jump the hell in, because I'll be rolling. I just saw a scorpion on one."

O'Neill stood outside the plane, smiling foolishly. Alan hit the ignition and the prop slowly turned, the whine of the starter rising, and then it coughed and caught and roared into life. He tried to adjust the mix, had the wrong lever, couldn't see anything because the only light was the flashlight; then he got it, and he listened for the hard-edged roar that meant the mix was right, and the engine settled and he advanced the throttle.

He looked back once to check Djalik. He looked dead, but he was there.

"Chocks!"

Harry was under the plane, and Alan had a stab of fear because he had forgotten to warn Harry about the prop, stay away from the prop—but Harry was smart, and he scrambled aboard and slammed the door, and Alan rolled the plane forward and turned it down the runway, and he wondered what direction the breeze was coming from or if it even mattered, because he was going *now* and nothing was going to stop him.

Harry was looking back. "That bitch is looking for her gun," he said. "That money-grubbing bitch!"

Alan ran the engine up to full power. The plane wanted to go. He checked gauges, switches, cursed because he couldn't read the French terms for the gauges and wasn't sure whether the measurements would be meters or feet, kilometers or miles. *Find out when we're up there.*

He was hyperventilating. His heart was beating as if he was going to do something terrifying and final—propose to a woman, go before a court. It *was* terrifying and final. He reached for the throttle.

"You want to share with me where we're going?" O'Neill shouted.

"Rangoon," he answered, and he pushed the engine up to a roar and released the brakes and they leaped toward the distant torches.

Before dawn, near Cannes.

Two big Renault sedans pulled up to the gate of Lascelles's villa in the darkness, the headlights out, the lead one putting its bumper right against the gate. The halogen light that always burned over the gate was not on; it had burned out, it seemed.

A flashlight blinked inside the gates; an answering blink came from the lead vehicle. The gates swung inward, and the dark car moved forward as if drawn by the gates themselves, accelerating as it went, and the man who grabbed the car's door and swung himself up was almost too slow to get a good hold before both cars were purring up the gravel drive, their tires crunching the little stones with a noise like rain. The guard dogs were not to be seen (all four were full of drugged meat behind the house); the two human guards were in the garage, watching a new pornographic video.

One car swung wide and went around through the *porte-cochère* and into the courtyard beyond, its doors opening and men in dark clothes jumping out. The lead car stopped at the front door; one man slammed a wad of adhesive plastique against it, jumped away, and the door blew in, the sound astonishing, to be followed by a stun grenade only seconds later, and then they were in.

Belloc came more slowly behind them. Hamy was up ahead, directing his men. Belloc heard some confused voices toward the back, one gunshot.

"Upstairs."

Hamy nodded. "LaGrange and Bejart are already up there." His hoarse whisper sounded conspiratorial, almost frightened. Was he in awe of Lascelles, after all, Belloc wondered?

Belloc moved up the stairs with more speed than his bulk would have seemed capable of. He was met at the top, conducted along as if he was being quick-marched to a cell. Lights were on everywhere now; he took in the signs of luxury—marble, memories of Louis Seize, paintings—and dismissed them.

Lascelles was standing by a bed big enough for six people. He was wearing silk pajamas, from which his

515

feet projected like roots. They were very old feet, Belloc thought, with something sad about them.

"This is an outrage!" Lascelles screamed. "This is an insult to the people of France! I demand— !"

Belloc slapped him, right hand to left cheek. The old man tottered and would have fallen if one of Belloc's men hadn't held him up. "No demands," Belloc said. "It's over." He turned to Hamy. "Get the medevac helo down here. That doctor had better be ready with his magic potions; I want to start working on him on the way."

"No—no— !" Lascelles screamed. "I am a citizen of the French—"

Belloc slapped him again, and he shut up.

"Check him for weapons and poisons—teeth, asshole, between the fingers and toes—Hamy, see it's done right. I don't want him dying on us." Belloc went out to a balcony as the first helo descended toward a grassy space beyond the garages. The grass looked a livid green in the aircraft's lights. Somebody called up to him from below: everything was secure; none of theirs hurt, one of Lascelles's men down. Should he go in the medevac?

"No. He can wait."

He left the bedroom and went down to the ground floor. Lascelles followed, carried by two big men. He was moaning, then weeping, but they paid no attention. As they reached the bottom of the wide staircase, the medical team trotted in the blown front door, and the two men deposited Lascelles in a chair and held him as a doctor prepared a syringe. Lascelles began to howl.

"Shut him up!" Belloc shouted.

"Oh, he'll shut up," the doctor said mildly. He plunged the syringe into Lascelles's arm. He was right; the old man stopped in mid-howl, staring at his arm. The doctor started the litany of drug-effect response: count backward from a hundred, please, now, please do it, sir—

"Local police are coming!" somebody shouted.

"Oh, fuck them. Hamy! Tell them to stay the fuck out of it." Belloc sat in a chair that was too delicate for him and watched the old man. His eyes had changed, no longer terrorized, almost childlike now, wide. "How long?" Belloc said.

"Give him three minutes."

"Get him in the helo." Belloc lumbered toward the door, stood back so they could carry Lascelles out. When he reached the stone steps, a tall man was waiting for him and handed him a headset. "Message from Paris, *Chef*."

"Belloc," he growled into the microphone.

"Belloc, Martin-Poisoneuve here." The boss. The *big* boss. "It went?"

"It went, it went. Now the hard part."

"Yes, your responsibility. This just in, Belloc: another message from the Libyans. In the interest of furthering international peace, they're putting this man, Zulu or whoever he is, on a commercial flight out of Tunis."

"They can't! We're to have him!"

"Well, there wasn't a formal arrangement—you've put all this together so fast, Belloc, there is this potential for surprises. Your responsibility." The minister sounded sleepy but pleased. "Anyway, they're putting him on the next flight out of Tunisia to his homeland."

"Shit! Excuse me, Minister. Well, yes, a surprise, but not unlike the Libyans. Trying to have it both ways, I suppose. Well, we'll work this out. Thank you for your concern." He managed to say the last words without irony, or he hoped he did. He handed back the headset, made sure that the interrogation team were on the helo and told them to get going. Moments later, Hamy was at his side and he told him about the Libyans' latest move.

"Shit," Hamy said.

"My response exactly. All right, here's what we're going to do. Get on to Pigoreau in Sarajevo. Tell him to contact Milintel in the French Zone, they are to select an unused airfield and provide a company of tough ones—say I prefer *Légion étrangère* if he can get them. How long does it take to fly from Tunis to Belgrade? Four hours? Six? Anyway, this has to go down very fast. Tell Pigoreau to get his man, this boss of his, the American—this is the bone we're throwing, Hamy, and it matters; we have to wipe the slate clean with the Americans—and when it comes together, they're to be in on it. Then—no, do this first—get to the Air Force, tell them to pick up the aircraft— Oh, Christ, we don't know the aircraft. All right, let me go backwards. Check Tunis and Tripoli and get the flight, the make of aircraft, the line—everything. You know what to do. Then get to the Air Force. We'll need at least four jet fighters, two out of Bosnia and two out of, oh, I suppose Marseille. Here's what we do—"

Wind rattled the dead leaves of the beautiful old trees above their heads, and both men looked up. The helos were already gone, the stars brilliant and hard. The gust caused the branches to sway like dancers, and then, as suddenly as it had come, it was gone.

"Winter," Belloc said.

35

December 9

Zaire.

He had started with full wing tanks and a partly full reserve, enough, he figured, to go more than twelve hundred miles at max conserve. The first hour in the air had blown the calculations. What the hell was the problem? He was above five thousand feet, he had got the plane level, his fuel mixture was not too rich— One hour's flying, and the gauge showed him a quarter down. Either the tanks had a leak or he was misreading the gauge, or had he figured wrong?

Because of the fuel problem, he couldn't settle down and fly. He tried altering the aircraft's angle of attack to see if it changed the fuel reading. He tried tapping the fuel gauge. *Being French, it'll be different from every other one in the world*, he thought. Still, it flew pretty much like a 182.

Harry was flaked out in the seat next to him, his dark face slack in the sleep of exhaustion. The takeoff had scared the shit out of them both; Harry was coming down from that by sleeping.

Djalik was even farther down. Alan couldn't get a good look at him because he was lying down with his head behind the pilot's seat, and every time Alan turned around, the plane would begin a gradual turn to the right. The turn to the right would lose airspeed and the plane would begin to descend, so that Alan had to get the nose up, increase the throttle, coax the plane back to altitude and then slow her down again, get back on course, and find the settings that kept her at constant speed and altitude. He found himself cursing the corrections and he found himself over-compensating. He had to fight the sine-wave effect that pushed the plane through gradual ascents and descents of about two hundred feet, wasting fuel. He knew, deep in his mind, that the sine wave was caused by his over-control on the yoke. For two harrowing minutes, he could not fix it.

He wanted to wake one of the sleepers, for the company. The reassurance that he was not alone. What he wanted most of all was to get there. The landing would be the worst. He wanted to do it now—right now, get it over with.

Nothing helped. He swung between wrestling with the yoke and brief periods of nodding off. Sleep was waiting for him, very close, even though he'd had as much sleep in the last twenty-four hours as he'd been getting on the boat.

He tried to sit straighter, to think of Rose, to play mind games that had kept him alert in the S-3. He squirmed and fidgeted and burned his energy and his nerves for two hours.

Then he found the auto-pilot, which was located in an unfamiliar place and labeled with French he didn't know. Worse, he'd forgotten to look for it.

Over the Med.
Far to the north and east of Zaire, an Air Libya 737 made the turn north that would take it out of Libyan air space. It had come from Tunis, the nearest airport to its own country where it could land because of sanctions.

Completing its turn, it started across the Mediterranean toward the European mainland.

Three thousand feet above, two SEPECAT Jaguar As of the French Escadron de Chasse 4/11 swung into position as the airliner crossed out of Libyan air space. They rode there like two guardian angels.

Sarajevo.

Far to the north of Libya, Sarajevo was coming to. Dukas, waking in his chilly flat, tasted the bitterness of a hangover and put his hand on the ringing telephone. He had meant to unplug it last night and had been too drunk to do it. Now he paid.

"Dukas."

"Michael, it's Pigoreau. Get dressed and meet me in fifteen minutes downstairs."

"What the hell for?"

"I'll tell you when I see you."

The line went dead. Dukas got up, drank three glasses of water and stared at his bloated face in the mirror. He really felt like hell. However, you don't die of a hangover, he knew from long experience; you just wish you did. He took four aspirin and a handful of vitamins and dressed as slowly as he dared—shirt without a tie, flannel pants, beat-up old tweed jacket with two buttons missing. Took the jacket off and put on his shoulder rig with the .357, wriggled back into the jacket, picked up his raincoat and went downstairs.

Pigoreau was there with a French jeep. The driver and a hawk-faced officer sat in the front. "You sober?" Pigoreau said.

"I don't know. Probably not a hundred percent. What's up?"

Pigoreau handed him a thermos. It was full of French

521

coffee, no cup. He drank straight from the thick-lipped mouth. "People survive drinking this stuff, do they?"

"Zulu's out."

Dukas looked up at him over the thermos. *Out?*

"He's in the air. Civilian flight, Air Libya, out of Tunis headed for Belgrade. Come on."

"Where to? Belgrade?"

"Michael— ! Get in the fucking car." As soon as Dukas was in, the jeep began to move.

"Where are we going?"

"We're going to meet Zulu."

Over western Africa.

Four hours after takeoff, Alan was down to the reserve tank. The auto-pilot had saved his energy; before the fuel situation became critical, he had twice snatched an hour of sleep and awakened to the three different alarms he had set; watch, GPS, auto-pilot. Harry woke with him the first time, drank some water and returned to sleep. Djalik did not wake.

Djalik's hand stank. Alan knew gangrene only as a disease that worried characters in C. S. Forester books, but he knew that it reached a point where it began to poison the blood and killed. He wondered if they should have tried to take the hand off. Probably not: he knew more about flying this aircraft than about surgery. O'Neill was no better. So Djalik had to get to a hospital. He planned to fly near Bata and Libreville, but he wasn't sure, wasn't sure of them at all—AIDS, Ebola, a continent of low tech and poverty, where needles got re-used— Any country he landed in now would demand visas and country clearances. And explanations—they had too many weapons in the plane, and too much blood on them. Maybe they

522

could ditch the plane, radio the boat, get them to fix it with the local embassy—

He had landed his Cessna on a virtual *Nimitz* dozens of times in the Microsoft universe—thus, in a sense, knew it could be done. But that was probably like saying that a child who had killed a bad guy in a fantasy knew it could be done. Knowing it could be done wasn't doing it, as he'd learn when he hit the ramp. Or the water.

The terrible truth was that he wanted to be back on the ship. He wanted to take O'Neill and Djalik home.

But the more immediate concern was that he didn't have the gas to make it to the *Rangoon*, much less the *Jackson*. He'd have to go down for fuel.

He woke Harry and set him to trying to locate a truck corridor in southern Cameroon on their big-scale map. Then he dialed a minute course change into the auto-pilot.

In one hour, he was going to try to land. On a road.

He practiced the lineup twice at low altitude. The third pass, he could see that he had drawn a crowd out of the pale brush that grew on both sides of the black-topped road, which ran like a straight black ribbon north toward Yaounde. Good: he wanted the attention of the people who lived along the truck route.

A small boy crouched at the edge of the brush, one hand shading his eyes, the other hand pulling his long red kilt up to make a better seat on the cool pavement. He had seen a plane before, but never one that flew low over his own house. Over and over! This was better than the trucks that roared down the highway. He wanted to drive a truck one day.

Idly, he traced the outline of the plane in the fine grit

on the surface of the road. The boy must have been a keen observer, because he traced a reasonable likeness of the plane with the flaps fully deployed. The plane had turned over the road four times now. The boy thought that the plane was going to land but did not say so, for fear that the older people around him would use ridicule. No plane had ever landed there.

Where the truckers often made their engines roar when they passed, especially when they passed a woman, this one seemed to make his engine quieter as he came down. The throaty roar of the first passes was now a muted rumble. The plane dropped like a stone. Then it dropped more slowly. Then it appeared to glide, and glide, and passed just a few thrilling feet over the boy. Down the road, close to Ab'jans path, the wheels touched, and the plane disappeared in a cloud of swirling grit. Many of the people ran back into the bush. The boy ran after the plane.

Alan pointed the nose back south by wheeling the plane in a trucker's turnaround. The stiff wind coming from the south was refreshing, but not nearly as refreshing as landing the plane and not meeting a truck head-on.

All over sub-Saharan Africa, the trucks on the bad old roads keep civilization together. The truckers are the captains of great ships that ply the spaces between towns. There are no gas stations. He and O'Neill knew that on any truck route, petrol was purchased out of the tall brush beside the road, and no tax was paid to the government. Where does the gas come from? How much is stored beside the road? What impurities does it have?

Alan couldn't answer any of those questions, but the plane was full of gas now and the engine ran. One boy had come to the plane first and run off and brought back the first gas. Then a crowd formed, seemingly from nowhere. Eventually there were a few women.

And then he had heard Harry talking to them in French. He was squatted by the road with the men and boys. It was more of what he had thought about in his confinement, more of what he had said to Djalik on the trail: about family and democracy and decent education for children. He had nothing to give them, he said, but words, because everything he owned had been taken. So he gave them what he had learned. The old men nodded. Boys looked on with widened eyes: a black man who said he was an American had dropped out of the sky to talk to them.

Alan paid for the fuel with American dollars and got into the plane and called for Harry. Twice. Waiting. At last, Harry broke loose and took his seat, and, after a few final words, closed the hatch. Alan pointed the aircraft into the wind and pushed the throttle and they roared down the black ribbon, an easy takeoff that made him think it was all going to work.

Beside him, Harry was twisted to look out and down. "That's what I thought it would be like," he said. *In Africa*, he meant. When Alan looked aside at him, Harry had his head down and was crying.

Alan began trying the handheld radio as soon as they crossed the coast. There had been no decision to by-pass the cities; the decision had been made back in Zaire, when he had first seen the plane. They were going to the *Rangoon*.

Alan's fatigue was a constant now. Djalik seemed to be going into a different phase, starting to twitch and mumble. Harry dabbled water on him and injected more antibiotics.

"How long?" he said.

"Hour. About."

He raised the *Rangoon* just after noon, local time. He told them what he intended. A senior officer came on, was stiff but resigned, maybe apologetic. It was *Rangoon*'s choppers that would have lifted them out.

"You a qualified pilot, Bear Cub?"

"Negative."

Silence. "We'll talk you in. Good luck. Over."

Even while they talked, *Rangoon* cleared her deck. Every plane and chopper that could be put in the hangar deck was hustled to the elevator. The two remaining choppers and one Harrier were readied for takeoff, the VSTOL jet to fly wing on him, the helos to be there if he went into the water. The aviators were canvassed for an LSO who knew light aircraft, but the Harrier skipper said it was his responsibility and he'd do it. Even though he sure didn't want to.

On the flag deck of the *Jackson*, Admiral Pilchard got the word from a breathless flag lieutenant who had run all the way from comm. He stared at the younger man; he had been listening to an evaluation of their sub contacts and had to shift gears.

"Where is he now?"

"Cleared the coast twenty minutes ago, sir."

"You mean—somebody extracted them, after all?"

"Apparently Craik got himself out, sir. That's what the message says—'LCDR Craik at controls.'"

"Of what?"

The lieutenant shook his head. "Not specified, sir. 'Light aircraft,' that's all."

The admiral looked at the startled faces around him. He put a hand on the lieutenant's shoulder. "You get the ship's chaplains together right now, you tell them this is from me personally, and you have them go on ship's PA with a prayer. You tell them I want this whole ship praying for somebody who needs all the help he can get."

"How far will he go to get his buddy, if he has to?"

"Pretty far. Real far."

The Harrier appeared off their wing twenty minutes later. Alan felt his heart leap at the sight. Almost home. Almost *home*.

Harry saw the little attack carrier first. He was craned up in his seat, trying to look over the canopy. It looked unnatural with its deck completely clear.

"They all look small, coming in," Alan said to comfort him.

"Al, don't shit me—how long is that flight deck, really?"

"Eight hundred feet."

"Can you land this thing in eight hundred feet?"

"Well— See, normal run-out is about thirteen hundred, but that's on a field. The theory here is that the carrier will be moving, so we subtract their speed from ours, and when we touch down we'll be going only twenty-five knots or so, relative. Get it?" He glanced aside. Harry was staring at the carrier. "We shouldn't need more than four or five hundred feet," Alan said.

"They got a net, like on the *Jefferson*?"

"No. Goddamit, Harry, in World War II they landed planes a hell of a lot bigger than this one on CVs just like that!"

"They had hooks."

"Well, yeah, they had tail-hooks. But that ship down there doesn't have a wire, even if we had a hook—Harriers and helos don't need wires. Harry—the principle is right! They'll get their speed up; I'll throttle down; it should be like landing at twenty-five knots!"

The carrier was closer now, and he could strain a little

and see it. At least the flight deck was *wide*. The island was well over. He'd have some flex in one direction, anyway.

He asked the Harrier to lead him through the break. He didn't want to have to think about distances and times; he wanted to concentrate on his lineup and his angle of attack.

There would be only the one attempt to land. He would have to get the wheels down and the brakes on in the first hundred feet of the deck if he was going to make it, even with the CV steaming. If he miscalculated and touched the wheels too far down the deck, the brakes wouldn't stop him in time to keep from rolling right off the bow. He had seen it in World War II films. He didn't mention those to Harry. And there would be no recovery if he bitched it: he wouldn't have the option available to Rafe of going to full power when he hit the deck, and either catching the wire or flying off for another try. Not enough deck, not enough power.

Into the break. The LSO had offered a straight-in, but that's not how he had done it in the simulator and he didn't want to do anything differently. The LSO had sounded a little strange when he had said, "I'm used to taking the break, sir," but he'd okayed it.

He followed the little jet around and lost him. The Harrier was way off ahead, far too fast to throttle down to his speed, and Alan called him off. "Thanks, Harrier One. Nice job." He risked hubris. "See you on deck."

The *Rangoon* was moving at twenty-nine knots. The little aircraft's stall speed with full flaps was somewhere around fifty-five knots, meaning that he could, if he did it right, have only twenty-six knots relative airspeed when he hit the deck, just as he'd told Harry.

Alan put his flaps to full and began his turn for lineup.

He didn't think about Harry, and he didn't think about Djalik. He didn't think about Rose, or Mikey, or even his father, who must have done this a thousand times in ten different aircraft. He thought about the landing.

He overshot the lineup and had to chase it.

"Good for lineup," said the LSO's voice from the radio, now in Harry's lap. The voice was trying to sound soothing.

He remembered to cut back on the throttle, which gave him more time and cost altitude. He pulled the throttle all the way to idle and let the plane sink.

The LSO watched the little plane wobble and wobble, chasing the flight deck, and he knew that this guy was new to the game. The problem was, the LSO was a Harrier pilot and had not landed the "long way" on a carrier since Pensacola and T-84s. They were both a little out of their depths here.

He called the lineup to steady the guy down.

He looked all right. No, he didn't look all right. Jesus, this is NOT the way you land on a Tarawa-class ship. Jesus, he's descending too fast. No, maybe not. Hard to tell. Not really qualified as an LSO for Cessnas.

"Power!"

Alan thought that it looked great, but he rammed the throttle forward. His angle of attack almost instantly became level flight, with a sag. He inched the throttle back out.

Nobody was on the flight deck except the Harrier skipper and the crash and fire crews; the ship itself was at general quarters and collision stations. The ad-hoc LSO was sweating buckets.

Fuck. Now the guy was too high. Now he'd caught it. Not bad, actually. *No!* Back to that steep descent. It was going to be close. He could see that the guy wanted the whole run of the deck to brake. He didn't seem to realize that the carrier was moving almost as fast as he was. It was close. Too close.

"Power!"

Alan gave the plane throttle again. The deck filled his vision and the island seemed to be rushing at him. What had seemed to be a long glide to certainty had become a scramble. Harry had the radio up for him. He couldn't see the deck edge, but it was close, close and he pulled up the nose too fast, to get a few more feet of glide, and the plane stalled. He felt it go. And the nose fell away underneath him.

The LSO saw the stall and thought it planned. He completely rewrote his view of this guy. The stall killed his airspeed and put him right on the deck. It was a beautiful, gutsy maneuver.

All three wheels hit the deck, and the plane jerked once as it bounced and went all of twenty feet before Alan recovered enough to set the brakes. The plane stopped. Ahead of them, the flight deck of the *Rangoon* stretched like two football fields.

He had taken a hundred and thirteen feet.

Alan sat and shook. Medics were running for the plane. Harry turned and smiled, sweat beading his dark, yellow-splotched, battered face. A warm hand curled around the back of Alan's neck.

When the medics opened the door, the two men were hugging each other and laughing like hyenas.

* * *

He hadn't figured that they would insist on putting him on a stretcher like the others, but he was wobbly-legged when he climbed out of the little airplane, and they made him lie down. The small carrier felt strange to him, the flight-deck proportions wrong, the sense of movement unstable after so long on land. Hands were holding him up and he was trying to fend them off, and then he was flat and grateful for it, and he craned his head and saw a stretcher with Harry on it moving into the hatch. He shouted. Harry turned his head so his good eye could look at him; Alan sat up on his stretcher, and the medics started to push him down.

"Harry!" he shouted. "Harry— !"

O'Neill waved. His words floated down the flight-deck wind: "Goin' to glory, man!" The hatch closed behind him.

"Where's Djalik? My other man—we brought in two guys—"

"He's already headed for sick bay, sir. Maybe you'll see him down there. Just lie back, okay? Everything's gonna be just fine. Lie back—that's m'man—"

And he was asleep. He woke when they put him on a gurney in the ship's hospital, and after he had argued long enough with a doctor, they wheeled him to the OR where they were already working on Djalik. A nurse went in, because he insisted, and she came out looking bland and untroubled, the way nurses make themselves look so they won't get too close to feeling, and she said brightly, "He's in surgery right now. They didn't lose a sec! He's going to be great."

"What are they doing?"

"They're operating, Commander. He'll be—"

"*What are they doing?*"

"They're removing part of his hand."

Alan sank back. "And O'Neill?" he said after a moment.

"I don't know. I think he's being prepped." She sounded slightly pissed-off now. Alan started to worry about that, about O'Neill and Djalik, and then he was asleep again.

He slept for two hours, he found later, and when he woke, O'Neill's eye had been "stabilized" and Djalik's left hand had been mostly amputated. Both men, he was told, were going to be flown to Germany for further treatment.

"You came through in pretty good shape, on the other hand," a preppy-looking doctor said. "Exhaustion, lot of insect bites, can't see much else. Take your malaria prophylaxis? You oughta be okay, then. We'll do a workup, check your stool, blood, the works. Had the crud? I put that stuff on your hands. Don't use them for a couple of days."

"I have to get to the *Andrew Jackson*." He was thinking about Rose.

"No, you don't."

"Yes, I do." He got off the gurney, almost fell, and fended off the doctor with a straightened right arm. "They got doctors on the *Jackson*, too. Come on, Doctor, I'm basically okay, and you know it. Show me where to get a shower, and I want to send a message to my admiral that I'm here."

The young doctor grinned. He held out a message paper. "This went out to the battle group two hours ago."

Alan read it. It was from Admiral Pilchard, to all hands: *LCDR Alan Craik, IS1 David Djalik, and civilian Harold French O'Neill landed on USS* Rangoon *seventeen minutes ago. Prayers are answered.*

The French zone of Bosnia.

The jeep had come down into a bowl among hills that swelled farther away into mountains that looked only like gray shadows in the rain. A potholed dirt road had led down into the bowl, where a French soldier in a rain cape had directed them down a muddy track with quick, seemingly angry gestures. Down there, Dukas had already seen, was an airfield.

Now, they sat in the jeep and waited. The rain was a constant, heavy drumming on the plastic roof, and Dukas felt his headache as a jab between his eyes and along the sides of his head. Cigarettes he had bummed from Pigoreau had left a terrible taste in his mouth; the answer to that was to smoke another.

"This is it?" he said.

Pigoreau said something to the man in the front passenger seat. He replied, only a couple of syllables. "This is it, yes. No farther."

Dukas spat out a piece of tobacco. "Old Yugo Air Force emergency field. Yes?"

"I suppose."

Dukas looked down the runway. It seemed endless, vanishing into the rain.

Pigoreau had told him that Zulu was in the air; it didn't take a genius to persuade him that they were at an airfield because that's where Zulu was going to land.

"Do we take him?" Dukas said.

"We wait and see, Michael."

There were several French trucks parked way down the runway, with portable radar gear off in the grass. This was the French zone; the evidence was everywhere, even if Dukas couldn't have guessed from the direction and the distance they'd come. He thought the signs weren't good—

too much French muscle, nothing of his own; Pigoreau was a friend, but—a French friend.

After they had been sitting there for a few minutes, he heard vehicles behind them, and he craned around the rear window and saw two military trucks and an armored car pulling in behind them, and then two civilian cars, one of them extremely handsome and flying French flags. *Diplomatic*, he thought.

The armored car pulled up behind them and sat there.

The trucks moved around them to the end of the runway and then went slowly up the runway itself. The officer in the passenger seat said something, and the driver started the jeep and they moved off after the trucks, the two civilian cars pulling in behind them, like a funeral procession. Six hundred meters along, they pulled to their right into a taxiway, then again parallel to the runway, then again to their right, and, after a quick turn, came to a stop facing the runway, a hundred feet from the trucks. Three squads of French soldiers were already out of the trucks, lining up, checking equipment. Dukas caught their shoulder flashes, thought, *Foreign Legion. Serious mothers.*

The two civilian cars went on past the trucks and then turned in on the far side of them. That left the jeep all by itself.

"You believe in body language?" he said to Pigoreau. Pigoreau raised his eyebrows in question. Dukas threw the cigarette out the window. "I think we're being ignored. Big-time."

"They know we're here."

"Oh, yeah, I know they know we're here—they couldn't make that plainer if they gave out cards marked 'We don't see you.' What the hell is this, the famous French *politesse*?" The man in the front seat seemed to find that a little amusing.

Then they heard the plane.

It took it several minutes to circle to the north, unseen, come around again, lower and louder but still up there in the cloud, then fade again to the north. The rain had eased off into a kind of soaking drizzle, and if anything the visibility was worse than before. Dukas thought the aircraft had given it up, but then there was a bustle among the French troops, and they were again lining up in front of their vehicles. To his surprise, an officer went along their lines, tugging now and then at a strap or a button, and Dukas thought, *Jesus, like a parade.*

Minutes after he expected to see it, the 737 ghosted down out of the clouds. It was hardly more than a speck between them and the low hills, and it seemed to hover there forever, neither growing larger nor dropping. Then suddenly it was an aircraft and it was descending at the far end of the runway, touching down, and he could hear the roar as the engines reversed. Spray rose from its wheels like bow waves as it tore over the puddled, cracked concrete, and, half-visible in the mist above it, two combat jets sailed overhead, their flaps dragging air to keep them slow.

Pigoreau cleared his throat. "The 737 was forced to land. Or, at least the pilot did what we asked. The passengers were told that Belgrade is closed."

A voice shouted a harsh command. The French soldiers came to attention. The diplomatic car with the flags opened and a small man with silver hair got out. He looked around, tugging at his suitcoat and shrugging his shoulders, then looked up into the drizzle and wiped his hand over his hair.

The airliner swung into the taxiway, still rolling fast, and came down the same way they had, swinging again toward them and seeming to threaten to rip right through

535

them. In the front seat of the jeep, the officer looked back at Pigoreau and jerked his head and then got out. Pigoreau pulled at Dukas's sleeve. "Come on."

"What the hell?"

"Come on, Michael."

He climbed out on his side and went around behind the jeep. There was water everywhere; he stepped in over his loafer-tops, felt the chill of the water, almost pleasant. Going behind the jeep, he touched his revolver, made sure he could get at it.

Somebody in ear protectors was standing in front of the aircraft, waving it forward with two light batons. She backed toward the troops, waving the batons back toward her shoulders—back, forward, back—until the aircraft was close, and then she shot both arms to their left and the plane turned and stopped. Dukas could see that all the window shades were drawn—SOP when landing anywhere in this part of the world because of snipers.

The engines kept running.

The diplomat started forward, and at the same time the cabin door opened, like a lower jaw making a yawn. A stair started down. The diplomat was on it as it touched the ground, going up with the nimbleness of quite a young man. He seemed in a hurry. He shot inside, then was back in only seconds. He hesitated in the doorway, then stood aside.

"He tells Zulu he is from Lascelles. Then we hope Zulu—" Pigoreau stopped.

Zulu was standing at the top of the stair. Dukas recognized him without question—the stance, the head, the powerful body, and that brutalized nose.

Another civilian moved toward the aircraft. He was smiling. He looked pleased with himself—good-looking, smooth. Pulling down the bottom of his suit-jacket so he would look his best.

Dukas looked around and saw that the French soldiers had deployed out of their line and were moving, half of them around the tail of the aircraft, some behind him and the jeep. They were all facing away from the aircraft. Guarding—whom? Zulu? From what—the Bosnians?

Zulu seemed to be wearing a white mitten—a bandaged hand and arm. After all this, that's what he had—a bandage on one hand. Dukas felt intense disgust, then hatred, and his own hand moved toward the .357.

"No, Michael." It was only a whisper, but Pigoreau had locked his fingers around Dukas's right wrist. They stood there, arms together like lovers.

The diplomat said something. Bobbed his head. Smiled. Zulu looked around—the low hills, the soldiers. Not seeming to take in Dukas and Pigoreau or not caring about two civilians who didn't have diplomatic flags on their vehicle.

He started down the steps.

The man at the bottom came forward, freeing his right hand for shaking hands.

Zulu came down.

The man at the bottom took one more step forward, his hand out, and Zulu took the hand and bent a little forward, as if he thought the Frenchman would probably kiss at this point. The man's other hand, his left, was on the side turned to Dukas, and Dukas saw it when it came out of his pocket with a pistol and came up smoothly and put the barrel against Zulu's throat, and at the same time the "diplomat" on the steps above him drew a semi-automatic and put it at Zulu's back, and Zulu's face turned angry.

Urged by the weapon behind him, Zulu started slowly across the wet concrete. Behind him, the steps of the aircraft swung upward and the clamshell jaw began to close; Zulu turned his head, despite the pistols, the soldiers, and watched the door close, that hope of home.

They marched him slowly to Dukas and Pigoreau. The soldiers stood with their backs turned; the aircraft sat on the taxiway. When the three men were a few meters from Dukas, they stopped. The one behind, the "diplomat," murmured something to Zulu, and his eyebrows went up and he stared at Dukas.

"I thought I killed you," Zulu said in English. He sounded like an American.

Dukas held up his International War Crimes Tribunal badge. "I arrest you for war crimes against—"

"Fuck you! You got no jurisdiction; this is bullshit! What is this, entrapment, I spit on this shit— !"

Dukas controlled his rage. Even Pigoreau must have felt that control; his grip on Dukas eased. "Zoltan Panic, deserter, US Marine Corps, war criminal, murderer of two African presidents. Pack it in, Panic."

But Zulu didn't move. He wasn't frightened; he was enraged. He was sure there was a way out, and he was going to take it. There was a sound behind him, and, astonishingly, the door of the aircraft opened again and the steps began to descend.

Zulu looked around. He was a brave man, and a desperate one; perhaps, too, he was disoriented—the soldiers, who did not have their guns trained on him, the "diplomat" who was supposed to be from Lascelles. Zulu muttered something to the man, and the two conferred, as if there was a decision to be made, options to be considered. To Dukas, there were no options. What was Zulu trying to do?

The "diplomat" smiled, and Zulu actually chuckled. What was it? Dukas felt he had lost control, if he had ever had control, and he made a half-step, and suddenly both the French pistols were pointed at him, and Zulu was grinning; Pigoreau clamped his hand on Dukas's wrist again, and the "diplomat" said, *"Allez!"* and Zulu swung around and began to run toward the aircraft. Dukas tried to shake Pigoreau off, but Pigoreau held on, only the one hand, but the second French gunman got between Dukas and the running man, and Dukas was blocked.

And then the "diplomat" turned, raising his semi-automatic like somebody target-shooting, one-handed, and he fired, fired again, and Zulu staggered. He fired again. Zulu put his arms out for balance, still trying to push himself toward the aircraft, and the "diplomat" fired again, and Zulu turned slowly, arms out, and fell backward on the rain-soaked, cracked paving.

The man with the pistol trotted forward, looked down, and shot Zulu in the head. Then he turned and looked straight at Dukas and Pigoreau and gave what could only have been a military salute and ran for his car.

"Tué pendant l'évasion," the other one said, stepping out of Dukas's way. He, too, gave a kind of salute and ran for his car. The aircraft's steps began to close upward and the plane began to roll.

Orders were being shouted. Soldiers were running for the trucks. The aircraft was taxiing out toward the runway, making the turn to the taxiway too fast. The truck engines were roaring to life. Soldiers started piling in. The aircraft roared out to the runway, spun, and without a pause began to roll away, its engines rising to a scream.

The diplomatic car was gone. The second civilian car ran out to the taxiway and began to accelerate, throwing spray, and the trucks rolled forward, engines loud, coughing, banging, their bodies rolling from side to side as they went straight through the scruffy grass and the mud and followed the cars.

Two minutes after Zulu had been shot, they were alone. Far down the runway, the portable radar was coming down. The armored car was trundling slowly toward them. Pigoreau's grip on Dukas's arm relaxed; the hand fell away.

Dukas walked to the body. It was sprawled on its back, the face washed clean of blood by the rain, but for a little pool under the left ear, from which a thin, watery red trickle was running away down a crack in the pavement. *A .380*, Dukas was thinking. *Europeans like these little guns.*

He knew what he was supposed to do. He knelt and felt in Zulu's throat for a pulse.

Dukas had not seen very many people killed. He wasn't a homicide cop. The smell of new blood sickened him. So did the sight. He decided he wouldn't be sick there, nonetheless, although it was an effort not to be sick on the dead man.

A French officer and a soldier were standing over him. The soldier had a body bag, already unzipped. "We take the body," the officer said in accented English. "It is the French Zone. A full report will be made." The soldier started to kneel with the bag, and Dukas waved him off. He felt in his pockets and found a sheet of paper that was clean on one side, and, using the blood behind Zulu's head instead of ink, he carefully rolled a print of each of Zulu's fingers and thumbs on the page.

The French officer, sounding offended, said something to Pigoreau, who answered, "*Taisez-vous. Il est flic formidable.*"

Dukas stood. Pigoreau and the other two backed away, as if they were giving him room for something private, some grief. Dukas walked a few feet toward the jeep, looked back at Zulu. His clothes were soaking up water, turning black. Dukas shivered. He started to feel sorry for Zulu, and then he thought of Mrs Obren. The soldier and the officer began to get the body into the bag.

"They didn't mean for me to take him, did they," Dukas said. It wasn't really a question, and Pigoreau only gave him a kind of wincing frown.

"Because he knew too much?" Dukas said.

Pigoreau shrugged. He took a step toward Dukas. "Michael, I didn't know about—the end of it. I thought they would—truly—"

"Yeah." Dukas sighed. "All three of us got fucked. What'd you say to the officer just now?"

"I told him to shut up."

"What else?"

"I said you were a real cop."

Dukas looked at the body bag, and three more men coming from the armored car, the only vehicle left besides their jeep. He looked at his hands, still red with Zulu's blood.

"You, too, Pig. You tried." He shivered. An icy wind flung little pellets of freezing rain at their faces. "Winter," he said, and they headed for the jeep.

Part Four

Weapons Free

36

December 9

At sea—aboard the *Jackson*.
Sneesen had written another letter to the chaplain, and
nothing had happened, and he was about at the end
of his tether, really ready to explode, frantic, and then
Commander Rafehausen called him into the squadron
office and sent everybody else away, and Sneesen knew
that at last everything was going to be okay and his prayers
had been answered.

Commander Rafehausen sat behind the desk and didn't
smile or anything when Sneesen came in, and he didn't ask
Sneesen to sit down. He had a manila file open in front of
him, and right on top was Sneesen's letter. That was okay.
That meant the chaplain was on their side.

Commander Rafehausen put his hands together on the
desk and looked down, reading the letter. Outside, everybody was coming and going, and there was noise in
the p'way.

Commander Rafehausen looked up. "Sneesen," he said,
"what the hell has happened to you?"

The question confused him. This didn't have anything to
do with him, really. This was about Commander Rafehausen
and the mud-bitch and the Jew. "Sir?" he said, hating it
because his voice squeaked like a kid's.

"Sneesen, what's *happened* to you? You were doing great

there, you were a worker, you saved our lives—and now, this." He put his hand on the file. *This?* "Did you write this letter?"

"I—" He started to say *no*, because something was wrong, and he knew the tone, knew when he ought to lie. But Borne had said you have to stand up for Truth, so he said, "Yes, sir, Commander Rafehausen, see, nobody was—"

"Sneesen, Jesus H. Christ! What the hell are you thinking of? My God! Sneesen—" Commander Rafehausen waved a hand, as if he was all of a sudden old or helpless. "Sneesen, is something going on at home? Is it your mom, or have you got worries—got a letter from your girl, anything—?"

Sneesen didn't have a girl. His mother wrote once a week. What did that have to do with anything? "I pray for you," Sneesen said. "I been praying for you all the time."

Commander Rafehausen rubbed his eyes and shook his head. He was burned out, everybody said so. Sneesen felt a lump swell in his throat, compassion for Commander Rafehausen bubbling up there.

"Sneesen, I don't get it. When you came aboard, you were one of the best new guys I've ever had. You got along. The squadron thought you were okay. Now—" He made the gesture again. "Half the guys in the squadron say you're *weird*. What's going on?"

Weird? That's what they'd say, of course. Sneesen started to tell Commander Rafehausen about the Jew and mud-people and Satan's Plan, going too fast because it excited him, and he could feel his face was hot and his underarms were sweating, but it was the Truth, and he was babbling it all out, okay, maybe some of it out of order but—

Commander Rafehausen stood up, taller than Sneesen by inches, and he closed the file and shut Sneesen up with a gesture. "I want you to see the doctor, and he'll put you

546

on a phone hookup with a psychologist on the beach. I'll try to keep this from going to a mast, but Sneesen, this is a real serious thing. You can't spread lies like this about people. You can't call people these names. Look, we're going into a really tight time now. I can't get everything done right now, but I want you to go to the doctor and talk about this. I'm relieving you from duty until—I dunno. Let's see what he says. But Jesus, Sneesen, get a grip, will you?"

When he heard "psychologist," Sneesen knew it was over. He couldn't face another one of them. They were too sneaky; they had drugs; they'd make him say things, and all the old stuff he'd lied about to join the Navy would come out. And then the rest—a captain's mast, for what? For telling the truth? And relieved, how could they relieve him? He was the best electronics man in the squadron, maybe on the whole boat!

Sneesen started to cry. Not because of the psychologist or the mast or being relieved; those made him sick and they frightened him, but it wasn't those things. It was Rafehausen. He was crying for Rafehausen, because he had been trying to save him, and now he saw that Rafehausen was just like the rest. He was one of *them*. They already had him, and Sneesen was too late. He was crying because his heart was broken.

Sneesen went down to his rack, feeling the sadness, the frustration turn to anger. He'd never been this angry. This was horrible. He went down to his rack and wrote about it in his secret diary, and then he went to the canteen and got two Cokes and poured them out in the head, and then, feeling the anger in him like ice, his whole inner self turned to ice, to hatred, he went to the shop and to the back, where they kept the epoxy pumps. There

547

were two, a big and a little; they gave five-to-one shots, epoxy and hardener. He pumped them into the cans and mixed the sticky fluids with a screwdriver he poked down through the drinking holes. Not perfect, but it would be good enough.

He put the cans on a steam pipe to harden and went back to his rack and wrote the rest of it in his diary, then put the diary right on top of his folded uniforms in his locker. Ice—a block of ice. Hard as ice. No reason to hide any more. He got out his white flight-deck jersey. The hell with them—yes, that was it, that was precisely it—to Hell with them!

And went and got the two cans, which were hot now, the epoxy inside hard, and they were heavy in his hands, like some kind of weapons. He walked the p'ways and the ladders with one in each hand, squeezing himself against the bulkheads, really pushing himself into the wall when the black guys went by. Not wanting to touch or be touched. He had a mission. He didn't want them touching him, contaminating it.

He crossed the hangar deck and went up to the catwalk. He had hearing protection so he'd look like everybody else. He'd brought his tool kit. Everybody saw him up there all the time, anyway.

The deck was a madhouse, but one that made sense to him now. He knew what it was all about. He didn't care about it any more.

He knew right where to look for Rafehausen's S-3, tucked down between elevators one and two, way outboard. Sneesen walked right to it. He looked at the radome—just looked at it; why would they think he was doing anything just because he was looking? *Weird— because they said he was weird.* Sneesen looked around and then went to the port engine intake and looked in, and, when he knew nobody was looking, reached way back and pushed one of the epoxy-filled Coke cans as far back as he could. He put some tools in after it. Then he strolled over to the starboard engine and did the same thing.

Then he walked to the number two elevator and walked off the edge. Nobody saw him go; one moment he was there, the next he was gone—down, down the height of a five-story building, to hit the water, sudden cold, shock, landing partly on his buttocks and back and feeling the air slammed from his lungs, then sinking and hearing the great noise of the ship going on, tumbling in its wake, sinking, drowning. Gone.

The Gulf of Sidra.

USNS *Philadelphia* was on station at 32.17 N, 17.04 E. Long swells were running, lifting the ship and then pointing it bow-down and running away under her; a strong wind blew out of the northeast, carrying away spray from the fringe of the surface chop. Everybody was seasick, but Rose and LaFond were on deck in foul-weather gear. LaFond unashamedly threw up when he had to and made no apology; Rose, perhaps feeling some constraint because of command, found shelter. It started to rain, hard drops that hit like blown sand, and she made her way aft to the bridge and the comm office. Despite the seasickness, she felt strong enough for anything. She hadn't known Alan had been missing, only that she hadn't heard from him; now, she had a special message from Admiral Pilchard that he was on the *Rangoon* and well.

Valdez was in his bunk. The marines were in their bunks. The IVI delegation—three company reps and two scientists—were in their bunks. There was little to do for sixteen hours except wait.

The captain was in his quarters just aft of the bridge.

Told that Rose was on the bridge, he came forward, a short, paunchy man in his forties. "Doing okay?" he said with the seaman's grin at the seasick.

"I've spent a lot of time at sea, Captain."

"Well, the *Philly* rides a little rougher than a CV."

"Yeah, but it isn't a chopper carrier, either. They stand on end. I'll be okay."

"I know you will. Well, our situation's good, except the weather. If this lasts, we're not gonna have fighter cover out of Aviano; they're socked in up there."

"I checked."

"Well, you know our situation. We're going to depend on what we can get out of Sigonella, but they tell me the F-18s can't do too much for us."

"Short legs, yeah. We'll be okay." She glanced at the surface radar display. "How's that Libyan Coast Guard cutter doing?" The Libyan gunboat had been shadowing them for hours, staying just over the visual horizon, but close enough so that its mast-mounted radar kept them in sight. But that worked both ways: the *Philadelphia*'s higher mast kept easy track of the Libyan, and the Libyans' choice of distance revealed the gunboat's mast height and probable size—a good deal smaller than a frigate.

"Still there." The captain tapped the greenish blip. "Holding station."

"Good."

"Game plan says we're supposed to have a destroyer within visual. Where is it?"

"Russians are playing some game up north; there's an Akula hanging around. Normally, they'd be running lines on it from the air, but the carrier's too far away. Shore-based P-3s are doing their thing. I guess Admiral Pilchard thinks he needs the destroyers up there more than we do down here."

They both looked up as a gust of wind blasted the nearest window with rain. The ship was climbing the swell, and it seemed to be heading up like an aircraft flying into the weather. Rose had to take half a step backward to steady herself, and she grabbed for the big command chair.

"Can you launch in this?" the captain shouted over the wind.

"No!" She pulled herself up the slope of the deck. "Van Nguyen, the civilian launch guy, says thirty-knot wind max plus some cockamamie scale he's got for wave action." She tried to grin. "We didn't rehearse for bad weather during Fleetex."

Without affectation, the captain said, "Oh, this isn't bad weather." Then he realized what she meant. "Bad for the launch, you mean, yeah. Well—we wait and see." He braced himself against the chair. "Between you and me, I'll be glad when that thing blasts off my deck and is gone. Nothing personal—I'll just be glad when we're rid of it." He looked at her. "You know the Chinese and the Italians both made some sort of speech against it today in the UN."

"Yeah?"

"They claimed it was a weapon of destabilization. It's all over the Italian radio."

Rose thought about Peretz, decided there was nothing she could do, and headed for the ladder. *Just do your job.* She went back down to the deck and joined LaFond and then made a tour of the sleeping spaces, trying to cheer people up. Things were really tight on the *Philadelphia*, which had not been configured to carry so many passengers. At that moment, nobody cared.

"Let me die, man," Valdez moaned.

"Aw, come on, Valdez! You're a sailor!"

"Take me back to Silicon Valley."

The updated weather predicted that the storm would slowly shift northward, meaning that the *Philadelphia* might get clear enough to launch next day. L-minus-8, the formal beginning of the countdown, would come at 0400. At best, it would be tight, with the civilian experts saying they had to stay on the cautious side of the judgment line and Rose and the captain saying they wanted to launch. Either way, air cover was going to be a problem, because, as the wind lessened, the ceiling might come right down to the water, and Aviano and Sigonella would be solidly socked in. As she rolled into her rack for a nap fully clothed (admitting the truth to herself; she was nauseated) Rose thought, *If it grounds us, it'll ground the Libyans, so it's zero-sum-game time.* She didn't let herself worry about the fact that the Libyans took off from south of her, where the weather would be improving first.

She woke and checked her watch. 1720—still early. She could feel the ship under her, tipped bow-down as the swell moved her. Wave action was the same, she decided, but what was the wind? She climbed a ladder and came up on the deck, but before she even got there she knew the sound of the wind was different. The high keening was gone, and with it the unpredictable blasts that smashed rain against the sides. On deck, she met fog and a reduced wind that was like a slap with sopping rags.

But it was better—it was better. It was going to be okay!

She wanted to tell somebody—Alan, most of all, but Valdez would do. It was going to be okay, and tomorrow at noon they would launch, and *Philadelphia* would turn north and head for Naples, and she would have done her job and done it well.

She hugged herself against the damp cold of the wind.

Then she felt the ship shudder and lurch, lifting stern-up and listing to port. A dull crunch and boom seemed to come from everywhere around her as she was thrown aside, trying to keep her balance, then falling to the steel deck and sliding ten feet over the wet surface. She was aware of water boiling by the rail, and her first thought was of some vagrant wave, and then she realized that the ship had been hit by an explosion, and she was sliding and tumbling and wondering if it was the missile or the ship's propulsion system or was it the Akula or—?

Blood was pouring from her nose, but she was alert. She clawed her way up the ladder and thrust her head through the steel door to the bridge. Somebody was shouting "Helm's not answering!" when she burst in.

"Get Cobb on the *Fort Klock*! Tell him I think we've been torpedoed!"

At sea—aboard the *Jackson*.

The Air Boss looked down over his kingdom and sipped at his twentieth cup of bad coffee since sitting down in the tower. He had launched two-thirds of the air wing in only two cycles; the leaders would be near Gibraltar, by now; the last planes in the chainsaw were below him, an S-3 and two F-14s. These three aircraft were the purpose of the entire launch, the actual payload that would travel up the thousands of miles of waiting tankers and defenders and do the job of the air wing. Two fighters and one big, dangerous grape.

If he hadn't had a major hard-ass image to maintain, he would have cracked a smile. This air wing had pulled itself together and now it was possible, just possible, that it might be something special. An air wing that could launch a four-thousand-mile chainsaw.

Behind him, there was movement, and two of his enlisted men had a brief conversation.

"What's up?" he asked, not taking his eyes off the deck.

"VS-49 has a sailor missing. They want us to check if he's on the deck."

The Air Boss watched the deck for a moment. "Okay, get it done. Don't make a fuss; we haven't got time to run a Man Overboard right now." He heard Petty Officer Dearing talk into the comm link to the deck chiefs. Some kid probably overslept; they were all bushed.

The Air Boss saw the signal he had been waiting for and raised his hand.

"Deck is clear. Commence the launch." Immediately, there was a little buzz behind him as the team began to inform the deck and the air wing. The S-3 was already on the cat. Rafehausen's plane; that didn't always mean much, but the Air Boss suspected that Rafehausen was the best pilot in the air wing, and when the chips are down, you send the best. He saw the plane quiver like a cat ready to pounce as the shuttle locked home, and then his trained eye saw a tiny flutter of metal near the left engine and he slapped at the button to hold the cat, but the catapult had already fired and the plane began to gather speed down the deck. *Something in the engine intake*, he knew. That engine was shredding itself even as—

The engine burst apart in a flash of brilliant white and silver, but the implacable catapult continued to fling the broken plane down the deck. The second engine went with a scream that was audible even on the bridge. A piece of turbofan blade, released from the cowling at full rotation, cut through a nearby F-18 and ripped upward and struck the Air Boss's armored window like a hammer. The tough glass starred but didn't hide the now wingless

S-3 as it was tossed forward by the catapult. The plane rotated sharply to the left, free of the deck with no engines, no lift. One seat fired straight out over the water at a height of sixty feet; the chute opened and it hit the water at once, the rocket-propelled seat skipping over the waves. Then, directly ahead of the ship, the plane hit the water upside down. It floated for almost two seconds, breaking up from the impact but still, somehow, game. Then it was gone.

The deck was chaos and a helicopter was launching, but the Air Boss knew it was too late for the crew of the plane. As he stood up, he and every member of the crew could hear the cruel rattle as the wreckage of the plane began to drag down the length of the ship's hull.

The con on the bridge was trying to turn away from the wreckage. It didn't matter. But there were lives at stake somewhere in the Mediterranean, and the air wing had stretched to the limit to get a package in the air, and the Air Boss swallowed his panic and his sorrow and did his duty.

"Tell VS-49 to get another plane on deck."

37

December 9

Off the African coast.

Alan got his way: they put him into an ancient CH-46 and he headed for the *Jackson*. By the time he lifted off, he had seen both Djalik and O'Neill again—both sedated, both alive, Djalik critical but "stabilized."

He was tired but up—too up, although he didn't know it yet. He still had that sense of urgency that had driven him on the flight, as if he had to get there, *get there, get there!* Even though *there* kept receding from him. Was there some new *there*, still over the horizon? Or was *there* the *Jackson*, duty, that life? Or was it Rose, some fear for her?

The helo winnowed down on the *Jackson*'s flight deck and he clambered out, humping his helmet bag with the stuff that had got him into and out of Zaire, and the ship looked strange to him, and at first he thought it was only its newness, and then it hit him: there were almost no aircraft. F-14s sat on the number one and two cats, but the deck behind them was dark and almost empty, and he wondered what was going on—ASW threat? An operation he didn't know about?

He ran to the catwalk, and half a dozen officers were there to pound his back and wring his hand, but each did it and got out of the way, too fast, something wrong, passing

556

him along; Captain Parsills last, until he passed him on, too, murmuring, "Great job, super job—the admiral wants to see you personally—"

And there was Rafe. And Rafe wasn't smiling.

Rafe put out his hand. Alan took it, and Rafe—most un-Rafe-like—put his left hand on Alan's shoulder. "Can you fly?" he said.

Alan thought it was a joke, a reference to his landing on the *Rangoon*, and he started to grin and then saw that Rafe wasn't joking; he was beyond seriousness. Parsills and the others were behind Alan; he could feel them there, hanging back. *What the hell?*

"We're running a chainsaw; I'm the last aircraft. I need a TACCO."

"Jesus, Rafe—?" *You never say you are too tired to fly.* He wanted to hold up his cotton-gloved hands and yell "I'm burned out—what do I look like?" But the look on Rafe's face stopped him.

"Somebody hit the *Philadelphia*. Rose is okay, but they need air cover. That's what the chainsaw is for. *Can you fly?*"

He felt stupidly slow. Rose—*Philadelphia*—it was almost launch day, must be, so the *Philadelphia* must be in the Gulf of Sidra. *Somebody hit the* Philadelphia. "Hit with what?"

"We don't know yet. Air cover's gone; Cobb's BG is focused on a Russian sub. She needs us, man."

He looked around. Parsills and the others were looking at him, waiting. They all knew, of course. He saw the one, lone S-3 on the deck. The last plane in a chainsaw. *Rose.*

Rafe still had his hand. Now, he dropped it and looked away. "We wouldn't be going, but—" He was having trouble speaking. "Last S-3 was supposed to be mine. Skipper Paneen took my plane and— Engines blew going off the cat about ten minutes ago."

Alan had never seen it happen, but he had heard about it. The aircraft launched, disappeared below the flight deck, and never came up. Into the water off the bow, the carrier plowing over it—

"Jesus, Rafe, did they—"

"Skipper, Dickson, Chief Rinehart." He swallowed. "Christy—" He swallowed again. "Christy may make it. She ejected, broke both— She may not walk, if she— You going or aren't you?"

"Of course. Jesus, Rafe, I'm—"

But Rafehausen had already turned away and was going through the hatch. He wasn't going to weep; he wasn't that kind, but he was on the edge of a crash, an abyss, and he wanted to face it his own way.

Alan turned to Parsills. "Nixon was the only one who got out alive?"

Parsills nodded. He gripped Alan's arm. "This is a tough time, Al—all the way up to the flag. BG's split, your wife's ship is in trouble, then this. You're the only bright spot. Come on, the admiral wants to see you."

Alan's "up" turned into a down, the down of waiting. He had lost a dozen pounds, and his flight gear all had to be rebuckled, and a parachute rigger was trying to take some webbing out of his harness and re-sew it so it would fit. That sort of trivia, and the time it took to get little things done, were fraying his temper. He still had that drive to *get there*, and re-fitting was preventing it. He wanted to be in the air *right now*. He had to get to Rose. The chainsaw was in the air. And he was holding up the plane waiting for his fucking flight gear to fit!

Rafe seemed calm enough now. He'd already gone up and pre-flighted the plane twice. He was too quiet, was Alan's thought, maybe because a lot had happened in the weeks he had been away and maybe because Christy Nixon was down in the ship's hospital with a broken back and smashed knees.

Alan finished his can of Coke and looked at the rigger, who seemed to be staring off into space.

"Goddamit, are you working on that thing or not?" Alan snapped. The rigger glanced at him, looked hurt. "I'm not going to a fucking fashion show."

"Measure twice, cut once, sir. Sorry it's taking so long."

Rafe grabbed his elbow. "Talk to you in the p'way, Alan?" he asked quietly. Alan followed him out of the rigger's shack to the passageway beyond the ready room. It was empty. The chainsaw was engaging almost every S-3 and its crew. All the gas the air wing had was in the air.

"Alan, are you okay for this mission? Because if you keep snapping at men and women trying to do their jobs, I'll leave you behind."

His fists clenched and the pain in his hands cleared his head. He counted to five. He knew, *knew* he was out of line, but the impatience was still there and his words were choked. "I'll be fine. I'll apologize." He stared at Rafe's too-calm eyes. "You need me." He meant, *You're hurting, too; I'm trying to help you.*

"Screw that." Rafe wouldn't look him in the eye, "That depth charge you asked for? McAllen says that's a good idea and the ordnance people are digging one out of stores. It's going to take fifteen minutes. I did your seat and McAllen did your computer. Go into the ready room and put your head down until I come for you. That's an order."

Alan thought of what he had been through with O'Neill and Djalik. Rafe's "order" existed in a context that made him smile. "Yes, sir."

Rafe walked back to the PR shack and poked his head

in. "Hey, Waller! Don't sweat it. His wife is on the *Philly* and he's a little tense."

Waller didn't look up. "I know, sir. Just can't do this any faster." Waller, like a lot of people on the boat, had some notion of how much Rafe must be worrying about Christy Nixon.

"You've got half an hour till the crew walks."

"Cool, sir. Thanks."

Rafe ducked out and went to the ready room for coffee. Alan was already asleep in a rear seat. Rafe, Cutter, and McAllen started the brief without him.

When Rafe woke him, he came awake thinking of Rose. Sick worry hit him; he tried to conquer it. Half an hour of sleep and the imminence of *getting there* gave him a rush of false energy. His flight gear was ready, and after he put it on he dashed into the rigger shack to thank Waller, who smiled and looked sheepish. Then he slipped into old habit: he flung himself into the ASW module, slugged down a mixture of coffee and chocolate, filled the thermos, and grabbed a plate of cookies from the chart table. He looked at the last locations of the supposed Russian sub and the other players. The Russian surface ships were closing in on the *Fort Klock* task force. Bad weather still hampered both communications and locations. The chainsaw had tankers extending almost fourteen hundred miles from the carrier. Two KA-6s full of gas were on their way to the last fuel point inside the Med, near Algiers, and a KC-10 was leaving Rota in two hours to meet them off Lampedusa. He studied all this, absorbed it, drank his hot drink, and he thought all the time about Rose and about Rafe: he could do something for Rose; Rafe could do nothing for Christy. How was Rafe going to get through the long hours of this flight? How was he, for that matter?

Before they walked, a sailor handed him a message

board. The top sheet was for him, from Dukas. *Zulu dead.* *"Shot while escaping."* You can't win 'em all.

He handed the message board back. *Zulu, dead.* He smiled, a smile that caused the sailor who had brought the message to flinch. For a moment, Alan's face was the face of barbarism. He wondered how Dukas had gotten Zulu, but it was remote now. As with a wound, the pressure would come later. He took a pen from his shoulder pocket, and scrawled "Pass to Mr Harry O'Neill onboard USS *Rangoon*."

He pointed at the note. "Can you do that?"

The sailor nodded and took the message board. Alan wondered why the sailor looked so scared and moved down the passageway toward the plane. Toward *getting there.*

Alan walked quickly around the plane. A buddy store to top off the two F-14s that would be trailing them one last time as they got close to the action area. A Harpoon missile. A full rack of sonobuoys, both active and passive types. A buddy store and gas. Several hydro-acoustic data buoys. Chaff and flare cartridges to deflect SAMs and air-to-air missiles. In the bomb bay, one Mk 46 torpedo and one conventional depth charge. It was the heaviest load that an S-3 could carry off the deck.

Serious business, he thought. It was serious for him because of Rose, but he wondered about the Russian sub and how much those guys wanted it to be serious business. If he had to use that depth charge on an Akula-class nuclear submarine, what would the next move be?

He climbed into an aircraft that was already running and warm. He checked his seat anyway, from habit, and strapped in. The moment he was in, Rafe had the plane rolling toward their spot on catapult two. The deck was strangely empty, the entire air wing deployed in order to get three planes across nineteen hundred miles of chainsaw, the F-14s that would fly with them already aloft and on the tanker, heading up the chain.

At top speed and with favorable winds, the S-3 should hit the KC-10 in eight hours, yet Rafe kept saying six. Alan suddenly got it: Rafe's *not going around; he's going to fly across Algeria and Tunisia.* He smiled. Rafe was the skipper, now, but he still had more balls than anyone Alan had ever known. *Six hours to Rose.* Bless Rafe Rafehausen and his balls. Six hours to Rose, and whatever had blown a hole in her ship. Alan had a hunch about that, and the hunch had led him to ask for the depth charge.

He thought about that hunch as they rolled onto the catapult and went into tension. His kneeboard cards were ready to hand, his procedures taped in little notes at three places on the screen. He already had emitter data on the Libyan patrol boat and the Russians. He thought again, fleetingly, of how close all of them might be to a real war, too many hulls in the water, too many planes in the air, Russian and American and Libyan.

Rafe gave a crisp salute to the cat officer and said, "On to glory!" and the plane tore down the deck. Alan thought of Christy Nixon, in this seat, hurtling off the deck and hearing the engines fail, feeling the loss of power, the water—

As AH 702 fought for a few meters of altitude with her load of fuel and weapons, Alan tried to picture his hunch as it appeared on a page of Jane's *Fighting Ships*. Terrorists had used them more than once. The Libyans might have one. Small, compact. Four-man crew.

Mini-sub.

But if he was right, what was a Russian nuke attack boat doing down there, as well?

Gulf of Sidra.

USNS *Philadelphia* was drifting broadside to a thirty-knot wind. The swells now struck her only slightly stern-on, seeming to threaten to broach her as seawater clawed at the upswell side and broke over the deck. Water battered the container that housed the missile; the three men assigned to checking its fittings and its condition wore survival suits, and they had lifelines that they snapped to strategically positioned holds as they tried to move around the wave-washed deck.

On the bridge, Rose and the captain tried to understand their situation. The ship was in contact with Captain Cobb on the cruiser, a hundred and thirty miles to the north. Rose had been in contact with the IVI watch officer and had been told that the In-Flight Command Executive—Ray Suter—was being called at home. Rose had also spoken to the Whiskey Bravo on the *Andrew Jackson*, who said they would launch aircraft within the hour. There didn't seem to be any more communication to be done.

The captain was in a yellow foul-weather jacket, with Merchant Marine pants showing beneath it. He looked haggard, more like a street-person than a ship's captain. Rose, dried blood from a broken nose still crusted on her upper lip, was scowling down at the black deck, where flashlights pierced the dark as the crewmen worked.

"What's the situation now?" she demanded. She had been below, trying to assess damage, and she had come up to the bridge because she had understood she was in the way down there.

"Steering gone, main propulsion gone. I've got lateral screws, and I'm trying to get us in the line of the swell with those, but if I do, we're going to be carried toward the coast."

"How far before we're in Libyan waters?"

"If you accept their definition, we're in Libyan waters now. International law, we're about twenty miles off." He cleared his throat. "Either way, we're inside their goddam Line of Death."

"How long?"

He shook his head. A crewman appeared and passed the captain a report from the ship's engineer: he was reversing one lateral screw to bring the ship around.

"How long?" she said again.

"Maybe three hours. I thought you were gonna have that nose looked at."

"How long if you use the lateral screws to fight the wind and the wave action?"

"We couldn't stay bow-on if we did that. See, we'd be broadside like now, and—"

"How long?"

He compressed his lips. "I guess I could keep us in international waters a day, maybe a day and a night. If those engines last—they're not made to run constantly." He turned on her. "You know what it'd be like to stay broadside to this shit for twenty-four hours?"

"We'd be real sick. What else?"

They stared at each other. He shook his head. "Maybe I could rig some kind of sea anchor," he said. "Slow down the drift. Then maybe use the laterals at an angle—"

There was an old sound-powered phone system on the ship, kept as a backup. Rose got on it now to Valdez, who had been snapped out of his sickness by the explosion and was now down with the damage-control crew. One of the civilian reps was down there, too; he was a former senior chief who had worked damage control on an Arleigh Burke-class destroyer. "What's going down?" she shouted into the antique headset.

"We got timbers up, pumps are working!" Valdez's voice seemed to come from another ship.

"What's Anson say about it?"

"He says not a torpedo. Something like a mine. He says, fucking lucky hit or somebody knew just where to put it!" Then Valdez shouted something she didn't get, and she had to ask him to repeat, and they talked over each other until she heard the words "limpet mine."

"Jesus Christ," she murmured.

"What now?" the captain groaned.

"Anson thinks maybe it was a limpet mine. That means—"

"I know what it means, Commander!" The captain's face was a mask of outrage. "It means somebody sabotaged my ship! It means the goddam Libyans or Russians planted a bomb on us so we'll drift into their waters and they can grab us. Well, I'm goddamned if they're going to do that to my ship!"

That made a kind of sense, she thought. Yes, the Libyans would like to grab this American ship that was in waters they claimed but didn't dare to defend against the Sixth Fleet; yes, it made sense that they would try to disable the ship and let it drift into water that even the US would acknowledge was theirs; yes, it made sense that they had that patrol boat just over the horizon, maybe waiting now for the moment to move in.

Rose went to the comm center and messaged the battle group that the explosion had come from outside the hull. She reported what Valdez had passed on to her from Anson: suspected sabotage, probably planted underwater by a diver. She asked that intel check Libyan order of battle to see what submersibles they had that would carry swimmers to this distance from their coast. In her mind—and now, she knew, in the minds of the battle group—was one question: had it been done from a submarine,

565

and, if so, was that submarine the Russian Akula? And if that question went unanswered, what would the cruiser and its destroyers, shorn of air cover, do?

Over Gibraltar.

Alan slept between refueling points on the chainsaw. They passed up the coast of Africa with a tailwind and passed Gibraltar without a hitch. The weather was getting worse, and Alan knew from meteorological reports how bad it was near the surface in the Gulf of Sidra. They got gas just east of Gibraltar as the moon rose over the dense cloud below them. The F-14s were ahead of them and had drained the other tanker. They had two more of Rafe's squadron's S-3s waiting north of Algiers, and then they would be on their own—the point and purpose of the chainsaw, one S-3 and its covering F-14s, which would take the combined aerial power of a super-carrier to get two thousand miles from her deck.

Rafe had redirected the KC-10 enough to reveal his plan to overfly North Africa to anybody who thought about it, but nobody challenged them. Alan took the opportunity between fuelings to share out coffee and cookies. Nobody talked much. Rafe said that *Klock* reported that Spain and Italy had forbidden armed US aircraft to take off from their territory or to overfly them. *There goes Air Force support for the BG*. A cynic would say that both countries had major trade with Libya to protect, but the outrage they had expressed at the Peacemaker launch seemed real. In fact, Peacemaker seemed to have stirred up an international movement against the US; Rafe told him that press traffic the night before had the Chinese ambassador to the UN making a speech about Peacemaker's being a terror weapon. That tickled something in Alan's memory, something way back when Abe Peretz had

566

done his Reserve duty at IVI. Peretz had hinted something about Peacemaker's being a weapon—was that it?

He'd been out of it a long time—what had the world learned while he was thrashing around in Africa—?

His head fell forward and almost hit his keyboard, but his parachute harness caught him and he didn't wake. He dreamed about crows.

Gulf of Sidra.

Back on the bridge again, Rose could see a work light shining on the deck and more figures darting in and out of its yellow glow.

"We're bringing up material to rig a sea anchor," the captain said. "Take an hour, anyway." He stared into the black sky.

"How much time have we got?"

"Well—if you're an optimist, you'll say that Sixth Fleet will have something down here to tow us out in six hours. That depends on what's available and how they're doing with the Russians up there. Y'know, I been thinking— this could of been the Russians and not the Libyans, or the two together, maybe to draw a couple ships down here and then—shit, I don't know. Maybe they're after your Peacemaker." The captain was both smarter and better informed than she had thought. His fears were in fact hers.

"And if I'm a pessimist?" she said.

"Worst case, we duke it out here by ourselves because Fleet has its plate full. I'll keep us out of Libyan waters for twelve hours, by God, if I have to tow the *Philadelphia* by swimming with a rope in my teeth, but after that, oh, shit— They'll get us. No way they won't get us if we just drift." Agonized, he glanced at her. "How soon can you launch that goddam thing off my deck?"

"Countdown is supposed to start in—one hour twenty."

"Any chance you can move it up?"

"Captain, we got two minds with but a single thought." She pressed the button on the sound-powered phone and ordered Valdez to the launch command module. "Spread the word down there, launch countdown has been moved up, it is now L minus eight-thirteen and counting. I want you in the module, in your seat, ready to go in thirteen minutes! Bring a bucket, because you're not going back to your rack!"

Before she could leave the bridge, the duty mate stuck his head in and shouted, "Captain!" and disappeared, and the captain shot after him. She hesitated, and after twenty seconds the captain put his head back around the doorframe and looked at her. "Libyan patrol boat is moving! We got confirmed radar they're heading this way—about fifteen miles out!"

Rose bit her lip. She tasted the blood that had dried there. She went back to communications and put her hand on the operator's shoulder. "Pass the word for Gunnery Sergeant LaFond. Marines to assemble in battle gear just aft of the launch module ASAP. All weapons on the deck and loaded. LaFond to report to me in the module." She patted the shoulder. "I'm moving there now."

On her way off the bridge, she passed the captain again. "You keep us in international waters. I'll take care of the Libyans."

"This is my ship, Commander!"

Her voice was soft. "Yeah, but it's my mission. You know how my orders read. You sail it, I use it—and defend it. Captain, if they take the *Philadelphia* we'll be in Benghazi for breakfast, and we could be stuck there for years. I don't mean to be the first naval officer since Decatur to rot on the Barbary Coast."

She went out into the dying storm.

24 NM north of Algiers.

Alan unstrapped before they reached the tanker, pissed into a bag, and lay down in the tunnel by the computer to stretch his legs, his hands burning by his sides. He smiled wryly. Djalik had lost a hand, Harry an eye, and he had blistered hands. When he was done, McAllen and Cutter followed suit. Then they hit the last two tankers just on schedule.

The F-14s were flying at max conserve, already gassed up. Rafe hit the funnel on his first try and took all the gas the other S-3 had left to give. Then he hit the second tanker and drank it dry, too. Both were supposed to land in Rota—would the Spanish let them in now? The whole maneuver was done without radio contact. They flashed flashlights on and off to make signals. It wasn't as well done as in Alan's first squadron, but it was a miracle to Rafe after the debacle of Fleetex. These guys were eager, and they were getting good.

Rafe got alongside the refueled F-14s and flashed his flashlight. When he had their attention, he held up his tiny rescue radio, supposed to have a range of less than two miles. He turned it on the guard frequency and pointed the antenna at the other plane.

"Pitcher calling Shortstop," he said slowly into the hand-held.

"Roger, Pitcher. I copy. What's up?"

"Change of plans, Shortstop. Just follow me."

"Roger, copy."

"Roger, out."

Rafe dove for the deck and turned toward the Algerian coast, because he was about to start an illegal over-flight from about Constantine, Algeria, to near Ben Gardane in

Tunisia—almost the point where the Tunisian–Libyan border met the Mediterranean. Alan handed forward a computerized map printout showing Algerian and Tunisian radar coverage.

"Thanks, Al."

Rafe had to unstrap to come back and take his turn in the tunnel while Cutter flew. He was still looking at the map.

Alan knew Rafe was hurting, had to be hurting. He touched Rafe's arm. "Thanks Rafe. For everything."

They pressed on into the dawn, five hundred feet off the deck.

38

December 9

The Gulf of Sidra.
It took the Libyan gunboat almost an hour to close the distance that had separated it from the *Philadelphia*. When it was within a quarter of a mile, it veered slightly northeast and slowed, and they could see it as a pale blur of light in the drizzle that had begun to fall. The wind was still dropping, so the chop and the spray were gone, but the long swells continued to roll the *Philadelphia* like a log.

On the bridge, Rose, in body armor, helmet, and night-vision goggles, was trying to goose the countdown along while marshaling the ship's meager defenses. She had already been on to IVI twice, demanding permission to slash the countdown. Unsatisfied by the well-just-let's-not-go-too-fast response, she had got Nguyen into the launch module to tell her exactly what they could cut and still be ninety percent certain of getting the thing off the deck and out of Libyan air space. He was working on it.

The marines were near the launch command module, the two tripod-mounted Mark 19s placed to cover a zone on each side of the ship. The LAW had been brought up as well. On the stern, six of the ship's crew were posted as lookouts, lightly armed with streetsweepers and side arms. The other civilian reps and scientists had been sent below. Valdez, also in helmet and Kevlar vest, was still in the module, honchoing computer readouts and fingering an AUG and trying to hurry the countdown over the objections of the civilians.

Rose triggered her handheld radio. "Report, Valdez."

"Okay at Launch minus seven-nineteen. Readouts normal; Peacemaker's awake and checking out. We're go on Raise to Vertical in twenty-seven minutes, but Nguyen finally admitted we can do it in sixteen-thirty-one and check the Readout Access after it's erect. New news, though, Boss—we gotta launch before seawater leakage changes the ship's trim. Anson gives an hour and a half on that, which is a laugher 'cause we got six hours of countdown to go. What's going down where you are?"

"Negative on Raise to Vertical until that Libyan boat drops off. Stop the count at Vert minus seven if we've got a no-change situation. They're now four hundred meters off the port side—can you see them?"

"I see a kind of blur. What's happening?"

"Situation stable. Hey, ask Nguyen if he can skip forward and then come back to Raise to Vert if the Libyans delay us. And keep at that goddam countdown!" She didn't want to take Valdez's focus away. In actuality, a lot was going on to worry her, but she didn't want to tell him: Suter had told her to push the countdown to Launch minus forty and hold there for orders—meaning that he wanted support at his end. From Shreed? she had wondered. Or was it from Touhey? Communication with the battle group continued but clarified nothing: Cobb had made it all too obvious that he was worried about the location of the Russian sub. Whiskey Bravo had reported that a mission package had launched from the carrier, ETA six hours, and that Rota, Spain was sending a KC-10 refueling tanker and two F-16s, but they were coming without weapons. She had just heard that Spain and Italy were refusing to let armed US aircraft take off, meaning she was being stripped of air cover.

"Message from the Libyan boat!" a voice cried at her elbow. She snatched for the paper, but the captain got to it first.

"'Prepare to accept inspection party. You are in Libyan waters.'" He scowled at Rose.

"Tell them we're in international waters and will not accept any party."

He didn't like her jumping into it, but it was exactly what he was going to say, anyway. He scribbled on the same sheet and handed it back to the comm operator.

"Bastards," the captain said. "Don't put that in the message, son."

"Just doing their job." She switched to the marines' channel. "LaFond, this is Lieutenant-Commander Craik. The Libyans messaged us to stand by for visitors. Be ready to repel any attempt to board this ship."

"Yes, ma'am!"

When she got in touch with the stern, a grim voice reported that they could see nothing from there.

"Keep an eagle eye *on* the water and *under* the water. They're going to try to board."

The captain grabbed another piece of paper. "Message." She saw that his hand was shaking. "'You are in Libyan territorial waters. Prepare to accept tow to nearest port for your protection.'"

"That means they may have something else waiting—an ocean-going tug, or some such," he muttered. "But maybe they're bluffing. Radar, do a wide sweep, surface, and see what you get."

"Nothing I can make out, sir. We're getting a lot of clutter near the coast."

"Air?" Rose said.

The *Philadelphia* didn't have much in the way of aerial-search capability, but the man could coax some coverage out of what he had.

"Maybe two choppers," he said. "Right against the coast. I'm sorry, ma'am—this gear isn't built for that kind of work."

The captain was writing another reply to the Libyan gunboat, but she put a hand on his arm and again got on the marines' channel.

"LaFond, we may have choppers incoming. What's the status on the LAW?"

"Caps are off, safety pin still in place, tube un-extended."

"Prep it to ready-to-fire and wait for my signal."

Another message arrived: *Prepare to be boarded.*

Brilliant light suddenly surrounded the Libyan gunboat, haloed by the drizzle into something like a cheaply staged religious vision. Two searchlights poked cones of dazzle through the murk. Rose took her hand off the captain's arm and tapped the message paper. "I'd like to message them simply, 'Reply follows.' Okay?"

The captain glanced down at the place on the deck where the marines were, then looked at Rose. Behind him, the sky was lightening. He scribbled and gave the paper to the operator.

Rose flashed LaFond. "Aim the LAW well ahead of the Libyan boat. You see it okay?"

"Affirmative."

"Don't aim at it! This is what's called a shot over the bow. On my signal."

"Roger."

The communications man muttered, "Message sent, Captain."

Reply follows.

The captain nodded at Rose.

574

"Fire."

The M72 LAW is a fairly crude rocket based on the bazooka. Intended for defense against tanks, it is not normally a weapon for use at sea. In the pre-dawn murk, however, its flaming tail is an impressive sight, and its twelve-hundred-meter range, rocket-powered the whole way, sends a distinctive message. Rose watched the orange flame fizz off the deck, rise in a low trajectory hardly higher than the Libyan's mast-borne radar, and roar across the bow at less distance than she thought was really safe.

The effect was almost instantaneous.

The Libyan doused his spotlights, surged forward, and veered sharply to his starboard, clawing up the water to put distance between himself and the *Philadelphia*. As it came stern-to, a twin 20mm started firing tracer over the American ship.

"Fire another, Commander?" LaFond shouted eagerly.

"Negative! Man the Mark 19s and load with frag." She switched channels. "Stern, prepare to repel boarders. We will join you." She switched again and wondered. *Repel boarders*. When did someone last say that in these waters? She needed Valdez—the countdown would have to take care of itself. "Valdez, join me on the after main deck, armed and ready. Ask—*ask*, don't order, he's got to volunteer, he's a civilian—ask Nguyen to continue the countdown. Let's go!"

She swung down out of her chair. "We'll do what we can, Captain."

The radar operator's voice caught her as she headed off the bridge. "I've got an airborne blip about two hundred miles out and closing on us, Commander. Due west."

"Tripoli direction?"

"No, ma'am. Over water, coming from the Med. Could be one of ours."

"Could be." She sounded casual; inside, she was praying, *Make it one of ours! Make it one of ours from the carrier! I'll even take an unarmed F-18 from Rota!*

Carrying the stubby Steyr AUG, she headed for the stern.

Outside the Line of Death.

The S-3 bored straight through the dark sky toward the bright line of dawn. It was making no deceptive maneuvers, dropping no chaff to confuse the radars that lit it every several minutes. The crew of four, knowing their vulnerability in the "big fat grape" that had taken off from the *Andrew Jackson* six hours before, were awake and tense despite a lack of sleep that, for one of them, stretched back more than a day. Flying the final tooth of the chainsaw, they had given the gas taken on at Gibraltar to the two F-14 Tomcats that nestled like oversized chicks under the S-3's stubby wings. On any radar, the three planes would show as a single blip. Behind them, out over the Mediterranean and well to the north and west, another S-3 was moving parallel, refueling two F-18s as it came. That arm of the chainsaw covered the *Jackson's* future path into the Med.

Rafe had overflown Algeria. Against international law. Now they had caught up to the KC-10 south of Lampedusa Island, both the S-3 and its chicks close to running out of fuel. Even as they climbed, Rafe was coaxing the giant tanker to meet them at 6,000 feet instead of 16,000.

Rafe didn't want to admit that he lacked the fuel to get up there, and he didn't want to tell the Air Force that he had just overflown two neutral countries at low altitude, and that if he'd come the long way around as he was supposed to, he'd be in the water now.

"With the gas, we'll be good to go for six more hours,"

Rafe muttered. "The Tomcats will only be good for a couple, and those pilots must be burned. Al, what's our situation?"

"Two-forty miles to the *Philadelphia*." His voice gave no indication that he had a personal stake in what might be happening on the crippled ship. Like the others, he was terse, barely audible. No jokes this morning. "Other blip is lying off the *Philadelphia* about two miles; hard to separate them on the screen. Just got lighted by another Libyan SAM site, but no launch. P-3 is on station eighty clicks east of Benghazi, still reporting he thinks he has contact with a quote large underwater target unquote, which could be the supposed Russian but which could also be a Libyan Whiskey-class. The P-3 reported a probable and a possible three hours ago and nothing since, and what they're doing is boring lines in the sky trying to fake out something they haven't identified on a bearing they haven't defined at a depth they haven't guessed. It sucks."

Before he was done, Rafe and Cutter had the S-3's probe drinking gas out of the KC-10, which loomed huge above them in the first gray smear of dawn. Extending multiple hoses, it tanked the two F-14s at the same time, turned gently and began to head east toward the *Philly*. Good thinking—every mile they got closer on this guy's nickel, the better. The S-3 crew drank more coffee and stretched again. By the time that they were done fueling, they were sixty miles closer to the *Philadelphia*, and Alan had identified the Libyan patrol craft as a Nanuchka-class guided-missile boat, which carried both a surface-to-surface missile and a SAM.

The KC-10 turned north, returning to the protection of the *Fort Klock*'s missiles.

Alan reported on the Nanuchka. "The good news is they've got a ship missile, but they aren't using it; the bad news is I think they're after the Peacemaker and don't want to bang it up. The other news is that they have a surface-to—"

"Hold it, Al—" Rafe was suddenly tense. He looked aside at Cutter, made a face, and switched his comm, listening to a message the rest couldn't hear. He switched back abruptly: "Al, the *Philadelphia* is quote under imminent threat of attack by boarders unquote. Fleet wants a hard fix on their position—get it for the record: are they inside the twelve-mile line, or aren't they?"

Alan didn't even have to look at the screen. "Roger. Wait one—" He studied the screen and used the radar cursor to measure. "Seventeen nautical miles *outside* the line. Not even close."

Rafe switched to the command frequency and relayed the message. Then, half-turning toward Alan, he said to the crew, "We're being patched to the captain of the *Philadelphia.*" He hesitated a moment. "Then we're standing by to talk directly to the Joint Chiefs." He cleared his throat. "Or to be talked to by the White House. Holy shit! The White House! What the hell's going on? Stand by—"

A new voice came faintly through the phones. "USNS *Philadelphia* bridge. Captain Gerault speaking. Do you read me?"

"Faint but clear. Go ahead, *Philadelphia.*"

"We are taking machine-gun fire from a Libyan cutter that has put two boats in the water. They appear to be heading toward the ship. US marines are responding. No attempt to board yet but we estimate three to five minutes for the boats to reach us. If they do—the marines are putting out a hell of a lot of firepower."

"Sir, please confirm that you are under direct attack? Please confirm."

"Two power boats, big inflatables, are headed toward

us. It's still pretty dark down here, but we can make out men, we think in battle gear. Yes, confirm hostile fire incoming. They've taken out one of our navigational radars and seem to be aiming mast-high. Confirm hostile action. Confirm!"

"Here's the CNO," Rafe muttered, then opened the comm to the *Philadelphia* again. "Sir, we'll be back to you. We're on our way."

A pause, a change in the static, and a new voice, sounding young and fresh—it was not yet midnight in Washington— said, "Are we through? Hello? Are we patched through?"

Rafe cleared his throat. "Go ahead, sir."

"Good evening. Or good morning. Stand by, please."

"Hello, have I got Chainsaw One? Or are you Pitcher now?" Hell, the CNO had both comm cards. Nice to know that he was organized.

"Yes, sir."

Pause. Rafe, sensing a cue, said, "Sir, we just had radio contact and learned that our ship is under direct attack. That was confirmed by the—"

"Roger, we listened in. Okay, are you drop-dead sure that ship is in international waters?"

"Affirmative."

"I copy affirmative. Wait one."

Alan felt what was coming, then. The Joint Chiefs, maybe the President, wanted to make sure they were covered, because the CNO was going to let them hit that Libyan boat. While the CNO had been speaking, Alan had isolated the Libyan on the screen and entered the range data into the Harpoon aiming system. As the CNO finished, Alan was beginning to enter the waypoint information that would take the block 1C missile far off-axis from the *Philadelphia* and bring it broadside on at the Nanuchka-class Libyan boat. He had practiced this so many times in the Gulf that it was like something he did without thought—fly-casting, maybe. Yet, he couldn't get his mind off how close the *Philadelphia* was to the Nanuchka, and how much bigger target the *Philadelphia* would make to the warhead. Nonetheless, he reached up, pushed back the plastic cover, and put his fingers on the arming switch.

"Sir," Rafe said, "do I hear you saying we have permission to take action as necessary?"

There was a moment's silence. Then: "I'm authorizing Admiral Pilchard to give you weapons free."

"Sir, are you saying—?"

A new voice came on. "Pitcher, you are weapons free to take retaliatory action against that Libyan Nanuchka as required." Alan could hear that it was Pilchard.

Rafe shook his helmeted head. "Okay, I guess that means weapons free. Alan?"

"Ready. Waypoints. Weapons hot."

There was a moment's silence. "Sir?" Rafe said. "You copy?"

Silence.

"Shoot!"

Alan's fingers thrust the arming switch into place, and his hand shot to the weapon switch and released the cover. He checked his screen, saw a SAM site come on along the coast, and said, "Harpoon away! Take immediate evasive action against possible SAM— !"

The bottom dropped out of the sky as Rafe put the nose down and banked harshly north. Alan's vision darkened, then focused, and he fought the Gs to watch the screen, surprised that no SAM launch showed and at the same time watching a blip separate itself from the coast near the *Philly*, then seem to merge again, then separate.

He struggled to change the radar picture. Rafe turned

east again, dove; Cutter was counting off chaff and flare and firing them. They were going right down on the deck, down where the radar horizon was small for both them and the coastal SAM sites.

"Possible aircraft leaving the coast bearing one-six-three, no reading on speed or direction." His voice shook as the aircraft shuddered. "Warn the *Philly*—possible incoming aircraft on one-six-three—" *Oh, Jesus, Rose*—

Rafe made one more evasive move to the south and put the S-3 down to three hundred feet above the water.

"Admiral?" he said into his mike. Alan had forgotten the command frequency was still open.

Alan was busy timing off the missile until impact. He had split his display screen to show a live radar image of the Nanuchka floating green and eerie in a dead black sea. On the other side of the screen her three fire-control radars showed him their emissions. Cutter was setting up comms between Shortstop—the Tomcats—and Captain Cobb—Catcher—on the *Fort Klock*. Stealth was finished now.

Nineteen seconds to impact. In nineteen seconds, the Libyans, the Russians, and everyone else awake on this gloomy morning would know that the Americans had some air cover.

Rafe switched channels. Cutter was working on a knee-pad; in the other back seat, McAllen was checking the weapons array. Rafe was talking to the *Philadelphia* again.

"Rose, get your head down. Harpoon impact in ten seconds!"

They all tensed as the captain's voice came on.

"This is the bridge of the *Philadelphia*. We have boarders at our stern. Marines hit one boat before it made contact, but the other went to the stern and there is fighting there. Repeat, we have boarders and I think they're on the deck—wait a minute—"

"Sir?" Rafe said. "Sir? Harpoon impact in five, sir? Sir?"

They waited. There was only silence, and then the sound of automatic-weapons fire. Then static.

By the magic of encrypted datalink, Alan's screen showed the same picture that the captain could see on the bridge of the *Philadelphia*, that Cobb could see on the *Fort Klock*, and that the captain could see on the bridge of the *Isaac Hull*. Far to the west, near Tenerife, Admiral Pilchard could sit on the flag bridge of the *Andrew Jackson* and see the same picture. The President could watch the same picture in the White House. Dozens of sources of information converged on the screens to plot the locations of friendly, neutral, and hostile ships all over the world. Radar and sonar, active and passive reception, signals intelligence and direct visual observation could be fed in to clarify and resolve the locations of every unit. Circles meant friendlies, squares neutrals, diamonds hostiles. Different codings indicated whether the contact was a ship, an airplane, or a submarine. A mouse click would bring up information on the contact's method of identification and classification. Another click would identify its circle of weapon coverage.

It was these circles that dominated Admiral Pilchard's screen. At the moment, he had the Nanuchka's surface-to-air missile circle showing; it differed sharply from her radar horizon. The half-circle representing AH 702, Rafe's S-3, moved jerkily toward the diamond representing the Nanuchka, which was so close to the circle representing the *Philadelphia* that, at this resolution, they overlapped. *Fort Klock*'s bold blue circle was almost fifty miles north of *Philadelphia*'s and showed her air-defense missile ranges and her radar horizon; near the *Fort Klock*'s circle and inside her protective ring was the half-circle of the KC-10.

Thirty miles north and west, three red squares marked the last known location of the Russian surface-action group. They were not emitting with radar, however, so they might be closer. Their circles represented their radar horizon against a tall-masted surface target like the *Fort Klock*. They had missiles capable of hitting at very long ranges, but, as always, the problem was targeting.

Suddenly one of the three Russian ships jumped several inches on the screen, moving it almost ten miles to the east. AH 702 had just been lighted by a radar emission and had identified the location of the source, a Sovremenny-class destroyer. Computers had examined the information and massaged it. They had decided. The symbol had jumped.

On board the Russian destroyer *Poltava* were several similar systems, but they lacked input from aircraft, and the Russians were moving almost in the dark, limited to their radars, which the long, heavy seas and sand-filled wind were degrading. The Americans were out there, to the south near Libya, they knew. One of the American ships—almost certainly the noncombatant *Philadelphia*—was damaged, given the frequencies they were broadcasting. The Russians knew, too, that the Americans had an S-3 Viking in the area, because it was using its targeting radar at intervals, illuminating the *Poltava* itself a minute earlier. There was also a large aircraft overhead the *Fort Klock*, which might be a tanker or a command and control plane.

Second Captain Lutovinov tried to remain calm. His orders were to remain close to the American group but to avoid direct contact. He was trying to shadow, but the only American unit he was sure of was the S-3 aircraft; he had elected to run east when it targeted him, to put his missile batteries broadside to the threat of the S-3, which was capable of carrying a Harpoon.

The other two Russian ships were in line behind him. Lutovinov had two very good helicopters with radar units that could illuminate the area, but using the helicopters would give his position away and escalate the electronic jab-and-parry another notch. Still, better to reveal himself than blunder into the Americans in this foul weather. He had to be able to see.

"Launch the helicopter."

Lutovinov had that feeling in the pit of his stomach. If it was fear, then he was a coward. He had the feeling all too often. He had been a junior officer in the heady days of the eighties, when this kind of game was played every day, all over the world. He knew how the game was played, but he had never been the man responsible before. Each action caused the consequent reaction. He also knew that his job did not include starting any form of conflict. His presence was a protest. Suvarov had been firm on that score.

On the other hand, Captain First Rank Suvarov was what the Americans called a "cowboy." And someone had hurt the American launch ship, not by protest but with a real weapon. Was Suvarov mad enough to do it? Lutovinov did not think so. He wanted more information. He also wanted guidance. That S-3 was primarily a subhunter. Was it looking for *Shark*?

"Prepare a message for North Fleet headquarters as follows . . ."

Rose was running up the port side toward the ladder to the bridge, gasping for air, trying to keep up with LaFond. Behind her, Valdez was pressing like a runner trying to surge, and he swung right and went around her. His chunky frame contained great speed, she found; he went by her like a sprinter, the AUG held vertically in front of him, his hands ready to fire.

The marines had dealt with one of the Libyan inflatables before it had ever reached the ship, holing it as it came in close so the air cells began to deflate. The fragmentation grenades went on through without exploding, but when the boat was only ten meters away, its blunt V-nose up, a bow wave surging below it, the M19 round went through the rubber walls and hit something beyond—a weapon, the motor, a helmet—and the inflatable seemed to push bottom-first toward the ship, then rip apart. Within seconds, the defenders on the *Philadelphia* were astonished to see the Libyan patrol boat also go up in a flash of light and smoke, the incoming Harpoon all but meaningless to them in the fog and gritty light of dawn.

Rose had been at the stern then with the civilian crew-members and Valdez. They were aware only of the explosion of the inflatable, then of the distant fire on the patrol boat. Rose had shouted into her handheld, bellowing LaFond's name over and over, and then the second inflatable had appeared under the stern and it was too late to find out what had happened.

Three of the civilians tried to shelter behind the steel rail and yet lean far enough over to fire down *Philadelphia*'s sloping stern to stop the second load of boarders. From her post by the superstructure, Rose had watched one of the men explode into flying blood as the Libyans sprayed the rail with automatic fire. The other two men fell into the scuppers. She was about to rush the rail when Valdez grabbed her arm and flung her against a steel bulkhead, pulling her back and away from the rail as two stun grenades were lobbed over from below, one bouncing wide and disappearing back into the water, the other concussing in the area where the defenders had tried to stand.

Deafened, Rose had leaned back against the bulkhead. Valdez's face was close to hers; he was shouting and she couldn't hear him. Then, as if he were shouting from a great distance over the noise of surf, she heard him say, "Okay? You okay—?" and she nodded, shaking her head to try to clear it.

"Commander!" somebody was whining at her. Some child—a child's voice. Tinny. Then Valdez was pushing the little radio against her ear and she heard LaFond, clearer now. "Commander! This is Gunny! What's going on aft? Commander?"

It had been a great effort to concentrate and to make her lips and tongue work. "Gunny— They're boarding at the stern. There's only two of us—"

Then she had been aware of a man pulling himself over the rail twenty feet away, and later she would realize that he had been coming up a line that he had grappled to the ship; but then, he seemed to be materializing from the sea, head, hands, shoulders, hips, a man in camo and a khaki watch cap and body armor; and Valdez had turned and shot him with bursts of full automatic, knocking him right off the rail as he started to swing his leg over. He went back and down, the force of the weapon enough to push him into the sea, armor or no armor.

Two more of them came on, and Valdez was firing, and then she had the stubby submachine gun up and felt it buck in her hands. She and Valdez had spent a day shooting the Steyrs at the Navy SEALS school at Little Creek, but that had been play and now her life was on the line, and when one of the boarders started to throw something, she cried aloud and turned the weapon on him and sprayed, ripping his vest armor apart, then his neck and chin.

Then LaFond and one other marine had come from the starboard side. They had shielded her, firing three-round bursts and throwing grenades over the stern at the unseen inflatable. It had already moved forward, however, because a voice started shouting over her handheld that they were headed for the bridge, that they were on the main deck and heading toward the ladder to the bridge.

LaFond had jumped toward the port walkway, plastered himself against the bulkhead and waved the other marine to the limit of protection, then shot a look up the walkway and immediately drew back as firing started. He tossed two grenades and ran, firing in burst mode, pulling the second marine with him. Rose followed; Valdez dropped in behind her as they heard one of the M19s chatter amidships, and that's where they were now, running up the deck like sprinters in a race.

LaFond turned and pushed her to her left, where she came up hard behind a steel stanchion, hyperventilating. Valdez hit the deck behind her, weapon extended. LaFond was tight up against the bulkhead across and a dozen feet ahead of them, with the other marine on the deck and bleeding. Thirty feet ahead of them, five men were clustered on the steel ladder to the bridge. It went up seven steps, turned across an eight-foot square landing, and then went up the other way. The stairs were open, so that the protection from the steel treads increased as the men went up but was minimal at deck level.

Valdez was craning his neck up from the prone firing position, then rolling on his side to aim the Steyr. Three men were already on the upper half of the ladder; at the top was a steel walkway with a waist-high bulkhead, and then a door to the bridge. "They're gonna get the bridge!" Valdez was shouting over and over as he fired. Mostly, the steel treads were protecting the men as they ran up the stairs; then one stumbled and seemed to fall and then caught himself. The other two were almost at the top when the door to the bridge opened and a man pushed himself out into the open space there. Rose had trouble recognizing him as the captain of the *Philadelphia*. He looked wild, even crazed. He was shouting.

The captain had one of the streetsweepers. He began firing as he got free of the doorway. He was going on adrenaline and rage, but he was a middle-aged man and he wasn't quick. He blew away the first man to reach the top, but the second put him down with one shot from a 9mm Helwan. He was a skilled commando, the leader of the assault, for whom the snap shot that killed the captain was pure reflex. It turned him away from Rose and Valdez and LaFond, however, and LaFond, who wasn't a SEAL or a commando but who also had honed reflexes and was an instinct shooter, put a three-shot burst into his head.

That left the man Valdez had hit on the upper half of the ladder, and two who were sheltering in the lower half, already separated from the leader and already hanging back in the protection of the steel bulkhead.

Behind them and far over the starboard side of the ship, the remains of the patrol boat were burning on the sea. Rose saw it all in one flash: the patrol boat was on fire; they had the boarders cornered; the boarders were done.

"Take them alive!" she shouted at LaFond.

He had a grenade. He hesitated.

Valdez rolled back behind her.

"Throw down your weapons!" she screamed. Nothing happened—but nobody fired. She shouted it again, cursed herself for knowing no Arabic (Alan would have, she knew) and remembered that Libya had close ties with

Italy. *"Finito!"* she bellowed. She didn't have much Italian, but both her parents had spoken it as children, and she hadn't been able, in the Italian neighborhoods of Utica, New York, to grow up without knowing some words. *"Finito! Tutto morte! A terra i fusili!"* *Terra* didn't make a lot of sense there on the water, but she didn't know the word for deck. And was *fusili* right for guns? Fusili was a kind of pasta, for God's sake. *"No piu! No piu! Fasciate la pace!"* She tried to put it together in her head—*Your boat is sinking, what the fuck—La vostra—oh shit, boat—marina—no—goddamit—* !

LaFond's hand came back a fraction of an inch, ready to throw, and then an AK fell to the deck from the second level and bounced and lay there. After a moment's silence, a voice shouted, *"Promesso dei lege della guerra? Promesso d'essere prigioneri della guerra?"*

Yes, she shouted at them, I, a senior *ufficiale* of the Navy of the *Stati Uniti*, I promise you that you will be prisoners of war under the rules of war. "Geneva Convention!" she shouted. She didn't know any Italian for that, either. *"Mani alla testa! Fasciate scendere coi mani alla testa!"* Surely *testa* meant head. Christ, if it meant testicles they were all going to look pretty stupid, guys surrendering with their hands on their crotches.

But they came down with their hands on their heads, frightened, probably thinking of Lockerbie—except for the guy on the second level, who had one of Valdez's bullets in his left knee and who was moaning. They were not young, these two, and they looked to her very much like Italians. She felt no hatred and no disgust: these were not intelligence agents who planted bombs on civilians, but soldiers who had tried to carry out a tough mission and had failed.

LaFond had them against the bulkhead with their heads on the painted steel before he would let her move, and then he ran up the ladder, weapon at the ready, and screamed for the wounded man. He was gone. There was a blood trail to a hatchway, but the hatchway was closed. "The fucker's gone down a ladder and screwed the hatch down, Commander! He's fucking bleeding! He's fucking crazy!"

"Valdez!"

"I'm with you, ma'am."

"Damage assessment. Get on to Aston, then check with Nguyen and the science team to see if anybody's hurt. I want status on that countdown, number-one priority. LaFond! Get help for this marine! And find the guy who crawled away!" She was running up the ladder. "Bridge! Hello, on the bridge!"

She tried not to look at the captain's body, then looked, saw that he had a hole just above the eye in the left eye socket. He still looked crazy. She stepped over his legs, noticing that he had changed into chinos and wondering when, an absurd thing to be thinking about, and she opened the door and she saw the first mate standing there with a shotgun pointed at her.

"Put that goddam thing down!" They stared at each other. "It's over! It's over!" He didn't recognize her, she realized. Her fingers tightened on the AUG and she was thinking that the buckshot from the sweeper might not do much of a job on her body armor before she killed him when he slowly lowered the gun, swayed, and fainted.

"Oh, shit!" she said. "Bridge watch! Who's got the goddam bridge watch?"

The engineer emerged from behind a console, holding a Ruger highway patrolman in her left hand, a comm mike in her right. Rose had barely seen her the whole mission but she seemed pretty cool.

"Commander Craik? There's an aircraft asking for you

590

They say they need to get some mini-sub now, and have you got any explosives you can put over as depth charges?"

"What mini-sub?" It didn't make sense. Depth charges? What the hell— !

"Commander?" The engineering officer was coming toward her with a funny look on her face, holding out the hand that didn't have the gun in it as if she thought she was going to have to hold something up. Then Rose realized she was shaking, that she was the thing that might have to be held up, and she pushed herself back against the bulkhead and slid down it until her butt whacked on the deck.

Her hands were shaking so bad she could hardly hold the radio. "LaFond—LaFond— Hello? LaFond—?"

On his screen, Alan saw the Russian helicopter launch from the destroyer, although he was really looking for any signs of emission from the Nanuchka. He was running the ESM program again, looking for data from other ships or other planes. Another Sovremenny-class destroyer rotated its air-search radar once, and he caught it and passed it on. Rafe was turning the plane and running in on the *Philadelphia*'s location. For an S-3, this was moving fast. Alan toggled the screen to look for signs of hostile radars, but the Nanuchka, which had had radars emitting on three frequencies a moment before, was silent. Unless he missed his guess, they had hit her hard.

He toggled the ISAR radar and placed the beam squarely on the Nanuchka. A huge radar return blossomed amidships, where a few seconds earlier she had shown only the normal returns of her canted bridge.

"Direct hit amidships. No signal, no radar."

Rafe said nothing. Alan watched the heading change on his screen and toggled back to his datalink display, which showed the relative position of the plane, the Nanuchka, and the *Philadelphia*. He didn't have to care, yet, about what lower resolution showed— other Libyan ships beyond the horizon, or the Russians, or Libyan aircraft. Not yet. And if the weather got any worse, he wouldn't see them coming, anyway.

Alan was too busy to think of how many men had died when the Harpoon hit. He was too busy to be glad it had hit at all. Somewhere, sometime, he would remember how close he might have come to putting the Harpoon into Rose's ship. He pressed his mike button.

"Okay, let's see who's under the *Philadelphia*. McAllen, ready with the sonobuoys? Everybody ready?"

"Alan, you sure that fucking SAM on the patrol boat is fried?"

"A-ffirmative!" Alan looked back at his ESM screen. Nothing. The Nanuchka was silent.

Petty Officer McAllen was laying out his sonobuoy pattern on his screen. Alan could only watch. He understood the basics and the theory of acoustics, but McAllen was an artist and Alan left him to his work.

McAllen spoke for the first time in what seemed hours.

"Sir, I need you to fly the course I've laid on. The 180 is the inbound radial. I'll drop sonobuoys along the whole path from the first mark. Then you turn west and follow the circle I've laid on and turn onto the 090 radial. When we're done, I'll have a cross-shaped pattern of buoys in the water covering two miles around the *Philadelphia*."

"You going active?" Rafe sounded like he had to be sure.

"That's Mr Craik's plan." Was that implied criticism?

They turned slightly and Alan felt, then heard, the 'ka-thunk' as the first sonobuoy launched. Sonobuoys began to come out in regular order, one every few seconds. Active, passive, passive, active. Eight buoys on each heading, five hundred meters apart, making a cross with the *Philadelphia* at the center.

Alan continued to play with the radio codes. Finally he gave up and asked Cutter to get him the *Philadelphia*. Between them they took almost a minute to discover that somebody had hit the reset on the radio, and Cutter reentered the frequency. The time seemed to drip by, punctuated by the relentless 'ka-thunk' of sonobuoy after sonobuoy. As Alan finally got a clear signal, Rafe threw the plane into a hard bank, and Alan watched the aircraft's course onscreen as Rafe stuck to the arc inscribed for him as if the plane had wheels and was on a road.

"Zulu Bravo, this is Pitcher, over?" Somebody had checked the comm card: Zulu Bravo was the *Philly*.

"Pitcher, I read you, where have you been, over?" Woman's voice from the *Philly*. Not Rose.

"Zulu Bravo, we had a little radio problem. We had to e-code. Zulu Bravo, what is the situation of the hostile ship, over?"

"Pitcher, this is Zulu Bravo, that ship is on fire and listing heavily to starboard, over."

"Thanks, Zulu Bravo. What is your situation, over?"

"Pitcher, this is Zulu Bravo. We have control of our ship but at least one bandit remains unlocated at this time, over."

"Roger, Zulu Bravo, I copy in control, at least one hostile unlocated."

"Roger that, Pitcher."

"Okay, Zulu Bravo, on to part two. We need to get whatever hit you. I think it's still there, either under you or nearby. Do you concur? Over."

"Roger, Pitcher, I copy and concur. One of the marines claims he saw a submarine a few minutes ago. What's the plan, over?"

"Zulu Bravo, we asked about explosives, have you got any?"

"Roger that, Pitcher. This is not my specialty; I'm passing you to uh Lieutenant-Commander—uh, God, I'm sorry, her name—the Navy officer in charge. Wait one."

And a new voice came on, a woman's again, and this time it was Rose, and Alan's heart lurched and he felt a bubble rise in his throat. "This is Lieutenant-Commander Siciliano. I have six, repeat six Claymore mines."

Rafe was straight-faced. "Roger, Zulu Bravo, I'm going to give you our ASW specialist, Lieutenant-Commander Craik. Hold one."

He went to intercom. "She's all yours, Al." And back suppressing whatever he might have thought just then about reunions, and Christy Nixon, and women.

Alan found his voice was husky. "I copy six Claymore mines. Six. Hi, Babe. I'm going to try to force him to run under you with active sonar. You drop the Claymore with different detonation depths; your gunny ought to be able to work out a way. If that doesn't get him, it might move him to where I can see him. He has to believe that under your vessel is not a safe place to hide, do you understand?"

A moment's silence, and he knew she was crying. "Roger, I copy and understand. I've missed you so much— !" Getting better control of her voice. "Pitcher, how are you planning to get him if the Claymores don't?"

"With a big, messy depth charge, so hold on."

"Roger. And I'm restarting the countdown on—you know."

"Concur." He checked his screen, trying to be dispassionate, trying to make it straightforward and flat, but wanting hard to wrap her in utter safety. "Rose, I have bandits closing from the south. Are you ready?"

"Roger, Pitcher. We'll have the tools on deck in zero five mikes. I'll rig the bug zappers."

Bug zappers? Alan hoped that Rose meant Claymores.

"Roger, Zulu Bravo. Stand by."

"Copy."

He took a deep breath, tried to sound normal. He switched to cockpit. "Cutter, what's the shallowest setting on a MK 46 torpedo?"

"Uh—!" Cutter was flustered. They all were. Everybody had been avoiding anything personal, because of Rafe, and now the personal had happened, right there, and they were all shaken. "Uh, that was on my mission-commander test. Sir, uh, Al. Ten meters."

"Can it get a lock on a small submersible like a swimmer-delivery vehicle or a mini-sub?"

Cutter's voice was faint. "No idea, sir."

Alan tried to push Rose out of his head. He had to re-think the problem. Rose was in the problem but thinking about her would just get in the way. The torpedo was probably useless if the target was really a mini-sub; worse, it might lock on the much larger *Philadelphia*. The depth charge was also likely to damage the *Philadelphia* if it was close, so the drop needed to be accurate, and it had to be well away from the ship. He would have to know exactly where the target was to have a chance.

He needed the target where he could *see* it. In the clear Mediterranean, even a small submersible would show in five meters of water. Maybe more, if it was a pale color.

He was counting on its fleeing from the active sonar by trying to hide right under the *Philadelphia*. A daring captain might try to hide under the burning Nanuchka, but the S-3 would probably see a mini-sub move if it did. To keep it moving, they had to make it feel helpless. If he was right, and there was a mini-sub at all. Well, something had set the mine.

He wished he had a couple of ASW frigates and another S-3 and the warrant officers who ran the ASW plot on the old *Jefferson*. This was like being the only cop in a big city.

McAllen was bringing the passive buoys on line one at a time, reading their information with slitted eyes. Rafe swung the plane around in another tight curve, and Alan saw the now smooth, gray swells just below his small window. Rafe was well down there, all right.

"That burning Libyan boat's making a lot of noise, sir," McAllen said. "*Philadelphia* ain't exactly quiet, either."

Alan wondered about the Russian sub that had been playing hide-and-seek. It didn't make sense to him that an Akula-class had sent out divers to plant a limpet on the *Philadelphia*. Would the Russians work closely enough with the Libyans nowadays to do such a thing, then hang around while a Libyan boat came in to board? Or could there be somebody else down there? He didn't want to find a Victor III or some third-generation attack boat in the area, too. A Libyan diesel boat? They had a few, but most were welded to the piers in their dockyards. What would be the consequence of dropping the depth charge and whacking a Russian? Or a Libyan, for that matter? Christ, he needed a lawyer. Or was that what had prompted the White House interest?

McAllen raised his head from his console. "This might be something, here at the 40 dB line. An auxiliary, maybe? A pump? It could be on *Philadelphia*. I've got it here on buoy six, and here on buoy twelve. It's not all that close and it's really, really quiet."

McAllen went back to his first buoy, a specialized type that gathered hydro-acoustic data for comparison. He was trying to filter out background noise and see where the thermal layer might be and how much salinity there was. Alan understood these things in a general way, but he didn't know the details, and McAllen seemed to have them by rote.

Alan hit the switch to communicate to the front seats.

"Rafe, we don't have time to piss around. We have to go active."

Rafe was silent for a moment. Today he had ordered the sinking of a Libyan patrol craft. He'd also flown three armed aircraft through neutral air space. Breaking the active sonar rule was scarcely going to get him in worse trouble, but staying off active was an ingrained habit. Alan was on top of the ASW situation, but Rafe was in command. It had to be his decision; that was the way things worked.

"Do it."

Shark was lying with her stern pitched down at a thirty-degree angle in fifty meters of water, a bow-up profile that allowed Suvarov to have his bow sonar above the thermal layer while the rest of the ship lay below it. The bow sonar was not as accurate as his towed array, but deploying the array meant movement and possible detection. The thermal layer would bounce acoustic signals like a mirror because of the steep change in temperature: he could listen, but he was invisible.

Because of the need for stealth and the difficulty of passing signals through water, however, Suvarov was blind except for his sonar. Because of a lack of satellite connection, he couldn't datalink his knowledge, however sketchy, to the *Poltava*, far to the north. He had no real idea of the location of the *Fort Klock* and her escort, although instinct suggested she was also to the north, probably closer than his own ships.

Lebedev was sitting in the sonarman's seat. His display was usually split to show data from both arrays, but with the towed array onboard, only the left side of the screen was illuminated. They had deduced from their acoustic data that the *Philadelphia* was crippled. The computer had said that a second set of engines near it had been a Nanuchka-class guided-missile patrol boat. Lebedev put that down to the Libyan Navy.

Something else was up there, too. It scarcely moved, scarcely registered, but at two kilometers, with the perfect aspect, *Shark* could hear it. Lebedev thought that the third craft was electric. Perhaps a very small submarine. North Korea and Germany both made them. It was not Russian, they knew that.

Suvarov continued to stare at his plotting board.

"So," he said, "here is *Philadelphia*. This unknown vessel hits her a few hours ago. She stops. Then the Nanuchka arrives when we do. They send a boat, right, Lebedev?"

"Two, sir. Two small inflatable rafts, each with one engine. Then the gunfire."

"So the Libyans have boarded the *Philadelphia*. *Da*. So then, a few minutes ago, the Nanuchka takes a missile hit."

"Yes, sir. Hit hard. The hull is coming apart. Wait, sir, I'm hearing splashes." He looked at Suvarov, his brows contracted. "Aircraft." A touch of worry in his voice.

Suvarov looked calm. Airborne ASW had been a joke to the old Soviet Navy. But if the Americans were sufficiently worried— Lebedev nodded: sonobuoys.

"Time to go. Engine room, give me revolutions for two knots. Stay quiet. Con, slip the bow back below the layer very, very gently and turn north at two knots."

If he had been there to fight, he would have taken the risk and stayed. The layer was good protection, even from active sonar. He'd have waited and taken his shot. But this was a different kind of mission, with different rules. If the Americans saw him at all, they were likely to misunder-stand. His greatest fear was that they might see him and not see the tiny electric boat. Americans were very good at leaping to conclusions. Suvarov felt comfortable, but he was troubled by one question above all others. If the Americans fired at him, should he return fire? His sense of professional honor suggested that he should. On the other hand, it went directly against the spirit of his orders. Suvarov did not have a weapon capable of engaging the American plane, and torpedoing the *Philadelphia* would only serve to confuse matters further. He chewed his lip and waited for the Americans to go active.

Before Alan could give the order for active, McAllen tensed.

"Something's moving. Quiet and deep. Quiet and deep—" His voice was singsong, tracing continuing movement for them. "Gone. Still got it on 12. That same line. Not much, but something—" His fingers flew as he entered the possible contact datum. "Maybe-e-e—"

McAllen projected the contact moving northwest at two knots.

Alan looked at it. If this was a Russian sub, it was one of the third-generation types, Akula- or Sierra-class. Could it be French? A diesel boat? Long way from home. Alan didn't think there had been an Akula in the Mediterranean before.

"Go active."

"Sir, I just want to put a few buoys in front of him."

"Screw that, McAllen. I have to see what's under *Phila-delphia*."

The AW looked across at Alan. He wasn't angry, only

curious. Here McAllen had a once-in-a-lifetime chance to register acoustic tracking time on a really quiet submarine, and he was being asked by an intelligence officer with no acoustic training to drop that for a hypothetical submersible under the *Philadelphia*! In his heart, McAllen believed that one quiet Russian was all there was. After all, the Russians were his hereditary enemies. He had grown up with that; why look further? But Mr Craik seemed so sure.

That sureness commanded response.

McAllen popped the switch that cycled the active buoys. Then he called the P-3 to his most recent contact with the unknown submarine. He hoped that Mr Craik appreciated what he was giving up.

The screech of the active sonar was audible everywhere on the big submarine. It sounded close, within a kilometer. Whether they were hunting him or the little bastard that had hit the *Philadelphia* was immaterial.

"Run," said Suvarov. The *Shark* leaped forward. Protest, not fight. Suvarov prayed the Americans had a man of talent at the sonar.

"Pos contact one is running at sixteen knots!" McAllen was excited. "I got him across the board, sir. Let me put more buoys down!"

"What else do you see?"

McAllen held his breath, having to take time to examine his sonograms. He was losing the equivalent of a unicorn— a mythical beast, a rarity of a rarity. He thought the sub running off might be a Sierra. He hadn't ever heard of anyone with acoustic data on a Sierra, and Sierras were rare and beautiful to AW2 McAllen.

It was a tribute to McAllen's sense of duty that he did a

professional job of looking after the other grams. The ones that were empty of his precious contact. He looked at all four quadrants of the acoustic trap he had built with his cross of buoys. And in the last place he looked, there it was—something small, only a little echo. Bigger than a torpedo, but not much. He'd seen those in training.

"By God, got it, sir. Right here!"

Alan leaned over, releasing his parachute harness in his eagerness to see the pinpoint on the screen. He slapped McAllen on the back. McAllen looked up.

"Let's put a couple of passive buoys on top of him, sir."

"Great," said Alan. "And an active to spook him. Close as you can."

Again the AW laid out a course for Rafe. The plane turned hard and came dead level within ten meters of McAllen's ideal position, and he dropped three buoys. Cutter was on the radio with the *Fort Klock*. As Rafe tilted the plane up on one wing to turn, Alan was able to look out over the burning wreck of the Libyan Nanuchka to the *Philadelphia*. There was smoke aft, but she seemed to be on an even keel. The wind held her naval ensign taut as a board above her bridge.

"Catcher, this is Pitcher, over."

"Pitcher, this is Catcher. I read you loud and clear, go ahead."

"Catcher, we have upgraded pos-contact one to probable contact, I repeat probable contact. Contact identified as Sly Fox, over."

Long pause as someone on the *Klock* groped for the comm card of the day and read through the codenames of possible hostile vessels.

"Pitcher, did I copy Sly Fox? Please say again."

"Roger, Catcher, that's Sly Fox. Last contact 0831 Zulu. Last location—Catcher, do you have this on datalink?"

"Roger, Pitcher, we have your last."

Another voice took over the radio. "Pitcher, this is the captain. Are you saying you have a probable contact with a Sierra-class Russian submarine at your datum?"

Cutter looked for the red light to make sure they were encrypted, but captains were always breaking rules that would get jgs arrested.

McAllen spoke from the back seat.

"Yes, sir. It's either an Akula or a Sierra." McAllen didn't bother to say, *And he's headed right toward you at sixteen knots.* They could see that on the datalink.

Alan spoke up. "There's another target—I think it's a mini-sub—about three hundred meters from the *Philadelphia*, sir. I don't think the Russian sub is a player."

"Pitcher, what are your intentions?"

"Catcher, this is Commander Rafehausen. I intend to sink or destroy the mini-sub and let the pos-con run."

"Pitcher, are you certain of this mini-sub? I recommend active pursuit of pos-contact one."

Alan hoped he was misreading the conversation. Catcher, on *Fort Klock*, seemed to think the Russian sub was responsible for the attack. Anyway, down here it was his call.

"Negative. Sir."

On the *Fort Klock*, they saw the Russian submarine as simply another ugly blip on a very dirty screen. Captain Cobb's computer terminal showed three Russian warships just over the horizon to the north, two Libyan patrol boats approaching his southern horizon, and the possible third-generation Russian submarine twenty miles to the south. It also showed a swarm of air activity over Libya as the weather over the Gulf of Sidra cleared enough to make his radar reliable. And *Fort Klock*, despite her position, had the equipment to locate aircraft much more accurately than the S-3 or even the F-14s that were flying CAP down there.

He had the sonar tail in the water and would get some data from it soon—maybe. His missiles were warm and his crew seemed hot to go. He was not. He was deeply worried that some old Fleetex exercise with Russians and Libyans combining to attack a US battle group near the Line of Death was in the process of coming true.

"Combat, this is the bridge. Launch the helo with decoys. Lay an ASW screen as indicated. Target is a possible third-generation Russian nuclear attack boat that has already fired on a US naval vessel."

"Captain, this is Combat. I have four probable Su-22 fighters outbound from Benghazi on course for the *Philadelphia*. Sir, the Su-22 does not carry an anti-ship missile. Uh, sir, do we *know* that this submarine fired on *Philadelphia*?"

"Thanks, Combat. No, we don't know. But treat as hostile." No anti-ship missile on the Su-22? Best news of the morning. "Give me his course. Order the *Isaac Hull* to point in a Fallow Drop formation. We're going to sprint and show our broadside to the fighters and the Russians. Get me those F-14s on line. Make twenty-four knots this course, 125 true."

"Sir, AC 101 is the flight leader. Codeword for the F-14s is Shortstop."

"Shortstop, this is Catcher, over."

"Roger, Catcher, this is Shortstop, over."

"Shortstop, we have four possible bogeys inbound on radial 175, do you copy?"

"Roger, we have them on datalink. We're not radiating. We're playing possum."

"Roger, Shortstop. Keep the P-3 and the S-3 covered. If the bogeys come within five miles of *Philadelphia*, you may engage. Repeat five miles, over."

"Roger, Catcher, I copy weapons free within five miles *Philadelphia*, over."

"Roger."

Captain Cobb watched the two F-14s turn north on his screen and come closer to his ship. They needed to be that far north of the *Philadelphia* to get good shots with their missiles at the Su-22s. This movement covered the P-3 but left the S-3 exposed, but the S-3 was low and would offer a tough target.

"Sir, one of the Russian ships has just launched a helicopter. Turning toward us. Now it's gone below the radar horizon."

Those were Sovremenny-class destroyers. They carried a missile as good as his Harpoon, if they could target it. Were they going to use a helicopter to do the targeting? Jesus, he was between a rock and a hard place—were these Russians really serious?

Well, if they were, he was. "Combat, if that helicopter uses a targeting radar, take him."

There. He was committed.

Now for sweet reason.

"Somebody try to get me the Russian commander, before we all get hurt."

"Captain?" The communications tech on the bridge sounded impressed. "Sir? The *Joint Chiefs* are on the command frequency. He wants a report from you and some lieutenant-commander on an S-3 that's—"

"Get me the Russians! Keep trying. Screw the Chiefs Get me the S-3." On another channel, a junior officer said "Admiral? The captain is a little busy right now—"

"Fuck, I didn't mean *that*." His voice changed. "Sir?"

Admiral Pilchard sat, surrounded by his staff, on the *Andrew Jackson*'s flag bridge, listening on the command frequency. Pilchard had already spoken to the President. He was too far away from the action to interfere: Cobb was the commander on-scene, and Cobb was the best of his captains. That's why he had the independent command, after all. Admiral Pilchard had trained his ships and picked his men and made his decisions; they had come a long way from Fleetex. Now the men on the spot would make the hard choices.

"Captain Cobb?"

"Yes, sir, I have you loud and clear."

"Commander Rafehausen?"

"Sir. Admiral, this is Commander Rafehausen. I'm asking Lieutenant-Commander Craik to do the talking from here."

"Explain what's going on absolutely as quickly as you can. Are we in a war situation?"

Cobb said, "Admiral, a probable Russian submarine has crippled the *Philadelphia*, and a Libyan vessel has attempted to board her. The boarding was resisted."

"Successfully."

"Who's that?"

"Craik, sir, on the S-3. Sir, the *Philadelphia* is reporting she's clear of boarders. And the submersible that crippled *Philadelphia* may have been Libyan, but she was not, repeat not a Russian, sir. I'll stake anything on it. The Russian is a bystander."

"Commander Craik, are you saying that there's *two* submarines out there?"

"Yes, Admiral. A mini-sub and a probable third-generation Russian."

Again, Cobb jumped in, and this time he sounded angry. Admiral, the Russian surface group to the north of me has just launched a helicopter and appears to be preparing to fire. The Russian submarine that was in the vicinity of the attack on the *Philadelphia* is now running toward me, as well. I am preparing to take defensive action, but, yes, sir, this is potentially a war situation. Sorry, sir, this is Cobb, of *Fort Klock*."

They heard rumbling from the Washington line, and then a new voice said, "We'll get back to you." Then silence. "Gone again," Rafe muttered, and he switched back to the channel and said, "Catcher, we seem to have lost the Washington line, over."

"Roger, Pitcher, we copy."

Alan looked over his and McAllen's screens one more time. The mini-sub seemed to be slipping under the *Philadelphia*, as he had hoped, and the Nanuchka was going down too fast to make cover for it if it ran. Alan cycled through his screens as quickly as he could. Two Libyan vessels were leaving the coast, but their speed showed as only twelve knots, way below max. Were they cautious, or did they know something he didn't? He switched again and looked at the four Su-22s and then brought up Strike Common.

"Red Leader, you see the Libyan air to the south?"

"Roger that. Four Su-22s climbing out at 400 knots."

"Their ETA on us is six minutes."

Rafe cut in.

"Alan, those Tomcats need gas soon." He looked at Cutter. "How soon?"

Cutter was way ahead of the action. "They need gas in one five minutes. One five. Less if they go to burner."

They all knew that in the crunch it was the *Fort Klock*, not the *Philadelphia* or the S-3, that had to be protected. Rafe went back up on Strike Common. "Shortstop, this is Pitcher, over?"

Chris Donitz's F-14 sounded as if it was alongside. "Roger, Pitcher, we got you loud and clear."

"Shortstop, I show you at one five minutes from refuel or bingo. Is that correct?"

"Roger, Pitcher."

"Copy, Shortstop. Shortstop, check in with Catcher and go tank now. I mean *now*. One plane at a time."

"Roger, I copy, Pitcher. Break, break. Catcher, this is Shortstop, over."

"Shortstop, this is Catcher, over. I copy the last exchange and concur. One at a time."

On the *Klock*, Cobb had been watching the time-to-refuel clock, but he had planned to let them get gas *after* they engaged the Su-22s. But Rafehausen sounded as if he had a good head on his shoulders, and he was probably right. The Su-22 radar wasn't worth much, and Rafehausen was almost too low to be seen, so that the F-14s could be spared without grave risk to the S-3. It wasn't an easy choice, but it was the right one.

Twenty miles to the south and twelve thousand feet up, the F-14s turned away from the threat to the south and raced for the tanker.

"Valdez, go to Vertical. I'm on my way down. Cut anything you can."

"Way ahead of you. We're checking Transmits and are gonna go back for Vert in about—five seconds—four—three—"

Rose raced down the ladder outside the bridge and sprinted across the deck plates and the non-skid toward the module. The missile was just emerging from its cover, rotating in all three axes simultaneously, like a cobra emerging from its basket. The damage control effort had barely slowed for the firefight, and the vessel now seemed stable and more or less level. Valdez and the geek with the wave-action graphs would know for sure.

She toggled the hatch and entered the module.

"Hey, you look like hell," Valdez said from the console. He was still in camos, tousled, sweaty—hardly a recruiting poster himself. "You okay, Commander?" He was worried about her, really worried.

"I'm fine. I threw up a couple times and I feel great!"

A new voice was on line.

"Gentlemen, the President of Russia has just assured our President that his forces in this area have not engaged our forces. We are assured that the Russian helicopter launched by the, um, destroyer—" His voice sank a little as he seemed to turn away from his mike. "—was that a destroyer, Jack?—" and it came to full voice again to say, "will be recovered and that the Russian surface group will turn away to the—" Then he was gone again, farther this time but still audible. "Jack, are we sure he said north— north? Well goddamit, somebody check— Jesus Christ." He came back. "Hello, Captain Cobb? Hold on a sec—' And was gone, talking to somebody else, "Well, it's about time!" And back: "Yes, north."

Cobb turned away and called Combat.

"Combat, this is the captain. Do *not* fire on the Russian group. Weapons locked."

Ten seconds later, the Russian helicopter's radar came on, illuminating the *Fort Klock*.

"Periscope depth. Bow up twelve. Come up slowly. Suvarov was perspiring, but he was in the game. On plane had followed the little submersible near the cripple American ship. Another, probably a P-3, had tried to fin him. The plane that was hunting him had continue to follow his straight, fast course toward the American surface ships. He had done a long sprint and then a sharp maneuver and a drift. It was a textbook stunt, executed perfectly, and the aircraft was still dropping sonobuoys somewhere several miles astern. At two knots, he was invisible to them.

Suvarov remained worried that the Americans believed that he was the one who had hurt the *Philadelphia*. Now that he had evaded their search, he felt free to correct that error, in part because it was insulting to be thought guilty of something so stupid.

"Periscope depth in thirty seconds."

"Dead slow. Radio mast up. Prepare to dive." Suvarov did not really believe that World War III was about to start, but it was best to be sure.

"Get me the American Guard frequency." He could see the distaste on Lebedev's face. To Lebedev, the Americans were the eternal enemy. Bred in the bone. Suvarov knew he would have a talk with the man. *Times change, and so do the tribe's enemies*, he thought.

"Ready, Captain."

Lt Chris Donitz got the tanker to turn south so his Radar Intercept Officer could keep the F-14's radar on the Su-22s. He didn't think anyone had ever started an air-to-air engagement from under a tanker, but he was willing to experiment. The second he came off the tanker, he would have to start toward a merge; the Libyan jets were that close. He brought his wingman back toward the tanker, detached the fuel line, and started his run.

Alan was watching the returns as the mini-sub moved into the shelter of the *Philadelphia*. His concern was that might try another attack. He busied himself setting the depth charge for its shallowest setting. It was pure rule of thumb, but he wanted the mini-sub at least five hundred meters from the *Philadelphia* before he tried it. And the weather was closing in again. If it got rough, he'd never see the damn thing even if Rose's marines managed to hurt it.

"American aircraft, this is Russian submarine on Guard frequency. American aircraft, this is Russian submarine on Guard frequency. Do you copy?"

Holy shit! Alan slammed his finger on the press-to-talk switch.

"Russian submarine, this is AH 702. I copy."

"AH 702, this is Russian Navy attack submarine *Shark*. I have not committed any hostile action, over."

"*Shark*, this is AH 702. I copy."

Suvarov smiled. *Should he tell them?* He should. Whoever was out there in the mini-sub had tried to involve him had at the very least taken advantage of his presence. The admiral would have told him if it was part of the plan. *Wouldn't he?* Suddenly Suvarov looked at Lebedev. An ugly thought had crossed his mind. He felt slow. He released the talk switch.

"Lebedev, do you have something to tell me?" There was steel, titanium in his voice.

Lebedev just looked at him, aghast. Good. Sergei might have sacrificed an old friend, but a son, never. And Sergei was not one of the old men who wanted the Cold War back. Suvarov thought of all the times he had wished for the old days. No. The Mafia was better than the other. Spare parts were not the only things to live for. Suvarov thought for perhaps five more seconds. Screw Moscow. Suvarov would not allow himself to be used. If some egghead in Moscow wanted a war, he could whistle for it. Besides, he could register the protest ver well this way. Yes. A little help for the poor, acoustically challenged Americans.

"AH 702, this is *Shark*. We detect a small submersible in the area of your damaged ship, over."

Alan smiled. If the Russians, with their superb sonar, said there was a mini-sub, then he and McAllen were not dreaming.

"Roger!" At that moment, Alan lost the mini-sub's blip. It must be right under *Philadelphia*'s hull. "*Shark*, do you have the submersible located?"

"Roger, AH 702. It is close under your damaged ship, at a depth of one-six meters."

"*Shark*, this is AH 702. I am commencing prosecution of the submersible. Please clear the area. Thank you for your help."

"AH 702, this is *Shark*. We will comply. Please note that we engaged in no hostile action and have aided in your resistance of this terrorist action, despite our feelings concerning your illegal launch." Suvarov smiled. There. It was like firing a torpedo.

Alan had no time for the last. He hoped he could remember it. Right, they were protesting the launch. Rafe seemed to have the gist, was relaying it to higher levels in front. Alan called the bridge of the *Philly* to pass the word to the marine gunny that the enemy depth was sixteen meters.

Rafe spoke up. "Where to now?"

"Stay right over the *Philadelphia*. I don't know where that little bastard'll go when the Claymores go off, but it'll go someplace. If this doesn't work, I'm going to ask Rose to try to move the *Philadelphia*."

"With what?

"I dunno. Swim fins?"

"Roger."

Cobb heard the conversation with the Russian on Guard. The Russian helicopter was gone from radar, and its radar signal was gone, as well. He was breathing, but not freely: the Libyan Su-22s were three minutes out from the *Philadelphia*, and the F-14s were moving toward an engagement.

He poked a button to get the ASW frequency.

"Pitcher, this is Catcher, over."

"Catcher, I read you. Go ahead." Cutter had the mike now. Alan was talking to the *Philadelphia* and Rafe was turning tight circles only a hundred feet over the *Philadelphia*'s bridge.

"Pitcher, what are your intentions?"

"Catcher, we are prosecuting the mini-sub. Do we have weapons free?"

Alan hadn't even thought to ask. *I thought we'd already been through that*, he thought.

"Roger, Pitcher. Confirm weapons free on the mini-sub."

McAllen had the depth charge ready. Alan handed him the release. Alan had never dropped one, and McAllen was known as a good hand with an accurate drop. Alan brought the *Philadelphia* back onscreen. He thought of how close he was to Rose, realized that it didn't feel close. It was a very relative distance, and "close" felt very far away just then.

"Zulu Bravo, this is Pitcher. Bug zappers *now*."

"Roger." It was a male voice talking. "Bug zappers firing NOW."

The Claymores went off with loud underwater pops that were clearly audible to McAllen on the passive buoys. Six pops, two more muffled than the rest. McAllen watched his sonograms like a kid watching a video game.

"Got him," he said softly. "Not a kill, but something's making more noise. I've got him on passive, now. He's moving-g-g-g—"

Rose hovered over Valdez as his fingers fluttered on the keyboard. He made several input errors; his adrenaline still had him pumped. The loud "whack" sounds of the Claymores detonating somewhere under them didn't help. Rose put one of the tech reps to checking Valdez's input, just in case.

Rose turned so that she could get the attention of all the scientists and technical people who had crammed into the launch module.

"Okay, folks, I need to get this thing off the deck ASAP. Like in minutes. Tell me what else we can skip in the sequence and still get a functional launch." She looked from face to face—Anson, calm, but it wasn't his specialty; Nguyen, eager, helpful now; Maulcker, always a pain in the ass. "We just tried to flush a submersible from under us. If it doesn't work, they may hit us again. Our mission is to get Peacemaker into orbit. Now, how do we do it the fastest?"

They looked at each other. Two guys began to speak at once; if anybody had bothered to listen, they would have turned out to be saying mutually contradictory things. Everybody wanted to protect his own area—engineering, telemetry, rockets. Behind her, she could hear Valdez's fingers clicking away at the keyboard. Nguyen broke from the group and came close to her and spoke up.

"Commander, I think we can cut immediately from Launch minus five minutes to the Launch-minus-one-point-two-minute hold, run a status check, and count her off. I did the figures. Everything else is redundant. At least, technically." He had the grace to wince at the last. Maulcker started to protest. She turned away. Valdez looked at her, his eyes eager. She nodded. Valdez counted down to Launch minus five and pulled a switch.

"Launch-minus-one-point-two-minute planned hold!" He looked over the launch board. Everything showed green. "Running final diagnostic. Shit, there *is* a lot of telemetry in that data stream, ma'am. Diagnostic good to go."

She nodded to him and spoke into the launch recorder.

"Launch minus one minute twelve seconds and we are go for launch. Countdown restarts at seventy-two seconds to launch." The lights still showed green. Rose crossed her fingers.

From ten kilometers away, Lebedev registered the small explosions. "They are attacking."

Suvarov smiled. "Get me the *Poltava*. Then let's get out of here." He did not want his beautiful boat lingering for further detection by the other American aircraft, which would be an embarrassment. He also did not want to tempt fate.

The Americans had been given the message about their launch. He had carried out his mission. His boat, and his group, had held to the line exactly.

"Message from Moscow via satellite, Captain."

Suvarov did not have to read it. *Stand down.*

As usual, he was way ahead.

He looked around the bridge with a deep satisfaction. His hand clasped Lebedev's shoulder. "Well done, every man. Let's go home."

The mini-sub seemed suddenly to move very quickly. She also seemed to be heading for the surface. *Wounded? Willing to surrender? They have a Stinger? Or a small torpedo for the Philadelphia?* Alan was chilled by the last thought. If the *Philadelphia* could not offer them refuge, they might try for a shot—but they'd need to get some distance from the target to arm the warhead.

McAllen had the mini-sub on several lines. He suspected that its outer hull was breached, and he was watching a line created by flow noise over the wounded area. Her six-knot surge suggested desperation.

Alan reached the same conclusion. She couldn't have a lot of power left if, as was almost certain, she was running on batteries. The sprint had to be a targeting run. Otherwise she would either surface and surrender or go deeper, look for the layer and try to limp home—or was it a suicide mission? No, this near-sprint on the surface had to lead to an attack.

"Sub is turning." McAllen was calm. Alan could feel the fatigue of Africa and the eight-hour flight behind his eyes and in his joints, his ravaged hands. "Rafe, I think he's going for a shot. We have to use the depth charge."

"Do it." Rafe sounded wiped out, too. He had been at minimal altitude for almost an hour, after all the other stunts in this flight. "Whack him, Mac. I don't have the gas to go back for another bomb." The plane leaned one wing down like a tired bird and stooped toward the spot in the ocean that McAllen had marked. Cutter craned to look over the windscreen.

"Visual. Dead ahead."

"Take him." That was Rafe.

Alan had a few seconds. He wasn't making the drop. He cycled through the screens and looked at the Libyan Su-22s. They were emitting radar and they were only fifteen miles away. Two were low—two thousand feet, going for the *Philly.* But no anti-ship missiles. The F-14s had just turned on them, noses hot.

The S-3 was trim and level one hundred feet above the swell. Rafe was no longer watching McAllen's mark on his console; he was able now to see what Cutter saw, a slender form hardly darker than the water.

McAllen couldn't see it, but he knew it was nearing the end of its turn, lining up a shot. He opened the Lucite cover and waited, hand on the switch. He counted under his breath. He had hit very small targets in practice. Five, four, three, two, one. He pulled the lever.

The plane rose as the weight of the depth charge fell away; Rafe pulled the nose up hard to gain altitude, counting seconds until the charge went off, putting the tail where he thought the explosion would come from, then leveling off. The blast wave hit them and rocked the wings, but they were five hundred feet off the water and Rafe kept it under control.

"Pitcher? This is Zulu Bravo, over." The voice sounded jubilant. "You got him. You got him. Wreckage visible." McAllen whooped and Alan gave him a high five. Rafe rocked the wings.

Rose watched the countdown flickering down an LCD readout. The depth charge's explosion and the thin cheering on deck told her their story, but it was distant, a different set of problems. She and Valdez were in the last seconds of the count. She knew the Libyan aircraft were close, but without a datalink or direct contact to Alan's plane, she had no way to measure. *12 . . . 11 . . . 10.* The deck rumbled as the hydraulic gantries pulled away, backing like praying mantises from the rocket. Valdez was talking into the mission recorder. Rose flipped on the ship's intercom.

"Secure for launch in ten seconds! Take cover! Take cover! Seven! Six! Five!"

Everybody should have got the message by now.

Three, two . . .

"Ignition. Starting mission count! Plus one, two, three, four—"

The engines were roaring. The rocket's effort to lift was actually pushing the ship's bow down.

"Liftoff—we got liftoff—nine, ten—"

Water was atomized on the deck and blew against the windows like a squall. White smoke and steam obscured the rocket, then opened, and, craning her neck and stooping, she could see the brilliant flash arcing away from the ship, up-range toward Venice. The white-hot light turned gold and seemed to pulse, then fade and tarnish to brass, then something like dull aluminum as the rocket soared into the low cloud cover.

Beside her, Valdez leaned forward and spoke into the mike.

"Launch sequence complete. Peacemaker launched at 0631 local, under goddam difficult conditions, if I do say so myself. This thing gotta be made easier. No way anybody gonna launch this thing with that eight-hour countdown under combat conditions. That's asinine."

Two of the tech reps were high-fiving; Maulcker, the bald one with the attitude, was being glum. He had said it wouldn't work without a full countdown. Now, seeing Rose's grin, he said, "It could go haywire downrange, you know. Telemetry is unchecked, absolutely unchecked! Computer banks could be damaged—goddamit, if that thing goes into the wrong orbit or crashes, it's your goddam fault!"

She went right on grinning. She had got Peacemaker off the deck before the Libyan aircraft got there, and that was all she wanted for now.

* * *

617

In suburban Washington, Ray Suter sat, telephone at his ear, watching the telemetry data. "Ignition—counting— Jesus, they've got lift—it's lifting— ! She did it. Goddamit, she did it!" He had thought it was all over. He had thought it was hopeless. "She did it!" he cried again. For that moment, he had forgotten that he hated her now. All he could think was, *We're good to go, we're good to go— !*

Alan watched the missile climb away from the *Philadelphia*. At a range of one kilometer, it was rising with deceptive slowness through the thick air and already disappearing into cloud, its blast light glowing like a silver sun. It seemed to be accelerating as it disappeared. When he looked down at his screen, its form was burned into his retinas and tracked around the screen with his eyes, and he had to look at the displays with peripheral vision.

He studied the datalink from the *Fort Klock*, which now, astonishingly, wonderfully, showed the Libyan aircraft turning away, barely five miles from the ship, eighteen miles from the avenging F-14s. Perhaps they had thought that the Peacemaker was a giant surface-to-air missile. Perhaps they had just thought better of facing the Tomcats. Or perhaps the Libyans had been told to stand down, too.

Rafe kept the S-3 a few feet above the surface.

"Checking gas," Cutter said. "How long we gonna hang around out here?"

Alan smiled. "The *Klock*'s forty miles away and steaming. *Philly*'s help is on the way."

Rafe was already on Strike Common, nagging the F-14s to suck gas and get back on station. "Roger, roger," he said finally in a tired voice, switched to intercom. "Twenty minutes. We'll hang around until they get back." He sighed. "Sorry, guys. I'm going to have to go into the Coast Guard field at Lampedusa. The K-10 hasn't got

618

enough for us to make it to the boat and fuel the F-14s coming off the chainsaw." A chorus of groans sounded, Alan's included, but he had been thinking of the same thing himself and hadn't yet dared to ask—that if they diverted to tiny Lampedusa Island, where the US Coast Guard kept a station on an Italian island that was really closer to Africa than to Europe, they could stay out and guard his wife for an extra half-hour. He groaned, but he was happy.

"We'll gas at Lampedusa, get a nap, and head for the boat." Rafe sounded numb.

Alan looked out his window at the sea. There was no sign of the mini-sub, and her identity and her story had probably vanished with her. Rose had two prisoners on the *Philadelphia* who could be interrogated, she said, plus a wounded guy who was holed up somewhere on the ship. That would be fun, flushing him out. Fun for him, too—maybe dead already in the chain locker or the double bottom. The other two might tell who planted the limpet mine.

Feeling another wave of exhaustion hit him like a blast of heat, Alan said, "How you doing, Rafe? I'm about vasted."

There was a grunt. A wave of a hand. Rafe was a little like Rose, he thought, holding himself together by keeping himself apart. Never calling in to the *Jackson* to check on Christy. Locking it all up.

Then the *Philadelphia* came into view out his window. She looked like a fairly normal ship, not one from which marines had been repelling boarders less than an hour before, or one that had survived a mine. The missile gantries might have been cranes for cargo, and the scorched launch pad could have been a chopper pad or just some weird part of the deck. Yet she had survived a lot—captain dead, several crewmen dead, hull holed. Damn good ship, even if she was a noncombatant.

Then the F-14s swung into place a couple of thousand feet above them, and Rafe gave them some parting words, and they twisted in tandem and were gone, up and west to begin a CAP above the *Philadelphia*. Well, he had wanted to wrap her in safety. Could he do better than this?

"—message to the battle group," a strange voice broke in on the comm. Rafe was waggling his fingers at them. Everybody listened up. "The White House has just released this message from the government of Libya as passed to them by the government of the Russian Republic, quote: The State of Libya regrets the misunderstanding that led to the sinking without warning of one of its patrol boats The government of Libya regrets that its attempts to help a stricken ship in international waters near its coast were misinterpreted, and it insists with all its moral force that it had no part in whatever events led to the crippling of the stricken ship, despite the fact that that ship engaged in serious provocation of all nations of the Mediterranean rim by launching a space vehicle in violation of the Anti Ballistic Missile Treaty and of the clearly stated wishes of all peace-loving nations. As proof of its peaceful intentions the government of the State of Libya has withdrawn all military units from the ship's immediate area. As further proof of its commitment to human rights and international peace, Libya has also ejected from its territory the international war criminal Zoltan Panic, also known as Colonel Zulu. The government of the state of Libya is joining with other nations of the Mediterranean rim to try to apprehend this great criminal before he escapes into sympathetic surroundings in Yugoslavia. Unquote." The voice stopped and another voice came on. "This is Admiral Pilchar speaking. Well done, guys."

Zulu. That snapped Alan's attention back from the *Philadelphia*. It was disorienting, as if the month he had spent in Africa and had been jerked so abruptly from had just as abruptly jerked him back. Dukas had messaged that Zulu was dead. Then he got it: the Libyans had let him go well before that message went out; they didn't know he was already dead. They simply wanted credit for turning him loose, now that it was all over.

39

December 9

In the IVI headquarters in suburban Maryland, Ray Suter was sweating. He had discarded his suit-jacket, which hung from his chair like part of a corpse. Despite the air-conditioning, Suter was soaked. He had thought it wouldn't work, and it had worked.

It was not quite three in the morning. IVI was all but deserted, only watch officers and security people and some night-staff security jocks. And Suter.

He was watching the telemetry data from Peacemaker. Despite the truncated countdown, despite whatever had happened to the *Philadelphia*, Peacemaker was in orbit, sailing over Franz-Josef Land, a moving spark in the night sky if you had the instruments with which to see it. Not quite in a polar orbit, it would cross over Alaska and start down the far side of the world, heading south over the Pacific, across a sliver of Antarctica. Then, Suter would command the computer to initiate an orbital-adjustment sequence that would move it east over the South Atlantic just far enough to bring it across the eastern tip of South Georgia Island. There, twenty-one miles east of the main island, an uninhabited pile of rock would receive Peacemaker's rain of depleted uranium rods, observed only by instruments set up weeks before, and by the feral goats that live there, descendants of animals left by whalers a century and a half ago.

Suter was smoking. He hadn't smoked in three years. Now he was chewing his lip and smoking and tapping the end of the cigarette pack on his mousepad, looking at his watch every half-minute, then at the big wall clock. Thirty-one minutes.

The telephone rang.

"Suter."

"Sir, this is the Duty Officer. We have a priority message from the White House, Code Red. Message reads, 'Stand down.' I repeat, the message is, 'Stand down.' Sir, you are to record data but put your console in Passive Mode. I refer you to page 1.12.47 of the operations manual, 'Levels of Command.' An officer will join you to—"

"What the fuck are you talking about?" Suddenly, Suter was screaming. Then he threw the telephone. *The White House! Who cared a shit about the White House?*

The green phone rang and he grabbed it, and before he could speak, a voice said, "A phone message from General Touhey in Houston, sir—please call him on the secure line at once."

"'Stand down?' That was the White House message? Confirm that, goddamit—get— !"

"It's been confirmed, sir."

Suter looked at the clock. Thirty minutes. *Stand down. What the hell! The White House had blinked! But why? There had been intense pressure for the last three days; they hadn't budged. The Chinese ambassador to the UN had made a scorching speech last night—so what? Stand down? Now?*

Touhey was waiting in Houston. He was terse, a sign that he was deeply angry. All he said was, "I've heard. Stand by." Then there was a lot of electronic garble, and suddenly a new voice was there, cold and ironic. It was Shreed. The three of them were on a conference call. "I hear the master said, 'Down, boy,'" Shreed said.

"That sonofabitch don't know strategy from ape-shit!" Touhey cried.

Shreed laughed. "My, my." He didn't really sound amused. "You there, Suter?"

"Yes, sir. I'm outraged! Devastated! They can't do this!"

"Of course they can."

"We can say we didn't receive the message," Touhey growled. He knew better. The message had already been logged.

Suter looked at the clock. Twenty-seven minutes. "If we don't do the test-drop, we've got no data and no video coverage." The video was what Shreed had been waiting to get, he knew. That was going to be the proof, which could be leaked to nations that wouldn't get into line. Suter didn't know that Shreed was going to turn the results directly over to the Chinese, but he knew that frightening China was part of the goal.

"I'll be at the Senate's front door when it opens tomorrow!" Touhey railed. "I'll get on the White House's ass about this, you can bet— !"

"It won't bring the test back." Shreed sounded cool. Distant. As if he didn't have a stake here. "The Brits have denied us use of South Georgia—three minutes ago. Just to make sure, they're jamming the island and cutting off the emitter. It's over."

"We can change targets!" Touhey shouted. "Goddamit, we'll go public with it now! We can adjust orbit another hundred klicks, do a minor re-adjust a little later, what the hell'd it be? Three minutes, four—Christ, we got all that goddam targeting data, it's in the goddam computer all we got to do is *apply* it—and we drop the rods and the President can go suck his dick about it!"

"And how would you and I explain that?" Shreed said. Then he sounded wistful. "It's going to be hard to get them to back another test any time soon, though. Maybe never." His voice took on a nasty quality. "'Touhey's Folly.'"

"We could drop on the goddam Libyan desert! Nobody'd object! People hate Libya—shit, they tried to sink our ship! They were out there, it was their mini-sub, the way I hear it!"

"You're not thinking. I am. It's over."

Touhey began to babble. He dropped a lot of names, used a lot of swear words, but it was all reaction, no action. It was Touhey's way of admitting it was over. That, maybe, his career was over. That he was mad as hell and he couldn't do a thing about it.

Suter was thinking. Touhey railed, and Suter thought. The clock ticked. Suter was thinking first of himself, of what it meant to be connected to failure. Maybe to a program that would be shut down, now. Touhey had lots of enemies; IVI had lots of competitors for money, or power. Next year, this building could have a different sign outside, different people in here.

Suter was thinking of Rose. *All those questions, right at the end. Not believing me. She turned against us. She turned against me.*

Suter was thinking about Peacemaker. No target, no data, no videos. No threat to the world. But if Peacemaker went ahead and dropped its rods, and the world knew it had done so, knew somehow that Peacemaker had hit a target—

Twenty minutes.

"I have an idea," Suter said. His throat was so tight

625

he could hardly speak. When he lifted a cigarette from the cup he'd been using as an ashtray, his hand was shaking.

"An idea!" Shreed crowed. "Well, well, an idea! I love ideas. What's your idea, Suter—we regroup and come back as the Three Stooges?"

"I'm serious." Suter realized how much he disliked Shreed. The dislike would make no difference to his working for the man, might even make things better by giving an edge, but he felt the stab of hatred, regardless. "I'm serious even if you're not," he said.

A little silence. "Ah," Shreed said. "The worm turns. Well, well. Okay, give us an idea."

"You have to give me cover." Suter eyed the clock. Nineteen minutes.

"For what?"

"You have to promise cover, both of you! Confiden- tiality. Absolute confidentiality. If it doesn't work, nothing shows anywhere."

Touhey started to mutter, but Shreed cut him off. "You *are* serious," he said, and it was clear he was talking to Suter, not Touhey.

"I'm damned serious."

"Then I'll take you seriously. If you can pull a diamond out of this shit-pile, you've got cover. Absolute. From both of us." Now Shreed was serious, too.

Suter swallowed and plunged ahead. "We change the target to the *Philadelphia*," he said.

Something muffled came over the telephone, probably Touhey. Suter ignored him.

"It's the perfect target: everybody's watching it. It's emitting, so Peacemaker has something to lock on to. It's isolated. It's not in a foreign country, so nobody will object."

Shreed waited a second or two, but he would be figuring it out, probably had already figured it out. Still, he went a step at a time. "Why would anybody believe that Peacemaker targeted the *Philadelphia*?" he said.

"Because the launch officer cut the countdown, without authorization, and fucked the pre-programmed data. In the rush to get the missile off the deck, she entered the ship's location in the target window."

"Jesus Christ," Touhey breathed.

"It would show in the tapes," Shreed said.

Sixteen minutes thirty.

Suter wiped sweat from his right eye. "I can rewrite the tapes. There might have to be a gap of a few seconds."

Touhey growled, "Boys, we're talking about killing Americans, here. Listen up, now—"

"Awkward if they hit the cruiser," Shreed said. He was simply thinking aloud. "Russian sub was around somewhere, but he won't be on the surface. Too bad. Or maybe not—complicated, if we hit a Russian sub. There's a Chinese spy ship hanging back by the Libyan coast; that would be—"

"Guys," Touhey said warningly, "I don't like what I'm hearing."

"So the rods come down," Shreed said, going on exactly as if Touhey hadn't spoken, "and they take out the ship and the computers and the witnesses. That is what you mean, isn't it, Suter—that we're going to take out the witnesses?"

"Yeah, that's what I mean."

"Because, if the witnesses survive, we're in deep shit—is that right?"

"That's right."

Fifteen minutes, nineteen seconds.

"Well." Shreed's voice sounded full of admiration. "You're one nasty piece of work. Nastier than I ever figured for." He changed to a harsher, almost nagging tone. "Touhey!" Shreed waited. "You there, Touhey?"

"Yeah, I'm here. And I ain't playing."

"Yes, you are. If I play, you play. Let me put it this way, General. If you don't play, I'll kill you in the Senate. I'll have the intel committees into IVI like the Ebola virus. You'll be lucky to get out without a prison term. I'm not going to repeat myself, because there's no time. Yes or no?"

Suter watched the clock tick and hated Touhey now, too, for holding them up.

"Shreed," he heard Touhey say, his voice now rough with some powerful emotion that made it like the rumble of a bad muffler. "Eat shit. That clear enough for you? You just take me to the committees, just go ahead! I don't give a rat's ass what you try to do to me. And you, Suter—you're fired. You go crawl back to the C-fucking-I-A and tell them that out here in the real world there's one general don't think much of killing Americans just because it'd help his fucking career. You got me? Goddamit, Suter, answer me! You get me?"

"But—"

"Then abort! Pull that fucking Abort switch in the next three seconds or I'll have Security in there to arrest you for treason. One! Two!—"

"You're a fucking idiot, Touhey!"

"Three!"

Suter reached up, flipped the red Lucite cover, and pulled the switch.

Nearing the Antarctic ice pack, Peacemaker erupted in flame, soundless in space, and the deadly rods, shattered blew out in a cloud like sticks scattered by wind, an began their long, erratic, meaningless, harmless fall to burn, unexpended, in the atmosphere.

The Med.
Rafe turned toward Lampedusa Island. The S-3 rocked its wings as he drew abreast of the *Philadelphia*, a greeting and a salute to a gallant ship. The Libyan Nanuchka was just slipping under the surface a quarter-mile away, her narrow stern going last, and Alan lifted his right hand to his forehead—a salute to another gallant ship, one that had done its best in a cause that had been different from his. He looked down at the *Philly* as they passed their closest. A small figure was standing on the *Philly*'s stern, waving. Alan deployed the infrared pod and moved it up and down as they passed overhead.

On the *Philadelphia*, Rose was up on the main deck, watching as Alan's S-3 became a dot in the north and then part of the sky. She was alive; he was alive. *Alive!*

A helicopter was just taking off with the wounded marine and one of the surviving crewmen from the battle at the stern. She held her hair as the wind gusted from the rotors. A chopper pilot herself, she saw it as if she was inside the aircraft, driving it up, turning, moving away toward the north where the cruiser and its hospital were waiting.

"We're okay, Gunny," she said, when she could be heard over the rotor noise. "We did it and we're okay!"

LaFond had his M-16 slung over his left shoulder, and a bandage on his cheek where something had hit him during the gun battle, probably metal or encrusted paint from the deck. The bandage was big and made him look swollen. When he grinned, it rode up on his face. "Kinda hairy here, once or twice." He spat a brown stream on the deck, stepped on the splatter and moved his foot around. He was chewing tobacco.

"What's happening with that third boarder?" The truth was, she couldn't have cared less about the third boarder; she was too happy. But she was being a good CO, doing it on automatic. Running down.

"Ship's company found him in a p'way. Bled to death." LaFond spat again. "You okay, Commander?"

"Never better!" In fact, she felt weak in the knees, silly in the head—happy and coming down all at once. A little like birth. It was over, and there was a letdown. *But this birth worked. I did this one right.*

LaFond touched her arm, pointed. Somebody was waving at her from the bridge—the woman engineering officer. Rose waved back. The woman waved more vigorously and beckoned her closer.

"Aw, Christ, what now?" she muttered. She felt it as a huge imposition, then remembered that this weight was the weight of command. She turned back to LaFond. "Get our weapons together, Gunny. Get them below decks someplace before the cruiser gets here, okay? Let's look a little shipshape."

The deck felt as big as a football field as she crossed it. Her thighs were stiff, her left calf so knotted that she hobbled. Where had she hurt herself? Seeing the engineering officer waving harder, she tried to run. *Belay that.* She hobbled up the ladder and to the bridge.

"Somebody wants you!" The woman pointed at the sound-powered phone.

"Yeah, Siciliano here."

"Hey, Commander, Jeez!" It was Valdez.

"Aw, Valdez, what now— !"

"I thought you'd want to know. Peacemaker aborted! Ka-boom! Gone."

She didn't get it. It made no sense. She was dizzy with fatigue, mild shock—what the hell?

"Hey, Commander, you there?"

"I—yeah. What?"

"They aborted Peacemaker. From IVI. White House order. I got it on the dedicated link, so I bring it up on the screen and one of the scientists, he goes ballistic. His career is in ruins, he says, which don't mean squat to me one way or the other, but I can tell you something that does mean squat to me: He goes, 'This was the greatest weapon in the world and they aborted it.' You like that—weapon, h'mm? *Weapon?*" He paused. "*Weapon,* as in that's the missing data?"

She thought of Abe Peretz. She thought about her own refusal to see what perhaps should have been obvious. What did that make her—a dedicated officer, or a fool?

"Come out on deck and tell me about it," she said. She stared down at the rolling gray water. The feeling of triumph had slipped from her like a coat that didn't fit. "Come talk to me, Valdez." She handed the sound-powered phone back and went out into the air, feeling it rouse her, pull her into the world, when all she wanted to do was sleep. She saw Valdez's small figure emerge from the module and start toward the bridge, and she went down the ladder that only an hour before they had been fighting over, and she turned toward the bow and went toward him, both slanted a little to one side to counter the list of the ship. New figures were moving around the decks, damage-control specialists flown in from the *Clock,* marines to back up LaFond's weary crew, more IVI technicians. She and Valdez ignored them, headed for each other.

Valdez stopped a few feet away from her. "You did your

631

goddam best! I don't want you to worry about this now, you hear me? Commander?"

She began to grin. "Oh, Valdez— !" Then she was laughing, and tears were running down her face. "Oh, Valdez— you're the best!"

40

In the S-3, the flight to Lampedusa was anti-climax and torture. Even moving around the tiny cabin didn't help after nine hours strapped into the ejection seat, and every man had experienced so many surges of fear and adrenaline that their suits stank, and the cabin stank with them. And the coffee was gone. Rafe announced that he suddenly wanted to smoke, a reaction he had not experienced in years. Cutter shared a bottle of water with everybody. Alan dozed, more like passed out. McAllen woke him a minute out from the landing.

"Straps and brace, sir. Jeez, what a flight, huh? Sure am sorry we didn't get to use that torpedo!" Alan, fuzzy from sleep, just looked at him. McAllen burbled on: "Well, we took a buddy store and drained it dry, right? We nailed the Nanuchka with the Harpoon, right? We killed the mini-sub with the depth charge, right? Pretty good mission. Too bad we didn't get to use the torpedo on that damned Sierra!" McAllen sounded as if he was ready to do it all over again. Cutter laughed. Alan wondered if McAllen really meant it. *The torpedo, on the Russian submarine?* Was he really that young?

They got a straight in from Lampedusa, and Rafe accepted it for a landing that was dramatic only in its absolute lack of flamboyance. He ran the engines down from full throttle and let Cutter lead him through the checklist as they taxied toward the minuscule Coast Guard tower.

"If the Italians make a stink about us having that tor-pedo aboard, just keep talking about no gas left. We're down, and that's what matters." Rafe sounded half-asleep. "Unless they won't let us take off again. Then we'll ditch the torpedo and pick it up some other time."

He and Alan were the last out of the plane, and they walked toward the tower together. Rafe was anxious to be in the air again, even though he was exhausted. He was the acting squadron skipper now; he'd have a bunch of things to deal with on the boat. The deaths of four squad-ron members, for starters. Alan walked silently beside him, his boots scuffing as if he were too tired to lift his feet. He pulled his helmet off and tucked it under his arm, thinking about O'Neill and Djalik and Christy. His shoulder whacked a doorframe as they reached the building, and he leaned against it, one hand on the doorknob. "I know you're hurting, Rafe."

Rafe simply looked his numbness: *Don't remind me.* No words. His jaws were covered with dark stubble; he had circles under his eyes; he smelled like a locker room.

"Had enough problems for one day." He started to push past Alan into the flight spaces. Alan held the doorknob and forced Rafe to look at him. "Thanks for saving Rose," he said.

Rafe met his eyes, only for a moment. "Yeah. No problem."

"I'm sorry about Christy. They got great doctors; they'll do everything for her."

Rafe stood there. He nodded. He didn't look at Alan but at the door—at nothing. Then he said something that suggested that he had been thinking, too. "If her plane had made it, we wouldn't have gone. And they wouldn't have done it as well as we did. Maybe these things—happen certain ways for certain reasons." He started to say something, stopped, then looked at Alan's eyes. His own showed a deep pain, perhaps a kind of pain he had never felt before. "I can't talk about her yet. If she makes it, I want to— I love her, Al." Alan put his hand on Rafe's shoulder. He nodded again. Alan opened the door and Rafe went through.

Coda

The Friends

Norfolk. June 1997.

Mikey Craik woke and felt the dog's big head on the bed beside him. The dog did that sometimes—just came in and put his head there while Mikey slept. Just checking. The sleepy child moved his hand to touch the wet muzzle, and the huge tail wagged, and the whole dog moved, and Mikey's bed moved with him. He chuckled.

Downstairs, the grownups were making noise. There hadn't been much noise like that in his life until his parents came back. Now there was noise, happy noise.

He slipped out of bed and padded to the door, the dog at his shoulder. They went down the hall and reached the top of the stairs, and the little boy went down the stairs step by step, holding on to the spindles of the banister until he was far enough down so that he and the dog could sit on the step and look through the spindles and watch the party.

Harry O'Neill looked wonderful. It was hard to see that he'd lost an eye. They'd made new lids from skin from the inside of one arm, and his artificial eye was a beautiful copy and even moved when the good one did. Of course, being blind on that side, he moved his head more to focus on things on his bad side.

He was wearing a new Oxxford suit and a pair of old Lobb shoes that were so beautiful that every other man in the room wanted to hide his own feet. Harry even smelled rich—some cologne that evoked leather and nutmeg and flowers and—well, sex.

Harry was laughing. He had an arm around Mike Dukas and an arm around Abe Peretz, squeezing them both and pulling them tight until their heads were close to his. He said, "How about it guys? You in?"

Dukas punched him in the ribs to make him let go. "Not me. I'm flattered, but I got a job for two more years."

"Mike, this is better!"

"I got a commitment. Things are moving now. We're making arrests."

Abe made a face. "Bea saw you on CNN! She wants to know who the sexy little guy with you was."

"Sexy? No, that was Pigoreau. He's just—" He frowned. *Pigoreau, sexy?* "Your wife's got lousy taste, Abe."

"Hey, thanks."

"Present company excepted! Anyway, Harry—thanks, but no thanks. Sounds interesting, sounds exciting, but—I'm in for the long haul where I am."

Harry squeezed his shoulder. "Thought I'd try." He looked at Peretz. "Abe?"

Abe cocked his head, rubbed his upper lip. "Give me your card. Let's talk about it. Lunch?"

"You bet. We'll find a place where you can hear me with your good ear, and I can watch the babes with my good eye." Their injuries had already become a bit of gallows humor between them. Abe had a hearing aid, barely visible, in his right ear, and the pink line of a scar still showed at his hairline, if you knew where to look.

"I heard that crack about babes," Rose called from across the room.

"This is guy talk."

"Guy talk is sexist bullshit."

Dukas detached himself from Harry and headed for

Rose. "Let's talk girl talk," he was heard to say when he got to her.

Harry had told them at dinner what he was recruiting for. He and the Agency had had an agreeable parting of the ways. "They could live with a black guy, but a one-eyed black guy was a bit much. I tried to tell them it could be worse; I could be Sammy Davis, Junior, but they didn't get it." He had looked around the dinner table. Nobody there got it, either. Harry had laughed. "One-eyed black guy who was also a convert to Judaism. If he'd been gay he'd have touched all the bases." Now he was a budding entrepreneur and was looking for what he called "associates," meaning employees, but he was looking only for specialized people with special talents.

Alan had smiled across the table at him. This was the new Harry O'Neill—quieter, tougher, elegant. The Agency had flown him from the *Rangoon* to an Air Force hospital in Germany and then to Washington, where his surgeries had started. When he was up and about, he had gone to his parents, brushed aside their hopes that now he had seen reason, that now he would go to law school, and he had told them that they were rich and he had an idea, and would they please give him a half million dollars; they could take it out of his share of their estate. It took them five days to accommodate their rather false notions of their son to the realities, and then they had begun to come around. Now Harry had his half million as seed money, and, with his father's and mother's help, he'd raised three million in venture capital among Washington's legal elite. Only Alan knew that he was still suffering flashbacks and nightmares, and that he faced an HIV test every three months for the next two years—or until he tested positive.

"So," he was saying now to Abe, "you're interested."

Abe shushed him with an eyebrow, looking at the kitchen, where Bea was moving back and forth past the doorway. "We'll talk. Let's say—the Bureau's a little staid."

Harry dropped his voice, turning his back to Rose. "What about what happened to you. You ever—?"

"There's some unfinished business there. I got some ideas. I assume that this new thing of yours wouldn't discourage an 'associate' from using resources to pursue his own wild hares now and then?"

"Shit, man, we'd—"

Alan joined them. "Talking the new shop?"

"We're comparing disability checks. Did I tell you I hired Dave Djalik?"

"You did, as a matter of fact, but not why."

Harry turned his head that fraction of an inch too much that revealed the failure of his left eye. "He has skills I want. And African experience."

"Djalik hated Africa."

"We-e-e-llll— It's a little more complex than that."

"He still hate my guts?"

"Let's say you're not his favorite person. He's grateful, Al, but—"

"I know. I know." He smiled. "At least he's one medal up now." Alan had made sure that Djalik was one medal up. He had recommended him for another Silver Star, and he had asked Parsills to see that no recommendation was made for Alan himself. Nothing. He had tried to explain. "What I did was for—friendship. What Djalik did was for duty—and then for something above and beyond duty. That's what they give medals for." Djalik had got his medal, but he hadn't forgiven Alan for Africa; he had a prosthesis where his left hand had been. They had seen each other once, but neither had been comfortable.

Abe, sensing the discomfort, said to O'Neill, "Aren'

642

you going to try to hire the great Craik away from the Navy?"

"Wouldn't even try! No point—is there, Alan?"

He gave them a slow, lopsided grin. "Harry knows me pretty well."

He looked across at Rose. She was flushed with pleasure and excitement. He had been home for two weeks, and they were rediscovering each other. She had been kicked upstairs at IVI and was on a completely different project; Peacemaker had pretty much disappeared; Suter had been sucked into the black hole of the Agency. Rose had been accepted into the astronaut program, with General Touhey pushing her application hard. He had written great things about her. Great things. Almost *too*-great things—as if he wanted to reward her by getting her out of his life.

Alan looked at Abe. "Let's talk sometime. I'm not entirely clear about—your doubts about Peacemaker." He and Abe looked at each other, letting silence communicate for them. "Rose told me yesterday you thought that Shreed was involved."

"Yeah, we need to talk. Sometime. Bea—"

He didn't finish, because Bea herself appeared from the kitchen, carrying a tray with glasses and a bottle of champagne. She put it down on a low table in their midst and hurried over to Abe and put an arm through his. Alan was surprised by this quieter woman who was so much more visibly dependent on her husband than he remembered.

"Who's doing a toast?" Rose said. They turned around. She was pouring champagne into six tall glasses.

"This is becoming a ritual," Harry said. "Once more, and we'll need special music."

They were all gathering around the table, half-consciously taking the same positions they had a year before. Rose and Bea passed around the glasses, and there was a little silence. Rose gripped Alan's hand and said, "I'm not going to make a toast, because I don't do that very well. But I want to say how great it is to have everybody back. Harry— Abe—Mike— Thank God we're all alive." She grinned, blinked at tears. "Harry, make a toast!"

And Harry was ready. He tapped the rim of his glass, looking down, then looked up and smiled. "We're a funny lot. One nigger—two kikes—a dago wop—a guinea Greek—and a WASP. Folks, if we can do it, anybody can." He raised his glass. "Here's to—" And he stopped himself before he said *us*, because he had looked beyond them and seen the face of the child between the stair banisters. Sleepy-eyed, dazzled, the little boy smiled down at them.

Harry raised his glass again. "Here's to the future."